The Crux of Eternity

The Eternal Dream, Book One

Natalie,
Your words show your
joy for life and your

Lane Trompeter

stories. I hope you love
these stories enough to
share them!

To my father, who fanned the flames when they were but an ember.

To my wife, who turned those flames into a bonfire.

THE CREATOR'S TEETH
COIN
DUSKBANK
ARDOR HEATH
KHALINTARI REPUBLIC
CARQOS
FORLORN CREST
SAIL
WAY OF THE WEST
BEDLAM'S JAW

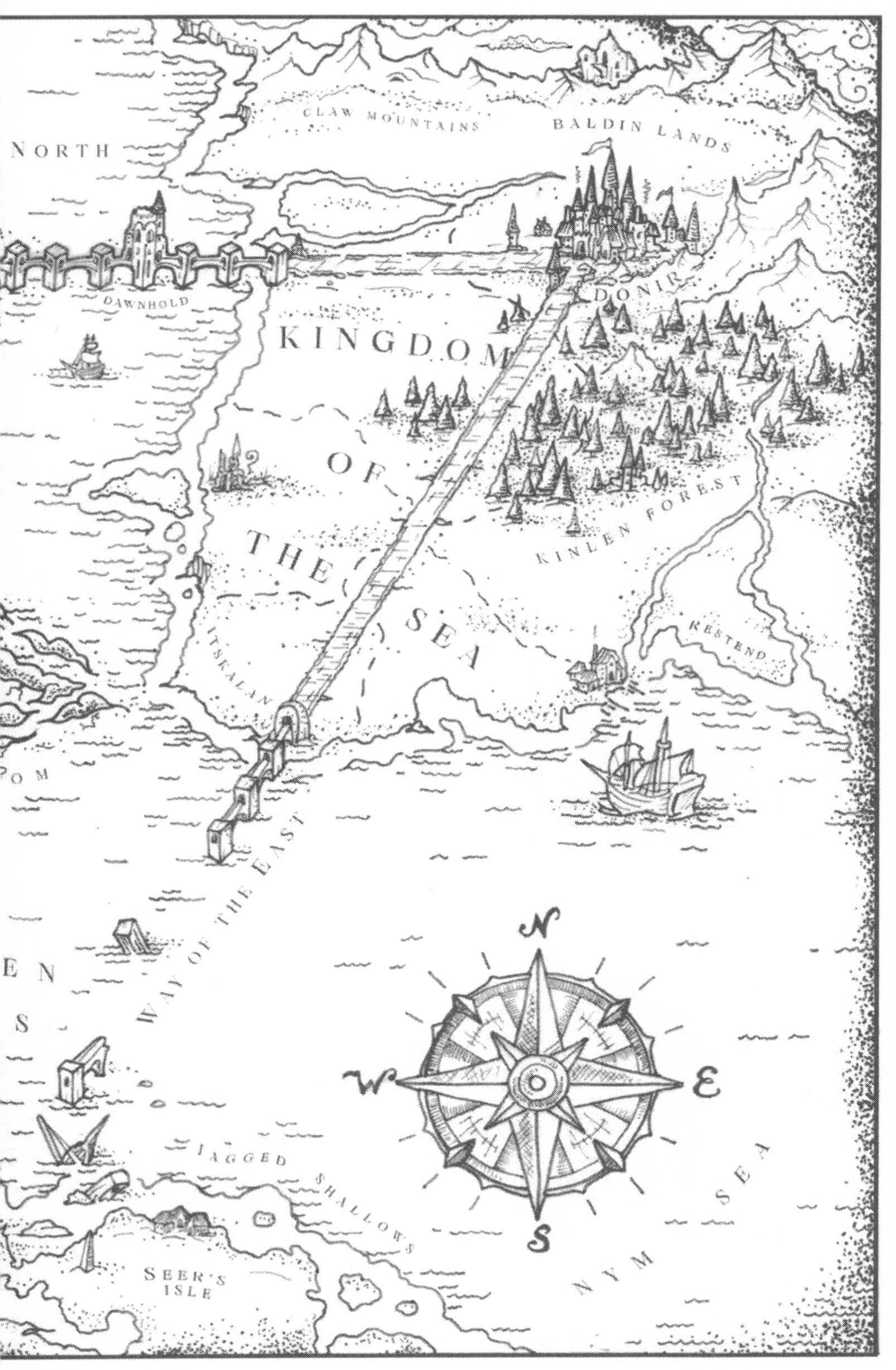
CLAW MOUNTAINS
BALDIN LANDS
NORTH
DAWNHOLD
DONIR
KINGDOM
OF
THE
SEA
KINLEN FOREST
RESTEND
ITSKALAN
OM
WAY OF THE EAST
EN
S
JAGGED SHALLOWS
SEER'S ISLE
NYM SEA
N
W
E
S

Prologue
The Coup

The Seventh Day of Winter
In the Year 5204, Council Reckoning

A thin, bright yellow flame balances on the air, hovering over the wick of a half-melted candle. The feeble light illuminates the inside of a stark, utilitarian tent. Noises of a martial gathering drift in through the open flap: the jingling of armor and harness, the rough tones of soldiers coarsely joking, the soft wicker of horses grumbling to one another. A cot stands pushed into a corner, dust from the dirt floor covering it from lack of use, while a table graces the center of the tent, maps hiding every inch like a patchwork tablecloth. A single chair is pulled up to the table. A man in a hooded black robe etched at the seams with bright reds and oranges bends over the maps, his posture hinting at advanced age.

The candle flickers as a draft of the cold Winter air spins into the tent. The light gutters and nearly goes out. The man snaps his hand out, and the candle flares briefly before settling back into its cheery glow. In that short burst of light, another figure appears, standing quietly in the shadows, and the sounds from without cut off as if sealed behind the great stone of a tomb.

"I knew you would come, old friend," the hooded man says from the table, his voice weary. It echoes weirdly in the sudden silence, as if the two men are lost in a deep vault.

"How could I not, Telias? Is it not my duty?"

"Hah, duty," Telias chuckles, his laughter mocking.

He reaches out, and the light from the candle jumps from the wick to his palm, remaining there and burning. The man in the corner tenses, his hand reaching above his shoulder for a sword sheathed diagonally across his back. The fire grows, soon a handful of glowing, crackling energy.

Telias spins his other hand around the flame, and it smooths, a perfect sphere of fire. The bright colors swirl inside the globe, contained by the man's iron will. The fire does not strain to assume its natural state, but floats calmly, sedately, as if content. The close flame illuminates Telias' face. He still appears to be in the blossoming of his youth, handsome behind his light brown beard. His eyes, however, belie his youthful features. In his gaze rests the heavy weight of the wise, the ancient, the broken.

From the sphere breaks the beak, then the dangerous eyes, of a miniature phoenix. The bird looks on the tent with the fierce gaze of a predator. Slowly, the flaming sphere shapes itself into the body, wings, and talons of the proud creature. The phoenix shakes, the excess sparks cascading off its tiny body and drifting to the floor in a bright shower of light. The bird paces in the air between Telias' hands, occasionally shaking or picking at itself. Always contained within the shape of the flawless little phoenix is the bright and hungry light of fire.

"Are you going to defend yourself, Telias?" the man in the shadows asks, his voice strained as he watches the performance.

"No, Altos. I won't. I'm just enjoying the last moments of life as I see fit."

The phoenix leaps from his hands, its flaming wings leaving behind a trail of bright cinders as it circles the room. The bird dives sharply for the figure in the shadows, who ducks and draws his sword in the blink of an eye. Telias doesn't press his advantage, though, too busy laughing as the bird returns to his grasp. He closes his hands on the tiny creature, and it disappears into his skin.

"No, I won't defend myself," Telias says again, staring down at his glowing hands with a sad smile.

The other man slowly walks forward. Sword held loosely in his hands, he stares down at the maps, studying them and shaking his head. The room darkens as Telias' hands lose their glow, and soon the entire tent is plunged into midnight blackness.

"Why are you doing this? Why are you forcing me to kill you?" Altos suddenly cries out in the darkness, his voice filled with agony.

"Why? Can you truly ask me that question? I won't be a part of what you're creating. I can't sit beneath that madman on the Council and listen to his ravings. Everything that we've defended, every truth we were raised on, is dead. I may as well die with them."

"Telias, please, reconsider. I'll speak for you before the Sealord. I can convince him to show mercy."

"No, old friend," Telias' voice reverberates through the darkness with finality. "My war is with Helikos. But I won't fight you if you stand with him."

Silence lasts in the tent for long moments, only the harsh scraping of Altos' breathing rasping against the quiet. The lack of noise is unnatural, artificial, something that can only be created by forces beyond normal ken. Neither man chooses to break it, and no sounds from the outside world can possibly pierce it. It becomes stifling, oppressive, a leaden weight that hangs upon the shoulders of both men as they wait, invisible mantles of burden. When Altos speaks, the tent shakes with the force of the gale arising outside.

"Telias of the Council of Shapers, sole Master of the Flame, your Vengeance stands ready to pass judgment on your deeds. Are you prepared to answer for your crimes?" The words are ceremonial, a shield to separate the man from the judgment, as if such is possible.

"I am."

"It is forbidden for a Shaper of the Council to lead and govern men. This army you have raised is a clear breach of our laws. It is forbidden for a Shaper, but not for a man."

A pause. The dull sound of a dagger slamming into wood echoes through the soundless space.

"Become a man."

Chapter 1
Kettle

The Second Day of Winter
In the Year 5219, Council Reckoning

"Just a little bit farther, Grace," I call down in a whisper.

The tiny waif clings to the hewn stone wall twenty feet above the ground with half again still to climb. I've gone first, the gaps between the stone practically broad paved steps to my questing fingers. My legs casually dangle over the side of the mark's stone balcony, swaying in the night breeze. Grace, however, is struggling. The moment of truth, as always, is when she glances at the ground below. The girl doesn't freeze, which shows promise, but her arms are trembling little sticks clinging to the stone. She reaches with uncertainty for the next handhold, her fingers brushing blindly against the mortar. Her small blonde head shakes back and forth, and her lips move as she mutters to herself.

Silently encouraging her, I try not to make any noise. Though the resident of the house is a light sleeper, we've scouted his patterns. He sleeps the deepest after his mistress leaves for the night, so the start of our climb coincided with the woman's emergence from the house. We have a reasonable window of opportunity, and the job is fairly low risk. Grace just needs to pick up the pace.

I uncoil a rope from around my chest, but she must hear something. She glances up, and, even in the gloom of the night, her eyes flash with anger and determination. Shaking her head resolutely, she reaches above her with renewed confidence. She levers herself over the balustrade, breath coming a bit heavier than the climb requires.

"I did it, Mother!" she whispers excitedly.

I grin and give her a nod, recoiling my rope. Though I've never actually brought life into the world, these pale little Donirian orphans are all I ever need. We turn towards the glass doors. I unfold a leather satchel that contains the tools of the trade and decide on a pick and tension wrench. We've lost a little time on the climb, so I can't waste time explaining. Still, she avidly follows my every move as I slide the oiled metal into the keyhole.

The lightest pressure, however, causes the door to swing open a crack. I frown as a prickle of danger creeps down my spine. The doors are locked every night; we do enough scouting to know that. The mistress was out on the balcony earlier that evening despite the chill in the Winter air, so she certainly could have forgotten to lock the doors again. Ignoring the pang of unease, I gently open the door.

The snores of the master of the house greet us. Spread-eagled on his bed, his round belly and hairy chest gleam white in the moonlight, along with some of his less... appealing features. Grace and I share a look, and she has to clamp her hand over her mouth to avoid bursting into laughter. Playfully, I cuff her on the head and she scowls, but her chest still shakes with mirth.

I beckon and lead the way, creeping silently across the room. With a hand motion, I send her towards the wardrobe in the corner. The fancy silks the merchant wears will fetch a pretty price from the right people. His girth just means there's more silk per shirt to sell. I creep closer to the bed, heading for the desk beside it. Papers cover every available space, some business missives, some love letters to woo back his wife. She'd left when she found out about the mistress. The merchant had seemed distraught, but he also hadn't stopped seeing the other woman.

As soon as we're fully in darkness, a rustle of movement slides along my skin underneath my clothes, familiar as the sun's warmth. Emotions not my own begin to well from the recesses of my mind, a yearning to move, to fly, to explore...

No. I'll let you out later.

The dim impression of disappointment echoes in my thoughts, but I push it aside and focus.

The merchant's snores cause the faintest rattle of the objects on his desk. Creator, what a fool. The stoppered ink bottle and golden quill tips slide into a pouch at my side. I reach for the first drawer, looking for the bags of coin for his mistress's 'allowance.' It's a surprisingly efficient way for the merchant to deal with having such a woman on the side. I don't respect either of them, but they certainly know their business. She provides him a service, and he pays her accordingly.

A creak sounds behind me, and I spin. Holding perhaps a dozen silk shirts bundled in her arms, Grace's panicked eyes find mine across the dim room. The wardrobe door still swings ever so slightly. I raise a placating hand, and she visibly relaxes, her breath leaving her in a sigh.

She's going to be a good one. I feel a motherly responsibility for the orphans that roam the streets. Many are so like me: rejected by their families, forced to work menial labor or beg just to survive. Donir is filled with them, far more than seems possible. I once heard a nobleman remark that he couldn't tell which was more numerous, the rats or the orphans. Taking his purse had been a matter of propriety.

Grace has a similar tragic story. Her mother died giving birth to her, and her wretched louse of a father never forgave her for the tragedy. He treated her poorly, ignored her, and beat her as she got older. Finally, as his debts mounted, he attempted to sell her to a brothel. Since the Simply burned, none of the others are generous enough to take a malnourished little runt like Grace.

When the brothels weren't an option, he turned to the Khalintari slavers. Luckily, that was when Grace decided to run.

There aren't many places for orphans like Grace to find a home. I know what it's like to have nowhere to go. I started the Family so that those with no reason to hope could find a place as long as they needed it. When we found Grace, an angry shopkeep was chasing her in the Pennies, a knife raised over his head and rage in his voice. She carried, of all things, a single strawberry, hardly enough to keep her alive another day, let alone work to hide the bones that stuck out through the rough cloth of her ragged tunic.

I trusted Timo to handle the man, and he had with his usual clumsy strength. Timo struck him with a right cross out of the middle of the crowd, and the man went down far faster than gravity would normally take you. I shadowed Grace to make sure the Watch didn't catch her. She eluded them, holing up in a hollow space between broken bits of masonry in a little-traveled alley. At that moment I knew she was one of us: nimble, smart, and desperate. Grace only joined the Family a month ago, but she's already pulling her weight.

The wood of the drawer hardly whispers, barely more than a snake sliding across the desert sands. The merchant's snores continue unabated, his corpulent belly rising and falling like the bellows in a smithy. My fingers quest into the dark opening for the sacks of carefully counted money. My hand hits the bottom of the drawer. I gently reach back and forth, but the drawer is empty, the one above also bare.

Odd. I watched the man reach into this drawer and casually toss his mistress a bag with my own eyes less than an hour before. We moved down from the roof across the way as the mistress left and were into the room less than a quarter of an hour later. Where is the money? I reach farther back, knocking as gently as possible for any secret compartments.

My arm is thrust into the desk almost to the shoulder when a sudden shout erupts from the floor below.

"Thief! There's a thief in the house!"

I jerk back on reflex. The desk rattles as I wrestle my arm free of the drawer. The merchant snaps awake, his florid face and grandiose mustachios whipping into view in the dim light.

"What?" he exclaims, his voice groggy and muffled by sleep.

I duck down, easing into a prone position beside the man's bed. I look for Grace's feet through the gap between the bed and the floor. She's standing, of all places, behind the drapes. I silently roll my eyes. Talk about finding the most idiotically obvious place to hide. I need to have a word with that girl.

"He's heading to the back of the house! On him, boys!"

The shout echoes up from below. Feet pound as the three men of the merchant's personal guard run past downstairs. By the forgotten Depths, there's *another* thief in the house? The merchant above me groans and rolls to the side, his bulk eclipsing the faint moonlight as he spins to get out of bed. Hardly daring to breathe, I scuttle underneath the bed like a spider, his feet missing my back by a hairsbreadth. The wooden floors groan under the man's weight as he staggers upright, and the whole bed springs upwards in relief.

My face warms in the dark. Talk about finding the most idiotically obvious places to hide... here I am, hiding under the man's damn *bed*. My reputation as the best thief in Donir fades before my eyes. My apprentice, hiding behind the drapes. Me, cowering under the bed. Hardly masters of our craft.

The merchant stumbles over to his desk, lighting a lamp and staggering towards the door. He doesn't glance around, though his steps look tentative from my limited angle. I figure he's going to go out to join the chase, but instead, he locks the door.

"They better catch the bastard," he mutters under his breath, his nasally voice instantly grating on my nerves. He's panting from the ten-step jaunt to his own bedroom door. How the mistress manages to come back night after night is beyond me. "Waking me at all hours of the night, ugh."

He settles back onto the bed, the mattress driving down and into my back. My eyes bug out of my skull and my breath leaves me in a quiet wheeze as the merchant's full weight settles above me. As he lays down, the pressure eases. I scramble silently to the side. Papers rustle, and he begins muttering unintelligibly to himself. It doesn't seem that our light sleeper is returning to his dreams. And he's left the lamp burning brightly.

Sighing, hoping the man doesn't look up and notice the pair of scuffed black shoes sticking out from under his drapes, I settle in for a long wait. I could get out easily, perhaps without the merchant even noticing, but I can't communicate with Grace, and I'm definitely not going to leave her behind. The Family looks after its own.

A crash from below sends a tremor flashing through the house, and a string of profanities echo up the stairs. The merchant sits up, the downward bulge of the bed luckily to my left.

"He's a quick one! Just stab him, forget trying to grab him. We'll sort it out later," a rough voice calls.

"He's run to the kitchens! Cut him off!"

Whoever the unlucky sod is down below, he's an idiot. Somehow, in the fifteen minutes it took us to come down from the building across the street and jump the garden wall, he snuck in through the balcony doors and stole the very stash we're here for. I should have known the unlocked door wasn't merely a coincidence. Why the man has been found after successfully completing the theft, and down in the main house of all places, is the true mystery. Had the bags been where they were supposed to be, Grace and I would have been gone before the door could finish swinging closed.

The sounds of continued pursuit rattle throughout the house, banging and slamming and the crunching of what sounds like porcelain. The master of the house curses under his breath, then louder as another horrendous crash interrupts the chase below. He levers himself out of bed and trots to the door. Fumbling with the key, he throws the door open and shouts down the stairs. His words are indistinct, something about his guards costing more than they're worth. Several insulting epithets are included for good measure.

You don't hesitate if you want to live in this business. I slip out from under the bed, the merchant's shouts adding to the cacophony below and hiding any sound of my movements. I grab Grace by the arm. Another crash covers her startled squeak. The balcony doors click shut quietly behind me, the merchant's shouts now muted. The rope on my back is too slow, it'll be noticed before we can make ourselves scarce. With a sigh, half regret and half joy, I call to the shadow.

The familiar, comforting smoke erupts from my clothes, noting my urgency. The darkness moves through the air like oil through water, absorbing the lamplight from within and the starlight from above in equal measure. It doesn't reflect light, an impenetrable darkness that defies the senses. Shadow is a poor word for my element, because it requires no light to live, but it's the only word that makes sense.

I will my shadow into a line, and it obeys. A black rope attaches itself neatly to the edge of the balcony without need of ties or support.

"Quick now, Grace," I say briskly, ignoring her wide-eyed shock. "It won't bite. In fact, should you fall, it will catch you."

"The rumors... the stories... they're true?" Grace whispers, her breath raising a cloud in the cool air. I roll my eyes and nudge her forward with my hip as I watch the man inside anxiously. She approaches the midnight strand like a wild animal. Grace hesitates.

"Now, *chela*, or your fear might capture us both," I mutter.

She glances back at me, and her eyes lock onto that now-familiar part of my face that has caused me so much trouble. Her gaze tracks across every whorl of the midnight black symbol, starting at the center of my forehead and wrapping down the left side of my face halfway to the corner of my jaw, all curves and flowing as if in some ancient, unfathomable script. The scar on my cheek is the only imperfection in the dark stain on my skin. It's a damned inconvenient place for the sign of my curse to show up whenever it's called. As if my Seer heritage isn't enough to make me stand out in this light-skinned city.

Luckily, I haven't misjudged Grace. She takes in the new information, her eyes growing resolute, and gives me a firm nod. With a deep breath, she clambers over the balcony. She lets the darkness take her weight and shimmies down the rope just like I taught her. As soon as her feet touch the ground, I abandon my vigil of the merchant and leap from the balcony.

I let myself fall for a few feet, reveling in the feel of the Winter air against my cheeks. With a thought, I resummon the shadow. The darkness cushions my fall and drops me smoothly to the ground to land gently on my feet. The shadow is eager, and my skin burns with unfettered joy. Hiding my curse is like walking through life blindfolded. Connecting to the shadow is like taking a deep breath after an eternity of illness.

Grace gawks at me, but I grab her hand and drag her towards the nearby garden hedge. She needs no prompting to begin scaling the short wall, a convenient trellis providing ample handholds. We reach the top of the wall safe and sound. None of the commotion occurring inside the manor is audible from our perch.

"I didn't think we were going to make it," Grace says breathlessly, turning to me and grinning. As I let the shadow go, the symbol on my face fades in return. Grace notices, but doesn't comment.

"Please. Family forever, *chela,*" I say, lounging back as if I hadn't been filled with the same fear a few moments before. "We always come through, together."

"What does *chela* mean? You keep calling me that," Grace asks, cocking her head quizzically.

"Where I'm from, it means 'little girl.' I say it because I like you. Now, we should be gone before whatever the Depths have brought us can come to light."

"Right," she says, nodding earnestly. "The Depths."

I laugh at her ignorance. Strange, people who have always been bound to the land. I ignore the pang of disquiet that goes through me when I think about how long I've been from the sea.

As I turn to go, a mighty crash echoes through the night. The sound of shattered glass tinkles across the lawn. A lithe form darts towards the same patch of wall we're sitting on, blood streaming from half a dozen small cuts. I recognize the man, no, the boy, just as he reaches the wall. He leaps high and clings to the stones like an insect, his whole body jingling with the sound of the purses he's stolen: Jace, the former apprentice of Jonah Defthands, proud scamp and independent from the Family. The distinctive clack of an arrow striking stone follows him, the sound startling me out of my surprise.

"Don't let him get away!"

I turn back to leave as the boy's hands grip the edge of the wall. Jumping down, I coil my legs and call for the barest hint of shadow to resist the pull of the earth. The shadow pushes upwards against the dark leather straps criss-crossing my torso in the traditional garb of the People, so much stronger and more flexible than the shoddy craftsmanship of the Donirian lands. Landing smoothly, I lift my hands up to Grace to catch her.

Stunned, Grace stares in amazement at the bleeding boy who vaults the wall next to her. He comes down easily, rolling into a dead sprint, at least half of the stolen coins rattling out onto the cobbled street. His skinny legs flash white through his threadbare clothing as he slides around the corner. I don't begrudge the little rogue the money; Creator knows he needs it more than we do.

"Sorry, Kettle!" he throws over his shoulder as he disappears from sight. Grace still sits stunned on the wall.

"Hurry, *chela*, jump!" I say desperately, clapping my hands together.

"Bring him down!"

The rough shout echoes through the night. She smiles at me, full of trust, and brings her hands up to push off. Her body jolts. The arrow bursts through her chest and mists my face with her blood. She falls, boneless, limp, all of the dainty elegance gone from her limbs. I catch her, spinning her over, praying to the Creator with all of my soul. Her lungs fight for air, but blood seeps from the corners of her mouth. Life already ebbs from her eyes as they vacantly reflect the stars. With a shudder, she falls still.

The shadow hiding under my clothes boils out without conscious thought. I can't look away, even when the starlight reflected in her eyes darkens under the cover of my curse.

The voices of the men from the merchant's personal guard drift in the night. They laugh and joke about confirming their kill and the reward they'll receive. My heart freezes like the frigid depths of the northern seas. I stand up, the shadow forming a sword in my hand. My steps don't raise so much as a whisper of sound. The dust on the streets lays quiet and still at my passing as if even the earth fears what treads upon it. I round the corner of the house to see the three men walking forward, a lantern held high. When they see me, they squint, their small brains desperately trying to make sense of the scene before them.

I don't raise my blade or make a noise. I just begin running. They glance at one another. In that moment of hesitation, I strike. I scythe through them before their eyes can register surprise. Twirling between them, my blade cuts high and low. The shadow knows no resistance. The men fall in pieces, the sound of their blood and bones hitting the ground unsatisfying. I glance at the house, thinking of the fat merchant, but the need for revenge evaporates as suddenly as it came. More death will serve no one. I step over three growing pools of blood on my way back to Grace.

The sword evaporates into smoke, the shadow rising up and gently wiping Grace's blood from my face. A kindness, what little the shadow can do to comfort me. I reach her body, bending down and slowly lifting her in my arms. She weighs nothing, as if her body is little more than a dream. If I squeeze too tightly, even this sad remnant of her life will disappear. I walk into the nearest alley, scaling it and calling on the shadow to draw Grace's body up. We set out across the rooftops, the tiny child cradled in my arms.

Even though it takes me half the night, even though I'm bone weary as I stagger up the steps, even though I know that her body means nothing now that the pure soul that animated it has fled, I carry her home. Because the Family looks after its own.

***

"I'll kill him for ya," Timo growls, his anger heating the room in waves. His gigantic hands curl into equally gigantic fists. "Tha' little bastard is meat."

"Wait," I say, my voice tired and dull.

Grace's body is freshly in the ground outside the city walls. The city cemetery is long since full, the few remaining spots designated for the nobility and the wealthy. The funeral was a somber, silent affair. As was fitting, we laid Grace into the ground at midnight. The twinkling stars were the only witnesses, the shadows welcoming Grace into the next life. We hadn't said anything but the simple words that bound us together: family forever.

Grace is the first we've lost in two months, perhaps a casualty to the speed at which we're growing. I can't train them all fast enough. You have to be careful, quiet, and above all decisive in the business. Grace failed at that final test, and she paid the heaviest price. My soul darkens at the thought of the little street rat who put us in this situation. Some part of me knows that he can't be blamed for this accidental convergence, but logic is often worth its weight in gold.

"Why?" Timo says, turning back to me. "He refused ta join the Family, spit in our face, and now he's killed one o' us!"

"He spit in *your* face, I believe," Corna drawls from the corner. "While I'm your sister and all that, I know the boy could have been convinced with a bit more... tact."

"Shut yer hole," Timo spits back. "What's done is done, and the boy has done it. He needs ta die."

"Do you have any idea how nonsensical what you just said is?" Corna rolls her eyes. "How many times can we fit the word 'done' in a single sentence? Perhaps if you weren't so dun, we would have already made up our minds what needs to be done."

Timo looks confused, as well he might, but I just close my eyes. My two lieutenants are as different as night and day. Corna was raised a noble of a minor house, her parents reasonably successful traders in fine cloth. When she was declared a woman at fifteen (a barbaric practice, in the Isles you become a woman when you damn well please), her parents arranged for her to marry a man who was two tiers above her in rank and four times her age. Being Corna, she would have none of that particular bargain, disappearing in the night and making her way to the capital. Her pretty smile and auburn locks allowed her to pass through doors that should have been closed to her. Over the course of two years, Corna danced and twirled her way through half of the high society in Donir, naturally keeping any gifts granted her by suitors and robbing them blind on the back end of each relationship. When I met her, she was the most wanted woman in the city, the reward on her head practically astronomical. We faked up a corpse and collected that money for good measure, putting the case of the Demonic Debutant to bed.

Timo, on the other hand, was born on the left side of a gutter, raised on the right, and taught to beg and steal before he had the strength to crawl out. His mother used him for as long as she could, back when he was young and reasonably adorable, but he grew so fast that soon she was forced to switch tacks. She convinced him to take up strong-arm robbery, mugging the drunk and the unwary. His giant fists pounded away, and each strike drained the big man of humanity. I found him drunk in an alley, two knife wounds festering high on his chest, closer to dead than alive. He couldn't have been more than seventeen at the time. I had been walking quietly through the alley when he began to shout, delirious and unaware, the words of a play: "What passes here but the long approach to silence? Only in the stillness of the grave can we finally rest." Somehow, a street tough from the desperate edge of the Abyss had learned the final words to *The Lost Lore of Isa*. I was confused enough to ask him how.

Both of them jumped at the opportunity to start again, despite their skepticism of something so intrinsically different from their lives as the idea of a family. But the nature of the Family is that we are all orphans, all cast aside, each of us lonely and desperate. We are all of us looking for something to belong to, someone to love and to trust and to sleep soundly next to. When I left the Isles, I vowed I would have that feeling, even if I had to fight and kill for it. So I *made* it happen.

The two of them are still bickering, their words like a gentle caress in the back of my head, comforting, reassuring. Grace's death cut me adrift, but the familiar arguing between the two returns me to ground. I still have the rest of my Family to look after. I can't dwell.

"Enough," I say quietly. Timo turns to me, mid-tirade, and drops his arms. Corna just cocks an eyebrow. "I would hear your thoughts. Take your time; think it through. What should we do about Jace?"

"Ya know what I want," Timo says. "It's tha' third job he's botched for us, and now he's killed Gracie! We canna let him live in our city."

"Regrettably, Kettle, I agree," Corna says reluctantly, shooting Timo a look as if the very act of agreeing with him is, well, disagreeable. "While I do think that he could have, at one time, become one of us, he has put his dirty little foot in our business far too many times. I don't know if we need to kill him, as my simple brother suggests, but something does need to be done."

"Is the answer to death more death?" I ask, shaking my head. "Very well. It's late. I'll sleep on it. The two of you do the same. Have Jeld go and watch the boy's nest in case we need to find him."

"He's a slippery one," Corna agrees. She stands, her silk nightgown leaving little to the imagination. It's a credit to Timo that he doesn't so much as glance at her as she stretches. The two really have become siblings. "Are we sure Jeld can mark him if he leaves?"

"Fine, let Sario and Ret tag along. They need the experience. Tell them that, if they're spotted, they'll sleep outside for a week."

Our manse looms innocuously in the middle of the Corpses, the set of dilapidated merchant and noble houses stuck on the wrong side of the Abyss from the market and the palace. The Abyss had been one of the many things I gawked at when I first walked Donir's streets three years before. Halfway to the walls on the northwestern side of the city, the Abyss is a gigantic circular pit in the cityscape, stretching down into impenetrable darkness. On the night of the Desolation fifteen years ago, tens of thousands of souls fell into the Abyss as the ground just dropped away underneath the city. Supposedly, the Sealord had killed the cursed Master of Earth, and his death unleashed the cataclysm.

Though the manse is as broken down and ugly as its fellows on the outside, the inside is the product of close to three highly successful years of theft and mischief, a display of opulence so absurd that it even makes me cringe from time to time: ornamental rugs spun so delicately you feel as if clouds cushion your feet, each piece of furniture carefully selected or crafted from exotic woods, each wall adorned with tapestries and art worth more than the rest combined. The Family lives like royalty, beyond the fathoming of anyone who has never entered the house.

My feet are silent on the extravagant rugs and even quieter on the polished hardwood. We could recruit every single orphan in the city if we showed them the inside of our home, but we don't. It's easy to choose to be a part of something beautiful. I don't want a child to come into the Family just because she sees the house and wants a warm place to sleep. I tell them nothing but that we're thieves, and the life is hard and dangerous. A child shows courage when she chooses to be a part of something difficult and frightening.

The quiet knock of wood draws my eyes to three young children playing with knick knacks in the corner. They are all fairly new, each less than three months living with the Family. I can't help but smile at their laughter and their tiny bodies. Already, Elan has filled out, his bones no longer peeking from beneath the skin. Tera is healthy for the first time in her short life, her cheeks bright and red from laughing. Kit is quiet, but stern, his gaze focused down on his hands as he plays. A flash of metal turns my grin to a frown.

"Children, what are you playing?" I call, walking over.

"It's a game Uncle Timo taught us!" Tera says. My heart sinks. This can*not* be good.

"Yeah," Elan says, eyes fixed on Kit's hands. "Timo said we need to learn if we want to start pulling our weight."

The way the boy says it makes me certain he has no idea what 'pulling our weight' really means. I reach the circle of children and suppress a sigh. Kit has a short knife in one hand, quickly and confidently jabbing the blade between his splayed fingers. Two shallow cuts gleam red on his fingers, and I can't hold in a groan at the bandages wrapped around the fingers of the other two.

I almost reach down and snatch the knife out of their hands, but I stop. Before tonight's events, I probably would have. But Grace's death reminds me that the children need to grow up far faster than I want them to. Kit begins to pick up the pace, the knife blurring as he slams it into the wooden board they've laid over the hardwood. His dexterity is impressive, the knife sure and true despite the speed. Both of the other children watch, eyes wide.

"Do you know how to play this game, Mother?" Kit asks, his voice calm and even despite the knife's continued play.

"I find it rather dull, but I've played with knives before, yes."

"Can you do it faster than me?" he asks, stopping suddenly and flipping the knife into his off hand. The boy can't be more than nine, but the glint in his eye, the challenge, shows that age is nothing but a number after the streets.

"Perhaps another time," I say, yawning. "I think we should all get to bed."

"Please, Mother!" Elan says, eagerly looking up at me. "Will you show us how to do it?"

"Yes, Mother, please," Tera joins in.

"Oh, all right," I mutter, sitting down in the circle. "But just once, and then we all head to sleep."

Kit slides me the board, offering me the knife and a smirk. The boy is certain of himself, I have to give him that. I take the knife from him and flip it quickly through the air a few times, testing the balance. I grimace. It's one of the steak knives from the kitchen, tip blunted and bent from the game. Timo and his stupid ideas.

Without preamble I begin, opening my fingers wide. Firmly, yet almost gently, I stab the wood beneath. Picking up the pace with each revolution, my grip remains certain and my aim impeccable. The countless tiny scars on my hands are mostly from a living a dangerous life, but a few are from the first moments after I learned this stupid game back in the Isles. Still. Kit feels like he's superior, like 'Mother' should be challenged? Let's see the look in his eyes when I finish.

Soon, I have the knife humming, the sound of each strike on the wood blending into one long knock, unbreaking. I flip the knife up, catch it in my left hand, and press my right to the wood. Before the sound can die, I resume the breakneck pace with my offhand. The children gasp in delight, and I smile to myself as the knife continues to work. I switch back and forth twice in rapid succession. Turning to look at Kit, my hands move even faster than before. He smiles at me, a self-conscious grin of self-reproach. Winking, I flip the knife and offer it to him with a flourish.

“Perhaps, one day, one of you will be better at the game than I am,” I offer as he takes the knife. “But not yet. Now, children, let's make sure that we use daggers from the arms closet, not knives from the kitchen, okay?”

“Yes, Mother,” they chorus.

“Good. Now, off to bed. I've heard that children don't get any taller if they don't sleep. You don't want to be tiny forever, do you?”

They break up the game obediently, heading towards their beds. The children stay together in the communal rooms where servants once slept. They are given a few simple rules: respect your elders, respect each other, and respect our house. They have to recognize they are one family, whether they want to or not. I walk them over to the entrance, patting each on the head before turning to leave.

"Mother," Elan calls, his freckled skin peeking out from a shock of carrot-orange hair. "What do I do if I get scared? I keep waking up, and I..."

His little blue eyes are shining, tears glistening in the dim lamplight. Who are these children? I almost never learn their whole story, at least not quickly. The scars of the past are too deep, too fresh. Each has a particular tragedy. I can do nothing for the past; human beings are never meant to fend for themselves alone. All I can do is help them move towards a brighter future.

"If you wake, I'll be there."

I hold out my hand. He grasps it tentatively, smiling through his fear. His white skin contrasts markedly with my own, so foreign to this pale city. Too pale to fit in at home, too dark to fit in here. With a heavy sigh, I walk with him into the narrow corridor that leads to his pallet, one among many. The orphans, ranging from children to adolescents, look up from their conversations or their games, but only for a moment.

Elan settles in under his blanket, pulling the soft white cotton to his chin. I smile and lay down next to him, cradling my head in the crook of my arm. The little man tries valiantly to keep his eyes open, but he loses the battle. The fear leaves his eyes as they flutter closed. His mouth opens, and his frail, wheezing breaths break my heart. I can't stop myself from glancing at the pallet Grace claimed in the corner a month ago. She came in so fearless, so determined to fit in and prove herself. Perhaps I rushed her into the job. She could have stayed here, learning and growing and healthy. Her death is on me.

A gentle hand comes to rest on my shoulder. Kit holds out a pillow solemnly, as if he is a king granting me a boon for some service. I take it gratefully, sliding it under my head. My black hair pools into my line of vision, and I adjust so it won't brush Elan's sleeping face. A blanket wraps around my shoulders, more than one pair of tiny hands smoothing the sheet over me and tucking me in.

"Goodnight, Mother," Kit whispers, the sound echoed by a dozen small voices.

I sigh. Grace probably wouldn't have lasted as long as she had if I hadn't taken her in. Some merchant would have caught her stealing, or the Watch would have gotten overenthusiastic in their punishment and thrown her in the sewers. My children need what I can give. They need someone who can watch out for them and keep them safe. Even as that word echoes through my thoughts, my jaw clenches. I *will* keep them safe. I can't let what happened to Grace happen again. My children deserve better.

Talan has been fighting again. Even though he comes home each day with a smile, it isn't hard to see when his face is puffy or he's moving more tentatively. I watch through the window as he walks up to our small house on the edge of the village. He's limping, wincing slightly as he takes the uneven wooden stairs. It wouldn't be so bad, if my brother wasn't normally such a gentle soul. It wouldn't be so bad, if it wasn't all my fault.

He staggers into the room, one of three in our tiny slice of paradise, and slowly puts his hands on his knees, breathing deeply. I watch him from the door to our room, fighting the tears that try desperately to flow, but I can't contain the smallest sob. He looks up sharply at the tiny break in the silence.

"No, chela, no. It is nothing," he says, his voice already deep and rich despite his age. He stands and gives me the winning smile which normally graces his face. His dark skin practically gleams in the setting sun, his teeth white against the midnight beauty of his complexion. The sight serves as a reminder that I am different. That my skin, so much lighter than that of my brother, is causing all of these problems. My hair, so much straighter, marks me as different.

I can't contain it any longer, and I burst into tears. He comes to me, trying to console me, as if I want to be another *burden on him once he comes home. I push his arms away. He tries to grab me, but the pain hunches him over. I run out the open front door, ignoring his shouts, voice hoarse against the stiff wind. My feet carry me through the tall grass that leads away from the village. I can't run anywhere else; I'm not welcome.*

I thread my way through the trees, ignoring the swarming bugs and the palm fronds that sway in my path. Tears blur my vision in the fading sunlight as I struggle through a particularly dense patch of undergrowth. Vines tangle around my body. With a growl of frustration, I force my way through, ripping the vines in two.

Perhaps I can run far enough. If I make it to the sea and follow the coast as far as the island allows, I can give Talan a chance. He deserves it. He is such a bright boy, his studies with the Seer a mark of pride and dignity. He's learning to become a leader of our people, one of the pillars of our society. It will only hurt him if I stay.

My bare feet grow dark and brown with mud as I run, my skin for once matching Talan's color. My breath comes in short, staccato bursts. The humidity soaks the soft linen strips of my shirt, the near-constant rain of the jungle unrelenting even in the dry season. I duck under a low-hanging vine, only afterwards realizing I have just avoided death. It was a noose snake, and a big one. The coils of the snake hang low as if just another vine in the thickness of the jungle, but if a creature touches those deadly scales, the noose will close, and the mighty serpent will drag them into the air, suffocating and broken.

With an internal shudder, I keep running, knowing it can't be far. I've been running for over an hour. Talan is hurt; he can't follow me in that state. The mud and crushed detritus of the jungle begin to grow sparser, patches of sand and empty space appearing between trees. Before long, I begin to hear the crash of the sea, a gentle and slow counterpoint to the thundering of my racing heart. The smell of salt in the air breaks through the dense forest, and I breathe deeply. I fight against the smile that tugs at my face. I shouldn't be happy to be running away, I know. But Talan deserves better.

And so do I.

I break through the treeline so suddenly I stumble to a stop, feet sinking into the deep sand of the beach. My eyes drink in the sight of the ocean. Waves race up to claim the land before bowing to the forces of nature and slinking away, defeated. The water stretches as far as I can see. The last bit of scarlet light from the setting sun glimmers like rubies on the surface. I stand until the sun retreats fully, allowing my breath to return and my heartbeat to slow.

I drop slowly onto the sand. My chin comes to rest on my knees and my arms wrap around my legs. Stars peek out in the sky, warily offering their beauty to the world below as darkness fully falls. The brilliant moon, nearly full, crests the horizon in a shimmer of silver. I sit for hours, my mind blank, accepting and joining with the beauty of the world. Crashing sounds in the forest behind me, the kind that only large animals make, but I don't turn around. No predator seeks out my people. We've made far too frightening an impression for such nonsense.

Finally, I close my eyes and slump onto the sand, resting my head against the crook of my arm. The cool ocean breeze caresses my skin, and I find the peace that so often eludes me in the comfort of my bed at home. The gentle voice of the ocean harmonizes with the quiet song of the wind, and my consciousness begins to drift.

Perhaps it won't be so bad, being alone. I'll only need to worry about myself. Talan can finally be free of me. He won't have to fight the other boys when they say mean things about our mother or me. He will be able to live his life, as it is meant to be. He will become the next Seer, and his world will be so much happier.

Without me.

I wake to shouts, distant but drawing closer. Blinking blearily, I stagger to my feet. My heart drops out of my chest. The freedom of the previous night evaporates, the lightness and harmony of the world dissipating before the familiar voice calling my name.

"Aea!" Talan shouts, his voice practically frantic with worry. "Aea!"

I turn to run, to hide, to drown myself in the sea if necessary, but he bursts out of the jungle and runs to me. His strong arms wrap around my chest. He sobs into my back, and I let him cry, stiffly enduring his embrace, hating myself for the comfort I feel.

"Talan..." I start, my face trying to be stone, but cracking under the weight of my grief. "I need to go. It is better this way."

"How can you say that, chela?" he whispers against my back. "We are all that remains. We are all that we have. What could I ever do without you?"

"You could live, as you were meant to live," I say, the words ringing true. "I am the cause of all your sorrow."

"You are wrong! You are so wrong," he gasps, squeezing me tighter. "You are the only source of my joy. Do not leave me, chela, please, Aea. When I am Seer, when we are grown, the others will have no choice but to accept us. We must survive, for now, together."

"I should have run farther," I say dully. The conflict in me threatens to tear open my soul and send it screaming into the Depths. I can't escape him. Not for his sake, and not for mine. I'm not strong enough.

"Do not say that, Aea. Come home with me. I will make us soup, and the day will be ours to spend together."

"You are better without me," I say, one last time, desperate to make him see. "I will hold you back, an anchor to your joy."

"Come," he responds, ignoring me and taking my hand. "Let us return. If we hurry, we will still be in the right hour for a midday meal."

I let him drag me back, my feet still caked in the dark mud of the jungle. They look good, dark like that. If only I had been born with skin like the rest of my people, perhaps life would have been normal. I might have had friends, and flirted with boys as the others did. The dimness of the jungle begins to close off the light of the sun, throwing the pair of us into gloom and shadow. I feel safe with Talan holding my hand. His strong back parts the undergrowth before me. I know even as I walk back that I am the worst form of coward.

I wake to a gentle hand on my face, small and soft. Elan wipes away the tears I've cried in my sleep. A small hand comes to rest on my back and another caresses my hair. The children gather around, doing their best to comfort me.

"Do not cry, Mother," Elan says, his high voice soft in the darkness. "We are with you."

"Sleep, Mother," I hear a voice say above my head. "We are here for you."

I sigh, their love quieting the turmoil of my spirit. With another deep breath, I fall back into sleep. Thankfully, I do not dream.

Chapter 2
Jace
The Third Day of Winter
In the Year 5219, Council Reckoning

Rain, unseasonable in the Kingdom of the Sea after the turn of the season, falls in fat dollops of ice, washing the filth of the streets of Donir out of the gates and down the long slopes leading up to the ancient city. I shiver violently, my soaked burlap shirt and ragged pants little shield against the frigid rain. The cold doesn't seem to bother Kettle where she stands, feet planted firmly on the edge of an apple cart. Her eyes find me across the square, her dark, delicate features pressed into a stoic mask. Turning to the crowd, she opens her mouth to speak.

"People of Donir, listen well. I am Kettle, Mother of the Family, and I come before you to announce–"

"Shut up, Isles witch!" a man cuts in angrily.

Timo, Kettle's muscle, a mountain of a man graced with all the subtlety of an avalanche, steps out from next to the apple cart and slams a giant fist into the stomach of the man who shouted. He crumples with a groan, splashing into the stream of water flowing towards the east gate. Corna, Kettle's beautiful lieutenant, kicks the man over onto his back and places the heel of her boot against his throat.

"Anyone else have a problem?" she asks pleasantly. The foot traffic halts as the sparse crowd of the Corpses turns to witness. No one dares speak.

"I come before you to announce the gravest of penalties," Kettle continues as if nothing happened. "The rogue thief known as Jace of the Simply is hereby banished from my domain on pain of death. His crimes are many and personal. Should he be found anywhere in this city come nightfall, that hour is his last."

Shit.

The majority of the people in the square have no idea who I am. Many are simply merchants or pedestrians, wending their way towards warmth and shelter. The ones who matter, though, the ones who have any idea who Kettle is, stare at my unfortunate self. Kettle has effectively signed my death warrant. My entire life has been lived in Donir, all fifteen years of it. I don't know where else to go or how to live.

After a long moment, even the random passersby are starting to notice so many people staring at the bedraggled boy in the corner. I dart forward and around the corner into a busier thoroughfare, losing myself as quickly and efficiently as I can in the heavier crowd of the cold Winter day. The entire Family will be after me come nightfall, and the sky is dark even at noon. The definition of 'night' might just get a little blurry to some of the overzealous looking to prove something to Kettle. I work my way as fast as I can to an alley some way down from the square, scaling the roughly-made gutter and scrambling over the lip of a tavern's roof. The warmth coming off the brick chimney nearby does nothing to quell the shakes rising in my chest, the shouts of laughter making a mockery of my desperation.

I'm dead. What chance does a beggared thief have of surviving outside the city? I can't do any honest work. I don't even know where the nearest city is. Sobs wrack my chest in paralyzing jerks and starts. I lost everything and everyone I had ever known when the Tide burned the Simply two years ago.

And now this.

Jonah wasn't a member of the Family, so why is this happening to me? Why-

Shaking myself back to the present, I do my best to stifle the sobs that well up in my chest. The sky has already grown noticeably darker. I curse, scrabbling up and looking around. My muscles are stiff with the cold, so I shake them out as I scan the rooftops. I can't see anyone watching me, but that doesn't mean no one is there. I take off over the rooftops, leaping over alleys and launching off of gutters.

Following a winding path to make sure I'm not followed, I slowly make my way back towards the dilapidated mansion I call home. Before I reach the familiar clay tiles, I drop down to a crawl, searching every shadow with care. They have to be there. The pronouncement is hours old. Even though I've been careful never to give away my hiding place, there are no secrets among thieves. At least none worth keeping.

With an inward shrug, I stand and let gravity slide me down the slick clay tiles of the roof. I have never been known for my patience. I gather speed as I approach the edge, a painful, perhaps fatal fall awaiting me if I mess up. Flying over the edge, I spin and latch on to the lip of the roof. Only seven of my fingers actually have purchase and the rest are hanging on air. My grip may not be perfect, but it is plenty. I swing my body gently backwards into the open air over the street twenty feet below me, then snap forward, my fingers absorbing the strain as I fly feet first into an open window.

I say open, but, honestly, there just isn't a window anymore. The building is decrepit, one of the stains on the beautiful cityscape of Donir. Paint stands out in a few patches in the corners, but the rest of the room is a mixture of stone and wood skeleton peeking through once-majestic walls. One of the Donir's Stars, the myriad of ever-burning lamps illuminating the streets, still flickers just a dozen yards down the street from the house, so whoever once lived here was wealthy. They just faced the misfortune of living on the wrong side of the Abyss. At least they hadn't been so unlucky as to live, you know, *above* the Abyss.

Dusty floorboards creak under my weight, but silence is my only greeting. Everything looks just as I left it...

I force my gaze to keep moving as I pass over the booted feet of someone hiding behind the rotten drapes of a window facing the alley. What an idiotic place to hide. I note a scuffing in the dust that indicates someone is behind my chest, as well, and the slight scrape of a foot sliding across wood announces someone standing by the window through which I've just entered.

The first attacker surges forward from behind. I drop down to my belly, kicking my feet out behind me and connecting squarely with his leading ankle. Something crunches and I wince inwardly, but my body, desperate and terrified, is already up and moving to the chest. As the shrill scream of the first attacker–a woman–pierces the room, I dive forward and kick the chest with all of my weight.

The massive thing skates back two paces, slamming into the man crouched behind it with enough force to send him bowling over and down a ragged hole in the floor. He disappears with a yelp of surprise and a rumble of breaking wood and mortar. I spin back to the man behind the drapes just as he steps out. Perhaps four seconds have passed.

We size each other up. He has dark hair and dark eyes sharply contrasted with skin the color of new parchment. He wears the dark leathers of a thief, and I acknowledge the dagger in his hand and the easy way he holds it. He takes me in, a burlap sack for a shirt and pants that barely reach my ankles, tattered and frayed without knees or a proper hem. He starts to smile, but then he notices the gibbering woman on the floor and the still-settling debris of his friend's descent. His grin fades.

"Won't be long, boy," he mutters low in his throat. "You can't beat all of us."

I wish there's something I can say, some rebuttal that will sting the man, but he's right.

In a flash of movement, he whips his arm forwards. I throw myself to the side. His thrown dagger cuts right through my worthless sack and the flesh beneath, and a long, wicked scour of welling blood burns along my ribs. When I look up, he's gone. The sound of his running feet slapping on the cobblestones fades into the distance.

Clutching my side, I walk over to the woman and strike her a square blow to the temple. She sags back onto the floorboards with a groan. Jonah taught me how to punch, but damn if her skull isn't harder than it should be. I suck my knuckles, though the pain of the cut is quickly overwhelming everything else.

Darkness has fallen fully. These three were overeager, but the rest of the thieves will begin the search before long. I want to care, Creator knows I want to, but I'm tired. I look down dully at the blood pouring out of my side, and I barely feel myself slump down to the rotten wood. Some part of me screams to get up, to run, to hide, but I'm just so damnably exhausted. And cold. If I can sleep, for just a few moments...

I jerk awake from dreams of grinning faces in dark hoods and the glitter of steel. My hands go to my side. I'm hurt, but it's practically nothing. My eyes pop wide when I notice the dark swathe of blood down my shirt, spreading into my pants and into a small pool on the floor.

How am I breathing? How can I possibly survive losing that much blood? Why do I feel so... alive?

The woman is still unconscious on the ground, but something else tickles at the back of my brain. I take a dozen breaths before it hits me: the room is dark. Not just the dark of night, but genuinely dark, as if... I scramble up, warily avoiding the pool of my own blood, and go to the window. My mouth falls open.

Impossible. One of the Stars of Donir has gone out. The flames have burned for so long they are considered eternal. A common saying of the city is that 'Donir's light will show the Creator home.' No one expects him to come home any time soon, either.

I can't worry about it, though. I've been asleep for less

than fifteen minutes, but the sky is true dark, not just the false night of cloud cover. I need to change my circumstances, and fast. If I stay, I'm dead. If I leave, I'm dead. What I need is a serious influx of wealth to give me a fighting chance of living beyond the city. The fat merchant's take mostly fell in my flight the night before, and the rest went to food. My plans for the Historian need to move up. The rain stops, I gather my materials, and I slip out the open window into the welcome cloak of the night.

***

My racing heart refuses to slow as I creep forward over the rooftops. My hands shake throughout my descent into the alley next to my target, hard enough I'm thankful I reach the bottom. I crouch down in front of the Historian's inset window and take a shaky breath. My entire life on one roll of the dice. If the man doesn't have what I need...

What I need, right now, is to focus.

I take a hundred long breaths to make myself a part of the stillness. The stillness isn't silence, which doesn't exist, but instead a kind of waiting, sleeping watchfulness. Although it can show itself at any time of day, the stillness most often manifests in the night. The clouds pass lethargically overhead, filtering the soft moonlight and obscuring the stars. Their slow, dreary movement only strengthens the stillness. A Star of Donir flickers at the corner of the alley, but the cheerful flame doesn't reach the window, leaving me placed within the deep, unblemished stillness. The house before me creaks under its own weight, a not-so-silent brick monolith. A black rat scrabbles at whatever lies in the corner between two clay bricks, though even its movements seem furtive. The wind whistles gently through the alley, stirring up the small pile of trash in the corner and raising up the hairs on my bare arms. Even so, the stillness remains.

You might feel it in the last sliver of consciousness before you fall asleep, when all the world is at peace and yet all the terror of the night rises in your chest. It skitters along at the edges of your thoughts as you walk alone at night, your footsteps muffled against the darkness and your eyes trained wide for the slightest movement. You've felt it break with the first gentle sob at a quiet funeral, when all of the emotion seems somehow false until it is given voice. It is there, waiting for the opportunity to creep, carefully, laying a quiet, tense gauze over the world.

I remember the first time I ever felt the stillness.

Jonah takes me up onto the roof of the Simply in the deep of the night. The evening is clear, and the moon shines brightly. He looks down at me, smiling and rustling my hair before his dark eyes turn back out over the city. I walk up and place my chin on the low stone wall at the edge of the building. If I could mirror his stance I would, but I'm not tall enough yet. The city is the same as always. The same buildings stretch too far for my eyes to reach, the same ten thousand Stars light up nearly every street. I don't understand what we're up here for. I want to be like Jonah more than anything, but I'm bored. I start to fidget, but just as I begin to move, Jonah's hand closes painfully around my shoulder.

"Don't move, Jace," Jonah says, his voice gentler than I expect. "I want you to listen."

"What am I listening to?"

"Just listen," he says again, turning back to the city and releasing me.

I try hard not to rub my shoulder, but my hand comes up against my will. Only for a minute. I love Jonah, so I still and stretch out onto my toes, craning my neck to the city to hear something, anything. I hear cats in the alley below, their droning wails the first sign of a fight. I hear boots marching as a passing patrol of the Watch make their weary rounds. I hear one of the girls in the rooms a floor below us, crying out in counterpoint to the grunts of a strange man.

Listening harder than I ever have before, I begin to hear other sounds, more subtle sounds. I hear the wind for the first time. I hear, barely, the guttering of the flame in the lamppost down below. Then, in the back of my mind, I begin to hear something else. More than hearing, it is feeling. Something is there, lurking in the dark recesses of the city and of my mind. A chill shoots down my spine, and I look up at Jonah with confusion.

"What is that?" I ask.

"That, Jace, is the stillness."

I don't understand, but I want to be like Jonah more than anything, so I nod seriously.

I wanted to be like him all the way up until the ax came down.

I snap back to the present as I feel myself begin to slip out of the stillness. I resume my deep, quiet breaths and push away the anger and sorrow in my heart. I can't afford mistakes. Jonah was like a father to me, and he taught me more than anyone else in my life. But he wasn't careful enough. It isn't that I don't want to be like Jonah anymore. It's that I have to be better.

When I'm ready again, I reach out and run my fingers gently along the glass. The touch doesn't illicit even the slightest whisper. I pull out a thin metal pick from along my scalp. The grease from my hair actually serves to make the pick's movements quieter, and no one ever searches a thief's dirty, 'lice-ridden' hair. I wedge my fingernails under the edge of the window and pull upwards gently. I've been by several times in the past few weeks to oil every available surface, so I'm a bit more comfortable as I increase the pressure. The window begins to slide upwards noiselessly. It catches abruptly after a short span as the chain holding the window closed stretches taut, a small lock holding each end together.

I bend forward, holding up the window with my left hand and slipping my right hand under the edge. I insert the pick into the lock by feel, and with a few twists it opens with a soft click.

The stillness fractures. I sense as the house becomes suddenly watchful. That click is a noise so foreign to the night that the world resists its intrusion. I struggle not to put the window down and run, but I can't afford to back down now. Better a swift death at the Wave's hands than whatever lies in store for me if the Family catches me. The lock itself remains in its original position, barely. The chain and the window all stand in perfect silence beneath my straining fingers.

Slowly, ever so hesitantly, the stillness creeps back. The cracked silence mends, and I breathe a sigh of relief. Delicately grabbing both ends of the thin chain, I relax my grip on the window and let the lock sag open onto the sill. Lowering the chain to rest as well, I lever the window silently upward and slip forward into the darkness.

My foot encounters the expected table underneath the window, and I maneuver myself around the knick knacks on its surface by patience and memory. I let the window shut, reattaching the chain but leaving the lock open for the way out. My calves are trembling, the effort of staying in a poised, crouched position weighing on my strength. I transfer my weight slowly to one foot, swinging the other down and onto the polished wood floor. Off the table, I survey my surroundings, noting the red velvet couches and their respective end tables as objects to avoid.

I'm here to rob the old Historian: the man whose life's work is compiling the entire history of the world. He does scribing on the side to support himself, and I first noticed the potential for a worthy take when I watched a nobleman pass him some real, actual gold for his services. Every time he is paid for his work, he retreats back to the same section of the house and comes back without the money in his possession. He doesn't live an extravagant life, so there's got to be a pile of gold somewhere back there.

I slip along the wall, stalking towards the door to my right. In the next room, the Historian does his scribbling, and the doorway in the back of his study leads to the reaches of the house that hold my interest. I pause for just a moment as I cross into the study, admiring the shelves and shelves of books lining every wall. My mother used to read me tales from *The Enchantress*, tales of nobles with generous hearts and men who save women from some dastardly fate. In my experience, both are myths. Nobles are nothing but greedy assholes, and men usually exploit women however they can. Still, the stories stuck with me.

I turn the handle of the door carefully. I haven't oiled these hinges, so I patiently exert pressure until I feel the door open to my touch. The heavy door swings open silently. As I take a step, however, the hairs on the back of my neck prickle. Something is different about the house. The stillness isn't broken, or even damaged as when the lock opened, but something has changed. I close my eyes and struggle to figure out what it is, but no sound reaches me. The stillness persists, so I ignore my instincts and close the door behind me silently.

And I'm immediately struck blind. No windows open onto this section of the house, so I lack even weak starlight to see by. I reach out with my left hand, finding the wall within easy reach. My right arm finds nothing but empty space. My head begins to spin in the impenetrable darkness, but I cling to the wall and take a silent step forward, then again, my pace so unbelievably slow I'm certain it'll be morning before I find anything, but I can't afford to run into an unexpected table.

My left hand trails around a smooth plaster corner. Still having no idea where the other walls are, or even what kind of room I'm in, I decide to stay on the left wall. I don't want to risk a light, both because I don't know if anyone lives in these rooms and because it will be difficult to see any other sources of light if I have my own.

My leading hand prevents me from running directly into a door in the darkness. I let go of the wall, reaching out and running my sensitive fingers over the wood. Something about the intricate carvings sends alarms jangling in the back of my head. I try the handle and find the door locked. Reaching forward and pushing, gently but purposefully, I smile as the door doesn't so much as rattle in its hinges. Nodding to the watchful darkness, I dig out a piece of flint and a small stone. Scraping the two together as gently as possible, I produce a few weak sparks to get a look at the door.

It's made out of a wood I've never seen before. Inlays of weaving flame decorate every bit of the vibrant auburn surface, and the solidity of the door is instantly obvious. The lock has me risking another slight scrape. The sparks reveal a contraption entirely foreign to me. The keyhole is perfectly round and relatively wide, but no other adornment gives me any hints as to what to do about it.

I shrug my shoulders, relaxing my muscles as I reach for the pick along my scalp. Its longer sibling emerges from its secret place on the back of my thigh. The two pick and tension wrench in hand, I take a deep breath and slide them quickly into the lock. I sweep the pick around the perimeter of the lock, counting as I feel the click of tumblers under pressure from my touch. Ten. A reasonably complex lock.

Something, though, gives me pause. I sit back, frowning at my invisible nemesis. I insert the longer pick back into the lock, pushing deeper this time. The lock swallows nearly the entire thing before it catches. I sweep the pick around, feeling a second ring of tumblers deeper into the door. Ten more. An impossibly complex lock.

I almost give up. The back of my neck still prickles from whatever aberration exists in the stillness, and the lock is so complex that, even though I'm confident, I'm not certain I can manage it.

But never say I back down from a challenge.

I don't know how many combinations I try. I don't know how many times I blink sweat out of my open, staring eyes. After an hour, perhaps two, perhaps four, I decide I need to risk a light. I gently tear off a strip of burlap from my shirt and hold it close to the flint. After a few moments, a tiny flame kindles. Even that miniature blaze sets my heart racing, my vision blurring, the sound of distant screams… swallowing heavily, I bring the light close to the dark circle of the lock, leaning forward to peer inside.

A throat clears behind me, deliberate and polite.

I jump backwards, falling down on my ass and strangling a terrified shout in my throat. The flame winks out. I blink. Somehow there is still light...

I snap around, my hands coming up into a defensive posture. Half-blinded by the light, I can only squint into the lamplight at the dark figure behind it. He holds his lamp closer to me, and I shy away. The flame is far too close, too bright, too hot, and I'm trapped in a narrow hallway, a shadowed silhouette holding forth the fire. Creator, anything but fire. There are no windows or doors, and the only way out is through the man behind the lamp.

"How did you get in here?" the man asks again, his voice still more curious than angry.

I can barely hear him through the roaring flames and the confused screams. I rear back and spit at him, more animal than man. He takes a step back to avoid the spittle, thankfully taking the lamp farther away as well. With a shuddering sigh, I try to control my racing breath.

"Don't spit on my floor again, boy," the man says, his voice suddenly icy, so cold I feel the urge to shiver. "Now I asked you a civilized question, despite our current situation. I'll give you one more chance to answer it. How did you get in here?"

"The window," I say, intimidated in spite of myself.

Some of the meanest, ugliest thugs to walk, sneak, prowl, or crawl through Donir's streets have tried to intimidate me. They've threatened, chased, and beaten me dozens of times, and I haven't shown fear to any of them in the two years since Jonah's death. The steel in this man's voice, however, has me struggling not to cower.

"Which window?" he asks, curious again, his anger evaporating immediately.

"The window in the sitting room, closest to the study," I say compliantly.

"That window has screeched like a dying cat for ten years. I haven't opened it in six."

"I oiled it three times in the last week," I respond, meekly answering questions he hasn't even asked. "Just in case."

"Then I have to thank you," the man says, inexplicable amusement lacing his voice.

He lowers the lantern, revealing his face for the first time. Long brown hair streaked with gray matches a trimmed and stylish beard. Lines of merriment war equally with the lines of sorrow etching his face, and his brown eye smolders. A black eye patch completes the image, giving the man a fearsome appearance. Well, it would be fearsome, but the man is grinning so broadly my face hurts just looking at him.

"It was luck," the man says, his grin still firmly in place. "How I caught you. Well, unluck for you. I woke up and had a bit of a thirst."

"You come back here for water?" I ask.

"Hah, boy, I'm not that kind of thirsty," he says with a chuckle, sweeping past me and through the door before I can turn.

Every fiber of my instinct screams for me to run. My muscles tense, my head drops, and I take my first step towards the window. But something holds me back. I'm curious, just like an idiotic cat. The man doesn't seem like he intends me any harm. In fact, he seems genuinely happy. The situation is so far outside my experience that I can't figure out what to do.

The door reopens after a moment; the light reappearing with it. I turn back to see the Historian standing, regarding me, a bottle full of amber liquid in his hand. He pops off the cap with his thumb, tilts the bottle back, and takes a long swig. He sighs softly, a look of contentment passing over his features.

"Would you care for some? I would offer you a glass, but, considering the venue…" he says, proffering the bottle and waving at the bare hall around us.

My nerves shot, my hands already shaking, and my life still somewhere up in the air, I shrug and grab the bottle. A large gulp sends the liquid fire of whiskey burning down my throat. He takes the bottle back without comment, taking another drink before regarding me with a half-lidded eye.

"Why did you stay?"

"I don't know," I say honestly. "I've never met anyone who treated me…" I trail off. I don't have the vocabulary to describe how I feel.

"Like a human being?" the Historian supplies, a twinkle in his eye.

"Something like that."

"Well, then. If you haven't already guessed, I'm not going to turn you in. I'm not happy, either, mind you. But, from the looks of you, you could use some of what I've got behind that door. I don't want you to come to my house uninvited ever again," he says, a trace of the coldness creeping back into his voice.

I just nod, struggling not to let my head droop down as I move past him towards the front of the house. I don't know what I was expecting, but something about the dismissal just leaves me deflated.

"Now, if you want to come to the front door and knock, that's another story," he calls from behind me.

I spin back around and narrow my eyes at his open, innocent expression.

"I have more windows that need oiling, and other tasks that a young man of your stature might be able to manage. If I like your work, I may even have a bed in one of the spare rooms."

I look down at the burlap sack that clings to me and the linen breeches that end at my calf, held up by a single dirty cord. The only things of value on me are my thieving tools, hidden about my person and in a pouch strapped to my chest.

"I'm afraid I'll ruin your sheets," I say, gesturing glumly.

"And he's considerate, too," the Historian says, a look of mild amusement crossing his face. "Your payment for oiling the sitting room window will be a bath. The next job you do for me will earn you some clothes."

I'm speechless. It has been two years since I've thought about having the money to buy enough food, let alone clothes. Ever since Jonah and the Simply… I shudder slightly. I can't believe his kindness after catching me red-handed in his house.

"I don't understand," I finally manage, the sense of weirdness refusing to leave the pit of my stomach. "Why are you doing this?"

"Perhaps I'm an old man in need of a friend. Perhaps I really do admire your ingenuity. Or perhaps you remind me of an old friend. Can you afford to know why?" he asks, no hint of accusation in his voice.

I'm not sure what to believe, but he's right. It doesn't matter why. If the man is genuine, and actually wants to help me, I need him. It doesn't mean I'm not going to watch him like a snake, or that I trust him. I've heard far too many stories of young children taken off the streets and never seen again. But it's a risk I have to take. I take a deep breath, straighten my back, and walk over to the man, offering him my hand.

"I'm Jace," I say, looking him in his lone eye intently.

He is half-taken by surprise, but the smile that spreads over his face is all warmth.

"Reknor," he responds, shaking my filthy hand without a hint of disgust. "The Historian. It's a pleasure to meet you, Jace. Is it just Jace, or do I have something else to call you?"

"Just Jace. My mother always told me that she'd tell me more about my past when I was ready. She died before I ever thought to ask again."

"A shame," he says, a strange look in his eye. "I would be very intrigued to know your past. How old are you?"

"Fifteen."

I deliberately leave off the fact that I was born on the Desolation. The Desolation is the day when half dozen natural disasters ravaged the world. The Conflagration wiped out acres of farmland in an unexpected wildfire. The Swordplague, a supremely efficacious rust, destroyed all of the metal in half of the Khalintars to the west. The Abyss opened and killed thousands of people in Donir. The day also marked the ascent of the Sealord to the rule of his kingdom. Considering Donir is the capital, officials tried to get the day called the Liberation. They blamed the Shapers and their treachery on the disasters, but the loss was so great that people refuse to call the day anything positive.

Far too many people show great interest in me after I tell them the day of my birth, and I don't like attention. Rosie raised me to keep my head down and remain invisible, and something in Reknor's tone gives me pause. I see the interest in his eye, but I can't fathom why.

"Well then, on the morrow? Or do you have more pressing engagements?"

I mime pulling out a book, tapping my chin as I open it.

"I can't promise anything tomorrow evening, but my morning appears to be free," I say, grinning at him.

Reknor barks out a good-natured laugh, taking another swig of the whiskey. My smile falters, though. In this brief moment of kindness, I forgot entirely about the thieves and their hatred. I won't be back, no matter how much I might want to be. My life is over.

"My life just got a lot more interesting," he says, nodding in farewell as he walks past. "Interesting indeed."

I jump out the window and bend back to lock the window closed again. What might have happened? What would my life have been like? Had I succeeded in my theft, had I found this generous old man before I pissed off Kettle so much that she called for my head, had the Simply just not burned... through the crack I hear the man murmuring to himself.

"More interesting, yes. But for good or ill?"

I scale the wall opposite the alley, fingers and toes digging into the spaces between bricks. Levering myself up to the top of the building, I set off over the rooftops, hardly pausing as I leap from building to building. The structures, save for a few exceptions, are all of a uniform size in the Meadows where merchants live, so roof travel is easy and convenient. I don't have the risk of running into a passing patrol of the Watch, and I don't have to deal with the odd looks and shouts a dirty boy would get in a clean part of Donir.

As I run my mind drifts free. The Historian is offering something I haven't had since I was a small child: security. My mother and I went to live at the Simply when she stopped having jewelry to sell. I may have been five. At first, Rosie seemed to hold herself above the other girls, and they resented her for it. Ultimately, though, desperation brings us all low. After living with the women, I would never dare to call the oldest profession 'low.' Those women have a nobility I could sense even when I was a child. The girls all doted on me, a son for women who could never have one of their own. For the last two years, though, I haven't been able to rely on that safety. I can hardly remember what it's like.

Reknor also offers something I've never had: honest work. My life has always been devoted to the streets. Others work so that you can work them, as Jonah always said, so the idea of being on the other side makes me cringe inwardly. Reknor's still just a mark in my head, despite how nice he's been. Besides, I don't know how to do anything else.

I struggle to make a jump onto a flat, higher roof with a lip, scrambling up and coming back to myself just in time to take a backhand to the face. I manage to spin slightly with the blow and take some of the sting out of it, but it still rocks me to the rooftop. I don't try to get up. Through the ringing in my ears, I hear feet shifting in the loose gravel on top of the building.

"Nothin' ta be done," a familiar voice says above. "He's got ta die."

Several large figures loom against the cloudy midnight sky. The voice is Timo's, and that only means one thing. Somehow, in my distraction, I've wandered into a party of the Family searching for me. It is, perhaps, the dumbest thing I could have done aside from jumping off a roof thinking I could fly.

The Family approached me after the King's soldiers burned down the Simply, knowing Jonah had trained me and hoping I was more amenable to their offer than Jonah had been. With Jonah's death still fresh in my mind and the Simply's ashes still warm, though, I told them, in as obscene a manner as my thirteen-year-old mind could imagine, to go away and leave me alone. If I had known I was starting a feud between us in the future, I probably would have used a little more tact.

Timo and I have tangled on two occasions, and both times I escaped because I'm smarter than he could ever be. He's a great brute of a man, however, so if he ever gets a hold of me I'm in trouble.

So I'm in trouble.

Jonah's voice drifts into my mind, coaching me as I slowly try to get to my feet. Immediately, someone kicks me sharply in the ribs. I tumble back down and curl up, playing up the hurt of the blows.

"Alright, Jace, when you're outnumbered, there're some things that can help even the score. You can act like you aren't intimidated, like there isn't anything in the world that could concern you less than certain death. It can cow them, mostly because when there isn't any reason they can see for you to be confident, their minds will supply them with something worse and better than you could ever imagine for them. Now, you gotta read the situation, Jace. Sometimes it's best to act crazy. I don't know what it is, but everyone is afraid of crazy people. This one is harder to pull off and has mixed results. But I'm still here, hey? The last one is to act weak and pretend they've already won. When you know you can't intimidate them, and they know you aren't crazy, if you make a man underestimate you, you can get the drop on him."

I tick off the facts. Can't be intimidated. Know I'm not crazy. Only one option left. I try to cry as I hold my belly where they kicked me, but really all I get is some weak, fake sobs. In the darkness, it will probably do.

"Oh come now, little Jacie. We told ya not ta come back. Ya know as much as us this is our city. I seem ta remember Kettle sayin 'If ya come back, ya are to die.' So here ya are, still in our city, and we gotta do what Kettle says. As much as we might not want ta."

The thieves all laugh around me, but all I can think is how terrible a job he's done quoting Kettle's very dire, proper announcement of my death sentence.

"Timo, look, I'm sorry, I didn't know, I was distracted, please don't—"

The same boot as before kicks me again, harder. Since I can count my ribs through a rip in my shirt, I can count how many he's damaging.

"Jacie, look, I'm sorry, but this is how things go. Ya didn't think we would fall for that crap again, did ya?"

I flash back to the last time we had fought. Remembering the weak act I played, I sigh inwardly. How could I have forgotten that? My brain just isn't keeping up with the events of my life, and they are moving far, far too fast for my liking. Two of the dark figures haul me up, and steel glints in the moonlight. It isn't supposed to work this way. He's supposed to keep talking until I manage to think up a way out of the situation. I'm supposed to have more time.

"Wait!" I blurt out. "I have a stash!"

"What's that?" Timo asks, his voice suddenly interested.

"I have a stash! I'll let you know where it is if you let me go."

"I don't believe ya. Look at the clothes. He canna have more than two pennies ta rub together."

"You think I would buy new clothes, look nice, if I had the money? You rats would come try to find me the first second I looked like I had anything. Are you guys stupid?"

Timo hates being called a rat, and he hates being called stupid even more. So I wheeze under the expected blow to the stomach. If they think that I'm letting them in on my secrets, that the kid who has proven himself smarter than the Family a dozen times over the last two years is giving up his stash to them, they'll go for it. Every thief is constantly in suspicion that someone else has a stash. It's considered the height of insult for a thief to find and steal another thief's money, so when they offer it to save their lives it is generally considered genuine.

They'll go for it.

Probably.

The group moves off a way to confer, leaving me with the two thugs holding my arms. I sag, letting my legs go to jelly. They curse as they hold my weight up. I groan, hoping it doesn't sound too theatrical. They get their arms under my shoulders, hauling me upright and setting me on my feet.

"Thanks," I tell them, putting all of the pain I can into my voice.

As I relax, taking my own weight again, they relax with me, gripping my arms loosely. I twist, snapping both my arms downward. Surprised, three of the hands lose their grip on me, though the fourth stays firmly gripping my upper right arm. I punch out, just like Jonah taught me, putting my free fist into an open throat. He chokes and falls away. I jump up and kick him, using my momentum to push against the other man.

He staggers backwards, my weight adding to his careening stumble. By the time I realize we are backing towards the edge, it's too late.

"What the—?" Timo shouts as we go over the lip of the roof. I pray with all of my being that those aren't the last words I ever hear.

Falling for three stories is a long, slow process. Oh, I'm sure it only takes a few seconds. But for anyone watching, that time is multiplied tenfold. For anyone who is actually falling, that time becomes something else entirely. The man behind me is so stupefied he doesn't know much else to do but flail. Quietly, calmly, panicked, I can't tell, I move so that I'll land directly on top of him. It's a false hope. A beggar's hope. But it's all I've got.

We hit a mound of trash with the force of a thundering bull. It slows us down, however slightly, and we slam to the bottom. Something sickening happens below me, all crunch and squish and warm... All of the breath jars loose from my body, and my head jerks with such force that my neck nearly separates. It might have. I lay there, in the trash, on top of the broken remains of a dead man, doing my best to breathe.

After a moment, I manage to move my fingers and toes a bit, or at least I think I do. I slowly pick up my head, neck screaming with pain. Staring back at me are the eyes of a very dead, very rotten cat. The urge to breathe disappears. I tell my arms to reach up and push the disgusting creature away from me, but all I get is a loose, flopping twitch, the very action I'm trying to replicate when Timo's ugly face emerges over the pile, his expression twisted into a weird mixture of disgust and hope. When he sees my arms flopping, his face opens up in a look of total surprise. He calls out to someone behind him, and they pick me up out of the trash.

"What about Jeld?" a woman asks.

"Trust me, ya don't want ta look," Timo answers slowly.

"Well, let's get this kid's stash and get back. This hasn't been a good night," another man says.

A chorus of assent rises up from the surrounding thieves, and Timo walks over to me.

"Catch your breath, boy," he says harshly. "We need ya to lead us."

If I thought they were stupid before, I underestimated them. We march down Castleberry Street, my feet dragging as two strong men hold me up. They follow the instructions of a breathless orphan who knows he's about to die, not a penny to his name and no reason to believe he has one... how the Creator made such idiots, I'll never know.

We pass the Historian's house, and I give it a slow, quiet moment of reflection. I was that close to a real life, a life where the Family can't just murder me on a rooftop or in an alley somewhere, a life with enough to eat and roof to keep off the rain. I sigh, letting my head drop as we trudge past.

"Where is't?" Timo demands, stopping the troupe. "No way ya have a stash on Castleberry. Everyone knows that the Watch comes here twice as much!"

"Why do you think I hid it here?" I gasp, letting my contempt show through. "I couldn't be seen going to the same place over and over on Threepenny, could I?"

The logic satisfies him, but the thieves continue to glance around into the shadows. We make it about a block towards the next intersection when we hear a throat clear behind us. That throat clear, so deliberate, so polite, is far too familiar.

"Out for a stroll?" the Historian's voice calls from behind.

"None of your business, old man," Timo sneers. "Go back ta yer bed."

"Ah, but you're mistaken. The boy is my business. Drop him."

"Wha?" Timo says. I can't see the look on his face because I'm turned around, but I smile. I don't know what the old man is thinking. They'll kill him in seconds. But it feels like I really do have a secret stash to have someone care enough to stick up for me.

"Just take him," Timo says dismissively.

Lightly placed feet scuff on the cobblestones as they close, the stealthy nature of thieves taking hold even in a fight. The distinctive grunt as Timo swings his fist is followed by the meaty thwack it always makes when it hits flesh. I wince. It's okay that I messed up, that I'm doomed. But the Historian has only been kind. I can't bear his pain in this misguided attempt to save me.

One of the men next to me curses, letting go of my arm and running towards the fight. The other man's grip loosens, and I would make a break for it, but they really are holding me up. The other man struggles to hold up my weight, then lets me fall with a snarl. He draws a dagger and heads towards the fight.

The old man is hearty, sure, but I heard Timo's fist hit him, and men don't often get up from something like that. I struggle to roll over so I can finally get a good view of the fight. Dancing and sliding in the darkness, a man moves smoothly between half a dozen thieves, kicking here, punching there, blocking, dodging, his movements snakelike and certain. Three are down, either unconscious or groaning. As I watch, a fourth comes flying out, having caught a solid kick to the chest. As another falls, the rest quickly lose stomach for the fight. They pound past me, dragging or carrying their fallen.

"Later, Jacie," Timo says as he runs by, breathing hard. "I'll find you later."

Chapter 3
Iliana
The Seventh Day of Winter
In the Year 5219, Council Reckoning

Dancers glide through my stomach as if a party is starting and my fear is the music. It's hard not to be afraid; they tell me I'm a woman, but, when I look inside, I don't notice anything different. I still feel like the girl Uncle threw gleefully screaming into the air, what seems but moments ago. My heart still yearns to explore the depths of the palace gardens, digging through the dirt and helping the flowers to grow. What seems the day before, my father had encouraged such things, telling me that a connection with the earth and all things that grow is critical.

Not anymore.

I'm fifteen, the pleasant years of childhood flitting past as an ephemeral dream. Father tells me I'll need to take up other pursuits, more difficult tasks. He's been vague, only telling me that I needn't worry about them until it's time. Well, it's time.

"Iliana!"

My name is like a ram battering against what little happiness I can take from the warm bed and dozen pillows that lay snuggled around me. I keep my eyes closed, dreading the moment when Yrena will force me up. Normally, if I feign sleep, she'll leave me alone for a few more moments. Those moments are some of the first ways Yrena managed to steal a piece of my heart.

She'd originally been a simple bedchamber maid, hired on in her old age to look after the princess and keep her happy. She tends to my every childish whim and serves as a surrogate mother, standing in for the faceless woman who died to give me life. Father still looks into the distance, misty-eyed and vulnerable, when she's mentioned. Nadine. Some exotic beauty from across the Way of the North, dark-skinned and dark-eyed. Whenever she comes up in conversation, usually through Uncle and Father's reminiscing, they always talk about her like she was perfect. Yrena can never genuinely replace the beautiful, caring, loving mother I envision in my dreams, but I've come to love her in her own special way.

"Iliana! Girl, you get up this instant! Today is not the day!" Yrena shouts, and her quick feet patter across the floor towards my bed.

"Go away," I mutter, eyes still closed. "If there is any day for sleeping in, it is my birthday."

"Not this one," Yrena says, and I can feel her staring at me right next to my bedside. "Last chance, little one."

"You wouldn't," I say accusingly, cracking one eye in warning.

Abruptly, she snatches the heavy blankets off of me, exposing my skin to the frigid Winter air that constantly drafts through the palace. I bolt upright like a cat splashed with water. Grabbing the blanket, we fight for the thick material that is the last of my peace of mind. Growling, I tear the sheets out of her hands. The cloth catches on one of her nails. She gasps and pulls her hand to her chest, cradling it in the other.

"I'm so sorry!" I exclaim, abandoning the blankets and coming to her side. She turns her shoulder away, huffing. "Yrena, you know I didn't intend to hurt you. Let me see."

Yrena glances over her shoulder at me. It's almost coquettish, a glimpse into the girl Yrena once was. I go as round-eyed and childlike as possible, and she fights back a smile. Reluctantly, she holds out her hand so I can inspect it. The middle nail has been ripped almost to the quick, and blood is already welling from the wound.

“Oh, Yrena, this is the worst! I shall get Uncle to fix it for you in a trice.”

“No, little one,” Yrena says, her wrinkled face crinkling with concern. “The Lord General does not need to be bothered with such a trifle. I shall heal the normal way.”

“If that is your wish,” I say skeptically.

“At any rate,” Yrena says, suddenly finding her stride again. “You don’t have time for any of this! So help me, if you’re late for the parade, I’ll tan your hide so that you won’t be able to sit for weeks!”

“You can’t do that anymore. I’m a woman now,” I say matter-of-factly.

“Try me.”

I’m out of the bed and in front of the mirror brushing my hair before she can say another word. She strides out of the room, muttering under her breath that she needs some bandaging before she bleeds on the royal person.

The brush glides through my tresses, only occasionally catching on a tangle. Though I inherited some of my mother’s darker skin, a deep olive that doesn’t fade despite the near-constant rain in Donir, my hair is unique: long, soft, and the deep, luxurious brown of polished jasper. I’ve never seen anything like it, even when foreign dignitaries come to visit from the Khalintars or, on rare occasions, the Broken Isles. Reaching down past my hips, it’s my pride and joy. I’ve no idea where my blue eyes came from, just lighter than the shade of a clear sky at noon. They don’t match descriptions of my mother whatsoever, and Father has deep brown eyes. Men call them enchanting at court—trying to flatter my father, no doubt—but I don’t tell them to stop.

Yrena bustles back in with three younger maids in tow. I don’t know any of their names, though I’ve seen them a few times before. Father always tells me not to bother learning the names of the staff. They come and go with such frequency it’s not worth the effort. Yrena, of course, is my exception.

They stand me up in front of the mirror, slipping off my nightclothes and drawing up the elaborate and, as it turns out, extraordinarily heavy dress I'm to wear for the Liberation parade. It looks as if waves flow up and crash against the high bodice, wrought from gems in various shades of blue and green to complement the colors of my house and match the banner of the Sealord. The dress is covered in precious and semi-precious stones, stiff and unyielding. The back will keep me upright even if I fall asleep on the horse.

I sigh, or try to, but the dress prevents the movement. In years past I was a bystander, gleefully watching as the soldiers rode by in their royal blue armor, matching in every detail down to the rippled edges of swords carried at parade rest on every shoulder. The Lord General Kranos inevitably followed, never wearing more than a tight sleeveless leather shirt, his unbelievable size and strength sending ladies in the crowd swooning and causing every man with a sword on his belt to look elsewhere.

Then, the elite soldiers of the Tide marched around my Father in perfect step. He would always do something spectacular with his Shaping. The previous year, he caused every fountain and trough in the city to empty with a gesture. The sudden absence of sound had been startling, as everyone looked around at the suddenly bare and dry streets. The water flowed from every cup, leaving witnesses with empty glasses and befuddled looks. Just as the first outcries of disbelief began, he raised his arms and the water exploded from the ground, launching into a spectacular flowing tunnel that rendered him nearly invisible as he rode. As the parade ended, the tunnel burst into mist, the mist turning to ice and snow in the cold Winter air, drifting onto the overawed crowd.

And this year, it's my turn.

I swallow nervously as the maids finish fixing my hair, piling it atop my head and weaving the longest strands through a clear crystal crown that reaches high and sets my hair to shimmering. Soft lantern light sets the crown afire, a rainbow of colors dancing through the room. As I take in at the sparkling light dancing about the room, I know what my part will be.

Father strides into the room, his royal robes the color of the deepest seas. He smiles, standing behind me in the mirror. His broad, callused hands come to rest gently on my shoulders.

"The spitting image of your mother," he says warmly. "You look stunning."

"As do you, Father," I say playfully, giving him a grin through the mirror. "Are you excited about the parade?"

"Iliana, it's time that you learned what the parade is truly for," he says, stepping back and turning me around. "You see, everyone is required to celebrate the Liberation from the tyranny of the Council of Shapers, and many wish to. The pageantry is for them: our loyal subjects who wish to bask in our reflected glory. Others, however, do not wish to come. We rouse them from their homes, drive them along the streets, and force them to stand among the crowds. It is for these few I truly Shape. We are the elite, blessed by the Creator himself to lead, granted long life and the power to rule. They must never think they can resist us. We are wolves, and they are sheep. When I show them my power, they remember their place."

"I think I understand," I say quietly. There are only a handful of Shapers walking, and each is a gift from the Creator. We are blessed above the common man. "So that is why I must as well, for one day I shall rule. The sheep must be kept in their place."

"Well, that time is, hopefully, hundreds of years hence. Perhaps we will conquer the Khalintars and I'll give them to you, but I plan to be around for quite some time."

"Of course!" I say, smiling. "I have plenty of time to learn."

"Do you know what you'll do today? How you'll impress the crowd?"

"I do."

Scant hours later, hours that pass in a nerve-wracking blur, Uncle lifts me onto my horse as if I, and my heavy dress, weigh nothing. I sit side-saddle, grasping the pommel gently with one hand and trusting my balance and experience to keep me upright. He nods at me calmly, his broad shoulders level with mine despite standing firmly on the ground.

"Are you ready?" he rumbles, his deep voice rattling my bones.

"Of course, Uncle," I say, offering him a nervous smile.

It's a lie. The dancers have upped the tempo of their jig, but I'll never admit fear to Uncle. He always says that fear is weakness. With a wink, he strides to his own massive destrier and steps smoothly into the saddle, somehow dwarfing the mighty horse with the breadth of his shoulders. He rides out quickly, chasing after the marching cadence of the regular soldiers of the Wave. The crowds outside the palace cheer at the sight of him, and I realize with a start that a contingent of the Tide has formed up around me. Creator save me, it's time.

With a gentle tap, my horse begins walking, the soldiers marching next to me in perfect time. The bright noonday sun glows down, giving off little heat but illuminating the vast sea of faces spread out before me in their multitudes. Uncle is still in their midst, but all eyes are focused on me. Silence falls over the crowd. I stare straight ahead, trusting my horse and the soldiers around me to keep me on track.

Despite trying to focus, my eyes drift to the unbroken ocean of humanity stretching as far as the eye can see, a shocking riot of blurred color and indistinct shapes. The people are still, quiet, regarding me with something akin to reverence, as if I'm something else, something more, something greater than I feel myself to be. Almost as if the Eternal herself rides before them. Their awe and their fear wash over me. Imagining myself, though, I see the girl in the mirror. A slight wisp of a girl stuck in a gaudy dress she can barely walk in, riding stiffly on a horse too magnificent for such a tiny person. I can feel it, as the illusion begins to break, as the people notice that I'm nothing more than I appear. It almost terrifies me.

Instead, I concentrate. I can feel the energies coursing through me as only a Shaper can, suffusing my flesh with the power of my soul. I reach out, and the earth responds, welcoming. The power of my spirit quests down and into the stones. Beneath the cobbled streets, beneath the hewn sewers, the fresh, strong earth pulses and breathes. I drag it up, the deep power of the untapped earth heeding my call. As it presses through the minute cracks in the rock, I force it to change, pouring more of my essence into the dirt, compressing it, transforming it. The glowing symbol of my power rises to the surface of my bare upper arm, glowing a bright and vibrant emerald.

The first any of the spectators notice, it seems that the air around me shimmers, glittering and winking in the bright Winter sun. I close my eyes. Silence reigns as I raise my arms, the force of my will lifting the tiny shards of glass high into the sky. I bring my hands together, and the slender shards form into a floating disc high above us. I smooth it, turn it just so, and smile as sudden gasps erupt through the crowds.

I open my eyes. Rainbows dance through the crowd, the light of the sun reflected and bent through the massive lens. Every color imaginable bathes their upturned faces, the radiant glow shifting and mesmerizing. A low rumble sounds through the people, and soon they're cheering, on and on until the noise is deafening. My grin broadens, and I wave to them, the myriad colors sparkling off the gems in my dress. Their adoration fills me in a way I've never experienced. The fear and anxiety disappears, and excitement takes their place. I'm eager to be a woman and take on the role of protecting my subjects.

A break in the crowd forms as a man forces his way through the soldiers lining the parade route. I smile, ready to accept his gracious adoration. His blonde hair takes the riot of color well, his handsome face warped with anger. He shouts something, nearly unintelligible through the noise, but I'm able to read his lips.

"The Vengeance sends his regards."

He raises his arms, a crossbow appearing from underneath his cloak. A punch in the chest knocks me clean off the horse. I hardly feel the impact with the ground, my head jarring against the smooth stones of the Way of the East. My lungs feel full and thick, unable to draw in the breath my chest longs for. I squint into the glowing rainbow of color, the prism shattering and fading into the cold light of the sun.

I lurch forward, reaching for the light and drawing breath in a grating rasp. The bright sun dissipates, replaced by the filigreed walls of my chambers in the palace. I gently grasp at my chest, reliving the sudden shock of a bolt blasting through me. My skin feels whole, unblemished. I lift my nightdress, but the same smooth surface I've grown accustomed to over fifteen years stares back at me. Was it a dream, an all-too-realistic nightmare?

Yrena bustles in. Seeing me awake, she throws herself into my startled embrace.

"My lady," she sobs out, gasping between each word. "I feared the worst. I saw you fall, and they said you'd live, but I've seen men thrice your size p-perish from less, so-"

"Peace, Yrena, peace!" I say, rubbing her back and cooing to her gently. She continues to sob, so I hold her loosely in my arms. So it's true. That man was real, blonde-haired, his elegant features twisted into such a rictus of rage I wince even in my memory. His words come back to me: "The Vengeance sends his regards."

My hands shake with cold fury where they meet around Yrena. The Vengeance is a nuisance, a constant threat to everything Father has built. Along with his ally the Mason, the Vengeance represents the last remnant of the Shaper Council to resist the Kingdom of the Sea. As the Shaper of Air and the

Shaper of Stone, the two men are more powerful than the entire might of the Khalintari Republic and the rest of the western continent and twice as troublesome. Father has dispersed two of their supposed rebellions already, scattering their armies like cockroaches before the approaching light.

If only I was old enough, perhaps we would have been able to crush them completely in the last resistance. No one has heard from them in seven years. Rumors abound: the Mason is currying favor with the Khalintar of the Coin, the Vengeance has been spotted flying over the deeper reaches of the Kinlen Forest, the pair of them have been seen treating with the Warcaptain of the Geledin, as if the people of the Broken Isles would ever accept or deal with a Shaper. After two high-profile defeats, it seems they are now resorting to subterfuge and assassination to accomplish their goals. I don't like the idea of killing another Shaper, but I'm certain that, for those two, it would be justice to allow their talents to pass on to another generation and finally wipe away the tyranny of the Council.

"Yrena," I begin curiously. She looks up at me, her tear-filled gaze joyful. "I was shot by a crossbow, correct?"

She bursts into tears again, and I roll my eyes as I gently pat her back.

"Come now, come now. I live. I breathe. I'm not even scarred. My question is, how?"

"The Lord General Kranos, blessed to possess the Creator's own hands, galloped back to you and ripped the bolt out of your chest. I feared that was the end of you, but he placed his hands over your heart. People are still spreading the story of how your skin sealed like it had never been injured, and your breath came back as if the Creator himself had gifted your lung with air."

"Did they kill him?" I ask calmly. "The man who shot me. Did they kill him?"

"I couldn't tell. Damn the Vengeance's eyes to the bottom of the Eternal's dark tomb! They beat him into the ground, and all was chaos as I tried to reach you. I didn't see him dead, but let us hope they killed him, little one."

"Don't call me that any more," I say, softly. "I'm a woman now. I'm no longer 'little.' It's time I acknowledged that fact. Where is my father?"

"You will always be 'little' to me, princess. Your father left to attend the Liberation Ball."

"The Ball is happening now?" I ask in surprise. "Get me up and dressed, Yrena."

"But, my lady, you have just been-"

"Enough. I am in perfect health," I cut her off curtly.

"As you wish," she says, eyes lowered. My heart aches at even this minor hurt I've caused her, but I ignore it. It's time to grow up.

She dresses me swiftly, procuring a deep blue gown of silk to match the robes my father often wears. She braids my hair in intricate swirls tight to my head, her fingers deft and practiced. Even as I watch her work, an unexpected sorrow echoes in my heart as I look on her wrinkled features and bony hands. She will be dust long before I show the first signs of age. Father is near a century and a half old, and he doesn't look a day past thirty.

"If only... If only you were one of us," I say quietly.

"Oh, no," Yrena sings out. "I would never want that responsibility. I've lived a full life, and should the Creator take me tomorrow, I'll be satisfied. Us normal humans are content to live and die our natural span."

"I cannot imagine."

"One day, when you've lived as long as I have, perhaps you will."

"No," I say, staring back at the reflection of my eyes through the mirror. Yrena finishes up, patting me gently on the back and looking at me over my shoulder. "I won't."

I sweep down the final flight of stairs to the main hall. Hundreds of people talk, eat, and dance throughout the room.

Dignitaries from every vassal state have come, individuals dressed in the supreme finery of their particular corner of the kingdom. The rustic military-inspired beauty of Hollen, the gorgeous lace and frills of the Tirans, the tightly woven straps that make up the dresses of the women of Itskalan; each person brings their own touch to the celebration. The grand hall of the palace is decked out in intricate blue and green stones in the shape of the mightiest oceans, much like my dress from the parade. The throne stands on a raised dais three steps above the floor. Pillars line each wall supporting balconies that stretch above the heads of the dancers.

The announcer sees me and hurries over before I can become lost in the crowd. He slams his staff on the marble flagstones three times.

"All hail Iliana, Princess of the Kingdom of the Sea, Creator's Blessed, Master of Earth."

Silence falls over the hall, and all eyes turn to me. I raise my chin and walk calmly forward. Whispers erupt, spreading like wildfire, rumors of my death and my miraculous recovery. The crowd parts before me, and I smile inwardly as I step confidently to my father and the throne. Just like sheep before a wolf. The people lower their eyes as I pass, the sound of my dress sliding on the marble a gentle harmony to the shocked murmurs. When I reach Father's right hand, I turn, gazing out on the nobility and wealthy of the kingdom. The Sealord stands and places a hand on my shoulder.

"As many of you know, my daughter has reached her majority. Today, we celebrate more than just the Liberation. Today, we celebrate the day your princess steps forward as a shining beacon to lead us into the future. Bow before your future queen."

He mentions nothing of the attempted assassination. The night will continue as if the parade has gone perfectly, as if my birthday is the only event of note. It's calculated, surely. These people can't know how close that bolt came. The guests begin to lower, each person casting eyes downward and bending. Exhilaration surges in my breast. Even if I can't play in the garden, even if I can no longer be Yrena's little one, even if my responsibility to rule and govern will be heavy... perhaps it's not so bad to be considered a woman. The entire celebration bows to honor me, to show their fealty and loyalty. I can get used to this.

The delegation from the Khalintari Republic, far across the Way of the North and still independent from the kingdom, are also showing their respect. They stand in the back, each of them decked out in an awe-inspiring amount of jewelry. Their heads are bowed, even though they refuse to bend the knee. I find the display to be acceptable, though a cold smile graces my lips when I think of my father's words: "Perhaps we will conquer the Khalintars and I'll give them to you."

Out of that group of olive-skinned men, I meet a set of eyes. Every other head is downcast and looking at the floor, but one of the Khalintari men stares steadily back at me. He can't be more than a few years older than me, and he's dressed in the simple (by Khalintari standards) silk vest and pants of a court scribe. He's handsome, his features angular but smooth, but his dark eyes are mocking, one eyebrow raised as if the display of my power is little more than a joke. A flush of anger darkens my cheeks, and I step forward just as Father begins to speak again.

"Let us celebrate!"

The guests all stand as musicians stationed on the upper balconies launch into a lively tune. I lose those mocking eyes in the shuffle as everyone stands. There are cheers, and I smile around at the crowd, but I have to clench my fists to stop their tremble. I need to find the insignificant scribe who would dare to exhibit such disrespect.

"May I be excused, father?"

"Of course, Iliana. This party is for you. Enjoy it," he says. As I start to walk down the steps of the dais he calls again. "Just remember. These people are temporary. We shall be here long after they are gone. Use them for your enjoyment and then discard them."

I nod, keeping my face smooth until he waves to dismiss me. As I turn away, my brow furrows in confusion. The closer I've come to the day of my majority, the more Father has dropped comments like that. Of how the Creator blesses us above the normal man. Of how they are inferior. Of how their lives are inconsequential. I'm not entirely sure I agree. The people of the kingdom have always been good to me. On those rare occasions I'm let out of the palace with Yrena, I've seen people laugh, love, and live with such ferocity I sometimes envy their joy. The palace life is a good one, as far as I can tell. I'm tutored, given freedom, and always granted playmates until I tire of them. But I still wonder what it would be like to be out among the people, as one of them.

Dignitaries amongst the revelers stop me as I walk through the crowd, smiling and bowing and wishing me great joy on my birthday. I respond in kind, but I don't bother to learn their names. I need to find that scribe. Every time I think about the derisive look in his eyes, my jaw clenches. I've almost reached the Khalintari delegation when a hand grabs my arm and spins me into the shadows under one of the balconies. I reach for the earth, the symbol of my power flaring up a bright emerald green. In the flash of light, I see the features of the scribe.

"You're angry," he says, his soft accent just noticeable in the Donirian tongue, his eyebrow cocked in the same mocking expression as before. He's even more attractive close up, his long black hair flowing past his shoulders. I shove the thought aside.

"I *am* angry," I say, still not letting go of my connection with the earth. I work some of the glass free from the mosaic behind him, slowly turning it until the sharp fragment is pointed squarely at the back of his head. "This is my home. This is my kingdom. How dare you show me disrespect?"

"Because you don't deserve respect," he says, waving a hand contemptuously. "Put your shiny toy away, girl. You might hurt yourself."

I blink once, shocked. My concentration wavers, and the piece of glass falls to the ground. The faint tinkle of shattering glass is just audible over the music.

"Good. That is no way to have a conversation, knowing someone is thinking about killing you. It makes it hard to be friends."

"What?" I say, my anger returning tenfold. "Friends? What in the Eternal's forgotten name makes you think I want to be friends with you?"

"You're only angry with me because I ruined your moment. All of those people, bowing to you, obsequious, spineless... boring. You do not yet understand, girl."

"Quit calling me that. My patience is growing thin. I could have you killed for this impertinence," I say, fighting not to stamp my foot. I know it would be childish. He smiles, as if he can guess exactly what I'm thinking.

"But you won't, will you, girl?" he says, his eyebrows raising slightly. "I interest you. I do not bow. I'm not a playmate that is forced to be in your presence, nor am I a servant who scrapes the marble at the first sign of your displeasure. No one has ever treated you this way, neh?"

"We are heading towards a crisis between the realms when I murder you in front of all these people," I say, mentally snatching up the shards of glass from the floor and sending them darting towards his neck. He doesn't move. He just smiles his mocking smile. Even when one of the tiny shards pierces his skin and draws a small bead of blood, his expression doesn't change.

"Your father is right. They are sheep. We are wolves."

My eyes widen, and the glass drops away from his neck. As far as I can tell, that phrase has never come up in any conversation that could be overheard. The man just seemed to pluck the phrase out of my mind. I look him up and down, but there is no tell-tale gleam of a symbol of power anywhere visible on his person. He's shirtless under his sleeveless silk vest, but none of his visible skin shows even the faintest hint of light.

"I don't know where you heard that from, but I don't believe you," I say, rolling my eyes. "You are not a Shaper. You're just trying to... I don't know what you're trying to do. Die an early death, I guess."

"Perhaps we can't be friends," he says, looking disappointed. "You are too young. You're just a pup, not a wolf. Why would you assume things you could never know?"

He grasps the fabric of his pants over his left leg, snapping it taut. A faint symbol in silver gleams through the silk, beautiful and mesmerizing in its shape. My eyes trace the intricate, weaving light. I start to feel dizzy, vision blurring at the edges. I finally tear my eyes away and meet his dark gaze. My breath comes shorter, my chest tight. We are halfway through a different song than when he last spoke. How long did I stare at that symbol?

"Perhaps, when you're older, you can come visit, neh?" he says, reaching out and patting me gently on the head. "I will be there. In the heart of Coin. Until then..."

He bends down, picking up a slender shard of glass. It gleams in the lamplight, a tiny bit of his blood adorning its edge. I blink, and he's gone. I glance around quickly, but there's no sign of him. In fact, I'm not sure what I'm looking for at all.

Confused, I wander back into the party. Something has just happened, something important, but my mind feels as if it's stuffed with mundane nonsense. I remember something about dark eyes, and a burst of anger burns through me, but there's nothing behind it. I don't even know what I'm angry about. How can you forget why you're angry?

In a daze, I blink slowly as a man comes into view. A boy dressed as a man. He's standing in front of me, a nervous look on his face. I squint at him.

"Right, well, I will just, uh, be going then, your highness," he says, scraping a bow and flushing red with embarrassment. It's clear he said something to me, and, in my befuddled state, I haven't registered the words. My brain catches back up.

"No, no, Torlas. I'm sorry. Something is up with my brain."

"Ah," he says, his expression clearing. "So nothing has changed, then."

"You... You... Blast it, Torlas. If my brain was working I would have come up with, I don't know, *something* mean to call you," I say, smiling in spite of myself.

Torlas is the first son of Duke Graevo. The Duke is one of the largest landholders in the kingdom, the head judge of the domestic court, and a close confidant to my father. Torlas himself is trying to follow in his father's footsteps, working as some sort of legal consultant in the courts. He's the only boy allowed near me since I turned nine, mainly because we've known each other since I was born (though he is four years my senior). Always around the castle, Torlas represents the most serious and dignified of fronts when exposed to anyone of importance or station, but I know him in an entirely different light. The boy is a prankster. He's constantly stealing things, hiding them, and playing practical jokes on everyone he won't die for offending. Sometimes, he toes even that line.

"Still the princess I know," he says, smirking. "Thinks far more highly of her abilities, mental or otherwise, than she should."

"You, sir, are an ass," I say, shaking my head and fighting back a laugh.

"Oh, you wound me!" he gasps, clutching at his chest.

"If you're going to die, Torlas, then please, do us all a favor and make it quiet."

He stands up straight suddenly, looking me seriously in the face.

"I find that I am much revived by the beauty that stands before me," he says, taking my hand and bowing gently, pressing his lips to my knuckles. I snatch my hand away, giggling.

"You can't say anything serious, can you?"

Something flashes across his face, something far from frivolity, but his smile is back in place before I can figure out what it is.

It has been six months since I've seen him last. He went with his father on a diplomatic trip to the southern province of Itskalan, something about ensuring the shipping lanes between the Broken Isles and our southern ports. The shipping lanes are a constant problem. My father being the Master of Water notwithstanding, the layout of the world, as designed by the Shapers of old, is not conducive to sea travel.

Before the fall of the Eternal and the Shattering of Isa, there had been three continents, brought together through the cooperation of generations of Shapers working out their lives. They moved islands, brought mountains together, flattened, crushed, and generally had their way with the land. In the end, the three great land bridges of the world were constructed: mighty edifices of stone and unshakable mortar that crossed the oceans to bring commerce and trade to all corners of the world. The land bridges formed a triangle which extended into the continents themselves, and the Ways travel straight and smooth to the largest city of each continent. Donir, the heart of the Sealord's kingdom, is an ancient city, existing at the confluence of the Way of the North and the once-mighty Way of the East, broken and mostly destroyed during the Shattering.

The Ways, however, still exist. Perfectly straight, they bore directly through mountains, hover above marshes, and delve through deserts and jungles. In each climate, the Ways are the safest places to be. With such an easy path available, the perils of crossing the open sea, especially the Maelstrom between the continents, never seem worth the effort. The only men and women who genuinely direct their energies to sailing are the people of the Broken Isles, the two Ways connecting their shattered continent to the others long destroyed. They rule the seas, and even the Sealord, Master of Water, can demand nothing from them.

As such, Torlas traveled down to the base of the Bridge of the East, as far south and west as the kingdom stretches. He and his father negotiate with the merchants, who then negotiate with the pirates, and, hopefully, the trade between the Broken Isles and Itskalan will continue.

The trip has hardened him, honing away some of the boyish curves and leaving the structure of a man, lean and tall, tanned face handsome and roguish.

"You're making me self-conscious, Iliana," he says. "You've been staring at me for entirely longer than is decent. Like what you see?"

"Of course. I see my oldest friend."

"Right," he says, sounding vaguely disappointed. "What mischief are we going to get into tonight?"

"Torlas, I don't know. I'm a woman now, or at least, that's what they keep telling me. I think it would be frowned upon for me to make a fool of myself now."

"Iliana," Torlas says, reaching forward and grabbing my elbows. He lowers his gaze until our eyes meet and holds me there for a long moment. "If you don't do anything fun for the rest of your life, I'll have to kill myself at the tragedy of it. I'm eighteen, nearly nineteen, my 'manhood' long established, and I'll never stop having fun. Now, damn it, follow me."

I let him lead me by the hand towards the doors, inwardly pleased. Maybe I'm not ready to be a full-on woman just yet. I glance back over my shoulder, just in time to see my father shake his head in disgust. I almost snatch my hand out of Torlas's, but before I can act on the thought, we're out of the hall.

He marches us towards the back of the palace. I have to wave a pair of guards back, assuring them I'm in no danger. Torlas ignores them and drags me into the first servant's passage we come across, threading our way to the kitchens.

"We shouldn't mess with the kitchen staff, Torlas. The dinner bell is an hour off and they are busy," I say, tugging back so that he comes about.

"We aren't going to mess with them. There's just something we need in the kitchen."

Shrugging uneasily, I let myself be led further. The sounds and smells of a busy kitchen begin to drift up the tight stone passageway, and I groan as I think about how hungry I am. The staff is preparing a meal for hundreds, and the fresh-baked bread, sizzling meat, and vast array of spices is mouth-watering.

We enter the kitchen proper. The clamor dies down as every single pair of eyes locks on me. My stomach twists in on itself. I look around desperately for a familiar face, but I don't have the faintest idea who any of these people are. It's clear, though, that they know exactly who I am. One of the men steps forward, grease matting what little remains of his hair to his head. His apron covers a generous belly, and his pants show the markings of countless swipes of dirty fingers across the cloth. His smile, though, is wide and genuine.

"Master Torlas, Princess Iliana. We were not expecting you this evening. With a thousand pardons, may I ask what you require?"

"Creator's hairy balls, Lucius, she isn't that much her father's daughter," Torlas exclaims, dragging me forward as he embraces the man with one arm. He steps back, gesturing to the man with a short bow. "Lucius Baker, the lead chef in the kitchens and the reason all of your food is divine. Lucius, meet Iliana."

He seems to have deliberately left off my title. I can't decide whether to be annoyed or elated.

"My lady," Lucius says, bowing deeply. "It is an honor."

"Thank you. If you are the creator of all of the works of art they call food in this palace, then the honor is mine."

His grin nearly splits his ears, his ruddy face deepening to a solid red.

"You humble me, my lady," he says, bowing again, but his grin belies his words. He's practically bursting with pride. "How did you get mixed up with our young master Torlas here? He's a shifty sort for such esteemed company as yourself."

"Oh, I fear I've been absconded with," I say, waving my hand over my brow as if I'm about to faint. "As you can see, the devil still hasn't let go of my hand."

Torlas, turning a bright shade of crimson himself, hurriedly releases me to the raucous laughter of the servants. Lucius turns and shouts at them to get back to work. They all shout back in mock outrage as they turn back to their tasks. Lucius leads us into the back corner of the kitchen, where a small table is tucked against the wall. He quickly clears the remnants of someone's snack from the surface, his movements swift, precise, and economical. In the blink of an eye, a chair presses at the back of my knees, and I sit as Lucius pushes it in for me.

"Torlas has been coming here since, oh, before you were born," Lucius says, looking down at us. "I first caught him trying to pinch a pastry from the cooling rack when he was three. The only reason I caught him, smooth as he is, is that the damned thing had just come out of the oven, and it burned him into crying! Even while he was crying, the little bugger was hiding the pastry behind his back, trying to pretend he'd stubbed his toe."

I laugh, picturing a tiny Torlas, stubbornly refusing to admit he has stolen anything despite the pain. Torlas looks embarrassed, but I just put my hand on top of his where they rest on the table. He glances up at me with a reassured grin.

"Come now, Lucius, tell her the truth. That's the *only* time you've ever caught me."

Even as he speaks, Torlas slides one hand out from under mine and throws a piece of chocolate high in the air, catching it cleanly in his mouth. Lucius' eyes practically bug out of his head. He spins around, staring at a mound of sweets artfully arranged for dessert. One piece of chocolate is conspicuously absent from the perfect presentation like a brilliant mosaic missing a tile.

"You rat!" Lucius growls, swatting Torlas on the back of the head as he swallows. Torlas chokes, coughing into his fist. "You deserve every bit of that, boy. Ruining my work."

"You have spares. I checked before I took one, you melodramatic ass," Torlas says, still coughing slightly.

"My lady Iliana," Lucius says, cleanly ignoring Torlas. "Is there anything that you require?"

"Well, Torlas, what do we require?"

"We require," Torlas says, mastering himself with a final cough. "Two glasses and a fine chilled wine."

"Very well," Lucius says. "Now, Torlas, if you'd come with me to fetch it, that'd be marvelous."

Torlas follows Lucius out of the kitchen and down the stairs into the cellars. The kitchen workers continue about their business, though several surreptitious glances dart my way. The time idle gives me a moment to think. Father always tells me that the staff doesn't matter, that they always change. From what Lucius said, though, he's been here since before I was even born. Why wouldn't my father want me to meet these people? Though mundane, they seem wonderful.

The door to the cellars swing wide again, and Lucius walks out with his arm around Torlas, pulling him close. He whispers something fiercely in Torlas' ear. I frown.

"Nothing is going to happen!" Torlas exclaims, pushing the man away. "I don't have a death wish."

"It had better not. Even your father couldn't protect you from that kind of slip up."

Rolling his eyes, Torlas walks back to our table. He has a large glass bottle filled with a translucent wine. A glass appears from behind his back with a flourish.

"Shall we retire to a more intimate setting?" he says, waggling his eyebrows in such an over-the-top salacious manner that he has to be kidding.

"That sounds grand," I say, taking my glass and following him.

Several flights of stairs and hallways in the servant's corridors later, he opens a door, seemingly at random. We come out into the lavish hallway where the royal apartments are located.

"How do you know this palace better than I do?" I ask, raising my eyebrows.

"My dear little princess, while you were being tutored and forced to follow our fathers around, I was exploring this labyrinth of a castle. I made friends with the servants, and you would be absolutely shocked if you ever realized how much they know."

We stroll down the hall until we come to my room. My palms go suddenly clammy. Torlas, in my room? We've been friends since childhood, but I'm not so sure about a grown, eighteen-year-old Torlas in my chambers. I grab his hand and move us down a few doors to one of the unoccupied rooms. Somehow, that feels better.

The only light in the room filters in through closed curtains. I throw the drapes open, smiling out at the night. The Stars of Donir dot the cityscape, glowing points amongst the velvet blackness of night. A near-full moon bathes everything in a gentle silver glow. Torlas stands beside me in the dark. He fumbles with the wine, finally wresting the cork from the neck and pouring a glass for us both. The wine is tart, but exquisitely sweet. Lucius, clearly, picked it.

A smile bubbles up from deep in my heart. Inexplicably, I'm content. I'm drinking a dazzling wine and looking out on the stunning city of my home, perhaps my only true friend standing by my side. The parade, the assassin, Yrena's tears, they all feel so far away, even though they happened in the morning. Tentatively, almost furtively, his hand comes to rest on the small of my back. I shiver, but I don't push him away. His hand is cool from handling the chilled wine, and my skin is hot and hyperaware.

"What a perfect view," I say.

"Indeed."

I glance at him, but he isn't looking at the view. He's staring at me, far too intently. His eyes are serious, focused, a gleam in them that never would have been there in the past. I sense more than see him begin to lean forward, his lips parted ever so slightly. A spike of adrenaline shoots through me, both fear and excitement warring for my attention.

"Torlas," I say, warning in my tone. "Can tonight just be... us? As friends? As we used to be? I'm not going to say we won't ever have a future, but for tonight, please?"

"Of course."

His expression clears and his hand falls away from my back. I fight a frown off of my face. The absence of his hand is even more pronounced than its presence. We drink for a while in silence. The darkness is inundated with thousands of shimmering lights, above and below. If I let my eyes unfocus, I can't tell where the sky ends and the city begins. Eventually, I sigh, regretfully turning back to the darkness of the empty chamber.

"Dinner will be served soon, and both of us will be missed, if we aren't already," I say.

"Yes, we'd better get back. Just promise me something, okay?"

"What?" I ask cautiously.

"Find the time to live for yourself, not just for your father or your title." Torlas' smile doesn't match the solemn fear in his eyes. "Your smile when you looked out at the city... that was a different smile from any I've seen lately. You relaxed, finally. Even the way you were standing changed. So, please, will you?"

"I'll try," I say, unsure if it's possible. Father told me that he has plans for me after this birthday.

"No, damn it, Iliana, promise me."

He scowls, his face open and determined.

"Fine, I promise," I say, trying not to make it a lie. "Now, can we go?"

"Yes," he says, straightening his coat and holding out his arm. I hook mine through his as we stroll back toward the main stairs, avoiding the servants' halls this time. "Yes, I'm satisfied. And I'll hold you to it."

Chapter 4
Bastian
The Thirty-Fifth Day of Winter
In the Year 5219, Council Reckoning

The girl stands, wiping her mouth and smiling at me vacantly. I cock an eyebrow and lazily wave her away. I send her a gentle urge that she would rather be helping with the cooking downstairs. Her little blonde head nods at me and leaves, grinning the whole way. I sigh, content and somehow sad at the same time. She will be the last Donirian girl I have before we return to the Republic. Pretty, in an impoverished sort of way, but she isn't exactly what I hoped for after the whirlwind trip this coronation has been. My final Donirian will be a serving girl in some nameless inn a few miles east of the Way of the North. The thought leaves me vaguely dissatisfied.

Serving girls are the best. When you're traveling, sometimes it's hard to find just the right woman to share your bed. You never know who is married, or who is going to cling to you long after you want them to leave. It would be a simple thing for me to just find out, but that isn't fun. Your typical passing beauty requires all sorts of mental energy to seduce. I've never been known to expend any more energy than necessary.

Serving girls, though. With the barest flicker of a suggestion from me, they practically jump out of their clothes and line up for inspection. As this was my first trip into the Kingdom of the Sea, I made sure to sample as many different variations of the local cuisine as I could. Most of the women in Coin are dark-haired, olive-skinned, fiery hellcats. I find the Donirian women to be fairer, tamer, and far more pliant. I'm used to working for my meals, but the women of Donir practically offer me everything I ask for on a platter made of gold.

The other diplomatic delegates and I stayed in the city long after the coronation of the princess. We left with trade agreements that the Kingdom would soon come to realize were in our favor, grossly so in fact. A small part of me feels guilty, especially because the Duke in charge of the negotiations seemed like an intelligent, savvy individual. If the bargaining had been real, we would probably have come off on even terms. Instead, the man never stood a chance. He might well lose his head considering how manifestly terrible the agreements are. Ah, well. As intelligent as he might be, this Paloran has served his purpose in enriching my kingdom.

The only unanticipated event of the trip had been the princess herself. Meeting her was... fascinating. Defying her will, there in her stronghold, brought with it a heady and delicious sense of recklessness. When she stood in front of me and threatened my life, I could have practically hugged her. It's been *so* long since I felt alive. The glass at my throat... the threat. I hold the tiny shard up to the morning light. She may be young, but she has all the markings of a classic beauty. I hope the suggestion I left her isn't too vague. It would be nice for one person to know who I really am.

I muster the energy to walk out on the balcony that attaches to my rooms. The gigantic towers marking the beginning of the Bridge of the North dominate the skyline next to the shimmering surface of the morning sea. I stretch, naked. The crisp breeze sends a shiver down my spine, but I lean on the railing, ignoring the cold. We'll soon be home. I can finally get back to Coin, where my presence is necessary. I'll need to reestablish myself; no doubt all sorts of mental insurrections have occurred in my absence.

A knock sounds at my door, so I shrug into a thin robe. The nervous sweat of the obsequious man on the other side practically soaks through the doorway. I open the door for Eledar Cortola, Minister of Finance in the Khalintar of the Coin, one of the three most powerful individuals in the entire city, one of the de facto rulers of the Khalintari Republic. He is a man known for his ruthless and cunning mind. This morning, he's donned the casual robes of his office: blue silk embroidered with cloth-of-gold thread and a dozen golden pendants marking his station.

Bending him to my will was all too easy. Cortola dotes on his daughter, a weakness for a man of such power. Whenever he thinks of me, a trigger I implanted in his mind blasts him with the irrational fear that I have total control over his daughter's life. It's not one of my finer moments, but Cortola has never gotten close to stepping out of line.

"My, uh, lord?" Cortola says, terror nearly stopping his speech. "The servants below have informed me your breakfast is prepared."

"Thank you, Eledar," I say, grinning and walking out in front of him.

As I place my foot on the first step down, a surge of elation rises behind me. I glance back, but Eledar is doing his best spineless impression, eyes on the floor. I narrow my eyes and cast out my senses. Half a dozen minds in the common room enjoy various meals and drinks. The staff in the kitchen also have normal thoughts, aside from the girl who recently left my room, who is far too enthusiastic about cooking. A wagon passes outside on the way towards the Bridge of the North, an old married couple bickering as they drive. Just as I'm about to give up, I catch a glimmer of hostile intent across the Path. Ah. Cortola hasn't ever stepped out of line.

Until now.

"Eledar, Eledar," I say, shaking my head. He shudders and clenches his eyes closed. The sound of my voice sends all sorts of terrifying images into his head. "I'm not going to eat down there, in the open, when you have so conveniently placed an assassin across the way with a clear view of my seat. That would be stupid. Do you think I'm stupid, Eledar?"

"N-No, my l-lord," Cortola answers. I wrinkle my nose as urine dribbles down his leg and stains his silk robes.

"Eledar, did you really think that ruse would work? How did you even come up with it?"

"I wanted," he gasps through his fear. "To protect my daughter."

I dive into his mind. The man is telling the truth. The constant fear he feels whenever he sees me has made me such an enemy that his hatred has overcome the terror. I underestimated his cunning. If I hadn't caught his elation, I would probably be dead, my face cooling in a Donirian stew.

"Eledar, I'm going to have to punish you for that," I say, a broad smile growing on my face.

"My lord, I'm sorry, please, I fear for Ilisa, she is everything-"

"Yes, I know," I cut him off.

I cast my senses back out, locating the assassin without difficulty this time. As another wagon rolls past, I jam my way into the assassin's consciousness and take over. He's so surprised he doesn't even have time to fight. We lift first one foot, then the other. Our body rises from a prone position into a crouch. With one last burst of will, we dive forward. Our head lines up perfectly with the front wagon wheel on the left.

Screams pierce the quiet of the morning as the assassin's head pops like an overripe cherry. I force my body not to sag as I come back to myself. Wrung-out and weary, the cold of the Winter air bites through my thin robe with a vengeance, my skin no longer feeling so resilient. The world is duller, the colors muted, even the grain of the wood in the walls less defined. Casting my mind that far is a trial, but it's worth it.

Cortola glances about in alarm. I brush past him on the way to my room. Despite dressing in my thickest shirt and functional trousers, I have to fight off shivers to buckle my belt. When I can steady my hands, I head back outside. Cortola remains in the hallway looking uncertain and afraid.

"Come, Eledar. Let's go to breakfast, shall we?"

"But, my lord-"

"Do shut up and follow," I snap in irritation. The man just can't play along.

I sit at the nicest table before the hearth. The warmth of the fire helps to drive the chill out of my bones, and life trickles back into my limbs. The serving girl from my room brings us two heavy plates heaped with food: roasted potatoes, a pair of boiled eggs, bacon still dripping with grease, and a hearty helping of oats mixed with cinnamon and honey. The girl lingers as she places my plate, but I ignore her along with the flash of hurt I sense as she flounces away.

Cortola has a perfect view of the street, where he can see the commotion outside. Realization dawns on his face, and his eyes flick from me to the street and back a dozen times. He chews his food slowly and struggles to swallow every bite. I, on the other hand, enjoy the meal immensely. No good Khalintari would ever be caught dead eating such rustic fare in Coin, but the hearty food fits the rugged people of Donir well. I sigh in contentment as I mop up the last of the oats with a final piece of bacon. The perfect bite.

"How old is your daughter, Eledar?" I ask. He still has most of his food on his plate.

"My lord, please."

"Now, now, you know better than that. What are you supposed to call me in public?"

"*Tarnas*," he grits the word out between his teeth. In the Khalin, it means 'servant.'

"Precisely. Now, Eledar, how old is your daughter?"

"Why do you want to know?" he asks, desperation filling his voice. When I look at him expectantly, he adds "*Tarnas*."

"Last I saw her, she seemed to be growing into a woman. That was several seasons ago. How old is your daughter?" With the third repetition of the question, I bring my will to bear. Though I'm still recovering from earlier, I am more than capable of influencing a familiar mind at close range.

"Fifteen, *tarnas*," he whimpers.

"Ah, then a woman indeed. Such a pretty little thing. Have you found her a husband, yet?"

"There are offers, but I've been allowing her to choose," he answers. His voice is steadier as the conversation turns to his daughter.

"How kind of you. Then she hasn't chosen yet?"

"She has her eyes on one man, the son of Khal Antarah of the Sword."

"Ah, young Junayd, is it? His reputation is that of an honorable man. He's acquitted himself well in the border skirmishes with the people of the Isles down south. The houses of the Minister of Finance and the Khal of the Sword coming together? That would be a mighty alliance, one to be respected and feared," I say, nodding in appreciation.

"Yes, *tarnas*. I am proud of my daughter."

He relaxes. It's as if he has forgotten who he's talking to, who he's just attempted to have killed. The fool.

"Good. When we get back to Coin, send Ilisa to me. We can't have her attempting to woo such a powerful man's son without some experience, can we?"

Eledar's face goes ashen. His limbs drop as if I've broken his spine. Slowly, his eyes find the table.

"You can't," he says, the word grating out of him through a fatal wound.

"I will," I snarl, leaning forward until he has to meet my gaze. "This is the least of the punishment you'll endure if you ever so much as think of defying me again. Your daughter *will* come to my chamber, willingly, or I will force her to come, and you will *watch*."

We set out the next day for the Bridge. Cortola keeps his distance from me aside from an occasional fearful glance, and I let him. I'm disgusted with myself for failing to notice his intentions earlier. I know he loves his daughter, but I never thought he would be so underhanded as to kill me at breakfast. Not a mistake I'll make again. None of the other dignitaries in our caravan notice or care that the Minister of Finance drops back and rides with the main body, leaving his scribe to ride alone up front with the vanguard. Normally, Cortola leads as his station dictates, but not today.

I keep my head up and admire the last vestiges of Donir before the long journey across the ocean commences. The land is so brown, not the light, gleaming copper of the desert but the deepness of mighty trees lacking their leaves. I didn't know trees could grow so high before I came to this land. We've ridden through forests that would make the stands of trees in the Khalintars seem as children grasping at the skirts of their elders. It leaves me feeling insignificant and downtrodden.

The feeling rises up in me again as we set out on the Bridge of the North. The massive edifice stretches farther than the eye can see, a constant in a world full of variables. The stone is seamless, so perfectly shaped as to defy nature and the senses. The structure is a mark of beauty and strength, arching over the waves passing far beneath the hooves of our horses. Every time I look out over the endless ocean, the feeling of insignificance surges again in my heart. The waves below us are the size of houses and would easily sweep us all aside but for the Bridge beneath our feet.

On the journey out, I forced one of the palanquins to accept another passenger. It's a simple matter to blank the minds of the guards as I climb in and force whatever important functionary that resides within to accept me as an honored guest.

It had been a comfortable, if boring, journey. For some reason, as I leave the untamed land of Donir, I want to experience the return trail from the back of a horse.

It's supposed to be my lot, as a scribe, to ride in the back of one of the wagons, but all of the servants know I'm no mere scribe. My station, as far as they can tell, is somewhere in between, above them but below the great lords. It leaves the servants in a state of confusion as to how to treat me, so I always act important and get what I want without much difficulty. It's exhausting to use my power for every tiny request, so I put forth a great deal of effort in appearing as mysterious as possible to the lower echelons. Thus, procuring a horse is as easy as asking.

The day is long. The irritable horse's hooves clatter against the smooth stones for miles on end. Riding was an Eternal-spawned notion which should never have entered my mind. I was alright while I was distracted by the sights and sounds and feelings of travel, but boredom quickly cured me of that. As we come to a stop, a burning pain ignites between my legs. The towers that mark the beginning of the Bridge are already out of sight. The long road stretches before us, the journey ahead one long unbreaking view of ocean and stone.

Our initial stopping point is the first aberration in the identical stone. An ingenious creation of the old builders, a well rises up in the middle of the road, fresh water bubbling to the surface through some unknown magic of the ancients. Twice daily, caravans can expect to find stops like this one, perfectly placed to make the journey simple and comfortable.

My back aches as I sit the horse. The beast occasionally flicks its tail at some unseen pest. I want to get off, but I dread the feeling I know is coming. With a sigh, I dismount, the chafing between my thighs sending shooting pains through my legs. The horse flicks its gaze towards me, then walks away without prompting. A pair of grooms intercept it and lead it towards the well, shooting me strange looks as I glare after the beast. The damnable horse wanted to let me know that it was in charge. It would be less annoying if it wasn't true.

I stagger over to the well, fighting for space with the cooks as they gather water to boil for the evening meal. I'm about to dunk my head in the bucket when a ladle appears in my line of sight. I look up into a pair of enchanting eyes, tilted ever-so-slightly upward and filled with mischief. My stomach wobbles in an unfamiliar way as she holds my gaze. I smile and accept the ladle. The smile feels unfamiliar, almost forced, and I struggle to figure out why. It's only after she turns away that I realize it's because the smile is genuine.

Her clothes mark her as a servant of the servants, one of the lowest in the entire party. She runs water, picks up horse shit, and participates in any of the other thankless jobs a caravan needs accomplished in order to operate. Perhaps I'll get to know her better on the journey home. The thought is pleasant, but leaves me with a sense of disquiet somewhere in a dark corner of my mind, like I shouldn't be thinking such uncouth thoughts towards someone who showed me kindness. It's not in my nature to dwell, though, so I shake it off without too much difficulty.

Winter holds a less tenacious grip the farther west you travel, and so the air feels just a hair warmer than on Donirian shores. It isn't much, but it's the first sign we are headed home. I scramble up onto the massive rail of the Bridge. The sun falls from the sky like a child's ball, dropped and forgotten before it can hit the ground. The sea becomes a sheet of blood red diamonds for the barest of heartbeats, the water glowing and alive. Darkness falls almost before I can process the majesty of the sunset. That feeling, so unwelcome, bulls its way into my thoughts again. All that I accomplish, all the power I wield, all the people I control.

Meaningless. Irrelevant.

I shudder. There is only one thing that can lift my spirits when the mood comes upon me.

Two other groups camp with us: a merchant caravan bringing what smells of tea back from Donir towards the Khalintars, and a small family of Donirians traveling in the same direction. The fires of the caravan push back the melancholy from my soul. When groups such as ours come together, tradition dictates campfires be set up for all parties to sit, trade news, and tell stories. I join one of the communal fires, sitting amongst perhaps a dozen others. I flick through their surface thoughts as I accept a bowl of stew from a passing servant. Most are engaged in the story of a fat merchant as he discusses how well he ripped off his Donirian counterpart. He's clearly trying to impress the official Khalintari delegation, but he isn't making much headway aside from a certain satisfaction at seeing the Donirians conned.

One mind, however, stands out. She's thinking sarcastically about how annoying the man's voice is. The blonde hair of the matriarch of the encamped Donirian family glimmers in the firelight. Her kids are just old enough to run around, and she ignores them aside from the occasional shout if they wander too far. She is still young and fairly attractive, youthful fire filling her cheeks and her eyes. I bring my will to bear.

Desire.

She glances around, and her eyes settle on me. Immediately, I can feel her passion, but thoughts of her husband subsume it in guilt. With a mental caress, I wash away the guilt. I turn the thought of her husband into a litany of all the annoying things he does, all the kindnesses he ignores. I sculpt her thoughts like a master with a chisel, turning away negative feelings and stoking her desire. Before long, she stands up and offers me a lingering look over her shoulder. The melancholy lifts from my shoulders as I follow her into the night, just like I knew it would. Some problems can only be solved by a woman.

The journey across the Bridge will take more than a season. Spring will have begun in earnest by the time we reach Coin again. To travel from Donir itself to Coin takes a total of a hundred days if you can manage twenty miles from dawn to dusk. Made up of the strongest palanquin bearers, horses, and wagons teams, our caravan can push twenty-five on the smooth and even Bridge. The days pass swiftly. The vista of the ocean from the top of the Bridge never changes. Sometimes, it's hard to tell if we're making any progress at all. Only as the first major landmark comes into view do the days again feel real.

Long ago, when Donir and the tribes of the Khalintars were in constant war, the Bridge of the North was the sight of countless battles. Over the centuries, each side constructed a pair of mighty castles to defend their half of the Bridge. The Donirians created the Dawnhold, a massive and utilitarian structure squatting malevolently across the Bridge. The Khals brought the Duskbank into being on the opposite side, an elegant and flowing structure that melds with the harmony of the Bridge itself. The keeps reflect their peoples.

As the Dawnhold rises into view, the masoned stone is a shock to the eyes after the perfect smoothness of the Bridge itself. Ancient and ugly, the castle is nonetheless impressive in its own way. The walls rise to the height of four men or more; the gates are constructed entirely of thick iron. When those gates close, only the Creator himself could force them open. The gates stand open as we approach, much like they have for several generations. The uneasy truce between the Khals and the Donirians has stood for nearly a century.

The watchful eyes of the garrison still look down on us with suspicion. Most of them are typical soldiers, garbed in the absurd blue chainmail of the Wave, as their pompous king calls them. Some, though, stand in the full seafoam green platemail of the Tide. Their eyes never stop moving. If battle is imminent, the Tide will be ready no matter what. I glance over at the lean silhouettes of our personal guard from the Khalintar of the Sword. They are members of the Edge, the most capable and dangerous of their isolated people. Wearing loose, flowing robes and no armor at all, they ride at total ease. Whenever they deign to glance at the Tide, they offer nothing but a confident smirk.

I'm able to relax again as we ride out the other side of the mighty keep. It's probably my imagination, but the Dawnhold marks a genuine border where even Winter dares not cross. The sun feels tangibly warmer than it was on the other side. Even so, I'm still tense until the castle passes out of sight. The itch in my back doesn't disappear until we pass out of arrow range.

A few days later, a haze of smoke begins to rise in the distance, blurring the clouds and setting the deep blue of the sky to shimmer. The clamor of civilization floats on the wind: the raucous cries of thousands of souls living in close quarters, the distinct rumble of smith's hammers, and the throated roar of a thousand arguments. As the first hovels appear spread across the Bridge like turds steaming in the sun, the smells hit. Food from a dozen countries, perfumes and spices from across the world, and, underlying everything, the unrelenting rank of man: our blood, our sweat, and our shit.

I smile as the myriad sensations of Halfway attack my senses. After being on the Bridge, alone but for the occasional traveler and with nothing but the sea for company, the city is a welcome break from the peace and monotony of the journey. There has long been a test of stupidity on either side of the Bridge. You simply ask someone to show you where Halfway is on a map.

The Bridge of the North widens out halfway across the ocean to create a large circle of land complete with soil and natural growth. Throughout the space, the dwellings and streets of a small town sit timeless and unweathered, created from the same stone as the Bridge itself. Finally, a long ramp and matching stone stairs lead northward and down to the surface of the sea, where a stretch of sheltered docks thrust out into the water. Great embankments rise from the depths of the ocean and encircle the peaceful Bay of Solace. Once upon a time, Halfway must have been a beautiful, sculpted little town over the ocean, a haven in the middle of the long journey.

Now, though, Halfway is an ugly stain of brothels, gambling houses, and thieves, each just waiting for the opportunity to rob you of every penny. Made of little more than spit, driftwood, and will, houses cling to the walls of the original stone buildings like tumors. Creative additions cover much of that stone, from additional stories reaching precariously into the sky to balconies and bridges stretching over the narrow, choked streets. Human filth stains what little of the original stone can be seen.

Yet Halfway is prosperous. Each of the predominant cultures in the world meet here to trade. It's obvious that the Kingdom and the Khalintars would use the neutral port, but the people of the Broken Isles also sail up and land at the harbor to trade for goods. Halfway is the only civilized part of the world where Islanders are a common sight. Most of the sailors of the Isles are dark-skinned, lean, and dangerous looking men. Curiously, though, every single one of the ships is captained by a woman.

Into the morass of scum we ride, our silks marking us as targets, sight of the Edge killing those thoughts as they are born. Beggars still reach up and attempt to grasp at our feet in supplication, and hawkers offer any number of products at the top of their lungs. The shouts die down as our soldiers begin to kick and drive off the crowd, forcing a path through the unfortunates and deeper into the city. We work our way south around the circle until we exit the outer ring of slums and enter the wealthier districts. The servants and slaves break off there, but the rest of us continue to the Southern Star, an inn as luxurious as can be found, rival even to the Falling Edge in Donir. Here, any human service can be found for the right price, whether it be companionship, assassination, or anything in between.

The thoughts swirling through the air are pure chaos, all of the combined hopes and desires of a hundred thousand people stacked on top of one another in a space meant for ten. There are countless flavors of fear, aggression, desperation, joy, hate, and love; a practical feast for my mind. The sun falls as I settle into the most luxurious and expensive rooms in the inn. The previous occupant mysteriously checked out, and our hostess was more than happy to open up her doors to 'someone of my importance.' A vague and powerful suggestion goes a long way.

I walk out onto the balcony, the reassuring solidity of ancient stone under my feet. I relish the emotions of the city as they sway along to unfamiliar tunes, darting this way and that, always changing, never ceasing, the complicated dance of humanity and all of our feeble hopes and ephemeral dreams. The churning tide of thought leaves me restless. Throwing on a cloak, I stride out of the inn, blanking the minds of everyone who notices me as I pass out into the city proper. My thoughts go forward to Coin, to a single room on the first floor of a lavish house near the center of the city, to the man sitting there. Tonight is for him.

I sip at passersby, stealing a few seconds from each. I laugh with a group of friends outside a tavern, a long joke coming to a final punchline. I wince as a man takes a powerful slap to the face, his clumsy attempts at courtship innocent but ill-received. I push aside the feeling of helplessness as two men take a whore in an alley, her thoughts on her family a thousand miles away. I swallow thickly as a child desperately tries to revive his father as alcohol still dribbles from his mouth. Finally, I find what I'm looking for.

Two young lovers walk hand in hand, their eyes bright as stars. Each looks on the other with total devotion, the kind of bond that can only be broken by death. His thoughts are of her, of how her hair sparkles in the moonlight, how the flush of her cheeks sends her beauty soaring beyond the sky, and how he can't wait for the night to be over so that she can lay in his arms. She thinks of him, how he makes her feel cherished, how nothing in the world can be better than being here, in this moment, holding his hand.

I study their feelings. Their joy doesn't touch me, not really, but the power of their emotion is vibrant and true. I need to understand where it comes from, how it can be so strong. Of every thought and emotion in the world, love has a hold on our minds beyond anything else. Hate, anger, sorrow, happiness, fear, wonder... whatever the feeling, love strengthens and magnifies each. The sorrow for a loved one's passing is far stronger than any remorse for a stranger. We fear our loved ones, both in that we make ourselves vulnerable to them and fear for them whenever they leave our sight. The hatred that can spawn from love is truly powerful, an ever-growing vine that chokes out all else. To genuinely hate someone, you must first have loved them.

I *feel* love, but I know I won't ever *experience* it. Every time I look into someone's mind, I find all of the distasteful shit they're never willing to speak aloud. All of their perversions, obsessions, hatreds, pettiness, righteousness, their misplaced faith and vast ignorance. It's impossible to love someone when you know every time they think you look ugly, or think of another, or lie.

It's hard to even like anyone when you know everything about them.

No, Lav, I do this for you.

The lovers continue, their thoughts intoxicating and sweet, a messy mush of care and dedication. I try to ingest their exact flavor of love, tasting it as I have so many before. I'm not sure that it'll work, especially not for what I intend, but I figure that any kind of love is better than none. I track them until they enter an inn in a decent part of Halfway. I think about continuing to follow their thoughts as they make it up to their rooms, but I don't have the heart. It isn't as fun if you don't get to participate. I'm also in public. It's amazing what'll happen to you when you experience two people's pleasure at once.

As I walk back, I try to hold on to the feeling of their love, try to figure out what makes it special compared to all others. My feet wander. The occasional person on the streets at this hour often entertains dangerous thoughts, but I don't really have to concentrate to direct their attention elsewhere and convince them I'm not worth it. Still, I'm distracted.

Hostile intent hones in on my silhouette. I try to direct the man's thoughts away, but his focus on my unprotected back only sharpens. I frown and turn. A man, pale skin bright in the moonlight, closes rapidly. His mind is such an inferno of anger my senses flinch back. He clutches a knife in his left hand, the blade barely visible in the darkness. The man seems familiar, in a vague way, almost as if I've met him before. *My* eyes have never seen him, but that doesn't mean I haven't seen him in someone else's memory.

Despite my surprise, I don't panic. It isn't the first time I've dealt with this kind of person. I dive into his brain, sliding past his feeble mental barriers and deep into the heart of his consciousness.

I go too deep.

Too fast.

My thoughts merge with his.

The towering rage of his purpose blinds me.

I'm not Bastian.

She's gone now. Asking around frantically in the morning, several of the Khalintari delegation witnessed her leaving the fire with a scribe. They told me she left with the kids while I was sleeping, heading back for Donir. I thought we were happily married. The scribe ruined everything.

I struggle to disengage my thoughts from his, but the surging power of his hate buffets me back and forth until I can hardly tell where I end and he begins.

I sharpened the knife for hours thinking of this moment. When I can make him pay. The blade drives into his stomach to the hilt, smooth as silk. I draw it forth and stab into him again. His blood darkens my hands. Finally. After half of a season, finally I'll be able to rest.

The part of me that remains behind jerks from the impact. A cold fire ignites in my belly. The rest of me shares in the man's elation, the release. We smile. The horrid haze of anger drifts away. His brain drops into an exhausted stupor.

My life drains from my body. The wounds are deep. No one will be looking for me. No one will find me. I'll bleed out, stuck here on the dirty stone, all of my power and arrogance nothing but a memory. The bitter thought does nothing to aid me. I'm even strangely happy about it. No, that's wrong. I shake my head, the edges of my vision already wavering. The man's joyous thoughts continue to bleed into mine.

Groaning, I assume control of the man's body. Turning the knife upwards, we pitch forward. Just before we land, I jump out of his brain. The distantly thud of the man hitting the ground accompanies the sickening squelch of the knife driving through his eye, but I don't care.

The full force of the pain roars through me. My skin burns. My stomach freezes. My heart pounds. Blood spills between my clutching fingers, so dark, so *much*. Darkness creeps into the edges of my vision. Soon all I can see is red.

A voice begins to buzz at the edge of my awareness, a sound of panic and concern. A touch, feather-light, on my shoulder. Another pushes my hands tighter to my stomach. The pain snaps my vision back into focus.

A pair of familiar eyes.

Tilted ever-so-slightly up at the edges, dark and deep and filled with concern.

I smile.

No one has touched me that way since I was a child. No one has cared about me. No one knows who I really am.

I don't let them.

"It's okay," I try to say, but my tongue feels thick and heavy.

The darkness begins to creep back into my vision. Her eyes are constantly moving, her head turning, her mouth opening. Soon, though, they are all that I can see. Those beautiful, kind eyes.

"It's okay."

Chapter 5
Kettle
The Thirty-Ninth Day of Winter
In the Year 5219, Council Reckoning

The search for Jace turns up nothing. The others are jumpy after the mysterious old man so thoroughly trounced them, and Jeld's screaming death isn't helping, either. I get the feeling Jace hasn't left the city, but something in me doesn't want to go looking myself. I might find him, and, despite the aggravation and sorrow he's caused, a small part of me always roots for the little bastard to live and succeed. He's just so proud and fearless, even covered in filth and without a penny to his name.

So, as the others grouse and nervously twitch and search, I read poems. The only aggravating thing about reading poems in Donirian is when I encounter the occasional word I don't know. Trying to figure out the word 'boisterous' without anyone around who actually knows the word is harder than you'd think. I occasionally glance up from my book when the Khalintari triplets giggle in the corner. Inia, Koli, and Ezil aren't really triplets, but they spend most of their time keeping to themselves and speaking in Khalin. They are challenging each other to new levels of flexibility. Ezil has her feet dangling over her own shoulders as she walks on her hands, the others already stretching to attempt the feat. The sight makes me shudder, and I look hurriedly back to my book.

The front door crashes open. I jump, then roll my eyes at the flash of a wide skirt just over the threshold.

"I've got it!" Corna shouts, jumping through the doorway and throwing her arms in the air in victory. I cock an eyebrow, lowering my book and lazily regarding her. Her eyes are bright and her cheeks flushed and vibrant. I smile almost against my will.

"What have you got?"

"Some real excitement!" she exclaims, strutting over and flopping into the chair next to me. She seems to deflate into the soft cushion, the petticoats of her skirt fluttering to rest. "We haven't done anything really interesting since the Graevo job. I'm about ready to burst."

The Graevo job *had* been interesting. We conned the Duke's servants into believing the Sealord himself sent us to inspect the lands of Graevo's summer home. We wore chainmail, and Corna spent dozens of hours painstakingly sewing the Wave crest into some cheap tabards we purchased in the Pennies. The guards stopped us at the gates to his estate, and Timo loomed as only huge men could while Corna sweetly explained what our purpose was. Between her adorable face and his gigantic arms, the men hardly dared to try to stop us. We didn't even have to tell them what we were inspecting.

As the two of them 'inspected,' I slipped away, headed to the stables, and saddled one of the Duke's most prized possessions: a Khalintari pureblood, breeding stock direct from the Khalintar of the Steed. The damned animal was worth roughly what the rest of the mansion combined could sell for. It was a stallion, virile, and the fastest and fiercest animal who ever lived. One of Graevo's entire business ventures was dependent on that particular animal's penis.

I unleashed the beast into the estate grounds, clinging desperately to its back. Timo doubled back and compromised the guard that wasn't following Corna through the house. Two hellish hours later, halfway through the Kinlen forest and two mountain passes later, the animal had finally run out of steam. Creator knows I don't know anything about riding horses; I just Shaped shadow around the animal's middle and endured the horrible jostling with my eyes closed.

"Come now, we work jobs all the time. The money is good, the margins are safe, and we want for nothing," I say, raising my book back to my eyes.

"Creator's hairy balls, Kettle, I'm *bored,"* Corna says. She slaps the book out of my hands. "I can tell you are, too. Your pores are practically oozing boredom. I can smell it. In fact, if you were any more bored, I would swear you decided to settle down and marry a tree! Either that, or you're *boring,* which is far worse, and I don't even think we can be friends." She sniffs delicately. "Please, Kettle! I need some excitement. Let's roll the dice, live on the edge, make a name for ourselves!"

"Don't you remember the last time you made a name for yourself? Every man in the city wanted to either bed you or kill you, and some of them didn't care which order those were in."

"Oh, Kettle, ew," she says, scrunching up her face. "That was an image I didn't need. But please, hear me out? If we continue as we are, we'll be forty and doting on our two hundred orphan children as we send them off to school, rocking in Eternal damned rocking chairs in the foyer!"

"Well, we call it the Family for a reason..." I trail off, seeing the look in her eye. She's close to tears, her lower lip trembling, such a picture of utter anguish that I roll my eyes at the performance. "Fine, tell me."

Her grin is miraculously restored.

"Okay, I heard a secret."

"And?" She frowns. "Oh, fine. What is it, Corna?" I ask sarcastically.

"You are so aggravating sometimes, you know that?"

I blink slowly. She sighs.

"I *heard,"* she says, drawing out the moment. "About a secret vault. In a very secret place."

"A vault? What is that?" I ask, confused.

"Oh, sometimes I forget that Donirian isn't your first language. You speak it so well. A vault is a place where you put things that are stupid expensive or valuable, locked away behind a giant door which is practically impenetrable." I make a face at the unfamiliar word. "Unbreakable. Un-unlockable. Only the richest and carefullest people have them, so I'm not surprised you haven't heard the word. Doesn't actually come up in conversation often, does it?" she muses, tapping her chin.

"Whose vault is it?"

I narrow my eyes. I have a sinking suspicion that the answer to my question is not one I want to hear. Corna has a way of finding the most insane and dangerous people to piss off.

"Um, well, I want you to know it's going to be one of the coolest jobs ever if we pull it off, and it's such a secret that no one even knows what's in it..." she looks away, playing with the frill of her skirts.

"Whose. Vault. Is. It?" I grind out, pinning her with my stare.

"Well, it's... Gordyn's," she says, wincing.

"Gordyn, as in Jon Gordyn, the head of the Imperial Bank and single richest man in the entire world?"

"Yeah, that's the one," she says, smiling weakly.

"The same Jon Gordyn who owns an army of mercenary guards and investigators, who patrol every piece of property he owns with constant vigilance, *killing* anyone who trespasses without even bothering to detain them? The same Jon Gordyn who, on the rumor that Count Lapiris was cheating at one of his gambling houses, showed up at his house in *Elderen, five hundred miles away,* and tortured him until he confessed? The same Jon Gordyn who escaped torturing and murdering a Count of the kingdom with a congratulations from the King for exacting justice?"

"Okay, okay," Corna says, waving her hands. "You're focusing on the wrong details. The wealthiest man in the world has a secret vault behind his office at the Bank, the contents of which no one has ever seen! Can you imagine what's in there? Starsilver ingots the length of your arm, diamonds the size of your fist, Timo's weight in precious stones? We could live forever on that kind of haul."

"Live for as long as it took him to find out who we were, with our newfound *name* for ourselves, and then die horrible deaths as he cut us into tiny, tiny pieces and fed us to the rest of the Family!"

"Wow, Kettle, you have a twisted mind," Corna says, shuddering. "Who thinks to feed people to people?"

"Jon Gordyn, should he catch us or find out who we are," I say wearily. "We can't risk the Family. The children have come to us in trust. We would be signing their death warrants."

"Not if we're really, really careful," Corna says, a twinkle in her eye. "And, just a little, aren't you discounting our trump card?"

"What's that?"

"You, silly. Do you really think a band of mercenaries could kill you? No matter how ruthless or well-trained or bug-eyed they are?"

"I think you added something to that list that doesn't fit," I mutter, smiling. "To be totally honest, I don't know. I'm afraid that, even if I could keep *me* safe, I couldn't keep us all safe."

"You know, it is sounding suspiciously like you're looking for an out rather than flat out refusing. I've got you intrigued, don't I? Secret vault, most heavily guarded bank in the world, stealing from the richest man who ever lived?"

When I came to Donir, I could have been anything. I could have been a seamstress, or a clerk, or apprenticed with a trade. It was a fresh start for me, the Broken Isles nothing but a memory. But the training I received didn't lend itself to domestic life, nor did my mindset. I chose to steal because the night was mine, the world had pissed me off, and it was just so damned exciting.

And, of course, Corna's right. I'm bored. I've slowed the training of the little ones after Grace's death. Timo extorts money from merchants in exchange for our 'protection' from thieves. Of course, we are the most likely people to steal from them. The Sealord runs a tight ship; there isn't much organized crime in Donir, at least none that dare to show their face. There are a few other outfits, but they ignore us, and I feel fine returning the favor. Extortion isn't exactly exciting though.

It's not enough, and I know it. Though I occasionally pick some pockets on the street or steal silks from a lady's wardrobe, I'm a Shaper of an element that isn't even supposed to exist. Shadow deserves its time in the sun.

"We need to know more," I find myself saying, a part of me instantly regretting the words as Corna leaps to her feet and throws her arms around my neck.

"I knew it! Kettle, we are going to be so infamous!"

"Corna," I start, carefully keeping my tone neutral. "You realize that, consequences aside, we are trying to sneak into perhaps the most secure room in the most secure building in the kingdom. It's going to take patience, planning, and time to even approach a feasible plan. We could be talking years."

"Kettle, if we plunder Jon Gordyn's secret vault, I will retire from the business, buy one of the Broken Isles, and live my life with servants tending to my every need. I'll occasionally throw coconuts at *your* island across the water. I don't care if it's our last job, and I don't care how long it takes. This is legendary."

"Well, we need to know more. Bring Rina here. She has a head for numbers, and she *looks* wealthy," I murmur, the wheels already turning in my head.

"What do those things matter?" Corna asks.

"You scamps need to start doing some work around here. I think Rina needs to get a job at the Imperial Bank."

***

Two weeks later, Timo stares at me. I stare back. He blinks. I blink. The routine has already lasted for long seconds stretching into minutes. He still hasn't reacted. I don't say anything, though, because I can see cogs moving behind his eyes. The mind of an intelligent man hides behind his rough veneer. Far behind. He opens his mouth to speak, then shuts it. Twice.

"You wan' me," he says finally, the words slowly rolling off his tongue. "Ta act?"

"That's what I said, isn't it?"

"As in, a play."

"Yes."

"Act."

"Yes."

"In a play."

"I think we've established that," I say, exasperated.

"I jus' wanted you ta have tha chance ta change yer mind," he says, shaking his head in confusion.

"We need you to be able to be more than just our muscle, my friend. We need you to be able to talk, to pretend, to act as if you are more than the thug that everyone thinks you are. You are big and strong and intimidating. But what if you could also be charming, smooth, and persuasive? Imagine if you could speak like you do, or speak like a noble? Don't you want to play more roles than just 'hulking brute' or 'ignorant tough'? You can be so much more than you are. Don't you remember how we met? Why we met?"

Timo doesn't respond aside from slowly nodding his head. He remembers *The Lost Lore of Isa*, whether he wants to admit it or not. A gleam kindles in his eyes. The challenge. He wants to learn, to be something more than he ever thought he would be.

"It's going to be hard work," I warn. "You will have to learn how to speak 'properly,' and how to carry yourself, and you'll have to memorize your lines. Just remember, this is practice for the big dance to come. We need you to play a role that isn't yourself for what's coming, and I believe you can do it."

He nods firmly. I give him the details of the playhouse, along with the name he can tell them to access his bunk backstage. He leaves in a daze, not even bothering to say goodbye. He's effectively beyond my control for the next two months. I just hope Master Tiolacco took it to heart when I described the man he would be molding.

I put thoughts of Timo from my mind as Corna bounces down the stairs, Rina at her side.

"I've forged some pretty decent stuff in my day," Corna says, slapping a rolled piece of parchment into her palm. "But this is my masterpiece. The Creator himself would swear Rina has been working for the Khalintar of the Coin for the last three years, on loan from her father in the Badlands."

Rina is short, snub-nosed, and red-headed. She looks as if she could have been born amongst people of the Baldinland; her cover as a wealthy daughter out of that northern province is perfect. The 'Badlands' are so named because they mark the northernmost border between the Kingdom of the Sea and the frozen tundra in the north. The people there are hardy, surly, and mistrusting of anyone whose name they don't already know. They have to deal with the occasional, though steady, raiding from the tribes of dark-haired barbarians to the north. The Sealord doesn't bother sending his true army up there, because the lands themselves are a desolate, frozen wasteland. Conquering the barbarian tribes would be both expensive and pointless. Instead, the Badlanders deal with the raids.

"So, Rina wants to join the Imperial Bank. What are the denominations of coin?" I ask.

"Bronze pennies, silver pennies, bronze marks, silver marks, gold marks, and starsilver marks," Rina rattles off, rolling her eyes. I have to give it to her, it isn't really a question.

"If I had thirty-three bronze marks, a dozen silver pennies, and forty-seven bronze pennies, how many gold marks do I have?"

"None," Rina says. "All of that adds up to less than half of a gold mark. You could only change that into three silver marks, four bronze marks, six silver pennies, and seven bronze pennies. Exchange rates for that tiny amount of money would be practically negligible, but I imagine you would lose those seven bronze pennies in the trade."

"A man walks into the bank with a bag full of starsilver marks, staggering under its weight. He pours the whole lot out onto your desk and demands you put his money in your vault. What do you do?"

"Well, after I palm one, I would beg the man's patience and go talk to my superior. Most likely, he will fetch Gordyn if the man is at the office, because the kind of money you just described would buy most castles, many towns, and some small cities."

"Good," I say, not really satisfied but forcing myself to be. Rina's smart; she's been running with us for nearly two years. She has quick hands, a faster mind, and no weaknesses other than money. "But don't palm a mark. The last we need is some shrewd fool who knows the exact count of marks that were in the bag. He'll notice on the receipt, make an accusation, and you'll be dead or worse. I can't impress upon you enough how very dangerous what we're asking you to do is."

"Yes, Mother," Rina says, sarcasm lacing her voice. "Teach me how to pick the pocket, will you? Teach me how to make the beast with two backs, will you?"

I roll my eyes, waving her away. She takes the formal letter of introduction and strolls out of the house, her official attire somehow hugging her curves in all the right places. I ignore the tiny pang of jealousy drifting through my heart. I'll never be described as curvy, but at least my assets - or lack thereof - are perfect for squeezing into tight places. I turn to Corna, who shrugs.

"A bit touchy, asking her that last question. Isn't pouring a bag of starsilver marks on her desk part of the plan?" Corna asks.

"Maybe. To get it all together, we might have to sell the house, *chela*."

"It'll be worth it, little girl."

"If we don't all die," I mutter, pinching the bridge of my nose and rubbing away a rising headache.

"You are *so* gloomy," Corna says, rolling her eyes and slapping me on the arm. "Don't we have something else to do today?'

"Yes, your contact. Don't forget: we need to intercept the messenger Gordyn is inevitably going to send to confirm Rina's identity. She may well be dead if we don't."

"Yes, Mother," Corna says. "Teach me how to pick the pocket, will you? Teach me how to make—" she cuts off with a huff as I elbow her lightly in the ribs.

"I want to go check in on the children before we meet with your friend. It feels strange without them."

***

Once I decided to rob Jon Gordyn, I immediately divided the Family. Even though we won't be ready for months, probably years, I want to remove our place of operations from the obvious estate in the Corpses and make us much harder to find. Almost every adult member of the Family is off on a task. I leave Hom and Yelden to watch the house. They have by far the easiest job; they just get to sit on their asses and make sure the house stays clean. The children, though, are now apprenticed to the Temple of Creation. The Creationists were glad to accept more than a dozen budding acolytes in worship of the Creator. For a reasonable donation.

I gave the little ones an offer when I dropped them off: if they enjoy the work and genuinely want to join the priesthood, I will allow them to stay on after the Gordyn job is over. Many of them barely know me or each other, so I expect several to take me up on that offer. It hurts to think about my children leaving me, but the life of a priest is often more satisfying and far less dangerous than to be a part of the Family.

So the house is silent. I walked into the broken-down confines of the mansion with Corna eight-hundred ninety days before. The money we earned for turning in her fake corpse purchased the estate along with several others throughout the Corpses. Corna and I explored every nook and cranny, grinning and laughing and starting at the smallest of sounds. It was the first day I called Corna my sister. It was the first day that we started the Family.

The silence of the house is unbearable as we walk out. The lack of laughter, the absence of children's feet and the scrape of chairs, the emptiness without Timo's booming laugh and Corna's slashing sarcasm. The stillness of a house breathing, breathing, breathing... exhaling. A weight settles on my soul as I glance back at the looming, crumbling facade. The paint is chipped, the wood timbers showing rot, and the sloping roof is bowed in places. The house is hideous, but beautiful. It has been a home for over a hundred souls in the last three years. It provided shelter, warmth, and love throughout those last eight-hundred ninety days. Walking away from it is one of the hardest things I've ever done.

When I left the Isles, I didn't have a single friend, nor did I have a family left. I was as bereft of humanity as is possible outside of the grave. I had no love, no friendship, no joy. The Family has helped to heal those wounds. Each soul we took in brought me further away from that dark precipice. The House represents all of the positives of friendship and love for me.

As we walk away, I can't shake the feeling the Family is never going to come together under that roof again.

***

We stroll across the city, arm in arm, our simple dresses finely made but difficult to place. As ever, the perfect disguises are those in which you allow people to see exactly what they want to see. A person of low means will see us as a half-step above them, two servants out on some errand for our master. They will see the calluses on our hands and the light muscle of our arms and assume we work for a living. A wealthy person will see the cut and quality in our attire and recognize some level of money, but they won't be able to tell how much. That lack of knowledge will leave them off-balance, and most affluent people would rather assume you a peer than be proven the opposite after they treat you poorly.

There are hundreds of Temples of Creation spread throughout Donir. I've spent time praying at each one over the last three years, begging for forgiveness I know will never come, though a part of me hopes the Creator hears me wherever he's gone. The Creationists will tell you he's still around, that he cares for us, but the People know better. Humanity killed him long ago.

Each temple possesses its own appeal. Some, like fire and water, have a constant stream of humanity coming and going. The wealthy love to pray at the altar dedicated to the Sealord's element. Some believe he might even be able to hear them. The poor pray to fire and the legend of the last good Shaper to exist in Telias the Warmheart. Since his death fifteen years ago, a dozen popular songs and stories have been composed expounding on his loyalty and honor. Other more obscure elements like thought and lightning hold the near-silence of an empty sanctuary, little more than the occasional devotee gracing the temple's peaceful halls. The vast majority of the temples are dedicated to one element, each providing a single altar at which supplicants can pray and connect to a single aspect of the Creator.

The grandest temple in the kingdom is located on the edge of the Palace District, standing proud right along the edge of the Pennies. Construction on the mighty edifice finished three years ago; a massive undertaking funded by the Creationists and the King together. The columns in front would take a dozen men linking hands to encompass, and the relief over the entrance is a stylized carving of each of the greatest Shapers in history, locked in moments of myth and legend. Anna the Wind-Daughter, carved impassive and beautiful, a gale rising behind her to signify the cleansing of the Bridge of the East. Heloren the Unceasing Flame, a stone clutched in his hands as he takes the heat from a volcano off the western coast of the Khalintars. Intiol the Wise, a scroll in his hands, who used Thought to bring the warring Khals together. And, of course, Helikos the Sealord himself, gravely and proudly displayed in the middle of the frieze, triumphant over the corrupt Council of Shapers. Although all fifteen of the elements are displayed in the grand temple, the altar of water is honored above all.

Supposedly, a larger, even more impressive temple exists in the Khalintar of the Coin, so large as to dwarf every other edifice ever raised to the Creator. It has existed for hundreds, maybe thousands of years, hearkening back to the first days after the fall of the Eternal. Conspicuously, that temple is said to have a full sixteen altars, one more than any other. No one knows what the last altar is supposed to symbolize. Some worship at it nonetheless. People have always had faith in absurdly ambiguous ideas.

Corna and I pass out of the Corpses and into the Pennies, but then we turn south, away from the temple at the palace and into one of the simpler districts of the city. The land south of the Pennies is filled with working class families and small shops. Nothing ever happens here, and the roofs are all a uniform shape and height. For the peace and quiet, it has been dubbed the Meadows. If you want specialty work from craftsmen not corrupted by the flow of gold, or if you desire a loaf of bread baked with love and time, you go to the Meadows.

Nestled along the edge of the city against the southern wall, a lone Temple of Creation was quietly constructed three years ago. Small, unattended, and out of the way, this particular temple is my favorite place to pray. It's dedicated to the Unknown, the element that has not been Shaped since the fall of the Eternal. The element is acknowledged as real because the Shapers of the Council were able to find many Shapers of the Unknown during their reign. Whenever a Shaper of the Unknown was discovered during the reign of the Council, their lifelong task was to travel the world and search for the element of their power. None had succeeded.

Until now.

I walk into *my* temple, smiling to see that the lights of the sanctuary muffled as I requested. The hooded lanterns and oddly-placed torches create a strange, flickering set of shadows that dance about the floor and walls as if alive. The living shadow under my dress shifts, recognizing the safe space. With a thought, I let it pool in my footsteps, and the darkness eagerly seeks out the corners of the room. The shadow seems just a darker part of the dim corners, but I can still feel it. The temple is in good repair despite the lack of congregants; I make sure that the only temple dedicated to my element is looked after.

The Priest of Creation in charge of the Temple of the Unknown, Nolan, was once a promising young member of the clergy, his intelligence and dedication to the Creator unsurpassed. But, as he learned the history of the fallen Council of Shapers and compared it to the alleged reasons for Helikos' coup, he had been unsatisfied. He began to speak out against the Sealord and his rule, but before he could gain more than a handful of followers, the Temple threatened to eject him from their ranks or send him to the Khalintars in exile. I offered him a third option: learn to be subtle and stay in charge of a small, out-of-the-way Temple. He can still preach, and I make sure he has a steady stream of listeners. The Family likes to go to temple together on feast days.

Nolan's voice echoes from the back rooms of the temple, though distance obscures the words. In a pause, a small, childlike voice raises a question. Nolan responds, and his words grow more distinct the closer we come.

"... never heard why you should be afraid?" Nolan asks, curiosity in his voice.

"All we know is that the Eternal has saggy tits," Kit's voice, entirely earnest. The other children all chorus in agreement.

"And a dried-up—" Tera begins.

"Right," Nolan cuts in, flustered. I hold up my hand to Corna, and we stop outside the room, grinning. I wonder if Nolan had any idea what he was getting into when he agreed to take them on. The door is shut, but it's made of thin wood and the sound carries easily. "Well then, a proper story is in order. Would you like to hear the true history of the Eternal?"

"Are there any thieves?" Elan asks, excited.

"Assassins?" Kit puts in.

"Bakers!" Tera shouts, and I can picture her tiny arms shooting up as she wriggles.

"Bakers? Why in the Eternal's dried-up-"

"Okay!" Nolan exclaims in a state of near-panic. Corna and I struggle to contain our laughter. "How about I just tell you. This story involves everyone. Thieves, assassins, and yes, bakers, too. No interruptions. Just listen."

When Nolan speaks, people listen. The timbre and rhythm of his voice is hypnotizing, entrancing. As he begins his story, we fall into the words, becoming a part of the fabric of the myth itself.

We know the day. We know the year. We know exactly how long it has been since the Eternal reigned. More than five thousand years ago, before the King and his new kingdom, before the Council of Shapers and their long rule, there was the Eternal.

Where she came from is legend. Her reign stretched as many years as it has been since her fall, for she could not die. She was the undisputed, unquestioned ruler of the world. Every nation bowed to her, every Shaper served her, and every man, woman, and child worshiped her. She was a woman of startling beauty, so that all who looked on her loved her. It was a good thing, because they had no choice. She ruled the world with an iron fist, and she was unafraid of enforcing the laws, her laws, to their fullest extent.

The reign of the Eternal was a glorious time for humanity. Her capital, Isa, was the wonder of the world. The city was staggering in size. Homes wrought of such size that they would make the palace look like a hovel, walls so high the clouds graced their tops, the city was crafted of shining, polished stone. Under the Eternal's rule, we made the Ways, connecting the world and all of its people. The land was reformed, the continents brought together. Shapers dedicated their lives, hundreds of years, to remaking the land in the image of the Eternal's vision. Art and writing and medicine flourished. There was no war, no famine, no strife. Everyone who opposed her was crushed. Every family that raised their voices disappeared. Even kings guarded their tongues and their thoughts, lest their rule be short.

For the Eternal had the greatest of advantages. She could look into the past, the present, and the future. The Eternal was the Master of Time.

She had the power to stop the flow of time in its tracks, even to reverse the events of the recent present. The Eternal could read the possible futures and change the course of history. She knew the thoughts of her opponents before they had them. She knew who would betray her, when, and how. With this power, she ended all opposition before it could begin.

For five thousand years, the Eternal's reign was gracious and benevolent. The world flourished, and the people loved her. Whenever she left Isa, parades followed, the multitudes groveling before the ancient queen. No one with a prayer of opposing her existed, and no one left alive cared to.

But there are consequences to a life that lasts so long. No human was meant to live so many years. After five thousand years of rule, the Eternal stopped leaving Isa. She stopped leaving her mighty palace. She stopped leaving even the throne. She grew distracted. Her eyes looked far into the distance, and her attention focused less and less on the world outside her throne room. Some believe that her mind snapped, having been alive for so much longer than human beings are meant to live. Others believe that she lost her way looking into the past or the future. In any case, she drifted away from the present.

A hundred years into her distraction, the Eternal's soldiers chased a young thief as he ran through the streets of Isa. They believed he had stolen a ring from a wealthy woman of the city. The men, having been the sole source of law for thousands of years, were arrogant and cruel. The soldiers executed the boy even as they caught him, for thieving was not tolerated in those days. But the boy had stolen back his own property. He had given a girl a token of his favor and took it back when she was unfaithful to him. In her spite, she had called on the Queen's soldiers. That boy was Fenril, the son of Eterian, the Shaper of Earth and Vengeance of the Eternal.

When Eterian returned from a long journey and discovered his son slain, the earth bucked so powerfully as to shake the very walls of mighty Isa. He stormed into the throne room and demanded justice for his son. He shouted. He raged. Anger and pain shattered his voice. But the Eternal never saw him, her eyes far away. He begged her, there on his knees before the throne, but she never acknowledged his presence. After two long days, he left.

Eterian believed her mind broken. His rage and sorrow drove him to speak out against the Eternal. For the first time in her long reign, she did not respond to an opponent's words. She did not see them coming. The Vengeance of the Eternal was a respected and feared position: he was her justice. He carried out her will as a judge, and as assassin when called upon. He had been at her side for many centuries.

Though most people loved the Eternal and ignored Eterian's words, others began to listen; those whose ancestors had been rounded up and executed in advance of crimes they would never get the chance to commit, those who wished for power or a kingdom of their own outside her domineering rule, even those who just wanted chaos to descend upon the world.

The first army since the beginning of the Eternal's rule was raised in Donir. None of the people had the faintest idea how to be soldiers, nor what war really entailed. The first army was made up of a mob of farmers, craftsman, laborers, and, yes, bakers. They picked up hammers and pitchforks, standing behind Eterian as they marched down from Donir towards Isa. A contingent of the Eternal's Immortals met them on the Bridge of the East, led by Genos, the Shaper of Wind. When asked to lay down their weapons, Eterian responded that they wanted to speak with the Eternal. They just wanted her to listen.

In response, the Immortals attacked.

Eterian fought against Genos, Shaper against Shaper, for the first time in millennia. While they fought, the Immortals fell on Eterian's civilian army and slaughtered them. They never stood a chance. The elite troops of the Eternal were merciless to those they viewed as traitors. Lightly armed and unarmored, they died in droves. Eventually, Eterian managed to kill Genos, sacrificing himself in the process, and their battle shattered the mighty Bridge of the East and cut Donir off from Isa.

The people of Donir rose as one in anger and righteous fury. The Bridge's destruction allowed them time to build, to train, and to simmer in their anger. Word spread. Shapers, friends of Eterian and angry over the death of so many innocents, joined the cause. While the Eternal's armies marched across the Bridge of the West along the Ways through ancient Canto, now Coin, the Donirians prepared. By the time the Immortals started across the Bridge of the North, the Donirians were ready. Though still not up to the level of their foes, who had been raised to fight from birth, the Donirians outnumbered the soldiers more than ten to one. Shapers fought on both sides, names that still echo down through history. Jendo the Mind Razor. Kelion the Crashing Wave. And the most well-known of all: Sherrine, the Breaker.

For a hundred years, the war raged across all the land, and no city was spared. By the time the final battle was joined before the gates of Isa, less than half of the population of the world survived. The siege of Isa lasted for two decades. Shapers died on either side, the inheritors of their power raised on war and thrown into the fray. At long last, Sherrine was born. She was the Master of Stone, one of the most powerful to have ever lived. She knelt before the gates of Isa for three days. The defenders looked on, glad for the respite and resting as Sherrine seemed to pray. In reality, she was Shaping.

The walls of Isa stood for five thousand years of history and two decades of constant war. The Breaking took a single day. The walls fell inward, the massive slabs crushing and decimating thousands of innocents inside. In the effort, Sherrine herself perished, the explosion of power upon her death breaking what was left of the southern continent. When the world finally took another shuddering breath, Isa was gone, and the Eternal along with it.

Or so the people thought.

Over the next few years, all of the people looked for the rise of a new Shaper of Time. They were terrified of a new Eternal rising. Every baby was tested, every child examined endlessly. The entire world came together to search, trying to avoid history's repeating. After a generation, people started to question. After a hundred years, people started to forget. After a thousand, the Shaper of Time became a legend, a myth to scare children. But the Temple has the records. The Eternal existed. And there is only one explanation: she still lives.

A cold chill creeps down my spine as Nolan's story comes to an end. The Eternal is a fanciful myth. I'm sure some queen had once been known as the Eternal, had fancied herself as such, but I always imagine the Eternal as a series of queens, each taking the name to follow the reputation. The Eternal was just a very long, very powerful dynasty.

Told in Nolan's voice, with his knowledge from the Creationists... it isn't enough to make me question, but it damn sure leaves an uneasy feeling in my gut as I open the door. The children sit in a small circle, still enraptured by the story. Nolan glances up and gives me a gentle nod. "Mother!" Kit shouts, leaping to his feet. The other children all scramble up and throw their arms around Corna and me. Neither of us can get a word in edgewise as the children chatter and laugh and smile.

"Come now, little ones, it has only been a week! How do you like Priest Nolan?"

"He tells us the best stories!" Elan says, his eyes glowing beneath his mop of orange hair.

"There are even bakers in them!" Tera shouts. "My dad was a baker, you see, and I always want to know stories about—"

"We even have our own bed! No more sleeping on the ground!" another chimes in.

"Isn't that great," Corna says in a tone struggling between warmth and annoyance. Tera squeezes her arm in a death grip, and Corna is doing her best to extricate herself. She's trying to be as gentle as possible, but Tera clings fiercely in her excitement.

"So, it'll be okay until we can come back for you?" I ask, grinning at their smiling faces.

Their voices mix into an incomprehensible babble in confirmation. Kit, though, stays quiet and serious. He pulls me aside, his face set in solemn lines.

"Mother, you know I'll stay here if you wish it, but I don't want to. I should be with you, helping with the job!"

"Whoa, Kit," I say, blinking at him. "What do you mean, helping? What do you know?"

"I know you guys are doing something dangerous! Otherwise you wouldn't have sent us away. We're the Family. We're only strong together."

"You're right," I say, pride surging in my breast. "And we'll be back together as soon as this has ended. But, because we're the Family, I have to protect my children. Allowing you to help would put you right in the sights of someone very, very dangerous."

"But I can help!"

"Think, Kit," I say, letting an edge creep into my voice. "Let's say we bring you in, and you do help. Then our safehouse gets raided. We have to run, but first we have to fight. A big, armored man comes at you with a sword. What will happen?"

"I'll dodge, or hide. I'm fast," he says, but I can see the hint of fear in his eyes.

"No, what will happen is that I'll be forced to protect you. I'll have to keep an eye out for myself, and you, and everyone else as we try to get out of a fight we can't win. So I turn to help you, and someone stabs Corna. Or I save Timo, and a soldier guts you while I'm distracted. I know you want to help, Kit, but you have to recognize you aren't ready. I know you will be, and it'll be sooner than I'd like, but it isn't today. Stay with the priest, learn what you can, and then come back to me ready to rejoin the Family."

Kit nods reluctantly. I can tell he doesn't agree, but he's willing to do as I ask. Whatever. He doesn't have to agree as long as he's safe. I chat with Nolan for a while, and he assures me that he will treat the kids as his own. I've only ever been honest, open, and generous with Nolan. He has no cause to fear me. But, as I shake his hand and wish him all the best with my children, I feel the tremor in his grip and the uncertainty in his eyes. He knows what they mean to me.

***

Corna and I trace our path back through the city, the masses parting around us like stones in a river. We walk to the Pennies, to a particular inn known as the Juggling Bear. The place is ordinary in the extreme. It makes just enough money to survive, but not enough to flourish. The sign is noticeable, but unremarkable. The patrons are day-to-day laborers and travelers. In essence, it's the most bland and forgettable place we can imagine to have a meeting about robbing the richest man alive. Secret meetings are not made for dark corners. Those have a tendency to be scrutinized. No, if you want to have a secret meeting, make it as open and obvious as possible. Two friends meeting a third at a nameless inn for a meal is hardly remarkable. Two thieves meeting an informant in a dark alley is instantly suspicious.

We walk in, our dresses blending with the few women present in the inn. The tables are remarkably full for the Juggling Bear. In the back corner sits the man we're there to see. I notice him immediately, which sends a flash of terror through me. If I can pick him out so fast, surely others will be able to as well. Though his clothing is made of fine material and in the latest fashion, he's unshaven, and sweat glistens on his brow. His leg taps incessantly, and his eyes dart to and fro. As if spotting an assassin will actually save him when he has jammed himself in a corner that has no easy means of escape.

As we walk over, I glance at the other patrons. None show any undue interest in our friend, but I keep a surreptitious eye on them as we take our seats. The man leans forward, a fevered intensity in his brown eyes. He would have been handsome, but his face is screwed into an expression of stress and fear. His strong jaw is better suited to smiles and roguish charm. The table is close to clean, though the stain of hundreds of spilled drinks mars the weathered wood.

"Do you have the money?" he says, his voice low but insistent.

"Why, darling, what are you so worried over?" Corna says, loudly, her musical laugh tinkling through the inn and quieting everyone else as they turn to look. "That poem you wrote her is lovely. I'm sure she'll say yes!"

"What are you doing?" the man says, his eyes practically bulging out of their sockets. "Don't call attention-"

"She's saving your ass," I answer, my eyes narrowed in growing anger. "If you keep acting like you are, you won't make it two blocks with Gordyn on your tail. Pretend what I just said to you was funny."

He stares at me askance for a moment, but Corna continues to simper and loudly talk about his imaginary betrothal, so he forces a laugh. Soon, everyone in the place looks back at their food or drinks, forgetting about the nervous man and his imminent proposal.

"Now, we have the money," I start, holding up a finger in warning when he leans forward again. He forces himself to relax and sit back in the booth. His features don't match the act, though. "Do you have what you claim to have?"

He reaches into his coat pocket and produces a sweat-stained and crumpled piece of parchment. With a shaking hand, he smooths the paper flat and slides it across the table to us. I glance at it quickly, seeing an unfamiliar, though detailed, floor plan, down to circles marking support columns and the location of the various vaults and side rooms. My gaze flicks back upwards.

"How is this special? I could draw this just from walking through the bank."

"Look," he mutters, stabbing his finger down at a point on the map. When he moves his hand, he reveals a blank space.

"Are you wasting my time?" I ask, venom entering my tone. Corna reaches forward, scooping up the paper with a warning look and loudly remarking about how beautiful it is to compare her to a rose.

The man snatches the paper back irritably, pointing first at the middle floor.

"See? Here, the second floor has a series of offices and meeting rooms. They extend throughout this floor. The third floor offices are bigger; only Gordyn's closest compatriots operate on the third floor. No client ever gets brought up there unless they are a serious investor or a personal acquaintance of Gordyn himself. But look." He points again to the blank space. "The *area* of the two floors should be identical, by outward appearances of the building, but this space behind Gordyn's office is empty. I checked the place visually. There are windows on the back side of the building, and Gordyn's office is the last in his hall. I have been in Gordyn's office, and it doesn't have any windows. If it was really the last room in that hall, it would. There is something *behind* Gordyn's office."

I sit back, the possibilities swirling through me. Whoever this guy is, and however Corna came in contact with him, he isn't a fool. I'm sure most people would have been too intimidated, actually being in Gordyn's personal office, to notice such things. But his words also send alarm bells ringing in the back of my mind. Gordyn *knows* this man? He's seen him, even invited him into his office?

"Corna, pay him," I say curtly, snatching the floor plan out of his hands and turning to go. An old man looms over me. A full mustache hides his thin cheekbones, but his clothes hang loosely about his bony frame. My hand drops to the dagger hidden in my skirt, but he looks behind me to the nervous man in the corner.

"I couldn't help but overhear, if you'll excuse me," he starts in a wavering voice. "I have to say, you need to be courageous! If you want her to say yes, you need to be brave, young man."

I sigh inwardly and let the dagger stay hidden.

"He will. He's going to do it in a few hours! He just sent me to get the money for the ring!" Corna says, plopping the fat purse down on the table conspicuously. Even I have to suppress a shudder at the flagrant display of wealth. It's best to keep anything from appearing secretive in such a public place, but the amount of money changing hands is staggering. Our friend will be able to have a good start on a new life with the gold in that purse.

"Ah, well, good luck, lad. I'm sure you don't need it!" the old man says, smiling and ambling away.

We leave as fast as we can, the information already tucked away in the folds of my dress. We stroll arm in arm, the perfect picture of two young ladies out for an afternoon walk. The Winter air starts to bite as the sun drops towards the horizon, so we hurry like many of the other passersby towards warmer climes.

“We are about to learn something very important,” I hiss at Corna under my breath, our heads barely an inch apart.

“What is that? Why are you clenching my arm so hard?”

“Jon Gordyn *met* that man. He was in Gordyn's Eternal-damned *office*. Do you think he could get away with what just happened?”

“Wait, you're saying...” Corna says, eyes growing wider.

“Yes. That man, and our money, is going to be in Gordyn's hands. Soon. It's our job to watch and observe. We need to know how long it takes Gordyn to find him, and what he does to our friend when he manages. What did that man do that he wants to betray Jon Gordyn of all people?”

“I don't know,” Corna says softly. “I met him at a party thrown by Duke Graevo. Some merchant got invited, and I went on his arm. Weeks later, he sees me in the street and knows me. As in, me, Corna of the Family, not Corna the merchant's date. He wanted to sell me something valuable, and I listened because he was desperate.”

“We're going back to the Temple,” I say, turning us around and heading south again.

“What? Why?” Corna asks.

“We need to pray.”

Chapter 6
Jace
The Fortieth Day of Winter
In the year 5219, Council Reckoning

The first I know is warmth. I shift towards the warmth, the life, that holds me to the world. Little more than that sensation, a glow of life and love that envelopes me entire. Air moves across my face, her breath. My arms strain to reach above me, struggling to touch, to feel, to know.

The warmth intensifies. Soon the heat is unbearable. The roar of fire swallows my cries. Yanked from the embrace around me, I plunge into a stinging, burning brightness I can't escape. I open my mouth to scream, but smoke rushes in.

I wake up on my side in a bed, covered in sheets and bandages. The same familiar dream rocks its way through my racing heart, and I shudder against the fear. The movement opens up entire avenues to pain. Every inch of me hurts, my neck a black pit of unrelenting agony. I can still feel the heat from my dream burning on my face. That's new. I snap open my eyes.

A blazing fire burns in front of me, flames licking up the wall and scorching bright orange and red. My nightmare made real. I gasp, trying to edge away, but the pain is too great. My heart beats erratically as the flame consumes the blue curtains in front of me. The fire eats with relentless appetite. I can't move. My body won't respond to my frantic commands. The flame grows, racing towards the walls. The fire is going to consume me as easily as the drapes, and all I can do is lie still and watch it come. My throat tries to scream.

I must make some kind of noise, for the silhouette of a man blocks the fire. Slender and graceful, the fire moves in accord with his movements, two dancers in perfect harmony. Time slows as if to allow the two their moment, the silent figure and the roaring fire moving in time. The moment breaks as he yanks the drapes down from the wall. The heat and smoke blazes brighter. My panic finally overwhelms the pain, I jerk back. My neck explodes, and oblivion takes me.

***

With a groan, my eyes open onto white linen illuminated by brilliant, liquid sunshine. I've never seen white sheets before. I bring my arm up painfully and stroke the soft, clean purity with reverence. It's a luxury too large for words, too rare for use. Even at an upper-scale establishment like the Simply, too much goes on between the sheets to ever worry about what they look like. I struggle to roll onto my back, but lancing pain strikes me all along my neck and lower body. With an audible groan, I give up the attempt. Footsteps approach my bed with quiet certainty as Reknor takes a chair next to the bed.

"Tried to move, did you?" he asks, smiling.

"Just fancied a little stretch."

"No doubt," Reknor says, grinning wider. "But you wouldn't lie on your back even when you were unconscious, so I don't think I'd try it now, either. Now, out with it. What happened after you left my house last night?"

"I fell off a roof." The charred and blackened wall across from my bed has peeled away to reveal the timbers beneath. "What happened to the drapes?"

"They caught fire," Reknor says, cocking an eyebrow.

"That's it? They caught fire? No elaboration, no detail? "

"Well, you just fell off a roof."

I get the hint.

"I fell three stories. And those thugs thought they would rob me, but they apparently were too thick to realize I'm as poor as yellow grass in Winter. You saved me before they could carry me off and do something nasty."

"Remarkably vague and light on detail." Reknor loses his smile. "I would recognize Timo's ugly face even in the dark. You think he hasn't tried to make me pay protection money to the Family?"

"Ah," I say tactfully. "The Family, well, banned me from their territory on pain of death. Kettle made the pronouncement in front of about a thousand people in a public square."

"Oh, you're *that* Jace. Word spreads fast when a secretive leader of a secretive group makes a public appearance. You went to their territory?" Reknor asks in a tone that questions my sanity.

"I was distracted," I say defensively. "You gave me a lot to think about. And the whole damn city is their territory now. It's your fault more than anything. If you hadn't been so nice to me this never would have happened."

Reknor looks at me incredulously. My anger fades, and I start to chuckle. Pretty soon we're both laughing, though I'm a bit more reserved because it hurts so much. It feels good regardless. It's a breath of relief after the past few days.

"Well," Reknor continues finally. "We're going to need to develop an appropriate identity for you if you're going to stay."

"What are you talking about? I can't stay. They even know who you are now, and that means they'll be coming. Creator's middle finger, they've got to be coming."

I start to move around in my panic, doing my best to ignore the shooting pains down my spine.

"No, they won't," Reknor says, leaning forward and gently restraining me. It doesn't take much. "It was dark, and I took my eye patch off and put up my hair. I also kicked the crap out of them. No one would expect that of a scribe."

"How *did* you beat them?"

"Tactics," Reknor answers, shrugging.

"Tactics?" I ask in disbelief.

"Tactics," he says matter-of-factly.

I glare at him, though the expression is probably softened by the bandages and the fact that I can't move off of my side. Reknor's face looks stricken, and he sits back in his chair.

"Damn me, boy, remind me never to make you angry. You look like you're about to open a gate into the Eternal's tomb and drop me into it."

My eyebrows shoot up, and I fight to keep myself from smiling.

"I've had a lot of practice," I say flippantly.

"Right. Well, if I think you're ready, and Creator forbid you never glare at me like that again, I'll teach you some of my tactics. Regardless, no one will ever recognize you now. While you were sleeping I had a doctor come in and look at you. Part of the process was bathing you so that we could even see your wounds."

"What do you mean, no one will recognize me?" I ask, skeptical.

"When was the last time you looked in a mirror?"

"I see myself in windows all the time," I say quietly.

It's a lie. It's been two years since I've gotten a proper look at myself. I can distance myself from reality looking down at my toes. I can imagine that those legs are a different person's, that I'm not actually wearing that burlap sack as a shirt. Looking in the mirror, though, even partially, would be looking at myself in reality.

Reknor pulls a hand mirror from a nearby drawer and angles it towards my face. The boy staring back at me in the mirror is a stranger. The roundness and childishness of my cheeks are gone, lean hollows showing between my jaw and cheekbone. My hair is the pleasant, deep red-brown of mahogany, not the black-brown of dirt, tar, and filth. Even my eyes have changed. Where once they were the light, pleasant blue of a clear summer sky, now they've deepened into the tones of a clear mountain lake.

I look up from the mirror and into Reknor's knowing smirk.

"I get your point," I admit through my shock.

Reknor begins ticking things off on his fingers.

"They don't know where you are, they don't know what you look like, they don't expect you to be clean and well-clothed. They certainly won't anticipate you living in a house on Castleberry Street with an old half-blind historian."

"Why are you doing this again?"

"As I said before, Jace. Can you afford to ask that question?" We both know that I can't, but he continues anyway. "I'm an old man. I may not look it, but I've been living on borrowed time for years. I *feel* my age. I have no living relatives, no heir, no partner. What's the point of all this when I'm gone?" he said, waving his arm around as if to encompass the house and the entire world itself.

The words 'but why me?' die on my lips. I want to know. Curiosity burns in my veins, for I can sense something behind his words, something deep and poignant. His deception, however honest, provokes mistrust. Yet it's enough.

"Okay, okay," I say, suddenly remembering. "I gave you the details you wanted. What about the fire? What happened?"

"Oh, I just left a candle lit by your bed last night," Reknor says flippantly. "You must have moved in your sleep and knocked it over."

"Really?" I say skeptically. "That seems... strange."

"I know. I didn't expect you to move that much. Especially with your injuries."

"Right," I say, feigning a yawn. "Well, I bet you can leave one by me right now. I'm going to sleep like the dead."

Reknor smiles and stands.

"Sleep well, Jace. Recover. Call if you need anything."

I nod, closing my eyes. As soon as I hear him retreat, they slowly open again. I stare hard at the blackened portion of the wall where the curtain used to hang. There isn't any wax on the floor, nor on the desk. I can hardly imagine even my unconscious mind allowing an open flame near enough for me to 'move in my sleep' and knock it over. That quick story is the only time that Reknor's words rang truly false in my ears. Why would he lie about that? What could have caused the fire?

What does he have to hide?

***

The hunt has long died down by the time I take my first faltering step under Reknor's care. When I can finally walk freely, the thieves have given me up for dead or gone. I barely think about the hunt, itching as I am to *move*. I'm young and full of energy. Injury and sickness have never brought me low. Not being able to leave a bed, even to relieve myself, is humbling and frightening and awfully boring at the same time. It's with blessed relief that I finally totter out of the room.

Reknor's house is larger than it looks from the outside. Directly in front of the door, an open area with a desk serves as the front of his scribing. The bell on the desk rings regularly from a steady stream of business. To the left of the opening foyer, decorated in a simple yet refined style, a sitting room furnished to greet wealthy clients provides guests a place to relax. The right holds Reknor's study and the hallway to the door. That blasted, intricately-carved, flame-inlaid door.

Further back holds the kitchens, worked by one extraordinarily crabby old woman who calls herself Pies. Pies hates to talk to anyone. Over the course of the first few weeks I realize that Reknor has no control over the woman at all. Meal times are set in stone: breakfast at literal dawn, half past noon for lunch, just after six for dinner. If you miss the meal, you go hungry. Pies creates the entire menu herself, and Reknor never gives her any input. He pays her a substantial sum of money, most of which she uses to buy the ingredients for the meals for the house. The one time she catches me in the kitchens, she scowls at me so fiercely that I stumble out like I've been struck.

For all that, the food is outstanding. In the first three weeks, I never eat the same thing twice. There are stews of vegetables and a deep, hearty cut of beef, and dozens of different kinds of bread. Fish, which I have only ever managed to eat as the castoffs of the wealthy, is a delicacy I'm wary of at first but soon learn to look forward to. Under Pies' careful ministrations, I gain weight. My ribs stop showing quite so clearly through my skin. I'm able to walk freely. Not that I do much with it but stare out over the city.

The window overlooking Reknor's street is a never-ending tapestry. Merchants bow and wring their hands and cater to the wealthy patrons in one moment, then scowl and throw up rude gestures as soon as they turn away. Nobles ride past in ornate, ostentatious carriages, stopping wherever they please and hardly pausing for pedestrians. Young men on horses canter past, doing their best to look pretty for the crowd. Occasionally, I pick out a cutpurse stalking the streets. They no doubt make a killing with the plethora of soft targets along Castleberry. I haven't ever been able to make a run at the wealthiest districts of the city. You have to look the part to even have a chance in places like the Meadows.

A memory, unbidden, creeps its way out of the recesses of my mind.

I shiver on the rooftop. The snow falls thicker than it has before, and I have to blink to clear the snow from my eyelashes. I've been staring down at a butcher shop on the outer edge of the Meadows for hours. If I'm patient, I might be able to sneak down once he throws away his scraps. Waiting in the cold might kill me, but starvation isn't a reasonable alternative.

A young girl, probably eleven, approaches, bolder than I ever would be. Her red hair is still relatively red, so she's eaten well recently, but the ragged state of her clothing and the hunched, world-weary way that she walks flags her as a fellow urchin. Like a hopeless romantic, the girl tries her luck at begging the butcher for his scraps.

"Please sir," she pleads, holding out her hands. "I'm starving and it's so snowing, can you please just-"

"Bugger off," the man snaps. He doesn't glance up, but continues to chop the delicate portions off of a haunch of venison. Experienced street rats would never beg the man, let alone stay after he tells them to leave.

"But sir, my parents died. I just-"

"Leave, you little shite, or I'll have the guard here before you can scream," the butcher growls, looking up with a practiced sneer.

The girl can't take the rejection. It happens to some: the last rejection, the last brush-away, the last look of disdain. Suddenly they snap. Some attack their attackers. Some run screaming through the streets shouting nonsense. Others, like the little redhead, just sit down and cry. Her knees crumple, and she slowly sinks down into the shallow, dirty snow and weeps.

The butcher looks up from his cutting and curses. He strides off down the street, shouting for the guard. I silently will the girl to get up and leave. She shouldn't beg in the Meadows. She definitely shouldn't sit there crying while the Watch is coming. But I know a snap when I see one, so I know that I'm wasting my time with my silent plea. Like I'm the hopeless romantic, I start to climb down from the roof to nudge her along when the sound of booted feet and clinking chainmail freeze me in place.

The men and women of the Watch surround the girl. They ask her a few cursory questions I can't make out. Apparently satisfied, the captain motions to one of his men, who steps forward impassively and picks the girl up. Suddenly coming back to herself, she screams, loud and long, but it doesn't do her any good. My body tenses, but I can't tell if my adrenaline is begging me to save her or run away before a similar fate can befall me.

The guardsman walks over to the nearest sewer grate. Two of the brawnier men in the group lift the heavy bars aside, and the guard shoves the thrashing, screaming girl into the darkness below. She clings with her arms and feet, desperately crying out in a wordless plea for help. Her face contorts into the desperate fear of a cornered animal. Her giant blue eyes, bigger than any girl has a right to, are filled with frightened tears. The guardsman curses as the girl clings to the edges of the sewer with ferocious tenacity. A second guard finally has to pry her fingers off the edges of the sewer, and she disappears as fast as blinking. Her shriek cuts off when the heavy grate slams closed.

The Watch walk away, ignoring the faintest of cries emanating from under the ground. The butcher returns to work. He cuts his meat with cool precision. He throws the scraps into the alley, closing up his shop and heading upstairs to sleep. My eyes lock on the sewer grate, and I pause, some dormant part of me begging to help her. My stomach rumbles, though, and I thaw quickly enough. Scampering down the brick wall, I dart over and lift the salvageable fat and scraps of meat from the snow before they freeze.

I ignore the tears that run down my face as I stuff the raw meat in my mouth. I can't acknowledge them or I'll have to acknowledge the awful truth. I'm not crying for the little redhead, thrown into darkness so that an arrogant man can stay arrogant. I'm not crying for the brutality of the Watch. No, I'm crying for myself because I don't feel like crying for the little urchin at all.

"What are you doing?"

I start from my reverie. Reknor leans in the doorway with his arms folded, the long sleeves of his shirt hanging loose around his arms, buttons undone. He has the eyebrow over his eye patch cocked, which is about as disconcerting as it sounds. I often wonder how he lost the eye. He hasn't offered, and I don't know him well enough to ask.

"I'm watching the people, seeing wealthy people get cutpursed in broad daylight and struggling to feel for them," I say wryly.

"No, Jace. What are you *doing*?"

I look at him, then pointedly out at the street, then back to him, then again at the street. On the third repetition he throws up his hands in frustration and storms towards me. I lean back in my chair, uncertain what I've done to provoke the man. He towers over me, and the warm wood of the chair is no comfort as he leans in close. I don't cower, but it isn't by much.

"You just... sit," Reknor says, disbelief coloring his voice. "You don't *do* anything. When I first saw you, I thought you were curious and intelligent and vibrant... what is this? What are you doing?"

"I do stuff," I start indignantly, but I stop.

I think about the weeks passed. Sitting at windows, lying in bed recovering, never leaving Reknor's house to venture out. The thought hasn't even crossed my mind. I'm surprised at the thought. Why hasn't the idea of outside, of the world, of people, entered my thoughts? Why am I just sitting here?

"I can see your eyes and know you aren't an idiot," Reknor says, staring intently at me. "I've seen your curiosity and your fire. What happened to it?"

"I... I don't know. I guess..."

I look out the window just in time to see a woman slip a purse and toss it discreetly to another thief passing by. A twinge of unease spikes in my gut, and I slide back farther from the window.

"What do you want out of this?" Reknor asks bluntly. "What do you want from me?"

"I don't want to be afraid anymore."

The words slip from my mouth before I can grab them back. Even as they leave my lips I know them to be true. A tenseness between my shoulder blades tightens my body in the grip of a quiet, subconscious terror. My mental fingers can't place *what* I'm afraid of, but the very notion of leaving the safety of Reknor's house debilitates me. Reknor doesn't say anything, but strokes his beard, his expression thoughtful.

"What are you afraid of?" he asks me, no hint of reproach in his voice.

"Knives, and hobnail boots, and nobles, and Timo," I say in a breathless rush. "And Kettle, and hunger, and the snow, and the Tide, and you, and... fire."

I bury my face in my hands as soon as I finish. What am I, some kind of coward? What does this man, practically a stranger, care about my fears?

"All reasonable fears. Especially me," he says, crouching down to my level. "What if I told you that I could take away all that fear, including the fears you haven't even thought to have? Let you live in confidence, free from what's holding you back?"

"How could you do that?" I ask skeptically, my hard-won pessimism showing through. It sounds like a fairy tale.

"Well, the fear won't be gone completely. A man without fear is insane. But a man who can conquer that fear is dangerous. It'll take work. Hard work. You'll have to do what I say, anything I say, no matter how crazy it sounds. You must do it as if I was your commander, your general. It won't be easy. You may want to quit halfway. You may even try to run. But, here and now, if you agree, I won't let you. We will either conquer your fears together or die trying."

I look into his smoldering brown eye and, Creator help me, believe. I probably should be terrified at his conditions, at the intensity in his voice, but I don't care. I can deal with hardship, work, and toil to be free of fear. I stand up and reach out my hand.

His hand engulfs mine as he shakes it with a firm grip.

***

Gripping the wooden practice sword carefully, I eye the post in front of me. It's painted a variety of colors, as if it has just come from a rural town celebrating the coming of Spring. Red, green, pink, purple, blue, yellow, orange, a random swath of vibrancy from top to bottom. The pole is taller than I am, which puts it about the height of a large man. A storeroom in the back of Reknor's house has been cleared for my use, the only adornment in the entire space this gaudily painted pole.

"This is my opponent?"

"Yep," Reknor says cheerily from his position off to the side. "Strike pink."

"But shouldn't I be fighting against some*one* if I am going to learn how to use a sword?"

"Nope," he responds in the same tone. "Strike pink."

I sigh, bringing the sword around and slapping the pink side squarely in the middle. Reknor appears an inch from my face, and I freeze.

"Did I say gently tap pink?"

"No," I say meekly.

"Then *strike pink*!" he shouts, a vein standing out on his forehead.

I bring the sword up and around and slam it full-force into the pink section. Or, I try to. In my haste and with the strength I've put behind the swing, I miss low and hit purple. The blow stings my hands, the vibrating blade trying to jump out of my hand from the impact.

"You missed. Are you color blind? Strike pink."

Growling in anger, I cut at the pole again. My blow strikes directly in the middle of the pink section. The blow is awkward, and my hands ache. Still, I look at Reknor triumphantly. 'Blue' is his only response.

I spend what feels like hours cutting the pole over and over, high and low and middle and low and middle and high. My arms start to shake after the tenth strike. After the twentieth, I can barely lift the blade. After the thirtieth, I can't even see which color I'm striking through the sweat stinging my eyes. I cut at the memory of the colors. I force sobs down deep into my chest as blood drips down my hands and my arms move with the lumbering speed of an ox.

It takes me a moment to realize that Reknor hasn't called out a color in several attacks. I stare over at him stupidly. My numb hands refuse to let go of the sword. He watches me with an expression somewhere between a grimace and a grin. He holds out his hand for the sword, but I shake my head wearily.

"You want to keep going?" he asks in surprise.

"No," I pant, letting the point of the blade drop and rest on the ground. "I can't make my hands let go."

He nods solemnly. With infinite tenderness, he pries my fingers off of the hilt of the wooden sword. I cry out as each finger tugs free with a wet squelch. The dried blood pulls at blisters that have already broken long before. The sword finally comes free, and I fall to my knees, staring at my once-strong hands in horror. Most of the blood is dried already, but new rivulets of crimson leak down my wrists. I swear I can see bone through the skin. Reknor lifts me up, still staring at my hands, and walks me out of the empty room and back into the livable sections of the house.

He leads me up the stairs and into his room, through his bedchamber, and into his bathing room. A large bowl of marble ten feet across dominates the room. He pulls a rope, and steaming-hot water pours from the fixture to fill up the smooth marble bowl. I haven't seen anything like it, though its use is obvious. When the tub is largely filled, Reknor motions for me to undress and get in the tub.

"Now, Jace," he says, forcing me to look him in the eyes. "This is going to hurt. A lot. But let your hands soak in the water. It will help them relax and begin to heal."

I nod dumbly. He starts to leave, but I must make a noise. He turns back and meets my eye. I plead with him silently, too proud to ask but scared enough to beg. My fingers are little better than frozen claws. He studies my hands again and walks back over, quietly helping me take off my clothes so that I won't have to put my hands to use.

"Even though it might not feel like it right now, that was a pretty damn impressive showing for your first time at the post. I threw my sword down after the fifth stroke on my first effort. Earned me a beating, but still," Reknor offers.

He gives me a half smile and leaves the room. I ease down into the steaming, deliciously hot water. Slowly, I submerge everything but my head and my hands. Sharp spikes of pain shoot up from underneath my arms, and I shy away. I grimace, but force myself back into the water. I take a hundred breaths, trying to find some semblance of the stillness. It doesn't work, but still my heart is calmer as I begin to lower my hands into the water. Fire erupts through my fingers. I hiss between my teeth as my hands dart back away from the warm water. Scowling, mentally hardening myself to what's to come, I shoot my hands down into the water with one swift motion. My calm breathing shatters, and I pant and grunt like an animal as the water slowly turns pink.

When I wake the next day, I can hardly lift my arms. My legs aren't much better off, and my back and abdomen are sheets of aching pain. My hands are wrapped in clean white linen, and I sigh. Reknor is always patching me up while I sleep. When I try to sit up, a splitting headache draws a groan of agony. More stagger than grace, I stumble towards the stairs, thudding with a grunt against the wall. I refuse to use my hands to push off for fear of what that particular experience might do to my sanity.

I take the stairs at an achingly slow pace, first one leg, then the other, each step taking longer than the last. Reknor strolls out of the kitchens carrying a clay jug of something that sloshes just as I reach the bottom. My tongue immediately goes dry in response to the sound. Reknor grins at my expression and offers me the jug.

"Thirsty?"

"You know everything," I say eagerly, reaching out and taking the jug gingerly. The wrappings make the motion awkward, but I bring it to my lips. At the first taste, my eyes pop wide, and I swing the jug down and gawk at the brown liquid within. "What *is* this?"

"Milk mixed with cocoa from the Talirese Islands. It promotes swift recovery."

"It's the Creator's drink itself," I gasp as I finish another long swallow of the ice cold milk. I've only had chocolate a few times in my life. Each other occasion was on my birthday when the girls at the Simply had given me gifts. Usually, it was a mouthful or a small sweet mixed with caramel or coconut. I loved those rare times when the girls relaxed and were more themselves.

"Come with me," Reknor says, beckoning with his hand as he walks past the scribing desk in the front room and into his study. He picks up a stack of tomes from a cracked, green leather chair and gestures for me to sit. "Can you read?"

"Some," I say as I let my trembling legs relax into the seat. "I know my letters, and Rosie taught me stories out of the *Enchantress* when I was young. I don't know that many words, but I know enough to get by."

"Rosie?" Reknor asks, glancing up at me sharply.

"My mother. She raised me and gave me a roof to live under."

"What happened to her?"

"Do you know of the Simply?"

"Oh," Reknor says. "*Oh.* Jace, I'm sorry."

Everyone in the city knows what happened to the Simply. It's hard to forget.

Soldiers surrounded the brothel one evening in Summer just before sundown. These were not just soldiers of the Wave, but the knights of the Tide: the best, the brightest, the most ruthless. They had tracked a wanted criminal to the building and demanded him on pain of death. They were after Jonah, of course. They claimed he stole from royal messengers, missives detailing troop movements, news of the Vengeance and the Mason, and much more besides.

Jonah was with Darzay, his favorite girl, when they arrived. I was away on an errand for Rosie, buying some green onions and spices for the stew that night. That errand saved my life. The women of the Simply weren't just going to give him up. Rosie walked out to tell them he wasn't there. I turned the corner just as they cut her down. She spun to the ground, her blood hanging in the air like drifting Spring rain. A scream strangled itself in my throat.

The Tide piled kindling on the building and set the whole thing on fire. Even where I was, a block away, I could feel the heat, feel the screams as they pierced the night like rapiers into flesh. Some of the women tried to run, and arrows found them before they made it two steps. Darzay crawled, a bolt through her spine, dragging herself forward with just her arms. Her bright red hair was wild and already stained a deeper crimson with blood. She looked up, her green eyes burning out through the night. She mouthed 'run' just as a soldier stepped up, laughing, and plunged his sword into her back.

They caught Jonah as he tried to slip out a window in the back. A crossbow bolt took him in the leg, and he fell to the street. He was hardly able to hobble. We never spoke again. I never found out if he actually took any messages or if the Sealord was just trying to make an example. The headsman executed him two days later, but when they brought him out, the whole crowd went silent. The festival jeers and cheers of a normal execution day ceased immediately. One look at Jonah and every man, woman, and child there knew that the execution was mercy compared to what they had done to him. He couldn't walk. He could hardly breathe. He didn't cry out when they roughly thrust him to the block. Jonah was already dead when the ax hit wood.

My memory is vivid of those times. The smell of burning flesh, the horrifying screams, my mother’s death. Of all of it, though, what I remember most is the soldier's laugh. It was blithe, carefree. It wasn't malicious or evil. It was just the laugh you laugh when a friend tells you a joke. What sort of man laughs a happy laugh as he stabs a woman through the back? What sort of person burns down a building full of people and is filled with joy? You can see where my fear of the Tide is derived.

Reknor reaches up and pulls down a heavy leather tome from his long wall of books. I look at the embossed gold cover and smile. It's the *Enchantress*, twice as thick and three times as long as the copy my mother read for me as a child.

"Wow," I mutter. "This is a few more than I remember."

"Let's start with this: something familiar, and yet more," Reknor agrees. He places the book carefully in my lap so I won't have to hold it in my broken hands.

"What happens if I don't know a word?" I ask him as he settles down at his desk.

"You try to figure it out. Look at all of the words around it and guess at the meaning. If you really can't tell, then ask me."

His voice is already far away as he picks up his quill and begins writing. I crack open the book, shocked to see beautiful, flowing script wrought in gold. Images of fairies cavorting and knights rearing on white chargers twine in and among the crafted words. I glance up at Reknor wordlessly. What kind of man spends this much gold on a book of fairy tales?

I turn the page, and the words sweep me away to a simpler time, a more magical time, a time of goodness and heroism that doesn't exist in the world anymore. The words take me back to the cradle of my mother's arms and the soft lilt of her voice, the trace of an accent I haven't heard before or sense. Her eyes shine, her silky brown hair swirled atop her head. The words carry me back to a time when I was lost in the warmth and love of a mother.

The first story concerns a knight who rescues a princess. I read through it quickly, almost impatiently. The story is secondary to the memories parading through my head. I haven't thought of her in such a light in so long that I almost forgot her like this. But here she is, laughing as she tells me of how the knight tricks the evil king.

The next page has no words, but instead a painting of the knight facing down an army on his own. The artist has claimed each minute detail for his own, a miniature masterpiece worthy of any collection. I almost feel myself there, heart drumming, eager to fight in the name of my lady.

A tale of a simple orphaned street girl follows. She discovers that she has the power to shape the wind. Shaping is every orphan's dream; to find out that you aren't ordinary, you aren't poor. You're just waiting to find your element and call its name.

There once was a girl of little worth or mettle. She had bright red hair turned gray. It lost its color as she lost her hope. Her bright blue eyes faded to the same slate gray as her hair, and the blush of youth left her cheeks. Her name was Anna.

Anna lost her parents early, and there was no one to look after her. She had to fend for herself, barely finding enough food to survive. She begged, she stole, and she fought tooth and nail to keep everything that came to her. She survived those times through luck. Hunger and cold were her constant companions. She was never comfortable. She slept little. The hunger and the cold took turns shaking her awake with fiery and icy fingers.

One night, as Anna lay on the cobbled streets unable to sleep from the cold, she heard a whisper. Now, it had been a terribly hard day. Anna hadn't had anything to eat, and the only water she'd had was the bitter, dirty snow of the street. Anna thought she was hallucinating the sound, the voice.

I nearly stop reading at this point. The words are too close to reality for me. I've been far too close to starvation to enjoy this story. I also have to break down and ask Reknor what 'hall-uck-in-ate-ing' means. He corrects me gently and goes back to his work.

The whisper came, beckoning, begging her to stand up. Anna was cold and hungry. She cried out that she couldn't. The strength had left her frail arms. She couldn't even sit up. The whisper echoed through the alley again, louder, calling for her to find the will. She closed her eyes and ignored the voice. She knew that if she listened to the dead, she would find herself beyond the bone door that very night.

Finally, the whisper turned to a shout. The wind stirred Anna's gray hair and picked up her tiny head with the force of its voice. She looked up in wonder. The voice was the voice of the air itself. She reached out to the waiting wind, arm trembling. The wind picked her up from the ground, caressed her, cushioned her, made her as light and as swift as the air itself.

She walked without a care, the wind bringing her warm drafts from the South. They swirled around her and chased away the cold. The wind brought her the smells of meat and cheese and wine. She followed those scents to a kindly old man who was down on his luck. He refused to open his door at first, but he saw that the wind was with Anna, so he welcomed her to eat her fill.

Anna followed where the wind led, across lands and kingdoms, seas and plains of ice. The wind always looked after her. She learned to ask the wind for its help, and the wind responded willingly, a glad companion and friend. Never forgetting her own misfortune, Anna helped all that she could. When she found suffering, she left behind joy. She left behind the legend of the Wind-Daughter.

After years of travel, Anna had followed the wind across the entire world, helping everyone who needed her. Finally, the wind led her back to the city of her birth. There, the legends of the gray-haired, gray-eyed child were powerful. They welcomed the Wind-Daughter with open arms as their queen.

"Surely that can't be right," I mutter quietly when I finish the story.

"What was that?" Reknor asks, looking up from his parchment.

"This story. About the little girl named Anna. Surely that isn't what Shaping is like," I say, exasperated.

"You'd be surprised," Reknor answers with a faraway look in his eyes. "Turn the page. The Wind-Daughter was a real person, Jace."

I flip the thick parchment and have to draw in a sharp breath. An angelic woman with silver hair graces the page. Her features are delicate and pale, surrounded by a halo of her gorgeous tresses as they float in the wind. I blink when I realize she is floating above the earth, her long hair flowing around her and a beatific smile on her face.

"To say she was beautiful is an understatement," Reknor says, smiling.

"You say that as if you knew her," I scoff. "This story has to be a thousand years old."

"Seven hundred and forty-three." I glance at him incredulously, and he shrugs. "I am a historian, after all."

"Okay, fine, she was a real person. But the wind just talked to her? The wind can't talk."

"Really? Have you ever heard the wind on a cold night? Have you listened as the wind blows through a cracked window, or over the mountain passes? The wind has a voice, alright. Most of us just can't understand it."

"I can't imagine that's how Shaping works."

"Why don't you tell me what you know about Shaping, and I'll tell you how wrong you are," Reknor answers in a reasonable tone.

"Fine. There's one Master for each element in the world at each time. They have mastery over their particular element, though no one knows how they manage it in the first place. A lot of people insert a bunch of religious nonsense into the story here, but I don't buy any of it," I pause to take a breath, looking at him expectantly, but he just nods and waves for me to continue.

"Another thing no one knows is how many elements there are that can be Shaped. Everyone knows the obvious ones, like earth and wind, fire and water, but there are supposed to be a bunch. The Mason is supposedly the Master of Stone, and there are rumors that the Lord General is the Master of Beasts, whatever that means. I don't know. How can flesh be an element?" Reknor remains impassive, just gesturing me onward.

"Uh, no one knows how the power gets passed on, just that there is one of them at a time... Ugh, I'm repeating myself now," I mutter, then I remember. "Oh, there used to be a Council of Shapers that made laws for them and normal people and generally lorded over everything. Sometime around when I was born the Sealord and his buddy the Lord General killed everybody else and took over for themselves. All of the imperial types say it's for the best, but I don't buy that. There aren't stories from before the Sealord took over of brothels being burned to the ground."

I say the last bitterly. Reknor walks over and puts his hand on my shoulder in sympathy. I nod my thanks, looking up at his craggy face with its eye patch.

"Is that it?"

"Right, well, the Vengeance and the Mason are supposed to be out there somewhere, plotting the King's downfall and raising all sorts of rebellions, but no one has ever seen them, and no one knows where they might be. And Telias the Warmheart was the last good Shaper of all of them. The last man to stand before the Kingdom of the Sea was formed and fight for what he believed in. He would have won, too, but the Vengeance betrayed him."

Reknor's grip tightens uncomfortably on my shoulder. I start to flinch away, but the pressure disappears. For a second, Reknor looks so shaken I think he might faint. He recovers quickly, though, his face sliding back into its normal cheerful grin. I stare at him hard to see if any signs remain, but his smiling mask is in place.

"That's about it," I say.

"That was a whole lot of 'no one knows' you threw in there, despite the fact that you're remarkably well-informed. Where did a boy who is just learning to read get all of that information?"

"I was raised by a thief named Jonah," I answer. "He seemed to be kind of fascinated with Shapers. He told me all the stories he knew whenever he got drunk."

"Defthands, eh?" Reknor says, cocking an eyebrow.

"You knew Jonah? How—"

"Everyone knew who Jonah Defthands was after the Simply burned," Reknor says, holding up his hand to cut me off. "They put up posters across the city proclaiming his execution. I make it my business to know everything, including prominent thieves and cutthroats in the city. Now, you aren't far off about the recent history of Shapers, nor about the fact that there is only one Shaper for each element existing at a time. The way Shaping works... that's kind of a tricky question. Think of it this way. All energy comes from somewhere. For Shapers, the power to control the elements comes from within, from their souls."

"Souls?" I ask skeptically. "Didn't you nod in agreement with the 'religious nonsense' part of my story?"

"Religion does come in, and the Creator's faith is critical to Shaping," Reknor says seriously. "Each element is an aspect of the Creator's power he gave up in the creation of our world. The power was passed to us, his creations, so that we could continue to Shape the world as we willed. Our soul powers us, both typical humans and Shapers. It's how we walk, how we breathe, how we jump and speak and swim. You most definitely have a soul. In fact, Shaping isn't all that different from a normal action. It just requires the right mental commands like walking and running. It uses up the same energy, just to fantastic effect."

"Shaping is like walking? I believe that less than I believe this," I scowl, shoving at the book in my lap.

"Not quite like walking. Nearly anyone can walk, but only a few can Shape. Shaping is passed from one to another by way of an unexplainable energy transference that travels directly to the next infant born."

"What?"

"The power goes to the next baby born, anywhere in the world," Reknor simplifies. "A lot of people will try to tell you that the Creator blesses infants deserving of the strength, but there have been as many Shapers you could call 'evil' as 'good.' The passing of power, though… that is a true mystery. It just happens. The power passes. When a Shaper is near his element and in the right state of mind, he can use the energy of his soul to Shape that element."

"Just like that," I say, smoothing my hand across the air.

"It's not easy, if that's what you are asking. But those are the basics."

In fact, Shapers focus their power through..." He trails off, and a pained expression flits across his face.

"Focus through what?"

"A symbol." He clears his throat. "A glowing symbol that appears on the body of the Shaper the first time they use their power, each a different color: blue for water, orange for fire, gray for stone, and the like."

"Gray?" I ask, trying to wrap my head around that idea. Gray light? "How do you know all this? Talked to many Shapers?"

"The question you should be asking, Jace," Reknor says with a smile. "Is not 'how do you know' but 'what *don't* you know.' I am the kingdom's premier historian, perhaps the most knowledgeable man on any continent, anywhere, ever. Didn't you know who I was when you broke into my house?"

“I thought I did,” I say, slowly shaking my head. “But I didn't.”

I go through several bouts with the pole and a dozen books over the next few weeks. After the first day, Reknor gives me genuine instruction in how to hold the blade, how to slice across and score the wood instead of slamming into it, how to cut from one height to another smoothly. I’m never going to be a large person, no matter how much muscle Reknor tries to pack on my slender frame, but even I notice the strength building in my arms and legs. I also devour story after story in Reknor's small library, practically spending every free moment reading. I love the stories where the heroes aren’t really heroes, where the ladies aren’t particularly ladies, and especially where the monsters aren’t actually monsters.

Just as I start to get comfortable, I walk into the training room to find, as if by magic, a second post sitting next to the first. I pull up short and glance at Reknor. It isn’t just the fact that I have two targets, but the colors on the new pole are all entirely different from the first.

“It’s time we elevated your training regimen,” he says firmly.

Chapter 7
Iliana
The Forty-First Day of Winter
In the Year 5219, Council Reckoning

I blend with the large mass of humanity as I leave the Palace District and join the markets of the Mercantile District. Anything in all of the kingdom or beyond can be purchased in the Mercantile District of Donir. The sights and sounds and smells of the place were overwhelming the first time I had ever come out with Yrena. I never imagined so many people could be crammed into one place. Their shouts mingle into a deafening cacophony: hawkers, buyers, sellers, guards, the angry, and the joyful, it doesn't matter. All raise their voices to be heard above the din, and all succeed in going equally unnoticed.

The smells are even more vivid, from the sewage and filth rotting in the gutters to the vast array of cooking from a dozen different cultures. Spiced meats, baked bread, rotting fish, and many other scents all swirl together in a combination that is nearly indescribably horrible. You might catch a good scent like one of the sweet vendor's chocolates, but the second you inhale, something vile will assault your nose in the next second.

I move as smoothly as I can through the cold streets, constantly jostled by the early morning crowd. The bumps and shoves are welcome. Every time I run into someone or brush in between them, their warm, living bodies remind me of my own. I feel alive, more than any time other than when I Shape, and it's exhilarating to go completely unnoticed for once. No one cares what I'm doing; they're all wrapped up in their own lives.

Though a man nearly succeeded in assassinating me less than five weeks before, I finally begged my father to allow me out into the city with Yrena. He agrees that I can't always be locked up behind stone walls. I need some human contact, especially the anonymous kind that allows me to feel as if I'm just one among many, just another tiny cog in the crowd.

I distantly hear Yrena muttering behind me. She struggles to keep up as I dance past a cart navigating its way through the rushing populace. The markets are so glorious! A man selling candies nuts smiles broadly at me, the smoke of his tiny oven dirtying his portly face.

"Would the lady enjoy some sweets to take on her way?" he asks warmly.

I'm wearing well-made but mundane clothing, hardly the ostentatious display I normally make when I appear in public, but he recognizes me for a person of wealth regardless. I've heard there are two main places where wealth can be most clearly seen: in the hands, and in the eyes. My hands have few callouses. When my father trains me to fight, my weapons generally float around where I command. As for my eyes... who can tell?

"I would love some," I respond, smiling at him. "Just give me a moment for my friend to show up. She'll definitely want to pick some of her own."

As if conjured by my words, the crowd ripples and spits out Yrena. She's huffing, red in the face, and clearly irate. She spots me and storms over with black clouds hovering over her brow. Before she can open her mouth, I wave her forward.

"Yrena, which kind of nut would you like? I see almonds and cashews and walnuts. Oh, sir, do you have pralines? Yrena is particularly partial to them."

"As the young lady pleases," he says, bending down under his counter and bringing forth a white cloth bag. He opens it just as Yrena arrives. She gasps with delight when she sees the sugar-crusted praline clusters nestled inside. Unfortunately, the distraction isn't enough, for she turns to glare at me again.

"Don't think that this excuses your behavior, little one! You cannot go running off in the markets without me. It's a dangerous place for young women, especially ones who look like you."

"I can take care of myself," I mutter defensively.

"You should listen to your mother, child," the vendor says, not unkindly. "I've seen some horrible things happen right here in the markets in broad daylight. Stick with her."

"Thank you, sir," Yrena says, cocking an eyebrow at me. I stifle my annoyance. As if this street peddler has any idea what constitutes danger for the Master of Earth. I direct Yrena to pay him and move on as she counts out the money, quickly disappearing into the crowd again with a grin.

I wander from stall to stall like a butterfly, flitting about and light as air. I forget the assassin and the alleged responsibilities my father is going to lay on me. I just smile at strangers, dodge through crowds, and bargain with store owners for trinkets I'll never buy. That last bit is probably only enjoyable to me, not the poor shopkeeps who have to deal with some girl who doesn't plan to spend a single coin in their stores. The palace life is good, but it's *great* to be out amongst the people. The markets are so large that I can't possibly meet every shop keeper if I spend a week walking. That suits me just fine. There should always be more people to meet, and more experiences to have. It's the perfect day.

My neck snaps to the side.

Pain sears through my scalp as something drags me by my hair into an alley. A hard shove sends me stumbling to the ground, and my white dress drags in the filthy snow. I spin from where I am on the ground. A bald, pale-skinned man in dirty black leather stands over me. His muscles ripple as he kneels down, and his breath smells of rancid meat. I struggle not to gag as the rotten stench washes over my face. A young woman alone on the streets of the market is always in danger, and it looks like I've found myself some.

"Look at this pretty little thing," he sneers, though I barely hear him over the din of the market.

"Yeah, she looks... soft," a deep voice rumbles over my head. "Must work for a noble, or somesuch."

Refusing to let panic take me, I quietly draw on the earth. The mud from my fall fortunately covers the symbol of my power. I will the earth in the alley to form into a thin, nearly invisible shard of glass. The blade floats up behind the pale-skinned man, narrowing in on the base of his neck. I tense to strike.

"Enough foreplay," the man behind me grunts.

A huge paw wraps around my hair and rips me down to the ground. The man drags me bodily into a pile of trash deeper into the alley. I lose my concentration on the shard of glass. The pain burns through my head as if my scalp tears from my skull. Stunned amongst humanity's waste, his hands slap at my legs and try to force them open. I clench every muscle in my body to keep him at bay. I squeeze my eyes shut. His hands roughly pull my legs apart. I whimper. There's nothing I can do. They're too strong, my thoughts too scattered. No one will help me even if I scream.

The man succeeds in forcing a hand down in between my legs. My mind races through fear and doubt and terror. As he tries to force his finger into me, something snaps in my chest.

I am the Creator-blessed Shaper of Earth. I am the princess of the Kingdom of the Sea. I could kill them for this. I *will* kill them for this.

Cutting them with mere glass that won't satisfy me. I call to the earth all at once, bringing all of the mud and dust together and willing it to coalesce. All of it becomes crystal as one, a shining spear floating in the air, ready to strike on my command.

Fury surges right below the surface of my chest as the imaged faces of all of the girls these men have preyed upon, all of the women whose lives they ruined, parade before my vision. Worse, much worse, is that he's dared to touch *me*. He's dared to defile *my* holy skin. How dare he lay a fucking *finger* on me?

"You want me?" I ask, a fey smile spreading my lips.

"Oh, so the bitch likes it," the big man grunts, raising his hand to slap me.

With a mental jerk, my spear strikes him under his arm. It rips straight through his chest and bursts out the other side of his rib cage. The spear is not smooth, so it catches on flesh like serrated barbs, dragging pieces of his heart and lungs violently into the open air. My rage is such that the weapon doesn't even slow in its passage. He falls to the ground beside me with a funny little groan, blood already draining from his gaping mouth.

I sit up, the spray of his blood across my face and chest. The pale-skinned man stares in horror. His eyes are so wide I can see them perfectly, framed by the look of utter shock pasted onto his face. A light pastel green, his eyes are strangely appealing, nearly beautiful. He stares into my eyes, frozen, as I command the glittering spear to hover silently in the air before him. I line up the point with the center of the man's chest.

"How many women have you raped?" I spit the words out. "How many girls have you murdered?"

"None, lady, goddess, none! That man made me do it! I just watched out for him. He was going to kill me if I didn't! Please, I have a wife, a child, please!"

The man's begging is a classic joke. Like panicked rats, his words climb over one another to flee from his mouth. It's almost like he's throwing darts blindly at a board, praying that one will hit a place of compassion or mercy somewhere in me. He doesn't realize that such a mark does not exist.

With a gesture, I drive the spear through his thigh. His scream is so high and long that it interrupts even the sounds of the market for a brief moment as people crane their necks in our direction. With a thought, I fling some excess mud from further down the alley into his mouth. His scream dies in a cough. I wave cheerfully to the few people who still look our way. A few wave back, and the market returns to its normal chaotic state.

He struggles to cough the dirt out of his throat, while at the same time fighting to keep his leg still where the spear is embedded. He succeeds at neither.

"This is far less than you deserve," I say. "I should drag you screaming to the dungeons and prolong your suffering."

I stalk closer and lift his chin with my hand. His eyes are wide with fear, but I notice as they harden. Just as he tenses to punch me, I break off the top half of the spear and impale his hand, jerking his arm around and slamming it into the ground. His scream is little more than a cough this time, and far less rewarding.

"Your pathetic measures were all too practiced to be anything but habit. That you dare touch any woman is beyond my ability to condone, but you touched *me*. The Master of Earth, your princess. For that crime, you should die far slower, but I am merciful."

The spear rips out of his leg and shoots through his heart before he can respond. The moment the spear strikes, the image of the assassin's hateful gaze flashes in my mind. I wish fervently that I could do the same to him. The man sags onto the dirty cobblestones, the growing pool of his blood staining the brown snow a sickly red. I'm gasping, but not from exertion or fear. I feel more alive in this moment than I ever have before. I'm drained, but exhilarated. These men weren't worth the air they were breathing. Blood spreads slowly from both bodies, mingling into a puddle that threatens to reach my sandals.

As I step back to avoid the blood, my adrenaline fades, and hollowness replaces satisfaction. My face drops slowly into my hands. I can feel the first rapist's blood sliding between my hands and the skin of my face. I have to fight the sudden urge to vomit.

In the moment, it was glorious. I delivered justice like a Shaper of old, ridding the streets of my kingdom of filth and depravity. But after...

I can feel nothing but disgust.

I bend to pick up my heavy shawl, now brown with muck. Wiping away as much of the blood as possible with the inside of the cloth, I wrap the shawl back around my shoulders to hide the stains on my upper body. The chill of the Winter air cuts straight through my damp clothing as I rejoin the crowd. Head down, I move slowly. No one notices me. I walk through their ranks, covered in the filth of my deeds, and no one deigns to glance in my direction. The people of the market are too busy worrying about their own problems to care about another.

When Yrena finds me, I'm walking aimlessly. She knows something's wrong immediately. She pulls me to her and leads me back towards the palace. I can hardly feel her warmth through the ice on my skin, can hardly listen as she directs me back to the castle. We plod through the gates together. The guards glance at us out of the corner of their eyes, but Yrena manages to get me to my room without being accosted. She leaves, calling for the other servants to draw a hot bath.

The chill of the day and the chill in my soul merge. A violent shiver racks my body, and my teeth chatter so fiercely my jaw hurts. I blink, waking with my face pressed against stone. Slowly, I draw up my knees until I can curl into a ball on the cold stone floor.

I killed two men. I killed them, and in the moment of their death, I exulted. Is that how I'm supposed to feel? It's my right to defend myself. Those men earned the death they received a hundred times over. I can still feel their hands on my legs, their creeping fingers... but should I enjoy it? Should I relish watching their bright lifeblood pump from their bodies?

By the Creator, I did.

Two strong arms lift me and gather me into a warm, muscled chest. I glance up at Uncle's face. He walks me gently to the waiting bath.

"I'll not be far," he breathes.

He sets me on my feet beside the steaming water and leaves. Yrena strips me down and guides me into the warm water. I almost cry out as the heat scorches my icy skin. Painful bursts of feeling blast into my numb extremities. Yrena scrubs at my skin, but I flinch away from her touch. I know it's Yrena, but the foreign hand is too much, far too much like the hands in the alley. Over long, slow, gentle minutes, showing infinite patience and persistence she manages to get me clean, carefully navigating around my torn scalp and cooing softly whenever I flinch. When I'm dried and dressed, Uncle returns.

"What happened?" he asks, blunt and terse.

"My Lord General, perhaps we should give her some time. Do you not see the state she's in?" Yrena asks, eyes lowered in deference. It takes a lot for Yrena to speak around Uncle, let alone challenge him, but the flicker of appreciation in my chest dies as he speaks again.

"Iliana is stronger than that. Tell me," he commands.

He refuses to lift his heavy gaze from mine. I swallow and nod. Under his direction, I begin to report. He taught me long ago not to add extraneous details or emotions to any question he poses. He is a man of healing and the world's premier strategist. He has no time for frills. After the story leaves me, the words do not seem so awful. There's a distance, as if it happened to someone else, as if a dream rather than a reality.

"They did not manage to hurt you?" he asks, his tone that of a doctor querying his patient for routine information.

"No. They died before they could."

"Good," he says. His face softens. "It's always difficult to kill for the first time. This experience will allow you to grow, to mature. It will not be so hard, next time."

I nod, a lie in physical form. The killing hadn't been hard. In fact, it was all too easy, the men barely more than ants beneath the vengeful heel of my power. My turmoil is drawn from the joy I felt at their deaths, not the deaths themselves. Uncle nods and graces me with a rare smile.

"My little girl. Tougher every day," he says, turning and disappearing out of my apartments.

A robe around my shoulders, I settle into my sheets. Yrena sits at my side, careful to leave distance between us. She reaches out tentatively and gently strokes my hair. When I don't react, she sits closer, slowly drawing me down to rest my head in her lap. My heart eases under her slow, caring caress.

"I'm not sorry I killed them," I say quietly. "They were bad men."

"They would have done the same to you, little one. And your end would have been far less pleasant."

"But... I enjoyed it," I admit, swallowing thickly. "I loved it when the man begged me for life, because I knew that... I don't know what I knew. But..."

"Little one, you've done nothing wrong. They deserved their deaths. I'm just glad you were able to save any other women from that fate."

My eyelids begin to droop under her hand, a lulling metronome. My last thought before I drift off almost shocks me awake. Will I have trouble sleeping? Are nightmares waiting? But I sleep long, and deep, and dreamless.

***

Two soldiers of the Tide in padded armor are doing their best to simulate an attack. I've fought against greater numbers before, but never at quite such a disadvantage. As I grow older, Uncle stacks the odds against me more and more. His deep voice echoes in my mind, though, quieting my nerves.

Remember the rules, and use them to your benefit.

Right.

First, you are nothing without your element.

The challenge I face applies directly to that first rule. Before, I was allowed to work in the gardens, where my connection to the earth is strongest. The banquet hall where we held the Liberation Ball, however, has remarkably little earth. We're surrounded by little more than marble and brightly colored stones. Aside from the thin panes of glass keeping the mosaic in place, the best earth I can find is the dust drifting through the air.

With every ounce of my concentration and all of my energy, I can lift one of the gemstones from the walls with my power, but I can do little more than that. There's a bit of overlap amongst the elements. My enemy, the Mason, is the Shaper of Stone, and I am the Shaper of Earth. The line where those two elements cross is blurry, at best. Should we ever come into direct conflict, we'll have the option to fight one another for control of the same materials, but Father warns against it. To mentally and spiritually dominate a Shaper so completely is near impossible; instead, I should stick to the parts of the world that call to me the strongest.

I've never felt more powerful than when my father took me to the far south of Itskalan and through the desert. Every night, I rose and gazed about at the unending earth, closing my eyes and feeling the sand's joyful call. In my urban life, I've come to have an affinity for glass. The material is just sand reconstituted, and my connection with it is strong. Dirt is plentiful, but difficult to use effectively, especially in trace amounts. Glass, however, can be used surgically with even the tiniest of shards.

I duck under a slash from one of the soldiers, kicking at her knee to keep her at bay while I send a blade of glittering glass to threaten the other. He shatters the fragile sword with a blow, ignoring the aftermath as he doggedly pursues me across the hall.

Second, you are only limited by your will and creativity.

The shards of my broken blade never fall. I direct them to pepper his back as I roll away from another cut from the first soldier. Had he not been wearing padding, the shards would have cut him to the bone. Surprised, he obediently falls to the ground as if dead. My second foe presses her advantage, and her cuts come fast and sure. I twist and dodge back, but she's always there, pressing, pressing, each blow cutting closer and closer. I almost scream as one slash nearly catches the glowing green symbol of my power.

Finally, your symbol is the source of all your strength. Protect it at all costs.

Desperate, I summon the dust from the floor and thrust it into her eyes. She blinks madly, trying to clear her eyes with her forearm. Glass soars to my hand, reforming into a narrow dagger, and I place it against her throat. She stills, her emerald eyes glinting and a slight smile tugging at her lips. For a long moment, we stare into each other's eyes, and I find myself grinning back.

"Again," I say finally, spinning away, a flush in my cheeks that has nothing to do with exertion.

I beckon to a third soldier waiting patiently against the wall. A throat clears nervously behind me. I spin to see a page in the Sealord's livery standing by the door.

"Yes?" I ask him, annoyed at the interruption.

"The Sealord begs your presence in the dungeons, my lady," he says, bowing so that his nose nearly touches the floor.

"The dungeons? Are you absolutely sure?"

"Y-yes, my lady," he says. His entire body is shaking. Why he is so afraid is beyond me. "Absolutely sure."

"Very well. You are relieved," I throw back over my shoulder.

The soldiers relax. Just as I cross over the threshold and out of the room, I hear them laughing. I pause, frowning. What stops them from relaxing around me? I haven't heard them laugh once in a dozen training sessions. Why are they so silent and serious?

I follow the page down through several levels of the palace, passing three separate guard posts. At each posting, the men stop talking and salute me formally. We continue until we reach the open portcullis that leads to the palace dungeons, somewhere underneath the south wall. The page halts, breathing heavily, and I regard him with concern. Sweat beads his brow, and his eyes roam everywhere but at the door leading onwards.

"What's the matter?"

"Do not make me go back in there, please, princess," he begs, eyes shining with tears. "I already can't unsee what little I saw."

"I never come here, page. I'm sorry, but you have to lead me."

"Yes, my lady."

He takes a ragged breath as if to master himself, then sets out at a firm march down the dimly-lit corridors. We pass dozens of cells, many of them full. The only prisoners kept at the palace proper are political, suspected spies, or dangers to the state of the kingdom. Most appear quite miserable, if in decent health. The prisoners on the upper level are treated with a certain level of dignity.

As we descend, however, the prisoners begin to show signs of abuse. The page never looks aside from his determined march through the dungeons, as if the tortured souls are only real if he sees them, but I'm drawn to study the prisoners and their prison. I've never been to this level before. Iron chains hold a woman with dark hair to the wall, her wrists raw and infected, lips broken and cracked. Her vacant eyes stare deeply into oblivion, and she makes no movement at our passage. Hers is not an uncommon plight throughout the second level, and part of me recoils at the abuse they've been levied, but I don't waver. These people have earned their punishments. I'm sure of it.

Finally, we come to a dark awning leading down, a spiral staircase descending into the deepest reaches. The natural water of the earth seeps through infinitesimal cracks in the stone and slicks the walk with slime and moisture. The sound of our footsteps breaks an unnatural silence as we place our feet carefully on the wet stone. Torches light the stairs, but the darkness seems to press against us whenever we pass between their light.

Four cells await us at the bottom, simple in shape, but constructed with complex materials. Each was designed, long ago, to hold a Shaper. Created from different alloys and mixtures of elements, their creators crafted these cages in such a way so that they no longer resemble the elements of their creation. A Shaper locked in these cells will be unable to Shape, unable to break free.

Three of the cells are empty, or appear so, but my father stands in the doorway of the fourth, two members of the Tide flanking him. When he sees me, he smiles warmly.

"Iliana. I have a gift for you," he says, beckoning me forward.

He indicates the open cell with a sweeping gesture as if presenting me a banquet on Mourningtide. Inside, chained hand and foot to the wall, is the assassin who shot me. He's seen better days. The socket of his left eye gapes dark and red, and chains preventing his unconscious body from sagging to the floor. I don't think he could support his weight if we freed him. The lone eye remaining to him drifts, unfocused. Even like this, a surge of revulsion and fear clinches my belly at the sight of him.

"He's told us all that he knows. Pitifully, he seems to have no connection to the Vengeance at all. He was acting on his own."

"How is this a gift?" I ask, turning back to my father. "Kill him."

"My dear, I thought you would like the honor. This man is a traitor to the kingdom, and he tried to kill you. He nearly succeeded. When one such as he steps out of line, he must be punished."

At the sound of our voices, the man's head perks up. The cruel fire of unabashed hatred returns to his eye. He sneers, and blood and pus leak from the gaping socket on his left. I shrink back to the wall, the man's hatred palpable and overwhelming. His one good eye darts back and forth between my father and me as if he can't decide who he hates more.

"So the bitch lives," he rasps, rearing back and weakly spitting in my direction. The spit barely clears his mouth, dangling on the ragged beard covering his cheeks. "I hoped to do the Vengeance a favor. The world has gone to shit ever since you and your band of happy murderers took over. The Shapers used to serve the people, not themselves. May you find a place with the Eternal."

"I don't want to be alone with him, Father. He scares me."

"I won't leave you, my dear. We'll punish him together," he says, his tone calm and steady. "Now, I know you have a talent for Shaping glass. How about we begin with that?"

He produces a long, jagged shard of a mirror and holds it out to me. Uncertain but obedient, I reach out with my mind and lift it. The blade shimmers in the dim torchlight, turning slightly in the air. The assassin's scowling face flits through the shard's reflection for the briefest moment, and I force it to still. The only sounds in the dim room are the soft clink of the prisoner's chains and the quickening gasps of terror from the forgotten page who led me down. I move the shard closer to the man. He quiets as the point hovers in front of his remaining eye.

"Whatever you do to me, bitch, know that the Creator damns you for this. The power of the Shapers was never meant—"

He cuts off with a hideous wail as I push the blade into his eye.

I stare at him, shocked at what I've done. The man writhes in unyielding chains, the glass jutting forth from his skull like a twisted mimicry of a horn. I didn't mean to hurt him so badly. I just had to stop his words. How dare he? How dare he say that the Creator damns me? I'm the Creator's blessed. I'm one of fifteen Shapers to grace the earth. How *dare* he? The rage from the alley rises up in my chest like a beast unchained. My fear of his hatred fades, and in its place, dark confidence soars.

I have power over this man. Over his life, and his death. Over his suffering, and his solace. He is mine.

To do with as I please.

With a thought, I yank the blade of glass out of his eye. He screams a ragged scream and hunches over as far as the chains will take him. The urge to laugh is overwhelming as I watch him squirm. Curiously I stab the blade into his shoulder, but he barely flinches. A short giggle escapes my lips, even though I try to hold it back. Part of me shouts that it is wrong to laugh, but the larger part of me can't resist.

"You're finally starting to learn, my dear," the Sealord says behind me, his voice filled with a strange satisfaction. "Now, why don't we try something new? It's nearly impossible to Shape inside another human's body. Otherwise, I would have supreme power, as water is the principal part of a man's blood. No, the human body is, largely, sacrosanct. Let's see if you are ready to pierce that protection."

He whispers in my ear. I turn back to the bleeding prisoner and break the mirror shard into a slender sliver. Bringing the narrow blade to the edge of his palm, I put every ounce of my focus into the sliver of earth, connecting to it with every fiber of my being. With a deep breath, I drive it into his hand. He jerks, and his throat wheezes little more than a whistling croak after his previous screams.

Immediately, my connection to the shard begins to falter, the man's own soul resisting my influence. I close my eyes to concentrate on driving the sliver deeper. As it burrows into his wrist, he begins gibbering. The sounds hold no meaning, any words lost in the echoes that reverberate from the stone walls. I push, weakly at first and then stronger. The sliver of glass worms its way through his flesh. I open my eyes to watch as his limbs twitch and convulse. The shard delves deeper into his arm towards his waiting heart. My limbs start trembling, my thoughts growing fuzzy. The power needed to maintain my connection to the earth wavers as I reach his chest. With a last powerful mental push, I drive the shard into his heart.

He falls limp. The outward sign of his death hardly even leaks any blood. I glance back at my father through the spots dancing before my eyes. My breath is ragged and uneven, and my vision darkens at the edges.

"I did it," I gasp, smiling up at Father. I feel light, like I could take off and fly at any moment. I've conquered my fear of the assassin, and in so doing pleased my father. Such... power, to own another so completely. It is intoxicating.

"Of course you did. You are my daughter," he says, smiling warmly and taking me into a big hug. I return it weakly. "I'm proud of you, Iliana."

***

I wake slowly, though my eyes remain clenched shut, the pressure in my head a bottled hurricane. Tears trace streams down my face, mere tributaries to a dark, wet ocean that spreads out on my pillow. I force my eyes open. A narrow slit of a window high above allows the half-moon glimmering through the clouds to break the darkness of midnight, but only just. It can't be far til dawn, I rub my eyes blearily, shattering the crust of dried tears.

An image flashes into my head, the assassin twitching as if seizing, sounds coming from his mouth far from human. I flinch and curl up tighter into a ball. I remember, distantly, the feeling of euphoria that came over me, the joy. It's long gone. Emptiness yawns, the pit that has taken the place of my heart deep and dark. I don't know why I'm crying. Justice is on my side. But the tears come from some place that doesn't touch my conscious self. The strange giddiness of the assassin's murder, the horror in the alley, nothing seems real.

I feel nothing.

The thought scares me, sending a spark of adrenaline coursing through my veins. The fear is good; it's something different, something real to latch on to. I lurch out of bed in the near-darkness, striding over to my wardrobe and fumbling out a simple cotton dress. While finely made, the dress is one of ten thousand being sold in the market. I purchased it for just this reason. Sliding my nightgown off, I slip the dress over my head and dig out some simple leather sandals. With a shiver at the chill air, I spin a heavy coat around my shoulders and slip out of my room.

The palace is not exactly difficult to sneak out of if you know where to go. Torlas taught me long ago, when the joy of disobeying outweighed the consequences. While the walls are sturdy and high around the palace proper, the walls surrounding the garden are short. Protected more by thorn hedges and guardsmen than real fortification, the gardens open practically into the royal apartments.

I nod to the guard at the entrance to the gardens, and she bows her head, letting me pass without comment. She bears the deep turquoise armor of the Tide, though her hair peeks out a vibrant auburn from the edges of her helmet. I don't know her name, but I know her face: the soldier who nearly beat me in the hall yesterday. When I stop next to her, her eyebrows rise in surprise. Her nose is slightly crooked, probably broken on a battlefield and forced roughly back into place. A breathless tension rises in my chest as our eyes meet again. Her green eyes, hard as steel, soften as she takes me in.

"Tide."

"Yes, my lady?"

"What is your name?" I ask, trying to paste a smile on my face. The emptiness inside of me makes the expression feel strange.

"I am called Poline, my lady," she says, trying to hide her confusion. "Is there anything my lady requires?"

"If anyone comes looking for me, you're to tell them I am communing with the earth. I'm not to be disturbed, even by a messenger of my father. If he wants to see me, he can fetch me himself."

"But, my lady, your father—"

"I have no intentions of causing you trouble," I say quickly, bowing my head to her. Her eyes widen further. "This is simply a favor I ask. If someone comes demanding me to present myself... tell them the truth."

"And what truth is that, lady?"

"That you have absolutely no idea where I am. You saw me enter, but you never saw me leave."

"I will expressly not tell them about the loose bar by the lily," Poline says, nodding seriously and returning to attention. I'm shocked to hear my secret spoken so openly, but mirth dances in her eyes.

"Precisely. Thank you, Poline," I say.

The brilliant green of the hedges are punctuated by the patches of early Winter snow clinging to healthy branches. When I play in the garden, I turn the earth, sifting it, imbuing it with power. I breathe life into the cold, frozen ground. The trees in the small orchard bear fruit all year round. The leaves never fall from the trees, no matter how cold the Winter or how fierce the storms. The living things of my garden stay beautiful and strong as they ignore the passing years.

Today, though, I feel none of the familiar pride and happiness as the soul of the earth calls to me. Only in this place, of all places, does the earth feel alive and well in the city. Elsewhere, the rock suffocates the soil under stone's long silence.

We're lucky, quite honestly, that the Mason does not wish harm upon the people of the kingdom. Practically the entire damn city is made of stone. He could crush the walls and buildings almost at will. It wouldn't take long to have another Breaking, another city destroyed for a Shaper's war.

Shaking off the unwelcome thought, I stride through the gardens and between two sections of the hedge to come to the fence. At first, Torlas and I tried to count to the loose bar, but, after forgetting half a dozen times which it was, I came up with another plan. Next to the bar, I planted a white lily. Unique to the gardens, the flower is a perfect marker.

With a quick moment of concentration, my arm not even glowing through the thick coat, I lift the dirt and grime from the bar and pull it easily from its moorings. I slip out through the fence and replace the bar behind me, making certain that the bar appears exactly as it had before. No point in advertising to thieves and assassins that there's something interesting in this particular spot.

I weave my way through the small copse that surrounds this half of the palace and divides it from the surrounding city. The trees are strange in the stone labyrinth of Donir, as most of the city is built upon other buildings and foundations, including a positively ancient set of sewers that honeycomb everything below the street level. This earth, though still alive, is cut off from the rest by layer upon layer of stone.

Sifting through the trees, I come upon the row of fences that mark the outside edge of the palace. The estates of important nobles border the treeline, the small patches of land owned by the nobility a sign of status in the overcrowded city. Another loose bar gives me access to the small backyard of the Graevo mansion. I glance up at the house nervously. Torlas shouldn't be home; he's working out in the city with his father. I don't want to catch the eyes of the serving staff, lest I be mistaken for a thief or, worse, recognized as myself. I hurry forward and walk out past the guards at the entrance, my chin tucked and coat pulled close. They murmur something about a stranger, when I risk a glance back, they remain complacently standing at their posts.

With a sigh of relief, I join the flow of foot traffic passing through the city. At this early hour and on this particular wealthy street, few people are walking, but the teeming masses of Donir are a few short blocks away. I let my chin come up, breathing in deeply. The icy wind burns my face and plunges deep into my lungs, the claws of Winter deliciously dragging across my skin. A bit of me revives in the stiff breeze as my soul rises back up to greet my stimulated flesh.

A smile graces my lips, but, even as I recognize the expression, it falls away. What do I have to be happy about? Something is wrong, whether with me or the world or the Eternal's own grave, I can't tell. My soul feels broken, tattered, as if the events of the previous day have cut ragged gashes in my very being. The assassin twitches in my mind's eye, and I jam my eyes shut tightly, trying to force the image away. It only grows more vivid, the feeling of the shard of glass creeping through his body, driving towards his heart... I shiver. The wind blows again, but this time the cold bites through my dress and chills me to the bone.

"Young lady, is something the matter?"

My eyes pop open, seeing an expression of concern painted over a fearsome visage. A long, flowing mane of brown hair streaked with gray flows past a thin, tightly groomed beard. A black eye patch barely manages to cover an old, ragged wound. His missing eye immediately recalls the assassin's wounds, and I step back quickly, raising my hands, cursing silently. I can't believe I let a man surprise me again. I can still feel the pawing hands of the thugs and the ache in my scalp.

"No, sir, nothing is the matter," I say coldly.

"Ah," he says, a knowing look coming into his lone eye. It glints, lively enough to make up for the lack of another. "The only time I look as pained as you is when I get out of bed. Creator damn these old bones, I wouldn't wish that kind of hurt on anyone."

I give him a once-over. He has broad, strong shoulders, smooth, fashionably cut clothing, and a surety in how he carries himself. Old, maybe. But he doesn't fool me. This man dreads getting *out* of bed about how much I dread getting *into* mine.

"I'm sure," I say, cocking an eyebrow at the man. "Well, good sir, if you'll excuse me, I'll be on my way."

I brush past him, but he gently grabs my arm. I nearly call on the earth to strike him down, but he smiles down on me warmly.

"A bit of advice, princess," he says quietly, smiling a little broader. I clench my jaw, refusing to give him the satisfaction of a confirmation or a denial. "One of the best things to do when facing something difficult is to look for help. Find someone who'll listen. Lighter is the burden of a trouble shared. Just an old man's wisdom."

He releases my arm, turns and strides down the street as if he owns it. His steps claim the ground he walks on, his polished leather shoes firmly pressing into the stones of the street. As he starts to distance himself from me, he begins to whistle, the melody familiar, but just outside of recognition. I blink as a snowflake settles on my eyelash, and he disappears around a corner in the distance.

His words… Who can I tell? My father won't understand what I'm going through; he's the one encouraging me to do it. Uncle will go with whatever Father says. Anyone who isn't family will... how will they view me? I try to look at myself from an outsider's perspective, but I can't place it. I'm a Shaper, chosen by the Creator himself. What would the worth be in considering the views of a lesser being?

The icy wind blowing straight through my coat, I wander. The turmoil of my soul is no closer to calming. The sun etches a dreary track across the sky, occasionally obscured by ragged gray clouds. The people of the city impart no warmth, no life, as they used to. The alley, and the assassin, and the impossible joy suffusing those moments: each has drained something of the essence of what my life once was. The sun finally drops towards the horizon. I know I will be missed; the Tide may be searching for me even now, but I have no desire to go back to the palace.

Weight seems to pile on my shoulders, and my steps slow to a crawl. Several people jostle me from behind as they pass, but I can't be bothered to care. I angle for the side of the street so that I can stop and breathe for a moment. If only I can breathe. Just for a moment. I raise my head for the first time in hours. Without realizing it, I'm less than a hundred steps from the courthouses. The courthouse where Torlas works.

Before I can even think about stopping, my feet carry me towards the steps. As I approach the marble columns that mark the courts, I slow. I can't go into a place of the law looking as I do. But, then again, what will they do? Arrest me? Head down, coat pulled tight, I pass between a pair of uninterested soldiers of the Wave, their uniforms immaculate and their faces apathetic. They don't so much as glance at me.

As soon as the doors swing shut behind me, it's like I enter into a different world. The warm, quiet interior is a blessing after the chaotic volume of the streets. A line of people wait to be received by a few clerks sitting behind desks. Most reach the front, describe their problem, and sit to await judgment. The few chairs on the side of the room are full, and several people are forced to stand awkwardly in the open space between the counters and the door.

I don't want to cause a scene, so I join the line with my head down. I let my long hair fall around my face, hopefully disguising me further. In these close quarters, it's possible for me to be recognized in a way that the markets don't allow. An elderly couple waits in front of me in line, the woman continually babbling into her husband's ear.

"I tell you, we had better be seen today. It's been far too long without a single whisper from our counsel. If they keep this up, then we'll rot away and die before they ever have to talk to us! Perhaps that's what they want. Lousy pennygrubbers, always there when you owe them fees, never around when you actually need them. Are you even listening to me, Nore? This girl is! She understands, right?"

It takes me a moment to realize that she's talking to me. Glancing up through my hair, I blink in surprise to see both of them staring at me expectantly.

"Uh, of course!" I say, trying to brighten and praying that they don't recognize my face. "Lousy pennygrubbers."

"See, Nore? Even the youth understand me. I've been around, Nore, you see, I've been on this earth and in this city longer than anyone. I know things. Even if the counselors are trying to wait me out! I'll not die before I see one of you, hear my vow!"

The old man – Nore, I presume – turns to me. He reaches into a bag at his hip and pulls out a small piece of chocolate. Popping it into his mouth, he grins like a child and snags another from the bag. He offers it to me surreptitiously, winking. I smile in spite of myself, gratefully taking the morsel. A bit of the coldness inside of me makes way for warmth. He winks again, ignoring his wife as he turns back to look at the line, munching happily.

It's strange. Every time I want to give up on humanity, someone finds a way to bring me back. Like magic, an old man named Nore has given me a small moment of happiness and a shared smile. It isn't much, but it's something. The crack in the ice in my chest is no relief. I can feel something lurking there, some darkness I don't know if I'm ready to face.

I come to the front of the line. A young female clerk, probably a few years my senior, flicks her eyes up to me from the paper she's transcribing. Uninterest practically oozes from her very pores.

"What is your complaint?" she asks in a flat monotone.

"I don't have one."

"Then what are you here for?"

"I'm here to see Torlas Graevo."

Now she glances up at me in annoyance, her blonde eyebrows disappearing under the curtain of bangs that lays artfully across her forehead.

"Why would a man like Torlas want to see a... *girl* like you?"

There is such a tide of condescension in her words that I might drown if I let it wash over me. I feel like the common dress I'm wearing is an affront to her; she stares straight through me and sees nothing but a foolish girl trying to reach a powerful lord. She might be annoyed that some stranger has walked up to her desk and is asking to see an important man, but that means nothing compared to how annoyed I'm quickly becoming.

"I imagine he would want to see *this* girl," I say carefully, gritting my teeth.

"Please, child. Rumors say that Torlas already has the run of every noblewoman he desires, all the way to the princess, if you would believe that. Some girl he whose virginity he stole is hardly worthy of his time. Move along."

I slide the coat down below the level of my right shoulder, arching an eyebrow at the woman and drawing on the faintest thread of power. The symbol of my strength rises to the surface of my skin, visible only to the two of us in the crowded room. The girl pales. She knows that it will be simple as breathing for me to have her imprisoned and beaten for showing me such disrespect. Just as she opens her mouth to speak, I hold up a finger.

"Don't say a word. To anyone. About even a hint of this conversation. If you can keep that wagging tongue of yours completely still, I'll forget what happened here. If I hear even the faintest rumor that the princess was anywhere near the courthouse, any courthouse in all of the kingdom, I'm going to find you. And I won't turn you over to the dungeons. No, *girl*, you will answer to me."

The girl gulps and nods, standing so abruptly that her chair screeches on the marble.

"Now, lead me to Torlas, and nothing will have changed about your pathetic existence," I say.

Amusement replaces my anger as she strides forward far too fast for decency. I pull my coat up high, lower my head, and follow. She leads me back through a level of opulent offices occupied by some of the premier legal minds of the kingdom. We ascend two flights of stairs and follow an exterior corridor, the windows shining inward with the bright, cold light of the Winter sun as it nears the horizon. She stops at one of the offices near the end of the hall, bowing before the door so low as to nearly tip over. I let her stand there for a moment holding the uncomfortable pose.

"Remember what will happen to you if you speak."

Her long legs take her around the corner before three heartbeats pass. With a sigh, I turn back to Torlas' door. I can hear movement inside, the soft scratch of a quill on paper and the occasional shuffling of papers. I hesitate. Dare I offer my burdens to this man? It's Torlas: joyful, playful, a man who actually sees me for me and tries to bring me happiness.

And to that, I'm bringing only sorrow.

I let my head come to rest against the door with a soft thump. The sounds inside cease.

"Is someone there?" Torlas calls from inside, his voice strong and confident.

I stay in that posture for a long moment, doing my very best to turn and walk away. I know our friendship will never be the same if I walk in. All I have to do is turn my back and continue to struggle with my demons on my own. I don't know if it's strength or weakness that calls for me to open the door, but I open it.

Torlas immediately brightens when he sees me, like a child offered a favorite treat. I take in his dim office from the threshold, noting that a flickering candle serves as his only illumination. He's not afforded a window, and the tangible darkness inside is oppressive. He can always walk outside for a moment of sunlight, but the office is not what I expected to be given to the heir to the most powerful duke in the entire kingdom.

I take a step into the candlelight and away from the sun silhouetting me to Torlas' eyes. Before I can open my mouth, he's standing. His arm wraps around my shoulders as he leads me to one of the two chairs set before his desk. I sink into one, and he takes the other. He gathers both of my hands in his.

"Iliana, I am here for you."

His words, so simple, so caring, the way he inflects my name, even the sound of his voice, all pummel at the void that fills my chest. He doesn't ask me what's wrong. He doesn't ask what he can do for me. He just declares, as a true friend should, that he will be what I need him to be. I don't deserve whatever Torlas feels for me, in friendship or beyond.

"I..." I begin, but I trail off as the moment of my confession comes upon me. Looking into the eyes of my only true friend, my spirit quails at the thought of losing him. The words stick in my throat. "I have something to tell you. I don't want you to speak or to ask me any questions. I just want you to listen, okay?"

Torlas nods seriously, already following my instructions. So I tell him. The words come falling from my mouth one after another in a monotone; the uncaring ashes of the pyre of my innocence. Torlas doesn't respond or react until I describe the torture of the assassin. Even then, he just closes his eyes and continues to hold my hands. My words end abruptly. The story of my deeds is not so long, but the sudden silence is louder and lasts far longer.

Finally, Torlas opens his eyes: guarded, uncertain, a look of such confusion and mistrust that my soul drops back into the void. It's just as I feared. I've ruined whatever friendship I had with Torlas; cut down any budding relationship before it can even begin. As Torlas searches my gaze, however, a light kindles in his eyes.

"I'm not going to... excuse what you've done, Iliana," he says, his tone as solemn as I've ever heard him. "Torturing the assassin, whether he tried to kill you or not, was wrong. I can't believe that you'd do something like that. I understand, I guess. If someone tried to kill me, I'd want revenge as well. The men in the alley, the rapists, they deserved every bit of their fate. I don't know if I want my fifteen-year-old friend being the face of justice, at least not yet, but all women deserve more than to have those men walk the earth. It may be hard to believe, but this changes nothing."

"But you don't understand!" I shout, tearing my hands out of his. "I enjoyed it! I laughed as they suffered! I exulted as they died!"

"Why? Why would you feel that way?"

"Because I had power over them. Because I was in control. Of my life and theirs. I finally started to realize that they are beneath me."

"No. Iliana, don't say that. That's the Sealord speaking, not you," Torlas responds, shaking his head. "No one is beneath you. You are human."

"You're wrong," I spit, acid in my voice. "I'm different. I am the Master of Earth, the only one who can claim that title. I'm blessed to be the Creator's chosen. We are set apart."

"You are human," Torlas says again, his voice growing stronger. "You breathe, you laugh, you cry, you hate. You... love. No matter what you've been taught, you're still human."

"I'm not like you, Torlas. I'm a Shaper."

"You are more like me than your father. I don't want to do this. But, if I have to, I must. I'm going to pit myself against your father, as much as the thought terrifies me to my core. I won't let you become like him. You need to be more. It isn't just that you can be human *and* a Shaper; they are one and the same. As long as you let me, I'll be here, reminding you."

"Torlas..." I say, clenching my eyes shut against his words. What was a void inside me crumbles before a torrent of confusion I can't conceal. My family on one side, my only friend the other. Torlas is setting himself against everything I've ever been taught, straining against my love for my family. How can he? What does he hope to achieve? As if he stands a chance of winning. As if my father is the cause of all of this.

"I just want you to know, Iliana. I'll always fight for you. I know you love your father, and I know you want his approval. But I won't let you stop being the Iliana I've always known. If your father makes you do these things, if you ever feel like you felt when you walked into my office today, I'll be there. Come to me. I'll listen. I'll be your touchstone. I'll keep you human."

Chapter 8
Bastian
Some Shitty Day in the Middle of an Eternal-Damned Winter
In the Year 5219, Council Reckoning

Waking up is a surprise. Feeling like someone stored their collection of cutlery in my stomach, not a surprise. Dim morning light filters through a swarming cloud of dust and a set of half-broken blinds, the string holding the slats together fraying. The walls, too, look ill-used, paint peeling back to reveal the skeletal bones of the structure. Even as awareness returns, the unwholesome tickle of tiny organisms crawling in my hair and along my skin is an unpleasant harmony with the rough blanket draped over me.

I manage to raise my head, the effort titanic and ultimately futile. I don't learn anything about the room, but the effort of moving my head requires muscles in the vicinity of my navel. The flash of agony has me gasping and blinking away flashes of light. Groaning, I close my eyes and try not to move. Oddly, the bugs crawling on my skin are a welcome distraction from the ungodly agony.

The door in the corner swings open at the sound of my groan. I don't have the strength or the inclination to raise my head again, and I can't focus enough to pick up surface thoughts. It's probably some brute looking to ransom me or a quack doctor trying to extort me for money before I succumb to my wounds.

One of the first times in my life I'm happy to be wrong.

"I thought I hallucinated you," I mumble, but I'm not sure I get the words out through my sandpaper tongue.

"Luckily for you, you didn't," the servant girl says, her eyebrow quirking over one exotic eye. She's wearing ill-fitting, rugged, and dirty clothing, her hair a bird's nest perched on her head. She's a far cry from the clean servant's uniform and manicured appearance she maintained during our travel over the Bridge.

"You look like hell," I say, or try to, but my mouth is so dry that the words hardly stir the air.

She rolls her eyes and strides over to my bedside. Picking up a rough clay cup, she holds the rim to my lips. My hand comes up and forces the cup closer even before the taste of water registers. Lukewarm water spills through the beginnings of a scruffy beard on my cheeks, but I don't care. I continue to gulp even as my stomach blazes in blinding pain. Finally, I sag back, panting, trying desperately to contain my shuddering stomach.

"*You*, my friend, look like hell," she says, leaning back into a crouch. She balances easily on the balls of her feet. The thick metal anklet of slavery shifts and settles, the runes declaring her to be the property of Eledar Cortola clearly standing out in silver against the cold iron.

"Who are you?" I gasp, squinting through the pain of my wounds. "I mean, obviously you're a slave, but…"

"I am Lentana, of the Tenkal clan," she responds woodenly, automatically. "My terms of service are for thirty years, of which I have served eight under contract to Minister Cortola."

"But, what, what is going on? Why are we here? Where is the rest of our train?"

"Gone. When I found you, you were bleeding out on the ground. I took you to the nearest doctor I could find at that time of night. He did his best to patch you up after seeing your fancy clothing, figuring his pay would be extravagant. After I determined you weren't going to die, I went out to find the other Khalintari. I was in the process of explaining what had happened to Tilinki when the Minister walked out. Apparently, he had been listening in from the balcony above. He told me to forget you existed and begin packing to leave. That was two weeks ago," she says, sighing. "I had to smuggle you out of the doctor's when I realized we weren't going to be able to pay. I was lucky to find this place. I had to evict a bum, who came back with friends. Luckily for us, they weren't willing to damage the Minister's property, so the anklet actually helped for a change..."

"Must I ask the obvious question?" I think about trying to reach out and pluck the answers from her mind, but I can't bear the thought of accessing my power just now\. I can still feel the hate, the unending torrent of red rage, the sickening feeling of a knife sliding into my own stomach from two perspectives... "Why are *you* here? Why are you defying the Minister to save me?"

"What has the Minister done for me? I've picked up horse shit from his baggage train for the past eight years. Literally, as an illustrious servant to the Minister of Finance, I serve exactly two purposes: picking up horse shit and occasionally being called to his chamber to 'serve' him. Leaving behind another servant, no matter how favored, just felt wrong to me. We look after our own," she says, shrugging.

"But won't they take your family? They'll owe the debt for the twenty-two years of service that you haven't completed..." I stop as she begins to shake her head.

"Those bastards? I've never known who my parents actually were. I was living in an alley in Sail when a young couple saw me. They had food. I was starving. They were clean. I was filthy. They took me back to their inn, bathed me, and fed me. I felt like a Minister. When I woke up, the slave mark was on my ankle and Cortola's steward was informing me of my terms of service, its required length, and expected duties."

It's a common enough story. Most slaves in the Republic are people who go into the service willingly, or, at least, of their own free will. The terms of service are quite lucrative, especially for young, strong, or attractive individuals. Most choose the life in order to provide for their family, to guarantee a roof and warm meals to eat, or to escape from debt or enemies. It's not unknown for some couples to literally farm children, popping out as many as possible in order to sell them to the highest bidder and live on the profits. Some are even less scrupulous, taking in urchins or orphans and giving them up in quasi-legal trades for a fraction of their normal cost. The dealers then 'legitimize' the child, bring their credentials up to date, fabricate a history for them, and sell them into expensive contracts. A thirty year contract for a young and beautiful girl could probably feed a family for nigh-on a decade.

"Why haven't you run before now, if you hate the people who sold you?" I ask, genuinely curious.

"Where would I go? This life is better than street life, most days. Cortola has dozens of slaves and professional concubines. The times when I'm called to his chamber are few and far between. Here I'm, well, I *was* fed. I had friends, after a fashion. A young girl with the slave mark of the Minister of Finance has a less than zero chance of escaping Coin, let alone making her way in the world."

"Right."

I sit back, staring at the dingy ceiling. So. Cortola has acted overtly against me. Again. I can't blame him, but, certain as the sun, I'm going to make him pay. I start to categorize my resources, but I realize the list is remarkably short: a slave girl and my mind. The girl will be useful cover if we manage to procure respectable clothing and a bath. I also need to heal. With a grimace, I lift my head and peek under the bandage. The wounds appear clean enough, though the deepest, just to the left of my navel, is still an angry red.

"How am I alive?" I mutter. My knowledge of human anatomy is a little shaky, but I can picture how many internal organs the blade must have pierced. My stomach should be in tatters, my subsequent death inevitable, painful, and slow. Instead, I look to be swiftly on the mend.

"I may have, well, understated the nature of the doctor I took you to," Lentana says. "His practice is as fancy as anything in the palace back in Coin, and his fees would probably beggar most merchant houses... We're also in this level of shithole because he probably has anklebreakers out looking for us."

"Right," I say again, sighing. The problems just keep adding up.

***

I spend the next two days slurping broth, sipping water, and trying not to flex my stomach. All of my work will be undone if Cortola manages to get back and reestablish himself outside of my control. It'll be extraordinarily difficult to regain influence over a mind so clearly ready to resist me. Though I can't be sure, I imagine Cortola is beginning to get an inkling of just exactly how I'm controlling him. There being only one Shaper of Thought in the whole damn world, the logical jump isn't exactly a taxing one.

On the third day, I've had enough. I can feel sores forming on my back from the extended stay in bed, and the itching from small and no-doubt infectious insects is driving me mad. I manage to sit up with Lentana's help, her arm strong around my back. I'm weak, but I can move. She brings me a dirty rag and a bucket. Together we manage to at least wipe a modicum of the grime from my person.

"Lentana, in all seriousness, why are you doing this?"

"My friends call me Tana," she responds, smiling. She has adorable dimples. I can use that. "When I saw you on that horse, I took a liking to you. You were pissed off and suffering, but you chose to be out with the rest of us. I know you could ride in the palanquins with the rest of the pampered, but you chose not to. I respect that. Honestly, though, I know what it's like to have no one and nothing. When the Minister turned his back on you, I knew you would be totally alone. No one deserves that, Bastian."

For the first time since my injury, I reach out with my mind. Tana's words are earnest, her fierce protectiveness a burning beacon. She really did give up her life and force herself into the regrettable existence of a runaway slave for me. She's certain to be branded if she's ever caught. All because she refuses to let someone else live helpless as she does. Her memories run through a litany of kindnesses she's paid to beggars in the street, saving her food, eating too little, risking punishment to steal a few crusts, ignoring the hunger to provide scraps for a small collection of urchins she gathered at the market.

The sentiment is powerful, I guess, but sickeningly noble. I can't help but be thankful to the girl for her naiveté. Those children are a drain on society. They could just take the slave mark for a decade and leave service as respectable young adults with the skills to work in a household or provide for a family. Instead, they are choosing to waste precious Khalintari resources by dirtying up the streets.

Tana gasps. The bright silver mark of my power glows out from beneath my thin and ragged pants. I almost reach out and blank the image from her mind, as I've done so many countless times in the past, but the flavor of her thoughts is interesting. I sense a reverence, a near-religious respect. There's also a familiarity I don't expect. She's seen the mark before. I dive into the memory.

I bunch the sheets around my fists and heave again. The muscles in my thighs are on fire. The weight of Bastian's unconscious form slides along the dirty street a few more feet. The muck has already stained the white brown, but the high-quality sheets aren't going to tear just because I'm dragging a body in them.

The flickering light cast by the torches of the closest patrol glow around the corner. I risk a glance back over my shoulder. The alley is another ten feet away. Grimacing, I growl and drive my feet into the ground. Bastian slides forward again, but my legs begin to collapse. After everything I've done, a routine fucking guard patrol is going to catch me because I'm too tired to go on. I moan and force myself to tug again. Bastian barely moves.

Getting him out of the doctor's house was relatively easy. Normally in a city like Halfway, the death wagon is busy cleaning up alleyways. Bodies are always plentiful from a healthy combination of drunks, muggings, and starvations. Each night, on the off chance a patient expired under their care, the wagon makes a routine stop at each medical establishment. The bodies are then walked to the edge of the platform and tipped over into the sea far below. Halfway is a fantastic place to assassinate someone. Pick any direction and walk, and you'll find yourself with an easy place to dispose of the evidence.

I waited until the death wagon was on its way, then came to 'visit' my friend. It was short work to wrap him in his sheets like a shroud and drag him to the back door when they came knocking. The doctor was asleep, and his manservant knew to expect the wagon and waved the men off with a few perfunctory words. I sweated out a few desperate moments in the closet near the back door as the servant went off to his bed, then hurriedly pulled Bastian into the street and called out to the wagon to stop just as they were rounding the corner. Luckily, those kind of men don't ask too many questions, especially at a doctor's. It was a simple matter to shadow the cart until they headed towards the dingier parts of the city, then sneak his body off the cart and into the nearest alley.

But now, here I am. Stuck in the middle of a deserted street, dragging an unconscious man with three ugly stab wounds in his stomach on stolen sheets. Even if I could somehow make up an explanation for the Governor's patrol, they'll want to check out my story. I force myself back onto my feet, pulling with everything I have left. He doesn't budge. That's it. I'm done. I collapse next to Bastian's inert form, trying unsuccessfully to force down the sobs erupting from my chest.

Great job, Tana. You set out to rescue somebody and don't even make it an hour. The ancient street is smooth beneath my side. Bastian's face has worked its way out of the sheets, his eyelids fluttering as if he's dreaming. I glance over at the approaching light. The first patrolman rounds the corner, his immaculate tabard proudly displaying the sigil of the Governor of Halfway: a simple motif of a bolt of lightning splitting a circle in two. He notices me and his hand goes to his sword, approaching with caution as he calls out to the man behind him.

I look back at Bastian dully. His eyes flicker, and I lean in close to see if he is going to awaken. He doesn't. On impulse, I give him a gentle kiss, his lips responding slightly to the soft contact.

"It would be really fantastic if we were invisible right now," I mutter sarcastically into his ear. Six damn feet from the alley and a chance to hide.

"Hold it—" a gruff voice begins, then cuts off. I glance up at the approaching men. The lead man, his sword out, freezes, his eyes darting back and forth rapidly. "What in the Eternal's saggy tits…"

"What, Bolen?" a weasel-faced man whines behind him. His greasy hair is tied back in a knot at the base of his skull, but a few strands have escaped to dangle against his face. His eyes pass over us, moving on without the slightest pause. "See something?"

"I thought I did," Bolen mutters, taking a ginger step forward and scrunching his eyebrows together in near-comical concentration. "There was just…"

Weasel-face steps up beside him, glancing around again and then looking askance at Bolen.

"There ain't nothing here," he says, slapping Bolen on the back of the head. "You been sucking barnacles again down by Solace?"

"You rat-faced bastard," Bolen sputters, turning to glare. "I don't suck barnacles! I saw your mother down there, and it warn't her mouth the barnacles was slippin in, neither."

"Ain't the worst thing that's been inside her," Weasel-face laughs.

"I'm looking *at the worst thing that's been inside her," Bolen says before turning back and staring at us. Through us. I swear our eyes meet, but no recognition shows in his dull gaze.*

"Let's go, shitstain. I'm not walking this whole damn night in the middle of Winter," Weasel-face groans, grabbing Bolen by the neck and dragging him forward.

It's impossible. That man saw us, stared at us, drew his sword to accost us, but then… I look over at Bastian, immediately squinting from the bright silver light glowing out from his form. His eyes remain closed, though fluttering rapidly. The light is shining from a symbol on his leg. The color is pure, a more enchanting silver than any I've ever seen. His features are angular and strong in the glow.

"Invisible?" I whisper.

Tana stares at me, her expression awed. She's relived the memory with me, knowing I'm there behind her eyes. She doesn't seem repulsed, as most do when another's presence intrudes in the recesses of their mind. She seems almost grateful. Who is this girl? I resist the urge to reach out and continue to delve. The effort is exhausting what little reserves I've managed to build up over my rest.

"Shaper," she quietly declares. As if the knowledge isn't obvious at this point.

"Of Thought, neh?"

No one knows. That's the trick to the level of my influence and the safety of my power. I haven't shared the knowledge with a single soul… at least none who can tell the tale. For some reason, the thought of blanking this girl's mind disquiets me, though. I don't know if it's because she saved my life or because of her reverence.

I almost do it. I almost destroy those memories, as I have with every person who's ever discovered my power. But it's a relief. The secret of my Shaping has been with me for so long I guard it by instinct. The weight of it is extraordinary, now that I can feel it. Now that I'm being forced to acknowledge it. A secret is a powerful thing; the longer you hold on to it, the more difficult it becomes to share. The easier it seems to keep. The harder it is to reveal. I thought, long ago, that I had grown used to solitude. I was wrong.

Shit.

"Thought?" Tana asks, brow furrowing.

"Imagine my surprise the first time I read my mother's mind, then got her to bring me the chocolate she was holding out of reach," I say wryly, closing my eyes.

"How do we not know about you? Why are you keeping your power a secret? I mean, a *scribe*?"

"A convenient excuse to be around the most powerful men and women in Coin," I say, the words coming easily despite my reluctance. Now that the spigot of information is open, the secrets just continue to flow. "I'm present at every negotiation, every meeting of the Khals, every foreign dignitary's introduction…"

"Everyone has said that Coin is reaching unprecedented heights of growth," Tana says, eyes widening. "All of our trade contracts are favorable. Every foreign negotiator leaves believing in the fairness of their deal, but they're ruined in the process. You?"

"Quite informed, for a slave girl," I say, smirking slightly.

"You hear things, spending time in the Minister's chamber," she retorts, gaze hardening. "I've ears as well."

The flatness of her gaze makes me squirm. It isn't because I've never been subjected to a disgruntled look. It's that I didn't even think about my comment before speaking. The lingering hurt I sense on the surface of her thoughts also plucks at a long-dormant portion of my mind. What the hell? I feel bad? The thought scares me.

"Tana, I'm sorry. I was actually impressed with your knowledge," I start, but the words feel awkward. When was the last time I've apologized to anyone?

"It's nothing," she says. She stretches her foot out and jangles the heavy metal anklet marking her as the Minister's property. "I *am* a slave. I shouldn't be offended at this point."

I consider saying more, but I can tell she doesn't want to talk about it anymore. With a titanic effort, I manage to roll out of the bed. I land on one knee and wince at the new pain that shoots through my leg. At least it isn't the damn stab wounds. They are just a dull ache in the back of my mind, easily ignored. I push off of my knee, forcing myself on my feet. Tana reaches for my arm, but I irritably slap her hands away. I'll damn well stand on my own. Tottering around the hovel, the few steps from one side to the other exhaust me.

"Good enough," I mutter, lowering myself slowly into a crouch with my back against the wall.

"Good enough for what?"

"To get out of this Creator-forsaken shithole."

***

Tana supports me as we creep out into the streets, gingerly stepping through the filth and human detritus that litters the path. Halfway is a fantastically wealthy city due to its convenience, but it is also the home of unbelievable overpopulation. The dregs of the two great societies joined by the Way leave their desperate lives behind and make their staggering, unruly way to Halfway, the city of wonder and opportunity far over the waves. The dream is real, for a few. A very few. Most quickly find themselves swindled, destitute, and tipped off the side of the Bridge by the very corpse wagons that saved my hide.

A ragged hood pulled low over my head, I don't bother to hide my limp, holding my stomach close. Our grime and general malaise provide fantastic cover in the slums. No one bothers to rob the destitute. I see a few uninterested gleams coming from alleys we pass, but nothing to even suggest any danger. The thoughts surrounding us echo of depression and lethargy, a glaze of hardened apathy that can't be cracked by so bedraggled a couple as we.

We pass swiftly out of the worst of the slums. The area is not very large simply because of the limited space of Halfway.

The poor and the wealthy are crammed in street by street. Walk a few steps in Halfway and you can leave behind a man starving to death and enter a restaurant serving swordfish from the Isles a thousand miles away. I head for the long ramp down to the water, dutifully avoiding locking eyes with anyone, keeping my head down and my thoughts close about me. I'm still too weak to monitor the thoughts of all passersby, so I have to trust anonymity to protect us. The thought sets my palms to sweating. Every person who brushes past us could be a threat.

We reach the top of the ramp heading down to the docks, though the word seems inadequate for the miles-long stone piers that stretch out into a calm bay. Titanic stone walls curve around to either side and create the peaceful water so suited to commerce: the Bay of Solace. Far in the distance, houses and hovels have been built up even on the curtain walls. The Governor routinely tries to clear out the walls of Solace so that his men can get to the gigantic towers guarding the entrance to the bay, but it's a never-ending endeavor. Made child's toys by distance and perspective, dozens of ships rest quietly in their berths. Solace offers the only safe anchorage within a thousand miles. The massive waves of the Maelstrom grow smaller north of the Way, but they're still large enough to eradicate any structure not blessed by the power of Shaping.

The crowd sweeps us forward, the river of humanity carrying us along almost to the bottom of the miles-long ramp. The gradient is so gradual that I'm surprised when I find the masts of ships at eye level. Many of the ships are simple fishing schooners meant for boating to the edge of Solace and no farther; the real waves of the North Sea would swallow them before they sailed for five minutes beyond the shelter of the walls. Only a few ships show the impressive masts of the seafaring. I squint up, trying to read flags as we pass. I need to find a ship that will head to the Republic, because I don't have the energy to discover the destination of the two dozen mighty ships in the bay.

Almost near the end of one of the largest stone piers, a distinctly recognizable flag stands out from the others: an eye, partially closed, a sunburst rising from above the lid. White on a field of blue. The flag of the Seer's Isle.

The Seers are an honest folk, more accepting than most, and some of the savviest traders to come out of the Isles. They put in at Sail often and are known hunters of pirates rather than the other way around. Of all the Isles tribes, the Seers are the most respected. I lead Tana over to the adjoining pier, closing my eyes.

"What are we doing here?" Tana hisses in my ear. "We don't have any money. How can we possibly afford passage on one of these ships?"

"We can't," I snap back. "Let me concentrate. If you want to be useful, stand so that my mark won't be visible."

Tana moves to stand in front of me, leaning against my leg just as I reach for my power. Her body, strong and soft, presses against my thigh. For a moment I can't concentrate. Her warmth, her dark hair swaying down her back, the scent of her, even after these long weeks in a hovel, like orange and something I can't place...

Do you want to die here, idiot?

I shove thoughts of Tana away and dive into my power, carefully avoiding the bright spot of Tana's mind next to mine. Overwhelming emotion and thought cascade around me, the swirling, seething mass of humanity an impossibly complex kaleidoscope. I grit my teeth and narrow my focus, seeking only the ship, the particular thought patterns of the Seers.

The ship is getting ready to leave, the crew's thoughts focused on their tasks, their excitement of departure, their respect for the captain… there.

The *Mason's Fall's* crewmen busy themselves with various tasks, but a few gather near the gangplank, speaking with a man whose smugness is just barely eclipsed by his apathy...

"Now," I say suddenly, limping forward as fast as my trembling legs will take me.

"What do I do?"

"Act as if I'm the Minister himself. You provide me legitimacy. Be that."

We approach the group. A tall, youthful man with midnight skin stands at the base of the plank, shoulders thrown back and chin raised proudly. His muscled chest contains lungs like a bellows, and he towers over the wiry, whipcord thin woman negotiating with a man in the Governor's employ. Thin leather straps cross dozens of times across her chest, her skin visible in occasional flashes as she throws up her arms to punctuate her speech. She's energy incarnate, the muscles of her bare arms gleaming in the cool sun. She wants to be on her way, the vibrant flash of her eyes evidence beyond the agitation in her surface thoughts. The man, by contrast, stands silent, his thoughts ordered and measured, patient as a spider. He will need to be watched.

He notices our approach and tenses, his huge hand going to a blade at his side. The sword looks like a knife in his grasp. I have to force myself to continue, ignoring the pain and turning my limp into a confident stride. The Governor's man scowls in annoyance when he sees us.

"Move on, you lot!" he shouts, brandishing his tablet as if it were a claymore.

The huge man steps forward, face set and careful, just like his mind. The woman at his side, the captain, lays a hand on his forearm.

"No, Talan," she says quietly, squinting at me. There's something like recognition in her eyes.

"Captain Te'ial!" I raise my voice in a friendly greeting, plucking the name from the customs agent's mind. "This man is trying to swindle you."

"Of course he is," she says, completely relaxed, a small smirk forming on her lips. Her accent in the Kingdom tongue is quiet, hardly noticeable. Probably better than mine. She makes a quick hand gesture as if to say *such is the way of things*.

"I think we can get you a better deal," I say, grinning, ignoring that face that I probably appear one step above a beggar and two below a decent human being.

"Like hell you can," the Governor's man says, stepping into my personal space and lowering his voice. "Bugger off, beggar, or I'll give you a reason to."

Once I'm sure his body blocks me from view of the captain and her protector, I reach out a hand and lay it on his shoulder. Physical contact makes it so much easier to work my particular brand of magic. Before he can recoil, I jump behind his eyes.

He is, of all things, a pretty decent fellow. Loyal wife, sick child, some kind of rash and fever spreading across her body. Doctors are struggling to help. He swindles people on the docks not for greed, but so that he can pay for medicine for his child. I shrug inwardly. One more casualty.

I dive into the present moment. He actually holds the Seers in some kind of awe. As a child, he listened to legends of the Seers' ability to read the dreamworld and come back with knowledge of the future. It's impossible, of course, unless they have the Shaper of Time reborn. Even so, I implant in him the certainty the Seers actually do have the mystical strength legends claim they have. They can see the future, and, if properly compensated, alter it. I fan those flames of hope in the man's heart until they shine as a beacon burning bright in his mind. I know I have him when that hope alights in his eyes.

I release his shoulder and step back, having seemed to whisper to him for a few moments, nothing more. He nods at me, a hopeful but brittle smile creeping onto his face. He turns back to the Seers and bows low before them. Captain Te'ial's eyebrows rise fractionally, her only reaction.

"Honored Seers, if you would accept your docking fee as a contribution to your noble cause, I would consider it a blessing," he says, never raising himself from his bow. "If you would be so kind as to look on us with mercy in your hearts, that would be thanks enough."

He stays in the bow as he leaves, shuffling backwards before abruptly swinging about and striding off through the flowing crowd. Te'ial gazes after him, impassive, then her eyes flick back to me.

"How by all the Depths did you manage that?" she asks, the question feeling more like an accusation.

"I'm a man gifted with both knowledge and the means to use it," I respond, tilting my head in a gentle nod.

"And what do you want for this… extravagant gift?"

"For this paltry display? Nothing."

"Nothing?" she asks, lips quirking into that same knowing smirk.

"What I seek is passage on your ship. To Sail, if you can be persuaded to head that direction," I say, knowing full well that Sail is already their destination.

"We do not take on passengers," she says curtly, spinning on her heel and turning to go.

"Not even personal retainers of Eledar Cortola?" I call, pulling Tana forward. Te'ial's eyes snap to the slave mark, tracing the whorls and symbols etched in the iron.

"I've dined with Minister Cortola," she answers, switching smoothly into Khalin as if she were born to the language. My respect for her rises another fraction. "And none of his retainers look quite so bedraggled."

"We've obviously fallen on hard times. We were left behind when the Minister's train moved on three weeks ago. I was presumed dead, this poor slave given the task of finding me. She was ultimately successful, but I was in too dire straits to be moved. I have since healed, and I'm eager to resume my place at the Minister's side. I'm quite certain that the Minister will reward any who give assistance. As a man of no small means myself, present situation excluded, I can call on the administrators in Coin to appropriately compensate you for your time."

Which is true, though whether the money is particularly *mine* or not is irrelevant. I have often found the truth to be the best honey to spread over bitter words.

Te'ial glances at the man at her side, Talan. His face remains impassive, and they carry on a silent conversation as if they both possess my power, thoughts and opinions passing on a level of understanding only granted by true friendship and love. Finally, Talan sighs, nods, and strides up the gangplank. Te'ial looks back at me, her expression guarded.

"The terms of your contract are simple," she begins. "I cannot offer you a cabin, nor will you pass the time idly. You will be expected to work as a member of the crew in the rudimentary tasks normally reserved for our children. When we reach Sail, you will be accompanied to the nearest Coin representative, who will then provide us with my weight in gold marks. Afterwards, our contract is ended."

My eyes bulge practically out of my head. Her weight in gold marks could buy the bloodline contract of a family of trained slaves. Bloodline, as in, the entire family tree and any future progeny. It could buy three ships the size of the *Mason's Fall*, though the Isles is the only place with the knowledge and material to build them. I open my mouth to argue when she raises her hand.

"If I find that you are trouble in any way, my price rises to Talan's weight in starsilver," she says, pointing her thumb back over her shoulder at the giant man prowling about the deck.

I swallow my arguments back, almost gagging on the taste. Even though I don't have to worry about money, as people find themselves strangely willing to part with their wealth when I'm around, my pride drives me never to lose on a deal.

"Who's doing the swindling now, eh?" I ask, shaking my head at her ruefully. She smirks her signature smirk and makes a quick hand gesture as if to say *such is the way of things.*

***

The ride out is smooth. Aside from some cursing and the occasional scraping of hull to hull with the swarm of fishing schooners, the *Mason's Fall* sails easily out to the open ocean. Immediately, the ship begins to rise and fall in a gut-wrenching rhythm. Solace opens north above the Great Sea. The ocean itself is so vast as to be largely incomprehensible. If we sail directly south for thousands of miles, we'll reach the Broken Isles and perhaps come to the land of the Seers. But no one is foolish enough to attempt to sail across the center of the Great Sea. The waves even far out on the Ways are so rough that none but the people of the Isles try to sail much from the mainland. The waves in the vast open space between the Ways scrape the bottom of the sea.

I manage to avoid work by promptly falling so sick as to be immobile. I vomit until I'm not certain whether bile or pieces of my tattered stomach are slapping into the bucket. In rare moments of lucidity, I catch sight of Tana running around the deck, trying to tie thick rope, laughing with some of the crew at the rail, or climbing the heavy rigging a few yards up before sliding back down. The happy people of the Isles teach her with endless patience.

The entire crew matches Talan's dark complexion and muscular build, though he is the darkest and most impressive of them all. He's built like a cross between a bull and a panther, all savage strength and feline grace. He moves with such surety across the massively swaying deck that it seems impossible he could fall. All of the crew fear and love him equally. I don't understand how he commands such loyalty, but he would own this ship completely if not for Te'ial, whose word is law.

Tana approaches me on the third day, teeth gleaming through the wet hair plastered to the side of her face. She doesn't even seem to notice, instead throwing her arms up and hugging me.

"Isn't this glorious?" she exclaims, laughing as I throw up another weak stream of seawater. "I've never been so excited in my life!"

"We made—" I cough, my throat raw from bile and salt. "We made a terrible decision coming on this Eternal-cursed piece of shit-ridden death. We should have just stolen horses."

Tana just rolls her eyes, taking my bucket and heading for the side. A wave slaps over the side and splashes into the bucket just as she readies herself to heave it overboard. She glances down and shrugs.

"The Depths have claimed your offering already," she says, eyes glinting mischievously.

"On a ship three days and already speaking like the People," Te'ial calls as she approaches.

"Do you people have a death wish?" I ask miserably, squinting up at her.

"Perhaps we just like to know what living feels like," she responds, smirking at me. I'm already tired of that damned quirk of her mouth. "It will be smooth sailing from here to the Khalintars. I hope you have not been lying to me, *bient'al*, because then we'll have more than words between us."

I pluck the meaning of the word out of her brain. Bient'al. Honored one. She's being sarcastic. Of course she is.

Vigor returns to me over the next day as the unceasing roll of the deck settles into a more manageable sway. We've sailed north of the Bridge far enough that the titanic waves begin to calm. I manage to keep food down and strength returns to my limbs. My incessant vomiting has aggravated the wounds in my stomach, but the salt water and clean air keep them from infection. The crew begins to practice on the deck, swinging swords about with gleeful abandon. I can't tell if they're any good or if they're just waving around shiny bits of metal, but two are clearly head and shoulders above the rest.

Talan and Te'ial move in a blur of motion, he with his toy of a sword and she with a pair of long knives curved just slightly at the edges. They dance across the deck for minutes at a time, their weapons scraping against one another with brief showers of sparks and dissonant shrieks. Eventually, they settle back, breathing heavily, and seem to agree on an unspoken draw. Te'ial's chest rises and falls with each of her breaths, the gleam of her skin, the strength in her arms, the shape of her legs… with my strength's return comes other needs.

I don't feel comfortable influencing Tana, as she saved me and all that. No, I need someone with no connections, no attachments. There are a few female crew, but only Te'ial draws my eye. Her superior attitude and annoying smirk grate on my nerves, so there will be a certain satisfaction in the conquest. I go to her cabin as night falls on the second week out from Halfway.

She invites me in, the leather straps of her clothing still firmly secured, and offers me a stool at a small desk in the corner and sits.

"So, *bient'al*, what do I owe the honor of your illustrious presence?"

"Can my intentions not just be to enjoy the company of a beautiful woman?" I respond, smiling.

"If that is your intent, I believe Talan would take exception. And, no offense to you, but you do not seem the type to match up well against an angry Talan," she says wryly.

"Ah, so the two of you are… involved?"

"In an official sense? No. He is not available to one such as me," she says, glancing down and away for a quick moment.

"Why is that?"

I place my hand squarely over my mark as I stroll through her surface thoughts. Talan is important to the Seers; Creator, he's in his final training to be the next Seer himself. Te'ial seems certain he will win, and thereby take over the shamanistic religion the Seers feed their followers. From what Te'ial's mind dredges up, it's nothing but strange portents and vague mumbo jumbo. Thoughts of Talan also come with a yearning so powerful it shocks me. Te'ial loves the man beyond words or understanding. I never would have guessed from her swaggering exterior, but the giant man holds the only soft spot in her heart.

"He is important to our People. That is all I am allowed to say," she says, shrugging one shoulder languidly. Her smooth skin is perfect in the lantern light.

"Tell me about him," I say, trying to keep the huskiness out of my voice. This woman, so exotic, so clearly unattainable, is driving me to the edge. "Tell me about Talan."

She begins to speak, her words meaningless, the emotions behind them all that concerns me. An endless succession of stolen looks, longing, bitterness, lust, tenderness. She catches Talan looking as well, knowing his thoughts are the same, knowing equally they can never act on their love. The bitterness wells up, overwhelming the longing for just a moment. Talan is *choosing* to stay in the running to be Seer. There.

Our lips part, my fingers digging into the strong muscles of his shoulder. I close my eyes. His breath tickles the hollow of my throat. His hands encircle my waist, his fingers nearly meeting behind. I feel so fragile, so happy, so his.

The touch disappears.

I open my eyes, shocked. He stands in the corner of the small cabin, his eyes watching me, the rest of him disappearing into shadow. Despite the heartbreaking anguish in his gaze, he doesn't come closer. His breathing is ragged, both from the closeness of our love and from sorrow, I can tell. I sit up from the bed, my clothes still on, my heart still racing.

"Talan? What is wrong?"

"You know that what we do is forbidden," he says, voice dead despite the look in his eyes.

"Then forfeit your right!" I say, standing suddenly. "We are in love, Talan. I can see it in your gaze, I can feel it in your hands, I know it in your heart! Give up the contest. Be with me. We can sail the world together!"

I try to go to him, but he holds out his hands, keeping me at bay. Those huge, gentle hands are filled with love even as they try to resist. I grab onto them, desperate, feeling him slipping away even as I watch.

"Love is worth fighting for. Love is worth more than some meaningless title!"

"It is not possible," he says, his voice a broken husk of the strong, deep melody I know so well.

"Of course it is. You can declare our love. This has happened before. Others have given up the right in order to marry. Please, Talan, we can be together."

"It is for *love that I cannot. I swore, long ago, that I would find her."*

The words strike me like a blow straight to my heart. I totter backwards, his hands falling from my lifeless grasp. I end up on the bed, tears in my eyes, a void opening inside me.

"Who is she?" I ask woodenly. The words come more from reflex than any genuine curiosity.

"It is not another woman, Te'ial," he says sadly. "It is Aea."

"What?" The word echoes in the silence. "Your sister? The half-breed Cursed?!"

"Do not call her that again in my presence," he growls, anger returning the deepness to his voice. "She is my sister, wholly, and no half-breed."

"But why? After what she has done?" I can't bring myself to apologize.

The very thought of her causes me to recoil inside. The curse, the taint. None had been found in our nation for generations beyond counting. When the girl was discovered, wielding the evil in its rarest and ugliest of forms, the elders had argued about whether to put her to death immediately. But Talan had argued for her, argued for leniency. All the way up until the real tragedy.

"I must save her," he says, the words childlike in their hope. "She is Cursed, but we can cure her. We can make her sane again. I just have to find her and convince her to come back with us. Why do you think I wish to be Seer? For the title? For the power?"

His face twists into a rictus of derision, as if the very thought of something so selfish disgusts him. Of course, the thought does *disgust him. He is a man of honor. Yet how can he not see that trying to save this Cursed is dishonorable? That becoming Seer to fight for a Cursed spits on the very title? But I cannot say that to him. I love him too much.*

"With the power of the Seer, the ability to See, I will be able to find Aea. I can save her. I must save her," he finishes in a whisper, the words trodden over like a well-worn path, the litany a torch sustaining him in darkness. "She is the only family I have."

"You could have me," I say, knowing even as I say the words that my love for him, no matter how strong or how true, will not compete with this obsession. I cannot love him enough for both of us.

His eyes close. With a shuddering sigh, he turns. Facing the door, back rigid and tense, the words come out almost inaudibly over the creak of the ship.

"I am sorry, Te'ial. I cannot."

Then he is truly gone.

The power of her emotion is raw and intoxicating. I take the yearning she feels, the desire for Talan, and fan that flame. The feel of him, the intense and overriding *need*… fire rises in her eyes, her own emotion working towards my ends. I turn it, subtly. She can't have Talan. She can't even be close to him. But that doesn't satisfy that overwhelming desire. Perhaps there is an outlet that would serve. Even if it won't fill the empty hole inside her, at least it might allow her to forget…

I smile inwardly as she begins to look at me hungrily, desperately. She leans forward, eyes never leaving mine. She makes a low sound in her throat. I reach up and caress her cheek, face a mask of sorrow and understanding. She leans forward, and our lips brush, just the slightest of motions, the most gentle of caresses. She trembles, the leather straps covering her chest straining under her labored breathing.

"I am sorry," I say in a whisper, my breath against her lips. "I wish I could do something to help, to ease that burden."

Her hand twists into the dark curls at the nape of my neck and draws me forward, her mouth mashing against mine with a primal need. I let her take control, losing myself in the feel of her, the strength of her hands, the power in her arms. I bring my arms up around her, pulling Te'ial close.

I try to break from her when the door rattles against the opposite wall, but she has me in a tight embrace. A pair of massive hands, dark against the tan of my shirt, fix that problem for me. I fly through the air, slamming against the bulkhead with bone crunching force. My teeth rattle. All thoughts Te'ial disappear in a jumble of confused shock.

My eyes focus on Talan's face, twisted like some abomination from the wastes of the desert. I reach desperately for my power, grasping at every ounce of focus. Just as the symbol of my strength begins to glow, Talan's eyes flicker down, widening further. Shit.

I dive into his mind, frantic, wrecking all I can in a desperate attempt to confuse him. For a moment, I manage to deflect his attention, but an overriding wall of hatred and disgust rises up and thrusts me out of his mind. His giant fist slams into my gut like a horse's kick square in the lungs. My breath and focus leave me in a weak gasp of air. I heave up a thin stream of bile. He lets me slump to the floor, all thoughts of resistance fled. I try to hold on to the tiniest portion of my power, tapping into their minds so I can understand the conversation when they switch back into their native tongue.

"Talan, by the Depths, I don't know what came over me," Te'ial says, distantly, sobs in her voice.

"I do," his voice rumbles like distant thunder in a cloudless sky. "He is Cursed."

"What?" she says dumbly. "Cursed?"

"I saw the mark as he tried to use it on me. He was in my head. I could feel him there. I still can," he says, growling. I tense weakly on the ground, trying to curl further into a ball.

"He was in your head?" Te'ial asks, more a confirmation than a question. "Ah. Damn my weakness to the forgotten Depths! How could I have let this happen? I thought it was you; I wanted it to be you!"

"There is no fault of yours," Talan says, his voice moving to be directly over me. "Only this piece of filth. We should kill him now, and let Eo back into the world, for it can only be him."

"Wait. Better the fin you can see, than the shark below."

"He cannot be allowed to recover. He almost had my mind. Only my anger saved me."

"Then don't let him."

I look up weakly. Talan crouches down onto his haunches. I try to reach out, to speak, to apologize, I don't know. He slaps my hand away like a parent scolding a disrespectful child. His fist comes down, a mountain of judgment I cannot avoid.

Chapter 9
Kettle

The Twenty-Third Day of Spring
In the Year 5222, Council Reckoning

I stride through the entrance of the Imperial Bank confidently. The flowing skirts of my station swirl about my legs, and my heels click against the polished marble floor loudly. The sound goes largely unnoticed in the bustling business of the bank on a warm day in Spring. I ignore the men stationed on either side of the entrance, and they ignore me, as is their duty. The front of the bank is comprised of a single expansive room of ornate marble, gold plating, and tasteful frescoes depicting legendary figures from history. A wall of golden bars separates the desks of the tellers and their charges from the stairwell leading to the offices above and the vaults below.

I pause when I hear a rattle of coins, glancing behind me with a withering stare.

"Forgive me, *bi'ental,*" Timo says smoothly, ducking his head. "I misstepped."

Inwardly, I smile, marveling at how confident and cultured his voice is, but outwardly I shake my head and move on, loose hair brushing the tops of my shoulders. Timo follows with the massive bag of coin in his hands, even his considerable strength straining under the load. With clothes cut to accentuate his broad frame and highlight the strength of his shoulders and hair smoothed back, his bold features border on handsome. His time in the theater serves him well.

Rina returns from a break at her desk, just as planned. I haven't laid eyes on her in over two years, but time seems to have been kind to her. She's lived the cushy life of a respected bank teller for so long that the hard lines of a thief are difficult to discern through her uniform. I glance back at Timo and give an imperious jerk of my head, the dark waves of my hair swaying. He dutifully brings the bag forward to Rina's desk.

"What can I do for you, my lady?" Rina says, her face scrunched into the typical disinterested smile of all bankers everywhere.

Wordlessly, I gesture to Timo. He raises the bag and begins pouring its contents out on the desk. Starsilver and gold mix in a shocking waterfall of wealth, the unending rattle temporarily drowning out the rest of the sounds in the bank. Several coins fall to the ground, plinking and rolling on the marble. When the sound dies, so do all others. I refuse to look around, knowing every single person in the bank is frozen in shock. I simply stare at Rina, quirking one eyebrow upward.

"The Seers would like to store some of this metal with you," I say, heightening my accent until my speech is difficult to understand. My dress, made of the finest silk is so pure a white that it glows in contrast with my darker skin. "We have seen Jon Gordyn is a man to be trusted."

Rina does a fantastic job looking shocked, and in all reality she probably is. While we couldn't muster the necessary weight in starsilver alone (turns out, even all of our assets pooled aren't worth a bag full of starsilver), the amount of money mounded on the table is quite honestly the more than I ever imagined would be in one place. As a joke, Corna and I had filled a bathtub with the coins. It was horribly uncomfortable, but we still threw the coins up in the air like water and laughed the night away.

"My lady, allow me to speak with my superiors," she manages to squeeze out, her voice barely above a croak.

She raises her hand and two men walk over, their muscles practically bulging out of their uniforms. They stand on either end of the desk as Rina walks hurriedly through a gate of golden bars and disappears behind a set of double doors. The business of the bank hesitantly restarts, but I can still feel eyes all over us. Cocking my hip to the side, I paint an expression of utter boredom on my face.

"*At'lo*, pick up the metal you dropped," I say absently, eyes fixed ahead on the doors.

Timo obediently scrambles about, plucking coins off the ground. I clasp my hands before me to hide their tremble, steadfastly ignoring the bead of sweat working its way down the back of my neck. Too much time is passing. Rina has been gone too long. My stomach tenses, and the shadow under my dress rustles in anticipation. I resist the urge to glance up at the window set in the wall high above us. Gordyn might be watching.

The door finally swings open, a man in a tailored suit walking forward calmly with Rina in tow. He's old, his hair thinning at the top, his gut sticking forward a hair too far for practicality. He is most definitely not Jon Gordyn. Rina gives me a subtle nod, and I relax. A bit. We're still in the thick of it, but we've passed the first test. The man approaches us, smiling and offering his hand. I allow him to take my fingers and kiss my knuckles.

"My lady, there is much we would discuss with you. Keagan Atlan, at your service," he begins, bowing and opening his hand towards the golden bars. We follow him as he leads through the gate. "The Imperial Bank has long desired commerce with the Isle of Seers. Your wisdom and wealth have been legend for time immemorial, though I can see now they were not exaggerated. May I ask who I have the honor of welcoming?"

"Aea Po'lial, sister to Talan Po'lial, soon to be first of his name to become Seer of the Isle," I respond, raising my chin.

He halts as his eyes widen, surprise and sudden avarice quickly veiled behind a cold calculation. Yes, Mister Atlan. I'm not just some fool with money. I matter in the Isles. His smile becomes more genuine, even as it also grows into something less savory. He bows deeper this time, holding out his arm for me to latch onto. I put my hand in the crook of his elbow and he leads me deeper into the bank.

He blathers on in a stream of pleasantries, seemingly unconcerned when I don't respond aside from an occasional platitude. We stroll into the golden cage and through the inlaid double doors, passing the office of minor officials and heading for a stairway at the back of the bank. After winding our way up two flights of stairs, we arrive at a sturdy and luxurious wooden door. I resist the urge to smile when we pass the first door on the right. I just pick out Corna's voice, smooth and sultry, speaking to another official behind a closed door.

Rina informed us of the protocol for sudden and unexpected meetings: Eldin Pentol, the most senior of the bank's executives and a serious, unrelentingly professional man, takes the first. His only significant weakness lies in his obsession with young and endearing women. Corna is perfect to play our first mysterious investor. She's supposed to be a woman fresh to Donir after inheriting a vast sum from her merchant father and mother, both tragically lost to pirates as they sailed south to inspect their holdings at the edge of the Broken Isles. Being a young girl unexpectedly in charge of a large sum of money, she decided to cash out everything she could and run to the city to start a new life. If only some amazing, smart and, gasp, handsome man could help her with the details?

The second unexpected meeting would be held by his underling, Keagan Atlan. He's ten years younger, but the third most powerful man at the Imperial Bank. He also envies Pentol his senior status. He is always seeking the next big windfall that might finally allow him to overcome his mentor. The bait we dangle in front of him is particularly juicy and enticing. Though the Seers maintain a facade of simplicity and what outsiders consider barbarism inside our borders, the People want for nothing. Our ships, our trade, and our warriors are coveted the world over.

Their ships, I guess. I'm no longer a part of the People.

Atlan ushers us into the second meeting room. A table of the richest mahogany dominates the center, surrounded by ornately carved lanterns whose shimmer sets the beautiful wood to glowing. Eight armchairs wrapped in supple leather are arrayed around the table. The ceiling is a polished marble, the corners shining so cleanly I can see my reflection in them. A rug of the softest weave and intricate embroidery bedecks the floor in a rich red. It's a room to embarrass other rooms.

I take a seat at the head of the table, crossing my legs and placing my hands before me. Timo stands at my beck, his broad chest moving with his breath, calm and slow. Timo's serenity helps me to remain still and stoic. His solid presence is a rock in a storm. Atlan seats himself next to me, a bit closer than decorum normally allows. Definitely eager.

"My lady Aea," he begins, his smile near predatory. "Your nation has been one of the most successful shipping industries the world has ever known. Your goods are met in every nation with the highest praise for quality—"

"Your words are as waves on a beach," I cut in, waving my hand in front of his face. "I have heard them a thousand times. They are pleasing, but familiar. I am here for that which is unfamiliar."

"Right," he begins again. "The wealth your man laid upon poor Rina's table was a fabulous sum, no doubt, but is it all that you plan to invest with us? Or perhaps is the Seer herself—"

"This metal is a gift to Jon Gordyn," I cut in again, smiling inwardly as his eyes flash in annoyance. "We have no use for such paltry amounts."

"A very generous gift, I'm sure, though most bring objects of value or art—"

"We know the giving of gifts. Jon Gordyn cares most for shining metal. He will accept our gift. We *know* he will be grateful."

Atlan sits back. His hand twitches slightly, and his eyes betray a sudden fear. Legend has it that the Seer can see the future, can predict through her dreams many of the certainties of the world. The People know that the Seer can indeed see the future, though her sight is limited to snippets and fragments. Regardless, those snippets have shaped the very fabric of the Seer society as the long line of Seers have guided the People towards a prosperous future. Before I left, however, the old Seer began speaking insanity. Of the world ending, and the death of all. So much nonsense. Atlan, however, has no idea whether the Seer has seen this meeting or not. He is wary of making a mistake.

"Very well. What is it you seek with this gift? What is your desire with the Imperial Bank?" he asks, his tone more deferential.

"We wish to use more of this metal to buy land. The Seer believes our future lies as a part of this kingdom, with the People living on the mainland," I declare, placing my fingers carefully on the tabletop. "Now, where is Jon Gordyn?"

"Let me assure you, I am fully able to negotiate on Mister Gordyn's behalf—"

"We wish to purchase Itskalan."

"The Bank has many holdings in Itskalan," he says, struggling to control his temper as I refuse to let him finish a sentence. "We would be more than happy to show you a catalogue of possible purchases, large tracts—"

"You see the shallows, but nothing of the depths," I say scornfully, wrinkling my nose at him in disgust. "We do not wish for a scale. We desire the fish."

His mouth moves as if he's chewing some particularly difficult piece of gristle, the words he desires to speak clearly held back by greed.

"You want," he says, slowly, then hesitates. When I don't cut him off, he continues. "To purchase… all of it? The former nation of Itskalan?"

"Yes."

"What of the cities? The people? It is impossible."

"Not for Jon Gordyn. The Seer is not wrong about him."

"Not even Jon Gordyn has the power to—"

"Do be quiet, little man," Timo cuts in, his words elegant and articulate. "Mistress Po'lial has made the desire of her People known. If you do not have the power, bring us the one who does."

I regard Atlan blandly. He starts to speak once, twice, but stops himself each time, his mouth gaping like a fish.

"Very well," he says finally. "Mister Gordyn is in a meeting, but I will bring your… proposition to him as soon as he is available."

"We will wait. If that door opens for anyone but Jon Gordyn, we will also leave, take our metal to Coin, and see what land can be purchased there."

Atlan nods once, sharply, his temper and bruised ego nearly getting the better of him. He shuts the door behind him with a quiet click. As soon as he's gone, I jump up from my chair and slip off my shoes, padding over to the door and pressing an ear against the thick wood. His exasperated sigh is audible through the door, but Atlan's footsteps fade as he heads off down the hallway. I smile as he snaps at someone in passing, damning them for being slow out of his way.

I turn back to Timo, who is already crouched on the table, his hands in a cup waiting for my foot. I nod, running forward and leaping in the whisper-thin dress. My shadow catches me and carries me to his waiting hand. He lifts me as easily as a child, my weight nothing to his broad shoulders. Standing on the table with his arms stretched above him, I'm just within reach of the gleaming ceiling. Perfect.

The shadow comes to my call, boiling out from underneath my dress. Carefully, quietly, I hone the darkness into a blade, thin as air, sharp as a careless word, a blade impossible to forge. Even as I focus on the blade, I plead with the shadow to make my vision true. I hold the weapon loosely, the form really more a personal affectation than a necessity. The blade will exist whether my hand touches it or not. When I think I've got it, I turn it in the air, and the blade disappears. I blink, confused, turning the blade again. It reappears. The sword is so thin as to be invisible in profile.

Looking upwards at the marble ceiling, I gauge my strike. The beautifully inlaid stone is perfectly crafted, not a speck of dust to be found even close up. Picking a spot, I stab upwards, bracing myself for the impact against the rock.

I almost fall forwards off of Timo's hands as the shadow slides straight through the marble as if it isn't there. Timo grunts below me, stepping to keep me in balance, a tiny bead of sweat tracking down his broad face. I whisper an apology and look back to the ceiling.

The blade has sunk nearly to my fingers into the rock without a whisper of sound or resistance. Cautiously, I wiggle the sword, and the thinnest stream of rock dust trickles down onto the polished wood table. Well, then. This is going to go much easier than I thought. With a smooth twirl on the solid base of Timo's massive hands, I spin a graceful circle. My blade cuts through the marble effortlessly. White dust sprinkles down on the table, but nothing more. There is the slightest tremor, almost invisible in the marble, but the ceiling holds itself in place.

"I'm through," I whisper down, and he nods. "Now comes the hard part."

I'm not an idiot. Cutting a circle over my head of heavy gold-inlaid marble is a fantastic way to become a thin, blood covered flatbread on the floor below. As exciting as that would have been for Jon Gordyn to open the door to, I like myself taller.

Instead, I've cut upwards at an angle, the rest of the ceiling serving as a natural funnel to hold the plug in place. I jump down, landing lightly in my dress. Timo and I dash around the room, extinguishing all of the lamps in the room but one to see by.

"Brace me," I say, eyeing the near-invisible line I've cut in the marble.

"You've got this," he answers softly.

He crouches behind me and puts his back to mine. I lean into him, his solidity comforting and calming. When I call on the shadow fully, the remaining darkness erupts from beneath my clothes and forms into a cloud over our heads. The light in the room dims as if passed through a dirty pane of glass. Long ago, I learned a critical lesson about my power: the shadow can and will do anything I ask it to, but it can't stand bright light or the direct rays of the sun.

For lack of a better idea, I form the shadow into a hand pressed against the marble like a server would carry a tray of heavy food. Narrowing my eyes and my focus, I push. The marble groans, and the room trembles slightly. My instincts beg me to hesitate, to run, most definitely not to stay under a ton of loose marble, but I drive the fear into the back of my mind where its whispers can't distract me. Sweat beads on my forehead, the shadow and I collectively straining against the weight of the stone. It shifts minutely. I redouble my focus, the weight of the rock pressing back so powerfully my bones shudder through my connection with the shadow. Timo gasps behind me as the weight settles on him as well.

Finally, the stone begins to lift. The marble wobbles, and I clench my eyes shut and force it to steady. Stale air leaks down into our room carrying a tide of dust. I struggle not to cough, holding the rock firm and sliding it to the side. With the utmost care, taking longer to set the stone down than it took to move it, I let the rock settle onto the floor of the room above us with a dull thud.

I lie on Timo's back for a long moment, breathing heavily, and he's content to let me. I jump up, forcing some energy into my leaden limbs. Time doesn't rest for the weary. I stumble, drained, my heart beating a lethargic rhythm and my thoughts slowing to a crawl. I shake my head, but it feels like a gauze has been placed over my eyes.

"Find a way to get rid of all this dust," I mumble, climbing gingerly onto the table. "And give me a lift."

"Tha'," Timo says as he climbed up, eyes fixed squarely on the new hole in the ceiling. "Is one hell of a way in."

I ignore the slip into his natural speech. I have to agree with him. At a pat on the shoulder, he compliantly bends down and makes a cup with his hands. I put my foot into the stirrup he makes, counting down from three silently with my fingers. He explodes smoothly from his crouch, throwing me upwards unerringly towards the hole. I wince as I fly, half-closing my eyes as I envision my shoulder cracking against the unyielding rock, but I pass through without so much as brushing the sides, twisting and landing noiselessly on the stone.

I smile. We're in. All our wealth, all our planning, everything we've done will finally pay off. He passes me up the remaining lit lantern. I swing it around slowly.

Then again.

Once more.

My smile falters.

I squint behind me.

The room is a few paces wide, perhaps ten long, the walls bare stone and mortar. It has nothing of the shining marble and exquisite woods of the rest of the bank. The door that opens into Gordyn's office is barely a crack, a simple lever to the side clearly the catch. The rest of the room, however...

Empty. Mostly.

My spirit flees down to my toes and lodges squarely in the soles of my feet. My shadow reacts to the sudden change in mood, twisting deep under my clothes and tight to my body. Risking the Family, throwing our lives like dice... for what? Nothing. There aren't piles of starsilver. There isn't a single precious stone. No papers, no bank accounts, nothing of any value. Just some wooden pedestals in the corner.

Despondently, I sulk to the end of the room. Not pedestals, but display cases. A flicker of hope ignites in my chest. Eagerly, I peer down into the case on the left. The tiny little flame of hope in my breast dies as quickly as it came, even its embers fading into darkness. Elaborately carved, the case's inner workings are expensive and intricate. The stand is crafted made of pure crystal, that alone worth… at least *something* compared to the empty air of the rest of the room.

Sitting on that stand, however, innocuous and depressing, are a pair of leather boots. They are in decent repair, polished and shining, but I can see a scuff on the side of the left one that couldn't be buffed out. They're nice boots, I guess, but they're just boots. They sit there, mocking me, laughing silently. I scowl down at them. Stupid boots.

There is a plate engraved with a block of words below:

"Found Spring 5214, body of dead thief, male, killed by trap in Khalintari manse. Higher and deeper than any thief found before, luck heavily involved. Sound suspected."

Shaking my head, I feel every bit the jackass. Standing in this ridiculously secret vault and risking the lives of dozens of people and all of our collective wealth, I've found an egomaniacal banker's trophies of dead thieves. Sighing deeply, I plod to the next pedestal, refusing to let my hope rise. This stand holds a necklace, a green gem glimmering under the flickering flame of my lantern. The metal is some dusky gray material I don't recognize, the gem large, as gems go, but no more than semi-precious. Simple and attractive... for a peasant on her first trip to the market.

Disgusted, I spin away. A flare of emerald light flashes in the corner of my vision. I turn back, eyes narrowed suspiciously. The gemstone in the middle looks as if it's glowing under the light of my lamp, gleaming as if alive with reflected sunlight. I blink, and the glow is gone. A trick of the light. The necklace is just a necklace. The plate below reads:

"Found Winter 5199, farmer, female, extraordinary crops even in Winter. Late husband purchased at a local market. Wild."

Even more confused, I turn to the final case. This case is empty. Not even a speck of dust covers the crystal surface of the stand. Dully, more for the sake thoroughness than curiosity, I read the engraved message:

"Found Summer 5201, deep in the excavated remains of the Bridge of the East. Adjacent to a pedestal, engraved with an identical symbol. Light."

I hold my lantern closer, squinting. I'm wrong; the finest coating of dust *does* mar the surface of the crystal. I can just see the outline of a small circle imprinted in the thin dust. A ring perhaps?

What the hell is this? Random trinkets? Trophies? To the Depths with this shit, and Gordyn too. I start back towards the hole in the floor. The whole scheme, two long years of planning, has been for nothing. Less than nothing. In fact, we've lost everything.

Just as I prepare to leap down, something tickles at the back of my brain, almost like someone runs a finger across the back of my neck. I glance back. The feeling grows, a silent call. I find myself staring at the pedestal on the left. The one holding the boots.

Well. If I'm going to have to rebuild everything the Family's lost, at least someone else can feel the sting of loss. The thought feels right, as if the silent air... agrees. I shake my head, trying to clear it. The stress and exhaustion are making me lose my wits. But still... Creator knows what value Jon Gordyn places in these meaningless items, but he's going to waltz into his secret vault and find them missing.

The glass of the display case is thin and no doubt easily broken, but I want the mystery of my coming to be complete. Eyeing the simple lock inset into the front of the wood, I slide a few picks out from under my skirts and get to work. A tingle of warning sounds in the same corner of my mind where the urge to return came from. I pause, examining the area briefly. Nothing disturbs the silence save for the muffled sounds of the busy bank far below. The lock is well-made, oiled, and sturdy, but I find the correct tumblers in a few swift turns of my fingers. The last tumbler snaps into place.

Click.

My heart slams against my chest. I jerk my hands back, but I'll never be in time. The needle trap is cunning, ejecting straight out from the wood on either side, exactly where any thief's hands have to be to pick the lock. My right hand, miraculously, is splayed in just such a way as to have the needle pass between two of my outstretched fingers. The left, however, is not so lucky.

The tiny prick is hardly noticeable, the pad of my middle finger welling with a single drop of blood. I hold it up before my eyes, mouth open, unbelieving. The simplest of traps. A needle trap. I allowed my frustration and my disappointment to blind me to simple caution. I can already feel a burning in the tip of my finger, the poison working its way through my blood. My own pumping heart is now my greatest enemy; the faster my blood works through my veins, the faster I will die. Jon Gordyn is not one to take a prisoner, especially in his inner sanctum. To have reached this point, the poison will inevitably be deadly.

The urge to reach in and look at my 'prize' itches at the back of my mind. With a shudder, I climb wearily to my feet and reach out for the black leather boots. My outstretched finger touches the leather—

Cut it off, you damn fool!

"What?" I say aloud, snapping my hand back from the smooth leather and glancing around. I'm still alone in the dark room. I frown, my head cloudy, either from poison or exhaustion, I can't tell. Did someone just speak to me? I reach out for the boots again, my fingers coming in contact-—

Last chance, girl. Use the shadow! Your finger! Cut it off. You have seconds. NOW!

Jolted into action, I jerk back and form a blade of the shadow in my good hand. The shadow writhes, and I can feel its distaste for what is to come. You and me both, buddy. After the briefest hesitation, I push the blade of darkness smoothly through the base of my finger. For the moment, there's no pain. I watch, bemused, as my middle finger drops to the ground with the quietest sound. I pull back and dismiss the blade.

As soon as the shadow dissipates, blood begins to pump out of the stump in time with my frantic heart. The pain jams its way into my brain like a sword thrust. I clutch at my wounded hand, my breath coming in hyperventilating gasps, still unsure if I've even been in time to stop the poison. Or where the idea came from in the first place. The itch in the back of my head starts again, the urge to look at the boots. The lantern is still upright next to the stand, so I struggle to my feet though the haze of pain. Sitting benignly where I left them, the polished leather gleams in the near darkness. I tentatively reach out my good hand. The tip of my finger touches the surface of the left boot.

You might want to wrap that thing up, a wry voice says in my head. The voice sounds distinctly male and definitely mocking. *Passing out from pain and blood loss would be a remarkably sad end to a Shaper of Shadow. You're also going to have to deal with the finger if you want us to make it out of here.*

"How are a pair of boots talking to me?" I mutter, more to myself than to the boots.

What do you mean, how am I talking? I am Ensouled.

"What?" I ask. Witty.

Ensouled... never mind. We don't have time to discuss how in the Creator's name a fledgling Shaper of Shadow doesn't know what Ensoulment is, because we have to get out of here. Form a cap for your finger out of shadow.

Squinting through the pain, I do so, the darkness creeping up and sealing away the wound. The stub still pulses out tendrils of agony, but the bleeding slows and then stops. I feel the distinct urge to hide the hand, protecting both the injury and the shadow holding me together.

"What do you mean, we?" I ask, the question suddenly striking me.

We. As in, you and me, the boots say, as if speaking to a tiny child.

"Why should I take you with me? You're, well, you're scuffed," I mutter, having no idea why I'm conversing with the boots when I should be getting out of there.

I know, the voice responds, a profound sadness ringing through his voice. *They were my favorite boots, but they were all I had on hand at the time. To think that I've been spending decades, perhaps even centuries in a pair of scuffed boots is the most unfortunate in a long line of unfortunate happenings. But you can't leave me. I saved your life.*

The boots have a point. I sigh, reaching in with my good hand and pulling them forth. I look at them askance. They're too big for me, and I need to hide them somehow.

Just put them on. I'll handle the rest.

I shrug, sliding the boots on underneath my dress. The leather is supple and soft. When I stand up, I'm surprised to feel a perfect fit. I flex my feet, and they fit even better, adjusting to the shape of my body, hugging my calf but leaving the flexibility I need to run or fight. I can tell, instantly, that they are the best pair of boots I've ever worn.

I'm touched. Now, pick up your finger and get us the hell out of here.

I resist the urge to vomit as I gather up the tiny little appendage, trying not to look as I slip it into the pouch with my thieves' tools under my skirts. I have nothing to wipe up the blood, so I leave it. A few spots mar my otherwise pristine white dress, which I can hide with a little artful maneuvering. I spin to head back towards the glimmering light from the massive hole in the ground.

I blink awake on the ground, my breathing still coming in sharp gasps. I've forgotten all about the insane exertion required to lift the damn ceiling. We have to get out of there, but I don't have the energy to put the stone back. I barely have the energy to walk. Groaning, I drag myself over to the hole. Timo's powerful arms catch me as I fall bonelessly into the room.

The boots sigh in the corner of my mind. How can a disembodied voice sigh?

Take some from me, he says, his voice tense. *You need it.*

"Take some what?" I say, my speech slurring. Timo cradles me in his arms, his face a sudden mask of panic.

"Wha's happened to ya, Kettle?" he says, stroking my hair like a babe.

You can stop talking to me out loud, fledgling. I can hear your thoughts. If you keep asking questions of the air, people will start to talk.

Fine, I snarl through the haze of pain and exhaustion. *Take what?*

Touchy, touchy. Reach down with your mind, just like if you were controlling the Shadow. Feel my energy, the light of my soul...

I do as he asks, letting Timo support my weight fully, focusing completely down towards my feet. At first, I feel silly. Nothing happens. I'm just staring dully at a pair of black leather boots. But then, I *reach.* I *feel* him. The energy of a soul, bright, burning, and powerful. The teeming energy crackles just behind the surface of some invisible barrier.

You have to let me in. The wall is your own.

Sudden fear strikes me – a prick of adrenaline sparking through the roiling clouds of my thoughts.

You're strong, I think, sharpening my focus as much as I can through the haze of exhaustion. *How do I know if I should let you in?*

If you knew more of the Ensouled, you would know better than to suspect me of such a crime. But, as it stands, you have little choice. You're hurt, weak, exhausted, and near death. The man who runs this bank, the man called Gordyn, will be here soon. Let me in, and we can fix this before it is too late.

If you try anything, I'll banish your scuffed-up boots to the bottom of the forgotten Depths. You will join the Eternal, I warn.

Sounds dire. Let me in.

I try to drop the wall, but I run into a problem – I have no idea how to do it. I feel the energy on the other side, but I can't reach across the invisible divide. I strain against it, but nothing happens. Nary a tremble.

Time's ticking, fledgling.

Then help me, I snap in response. *How do I lower it?*

The wall is made of your own mental defenses. It's the divide between your soul and the rest of the world. You have to accept another soul into your own. It's a daunting prospect even for the prepared, but you don't have a choice. Lower the wall, or die a gruesome death.

Trust. It will require me to trust. It will require the boots... to be family. Family. I think of Timo. I would let him into my body to save him. His strong arms are wrapped around me, the support of a person who loves me beyond reason. I think of Corna, a dozen feet away across the hall, her unwavering faith and trust in me. I will have to find it in me to give these boots the same trust.

Desperation isn't enough, I say. *Speak trust into me. Give me a truth.*

He hesitates. A second slides past. Another.

I was once a man. Living. Breathing. But I gave up my soul to save the woman I loved. The last thing I ever witnessed with my living eyes was her heartbroken, panicked stare.

What is your name? I ask.

Yatan Tecarim.

The name is familiar, but distantly, as if I've heard it in passing. His words ring with undeniable truth. I consider this man. Yatan. As I would give my life for my family, he had for his. A man who had paid the sacrifice I pay daily, ignoring the hole in my heart where my brother still lurks. The hole where Talan's sheepish grin and his strong arms lay in wait to ambush me in moments of weakness. Both of us have to live with giving up the ones we love in order to save them.

I hope they both forgive us, Yatan, I say, quiet even in the depths of my mind. Echoing. The wall begins to erode, the crackling, living energy tentatively reaching across. I reach as well, and the energy of Yatan's soul dives forward into mine.

My back arches out of Timo's grasp, every muscle clenching as one. The exhaustion burns away before an unending tide of power. My thoughts sharpen, my heart the bellows of a citywide smithy, my eyes track dust falling in unfathomable patterns. I've never felt so alive. We've never felt so alive.

A craving forms, not my own, a surging *desire* to possess, to claim. The energy is everywhere, in every part of me, but it is not me. I stop seeing as he claims my eyes. I stop hearing as he claims my ears. Part by part, piece by piece, I lose my body in a war I have no idea how to fight. I feel my arm raise without giving the command. Something, some*one* else stares at my own hand in wonder.

Deep within my core, however, I'm still me. An alien presence scratches at the will of my resolve, demanding possession of my body, digging at the will in me to live, to fight, to act. It's like fighting a hurricane. I can't harm him. I'm trapped in my own body, and I can feel him clawing at the barrier, ripping down the last defenses I have left.

He blinks our eyes. We focus on Timo.

No! I scream in the darkness of my thoughts.

I drive my mind like knives into him. The energy flinches back. I cut away a piece of him and isolate the power. When I reach for it, absent his will to control it, my soul consumes the energy for myself.

Images pass before me, memories, faces I don't recognize, but do. Cities that don't exist, but once did. The face of a woman hovers over me, her eyes pleading, perfect blue and deep beyond measure, her mouth open in horror, lips quivering. The image is burned through every piece of energy I consume, every part of my body I recover. Cutting him off, piece by piece, I consume him. Slowly, fighting back every inch, I drive him back into the boots, using his own energy against him and walling him away.

I gasp.

Again.

Again.

My body responds. My limbs relax, falling dormant in Timo's care, his arms still gentle as I distantly hear him pleading with the voice of the lost. I sit up, my eyes still sharper than ever before, my heart still churning at a racing stroke. My body is alive in ways it never has been before, but I don't have time to wonder. I have seconds, maybe less, until Gordyn walks in.

I should never have trusted a pair of Eternal-damned talking boots. How insane am I? How gullible? At least I have control. For now.

The shadow comes to my call, easy as breathing. I need less than an ounce of the focus I normally use to Shape. A thin tendril of shadow wraps around the handle of the lantern, bringing it down and passing it off to Timo. He grabs the floating lantern from the air without a word. With a thought, I lift the stone plug above us and settle it silently into place. The ceiling groans as it accepts the weight again. A line, so thin as to be nearly invisible, is the only sign of my entry. With a thought, the shadow covers the table in a thin sheen, then sweeps away, any trace of dust scattered to the floor and the corners.

"Light the lanterns and stand behind me," I say, the words quick and clipped.

I sit down at the table, satisfied as Timo takes his place over my shoulder. I glance around the room one final time. It will have to be enough. The shadow hasn't left the stub of my finger, and no blood leaks through. I definitely don't have the concentration for that, but somehow the shadow remains. I rip off a small strip of cloth from the interior of the skirt, mentally releasing the shadow and wrapping the wound tightly. The symbol on my face needs to fade.

Just in time. The door clicks open, and Atlan walks in and smiles at us, the fake smile of all sycophants. He moves aside to reveal a different kind of man entirely. The man wears a similar suit, but it *fits* in a way no suit will ever fit Atlan. Not like the suit has been tailored and cut for him, but as if the style itself was designed for him. His walking stick, clearly an affectation, is carved to resemble a stylized wolf. He exudes a confidence that is palpable just by seeing his first step, as if that step has no need to claim the ground, because it is already his.

He could pass for thirty, but I know him to be somewhere closer to forty. In any other situation, he might be attractive, ridiculously so. His rakish beard is perfectly trimmed, his enormous confidence beyond compare. But then, I look into his eyes. So pale a blue as to be mistaken for white, they appear open and welcoming. A complete and bald-faced lie.

His eyes, in the shallows, are warm, living, humane. Beneath... this kind of man has clawed his way from the Depths. There is nothing there but darkness, murky pools to which a bottom cannot be found, no matter the seeker. I stare into them, near-mesmerized, willing my own panic to remain buried deep.

Gordyn marches firmly over to the other end of the long table, taking his seat at the opposite head. For long moments, we simply eye each other like duelists, our respective seconds hovering over our shoulders. I slowly quirk one eyebrow, holding my posture rigid. His hands rest gently on the table before him, his eyes appraising, weighing, measuring. I break the silence first.

"Jon Gordyn," I say, bowing my head slightly.

"Aea Po'lial," he returns the nod, the perfect measure of respect. "I was not aware of your arrival. I know with certainty that you've been absent from the Seers Isle for a decade at least. How have you come to my city, claiming to represent your nation, no less?"

"A decade ago, the Seer sent me on a task of which I may not speak," I say, my stomach lurching downward. "I have but recently returned. Though I did not get to stay long… as one of the People, I do as the Seer commands."

"I see," he says, his tone identical, offering nothing. "My associate has come to me with a rather weighty claim."

"The Seers have need of the land once known as Itskalan. The Seer herself has Seen that you, and perhaps only you, can deal in such things."

"I have some power over certain portions of Itskalan," he agrees, brow furrowing ever so slightly. "But I would have to bring your offer before the Sealord in order to work out any lasting deal. Provided I like the arrangement and believe I can sell it to him. You may have heard, but the Sealord is somewhat jealous of his territory."

"Our offer is simple," I say, hardly knowing what I'm going to say next. The plan had been to leave before Gordyn ever knew we were there. I never banked on seeing his manicured little beard. "You are aware of the might of our ships."

"Of course. Your people have perhaps the most powerful navy in the known world."

"Do not insult me with 'perhaps,'" I say calmly. As if I haven't just contradicted one of the most powerful and terrifying men in the world. "We offer ships."

"While valuable, ships, even many ships, could not possibly—"

"You misunderstand," I cut in. I see Atlan behind him, a look of relief in his eyes that he isn't the only target of my rudeness. Atlan's eyes flick to Gordyn to see his reaction. For Gordyn's part, he gives away nothing. He doesn't react other than to close his mouth. I don't see even the slightest hint of anger or annoyance.

"We will not give you ships. We offer the use of ships. In their entirety. For a period to be determined by our negotiations."

"Their use," Gordyn says, his voice making the words a question.

"Unlimited," I respond, knowing the value of what I offer. The ships of the Seers are massive, unparalleled monstrosities that can as easily plow through heavy waves as cut around them. The People account for a significant portion of all worthwhile shipping traffic through the Great Sea, connecting the exotic goods of the Broken Isles to the Khalintars and the Kingdom of the Sea. Our rumored wealth is directly tied to our ships. "If you wish to hire them to the Sealord, and let him move his little armies across the face of the Blue, you may. The ships would be yours to command, yours to spend. They will come crewed and ready to obey the whim of the architect who builds us a new land in Itskalan."

"What period of time would we be negotiating?" Gordyn says, leaning forward ever so slightly. It's the first sign of his intrigue in the impossible deal. As if the man can actually sell us a country out of the kingdom. The brass balls on him...

"Our first offer will be for a period of twenty years."

Gordyn's eyes widen almost imperceptibly, his shoulders moving ever so slightly, tensing and relaxing. His eyes don't change, but the look they cast out is almost... feral. I'm uncomfortable under that gaze, more so than before, but the hunger shows I'm speaking to something below that calm and careful facade.

"I can promise nothing," he says. He stands abruptly and walks around the table, offering his hand to help me stand. Before he can reach me, I stand on my own, hiding my wounded hand in the folds of my skirt and accepting the proffered hand gently. "Save to consider your offer and, perhaps, bring it before the Sealord."

"The Seer knows more than any of us could imagine. She has Seen this and knows of our success. I thank you, Jon Gordyn."

I let him lead me towards the door. As we move, the air swirls through the room, the sudden swaying of my skirts and the passage of bodies kicking up a fine dust. Atlan sneezes, violently, then begins to cough.

At first, Gordyn regards him with a measured look that hints at scorn, but then his gaze sharpens. He glances around, his brow furrowed slightly. His fingers grip mine ever-so-slightly, as if in tension or warning. I struggle to remain calm, painting a mildly concerned expression on my face.

"Can nothing be done for Keagan Atlan?" I ask, glancing at Gordyn. "He seems disturbed."

"I have—" He coughs another few times, holding a silken kerchief to his nose. "I am highly agitated by dust, and particles of any kind, really. The air in the bank has always been clean—" he breaks off, panting, and makes a hasty exit.

We hear his distant cough as the door swings closed. Gordyn's eyes search every corner of the room. The hairline seam in the ceiling of the room is barely noticeable, but my gut tightens as his eyes rake the ceiling. He reaches for the ornate handle of the door and pauses, looking back at me. Some part of him recognizes that not all is as it should be. I can almost feel his suspicion, his calculation, as he tries to do the arithmetic. For my part, I simply stare at him, my expression bored. I hope. The tension in the room eases, slightly, as he steps into the hall.

"I will begin to make overtures to the Sealord," he says. "This will take time. Would you perhaps allow me to know where you're staying, you and your... associate?"

"The Falling Edge," I answer carefully.

I ignore the talk of Timo, and he is wise enough to keep his mouth shut as well. The Falling Edge is one of the most expensive and chic establishments in the city. Situated on the Pennies side of the Abyss and built right up to the edge of that chasm, its most expensive rooms dangle over the precipice, defying the will of the winds and the earth.

"Ah," Gordyn says, nodding. "Then I'll provide you with the best. You can stay in my personal room for the duration of your stay."

"We are honored by your generosity, Jon Gordyn."

"Mistress Po'lial, I look forward to seeing you again."

One of the bank's many security personnel takes his place by my side at the top of the stairs. I allow him to take my hand, lifting my skirts with the other. As we walk down, I feel Gordyn's eyes boring into my back. My skin crawls, knowing how close I came to being exposed.

I'm sorry.

The sudden return of the voice shocks me. I lurch to the side in surprise, so wound up I'm dodging aside at the slightest hint of danger. Creator-forsaken boots. I lean heavily on my escort and pull at my skirts for balance. Timo steadies me, for which I give him a nod of thanks.

It had been so long... I believed myself in control...

Shut up, I snap in my mind, trying to drown out his sullen voice with anger.

"Hold."

The word, spoken so gently from above, nevertheless has its desired effect. I glance back. Gordyn stares down at me, his ice white eyes sharp with a new and unwelcome intensity. He doesn't come closer, but instead makes a sharp gesture to his guard. The man steps away from me, his sword clearing his scabbard with a whisper of well-oiled leather.

"What is the meaning of this, Jon Gordyn?" I say, pointedly ignoring the man poised next to me with a blade.

"Mistress Po'lial. Would you do me one favor before you go?" Gordyn asks, his voice dangerously soft and slow.

"Yes, Jon Gordyn?" I ask, feeling the perspiration beading on my brow, fighting the sudden urge to turn and run.

"Will you show me your footwear?"

Time slows. The boots betrayed me again. In my slip, shocked by the voice echoing in my head, my skirts must have come too high. Whatever these boots are, they are precious to him. His eyes are angry, but also show a certain admiration... and a certain smugness. As if, despite losing his boots, he still holds all the cards.

I let my hand drop, flicking a quick sign to Timo. Gordyn opens his mouth, no doubt to call some order, but I bring my hand up, and a tiny jet of shadow shoots towards his face. He jerks aside, and the darkness cuts a thin line across his jaw. He wisely drops to the ground, the return arc of the shadow missing him by a hairsbreadth. I spin, my heel digging into the soft carpet, my arm already coming up to block the guard's blow. I shouldn't have worried. Timo already has him down, his jaw probably broken, the sword tiny in Timo's paws.

"Run."

My shadow cuts the flowing skirts away from my legs with each stride, strips of expensive cloth fluttering down behind me like fallen leaves until my bare skin shimmers in the lamplight. Timo keeps pace, shooting me a crazy grin.

"Back in the shit," he says, his voice almost gleeful. These are the moments when Timo loves life. Crazy bastard.

As if I don't feel the same.

We race out the stairwell entrance. Distance muffles Gordyn's shouts of alarm. People can't hear him over the bustle of the bank, so our entrance serves as the first sign that something is amiss. We burst through the cage just as a clerk attempts to close it behind him. The man tumbles away, and the coins he carries roll in all directions. The crowd explodes into chaos as some scramble for coins and others fight for the exit.

Timo clears the way, his massive size demanding the crowd to melt before him. The people begin to settle as we near the entrance to the busy bank, the bustle behind us dying down as the last of the coins either return or disappear. Unfortunately, the sudden quiet allows Gordyn's voice to finally clear the crowd noise.

"Doors," he calls, his voice as calm as ever.

I glance back. A veritable army of personal guards surrounds him, some pushing forward towards us and others surrounding him in a tight cordon. Guards near the entrance immediately leap to action. The doors begin to close. The giant stone monoliths are impregnable, their weight ridiculous in the face of human power. If they close, we are never leaving this bank.

Under normal circumstances, the Imperial Bank has so much security and vigilance that the only reasonable threat will come from outside, some armed force powerful enough to feel that they can rumble with the mercenary army Gordyn employs. No one has ever successfully stolen anything after having willingly walked *into* the damn place. So the doors open outward. Strategically sound, as Gordyn appears to only fear a threat from the outside.

In this instance, however...

Timo picks up his pace, lowering his head and shoulder as he thunders forward. The Creator-blessed sunlight and freedom disappear in front of us as the doors slam closed. A man stands with a steel locking bar, ready to lower it into place the moment the way completely shuts. The bar starts to drop.

Timo strikes the guard like an irate bull, the man's weight only adding to Timo's own unbelievable force. The doors explode open, the men pushing them closed erupting into short screams before the mighty edifices crush them against the exterior walls. Everyone in the street turns to look, the sound of several tons of stone slamming against the carefully manicured facade of the building louder than thunder. We don't pause. Timo immediately favors his right shoulder, so I pull his arm over my shoulders and lurch forward.

Some people follow us with their eyes, talking excitedly, but many are far more interested in what is happening at the bank proper. Our exit, fast as it is, serves to give us a head start on anyone attempting to tail us. We duck into the line of people, twisting and turning through the growing crowd pushing forward to see what's happening. The thickening crowd only serves to hide our escape.

"Well, that got exciting pretty fast," Timo says from over my head as we walk, but I can hear the grin in his voice. "Wasn't there anything in the vault? You came back empty handed."

"There were just..." I trail off, having difficulty coming up with any explanation for the boots. The man inside them stirs, but I send him such a mental glare that he subsides again. I check the mental wall separating our energy, and it seems to be intact. Not that I trust it, or him, for a second. I'll have to deal with him later.

"Nothing of value," I say, smugly. That's right, boots.

"Pity," Timo says, momentarily despondent. Then, he brightens just as quickly. "We'll just have to come up with something better next time. At least we have a story to tell the kids!"

I smile, hugging the big man closer to me. As soon as we can, I'm going to get the kids together again. We might have to leave Donir, what with Gordyn having seen my face. There aren't exactly a wide variety of dark-skinned thieves wandering the streets. The connection between 'Kettle' and 'Aea Po'lial' doesn't take a massive leap. We need to bring the Family back together and head for greener pastures. As soon as we can get Rita—

"Shit."

"What?" Timo asks, suddenly alarmed and alert.

"Corna's still in there."

"She'll be fine," Timo says, though his voice sounds decidedly unconvinced. "She's gotten out of worse."

"Right. Of course," I say aloud, but an ominous chill creeps down my spine.

Chapter 10
Jace
The Thirtieth Day of Spring
In the Year 5222, Council Reckoning

"Am I ever going to get to learn how to fight?" I ask, breathing smoothly and easily after an hour of steady work against eight poles. I haven't missed a single slash, every attack slicing precisely through the appropriate color, every blow coming swift and certain.

"What do you think you've been doing all this time?" Reknor asks quizzically. "Learning to dance?"

"Practically," I mutter, letting my fourth cracked practice sword drop to the ground with a clatter, so much kindling for the fire. "I can't imagine using *this* to defend myself against anyone. But I could definitely win against a tree."

"Fine," Reknor says, impatience in his voice. "You want to learn how to fight? How to kill a man? Then pass one more test. If you pass, I'll teach you how to fight another person."

"Done," I say instantly. "What's your test?"

"Wait here," Reknor says over his shoulder as he leaves the room.

He returns in a moment with a cloth that can only be meant for one thing. A blindfold. When he has the cloth firmly settled over my eyes, tied tight enough to practically cut off the circulation to my brain, a set of thuds and scrapes immediately draw my interest like a bear to honey. No matter how I think, though, I can't imagine what he's doing.

"Do you remember where the poles are?" Reknor asks from behind me.

"Of course," I say, shrugging my shoulders. The hilt of a sword slaps into my palm, and I almost rip the blindfold off immediately. This is no wooden practice sword. I can feel the heft of it, so much lighter and sleeker than what my hands are used to. I can't properly describe how I know, but I'm holding a sword of sharp and deadly metal.

"Green four!" Reknor shouts.

I react by instinct, bringing the blade up and around in a cut at waist height. The sword slams into something with the sound of screeching metal. Before I have time to think, he shouts again.

"Cyan eight!"

I swing down in a crouch, low, my blade again screeching across metal. The shouts come frequently, practically as fast as I can recover, and each time the scream of metal on metal meeting my attack. Finally, Reknor begins to rapidly shout the colors of two of the poles, and I square up and strike blow after blow against my unseen metal foes.

When Reknor stops calling out colors, the sudden silence leaves me breathless. The clamor of the sword is a banshee's wail that drowns out all else. I breathe in once, deeply, then let the sword's point come to rest on the floor.

"Red one!" Reknor shouts, and I snap my sword up. It clashes against the metal one final time. "Take off your blindfold."

I rip it off to see Reknor standing there with sweat running down his face. His sword strains against mine. My blade is in perfect position to block his overhead strike. I could easily cut downwards from the block and into his throat or unprotected chest.

"But..." I breathe, my mind struggling to catch up. "But they are just poles!"

"Green two," he says, swinging his blade around in a horizontal slash at my torso. My arms move automatically into position to block. My sword rings against his with precision. He doesn't say anything, but sends a blurring attack at my neck. His blade meets mine, perfectly positioned in pink one. We exchange several more lightning fast blows, but nothing comes close to me as I bat away each strike with ease.

"Okay," I say, stepping back. "I get your point."

"Now remember this one. I taught you to use a sword so that you won't be afraid of knives, or guards, or thieves. I did not teach you the sword to kill anyone."

"Isn't that the point of a sword?"

Wordlessly, he drops his sword, moves in to grasps my arm. In my confusion, I don't resist. He flips me over and kicks the sword away, twisting my arm behind my back. My bones creak under the pressure like a branch under snow. A bit more pressure and my arm will be a flapping, useless wing on a flightless bird.

"Have I done wrong?" Reknor asks calmly, coldly. I can tell that the question is more to himself than to me. "I saw goodness in you. I could have sworn you would turn out to be a decent man. If not, I should end this right now."

He puts a bit more pressure on my sword arm, and I gag from the pain. I can't say anything; the agony shoots up my arm and rips into my soul like a lance driven by the Creator's own hand. For a long moment, he presses silently, weighing my fate. Finally, endlessly, the pressure eases a bit and I can breathe again. Tears stream down my face as he continues to hold me face-down on the floor.

"Why did I teach you the sword?"

"To take away my fear," I say breathlessly.

"When do you use a sword?"

"I don't know!" I blurt out, desperate.

His grip vanishes. I roll onto my good side, cradling my injured arm and fighting back the tears. Reknor crouches next to me.

“I'm sorry, Jace,” he says quietly, raking his fingers through his unkempt hair. “You only use a sword when there are no other options. It is the last option of all good men to resort to violence. Even then, you do not kill without necessity or good cause. It is the one act you can never take back, and leaves your soul stained in ways you cannot imagine.”

I don’t say anything. Somewhere in my mind, deep inside, I’ve always held Reknor in fear. The vast majority of the time, he’s as gentle as a kitten, playful and joyful. He teaches me with unending patience, and I’ve grown to respect and admire him on many levels.

But a small part of me remembers the ice in his voice when I spit on his floors in the first seconds of our relationship. The same part remembers the ease with which he dispatched seemingly insurmountable foes—unarmed—to save my life. My street self, buried under the gentle curiosity and education of my new life, reawakens to remind me: Reknor is not a man to cross.

“Do you understand, Jace?”

“Yes.”

“Fine,” Reknor says distractedly, standing with an explosive sigh. “Fine. This has been coming on for a few weeks now. For the last two years, you’ve been progressing at a remarkable rate. You’ve picked up swordplay like a prodigy and have taken to learning like a drowning man to the sight of land. You’ve nearly finished my library already, and soon I won't be able to touch you with a blade, either.”

I sit up straighter with a mixture of embarrassment and pride, the ache in my shoulder forgotten. Reknor hasn’t ever said anything even remotely this glowing in the past two years.

“But,” he says, raising a finger. “Your education is lacking in one specific area.”

“And what is that?”

“Real experience. Fighting in a controlled environment against the same opponent, no matter how cunning or capable, will not make you the elite swordsman you could be. Reading a book can't teach you about love or anger, just the theory of it. Are you still afraid of knives? Thieves? Fire? The Tide?"

"I..." I stop, thinking hard on my education, the knowledge and confidence I've gained. The image of Rosie's blood hanging in the air comes back to me, and I suppress a shudder, but it's easier than I imagined it would be. "I have no idea."

"Exactly. You'll only learn that back out in the world. No more avoiding the streets. No more locking yourself in this house. In fact, I'm going to force you into situations where you can really... learn," Reknor says with a grin. "Learn things that no one else has the opportunity to learn. You know the theories now, Jace. Let's put them to the test."

***

"To know a man, you have to walk and fight in his shoes. Tenfold for women," Reknor says, shoving me towards the door.

Before I can hesitate, I slip out the front and shuffle down the cobbled road. I've reached hardly halfway to my destination in agonizingly slow steps before my back begins to burn and my calves begin to chafe. I haven't passed anyone, and already, I can feel eyes crawling on me. I want to run, to climb, but I force myself to maintain my infernal pace as I near the end of the bustling intersection at the end of the street. Slowing further, I peer upward at the dozens of men and women who pass to and fro across my narrow line of sight. No matter how hard I try, I can't force myself to move the last few paces and step into the light.

Reknor's idea of education is, to put it frankly, ludicrous.

I'm wrapped feet to brow in itchy rags, shuffling along in my best imitation of the oppressed and downtrodden. Reknor has decided that my first experience won't have anything to do with either fighting or learning, but survival. I'm supposed to be a leprous beggar.

Leprosy. Mankind's worst nightmare.

To have your flesh stop responding, portions of your body rotting away and falling off, turning swiftly grotesque and horrifying. It says a lot about my respect for Reknor that I even let him wrap me up, let alone turn me loose in the streets to beg for coins. I've always hated begging. Even as a homeless child I could barely stoop to groveling for passersby like a worm. My pride and Jonah's teachings were the only thing that kept me from that ignoble life.

Ahead of me, a man turns down the street with a parcel under his arm. The sight of me brings him up short. He's in his middle years, with brown hair and a long overcoat with a paired top hat. His face morphs swiftly through surprise, pity, and revulsion as he stares at me. He swiftly crosses to the far side of the street and strides as quickly as possible away from me.

I recover my wits in time to feel a flash of anger at the man's callous reaction. How dare he look at me like that? Something shoves me in the back as I'm glaring at the man's back. I stumble and fall to the ground.

"How did you get out of your filthy little colony, I wonder?" a man's voice says, his voice close.

I struggle to turn over in the constricting wrappings. A man of the Watch stands over me, his expression reeking of disgust. Creator's saggy balls, I left the house five minutes ago. Of all the luck… shit. The cloth of my head dressings catches in my mouth and stops up my tongue, so I can't even speak. All that emerges from my mouth are frantic grunts as he bends down to lift me up, careful not to let me touch his skin.

"Stop squirming now, boy, or I'll be forced to lay you out."

I twist to free my arm, if only to clear my dressings and speak. My right arm rips free, and I reach my hand to my face in an attempt to rip the cloth from my mouth. Just as it begins to give way something crushes against the side of my head. I stagger, wavering in and out. I fight against the waves of weariness crashing over me long enough to hear another man speak.

"Wouldn't want to catch anything. Thank the Creator you're wearing gloves."

"Take this thing back to the leper colony in the Corpses."

"We'll be..." The blackness overcomes me.

***

Pain. I ache from a dozen deep bruises and a deep-rooted pain in my skull. A woman, brilliant blonde and beautiful, wavers in front of my eyes. I reach out to try to steady her and get a closer look, grasping feebly in an attempt to stop the rocking motion of the two, no, four women floating in front of me. The motion sets my brain to rocking. I close my eyes and sink back with a soft moan. The world spins behind my eyelids, and I turn sharply and retch. A weak spume streams out from between my lips, and my stomach tries to climb out of my throat. I squeeze my eyes shut tightly and concentrate on the deep and total darkness. After a minute or so, the dizziness begins to abate, so I force my eyes open once again. A small mound of straw lies beside me, and I promptly sneeze. My head strikes up another round of glorious combat with consciousness, forcing me to swallow back the bile that rises in my throat. I groan and attempt to curl up into a tighter ball.

The world does not exist. The pain is just a figment of a tortured imagination. For some reason, the insistent litany works, calming my head and my heaving innards. A female voice is speaking.

"...should be alright, but the lad seems to have taken quite a blow."

"You can see the blood, yes. I would have attempted to treat him already, but head wounds are some of the trickiest ailments to diagnose."

I latch on to the woman's voice as my sole source of hope for a return to humanity. Her voice is a sweet melody with just the faintest trace of an accent. Withholding a second sneeze, I slowly flex each of my muscles to assess the damage. My legs are largely unharmed, but both my torso and my arms feel as if someone has driven sledgehammers into them for a week. I groan and force myself upright, with surprising success.

I'm in the corner of a dilapidated single-roomed hut bricked in clay on a mound of straw obviously used for a bed. A few ramshackle chairs surround a small circular table in another corner, the only other object of note a faded medical bag propped against the far wall. A woman stands in the threshold of the cottage speaking to someone without. Her hair is a lusterless blonde, matted and filthy. As she concludes her conversation, she turns to face me.

We both jump simultaneously as our eyes meet, my stomach twisting in immediate revulsion. Her face is a deformed mass, as if something has eaten a critical portion of her face. One of her eye sockets gapes dark and empty. I gag by reflex and instantly she comes to my side. I scrabble at the earth to get away from her and in my terror bump the back of my head into the wall behind me. The room once again takes up its unfortunate dance with my eyesight. I vomit weakly, but still I clutch vainly at the straw in an attempt to drag myself farther from her. Whatever this monster is, it's coming for me, and there's nowhere I can go.

My panic cracks as I register the expression on what remains of her face. She's not coming any closer. I've crammed myself so tightly in a corner that I can't move. The fact that she remains sitting, quietly and somehow sadly watching, forces my gaze from her deformed features to her remaining eye. In its depths lurk intelligence… and sorrow. Behind her grotesque visage lies an infinite sadness and bitterness. To be condemned to this…life, this prison of leprosy, is beyond my understanding. I open my mouth to speak, and she raises what remains of her eyebrow in anticipation.

"I… I'm sorry for my reaction and to your… ah…well," I trail off into awkward silence. I can't find the words.

"Don't worry," she says with a smile somewhere in her still-musical voice. "I get that a lot."

She says it as a joke, but my heart breaks for her.

"I'm Jace," I say hesitantly and slowly, but deliberately, and reach out my hand for her to shake. Surprise kindles in her eye, but then she claps her hands, the sound dulled by the wrappings around her fingers.

"Oh, how crude of me! Here you are a guest in my home and you don't even know my name. I am Juliet, and a pleasure to meet you."

I can't suppress a chuckle, and she joins in after a moment. I deliberately refuse to look anywhere but her sparkling blue eye. Anything else might invite the crack in my heart to widen. I've known her for seconds, but I can't bear the thought of what she is… and what she might have been. Small talk seems pointless considering our situation, so I just rest and concentrate on a room spinning with slightly less authority. Her posture sings of uncertainty as she opens her mouth to speak.

"I… if it's too hard to talk about, or you don't want to, I completely understand, but I was wondering how long you've been…" she gestures lamely at my dressings.

I don't understand for a second. Oh.

Shit.

"Juliet. I'm…" I trail off.

I honestly started to say untainted. How callous. How ignorant. I struggle to find the words, but I can't find any that don't demean the woman sitting before me. How can I explain? What can I even say?

"I understand," she says, reaching out and patting my hand gently.

I laugh, the sound strangled and strange in the tiny room.

"I'm not sick," I finally say.

"None of us are," she answers, canting her head curiously.

"No, I don't mean sick, I mean I'm healthy…" I stop when I see her growing both more hurt and confused.

Words aren't going to bridge this gulf. Instead, I simply begin to unwind the cloth wrapped around my head. She watches in silence, expecting perhaps a mirror image of her own mutations. I expose my forehead, followed by my nose and cheeks. I grimace when the cloth sticks to the blood crusted on the back of my head, but I persevere and soon hold the wrappings in my hands.

She opens her mouth and lets loose a soft and nearly inaudible "Oh."

When my arms and legs are bare, I expect to see ugly, dark bruises mottling my flesh. Instead, a thin ointment covers my skin, something that smells of mint soaking through my wrappings. I twist my torso slightly, surprised. The pain has already lessened since I've awoken. I glance up to thank her, but the words die on my lips. Her gaze bears the heavy weight of betrayal, as if a friend has confessed to a crime. Although I am healthy and she is not, I've never felt less whole.

Juliet stands and bends to gather her things, shoving them hurriedly into her bag. That she refuses to look at me is worse than the accusatory glare.

"You appear to be feeling better, and you obviously don't belong here. If you go to the gates perhaps our *generous* guards will grant you passage home."

"Wait. I'm sorry," I say. the words are woefully inadequate, and I know it. "Isn't there any way I can thank you? Is there something I could do for you?"

She stops and I watch her frail shoulders rise and fall in a soft sigh.

"It would probably be better if you go."

"Really, I would like to do something in return for…"

"Stop it," she snaps sharply. She turns and advances on me, railing. "Just stop it. I see now why you looked so disgusted and horrified when you first saw me. I know I'm ugly, and I know that this… *disease* has ruined my life. I'm forced to deal with that every day, but I have no need for you to *help* me. I'm beyond help, so spare me your sympathy and get out."

The last words nearly stick in her throat as she chokes off a sob. Her trembling finger points at the door. I'm frozen. After a moment, she drops to her knees and resumes shoveling things into her bag. I can't tear my eyes away from her furious motions. Her hands shake so badly the clay jar she's holding catches on the lip of the bag. The jar slips from her fingers, falling to the earthen floor and shattering.

The sound seems to break her, and she covers her face, her slender shoulders wracked by bitter, uncontrollable sobs. I find myself walking forward. Before I know it, my arm wraps around her shoulders. She stiffens and resists when I try to draw her to me, so I sit and will comfort through our tenuous physical connection. After a few moments, she relents to another gentle tug and allows herself to be pulled gently to my chest. She buries her face into my shoulder, her violent sobs wrack me to the core. My own tears silently fall down my cheeks.

"You won't just leave?" she says in a small voice.

"I will if you really want me to."

Disengaging herself from my arms, she silently walks outside and beckons for me to follow. We stand in the cool predawn light. A small part of me wonders if Reknor is worried, if he has any idea where I am, but I figure I'm learning more right where I am than he imagined when he sent me out for this stupid role. I'm not in a hurry, either. The spinning between my ears still haunts my steps, so walking the long distance back around the Abyss and home seems like a titanic feat of strength.

The sun's rays trickle over the mountains on the far eastern horizon, the first innocent peek of an uncertain lover.

Normally, the city blocks any sight of the mountains, but the half-cleared mansions of the Corpses and the wide berth the colony is given offers an unobstructed view. At first glance the leper's dwellings look no better than a shanty town, a mixture of shacks and hovels spread chaotically over the small plot of land given over to their use. Looking closer, however, the small town bears a distinct order. A latrine trench lies close to the fence, perhaps a punishment for the guards who hem these people in. The light from the sun stings my eyes and sets my head to aching, but Juliet and I stand side by side until the sun finishes its inexorable march into the sky.

Eyeing her out of the corner of my eye, I try to imagine who she was. Her jaw is still strong, her posture erect and proper. Was she beautiful? How old is she? As her brilliant sapphire eye meets mine, my heart skips a beat. Juliet generates her own energy that has nothing to do with the sun. Her eye narrows as she regards me, and I raise my eyebrows.

"My lady?"

"First," she says. "You'll fix my roof."

I gather up an armload of thatch from the neat stacked on the side of her simple dwelling and scramble onto the roof. From this vantage, the fence of the colony is clearly visible. A patrol of the Watch walks the fenceline, ensuring that none of the lepers manage to escape. As if any can climb the high and sharpened stakes.

"So you built this?" I ask with a gesture towards the house. Sturdy and comely, the little hut looks like it could weather storms.

"Yes. I was reasonably well educated before this happened, and that education included architecture."

"How did you get to build your home so far from the others?" I ask, noticing that the others are packed in tight enough to foster disease, but Juliet has space.

"I was considered beautiful once. When I first came here, my face was intact. The leader of this small establishment took to me immediately, so I used him for as long as my beauty held," she says in a soft tone. A wistful sorrow taints her voice. "He was a loving and generous man. I never gave him anything for his favor, just a few cunning smiles."

I thought at first that she was bemoaning her lost beauty. But this? What kind of person gets dealt the worst of hands and still manages to feel sorry for others?

"Such a transient thing," she says, doing her best to smile. Abruptly, her smile turns wicked. "Now, get to work."

"Just what, my lady, are you going to do while I work?"

"Why direct, of course. I can't have you fucking up my roof."

I can only laugh helplessly and reach for the nearest bundle of thatch. I'm glad for her company as I do my best to patch the leaky holes in her roof. Her fastidious nature comes to the fore, and under her discerning eye I have to thatch and re-thatch the entire roof what feels like twice over.

As I work, we talk. Or rather, I listen. Juliet Perrea was once a bright and capable young medical student. She grew up a wealthy merchant's daughter and spent her childhood surrounded by tutors. She devoured mathematics, architecture, astronomy, and read books on love, war, history, and economics. Her father supported all of her endeavors, because he was a proud, vain man. The brilliance of his young daughter was simply another trophy to hold up to his rivals. Before she turned fourteen, she was apprenticed to the greatest doctor in the kingdom. She even met the Lord General Kranos himself. A few years ago, the first sign of her disease appeared. Juliet tried her hardest to ignore the pain and faint decay. Before long her teacher recognized the signs. It was rumored that Kranos could cure even leprosy using the Healing Hand.

"He found me 'interesting,' but hardly worth the time and effort necessary to cure. Many people get leprosy, was he to heal them all?"

A potent and toxic bitterness poisons these words. To be so close to a cure, yet to be summarily sentenced to exile and certain death, slowly wasting away, disfigured and alone, all from being found… wanting. Her father, after receiving word of Kranos' rejection, pretended she never existed.

"So they put me here," she says as I climb down from the roof. "I've been using what medical knowledge I have to ease the pain, and eventually the passing, of my neighbors."

"At least your skills have come to some use," I say hopefully. "Since you decided to learn medicine to help people, I can't imagine a set of people more in need of you."

She perks up slightly and gives me what remains of her smile. Just hours previous, I would have recoiled at the horrible grimace that results from the attempt. But my lips tug into a returning grin.

"Thank you," she says in complete earnest. "I needed that."

I pat her hand, but she winces and recoils.

"I'm sorry, so sorry," I say in instant contrition, stepping back in alarm. She waves my concern off with a casual motion.

"Be gentle, is all," she says wryly. "I'm not as strong as I once was."

She reaches out and tentatively grasps my hand, her grip feeble.

"How are you feeling?" she asks, reaching up to touch my head.

"I feel fine. No doubt thanks to you."

"Good," she replies, laughing. "You can work on my garden."

As the sun reaches its zenith, I dig yet another hole, listening to Juliet talk. She regales me with stories of her childhood and tales of her experience in the High Court. Her mixture of wit and humor keep me laughing and amused despite the monotonous work. She tells me of her favorite things, of the music and the art that she cherishes.

"Caldero's art was the highlight of my fifteenth Spring," Juliet says, obviously reminiscing. She says it like I should know who Caldero is, but I've never heard of the man. "He creates such fascinating images, so discordant, so despairing, and yet so... hopeful."

I reach the end of the line, and she places the final seed. She glances up at the sun and gives a small start.

"I didn't realize how long it's been. I need to go make my rounds," she says as she shuffles back to the little cottage.

"Do you want my help?" I ask, albeit reluctantly. I don't want to part with Juliet, but I'm unsure of my ability to help treat her leprous patients without revealing both my inexperience and my distaste for blood. She takes one look at my face and laughs.

"I think you would be more of a hindrance than a help," she says graciously. "It would be better if you head home. Someone has to be missing you..." she trails off leadingly. I shake my head solemnly.

"I'm woefully alone. I lay all day moping and ..." She rolls her remaining eye and heads back into the house. "Can I come back?"

She stops with her back to me. She doesn't say anything, the silence stretching like a coiled spring between us. Just as I resolve to ask again she speaks.

"Yes. You may."

She closes the door behind her. Satisfied, I move to the latrine pit and leap it lightly. I walk along the fence in search of either a guard or the gates. A patrol of the Watch comes into view, and I lift my arm to hail them. Immediately, a crossbow levels at me. I stop in my tracks.

"Hold right there," the man orders as the others look at me warily, hands on the hilts of their swords. I slowly, calmly raise my hands from my side and show they are empty.

"Sir," I begin. "I was thrown into this colony yesterday while I was unconscious, and I'm here to assure you I am not infected with any sort of disease whatsoever. Is it possible to secure my release?"

"Back away from the fence," the guard says, and his crossbow does not lower an inch.

"Sir, honestly, this is just a misunderstanding."

"This is your final warning. Back away from the fence and cross over the trench to where you belong, or I'll be forced to loose."

I consider trying again, but I come to the quick conclusion that my life isn't worth the trouble. The guard shoulders his crossbow, and the patrol resumes their march the second I'm back on the colony side.

"Sir, since you did not seem inclined to listen to me there, I would like to make a request of you from this side of the trench."

I make sure to put the proper venom in my inflection to get my point across. The men set to keep watch on the unfortunates interred within the confines of the leper colony should not treat its inmates like animals. They ignore me, but the man with the crossbow's jaw clenches slightly. I walk alongside them as they march, spewing a constant stream of sarcastic courtesy.

"As I have returned to my proper place, safely four paces farther away than I was before, I was wondering if you would stop a moment and answer my query." They continue to walk, and I pace them. "In all truth, I've never met men quite so polite as you. You're willing to join a poor man on his walk in the fresh air. I assure you I am more than capable of providing for my own safety."

I blather on for more than a quarter of the length of the fence in my best imitation of a conversation with a stone. I've been talking for more than half an hour before the captain finally turns on me.

"What is it you want?" he shouts. His face is red, but I just give him my most winning smile.

"Sir," I say in the same tone of the last half hour. "I was just wondering if you would answer a simple question." The man glares at me for a few long moments.

"What in the Eternal's forgotten name is your question?" he finally growls.

"How could I get a message sent out to someone in the city? I need to get word to Reknor the Historian, as I am wrongfully imprisoned, and I apparently need some form of corroboration in order to be released."

"Why, I'll take your message. Word to Reknor, eh? The Historian? Lives on Castleberry Street?"

"Yes, exactly."

"Never heard of him," the man says with a sneer.

He makes several loud comments about the tainted getting "uppity" as they stalk away, and I let them go. The retreating sun lengthens my shadow ahead as I begin the long walk back to Juliet's house. I need to wait for nightfall if I'm going to sneak out of here, so I have time to kill. Her house is still empty, so I scramble onto the roof to watch the sun fall over the horizon.

Just as the sun disappears behind the western walls of Donir, Juliet reappears, her shuffling step achingly slow as she ascends the gentle slope to her cottage. She has to stop twice to rest in the attempt, and my heart goes out to her. This woman, so ill herself, has spent the last four hours tending to her fellow inmates when she can hardly walk herself. The strength that act must take is beyond my understanding. She doesn't see me on my perch, but her steps slow and halt just before the door. She doesn't enter, but paces back to the edge of the slope, where she slowly, agonizingly, lowers herself to the ground. I study her frail frame for a few moments before I slip silently from my place on the roof.

"No luck?" her voice interrupts the stillness of the night and I jump.

"No luck," I say. I can't keep the bitterness out of my voice. We sit for a few moments before she glances towards me.

"It's easy to pretend to be like me, but it isn't so easy to be treated that way, is it?"

I turn and meet her gaze. This time, her gaze gives me nothing. No sparkle. No mirth. I swallow heavily.

"No," I say softly. She cocks her head quizzically.

"No, it isn't," I say louder. "It was never my idea to pretend to be sick. My master made me. I'm supposed to learn something from the experience, I guess."

"What it's like to be treated as an animal, most like. To see how you've treated others before you can learn how to treat them properly."

An angry rebuttal rises in me, but it dies on my lips. If, not a day ago, I'd seen Juliet on the streets, I would've shunned her as tainted and diseased along with every other person that crossed her path. For her part, she sits silently, staring off into the ever-deepening gloom. She gives me the benefit of time to come to my own conclusions.

Creator, I *did* recoil in fear and horror at the sight of a woman who, quite possibly, saved my life through her ministrations. I judged before I truly knew. Well then.

No longer.

"Thank you," I say, smiling. "Regardless of what Reknor's intentions were, I'm glad I met you. I think… I *know* you've taught me far more than I ever would have learned being kicked about and shunned on the streets."

We sit in silence for a time, but eventually she shivers.

"I'm going to head out. You go inside and warm up. I've got things to do, you know, on the other side," I say with a bit of chagrin.

Juliet nods as if my words are predictable. Which I guess they are.

"Good luck, and be careful," she says, reaching up and patting my wounded head gingerly. Her tone indicates she doesn't expect to see me again.

I smirk inwardly. You won't get away from me that easily.

"I'll be back around to visit before too long," I say, smiling.

***

"Well, boy, what trouble have you gotten yourself into? It looks like a bunch of crazy gorillas ran rampant on your face."

Peering blearily up at him, I scowl at Reknor in the morning light.

"Leprosy, Reknor?" I say, shaking my head. "You brought this on, not me."

I briefly recount my adventures, though I hold back any mention of Juliet, almost as if she's a secret I'd rather keep.

"Good."

"Good? That's it?" I ask.

"What, do you want me to worry over you like a tiny child who's skinned his knee? You handled yourself well. Perhaps you're ready for more?"

He hands me a tiny parchment roll. Written in Reknor's flowing, beautiful calligraphy are the words "The Silent Philosopher." In sparse detail, the order commands me to go to the listed address and be entirely silent. Should the opportunity arise to speak to someone, I'm to conduct my conversation in total silence. A hastily scrawled postscript advises me to start a fight. Without actually attacking anyone. I throw my pillow over my head and question Reknor's sanity for a long, solemn moment.

Arriving at the address, I wince. A sign for a coffee shop stares at me malevolently, and not just any coffee shop, but the

Tavern of Fours. The most brilliant political and intellectual minds in the Kingdom of the Sea come here to argue and debate. The Tavern of Fours is the place to go to speak freely, openly, and strongly for or against any topic that crosses your mind. And I'm supposed to argue with these people without speaking.

Part of me wants to feel cowed, to hunker down and slink into the shop, but humility just won't do in a place like the Tavern of Fours. I saunter in, full of arrogance and bravado. The sound of eager debate quiets slightly as I thrust open the door, but only slightly and only for a moment. Tables all over are filled with combatants and friends, smoking pipes and sipping various concoctions as they argue. Polished to a gleaming obsession, a circular wooden bar fills the center of the establishment. The proprietor, a thin, mousy man in an elegant if muted brown suit, nods at me as I enter.

He has no customers at the moment, so I stroll up to the counter. Offering my cheekiest grin and a wink, I set down just over exact change for the man's highest quality coffee. He regards me warily for a moment, then dips down under the bar. At my encouraging nod, he brews the cup, then hesitantly smiles as he hands it over.

I flip him another coin and glance around. There's only one open seat, and it looms across from the pinched face of nobility. The chair scrapes as I settle down across from the noble near the window. His pointed beard and slick mustache are in line with the current style, his strong jaw no doubt a testament to his bloodline or some other nonsense. His clothes suggest wealth, so I eye him with due respect as he eyes me with the exact opposite. He may be a few years older than I am, but he's not some elder statesman.

"Thanks!" the bartender calls behind me. My tip was generous.

Without turning from the man across from me, I give him an affable wave of my hand. I cock an eyebrow at the man, then turn and put my back to the wall, stretching my legs out into the aisle between the tables.

"I'm waiting for someone," the man says, his voice cutting clearly through the ambient sound. It's a voice that is accustomed to being paid the highest of attention, deep and confident. I glance at him, nodding, and sip my coffee with a contented sigh. "That means your seat is taken."

I look at him again, then down at myself. With an incredulous look on my face, I nod slowly. Of course it's taken.

"Oh, ha ha," he says with annoyance. He stares at me for a long moment in silence. "Alright then, boy, what are you doing here?"

I place my hand on my chin and gaze off into the distance.

"Thinking? Philosophizing? Can you speak?"

I nod my head, a helpful smile on my face. His eyes narrow thoughtfully.

"Are you going to speak?"

I shake my head ruefully, and he sighs theatrically. I take another sip of my coffee, starting to enjoy myself. He studies me for a moment.

"What would you do about the growing rat problem in the city? They appear to have moved out of the Corpses and into the city proper," he asks suddenly.

It's just the kind of pointless question they ask in the Tavern of Fours. Who cares about rats? Regardless, I adopt a thoughtful look, then blink, sticking my finger in the air. I stand up and hunch over, madly stomping my feet all over the floor. The man struggles to contain a smile.

"As useful as that might be, somehow I don't think we have enough feet between us," he says, spicing his voice with languid sarcasm. "My people are developing a new type of poison, but tests have shown that it could hurt us as well as the rats, so the inhumanity of it all has set back my plans weeks."

He waves his hands frivolously, but I see through his façade. The man genuinely cares about the safety of the people in the city. He has no real reason to care aside from, I don't know, possessing a small modicum of humanity, which places him squarely outside of my experience of nobility. I find myself warming to him. He stares at me pointedly, and a superior smirk spreads across his face.

"What, my dear friend, do you believe the stars are made of?"

I frown. I have absolutely no idea. I've heard stories from religion to suns to the souls of the dead. After a moment's thought, I elect to go with the one I can explain with hand motions the best. I mime a dagger to the heart, then raise my arms, fingers waving, staring at the ceiling with rapture on my face. The man laughs out loud, slapping his thigh.

"I thought I had you with that one. Yes, I've heard the departed theory. I fall somewhere closer to the small suns myself, but I do find something quaintly romantic about the idea we live on in the stars..."

From there we're off, our conversation ranging from petty politics to the nature of the Creator. I waggle my eyebrows, shift uncomfortably, and even flash the occasional rude gesture to explore my means of communication. A crowd forms. One by one, the other conversations in the room stop as I continue to argue in absolute silence. We move to a new table as our audience grows to nearly a dozen. Suddenly, he asks me a pointed question in front of the ever-growing crowd.

"What do you think of our illustrious Sealord?"

I grimace. If the man is a royalist, I should probably lie and try to appease him. If he isn't, I'll lose his trust. I glance around at the crowd, each of them focused on me, and I cringe inwardly. Any one of them could be a spy. This might be a decent chance to start that fight, though. Throwing caution to the winds, I make an exaggerated frown, slump my shoulders, and mime a whip cracking across my back.

"Strong words. Not many are bold enough to speak out like that," he says, a thoughtful look on his face.

I start shaking, silent laughter reverberating through my entire body. Words.

"Oh, ha ha," he says again, a smile twitching its way onto his face. He leans in a bit closer. "Sadly enough, I agree with you. While science and medicine may be flourishing, the constant censorship and oppression is starting to wear even on the upper classes. The free movement of ideas was open, even encouraged under the Shaper regime. This king, however, has restricted everyone who isn't writing propaganda for him. There are murmurs of rebellion in other parts of the kingdom."

I nod gently, my respect for this man growing. The faces of the men around us are thoughtful, and I don't detect any hostility directed at my new friend. I genuinely like this man, and our conversation has proven that we are of like mind. I respect Reknor enough to follow his wish, though. So, Eternal damn it, fight it is.

A man is leaning particularly close over my companion's shoulder, closer than is necessary. I hold up my hand for silence, and all eyes settle on me. I point at my adversary, then at the man leaning over him. Making a circle with my hand, I move my other finger towards it, a question in my eyes. The man beside him doesn't get it, but several men in the surrounding crowd do. They cough out laughs behind closed fists. Caution? From these men? My course is set, however, and my companion answers with a slightly clenched jaw.

"I do not know what you do behind closed doors," he says, and the men chuckle lightly. "But I am happily engaged to the Lady Eleanor Torgue."

I recognize the name, though I can't place it. Mind racing, I adopt a shocked expression. I point at him, then at three or four other men around the circle. With a conspiratorial glance around the room, I point at myself. Everyone looks confused, so I indicate my opponent and make horns upon my head, the universal sign of a cuckold. I grin arrogantly, leaning back in my chair. The muscle in his jaw begins to jump reflexively.

"I'll ignore that slight. This time. I know her true fidelity. But watch your tongue."

I stick out my tongue and cross my eyes, doing my best to watch it. The room erupts into nervous laughter, and his cheeks turn crimson. It won't take much more. I meet his angry gaze and deliberately roll my eyes. I hardly hear the chair screech before he's coming over the table, murder in his eyes.

***

Outside the coffee shop, my entire body aches and the corner of my jaw throbs in time with my pulse. My assailant, or friend, or whatever he is, sits next to me. We lean against each other for support. I still haven't spoken, and he's fallen into a reticent mood himself. When the brawl finally got going, a dozen other men joined in and the place was close to wrecked. All of the pretty boys with their elegant fashion actually ground out a fair imitation of a bar room brawl, though broken coffee mugs and distress over soiled cloaks are generally not a part of your typical taproom fight. The owner didn't complain once, however, as the soldiers came and dragged our useless carcasses outside. They recognized who my companion was, and they immediately backed away, bowing and scraping furiously with several 'milords' thrown in.

So we sit in front of the coffee shop. He glances over at me, and I look back at him, eyebrows raised. I have to blink once to get a bit of blood out of my eyes. He smiles to himself and shakes his head, looking back down at the cobblestone street.

"Thank you," he says, not looking up. "There are few men who'll act like I am a person, instead of a title. For good reason, granted, but still. There are even fewer who would insult me. Again, thank you."

I give him a short shrug and a smile. Whoever he is, I get the feeling I should be bowing, scraping, and begging for forgiveness, too. But… this man is genuine. He really is thanking me for giving him the black eye already swelling to puffy fruition. Even the high and mighty, no matter how high and mighty they might be, are just human. Something about this moment echoes faintly of the lesson I learned from Juliet. A man may look one way on the outside, but it's surprising how little his appearance may reflect his soul, good or ill. Just as not all evil is ugly, not all good is pretty either. Even though I judged him to be a sniveling noble who had been gifted a perfect life, he's still a man, one way or another.

"Well then," he begins. "As much as I've enjoyed our exercise, I have other responsibilities to attend to. Unless you would be amenable to a short luncheon?"

What could the harm be? I don't have anything else to do, and it feels like this man just needs a friend. I nod, standing with a quiet groan and offering him my hand. He takes it with a grimace, gingerly leaning on me as he sets off down the street towards the intersection at the center of the city. I pace him, not bothering to conceal my limp as my knee jolts with each step.

"Did you have to hit me with that chair? I always thought they broke when they struck people," he grumbles, rubbing at his lower back.

I nod, miming a breaking and shrugging. I always thought they broke, too. Pointing at my knee, I adopt an outraged expression.

"Well, can you blame me for retaliating? I admit the table leg was a bit under the belt, so to speak, but you had just hit me with a chair."

I chuckle, throwing an arm across his shoulders and pulling him a bit more upright. He gives me a pained smile and brings his arm up over mine. We lean heavily against one another, and our aching bodies offset, allowing us to walk in a reasonably straight line as we slip into the stream of humanity. A dozen steps in he straightens to his full height, glancing around in the crowd.

"Those damnable attendants are always underfoot when you're trying to get anything done, but they aren't around when you actually need them!" he mutters, pushing himself up for a better vantage with my shoulder as his leverage. I groan as my wounded knee buckles, and we both stumble and fall. Lying in a tangle on the ground, the crowd parting to either side of us, we don't bother moving.

"Is it bad that I don't want to get up?" he muses, staring up at the sky.

I shrug awkwardly as I lay on the ground.

"My lord!" The voice is distant, but urgent.

"Funny how you never look at the clouds. They really are peaceful, if you take the time to look. I'll have to remember that," he says, a smile on his face.

"My lord! My lord!" the shouts grow louder, and I crane my neck to see what's going on. The crowd regurgitates a man in fine blue servant's clothing with a mostly bald head and a thick white beard.

"My lord!" he gasps as he falls to his knees.

"Watkins!" my friend says, his voice cheery. "Just the man I was looking for. Would you be so kind as to bring the carriage? My legs aren't working quite right at the moment, and I'm growing ever later for a luncheon at Miranda's."

"Sir! Are you hurt? Can you move them? Are you well?"

"No, Watkins," he says solemnly. "I've lost the use of my legs entirely. In fact, I'm dying. My last wish is to taste something truly sublime, and Miranda's is the only place close enough for me to make it."

"My lord! What has happened?" Watkins cries, kneeling down and cradling my friend's head. He grabs Watkins' collar, pulling him close.

"Nothing, my dear man. I am in perfect health. I'm just, well, resting here. But I really do have a luncheon planned at Miranda's, and I really would love for you to bring the carriage here."

Watkins shoots him a betrayed look, but stands and melts away into the crowd.

"Wonderful fellow, isn't he? The carriage will be along shortly, and so we are left here to gaze in wonder at the clouds. Ah, do you see? That one is a bear. Even down to the claws. Remarkable."

I look up and see, for all intents and purposes, a few puffy white clouds. Nothing resembles anything like a bear, so I just nod amiably and close my eyes.

***

Miranda's establishment resembles a nobleman's estate more than a restaurant. In my thieving days, I would have been happy just chipping some of the golden paint off the doorframe. The place is opulence incarnate. I couldn't be more out of place if I ended up at the King's Ball.

Watkins runs before us and opens the door, disappearing inside. My friend and I continue at a more sedate pace, and I gawk in open wonder at the manicured gardens and an aisle of elegant marble statues. Every petal is perfectly arranged, every lead in its proper place, a fountain burbling on either side. I've just entered a dream of paradise. Reaching down my shirt, I pat my purse and struggle not to frown. Something tells me I don't have nearly enough money to eat here.

The door opens again as we approach the step, and a man in pressed satin holds the door open and bows low. I have to struggle not to turn away and run. What the hell is this place? I haven't ever been treated as much of anything beyond, occasionally, a normal person. No one bows to normal people. As we enter the foyer, a striking, enormous woman in luxurious silk who can only be Miranda swings down a sweeping staircase, elegant in spite of her bulk.

"My lord!" she calls, her throaty voice appealing and, subtly, seductive. "We have reserved our best room for you! Right this way."

"Thank you, Miranda. You're the only reason I continue to return, of course," my companion says, taking her hand and kissing it. Miranda blushes even through her white makeup, and I grin. He's suave, I have to give him that.

"It's not the food or the service?" she asks, playfulness stealing into her voice.

"Mere icing on the delicious cake," he says, winking.

Miranda fans herself frantically as she turns back. Her hand comes up like she wants to touch his face, but stops just short.

"What in the Creator's name happened to you, love? Your beautiful face..."

"Nothing, Miranda. Just a bit of sport," he says, turning to me and mock-scowling.

"Is the duke's room prepared?" she calls up, and a servant appears at the top of the stairs, bows low, and nods.

Duke… Engaged to the 'the Lady Eleanor Torgue'… I'm standing next to Duke Torlas Graevo. One of the most respected, wealthy, and powerful men in the entire kingdom. He sits as one of the eight men on Helikos' inner council. And that number includes Helikos and Kranos. He could not only have me arrested, but could stab me in a public place, wave his hand, and porters would run up to make my body disappear. He's considered 'untouchable.' I sway slightly, and I have to take some deep breaths through my nose to clear my spinning head. I hit a duke with a chair. I insulted him, degraded him, and hit him with a chair. My knees go weak as my body tries to force me to my knees and pray to thank the Creator.

"Well, shall we?" Torlas asks me, elegantly gesturing towards the stairs.

I struggle not to change how I've been acting. I'm utterly shocked that he hasn't challenged me to a duel or had me killed after some of what I implied. We'd even brawled like common folk… Creator save me, if he's going to be honest and well, actually seem to like me, then I won't change.

The room itself establishes a new bar for wealthy waste. Every fixture, from the candlesticks to the plates to the glasses, is made from some sort of precious metal. Gold dominates, but silver, platinum, and metals I don't recognize make shining appearances. The walls are a deep blood red, and the chairs themselves are crafted works of art. No less than eight servants stand at various points around the room, and each of them wear a uniform to beggar anything that I've ever *touched,* let alone worn. A man steps out and slides chairs from the small, two-person table in the center of the room. Torlas' hand comes down on my shoulder.

"I understand. The first time I ate here, I was too busy admiring everything around me to speak," he says.

I shoot him a look and smirk with confidence I don't feel. His eyes light up, and he throws his head back and laughs in such a genuine way that I can't help but relax. We take our places, the chairs drawing in behind us perfectly, cloth of gold napkins in our laps and a glass filled with an opaque amber liquid in our hands before I can blink. Torlas hefts his glass, inclines his head to me, and drains it in one swallow. I follow suit, and liquid fire ignites my tongue with the tastes of caramel, coffee, and a wooden nuttiness I can't place. When I swallow, the fire races down and warms me to the tips of my fingers. I sigh audibly, and Torlas grins.

"And all we did is prepare the pallet..." he says, nodding over my shoulder.

A dozen men file in with golden platters covered in golden domes. They set them in a dizzying pattern on the table. With a careful flourish, the lids spin away to reveal a dozen small, crafted dishes. A halved tart allows an unfamiliar spiced fish to spill out in a steaming yellow cream sauce. Exotic noodles wrap around a sausage bursting with juice and spices. A pheasant crafted to hold a cinnamon-baked apple lies posed among a heap of hearty vegetables. Each dish is a work of art beyond my imagination.

"The privileges of rank," Torlas says, slicing a bite off of a steak so rare it bleeds. "And to think, Miranda's normally requires reservations to be made months in advance."

I want to ask 'we weren't expected?' but I can't figure out how to get that message across without speaking. Instead, I look over at Watkins in the corner. Raising my eyebrows at Torlas, I motion towards him and indicate a space in between us.

"You want Watkins to dine with us?" Torlas says in a kind of bemused tone, looking over. Watkins just stands, looking as attentive and disinterested as possible, but I can tell that he's praying to whatever god, entity, or power he worships. "I suppose the two of us can't possibly eat all of this on our own. Watkins, come over here and partake."

Watkins doesn't bother to hide his excitement, practically running over. A servant with a chair is there ahead of him, however, and he falls into it awkwardly in his rush.

"Oh, thank you milord, milords," he says, nodding at Torlas and me. Torlas and I both give identical flippant waves, and we look at each other and laugh.

"It's wonderful that you've found a new... associate, milord. May I ask who I have the pleasure of dining with?" Watkins says, addressing Torlas but glancing at me.

"Ask him yourself, Watkins," Torlas says, a laugh in his voice. I turn to Watkins, my eyebrows raised.

"Uh, yes," Watkins begins. "Well, if I may be plain, sir, who are you?"

I make a show of deliberating whether or not I'll tell them, but then I just shrug and smile. My reticence perturbs Watkins, but Torlas just laughs.

"When our friend is ready, I'm sure he'll tell us who he is," Torlas says, his tone leading.

I nod as I cut off a piece of the sausage and pop it in my mouth, groaning aloud. The spices mix perfectly with whatever unholy concoction is in the center, taking the bite out of the pepper but complementing its taste. It's blasphemy to swallow, but I do, looking down at the dozen dishes in wonder. What other joys will I find in this sumptuous banquet?

We continue to chat in our one-sided manner, eating the entire feast with Watkins' assistance. As the meal winds down, Watkins appears more and more uncomfortable. He hasn't adjusted well to my silence.

"Well, my friend," Torlas says. "I've had a splendid time today. I'd love to do this again, minus the chair to the back, at another time. I do, however, require a way to contact you. Is it possible I could have your name, or your residence, or something of that nature?"

I don't hesitate for long. I know Reknor planned for me to spend the day silent, but the potential to create a lasting relationship with a duke on the inner council is too good of an opportunity to pass up.

"My name is Jace," I say, standing and reaching across the table to shake Torlas' hand. "I'm a ward of Reknor the Historian, on Castleberry Street."

Torlas rises smoothly, taking my hand in his own in a firm grip.

"I am Torlas Graevo, Duke of Donir. But I'm sure you already knew that."

"Not until we got here and they called you by your title," I say honestly, shrugging.

"Truthfully? Intriguing. I knew you weren't of the nobility, otherwise I would've seen you at one time or another in the court. A ward of the Historian, eh? Let me ask you something. Would our conversation have gone quite the same if you had known who I was from the beginning?"

There's a test somewhere in those words, and I can't be sure what the correct answer is.

"I'd like to think so, Torlas," I say, purposefully leaving off his expected honorific. Watkins looks horrified, but Torlas smiles.

"Good. I don't know if you've realized this, Jace, but I've already come to rely on you. No titles between us. Ever. Agreed?"

"Agreed," I say, grinning. "I *am* sorry I hit you with that chair, though."

Watkins gasps, shooting me a murderous look.

"Apology accepted. I hope your knee recovers apace," Torlas says, laughing. "I'll call on you as soon as I am able. And don't be afraid to call on me, either."

"Torlas, it has been a pleasure."

"For me as well, Jace. Until later."

Chapter 11
Iliana
The Thirty-First Day of Spring
In the year 5222, Council Reckoning

My eyes open to darkness. I never sleep until sunrise. Not anymore. There is too much to do, between lessons in court and politics, combat and Shaping, history and literature, the list feels endless. The darkness of my room embraces me in the quilt of night, but I ignore the tiny part of me begging to stay in bed. I shrug into a dress and fight back a yawn. I've been training ceaselessly, the members of the Tide no doubt weary of constantly feeling the bite of glass. Eventually, Father demanded that we ramp up the violence of my training. Uncle attends my sessions, Shaping shut the wounds the Tide incur. I try to avoid killing anyone, but I'm being pushed to the brink. I'm not sure I have the control to keep preserving the lives of my enemies, temporary or otherwise.

I glance over at Yrena. Her soft snores pierce the silence of the night. She's taken to sleeping in my room, and many nights I wake to feel the soft stroke of her hand running through my hair. Uncle suggested I cut off the long locks, as they are a liability in battle, but I can't bring myself to do it, not with Yrena still combing it every night, sliding the brush carefully through the tangled snarls I accrue throughout the day. It's a last ray of my childhood that I cling to with silent desperation.

I slip out the door, nodding once to Poline. Many members of the Tide would have balked at the suggestion that they spend their hard-won training and skills solely protecting a girl who never gets into danger, but Poline is different. She smiles in greeting, winks at me, and falls into step just behind. The empty hallways of the palace take us on our short daily journey to my garden.

"Sleep well, milady?"

"Naturally," I respond, and I can tell she rolls her eyes behind me. It's always the same question, asked at that time when night and day war for dominance, night ever reluctant to release its grip upon the world. I always provide the same answer, spoken with the soul-weary resignation of a woman three times my age.

I breathe deeply as we cross the threshold, the scents of life bringing peace. As we round the trunk of the mighty oak towering above the rest of the garden, however, my eyes fall on Father. The Sealord's brow is furrowed and his eyes distant. He doesn't acknowledge us for the briefest of moments, though he can only be here to speak with me. When his eyes focus, his face clears, and he smiles the same genuine smile he always has.

"Iliana!" he says brightly. "I've heard you often come here before sunrise. It is indeed a place of peace."

"Of course, Father," I say, but my voice comes out flat. It *was* a place of peace. Peace the Sealord is no doubt here to break. I love him, but he's been the harbinger of ill tidings recently. "To what do we owe the honor of your presence?"

"Can a man not just look in on his daughter?" he asks, his smile faltering. "It would seem to indicate an unsettled mind, to rise so early. Is something the matter?"

"No, Father," I respond, feeling a brief stirring of warmth. I go to his open arms, letting him enfold me in a hug. No matter how old I get, the comforting arms of my father will always bring me joy. For a moment, I close my eyes, breathing in the pleasant scent of him, the fresh smell of lake water and love. My mind wanders back to those memories of my childhood, his constant presence, the *safety*. "I have everything I need here."

"I'm glad to hear it," he murmurs, stroking my hair. His broad frame makes me feel so small. "I have ill news." And there it is. "Do you remember Markis Calladan? He was at your coming of age. He hasn't graced the capital with his presence since, but..."

A brief memory of a man's face, one among many. Brown hair, narrow face, open smile.

"Vaguely. Does Calladan not serve as Earl of Firdana? Has something happened to him?"

"No. Well, nothing has happened to him *yet*. His wife traveled in secret to Donir and sought an audience with me in private. Apparently, her husband has allied himself with the Vengeance," the Sealord's voice is heavy with sorrow. "I always respected Markis. I've no idea why he would see fit to betray me now."

"Can you be sure? Is his wife trustworthy?"

"She brought proof. Missives, in the Vengeance's own hand, directing him on where and when to drop off supplies to aid the rebels."

My father once knew the Vengeance, had even been friends with him in the days of the Council of Shapers. Then, the Vengeance betrayed them all, embarking on a killing spree of the other Shapers, fabricating evidence and punishing his peers for perceived wrongdoing. The Vengeance wasn't just a nickname for the man, but in fact the title given to the Shaper charged with keeping others in line. The Council of Shapers had lived by an ironclad series of laws which prevented them from ever taking part in the government or affairs of normal man. The Vengeance's purpose was to enforce those laws, keeping the might of the Shapers from ruining the budding civilizations of the world. Those laws had stood, untarnished, for over five thousand years. Ever since the fall of the Eternal, the Council of Shapers had resisted becoming involved in the workings of the world.

The Vengeance ruined the tenuous peace, slaughtering his fellows and eventually forcing Telias, the Warmheart, to raise an army to resist him. The Vengeance attacked him and defeated him despite his human allies. Father and Uncle were the last two surviving members of the Council save for the Mason, who was away from civilization out in the wastes of the west, unaware of the turmoil he left behind. They acted in concert before the Vengeance could return and finish them. In desperation, they warned the common people of Donir about the Vengeance's heinous crimes. The Donirians gladly accepted the protection of the Sealord and his friend, the Healing Hand.

One mystery remains: why did the Mason join with the Vengeance? Father sent messengers seeking the Mason, but they were unable to find him in the desert. The next he surfaced, rumors pointed him directly in league with the Vengeance. The silent war has been waged ever since, seventeen years gone. My hands curl into fists.

"How could he? His supplies are used to feed the people of Donir! His grain is what provides us with bread!" I exclaim, my voice rising. Poline shifts behind me, her armor clinking slightly. She agrees.

"I've always treated him with dignity. His treason stings worse because of that trust," Father says, sighing.

"We must invade his lands and depose him," I declare. "Men such as him cannot be left in power."

"I had hoped, perhaps, to reason with him, to ask him *why*, but he hasn't responded to my messenger. In fact, the man I sent has not returned nor reported back. I fear for his safety."

"Let me go and bring him before you." The words tumble out of my lips. Even as I say them, my resolve grows steadier. "I will ascertain what has befallen your messenger and bring back the Earl for your questions."

A glimmer sparks in my father's eyes, brief and gone before I can register it. He begins to shake his head.

"I cannot risk you for such a task," he says, grabbing my shoulders. "You are far more important to me than the treason of one man, no matter how serious."

"You've trained me for years, ceaselessly, so that I may be of use to you," I say, grabbing his hands and looking into his eyes. I won't beg. The Sealord will never soften to such methods. But a righteous fire burns in me, a need to bring this man to justice. To betray the kingdom, for whatever reason, earns him my disdain. But to imprison, or, worse, murder innocent messengers just because they serve the King... I will not stand for it. "Let me be the woman you claim I am."

He pauses, appraising me silently. I refuse to wilt under his scrutiny.

"Very well," he says begrudgingly. "But take a contingent of the Tide with you. They will look after your safety, in the event that word of your leaving the capital leaks out."

"I have no need of an entire contingent," I growl. This is my mission. If I take an entire army with me, Father will never respect me for it.

"My dear, you simply can't leave Donir without someone to watch your back while you sleep! Your uncle and I are both busy with a delicate matter, or we would travel with you."

Poline takes that moment to gently clear her throat. I glance over at her, and she gives me a wink, her eyes twinkling.

"I'll deign to take one of the Tide..." I say in a leading tone, letting my eyes drift to Poline. Father glances back at her, grunting under his breath.

"Your pet guardswoman," he says, disgruntled. "One guard is not enough-"

"But it's all I'll allow. You know she'll watch me carefully. She's been outside my door for years now, and I trust her. I don't know if I could even sleep around a bunch of strange soldiers. Poline will do nicely."

"Very well," he says with grudging acquiescence. "Tide, do you know that area of Firdana? Would you be able to guide and protect the princess?"

The Tide are always referred to as the singular and unrelenting Tide. The humanity and personality that make soldiers human is supposed to be subsumed by the will of the collective. They don't need specific names, as they act and respond as one. Poline is different. Her relationship with me throughout the previous two years has helped to break her further out of the shell her training created. The callous way Father addresses her sends a ripple of discontent through the back of my mind.

"I was raised in Firdana, my lord. I know the area well. I am Shorn, of the second echelon, as well as Tide," she responds, baring her wrist to the Sealord. He grunts in surprise as he witnesses her trio of tattoos and the clean scar of the fourth. I frown. What nonsense is this? Shorn? "I'll guard the princess with my life, and more, if necessary."

"You had better," the Sealord answers, his voice carrying none of the warmth he shares with me. Poline doesn't dignify the threat with a response. She is a member of the Tide, and will damn well do her job. She's told me enough in the last two years. "Iliana, remember. It would be ideal if you brought Markis and anyone in league with him back alive, but do not hesitate to defend yourself. If they would dare attack you, respond without mercy."

***

We need a certain amount of tact if we're going to discover who is really involved, and especially if we're going to rescue the hapless messenger. If he's still alive, I'm going to bring him home. That much is certain. Father wishes me to travel in all of the pomp and circumstance of the princess of the kingdom, but such ridiculous measures will only send Calladan and his people scurrying into hiding.

Instead, Poline and I head out of the south gate and join the heaving multitudes traveling the Way of the East. I've packed a few of my blending-in dresses to wear on the journey, along with a hooded brown cloak to cover my hair and hide my face, should the need arise. I almost stopped in to see Torlas before I left, just in case, but I received a note from him early this morning detailing how he will be out and about with a new friend. Despite the tiny pang of jealousy at the thought of Torlas being too busy to see me, I'm happy to hear he's met someone new.

As long as that new person is male.

Poline arrives in sensible pants and a tunic, though the quality is barely above peasant attire. I narrow my eyes. I've never seen the woman unpeeled from her carapace, so I look her up and down with a critical eye. Curvy outside of her armor, her broken nose only adds to her quaint charm. Her fiery hair and athletic body, honed from decades of training, make her striking. When she sees me, she smiles, and I can't help but smile in return.

"Poline!"

"What, milady?" she snaps, her hand dropping to her sword, her eyes roving the crowd.

"Poline, by the Creator's forgotten name, you're beautiful!"

"Milady..." she says, blushing a cute shade of crimson.

"You know, we may have to put you in a dress for the next ball," I begin, tapping my chin thoughtfully. "You'll be better able to guard me when all of the eyes in the room are squarely on *you.*"

"I... well, no, absolutely not," she says, shaking her head firmly. She can't fool me though. I can tell the idea of wearing a dress to a ball isn't quite so horrendous, and catching the eyes of men wouldn't quite be the end of the world, but I let the matter drop. For now.

"Well, let's be off, then," I say, spinning about gaily towards the open road. My dress swirls around my knees, my pale calves free in the Spring warmth. It feels *good* to be out of the palace and breathing fresh air, even *better* to stop Eternal-damned training my power and my skills, and the *best* because I have a mission. Father has finally trusted me with *doing* something.

"By the way," I toss back over my shoulder as Poline hurries to catch up. "You're going to have to drop the whole 'milady' thing. We're supposed to be incognito, neh?"

I stop, my eyes blurring, my senses scattered to the winds. I feel something, itching, clawing at the back of my mind. As if I should remember something, something that makes me both angry and terribly excited... I shake my head, trying to clear it, reaching up and grasping my skull. Why had that ending to such a simple sentence, such a strange little addition, caused my head so much pain? Why can't I remember?

"Milady, uh, I mean, Ily, are you well?" Poline says, the unfamiliar nickname skittering strangely off her tongue.

"Fine," I mutter, scratching at my hair and squinting in the strange brightness. Whatever spell I'm under, the feeling is fading.

"Perhaps we should go back. This journey was a mistake. I'll contact my commander—"

"No, Poline," I command, my voice snapping like a whip. "I'm fine. We proceed."

People are beginning to look at us strangely, our odd conversation and the dam we create in the flow of humanity distracting others from their business. I shake my head a final time, feeling the loose bun on the back of my head sway underneath my hood, and set forth again. Poline walks beside me, her hand on her sword and her glaring eyes meeting any who dare to look at us. I can tell she's on a razor's edge with so many strangers within arm's reach of me.

"Dearest," I whisper into her ear, gently grabbing her arm. "Please, the people in the crowd are harmless. People are looking at you *because* you're looking at them."

Poline tries to relax and does a decent job of it. We stroll for a while, my hand on her arm. Any glances our way are merely curious. Who is this young girl, hood up in the unseasonable warmth, hiding her features but walking with unmistakable refinement? Who is the woman that marches next to her with a distinct military bearing, her armaments and posture unmistakable? Whatever conclusions they draw, none could dare to venture that the princess of the Kingdom of the Sea is traveling in secret with a single guard. Such a thing would be impossible.

"If we're going to pull this off," Poline says after a few minutes. "You'll have to stop giving me commands."

"Then stop walking like a soldier," I shoot back.

"Then stop walking like a princess."

Shrugging, I slump my shoulders, trying to mimic the thinning crowd pushing to or from the gates of Donir. Some peasants swing their arms around as if they have no idea where their hands will end up, and their walks vary from carefree to plodding and weary. I let my arms swing, my shoulders swaying with the motion, my feet plopping onto the ground with what I hope is a casual stroll. No one looks at me funny, so I figure I'm not doing too bad of a job.

Glancing over, I nearly burst into laughter. Poline looks an absolute fool, her head back, her arms swinging far too high, her feet far too loose. She looks over at me, her eyes widening.

"You look ridiculous," we say in tandem, dissolving into gales of laughter. Now passersby actively avoid us, these loons pacing around like idiots, giggling maniacally in the middle of the road.

"We're hopeless."

"Utterly," Poline says, shaking her head. "So much for subterfuge. I imagine everyone on the road knows something strange is going on. We'll never get the jump on Calladan this way."

The grin fades from my cheeks, the reminder of our mission sucking the wind out of my sails, the gravity of the situation murder to my levity. We are on the way to seize a traitor, a landed noble treasonous to the crown, a man who would dare to imprison or murder innocent people to keep his secret. The brief sense of freedom at the start of our road disappears, mist before a strong wind. In its place, duty.

"We'll have to walk as naturally as we can," I say. "And stop drawing attention to ourselves. I look forward to the surprise in Calladan's eyes when we arrive."

***

The journey from Donir to Firdana takes a week's hard march. We could have ridden horses, but it would have made us all the more conspicuous. All of the flowers are in bloom and the crops just beginning to peek out from the soil with the onset of Spring. The crowd on the Way grows sparser the farther we travel from the capitol, but the Way of the East is never truly empty. As far and away the easiest method of travel between several of the major cities on the continent, the Way provides a steady stream of humanity traveling in both directions. The stones of the Way don't appear worn despite the millions of feet it has weathered over the past millennia.

No one gives us undue attention. The occasional group of ruffians leer at us from time to time, but one closer look at Poline and the worn grip of her sword seems to satisfy any curiosity as to whether or not we are amenable to their... advances. We move at a good clip, outpacing most people on our way. Both Poline and I are in significant athletic shape, having trained together every day for years. We are also well-furnished with supplies, though we stop occasionally for fresh fruit or squeezed lemonade from an enterprising vendor who has set up a stand along the busy Way.

We sleep the first night under the stars. I lie on my back, the roll of cloth Poline lays out for me genuinely comfortable in the tall grass beside the Way. We don't bother with a fire; I snuggle in my bedroll, staring up at the unending multitude of stars in awe. The ten thousand ever-burning Stars of Donir dim the stars over the city, their light stronger than the firmament. Out here, a simple day's walk from the city, the stars blanket the sky, and their light illuminates the sweeping farmland and the dark mass of the Kinlen Forest to the east. Drowsy and warm, I drift away.

A familiar nightmare shakes me awake. The scenario changes, but always I'm helpless, bound, unable to move and unable to scream.

A scant few hours have passed since I fell asleep. The stars still glitter in the dark cloak of midnight. Poline's silhouette is off by the Way, ever alert, ever watchful. She shifts and glances back at me, somehow recognizing my return to consciousness. The air has grown chill absent the sun, the cold Winter air only reluctantly surrendering to the warmth of Spring.

"Poline," I call quietly, and she lopes over to me.

"Yes, milady?" she asks in a whisper, her voice tender in the still night.

"Could you guard from, well, over here?"

"It will reduce the effectiveness of my—"

"Poline," I say again, gently cutting her off. Some of the young girl I once was creeps into the edges of my speech.

Poline doesn't respond, but sits next to me, turning away but leaving her back close to my bedroll. I roll over and snuggle up close to her. She stiffens, the gentle contact so unlike the violence and physical abuse we normally deal to one another. After a long few moments, she relaxes, at least as much as a Tide guarding a royal can possibly relax. Her muscles move underneath her shirt, her firm and powerful back comforting in the night, her warmth stilling the shivers before they can begin.

My heart slows into a steady rhythm. The responsibilities of my station, my title, and my power are far away. I feel like Iliana, the girl who loved for her old maid to comb her hair, the girl who could cause mischief with her young friend and laugh about it, the girl who I thought I buried with a tortured assassin…

I drift to sleep, curled halfway around Poline, who watches the night and does not tremble.

***

Three days pass largely uneventfully, though I grow a bit disgusted with my own smell. I haven't had the chance to bathe, and my skin is crusted with old sweat.

Something begins to trouble me as we walk. A lot of the people on the roads seem more haggard than normal. Men and women walk with their clothes ripped and hanging from their bones like sails after storms. Although some people have the desperate gleam of those willing to toe the line of the law, most just appear downtrodden and soul-worn. Women loosely hold the hands of children that don't have the energy to seek freedom. Any conversation is hushed and private. No one waves or smiles.

We pass a vendor selling strawberries near midday on the fourth day. Part of me wants to stop, but I'd rather not expose my face to anyone I don't have to. Just as we pass, the vendor shouts and kicks a sullen little boy who comes too close to his stall. Anger kindles in my chest, and I start to turn aside and give that vendor a piece of my mind, but Poline lightly grasps my arm. In response to my silent question, she nods back at the spectacle. The boy scampers back to the stall, flashing a rude gesture to the man, then dodges another kick as he cheekily pops a large strawberry into his mouth. The vendor's cries pierce the quiet morning, but few of the Way's desultory travelers show interest in the exchange.

"What is this?" I murmur, more to myself than Poline.

"I don't know," Poline says, her eyes roving across the sparse crowd with unease.

"So the Way isn't normally like this? I thought I was imagining it, or too sheltered to understand..."

"No," Poline says, her voice heavy. "Something is very wrong. Every kingdom has its own share of the destitute, but this... even in my early days with the Wave, I never saw so many like this. It feels like these people are refugees, fleeing war or famine."

"And we aren't at war," I say, frowning. "All reports show the kingdom as being fantastically prosperous. Every year we've seen signs of a flourishing economy. The poor are supposed to be disappearing, not gaining in number."

"Perhaps it has to do with our mission? Could the treason of one man cause something like this?"

"Not of one man, even a man in a position of power like Calladan. He holds dominion, yes, over large tracts of farmland, but we would have noticed earlier if his crop yields were significantly down. His betrayal would have been far too obvious. By all rights, the only mistake the man made was in trusting his wife."

We travel in troubled silence for a time. A patrol of the Wave rides past, their blue armor shining, magnificent in the morning sun. The soldiers appear nervous, their hands clutching the hilts of their swords, their captain taking them along the Way at a solid clip. People shy away from the horses, but some move aside with less haste. A few shout at the soldiers, their words angry but indistinct. The crowd has an ugly feel to it, as if some bitter poison creeps beneath the forlorn facade of the people. The Way feels suddenly busy, as if the traffic has picked up, but, glancing around, I can tell the feeling is false, derived more from my own anxiety than reality.

No violence breaks out, so we move on, but Poline keeps her hand on her sword, and I keep my hood pulled low over my face. People leave us alone, but more pointed glances come our way as if our gender and well-made clothing make us targets. The tension eases as the patrol passes out of sight, but only a little.

Soon, the farmland gives way to an offshoot of the Kinlen Forest, the trees encroaching almost to the edge of the Way. The distant sound of shouts echo back from ahead, but the voices ring jubilant, a marked difference from the anger directed at the Wave. Poline and I exchange uncertain looks. We are nearly to the point where we will diverge from the Way and head east towards Firdana, and the last thing we need is a distraction.

An open wagon trundles into sight, people crowding around and holding out their hands. A woman wearing well-fitted armor of leather drives, a bow comfortably balanced at her side. Two men stand in the back, tossing down something to the pack of people below: bread. The men are not accepting money, but instead gifting food to the desperate masses. They, too, are armored in quality leather, slightly worn from use, but well-cared for.

"Who are these people?" I ask.

Poline goes rigid next to me, the muscles of her jaw jumping under the skin as she grinds her teeth.

"Held," she grits out.

"I don't follow," I say, looking at her with concern. "What is being held?"

Poline ducks aside, drawing me gently after her. The wagon draws abreast of us, and I glance up at the men above. I meet the eye of one of them from under my hood, and he pauses, staring back for the briefest of moments. His thin cheekbones stand prominent and striking against his hair, the lustrous deep brown of coffee. Poline studiously looks the other way, slouching and using me as a shield from the wagon. An outcry distracts him, and he jolts back to his task, throwing some of the last loaves of bread to the waiting people.

"Held is a man," Poline speaks into my ear, her voice trembling with anger. "He was of the Tide."

"Was?" I ask, confused. "Members of the Tide swear their oaths for life."

People cheer and talk excitedly even after the food runs out. The edge of desperation has been dulled amongst the crowd as they revel in the unexpected gifts.

"Was. We came up through the training together, living and breathing and fighting beside one another. Even so, I was barely able to recognize him in time. He has changed much."

"How? Did he desert?"

"It's obvious now," Poline snarls. "He disappeared on a routine mission enforcing the will of the kingdom in the south near Itskalan. The kingdom refused to tell us much, but I spent a year trying to figure out what happened to them, what happened to my *brother,* as close to me as blood. A few members of his patrol were found dead, the cuts deep and precise, so perfect as to be impossible. The consensus was that the Vengeance had struck, murdering a patrol to weaken our hold on the region. The missing bodies were assumed to have been taken for torture, Held included."

"But that isn't what happened to him," I slowly say, my heart dropping into my shoes. I glance at Poline, but she only glares after the wagon.

"No," she says, not seeming to notice the tears gathering in the corner of her eyes. "He must have been part of it. He murdered our brothers and sisters and joined the Vengeance."

"Then why in the Creator's name are we letting him go?" I say, setting out after the wagon. I haven't gone a step when Poline's hand again grasps my arm. "What? They are traitors, members of the Vengeance's army."

"As much as I agree with you," Poline begins, her voice quavering between sorrow and anger. "Our mission is paramount. Held, for all his training, is just a soldier. A good one, but no more than a sword. Calladan represents something else entirely. We can't allow anyone of real power to defect, or we will soon find ourselves in civil war."

As logical and sound as Poline's reasoning is, I struggle not to run after the rebel soldiers myself. I've never met any real rebels face to face. I want to learn what makes them false, what can possibly force them to betray their oaths and everything they once held dear. I want to punish them, not only for daring to fight against my birthright and my father, but for daring to hurt Poline.

But she's right.

"Damn it," I spit, turning back roughly and heading off down the road. To Firdana.

***

The Kinlen Forest drops away behind us, the ominous mountain at its center the only indication of its dark depths. We leave the Way and follow the road to Elaren. Though well-maintained, the road is not so intricate or timeless as the Way of the East. The land grows more wild and untamed the farther we travel. The rolling meadows are lush and green in the fresh covering of Spring, gigantic wildflowers peeking over unending seas of tall grass as far as the eye can see. Occasional farmland encroaches on the shifting waves of grass, hugging the road as if afraid the wild will swallow them whole if built out of sight of civilization.

Our journey is peaceful and uneventful to Elaren, the only sizable town in Firdana. Elaren sprawls over several miles of land, streets broad and paved with flat flagstones. The roads curve gently around a motley assortment of homes and shops, mostly built of rustic wood but for the occasional cherry red of brick. Broad sweeping pastures and fallow fields surround the town. The town seems to have grown naturally around the wilderness rather than the reverse, and the quaint beauty of the place creates a natural peace. Oaks conquer a dozen town squares, their massive branches stretching over and around the homes, lending shade to the broad pathways under the gray beards of drooping moss.

A few farmers greet us pleasantly and smile as we move into the city. The people all move slowly, their gaits rolling and unconcerned, the clipped speed and stress of Donir entirely absent from the streets of Elaren. While the town itself can muster a fraction of the population of Donir, the sheer area the town occupies is nearly identical, so the people have the space to breathe.

I consider driving straight towards the Calladan estate, which stands on the opposite edge of town abutting a vast series of fields devoted solely to the training of Firdana's magnificent horses, but I reconsider after seeing myself in the clean glass of a shop window. Grime smudges my face, and my hair is a tangled mess. Though I don't need to look presentable in order to apprehend a criminal, a princess should still look the part. While I don't want to draw attention to us by walking into the most expensive establishment in Elaren and flagrantly flashing starsilver coins to the patrons, I also don't want to spend my time wondering if I'll be cohabitating with fleas and lice, so we rent a room at a decent, but far-from-ostentatious inn near the center of town. The woman running the inn is deliciously plump and cheerful, welcoming us and showing us to our room personally.

"Is there anything I could get the two of you ladies, aside from a hot bath?" the innkeep asks, smiling. I've just begun to settle onto my bed, letting my pack drop onto the polished wood floor, when I snap back to attention.

"Good lady, please, bring us twice the water you normally would. I want to *clean* myself, *then* take a bath," I say eagerly.

"Oh, darling, you do look tired. Have you walked far?" the woman asks, her smile understanding.

"We've come from—"

"All the way from Itskalan," Poline cuts in, affecting weariness. "We need the bath more than I would ever admit to anyone in public."

I blush, shooting Poline a look out of the corner of my eyes. The innkeep's friendly manner set me at ease, and, for a brief moment, I forgot entirely our purpose for being in Elaren. We can't be sure who might warn Calladan, as reports indicate he is well-loved amongst the people of Firdana. The woman doesn't seem to notice, but thanks us for our patronage and promises us warm baths in no time.

"Thanks for that," I say sheepishly, plopping down onto my bed.

"It's what I'm here for," Poline says languidly, already stretched out on the wooden floor next to her bed, hands behind her head.

"What are you doing?" I ask, amused. "You realize you have a bed right next to you."

"With the grime from the road and this thick layer of sweat caked in my hair? I'm most definitely waiting for the bath before I touch those clean sheets."

Jumping up, I groan aloud, scowling at my sheets, now slightly rumpled and most definitely dirtier than a moment ago. Poline cracks an eye and bursts into laughter.

"What?" I snap, annoyed.

"You should see the look on your face, Ily."

I open my mouth to give her a piece of my mind, but a knock interrupts me before I can get going. A pair of maids set up two copper tubs side by side, then scurry out the door. After a moment, they return with buckets, dumping the water in scalding hot. Steam fills the tiny room as the girls make a dozen trips up and down the stairs. I scarcely allow the water to cool enough not to outright burn me before I slip off my clothes and into the steaming water, sighing instantly in relief. My skin opens, my pores awaken, and a week of hard travel slides off my skin. Halfway through a thorough scrubbing, I notice Poline, still in her clothes.

"Poline, what in the Eternal's hell are you doing?"

"One of us must remain vigilant, *Ily*, or this adventure could quickly go awry."

"Poline," I say with all the dignity and authority I can muster whilst naked and half-covered in soap. "I command you into that water before it cools. I will take responsibility for our safety while we bathe. There is enough... in this room to serve should we have need."

She hesitates, briefly, but she can't hide her eagerness as she removes her clothing and efficiently folds each item into a neat pile. I can't look away from her, the scrubbing cloth in my hand forgotten. Her body is twisted, lean, *solid* muscle, various scars marring the otherwise pristine marble of her skin. Everything about her body screams warrior. It's remarkable that she manages to remain so innocuous in street clothes, like she's just another passing mercenary. Nude, no one could mistake Poline for anything but a trained and tested fighter.

She eases into the warm water, briefly groaning in happiness as tense muscles release under the water's steaming grip. I resume scrubbing, drawing on a tiny bit of the earth. My arm hardly glimmers in the bright light as a screen of particles, so small as to be invisible to the naked eye, form into a screen outside our door. I'll know if anything more solid than air disturbs them. Satisfied, I dunk my head deep under water, scrubbing furiously at my hair, my long locks floating in a halo around my head. At last feeling clean, I reach over and ring the bell.

The maids come to empty the tubs and bring us another batch of hot water. They don't comment on Poline's physique, though their eyes hardly leave her as they work. Good. Better Poline the center of attention than me. The second bath is even better, the heat of the water sinking deep into my bones.

"How do you wish to proceed?" Poline asks, her voice low. I sigh before I can stop myself. Back to business. "I believe we should announce our presence by walking straight through the front doors. Give Calladan no time to react, and take him into custody. His guards will not expect two women to be his jailers, and he will be helpless before your power. Any threat on his life will cause his retainers to hesitate."

"It won't be as simple as you claim; I'm sure of it. If we go in and he isn't at home, we could be ruining our chance to find him. Also, I don't want to endanger the life of the messenger, if he still lives," I respond in a whisper. "We need a covert reason to enter his estate, and some time to find his prison."

"The messenger is either dead or imprisoned, and our interference will change neither."

"How do you figure? Wouldn't you threaten a hostage if put in danger yourself?" I ask, curious.

"Ily... I don't mean to presume, but no one would ever believe a representative of your father would care the least for a simple messenger. A soldier's life would be a concern for... typical people. The Sealord and the Lord General do not constitute anything resembling typical. In fact, Ily, I'm surprised you care, considering. He is just a man, yes?"

Poline's sharp eyes search my face from under half-closed eyelids.

Why do I care? *Do* I care? A messenger, a soldier commanded to deliver paper from one place to another, is hardly worthy of my attention. My father's voice resonates behind the words, and I nod in time. The soldier had to know that not all messages he delivered would be pleasant to the listener, and to act accordingly. He's just a man. He's not a Shaper.

So why am I hesitating? The man doesn't deserve to die just because he delivered a message, but, as Father always says, normal people are as numerous as insects, and only marginally more important. Just as a maggot serves its function in the natural order, so do a farmer and a soldier and a merchant. A messenger knows the risks inherent in his position, especially in speaking for the Sealord. Poline is right.

"You're right," I say slowly. The rejuvenated feeling fades. Standing suddenly, I let the water cascade back into the tub as I reach for the drying cloth. "He's just a messenger."

Poline's posture shifts in the corner of my eye, as if she tenses. I try to meet her eye, but she shies away from my gaze. I rub the cloth against my skin, but the water no longer feels cleansing. Frowning, I step out of the tub to retrieve some clean clothes. I can feel something, there on the edge of my awareness.

Carefully, ever-so-slowly, I swirl the dust through the room. The particles of dust, so fine as to float on the air, caress Poline's face. She's watching me. I trace the contours of her face, mapping her expression through the path of the dust. I imagine it, my eyes planted firmly on the bed, my back turned to her view.

A look of melancholy paints her face, tinged with anger, a grimace of such disappointment and anguish I almost spin to see if the earth tells me true. But I don't need to. Poline is not looking at me as a friend, as we've pretended the last few weeks. She's not watching as a guardian would, protecting my back. She glares in betrayal, and I feel dirty under the weight of her eyes. My mind flits to Torlas. I try to imagine his face, smiling. Instead, I only see his eyes after I described the torture of the assassin.

A look of melancholy painting his face, tinged with anger, a grimace of total disappointment and anguish.

***

Despite the comfort of the inn, I don't sleep well. My relationship with Poline has grown over the years, both as my guard and sparring partner. I can count the number of people that I feel comfortable talking to on one hand, and I don't need all my fingers. Granted, Poline rarely has a choice in whether or not she desires to counsel a princess, but she's always been understanding, offering succinct advice that never crosses the border between soldier and royalty. The look on her face haunts my dreams, imagined or otherwise.

The harsh scrape of stone on metal awakens me. Sitting down on the bed, Poline slowly runs a whetstone along her sword, the rhythmic scrape grinding against my already-worn nerves. She refuses to meet my eye, an invisible wall erected between us in the night.

Hadn't I just agreed with her? She made a point, a valid one, that I was placing unimportant details before the completion of the mission as a whole. It had been Poline who argued for the direct approach, and innocent lives be damned. How can she blame me for agreeing with the very course of action she proposed?

"I think your sword is sharp enough," I snap, more peevishly than I intend. She doesn't react, just nods and slips the whetstone back into her pack.

"Well?" she says, standing and sheathing the weapon.

"I trust you to know when we have gone past peace and need to stray into violence," I say, turning and heading for the door. "The guards may allow us into the foyer, but we need to head for Calladan before he can mount any defense."

Despite the agreed-upon insignificance of the messenger, I still hope to find him alive. I know his name is Locke, and that Uncle values him for his talent and loyalty. Most official messengers serve as low-ranking members of the Wave, but Uncle knows this Locke personally. If we move fast enough, perhaps nothing untoward will happen at all. Uncle will be glad if the man is returned whole and hearty.

And I'll be glad, too.

Calladan's estate is impossible to miss. On the eastern edge of Elaren, the manse is a gorgeous representation of the aesthetic of the town. Trees weave in and around the washed white walls of the house itself, branches seeming to disappear into the upper floor's windows, though I'm sure that is an illusion in the dawn light. A low wall surrounds the house, ancient trees thrusting right up to the edge of lush green fields, horses galloping together in wild herds off in the distance. Nearer, stables many times the size of the estate flow organically around the ubiquitous oaks, stablehands of various ages leading horses to exercise in the morning light rising off the distant horizon. They each wear the forest green and silver of the Calladan household, as do the pair of guards standing at the gate.

They squint at us suspiciously, but don't reach for weapons. While Poline is well-armed, I appear to be little more than a girl, a simple brown dress swaying under my drab cloak.

"State your business," a guardswoman commands, gently holding a hand up to halt our progress. "What brings you so early to the Earl's estate?"

"We seek an audience with the Earl," I respond, bowing into a simple curtsy. "We have news of bandits in the south of his land."

"Bandits?" the woman asks, surprised. She exchanges a look with her compatriot. "How have you heard these rumors?"

"They are more than rumors," I answer, jutting out my lower lip slightly. "My father—"

"Her father was killed two weeks ago," Poline cuts in. "I was guarding a caravan visiting Piel, when we saw the smoke rising from the farmsteads to the south. By the time we arrived, the bandits were gone, and Serrah was the only survivor we could find. She hid in the bales of her family's hay."

"I'm sorry for your loss," the woman says, not without feeling. "I'll send word of this to the Earl."

"That's not good enough," I declare forcefully, stepping forward. "My family pays their taxes. We were deserving of protection. I want to speak with the Earl, to convince him to send men after those bandits."

"I can assure you that the Earl—"

"Let the girl speak to him," Poline interrupts. Her tone brooks no question and has the whip of a commander's displeasure behind it. The guards straighten subconsciously, barely avoiding saluting. "She deserves that much at least."

"Very well. We'll ask if the Earl can see you. In the meantime, I'll see if any refreshments can be brought to you. It's a long journey from Piel," the woman says, motioning to her partner to wait. The man on the left, more of a boy, really, squirms uncomfortably, but stays at attention until the woman returns a few minutes later and beckons for us to follow.

The interior of Calladan's estate matches the exterior: filled with rustic charm and a simple sort of beauty. Rich woods and delicate potted plants decorate every surface, creating a lush and vibrant atmosphere. The seats the guardswoman directs us to are of warm leather, the earthy brown perfectly complementing the natural tones throughout the house. I struggle not to feel at ease; the house seems as if it was designed for a Shaper of Earth to be comfortable.

Thinking about the clear signs of prosperity, understated as they might be, brings me back to the mission. Calladan is deliberately diverting food from hungry mouths throughout the kingdom to feed the rebels. The results of his efforts are more than apparent in our encounter on the Way. The common folk should be cheering the Wave and the Tide, not the damned rebels.

The guardswoman disappears through a door, and her footsteps retreat further into the house. She doesn't ascend any stairs. The Earl must be on our level. I catch Poline's eye, motioning with my chin towards the entrance. She rises silently, standing sentinel as she always has. I need her, because I'm going to try something that will require all my focus.

The earth comes willingly to my call, the shawl wrapped around my shoulders providing cover for the muted green glow. I don't command the earth, not in the usual way. I ignore the yearning to touch it, to Shape it, to command and have those commands answered. Instead, I simply feel. The sensation is instantly overwhelming. The earth permeates everything, from the dust particles floating through the air, the glass of the windows, the rich loam of the soil outside, the trace dirt on our clothes… I swirl in the eddying pockets of open space disturbed by our breathing. I grind against the wooden floors under Poline's boots as she shifts on the polished timbers. I vibrate ever so slightly from the early morning breeze shaking a window loose in its sill. I drift with the unceasing currents of the air.

I force myself to concentrate, to block out as much as possible so as not to get lost in the sensations of the earth. I narrow my focus, shutting out the myriad sensations around me and questing forth with my senses in the direction the guardswoman has gone. I ignore the dust built up in the corners, the tremor in the rich earth of a tree potted in the hall, the healthy soil falling from the boots of the...

I latch on to the dirt on the bottom of the guardswoman's boots. I rise, fall, rise, fall... I clench my eyes shut tightly, holding loosely to the feeling of the dirt but distancing myself from the actual sensation of *being* the earth. The movement stops, perhaps two dozen yards down the hall, and I let my senses drift outward from the woman's boots and onto the dust in the air. I follow the dust sucked into a room from a door's opening, slowly allowing my awareness to expand and fill the new room. It's large, with pieces of furniture difficult to discern through such a tenuous connection. I can feel the shape of two individuals through the dust, one seated, the other standing beside...

A window. Finally. I settle my focus on the window just as the door closes and the footsteps of the guardswoman sound in the hall back towards our sitting room. Distantly, I hear her enter, keeping my eyes closed, and Poline's reply, some explanation of stress and how long we've traveled...

My real focus, however, remains with the window. This particular skill is one my father doesn't know about, mainly because I'll lose my most effective means of spying on *his* secret meetings if I reveal it. Over the course of two years, playing around and experimenting with Torlas, I developed the ability to understand words through the vibrations of sound against glass. At first, it had been a joke between Torlas and me, him attempting to whisper against a pane of glass on the edge of the courtyard, me simply trying to understand what he spoke through the rhythms and cadences of his voice. As I got better, however, I realized how valuable a skill it could be to listen to someone from afar.

"...forget our strength remains thin."

The man at the window, his words clear, in control, close. His companion is too far from the glass, and I can't pick out his reply.

"We need to get you to safety. You know they'll send another assassin before long, if they don't show up with a contingent of the Tide and take you overtly."

Another assassin? I frown, confused. The other man's voice drifts closer. He approaches the window.

"...little good to anyone hiding out in the woods with the rest of you. My value—"

"Lies in your life. Dead, you serve no one, and do good for no one. This cause has enough martyrs, Markis. They've never galvanized the people to action. We need the living far more than the dead."

"But my people... Will there not be repercussions? Will the Sealord not strike at them for assisting me? I cannot protect them if I run."

"And you can protect them even less if you die. Or, worse, if you're taken. The longer you wait, the more likely you are to make them *a target for Helikos to use against* you. *Your love of Firdana is well known."*

"Very well, Altos. I'll—"

I snap back to the present, sucking in a lungful of air in a sudden gasp. Poline turns to me, alarmed, but I can't speak for a moment. Altos. Altos. The Eternal-damned *Vengeance* is a dozen yards from me. What in the Creator's name am I supposed to do? The Vengeance. The Scourge of the Council. The Master of Air. My enemy. Should I strike? Should I run? My heart races, my pulse thrumming at a breakneck speed.

"Poline," I gasp in a strangled whisper. "Come here, please."

“Ily?” Poline says in concern, sitting down next to me. My hand finds hers of its own accord, my wide eyes meeting her brilliant emerald gaze, seeking answers.

“He is here,” I whisper.

“Good...” Poline begins, eyebrows raising. “According to plan...”

“No, Poline. *He* is here. Our enemy.”

Poline's eyes widen to match my own, glancing around and taking in everything in a heartbeat. The guard waits just outside, her back to us, having told us we’ll have to wait half an hour before Calladan can see us. Poline stands, her hand grasping the hilt of her sword. I grab her arm.

“What are you doing?” I hiss in.

“I...” Poline trails off, looking down at the hand grasping her sword. That sword has been through much, I’m sure. She fought in a half dozen engagements with the barbarian tribes to the north before being promoted to the Tide by the Lord General. Poline fears little, but what can mere steel do against the power of the air, when so many of her own brothers and sisters have fallen to his cursed power? She looks to me. “What do we do? Can you, well?”

“I have no idea.”

How do you know when you’re ready? When you can surmount the greatest obstacle of your life? Can you ever? Some people wilt beneath the pressure or leave the task to others. Some people bravely stand and just as bravely fall. And a very lucky few succeed. I’m in my crucible, my trial. Who will I be? I peer into Poline's eyes, and she slowly nods. Our time. Our chance. To end the greatest threat to my life and my kingdom.

Our whispered conversation attracts the attention of the guard, who frowns. She starts to come over, our jerky and frantic movements no doubt suspicious. My eyes flick towards her. Poline moves so quickly that, between heartbeats, the guard drops to become an unconscious ornament on the floor. Poline lowers her to the ground almost gently, the corner of her jaw already swelling with the imprint of the Tide's sword pommel. I spin my hair into a tight bun, only a few locks escaping in my haste. With a deep breath, I lead us towards the back room.

We creep through the open doorway, moving as silently as we can. I command the earth to me, the soil from the plants potted throughout the hallway coming silently to my call. Some of it becomes daggers of glass, more than a dozen floating and moving about my person, more drifts under my clothing, a thin layer of moving, living armor. The Vengeance is a famed swordsman and one of the most legendary Shapers of the last thousand years. Sweat clings to the stray locks of my hair, and I lick suddenly dry lips. Who am I to challenge the Vengeance? Why can't it have happened in five years? A decade? With more time to hone my skills, to scratch and pull and fight for more power and control?

You are the Creator-blessed Shaper of Earth. You've lived for this moment, trained for it, fought for it. He won't expect an attack in his ally's own home. Even if he does, he cannot expect to be faced with you.

Gritting my teeth, my feet silently slide along the polished wooden floors. The distant sound of other activity strays into the hall from other parts of the estate. We don't need to remain in secret long, just a precious few moments.

I pull up a few steps short of the door. Something, some instinct, tells me to stop before. Poline halts with me, her sword gleaming in the dim hallway.

Something feels... off. I reach forward with the dust circling us, and it swirls back into my face. I blink. I push the dust forward again, and again, the dust drifts back to me instead of moving forward. It's almost as if the air itself...

"Go," I say, and turn my stalk into a sprint. An invisible wall of air, nearly imperceptible to my skin, shatters as I dash the final few steps to the door. The Vengeance maintains a barrier across the hall, much like the near-invisible wall of dust I utilized at the inn. As soon as anyone breaks through the barrier, he'll know. We can't give him time to react.

A thick clod of dirt breaks free from my natural armor, forming into a compact and heavy fist, which pummels the door just next to the handle. With a crunch of shattering wood, the door bursts asunder. I dive in when it springs open, rolling into a crouch as the door slams closed from a powerful gust of wind just behind me, clipping Poline on the shoulder and sending her graceful dive into a headlong crash. I won't be able to count on her for precious seconds.

Wide windows let in a gorgeous view of the rising sun to the east. A desk, over which Poline awkwardly sprawls, occupies the far wall, and a pair of leather chairs sit near the windows. Calladan sits in the chair on the left, his mouth agape. With his brown hair cut short, a trimmed beard lends his face a bit of natural charm he would otherwise lack. My eyes leave him almost before they finish seeing him, the level of threat he represents so low that he doesn't bear a second thought.

The Vengeance, however, carries all my attention. A slender man, his hair is blond, long, and unruly. His fair skin is tanned dark from the sun, and a few wrinkles around his eyes mar an otherwise youthful face. He could be anywhere from twenty to thirty-five, but I know the weight of centuries sits behind those eyes. His hands loosely hold a sword of a design I've never seen. Reaching nearly to the floor, the blade is long and single-edged, a gentle curve gliding into a deadly point. The edge catches the light in the rising sun, bursting into sparkles unnatural to steel, almost as if the blade is crafted of gemstones.

A piercing gray the color of the ocean in storm, his eyes hold less feeling than nature has for man. There's no surprise or alarm, no confidence or arrogance; the Vengeance reveals nothing. He just... is. If I thought I was going to surprise this man, this Shaper who has existed for three hundred years of long and perilous life, I was grossly mistaken. His left hand glimmers a shimmering white, a rune of power quietly awakened and prominently displayed. My own shoulder blazes, green light warring with the rays of the rising sun.

"The princess..." Calladan says, his voice strangled. "I never thought he would send *her*."

The Vengeance and I ignore him, even as Poline rights herself and holds her blade at the ready to defend me.

"Vengeance," I say, damning myself for the tremor in my voice. I *will* stand firm before my enemy. "You will surrender and come with me to face judgment before my father."

He doesn't outwardly react, but in his eyes kindle a flame beyond anger. A simmering, palpable hatred, almost as if he can reach across and slay me just with the power of his loathing. His mouth opens, revealing perfect teeth.

"Not likely," he says, as if discussing the weather. "You'll be coming with me. I'd never thought to find you so lightly protected. Helikos is a fool to let you out of his control."

"Do not speak my father's name so blithely, bastard," I spit. "Address him with the proper respect, as is due your king."

"Father?" the Vengeance answers, his tone just as mild. "King? These are titles that madman has never earned."

I'm done talking to the man. He murdered half a dozen Shapers of the Council and precipitated the dissolution of a government that lasted for five millennia. Words will do nothing to break his careful facade. Perhaps actions can serve.

In a blaze of renewed emerald light, the window behind him shatters into a dozen razor-sharp shards, speeding at his back as quickly as thought. Gracefully, almost casually, he slides to the side, his own mark of power still faint, the shards missing him by inches. I reverse their course, ignoring Calladan as he engages Poline. The glimmering shards dart at the Vengeance from every direction. He spins in place, his sword licking out and shattering the blades. Before long, all of my shards of glass are little more than glittering dust. His hand twirls in a brief motion. The wind picks up, carrying the broken shards out into the morning light no matter how hard I drive my will against his.

His symbol remains dim.

He isn't even exerting himself.

With a growl, I dart forward, glittering blades swirling around me, earthen armor shifting and moving. I leap into the air and come down swinging, a flashy distraction. A pair of glass blades slide along the floor and strike the Vengeance in each calf. Or, at least, that's what's supposed to happen. As soon as my feet leave the floor, he raises his hand. A fist of solid air blasts into my chest, and my breath leaves in a whoosh. My momentum halted, I drop to the ground clumsily, struggling to breathe. Even through my armor, the blow *hurts*.

Scrambling to my feet, I warily edge nearer to the Vengeance, who still holds his blade as if it's an umbrella and he's out for a casual stroll. I spin forward, throwing dust towards his eyes, sending blades at his back, and lunging with my own tightly grasped daggers. He lithely spins in place, the blades missing him by a hairsbreadth, his sword almost as an afterthought, deflecting aside occasional ineffectual attacks. A lunge carries me past the man, then again. He's a ghost. In three strikes, he's never where I expect him to be. I have to turn the next attack into a forward roll to avoid his blade slicing where my head would have been.

I spin back to face him in a crouch. He still stands calmly, his expression unchanged. I'm gasping, my heart thudding deep in my chest. I force myself to take a calm, deep breath. My pulse slows. Well. I didn't expect to beat the man fairly, did I? I'll need to cheat, to do something he can't anticipate.

Wading back in, I offer a few more lackluster blows, trying to lull him into believing that yes, these attacks are the best I can do, yes, I really am just a girl playing with her power, yes, I'm beginning to tire, to fear...

As he blocks another attack, I send my energy into the glass. The blade elongates instantly, turning from a dagger into a sword. The man's eyes widen minutely, his face mirrored in the reflection of the swiftly approaching point. At the last moment, Creator, *after* the last moment, the man moves his head aside, smooth, controlled, and hellishly fast. The edge draws a thin line of blood down his left cheek, missing his eye by the width of a finger.

Just as a feeling of triumph wells in my breast, the Vengeance's sword sweeps up faster than I can register. I blink, and my cheek kisses wood, my eyes now studying the grain of the floor. I struggle to move, some distant part of me recognizing how very dangerous my position is. My vision crosses, then drifts, coming to rest on the sun rising high enough over the windowsill to be seen from the floor. Creator. He hit me so hard I'm facing the opposite direction.

But somehow, I'm not dead. Awareness starts to return to my body, beginning with the trickle of blood wending its way down my cheek. My hands twitch, one twisted awkwardly behind and under my body. Groaning, I lever myself onto my back, spots swimming in front of my eyes like flies around a corpse wagon. The sound of steel clashing brings me rushing back to the present. My head lolls to the side, focusing blearily on a pair of figures dancing back and forth. Their movements are too fast to follow through the blurriness of my vision.

Narrowing my eyes, I manage to sharpen my vision enough to make out how the fight is going. Not well. Poline retreats constantly before the Vengeance's attack, somehow avoiding putting her back to a wall by experience, speed, and luck. She works for more room, using the chairs and the table to avoid being trapped. but the Vengeance is fast, too fast, his sword gleaming and darting, always in motion, always flowing, less predictable than the zephyrs the man controls.

I need to get up. I *have* to get back into the fight. Calling on reserves I'm not sure I possess, I sit up and shake my head through the pain. A grunt from the side snaps my focus back to the fight. Poline staggers back from a square shot to the temple, blood streaming down her face from the blow. She manages to fend off one attack, her sword desperately sticking in the wooden floor and defeating the Vengeance's strike with a screech of metal grinding.

He spins, impossibly fluid, and kicks the blade out of her hand. It sails cleanly through the broken window, catching the morning sunshine in a flash of liquid gold. The Vengeance raises his sword, quickly, efficiently. Poline glares up at him, blinking blood out of her eye and refusing to look away. He pauses. Offers the soldier of the Tide a brief nod of respect. Then, he strikes.

"Poline!" I scream, my voice tearing, my heart burning, my lungs locking.

I don't know what debilitating, racing fire suddenly arcs through me. The need, the horrible despair, knowing that perhaps the one friend I have in this Eternal-stained world will be gone, never again to stand at my side. I can never be in time, the sword will strike whatever I do, but still I beg the earth to save Poline regardless, casting my entire soul into that aching, burning *need.* The earth groans, as if the very world will break at my command. The house shakes, the ground splitting asunder, and an unending torrent of earth drives up through the foundations and crashes into the ceiling, a living wall between my friend and the Vengeance.

The explosion of earth clips the Vengeance, spinning him away and slamming his back into the far wall. He lands, somehow still on his feet, sword still in hand. My need to protect Poline turns into a blinding, desperate *hatred* of the man who would *dare* to threaten my friend. The wall of earth seeks to smother, to crush, to obliterate the bones and sinews of this enemy before he can recover, before he can ever cause me such pain again.

Quick as lightning, sliding just on the edge of the wall, propelled by a gale of rising wind which drives me flat, just before the edge of the collapsing wall of raw earth, he darts out of the broken window and into the open air. I fight against the wind, struggling to my feet and glaring after him. Unbelievably, the man is nowhere to be seen. The empty grounds beyond the window mock me with their serenity. The grass is no longer even and smooth, but rumpled and broken from the shock of the wall of earth now occupying Calladan's study. Somehow, the Vengeance is gone, no trace of his lean figure on the uneven grass.

I sag, exhaustion striking me as surely as any blade, nearly falling if not for a desperate grab at the windowsill. The action forces my eyes upward, and there he is. Already small and growing smaller by the second, he literally *flies* through the morning air. His hair flows behind him, his head leading, his sword gleaming like the trail of a comet behind him. He grows to be a speck, then disappears before he crests the horizon, moving so fast that in the space of a dozen heartbeats, he's gone.

I shake my head in disbelief. The man is legend incarnate. No Master of Air has flown since the days of the Eternal. He could have crushed me under heel with that kind of power. I shudder to think of how close I've come to being his prisoner. I would never have seen Donir again, never have seen my father again.

The act of standing up after the massive outburst of power is too much for my drained body. Even as I fall, a pair of strong arms wrap around me and hold me up. I meet Poline's beautiful emerald eyes.

"I thought I was too late," I say, wonder in my voice.

"You were," Poline answers, voice thick with emotion.

"What?" I ask, my mind muddled, darkness creeping into the corners of my vision.

"He hesitated. When you screamed my name, he stopped his strike. He... spared me."

Chapter 12
Bastian
A Day.
A Year.

"We cannot let him live," a voice echoes, elegant, refined, with an accent I can't place. Female.

"You know we can't let him die," another answers, male, with a recognizable Khalintari accent, though it is... off somehow.

"He is loathsome. He abuses the blessing he has been gifted. He is an abomination," the first voice continues.

"Yes, yes, and in your day, he would have been hunted like a dog. We've been over this," a third voice cuts in, young, spunky, the voice of a girl.

"Elitrea's vision is clear," the second voice picks up again. "As distasteful as it may be... he is critical."

"Pah, bullshit," a fourth voice, deep and aggressively masculine. Though I understand every word, he's speaking a language foreign to me. "Her damned visions are not infallible. For all we know, she foresaw this time period and began dreaming of just these very futures in order to convince us to spare him. He could very well be the reason we lose."

"That is far-fetched, even for you," the Khalintari says, an eye-roll in his voice. "Elitrea is cunning, yes, but we know she lost her sanity long ago."

"As hesitant as I am to admit it, I agree with the Dedarian," the first woman again. "To be safe, we should wipe this thing from—"

"Enough," a girl, her voice cracking like a whip. The command, spoken so powerfully in the voice of a tiny child, is jarring. "We have argued about this long enough. He's a terrible person, yes. He abuses

women, terrifies men, and uses his power for selfish ends. But. He is powerful. We have trusted the Queen's visions for all this time. We will not falter now. He lives."

"I demand a vote, for posterity," the first woman declares, miffed to be out maneuvered.

"Very well," the girl answers with a resigned sigh. "Those in favor of sparing the boy and staying true to the Queen's visions?"

A dozen voices, no, two dozen or more echo suddenly into being, overlapping one another and swirling back and forth like waves before finally subsiding into silence.

"He lives," the girl says quietly. "Wake up, Bastian."

The glare of sunlight burns through my eyelids. I send the message to open my eyes, but they refuse. In fact, no muscle responds to my commands, like someone shattered my spine and left me for dead. Slowly, as if from a great distance, the sound of distant children's laughter floats to my ears, along with the creak of wood flexing in the heat of the sun nearby. My skin is hot, clammy, as if I've run a long race or languished in a sauna. The air itself moves listlessly across my skin, the gentlest of breezes hardly stirring the hairs on my bare arms. The smells are foreign, wild, yet intoxicating, something of citrus and sunlight.

Finally, my eyes open. They close instantly as I squint against a rising tide of tears. Blast it, that *hurt*. What I saw isn't encouraging, either. Slowly, I crack my left eye, enduring a splitting headache as I adjust to even the tiniest bit of light. After a few minutes, I can open my eyes fully, though my head lolls weakly, as if I'm little more than a newborn child.

The sound of wood is a cage, not metal, sinister contraption built of bars and cold steel, but a cage woven of bamboo and held together with what looks like long, durable grass. The sun peeks through large gaps in the bars, large enough I imagine I could slip out with a bit of creative stretching. If I can get my legs and arms to obey my commands, that is. Or even my damn neck. I throw my head forward, or try to, but all I manage is a twitch. My face swings to face the other side of the cage.

The air saturates my skin in a suffocating blanket of humidity and heat. A short clearing of brilliant emerald ferns wave in the gentle breeze before abruptly ending at a forbidding wall of tropical greenery. Trees stretch up and out of sight into the sky, the space between them choked with an endless variety of plants: flowers, ferns, reeds, bushes, vines, and the like.

A tingling starts in my left hand, slowly spreading upwards to encompass my forearm. Finally, perhaps I'm getting back some of the feeling. I manage to roll my head over and glance down to see if the desperate desire to move is having any effect on my limp fingers.

A thick, hideous worm with a warlike carapace and an endless series of legs crawls up my arm, the arm that remains perfectly peaceful despite my frantic internal screams to move, to fling this horrifying thing off of me, to save myself before the damned thing *eats* me... I whimper as the ugly creature continues to crawl up, reaching my chest. More than half of its length is still on the ground, its innumerable legs driving its thick mass further onto my body. Two massive antennae stretch from its face, brushing the bottom of my jaw and eliciting a squeal from deep in my chest. It pauses, turning towards me and dragging its feelers up and down my bobbing, vulnerable neck.

It's going to eat me, it's going to rear up and bite my throat, and I'll never have any idea where this Creator-forsaken jungle is or why I'm in a cage or what in the ever-loving *fuck* happened to paralyze me and allow an Eternal-kissing *monster* to devour—

The creature disappears as if by magic. One moment, it was preparing to chomp down on my throat, the next it's gone, the only sign of its disappearance a brown pole bisecting my vision and blocking out the sun. I twitch, sending my dysfunctional head rolling around. My eyes follow the line of the pole, and my dull mind finally recognizes the well-worn haft of a spear. A pair of slender hands grip it, connected to a pair of powerful arms, over which hovers a sneering face.

"Captain," I say, though my tongue seems to stick in my mouth. I swallow thickly, feeling lucky to be able to do so. "How nice to see you."

"I wish I could say the same, Cursed," she says in her musical accent, turning and spitting off to the side. "I regret to the bottom of my cherished heart that I was just forced to save your life. Again."

"Captain, could you perhaps answer me a single question?"

Te'ial doesn't respond other than to twist her spear, and the unfortunate crunch off to the side seems to signal the end of the horrible monster. Te'ial looks the same, and yet... somehow different. I can't place the change, but something about the woman is clearly off.

"Why can't I move my body?"

"You've been drugged. Your mind has recovered, as the Seer has foreseen. Your body will soon follow. Though you may find yourself weaker than you remember," Te'ial answers through gritted teeth, as if being anywhere near me is an affront. Even as she speaks, my fingers begin to tingle. Terrified, I glance down, but this time, my fingers move in accordance with my commands. No monster. I sigh in relief.

Te'ial sees the motion, but wordlessly turns and strides away, her lithe form swaying as if she still walks on her ship. I want to call after her, but I'm more preoccupied with the sudden return of sensation to my body. The tingling shifts into a thousand needles jabbing my flesh, and I cough out a strangled cry of pain, curling up on the dirt floor of my cage and clawing at the earth and straw. My entire body trembles, from the skin of my back to the edge of my fingernails, the needles rising to an unending crescendo of pain and overwhelming sensation.

I shudder through endless shallow breaths, even my lungs abused and disoriented. Creator knows how long it takes, but the pain abates, the unending sharp waves of agony fading into nothing. Its absence is almost as shocking as the pain itself. I dully roll onto my back, my thoughts jumbled and slow. My mind is a difficult terrain to traverse, the edges rocky and uneven.

The setting sun dips behind the jungle to the west. The entire day was spent in shuddering misery. My muscles respond lethargically at best, twinging and rippling strangely at my commands. I make it halfway to a sitting position before I collapse back and to the ground, my stomach muscles burning. I lift my arm, holding my hand before my face. The fingers are slender, too slender, the nails dirty and untrimmed, longer than I'd ever let them grow. My arm trembles even at that pathetic effort, sinking against my will to rest on my chest. I feel like a stack of bones with too-little skin stretched too-tightly overtop. A beard adorns my face, and I twitch with shock as my hand, near the center of my chest, brushes the edges of that beard.

"Food, Cursed," Te'ial's voice rings from above my head, the scorn and hate practically crawling along my scalp, as if she would rather be cutting out my eyes than feeding me.

She carefully places a wooden bowl on the ground between us. The smell of something warm and hearty with just a bite of spice drifts on the air. I roll over, suddenly ravenous, and reach a shivering hand out towards the food. My hand knocks against the bowl clumsily, but Te'ial is there, steadying my hand so that the soup won't be wasted. After my third attempt fails as miserably as the first, she pulls it out of my reach. I loathe myself for whimpering as the food leaves my sight.

"*El'ti'raniuk,* Cursed. You are worthless," Te'ial spits, the unfamiliar word carrying such vitriol I've no doubt she's insulting me.

A strong hand grabs my tunic and drags me over to the edge of the cage. With a grunt, she props me up, threading her arms through the bars and bringing the bowl to my lips. Greedily, I suck at the broth, choking on the spice and the unfamiliar flavors but unable to stop. She pulls the bowl away, bringing a cloth to my face and wiping my soiled beard clean. The gesture could almost be interpreted as tender, but she jams the bowl back to my lips and forces more of the burning liquid down my throat.

When I finish the bowl, she walks away without a second glance. I turn to roll after her, but instead just slump to the ground. Creator, even my heart beats strangely, and my body refuses to respond to my call. My legs twist about on the ground, useless, dancing to an unheard beat. My arms tremble at the barest sign of activity, my once-nimble fingers reduced to clubs wielded by thugs at midnight. I'm a prisoner in my own body, screaming silently.

With extraordinary effort, I manage to lock one hand awkwardly around one of the bars, pulling myself halfway to my feet. My legs strain, lifting my body partly off the ground. I feel light, far too light, but my weight is still too much for my quivering legs to bear. I flop back to the ground painfully, what little I have that passes for muscles burning and overexerted.

What have they done to me?

Te'ial stopped her walk at the sound of my efforts, turning to watch my pitiful efforts. I whimper, more beaten dog than man. A spark of the man I was tries to catch in the ashes of my pride, but can find no kindling. Let her watch. The first tear, when it comes, is long into the minutes of dry sobs that wrack my emaciated body.

***

The morning dawns, muggy and humid. Misery mounted me and rode me mercilessly into unconsciousness some time after midnight. With a titanic effort, straining for five minutes or more, I manage to drag myself into a sitting position, back against the bars. My neck muscles soon protest, and I have to let my head loll against my chest. The sights aren't exactly compelling, anyway. A village, made mostly of wood and thatch, stands in the near distance. All other directions are blocked by impenetrable jungle.

My mind, once a keen blade, is now a dull razor, sliding roughly over the surface of my thoughts. It's painful to think, painful to breathe, painful to even exist. I'm clearly far to the south, deep in the Broken Isles, either on the Isle of the Seers or nearby. How the Seers kept me from waking for the journey is beyond me, because the journey from north of Halfway back to the far southern continent takes months.

Hang in there, Lav. I'll get out of here before anything can happen to you.

When Te'ial brings my breakfast, she initially pulls back, her nose wrinkling. Of course, with no ability to move, I pissed and shit all over myself in the night. Despite the stench, she dutifully kneels and offers me the bowl. She has to hold the bowl to my lips again, coddling me like a wounded fawn. She gets up to leave, half of the soup spilled in my beard or on my chest, but I reach out, grasping at her hand.

"Captain," I say, my voice sore from the unrelenting sobs of the previous night. "Where am I?"

"You are in the care," she spits the word like a curse. "Of the People. Let me be the first and the last to welcome you to Oti'lent."

"Thank you for the welcome, however begrudged. I know it can't be... easy, looking after someone you so clearly despise."

"I will do my duty as the Seer commands," Te'ial says woodenly, her words more rehearsed than genuine. "No matter how distasteful."

"Captain."

"Stop calling me that, *thriska* Cursed," she growls. "Your taint has cost me my ship."

"What?"

"The Seer foresaw the day in which I would discover a Cursed and bring him before her," she says, her voice distant. "When that day came, I would lose my ability to sail free. I would only sail when and where the Seer commands."

"Why would you allow someone to take your ship from you? You were a fantastic captain, from what I could see."

"When you meet the Seer, you will understand," she responds, shaking her head. She glances at me, her lip curling, and the moment of vulnerability closes as surely as a slammed door. "Work your limbs, Cursed. Recover your strength. You are to meet the Seer soon, and she will not demean herself by walking out to your... sty."

"Wait, Captain, one last thing," I call to her, and she turns. "How long have I been out? I've never been to this part of the world, so I do not know the season."

"It is Spring, though it shall quickly move to Summer. The year's long day approaches," Te'ial says, and I sag in relief. It's only been a few weeks. I can make it back to Lav and make things right in time, but Te'ial lingers. She stares at me with a sudden hunger in her gaze. Fear starts to worm its way into my belly, curling around my spine and clenching there tightly.

"You didn't answer my question," I say, the words grinding out of me, the impossible truth slowly beginning to dawn on my cracked and unsteady mind. "How long have I been out?"

"It is Spring," Te'ial says again, smiling a wicked smile. "In the year 5222, Council reckoning. You have been sleeping for more than two years."

Feeling fades. Sense fades. My vision narrows to a point, then disappears. Two years. Two long years. Two years and the months I spent on the journey to Donir, the weeks I wasted feasting. Two years. Lav... Eternal damn my soul... Lav... What have they done to you? Have they taken care of you? Is it even possible?

"Let me out."

The words come from a distance, grating against the back of my throat like a rusted razor over stone. Raw, broken my voice is little more than a whisper.

"You will meet the Seer, and she will determine your fate," Te'ial calls, almost crowing in her awful jubilation.

"Let me out."

"Listen, Cursed, our conversation is over—"

"LET ME OUT," I scream, my eyes focusing, my hands drawing up to squeeze the bars of my pathetic little cage. "I NEED TO LEAVE."

My arms lose their tremble. My mind burns away the mist smothering my thoughts. I scramble up, one hand squeezing the wooden bar so hard it cracks, lunging forward with the other hand and reaching out into the open air.

I can barely focus. My breath comes in ragged gasps. My vision wavers between a red haze and the startled brown face in front of me. I strain, slamming my shoulder again and again against the small gap in the bars, more beast than man, scrabbling mindlessly at a trap. A silver glow pierces the early morning air, and the woman squints, raising a hand before her eyes.

Her thoughts lay themselves out before me, a churning cauldron of hatred, a fading glee, and a rising tide of fear. I growl, crushing the pitiful thoughts that dance across the surface of her brain, slamming my own desire, my need, over and over again at her faltering brain like a hammer on an unwitting nail.

LET ME FREE. LET ME FREE. LET ME FREE.

She falls to her knees, grasping at her head, hands pressed against her eyes as she screams out her pain on the ground. Even so, she starts to crawl towards me, whimpering and rolling, her mind begging her body to bring her forward so she can do as commanded. Anything to stop the pain, anything to stop the unceasing command.

LET ME FREE. LET ME FREE. LET ME FREE.

Others appear, dark faces in the light of my silver glow, shock and fear blanketing their expressions. I shout, reaching for their minds, but...

The silver light winks out, the sudden silence as deep as the roar of my thoughts the moment before, my energy completely spent. My body drops out from under me like a puppet with cut strings. My muscles refuse all commands, twitching and rippling weakly under my too-tight skin. Te'ial moans in agony nearby, though I can't stir myself even to roll my head to the side. Instead, my eyes stare sightlessly upward, not even squinting as the sun finally crests the jungle trees.

Lav, how could this have happened? After everything I've done, after all this time... Oh, Lav, can you forgive me? Does your soul look down with hatred? I abandoned you. I let *them* abandon you. You never stood a chance without me, and now... now... I break into quiet tears, the weeping so gentle as to be impossible to separate from my ragged breathing. No matter how physically gentle they remain, the tiny tremors reverberate a hellish pulse of agony with each trembling sob. My spirit wilts before the onslaught, the grief like bitter swords piercing, piercing.

The light of the sun breaks before a shadow. My eyes struggle to focus, the burning orb of morning scorched into my sight for long moments. Finally, my watering gaze focuses on the source of my shade: a woman, tall and proud, her frame powerful and intimidating despite the gray of her hair and the wrinkles on her face. She wears an elaborate series of sashes pinned with various trinkets and adornments, a strange, incongruous collection of odds and ends. A pair of feathers, old and yellowed with age. A knife no larger than a child's thumb, the grip made of curling gold. A silver ring, reflecting the light of the sun in a burning gleam. A hook, ornately carved from the bone of some long dead creature.

Her eyes are liquid pools of the deepest umber. Reflected there... compassion. Sympathy. A depth of understanding I never imagined could exist. Those eyes hold me, stilling the sobs deep in the confines of my chest before they can wrack my spirit any further. She smiles, a deep dimple appearing in her ebony skin.

"Who are you?" I ask, hoarse and shattered.

"I am the Seer," she answers, her voice deep, melodious and certain the sound a distant bell, sonorous, somber, yet welcoming. My mind quiets before the presence of this stranger. "What causes you such pain?"

She knows the answer. The cant of her eyes, the gentle tilt of her head, the barest impression of her thoughts… she knows why I've lost my mind, part of me still sobbing out the unrelenting pain of it. Even so, my mouth opens, my abused vocal cords straining to tell her, to let someone else feel this mountain of pain.

"Lav," I whisper, the sorrow so powerful it almost overcomes the serenity this woman bears. "My brother. I've failed him."

"How have you failed him, Bastian?" the woman asks, her eyes full of all the sympathy the world can express, the tenderness a mother holds for a babe.

"He can't look after himself," I manage, my eyes closing, tears squeezing out to patter uselessly on the earth. "He needs me."

"Why?" her voice approaches, forcing my eyes open, forcing me to focus on the present and forget the grief, if only for a moment.

"Our parents... they..." I can't force the words out through the lump in my throat.

Don't tell me, a voice speaks in my mind, but not just a single voice. Another voice, hidden and practically in sync, echoes behind the words of the Seer. Someone strangely familiar, higher and more feminine than the Seer herself. *Show me.*

"Bastian!" Elina calls from the kitchen in surprise, a smile broadening on her beautiful features. "We didn't expect you for another month. I thought you were on a trip with your master?"

"We were able to conclude our business before we anticipated," I mutter, struggling not to slam the door behind me. I hate coming back home, especially for visits like this.

"Nomman!" Elina calls, her voice echoing cheerfully through the house. "Our son has come back to visit!"

Nomman stirs upstairs, rousing himself from a nap at the sudden activity.

The furniture remains the same, placed the same, worn the same, exactly as has been frozen in my memory for the past decade. The house is a small, two-story affair, but few can afford even this paltry modicum of space and comfort in Coin. We have a tiny piece of lawn behind the house, a washline of clothes fluttering there gently in the breeze, the bright reds and blues of Khalintari garb. Elina still cooks the same meals; the aroma of her crab soup drifts through the house like some tantalizing reminder of better times. The sound of the same stone bowls rings off of the same stone counter.

Nomman walks down the stairs, smile falling away from his face at the sight of my scowl. A glimmer of fear thrills through him, the plucking of the first string of a symphony of terror. I leaf idly through his thoughts. He knows something is wrong, though he has no idea why a singular look at my face should send such a spasm of horror through him. Still, he feels it.

As well he should.

"Son," Nomman says anyway, recovering his smile. He enfolds me in a hug, which I return, squeezing too tightly to be comfortable. He extricates himself shakily, keeping his wooden smile plastered on his face. "How was the trip?"

"It was lucrative. The Sealord's negotiators were remarkably apt to agree to our terms."

"That's great!" Nomman says, grabbing my shoulders and shaking me slightly. I resist the urge to hit him. "Elina, did you hear?"

"What, Nomman?"

"Bastian's work went well again! As we always knew it would. Our prodigy," Nomman says, leaning back and looking on me with pride.

"And what of your other son?" I bite out, rage lurking far too close to the surface. "Where is Lav?"

"Lavilion is fine, Bastian," Nomman says, glancing behind him towards the common room. "He is resting, but we took him out earlier today. The wheeled chair you sent back from your travels was perfect."

"We'll see," I say, brushing past Nomman and walking farther into the house.

"Bastian," Elina calls. "Should I add to the soup? Will you be staying for dinner?"

"Yes, Bastian, please stay. We would love to hear the story of your journey," Nomman adds behind me.

"I'll stay for dinner," I say over my shoulder. "I wouldn't miss it for the world."

I ignore their excited chatter, their damning lies, their casual disregard. My brother's room is in disarray: disheveled sheets, cobwebs in the corner, curtains drawn against the evening sun, offering barely a glimmer of light to illuminate the cramped little room. I stalk to the window, stepping past several stains on the floor. Healthy light filters in as I spread the drapes.

A grunt sounds from the corner. A man sits, thin as glass, frail as flowers, huddling in a polished wooden chair attached to a pair of large wheels. His shirt is soiled from a dozen spilled meals, his chin still bearing the remnants of their last attempt. His eyes squint against the light, though they focus on nothing. An unruly mop of black, matted hair hides most of his face.

Lav. My big brother.

I stalk out the back door, grabbing a clean towel from the line out back, slinging a heavy bucket over to the water pump. Slowly, carefully ignoring the eyes regarding me from the kitchen, I pump the bucket full and stagger back under the load.

"Let's get you cleaned up," I say, my voice soft.

Absently, I reach out to his thoughts. They are the same: the familiar fear and hunger and weariness, emotions a flickering kaleidoscope, merging into and around one another, an unruly mess of feeling for a broken mind. The flashes of memory are similarly shattered, brief images of three faces: Elina's, Nomman's, and my own, but only as if time has been reversed. Elina and Nomman look happy, content, even joyful in the brief but lucid image in Lav's memory. My face is young, no more than three years old, and I am the only one who does not seem happy in Lav's tortured mind. My face twists in pain, a look I rarely wore as a child. I can't place what moment Lav remembers of me, but I wish it were happy.

I gently wipe away the accumulated grime on Lav's face. His chin has never been able to grow much hair, luckily, and his skin wipes away an unnatural alabaster beneath the scraggly growth clinging precariously to his face. They haven't taken him outside, not for months. I make gentle noises in the back of my throat, as if he's a skittish horse, but outside stimuli changes nothing. He barely feels the hunger that has to be burning through him. His delicate cheekbones stand out sharp and prominent from his hollow cheeks. Sores fester on his back and legs.

Once I have him in new clothes and his chair gleaming again, I wash the floors and change his bedding. Halfway through, Nomman comes to the door, hesitates, and then retreats, though his shame floats through the air. Elina adds spices to the stew as she hums, her thoughts on herself rather than her sons.

When I finish, my fingers are raw and chafed, but the floor is spotless, Lav is clean, and the room feels like a room again instead of a cave. I wheel him out, the expensive chair paying for itself a dozen times over. Regardless of how light and frail he may be, lifting him from place to place was a trial. We make it to the table, Lav's place at the head of the table both a necessity and a symbol.

My lips twist. He's at the head because his chair slides easily into the space, but it's so much more than that. He's at the head because, by the Creator, he's the only reason I return to these awful memories. He's at the head because this family would long ago have broken apart and scattered to the winds if not for the tortured soul slumped wearily in his chair. Nomman settles across from him at the other side of the table. While I view him as sitting at the head of the table, perhaps my father *views the opposite, that he's as the foot, as low as he can be placed. Judging by the condition I found him in, they haven't even bothered to put forth the effort to wheel him to the table.*

The soup has grown cold, having sat too long while I finished my ministrations, and the meal is silent. A few times, Elina exchanges a pleasant word with Nomman, but I resist all efforts to be dragged into the conversation as I sip at the soup.

"I have a new form of love to try. I met an elderly couple from the Donirian envoy to the Khalintars," I say suddenly into the silence. "Their love has lasted nearly five decades, almost fifty long years of dedication. Not once did I notice a negative thought, a single notion of enmity. Their love was beautiful."

"When did you meet them?" Nomman asks, genuinely curious. "I thought you spent the last few months traveling to Donir with your master, not speaking with people here in Coin."

"Do you really think I would ever travel to that shit hole of a kingdom?" I ask mildly. "I've been in Coin the entire time. The coalition would fall apart without me controlling the wayward idiots you've named Khals."

"What?" Elina asks dumbly. I've had this conversation with my parents before. Eleven times before.

"Mother. Father," I say after a moment, the words cutting off some vapid thing Elina drones on about, the words entirely devoid of the warmth that should accompany those titles. "You have... disappointed me."

"Is this about Lav? We do everything that boy needs to survive, just like you ask," Elina says, overly loud, as if speaking the words with volume somehow lends them validity, but her thoughts betray her. She secretly hopes he dies, as she always has. She can't bear to think of Lav as her son anymore. He's a broken husk, nothing but a drain of

resources. Everything would be better without him; she could travel, she could go with me on my journeys, she could really live again. Nomman doesn't feature prominently in those thoughts.

Nomman shoots Elina a glance, but hesitates. He knows shame, a deep and abiding guilt that he should be doing better by his oldest son. But he loves his wife, always has, and he believes that going along with her whims provides him the only path to happiness. Much of Lav's condition stems from the bitch seated across from me, but Nomman's guilt does little to satisfy the cold fire in my gut.

"You are going to do a better job," I say, calm despite the storm raging in my breast. I reach into my mother's thoughts, excising those negative emotions, ripping them out like pages from a book. She cries out and clutches her head, and I ignore Nomman as he tries to comfort her. He doesn't understand why the woman he loves is doubled over, squeezing her temples as if any physical act could help with the feeling of having your mind brutalized. I understand the pain, distantly, a disquieting echo in the back of my thoughts: I have felt this pain as well. Someone once did the same to me, ripped thoughts and memories from my head. The pain is sickening, overwhelming.

I relish *it.*

The only person with the power to alter the minds and thoughts of others is the Shaper of Thought. Me. So I altered my own memories, taking things from myself. Why would I do so? The answer is plain. I'm protecting myself from something awful, or removing something unpleasant. Unlike most people in this world, I trust myself, and I know better than to meddle and pry into the memories I once deemed too unpleasant or powerful to exist.

I relish the pain because I can remember, even distantly, how awful it feels. So I know exactly what this bitch is going through as I yank out her dreams by the roots, burning away all emotion and leaving a void behind.

How could she cast aside her eldest son? How could she?

Into that absence, I pour my own love for Lav, my abiding sense of duty and purpose to the kin seated at the end of the table. I've tried this before. It will not last. The mind is resilient; no matter how powerful the blow, given enough time and the right circumstances, any mind can recover. Elina's mind has rediscovered this selfish, uncaring attitude half a dozen times despite my best effort to root it out and burn even the ashes of the ashes. Still, her mind recovers.

I dredge up the feelings of attraction she once held for Nomman. Of love, there is no sign, as there has never been. She married him because he was young, handsome, and owned a plot of land in Coin itself. She wants to be powerful, to live a life of luxury and decadence amongst the elite of Coin. Nomman, however, has no ambitions. He can't be pushed beyond a managerial position at the port office. He enjoys his work: the endless task of managing the ebb and flow of ships in the harbor, finding the space and the pattern in the myriad ships that sail up and down the Vein into Coin for trade or travel. Nomman loves his job, his wife, and his children; he's content.

I bring to the fore the feeling of the elderly Donirian couple's love, pouring into Elina their unceasing regard for one another, their patience, and their happiness, the satisfaction the man feels looking on his wife, the way his eyes soften whenever they hold her, how his awareness and uncertainties fade in her presence. I take that feeling, the best I can, and insinuate it into Elina's thoughts, carefully, quietly, weaving the love and affection into her old attraction, subtly urging her mind to accept the emotion in all its wonder.

Once, I would have jammed the love into her brain as viciously as I ripped out her previous thoughts. I've tried my hand at pruning, carefully snipping away each emotion. That works, to varying degrees of success, but rarely do the feelings remain absent. It's far more effective to torment the brain, scarring it so that the mind, as resilient as it is, resists even attempting to go near the source of that pain.

The removal of memories and thoughts must be brutal and swift, but the introduction of new thoughts and feelings... far from it. Forcing the mind to believe something it has never thought is nigh-on impossible. Instead, I use gentle, subtle nudges and suggestions.

It is almost as if I'm tending a forest, wild and untamed. A searing blaze in certain parts of the forest burns the vines and trees to their stubs. Left behind is little more than roots and ashes, empty and barren. In its place... I plant seeds. Shoving a foreign flower into an unfamiliar landscape will often result in growth native to the forest smothering the stranger before it can grow. Instead, I sow seeds in the scorched sections of the forest, hoping that one or two will grow into being and finally take over the native flora.

Perhaps this love, a love tempered and strengthened over decades, a love that has never known betrayal, will finally be the seed that catches. Perhaps she will finally love her husband and her son over herself.

I finish after a few minutes, leaving Elina asleep on the table, her bowl of soup seeping out onto the ground. Nomman shakes her, frantically trying to wake his wife. I reach into his mind, burning away the surface thoughts and the last few moments carefully, then nudge him to sleep. He slumps down next to her, his head coming to rest on her shoulder. I stand, glancing around the homely little house.

Lav stares vacantly forward, his thoughts unchanging and unchangeable. I sigh, leaning over and kissing his forehead before standing and tousling his hair absently. He'll be alright, for a while at least. Without a backward glance, I stride from the house.

***

"What happened to your brother, Bastian?" the Seer asks compassionately. I blink once, twice, adjusting to the sudden return to the present. "How did he come to be so broken?"

"I don't know," I say honestly, but my mind turns from the conversation. The woman just did something to me. She read my memory as if I played the images before her, as if she hijacked my power and reversed it. It's almost as if *she* has the power of the Shaper of Thought... "How did you do that?"

The Seer smiles down at me, her face just as magnanimous and welcoming as before. But something else lurks behind her eyes, a calculation, a guarded uncertainty that wasn't evident before. I try to reach for my power, to read the thoughts behind that strange look, but my body is too weak. I can't even lift my arm, let alone draw energy to Shape.

"I am a Seer of many things," she finally responds. "I can See things of the past, things of the present, and many things of the future. When I am in the presence of one with such strong emotions, I can often See the past they have lived. Your life has been one of misery and deceit, Bastian. And not just for those you have manipulated. I pity you."

"You pity me?" I say with a trembling voice. "I pity you when your people realize who they have been harboring. Who they have been raising up. There is only one who can see into the past. There is only one who can grasp the events of the present. There is only one who can peer into the future. I know you, Master of Time."

The woman looks taken aback for a moment, as if the accusation is so surprising she can't even comprehend it. Then, she laughs, a deep belly laugh of the kind that can only be gifted by genuine humor. She wipes tears from her eyes as she stands.

"For one so clever, you see so little," she says. She turns, shoulders shaking with humor, and strides away.

That evening, Te'ial comes to me again, her face more guarded and her manner more reserved. I've hardly twitched a muscle since my confrontation with the Seer. The overwhelming anger allowed me to draw on Thought for a few moments, but my body and soul need far more time to recover than a day of soup and rest. I'm worse off than when I awoke, the last dregs of my energy drained and gone.

The captain reaches in with her strong arms and rights me, bringing the accustomed bowl to my lips. I try to find it in me to hate her, prodding at what remains of my pride, but I can't muster the effort. The landscape of my mind feels much like the ashes of Elina's mind after my visits, save for the fact that the entire forest has burned. I can't feel the emotions behind a thought, but rather they come to me raw, uninhibited, untainted by sentiment or sorrow. Even thoughts of Lav are clean and sharp, none of the old familiar despair rising to the fore.

I eat in the desultory fashion of the depressed, allowing Te'ial to put the sustenance in my body but uncaring as to why. She handles me gently, the bowl carefully pressed to my lips, the soup doled out in small, manageable swallows. When she finishes, she props me more comfortably against the bars facing the village.

"The Seer told me..." Te'ial begins, her voice strange in the growing twilight. "I am better than my actions, Cursed. I grieve for your family. I grieve for my own. Though I will not like you... I cannot hate you."

"Then call me by my name," I say, meeting her eyes through the bars.

"I do not respect you that much, Cursed," she says, a pale shadow of her customary smirk on her face. "I feel as if my head will hurt for weeks."

"Worth a shot. I don't like you either. And yet, even after all this," I mutter, wishing, though unable, to wave my arm around expansively to indicate the village, the captivity, the time... "I can't bring myself to hate you either. I'll see you in the morning. Captain."

Her eyes narrow, but she merely nods.

"In the morning, Cursed."

My eyes are already closed. I don't hear her walk away before I sleep.

***

"This is... unexpected," the elegant woman speaks. "How can the boy hide such altruism behind the despicable facade he presents?"

"He is more complex than we realized," the girl answers, her voice thoughtful. "Did you notice, in that memory, what he's done? He took some of his own knowledge and buried it inside his mind. There

are memories and thoughts Bastian has lived that he can't remember. He removed them."

"His sanity should be questioned," the brutish foreign man responds. "Who willingly destroys their own thoughts?"

"If you never wanted to remove your own memories, you lived a life completely devoid of sorrow," the Khalintari says wryly. "The impressive thing about it is the control. Who among us would have been comfortable breaking our own minds apart?"

Silence answers him for long moments, infinitely long in this place which is no place.

"Impressive or not, this revelation is perhaps more disquieting than our initial analysis," the elegant woman picks back up. "At least before we knew who he was and could reasonably predict his actions. Now, we have no idea who this boy is."

"Exactly," the girl answers. Her voice is young, barely past adolescence. Even so, she speaks with the quiet authority of someone used to giving commands. And having them followed. "We don't have any idea. We haven't the faintest, for all our alleged omniscience. You wanted him killed before we knew anything about him at all. I would expect a more judicious approach in the future, Ulia."

"Very well, Jynn," the woman responds, somehow conveying the sense of being both chastened and rebellious.

"Who are you?" I ask.

The voices all cut off abruptly. I reach around blindly without knowing what I reach for. I feel foolish after a moment. The physical constraints of my flesh clearly have no meaning here. What does it mean to reach out a hand in a place where my body doesn't exist? Instead, I conjure the memory of the voice of the girl, Jynn. I stretch out my mind and **pull**.

A flicker of an image, there and gone almost before my mind can comprehend it. A girl, a young woman, perhaps eighteen Summers, dressed in silver armor under a warlike black robe etched with silver inlay, her light brown hair bound in a long braid stretching out behind her. The girl flinches back, the light of her soul twisting free of my *mental grasp without much difficulty. Still, I read surprise and the barest hint of fear before she can flit away.*

"Who are you?" I shout into the darkness. I get the feeling of being watched, as if an entire multitude waits just outside the range of my sight. I stretch forward, but the feeling doesn't fade. The voices remain quiet, but their silence is as conspicuous as their speech. I can feel them in their absence as much as their presence. "You won't hide from me forever. I'll figure it out before long."

"Wake up, Bastian," the girl says, her voice very close behind. Even as I try to spin—

My eyes flutter, then open, the predawn light doing little to illuminate the dark jungle around me. The mark of my power glimmers fitfully on my thigh, but it soon fades into my skin and leaves me exhausted. The exhaustion is good, though. It's the weariness of honest toil, the wholesome tiredness that comes with stretching yourself beyond your limits. I don't feel the soul-wrenching despair in my bones. My muscles respond to my command, bringing my hands up before my eyes. Though my filthy hands shake, I hold them up for several minutes before the trembling grows too great. I switch to my legs, raising them as high as I can, holding them aloft with the muscles of my stomach. I flex my legs at the knee and force every bit of my will into demanding they fold on my command.

Te'ial finds me with my arms up in the air, trembling mightily, but grimly satisfied as they hang longer than before.

"You know," I say conversationally, my voice still a rasp from disuse. "You never recognize how much you take movement for granted until it's gone."

"I wouldn't know," she says, sitting down with the bowl. She watches me for long moments, not interrupting as I return to bending my legs.

"I wish I didn't," I mutter, shoving at the ground and managing to prop myself up against the bars of my cage. She rearranges me a bit more to her liking, then brings the bowl to my lips again. I slurp the soup greedily. "Is there more?"

"You are to be given whatever you ask, aside from your freedom," Te'ial responds, shrugging. "Do you wish for more soup?"

"And bread. We can soak it so that my jaw can grow used to chewing again. Also, could you perhaps bring me clean water and a cloth?"

"It will take more than that to get you clean," Te'ial says, wrinkling her nose in disgust. Of course, I shit myself again in the night.

"Trust me," I say, trying a smile but probably coming far closer to a grimace. "I have never smelled anything worse than me right now. Wiping myself clean is a start."

"Very well. I will get Ton'kapu to bring you water and a cloth."

"Ton'kapu?" I ask, brow furrowed.

"He is the only one the Seer deemed you could not corrupt, aside from me."

"What makes him so damnably pure?"

"Not pure. Quite the opposite. He hates the Cursed more than anyone else among our people. The rest of his... faults do not prevent him from following the Seer's will. He and Talan have tangled in the past."

"Where is Talan? I have to thank him for introducing his fist to my face."

Te'ial laughs, a genuine laugh that comes from her belly. It's a pleasant sound that cuts through the omnipresent humidity and carries outward into the jungle.

"Talan has duties other than striking Cursed," Te'ial says, her eyes dipping down and away. "He is not here."

"Where has he gone?"

"Enough, Cursed," she cuts off, turning and striding briskly away.

I don't have to wait long. Te'ial doesn't return, but a portly, bedraggled looking old man with gray hair and midnight skin trots up with a bucket and a cloth that can generously be called clean. He steps up to the bars, looking down on me impassively. Then, inexplicably, he smiles broadly, his teeth yellowed and broken in his mouth. Perhaps his hatred isn't so deep...

He starts to speak, a stream of words in his native tongue. The words don't flow, as well-spoken sentences in Khalintari do, but instead seem to abruptly stop and start. The language is a series of staccato bursts, sometimes continuing for the space of three heartbeats, sometimes pausing every syllable in short but noticeable breaks. He nods as he speaks, the grin almost touching his ears.

Reassured, I smile and nod back. This seems to encourage him, and he gestures expansively. He points at the trees, spreads his arms wide, and tilts his eyes to the heavens. All the while he speaks in the fits and starts of the Seer tongue.

"Ton'kapu *as'idie'laran'costrien,"* Te'ial calls, or that's how it sounds, her pauses just as noticeable and jagged as his. I was concerned Ton'kapu was a madman, but the captain's speech patterns match him. She trots over with soup and bread.

Ton'kapu turns and speaks to her, his tone remarkably merry. She mutters a few more words in return, her tone sharp and rebuking. He merely shrugs, looking down at me and then back to her, laughing a great booming laugh. She rolls her eyes, ignoring him. He sets the bucket down, hands her the towel, and walks away, his laugh rumbling through my chest.

"I have never seen him so happy in his life," she says, wetting the cloth before handing it to me.

"I think I've made a friend," I say, then put my lips to the bowl, and Te'ial bursts out into laughter again. The bowl jumps in her hands, sloshing hot soup down my chin, and I squirm, unable to get away. The bowl disappears, and I lever myself around to see her on the ground, her chest heaving in great bouts of hilarity, tears streaming down her face.

"What did I say this time?" I ask, unsure if I should be offended or not.

"If—" she cuts off, shaking her hands in surrender, her skin glistening as dawn turns to full morning. She wipes away tears, trying valiantly to regain control of herself. "If Ton'kapu—if *anyone*—spoke to me like Ton'kapu just spoke to you, even the Seer herself, one of us would be buried before the sun reaches noon."

"But," I begin, confused. "He was so happy. He was laughing!"

"Exactly!" Te'ial says, fighting back a grin. "He was absolutely overjoyed to see a Cursed brought so low. He was so satisfied that a tainted soul was brought to cleaning the shit from themselves with rags, fed by his enemies. He called you and your ancestors and your bloodline more despicable and insulting things than I have ever heard used by anyone in the *I'wia*."

"Oh."

"If even an eighth of those insults were remotely *implied* about my family, I would have killed him for even having the thought in the first place!" Te'ial says, bursting into laughter again.

"What did he say?" I ask, more curious than anything. The insults can't have been that bad.

"The least of them was declaring your mother a—" she cuts off, shaking her head before she can master herself. "He called your mother a tongue-cleaner of the anus gland of diarrhea sick monkeys who—"

"Right," I say, interrupting her before she can keep going. "Well, he'll have to do better than insulting my mother. She *was* a... how did he put it? Cleaner of the anus gland?"

"It is not good to speak ill of your family," Te'ial says, growing a bit more somber.

"You don't know them," I say, more bitterly than I intend.

"Nor shall I," she says softly, but with certainty.

"What is your language? Did you call it the *Iwia?"*

"No, Cursed, the *I'wia*."

"That's what I said."

"No, you called it the *Iwia,* which is different. It is the *I'wia,"* she says, slowing down the word. I notice the nearly imperceptible pause between the first syllable and the others.

"I'wia," I say slowly, trying the unfamiliar word out. My tongue feels clumsy during the pause. She grimaces, but nods, as if the very sound of my voice butchering her language is sickening. "What does that mean?"

"The closest translation in your crude speech is the Voice of the World," she answers, shrugging with one shoulder. "But it is an ugly translation at best."

"And what does the other mean? *Iwia*?"

"Well..." she glances away, then looks back at me with her customary smirk. "It is a word that is not proper for polite company."

"You know better than any how far I am from polite," I respond, forcing my face into the aching lines of a smirk of my own.

"It's a name for a woman's secret flower," she says, rolling her eyes.

"Wait, wait, wait," I say, narrowing my eyes. "Your name for your language is that close to your name for your..."

"Naturally. The translation for *I'wia* is Voice of the World. The translation for *Iwia*... closer to Cradle of the World."

I open my mouth to respond, then pause, my brow furrowing. I can't exactly fault the logic.

"How could that pause mean so much? You barely even broke up the letters."

"Enough, *thriska* Cursed," Te'ial says, her demeanor suddenly changing, closing, as if someone slams a book shut. Her face becomes unreadable and remote. "Your questions bore me. I do not like you. I will not tell you the secrets of the *I'wia*."

"Fine," I snap peevishly, more disappointed at her reaction than I expect to be. "Can you tell me then what *thriska* means? If I am going to be insulted, I would rather know."

"It means tainted," she says, turning and walking away. She doesn't look back.

The sun falls quickly into the sky, far more quickly than it does in the north. My heart aches, distantly, the same way an old wound aches when you wake, having slept at just the wrong angle. The pain is fresh, but dulled, the echoes of a loss long since gone returning to plague me once again. I don't understand how the pain of losing Lav can ever feel this way, so distant and... forgettable. The pain is not enough to hold my consciousness; in fact, it's barely enough to occupy my attention. I remember the immediacy of knowing in my heart that Lav must have died after two years, that those cretins that pass for parents would never have taken care of him without me there to *make* them. I remember the pain... but it's a pain I am long familiar with. How can that be? I've held the knowledge in my heart for less than a day.

I shudder, forcing down tears that come unwillingly to my eyes. What is wrong with me? Why don't I feel the sorrow of Lav's loss? Shouldn't it still be fresh? I blink the tears away, realizing with disgust they exist more for myself than for Lav. I gaze up at the unfamiliar stars. I snort. Unfamiliar. As if I ever bother to look at those unreachable glimmers of light. As if I would ever be able to see a tapestry of stars and recognize it. As if I have a home for stars to shine over.

My brother is dead, I'm sure. The bickering Khals will no doubt have ruined all the careful work of years. I can barely move, and my muscles might never recover from the atrophy which has so thoroughly decimated my strength. Perhaps I should just stop eating, no matter what Te'ial demands. Perhaps I should just let my weakened body finish the job and slip quietly into death.

What do I have to live for?

The passing of my soul may also drive all of the people in the Seer's nation mad, as my predecessor's death did to the people of Tiran twenty-one years before. They still call it the City of Ghosts. No one returns for fear that they, too, will be driven insane. The thought is strangely satisfying. Perhaps my death will serve as my revenge. I close my eyes and sleep, head pressed to the bars.

Something wakes me, a looming presence in the darkness. A black silhouette silently stands beside my cage. Fear claws at my belly and grips me by the spine. The moon rises from the surrounding trees, and its silver light illuminates the weathered face of Ton'kapu. He's grinning, same as before, his teeth gleaming in the darkness, his eyes full of merriment and joy. The friendly look does nothing to curb my terror. I shy away from him, but he paces me around the cage.

"*Et'inie'te'ial,"* he says, his resonant voice muted and quiet.

"You know I don't understand you," I say, annoyed, both at him for sneaking up on me and myself for giving in to fear. "Piss off."

He laughs. It is nothing approaching human. There is something wild... something untamed and dark in that laugh.

"*Niope'lesti?"* he says, tilting his head to the side and grinning his toothy grin. With a broad gesture, he indicates the dark trees away from the village. The cage is open. The ever-present bars are gone, only the damp island air between me and freedom. I crawl before I can even think, muttering a thanks to Ton'kapu and pushing my elbows into the dirt. I'm almost to the edge of the cage when I pause.

What am I doing? I can't make it anywhere in my condition. What is Ton'kapu trying to pull? I glance up at him, only then noticing the gleam of steel in the night. He holds a dagger, bright and sharp, his other hand open in a gesture of welcome. Slowly, not taking my eyes off of Ton'kapu, I push my aching body back into the cage. He doesn't move, though he does seem to relax. Rather than disappointment, a grin flashes across his face, his eyes crinkling at the edges. He puts the cage back into place and presses his face against the bars, almost touching mine.

"Niope'lesti."

The words are not a question this time, but a statement. He's gone before I can blink, the darkness swallowing his dark silhouette before he travels two paces. I shudder, eyes wide and staring. The moon drifts behind a distant cloud, plunging my little corner of the world into total blackness. I gasp and jump at every noise in the night, and in the jungle, there are many noises. The morning can't come fast enough.

Te'ial arrives at her normal time, her confident swagger returning as the days pass. She holds my bowl as well as a piece of warm bread. I lever myself up, not having slept a wink since Ton'kapu's visit. She reaches in to feed me, but I nudge her hand aside.

"Captain. Can I ask you a question?"

"What, Cursed?" she asks, clearly annoyed at the delay.

"What does *niope'lesti* mean?"

I make sure to include the appropriate pause, counting on the acuity granted by fear to get the intonation right. By Te'ial's frown, I haven't spoken the words correctly.

"In your tongue... it means death-wishing. Where did you hear this phrase?" she asks, her brow furrowing in concern.

"Nowhere," I say, shaking my head. So I *did* speak the words correctly. "Something someone said to me once in Halfway."

"You have a good memory to remember the inflection so well. It means almost... what is the word for death-wishing in your tongue?"

"Suicide."

"Yes!" Te'ial responds, brightening. "To kill oneself."

Letting the morbid topic drop, I eat all of my breakfast, even reaching for the bread and forcing my aching fingers to grasp at it. I eventually manage to eat about half the bread, though the rest ends up in crumbs down my shirt. Te'ial doesn't complain about the waste, but simply watches through my struggles. After she leaves, I grind my teeth together.

It's one thing to think about suicide in your own damn head. It's entirely another for some ignorant savage to try to murder you in the night. Ton'kapu wants me to kill myself, does he? Well fuck him. I need to learn how to say that in the *I'wia.*

Chapter 13
Kettle

The Forty-Second Day of Spring
In the Year 5222, Council Reckoning

A distant rumble of thunder rolls through the slate gray sky. I pause. My eyes seek out the remote flashes of light, the brilliant twin to the sullen sibling trembling through the clay tiles of the rooftop supporting my feet. The first drops of rain, large and fat, take up a drumming rattle that only grows into a cacophony of nature's roaring voice. My hood is already up; my anonymity critical until I choose to be recognized. Even so, the rain quickly soaks through the material and traces its cold fingers down my spine.

I hardly notice.

I hardly blink.

My eyes are far too focused to be bothered by a sudden spring shower. The doorway across the street from my rooftop, a cheery and wholesome green, remains stubbornly closed despite my urges for it to open already. Despite my *hunger* for it. The man's late. Keagan Atlan is never late. The old, familiar chill of warning echoes in the back of my mind, an instinct whispering of danger, but I ignore it as easily as I ignore the sleepless nights and aching bones that accompanied the task of the past two weeks.

I blink away the rain to be certain I'm not imagining it when Atlan's door finally swings open. A vagary of the wind catches the edge of the door and whips it out of his hand to crash against the front facade of his house. He curses, the words just barely penetrating the curtain of rain between us. He scrambles to slam the door closed before belatedly opening up a cloth umbrella. Under other circumstances, I might have smiled, maybe even laughed at the fool's predicament. Instead, I merely continue my vigil. I come up on the balls of my feet, leaning towards the man eagerly.

He's not my target. Of course he isn't. But he might take me to *him*.

The rumors of Jon Gordyn's mercenary army, as it turns out, were not overblown. The day after our botched job, dozens of men had turned over the streets, raiding every location the Family was ever rumored to frequent. Tal and Bulo were killed in a safe house we were flatly certain was unknown to anyone outside the Family. The fire brigade in the Corpses had given up on the house when the flames that gutted it reached the clouds, and instead focused on saving the other derelict estates around it. The embers still smoldered a week later.

Luckily, the children remain safely tucked away in the Temple of Shadow on the edge of the city. So far, we haven't seen even a sliver of interest in the priest and his charges. Regardless, half a dozen thieves watch over it night and day. The rest of us search for Corna. She didn't emerge from the bank. Rina walked out of work that night while they were still investigating and simply never returned. But Corna...

Atlan glances suspiciously up and down the street. He doesn't look up, though there's scant chance he would see me through the downpour. He probably wouldn't notice me even if the sun was shining brightly, as it no doubt is behind the oppressive gray clouds. I follow him along the rooftops, lightly leaping over the gaps between the tightly packed houses. The task is simple enough that I'm able to think through my next few moves in this deadly game while I run.

Ultimately, the children are targets I can't afford to leave in danger, both due to my love for them and their use as a weapon against me. The secret of their whereabouts has a swiftly approaching demise: everyone, even the most dedicated, the most powerful, the most disciplined, everyone has a limit. I can't imagine a situation in which they aren't torturing Corna to learn about me, to use her knowledge against us. I've slaughtered a dozen of Gordyn's mercenaries in ambushes throughout the city, learning what information I can from them before making their bodies disappear. The unending chorus, no matter how... creatively I ask, is that no one knows where Gordyn is. No one knows where he keeps his prisoners. No one knows where his second hides. The only high-ranking member of the Bank left working is Keagan Atlan.

Gordyn's left Atlan exposed as retaliation for his failure to recognize that he was being swindled. Clearly expendable, he's either a pawn to be sacrificed or a trap to lure me in. I don't particularly care which. He's the only important man left in the city, and I'm damn well going to get what information I can out of him. Corna is running out of time.

Eight mercenaries jog up to meet him at the first busy intersection. I haven't been able to tell if Atlan or Gordyn hired them, but they're good at their jobs. I duck behind the eves of the house I stand on, narrowly avoiding the gaze of one of the men raking his eyes across the rooftops. They have crossbows and swords, and every inch of them screams how well they can use them. They exude a confidence and a competence that is borderline intimidating. For all of their willingness to throw themselves into the fray, the Family has little experience in fighting outside of ambush or subterfuge, and something tells me these men will not be taken unawares.

Which is why I reserve this task for myself. Alone.

The men set off, Atlan walking swiftly at their center, their eyes constantly roving the streets and the rooftops in equal measure. After a block and at least three close calls, I realize they'll spot me if I continue to pursue them over the rooftops. I need a new plan.

I turn my easy stalk into a sprint, heading out in a wide arc. The rain hammers down unrelentingly, thick sheets of water rattling like hail. I nearly stumble twice as I leap between rooftops at breakneck speed, but each time, my boots turn in just such a way as to let me recover.

I flat refuse to think any gratitude towards the soul trapped in them. He is walled carefully away behind half a dozen mental barriers so that I can't hear any annoying and distracting thoughts echoing through my brain. I probably should just take them off, but I'm not going to let them out of my sight. They represent the only bargaining chip I possess with Gordyn. He clearly knows what they are, and further believes them to be quite valuable. If I'm being honest with myself, I should marvel at the fact that a soul exists in the boots on my feet, but I'm angry. Tecarim tried to steal the only thing no one has ever been able to take from me: my very body. I'll never trust him again, and I certainly won't be thanking him for being an exceptional pair of boots.

Bastard. The stub of my middle finger throbs once, and I scowl. Even if he saved my life.

A few tense minutes pass as I run. The window to take Atlan is closing swiftly. At the pace the mercenaries set, he'll be approaching the bank in minutes. I jump over the eve of the next roof, falling and allowing the shadow to cushion me under my clothes, easing my descent. A beggar huddles away from the rain in the entryway to the ovens of the bakery across the alley, and his jaw drops at the sight of my freefall. I glance at him, and he snaps his eyes down, raising a hand in shaking greeting. I almost smile.

I dart out into the thin flow of traffic on the street. The Way of the East is busy even in the deluge, though most sane people are tucked safely indoors. The others all hurry, their heads down, hoods up. I blend in instantly, simply another soaked pedestrian surly to be caught in the rain. Scant seconds later, Atlan and his guards round a corner and march purposefully down the street. The mercenaries distinctly do not have hoods; they prefer clear peripheral vision over dry heads. I angle towards them, the cautious voice in my head shuddering at the blank space where my plans usually reside. Instead of the elaborate scheme I might have executed a few weeks ago, my thoughts are far more primal.

Kill the guards. Take the prize.

A covered carriage rounds the corner behind them, and I smile for the first time that day. Perhaps the Creator is looking down on me after all. People dart out of the way as the carriage, no doubt going far too fast for the downpour, sends a wave cascading to either side of its wheels. Even though everyone on the street is already wet, the ignominy of some snide, dry noble resoaking you is too much to bear. At least two people pick up stones from the street and hurl them ineffectually after the carriage, and several others make rude gestures universal to all cultures.

I glide forward as the vehicle approaches. The wall of water the carriage kicks up covers my approach. Half of the guards turn to glare malevolently at the carriage, while the other half gather closer around Atlan and usher him forward. The Way of the East is smooth and slick, not cobblestones like many parts of the city, or my next maneuver would hurt far more. As the carriage passes, I drop to my knees and slide along the slick stones, riding low as the guards raise their arms to block the encroaching wave of water. The first two die before the others even realize they are under attack, narrow slivers of shadow punching through the soft skin under the jaw and up into the brain. The others react instantly, swords drawn and attacking in the blink of an eye. I backpedal, barely dodging aside from expert sword thrusts from two opponents while the other four usher Atlan farther on the street.

Atlan calls out, some kind of protest at the treatment he's receiving, but my mind barely registers my surroundings. The mercenaries press me, working in concert, darting in and out of reach, constantly attacking, forcing me to block or roll to the side without pause. I can hardly even maintain the concentration to keep the shadow between my vulnerable flesh and their cold steel, let alone turn things back to the offensive. A shallow cut opens high on my shoulder, and the very tip of the woman's sword punctures my thigh as my blocks keep the wounds superficial, but only just. The cuts won't stay that way for long. Who are these people? As the man lunges, the sleeve of his shirt rides high, revealing a telltale series of dark black lines tattooed on the inside of his wrist. Shorn? Who in the forgotten Depths is Atlan to be able to afford the A'kai'ano'ri?

With every passing second, Atlan hurries farther away. My chance at finding Corna is disappearing with every gasping breath.

I jerk my hands up, throwing a thin screen of darkness between us. Two blades dart through on either side, one high, one low, cutting through the living shadow like smoke on the wind. If I was any ordinary person, their attacks would be deadly; I shouldn't be able to move before their swords catch me. But, in the instant I'm hidden from their eyes, the instant they have to trust their knowledge and experience to guide them, the very nature of how different an opponent I am becomes apparent. I'm already leaping, my feet clearing the higher blade by inches, the shadow drawing me smoothly upwards higher than any normal human could hope to fly. I come down before they can recover, hands darting to either side, and leave them falling in my wake.

I put on a burst of speed. Atlan has already disappeared around the corner with his guards. *Shorn*, I remind myself dourly. My gut clenches with worry even as I near the corner. Fighting two of them fairly was almost too much for me. The warmth of blood drips from my wounds and mixes with the cold rain, and the focus I need to Shape the shadow to my will is fading.

At the back of my mind, I feel a tiny urge, a nudge. I glance down at my boots as I run, scowling. There's no way I'm going to open myself up to Tecarim again. He, whatever he is, has proven himself far from trustworthy. I shake off a shudder even as the memory of his alien energy racing through my body resurfaces. I almost lost control, lost the very vessel of my soul. No, not again.

Take some from me. His voice is distant, drifting up through the walls I built in my mind, an uncertain echo.

Never, I declare firmly.

You're wasting your focus and your energy keeping these walls between us. Your natural will was more than enough to hold me back before, remember?

I can't trust anything you say, I growl back, trying to wrest my focus back to the present. I'm wearier than I believed if I'm wavering enough to allow his annoying voice back into my thoughts. That damn voice is the reason Corna was captured in the first place.

I'm sorry for that, Tecarim responds, sounding entirely sincere. *It had been so long since anyone had opened themselves to me with the Creator in their veins. I condemn myself for the sacrilege.*

I wish I cared how you felt, I snarl back.

You will not do this, even to save yourself?

Especially not for that.

Not even to save your friend?

The words are a silent reverberation that shakes me to my core. Am I being selfish? If I embrace the energy Tecarim offers, I will be in control, surely. I won in that battle of wills, before I even knew to expect treachery. Certainly, this time, wary and prepared, I can use that power, just a trickle…

My walls start to erode as I consider it, that feeling of being so very *alive,* of every bit of me down to the tiniest part thrumming with energy, so sweet and—

I skid to a halt as I turn the corner, nearly losing my balance. The four remaining Shorn wait, swords ready, perhaps ten paces around the corner. Atlan's pasty face peeks out from behind their tense shoulders. I tense myself, dropping into a crouch and preparing to spring into action, consequences be damned. Corna needs me.

"My lady Po'lial," Atlan calls from under his umbrella. "Let us end this without any further bloodshed, yes?"

Neither his Shorn nor I relax.

"I'm here with a proposition for you," he continues, picking at his damp collar and swallowing nervously behind his teeth. "A meeting, if you will."

"Having your mercenaries attempt to kill me on sight is a strange way to set up a meeting," I shoot back, eyes gazing into the flat and deadly eyes of the Shorn. "Not exactly the best way to engender trust."

"Ah, well, yes," he says. "They were perhaps overzealous—"

"What has become of them, Lady Shaper?" the thin man to Atlan's left suddenly cuts in. His eyes are serious, tense, but his tone holds nothing but respect. He has grey hair and the lined face of an older man well past his prime, but his body looks to be in superb condition. I almost spit out the first dismissive insult that springs to mind, but the earnest curiosity in his face cools my anger.

"They have joined the Creator," I say, meeting his eye. "They fought well, and died for their duty."

"They were fools who yearned to test themselves against the rarest of foes," he answers, shaking his head. "Our orders were clear. You were not to be harmed. That they fought well is immaterial next to the shame of their disobedience."

"Even so," I answer, unsure why I continue the conversation when all I care about is finding Corna.

"Your words are a kindness. Why youth always seeks its end so swiftly has ever mystified me."

"You were not the same?"

His eyes crinkle, a mournful kind of merriment dancing behind his gaze, but he doesn't respond. Atlan looks confused by the entire conversation, but he takes our silence as his cue.

"My employer wishes to meet," he begins. "He has no more desire for bloodshed, nor for any further—"

"Where is my friend?" His eyes flash with annoyance. Just because I'm no longer playing a role doesn't mean I have to let the man finish a sentence.

"Mr. Gordyn sends you his assurance that she has not been harmed. She—"

"What good is Jon Gordyn's assurance? I need to see her, alive and well. Tell him the conflict between us will end when she is returned to me. In return, I will offer him his... property."

"I don't have the power to negotiate on Mr. Gordyn's behalf," Atlan says, a bit of fear creeping into his voice. It's almost as if, just like wild prey stalked by a true predator, he can sense the danger behind my growing impatience. "He told me to simply give you a time and a place. He desires to meet with you in person. You may bring a second, for he will have one as well. He requests that, for the sake of your friend, you do not test the parameters he has laid out for this meeting."

"Where? When?" I ask, resigned to the fact that Gordyn holds the better cards in this game. For now.

"The Falling Edge. His personal room. Tomorrow night at half past six. Come dressed for dinner."

Cheeky bastard. The very room he offered to me when he believed me to be Aea Po'lial. Of course he wouldn't forget.

"You may not have the power to negotiate, Atlan, just as you lacked that power at our first meeting. But tell Jon Gordyn this: bring her, show her to me alive and unharmed, and our meeting can be cordial. If he tests that *singular* parameter I've laid out for this meeting, I can't promise what will happen."

***

The Abyss isn't something you easily forget. More than a mile wide, almost a perfect circle, the gaping maw is enough to drive people to vacate the land for blocks around, just so that the impenetrable darkness doesn't catch their eye as they go about their daily business. It's a sobering and unhappy event to consider. One day, tens of thousands of souls had been bustling about, chasing their dreams, fleeing their nightmares, loving their families, hating their enemies, but *living*. From one instant to the next, all of that changed. The city just dropped out from beneath them, their final moments comprised of terror and a long, unmeasured fall deep into the earth.

All from the death of one man.

The cataclysms when Shapers die did not occur prior to the war with the Eternal. It used to be that the power passed seamlessly, a simple transference of a soul to its next body. Unlike the rest of the heathen world, who believe Shapers are something to be venerated, souls to be worshipped due to their extraordinary power, the People remember the names of those souls, the men and women who slew the Creator and so carry the Curse from one body to the next, never able to pass on, never able to move beyond and rejoin their maker. I listened to those stories with the same mixture of fervent terror and wonder with the rest of the students seated at the feet of the Seer. The thought of a soul flitting from body to body, wandering through hundreds of pairs of eyes, always Cursed, never satisfied… I shuddered myself awake for a fortnight wondering what those horrible parasites experience in their unending torment. I never thought I could be one of them.

Still, they used to pass to their next host quickly, harmlessly. Now, however, the deaths of the Cursed wreak destruction on unimaginable levels, and the extent to which they fight to stay among the living only serves to heighten the desolation of their death. The lives in which they live the longest, use their stolen power the most, are the deadliest. The cataclysms they leave behind are legendary.

Eo, Cursed of Thought. He lived for five hundred years before he passed again. His last death twenty-one years ago had driven an entire city mad, Tarin transforming from a bustling trading post on the west coast of Donir into a set of empty buildings, abandoned even now. The people had killed and eaten one another, speaking strange languages never heard before nor since, their gibbering unintelligible even to one another. Stories of horror still abound of mothers spitting their babies and roasting them slowly over fires, of fathers quieting their daughters with hands over their mouths to disguise their screams as they were violated. Thousands died in the first day, and none ever recovered. The living victims of Eo's death are still being cared for in places, their madness making them a danger to themselves and everyone around them.

Yali, Cursed of Earth. She is one of the more powerful of the Cursed, the element she stole so much stronger than most. She last lived as the man Belden for three hundred years, her soul behind his eyes on the so-called Council of the Shapers. The gathering of the Cursed. Her death at the hands of the Sealord created the Abyss. Tens of thousands, perhaps hundreds of thousands of innocent souls fell to their deaths, the unholy grating and rumbling of the earth drowning out their screams. The Abyss blights the landscape of beautiful Donir, and the proud city can do little but ignore the ugly scar of that deadliest of days.

After the Eternal's death, either the souls of the Cursed desired vengeance for the death of their queen, or some knowledge has been lost preventing such catastrophes. Ever since, the deaths of the Cursed have caused immeasurable tragedy.

Of course, there is one Cursed my people do not mind so much. We know of the sixteen souls, their betrayal of the Creator, all of the evil they wrought… but R'hea, Cursed of Nothing, is pitied rather than hated. She has not been seen for thousands of years, has not been active in the world since long before even the Eternal's fall. Her element was little more than a rumor even before Isa fell. Her death never causes a cataclysm. There are no tragedies surrounding R'hea, only the unhappy story of a misguided follower, a young girl who did not understand what her brother was leading her towards. No, my people only tell tales of her unending loneliness, her unceasing regret.

As it turns out… R'hea is Cursed with *something* after all. Even the long storytelling tradition of the People has not been able to keep up with R'hea's long absence. The element of her Curse has long since been forgotten. Luck, for good or ill, led me to rediscover it. Even so, I don't feel like I possess any memories of a long-forgotten life. I don't feel as if evil flows through my veins, as if my actions murdered the very being who gave me life eons ago. I am Aea turned Kettle. A young girl who found something she never should have found, but who embraced a new life after her old passed. No, I do not fear that I am evil.

But…

I understand her loneliness.

I live her solitude.

I refuse to spend my life, our life, alone.

Even if I don't believe the stories, I will give my soul, new or old or both, a chance at companionship, a chance at a family. We—R'hea and I—whether myth or truth, will live a life surrounded by friends.

Jon Gordyn will not take that from me.

***

The Falling Edge is far too expensive a place to stay for me to have considered it for a meeting. Despite that, the dangling structure and tiered terraces were visible from the roof of the

House, when it existed, and we used to jokingly throw rocks at the structure from afar, imagining the thrill seekers among the wealthy toppling to their doom deep in the darkness. That Jon Gordyn keeps a personal room on the Edge is proof enough that the hotel isn't for people of my means. For all I know, he owns the damn place.

And yet, as I walk up the steps in a brilliant white dress, a functional twin to the dress I ruined when Gordyn and I tangled the first time, I struggle not to be impressed. The servant at the entrance bows low before us, the filigreed doors swinging open so smoothly it seems like magic. The foyer is as ostentatious and ridiculously opulent as expected, though Timo and I both pause for a moment and admire the display. The chandelier alone would keep the Temple and my children fed for a year, and that's a conservative estimate. We glance at each other, and I almost laugh at the hunger in his gaze.

Timo, of course, wears the same suit he wore to the bank. If Gordyn can be petty and bring me to the Falling Edge, I can give him a taste of the same. The boots are hidden away, guarded by no less than five members of the Family. If he wants to make a run at my life at this meeting, he won't ever find the boots again.

Tecarim was almost inconsolable when I mentally told him to get off my feet. The whispers of his words in the back of my mind spoke of helping, of lending me strength, of providing another perspective… but, in the end, he agreed to stay. While the prospect of having an ace in the hole for the coming confrontation is appealing, tempting Gordyn seems less than wise considering Corna's life hangs in the balance. Even though Tecarim is a rat bastard who tried to steal my body, he's reasonable when you present him with logic.

"We should have been robbing this place," he mutters under his breath. "Way easier than the bank."

"Agreed," I say, but I push down a pang of sadness at the thought. It had been Corna's idea to go after Gordyn's vault,

Corna's fast talking which earned us entrance. Her enthusiasm never faded over the long two years of planning. It would have been safer to rob the Falling Edge, no doubt. But Corna would have told me it was boring. Looking around, seeing the light security and the wide windows, I know I would have agreed.

"Miss Po'lial?" a voice interrupts my musings.

I turn to see an elegant young man in a pressed black suit that fits him perfectly, accentuating the lines of his broad shoulders and slender waist. His face is clean shaven, his features sharp but pleasing. He smiles, and I catch my breath. His full lips look… well. He isn't the first pretty man I've ever seen, but I could lose myself in his bright copper eyes without too much trouble. A flush rises to my cheeks that has nothing to do with the warmth of the Spring evening.

"Yes?" I ask, feeling slightly breathless.

"Mr. Gordyn will see you now," he says, offering me his arm.

"Right," I say, trying to shake off the effect the man has on me.

Timo grunts something almost like a laugh out of the back of his throat. I shoot him a dirty look as I slip my hand into the crook of the man's arm, his muscular, firm arm. Damn it. I shouldn't be noticing those kinds of things. Now is most definitely *not* the time.

He leads us back and out a glass doorway onto the elegant deck behind the hotel. He pauses, briefly, letting me drink in the beauty of Donir spread out before the yawning blackness of the pit in front of me. The lamps of the city set the rooftops ablaze, the lights of windows sparkling in the darkness of the clear night. I glance at him, surprised to meet his gaze staring back at me. My breathing goes a little erratic again, so I glance back at the skyline.

"We shouldn't keep Gordyn waiting," I say in my best bored voice. I can't help but assume I'm fooling no one.

"Of course not, Miss Po'lial," he says, leading us to a staircase spiraling downwards into the Abyss. The stairs have no railing and no supports; they just seem to drop off into the umbra of the night. Grinning, I lean out over the edge, feeling the coolness of a distant breeze rising from the depths. Hanging from the arm of Gordyn's mysterious associate, I let his strength take some of my weight so that I can look down into the deep.

He waits, patient, his arm solid as rock. If Gordyn means to kill me, this is the perfect opportunity for his associate to simply let go. Not that I'm in any particular danger. The shadow will always catch me.

As I stare down into the darkness, I feel… something. A tug, almost as if an invisible finger has hooked into my chest and gives me a gentle, subtle pull towards the blackness below. I frown, but I can't get a grasp on the feeling. The shadow under my clothes twists, moving about and agitated. It's almost… almost as if…

"I do believe you were right before," the man says suddenly, breaking my reverie. "We shouldn't keep Mr. Gordyn waiting."

I blink, and the feeling disappears.

"Right," I say, allowing him to draw me back over the ledge and onto firm footing again.

We descend, Timo stepping quietly behind us. I glance back, and he raises his eyebrows, a question in his eyes. I shake my head. I'm acting erratically and I know it, but I'm alright. The horizon of Donir rises out of sight as we drop past the lip of the Abyss. Soon, the watchful stars are the only illumination aside from a few regularly-placed lamps, drops of sunlight in a lightless void. We're suspended in an unending sea of darkness, the lanterns little more than tiny islands in an uncaring ocean. I shiver, whether from delight or apprehension, I can't tell.

Finally, after what seems an age, we reach a building built into the side of the rock wall. We passed half a dozen rooms on our way down, each more ostentatious than the last, each occupied with the tinkling of glasses and the raucous laughter of the rich and the entitled. At our destination, though, a suite of at least five rooms spreads out against the wall. The structure gives off a sense of such solidity that the feeling of weightlessness given by the spiraling stairs dissipates like so much mist before a stiff breeze. The stairs end here, of course. Gordyn owns the lowest and most obviously expensive of the rooms.

My escort reaches forward to open the door for us, and my eyes latch onto a pair of scars on his wrist, matched with a pair of simple black lines tattooed to his skin. Shorn. Just like before. But this one… this man, no matter how young he looks, vastly outclasses the mercenaries I faced before. The Shorn, or as the People know of them, the A'kai'ano'ri, are given their four lines when they join the brotherhood, and it is only through their mysterious advancement that their tattoos are removed, instead becoming scars to show the growth of their ability and their wisdom. Two scars mean the man has advanced from the lowest ranks of the Shorn, who are already formidable fighters in the extreme, and into the upper echelon of the Tempered. Only the Blades are higher.

The information was intentionally given. I ignore his eyes, and instead wait patiently for him to open the door. As he turns the handle, a nervous twinge flutters through my stomach, a sudden fear that wasn't there before. It isn't just the man next to me, though he's certainly dangerous. I have no idea what's going to happen when I cross through this door. There could be a hundred mercenaries waiting to pepper me with bolts the second the door opens. Corna could be dead, or, worse, bound and tortured there in front of me. I'll do anything to save her, regardless of what it costs me. Hopefully, Gordyn doesn't know how much she means to me.

The door swings open to reveal a long cedar table, highly polished and beautifully wrought, the intricate whorls and knots of its parent preserved in the shining surface. Places are set for five to eat, two on either end at the heads of the table, each with a second place at their right hand, with one place set squarely in the middle on the left side. A twin to the chandelier in the opening foyer fills the room, its many facets reflecting a gentle rainbow of light from the lanterns hanging from the walls. Gordyn is not seated, but instead stands at a window across the fabulous room, cradling a glass of some liquor, gently clinking ice cubes together as he muses on the darkness. His form, so slight, nonetheless sends a tremor of fear down to the tips of my toes. He didn't become the richest man in the world through stupidity.

He turns at the sound of us entering, his lips quirking into a small smile. For once, the smile actually does seem to reach his eyes. When we met before, I was scared of the predator lurking under the gentleman's facade, but none of that wolf is in evidence here. Gordyn looks relaxed, confident, almost happy. I immediately feel worse about my chances.

"Mistress Po'lial," he begins, beckoning me forward. "I'm so glad you accepted my invitation."

"I prefer Kettle these days," I answer, allowing him to take my hand and press a kiss to my knuckles. "You know as well as I do that I haven't been back to the Isles in over a decade."

"Very well, Kettle," he says, nodding once. "I would like to welcome you—"

"Where is Corna?" I cut in. "I trust Atlan did an adequate enough job relaying my words for you to know my terms for this meeting."

"Can we not be pleasant to one another?" he asks, frowning slightly. "I've treated you with respect and offered to negotiate with you despite the fact that you robbed me and killed more than a dozen of my employees. I feel like we can observe some niceties, considering how... lenient I am being."

"The scales are not balanced between us."

“No, but we will have a plan in place to rectify that situation before the night is out. Until then, could we please be civil?” he asks, his expression open and reasonable. At my grudging nod, he rings a bell and walks me over to my seat, drawing out my chair. “Now, I assume introductions are in order? Kettle, would you do me the honor of introducing me to your compatriot?”

“Jon Gordyn, meet Timo of the Family,” I say, feeling ridiculous as the only person seated.

Timo has no surname, nor does he have any family but ours. I blink in surprise as Gordyn offers Timo his hand to shake. Timo, too, seems taken aback for a moment, but he engulfs Gordyn’s hand in his own. Since I don’t see Gordyn wince or react in any way, I assume Timo didn’t do the barbaric thing and squeeze harder than necessary. He’s come a long way in the last two years.

“A pleasure. And I assume you have already made introductions with Mr. Kraft?” he says as the three men settle into their seats, gesturing to his associate.

“We have not. Mr. Kraft, is it?” I ask, careful to keep my expression neutral.

“Aurelion Kraft, my lady Kettle,” he says, smiling a gentle smile that sets my heart to fluttering. “Rumors of your beauty were clearly inadequate. Jon only worries for the facts; he told me only to be careful of you. I had no idea I needed to be careful of my heart.”

“You are too kind. I do have to wonder, though, how I’ve never heard any such rumors concerning you. You are far too memorable a figure yourself not to spark discussion, Mr. Kraft.”

“Please, if I’m to call you Kettle, call me Aurelion. I keep a low profile in Donir. My work for Jon requires me to be careful of my reputation.”

He glances at Gordyn out of the corners of his eyes, but otherwise stares intently at me.

"And what do you do for Mr. Gordyn?"

"Well, I handle some of his more… delicate matters. Those that aren't meant to see the light of day."

"He has been a valuable asset for many years," Gordyn interrupts our banter. "Mr. Kraft has traveled all over the world on business for the bank. He's never failed to fulfil any contract I've given him."

"Never?" I ask, keeping my eyes squarely on Aurelion. The smile on his face is as much predatory as congenial. "You must be a man of extraordinary talent."

"You have no idea."

A polite knock sounds at the door, and servants file in, platters and bottles glittering in their hands. Before I can process their arrival, they're leaving, my glass full of wine and a delicate and artistic meal laid out in front of me. It's the kind of food that only the wealthy eat: far too small, far too expensive, and more about presentation than function. On my plate, a thin fillet of tuna rests on greens and a swirling array of sauces, grilled in softened peppercorns with a portion of rice mixed with diced mango and chili peppers: foods of the People, specialties nearly impossible to find in Donir. I haven't tasted fresh tuna in a decade.

I glance around. Each of the plates seems to cater to our particular backgrounds. Timo has a massive, rustic steak, a generous portion of roasted potatoes and carrots in an artistic pile relegated to one small corner of his plate. He's clearly a lowborn commoner, so the fare is no doubt a dream for his simple tastes. Gordyn has a delicate cut of salmon over a bed of rice topped with tiny shrimp in a cream sauce. I've heard of a similar dish served in a restaurant alleging to emulate the peculiar tastes of residents of Halfway. If our meals do represent our origins, Jon Gordyn seems to be claiming the one place no one claims as homeland. Aurelion stares down at his plate, a half-smile on his full lips. His plate holds two long, dark vegetables stuffed with some sort of meat, cheese, and a white sauce flecked with green spices. I don't recognize any of it, despite long experience with the Donirian markets in the Pennies. Where is he from?

He meets my eyes, his smile broadening. I fight the urge to look away quickly, as if I've done something wrong, and instead meet the liquid copper of his eyes unafraid. He looks away first, and I suppress the tingle working its way down my spine. What in all the Depths is wrong with me? I'm here to negotiate for Corna's life. I've walked into the lion's den, and here I am ogling his cub like some lovestruck fool. I need to focus.

We eat our meals, chatting about inane nonsense, Gordyn expounding on financial and trade advice that would most likely be valuable if I hadn't put every penny of my hard-won coin into his hands during the theft. The two men are clever, cordial, their words weaving in and out of one another in a mesmerizing dance. I keep up, barely, doing my best to focus on the conversation and not on the tension building between my shoulder blades. Aurelion makes a joke, and I laugh, letting my eyes drop to the table.

Which is when I remember the fifth plate set at the table. A wide and flat bowl filled with a red soup and diced tomatoes and greens. A chill rushes down my skin. *Gazpacho*. Corna is from the western coast, and she always complained about not being able to find a proper recipe since she left her parents all those years ago. I remember joking with her about the ridiculousness of a cold soup. I can see her affronted face, as if I was the barbarian for believing soup should be hot. I look up with narrowed eyes. Gordyn stares back at me, a smirk on his face.

"Is she here?" I ask, ending the pleasant small talk as swiftly as dousing lamp.

"Of course she is. She's been listening the entire time. Corna, darling, please come in," Gordyn calls cheerily.

And there she is.

She walks in from one of the rooms off this main foyer, every inch the beautiful queen I know she is. She wears a sleek midnight blue dress as only Corna can, the delicate silk falling off her body in a liquid sheen of silver highlights. Her hair spirals up on top of her head, her eyes and face clear of blemish or harm. My heart leaps into my throat, my eyes drinking in the sight of her. She's alive. If nothing else, she's breathing. Thank the Creator.

I feel more than hear Timo growl a low growl beside me. I glance at him, concerned, but he has eyes only for Corna. I look back, really *look*, and the feeling of excitement burgeoning in my breast dies. She's moving gingerly, favoring her ribs on the left side, doing her best to disguise the limp in her step. Her visible skin, of which plenty is showing, appears healthy, but cosmetics can serve to hide much, and Corna is wearing thick powder. The carefree grace of her movements is absent, instead each step placed carefully and each movement truncated and slow. She meets my eyes for the briefest of moments before she glances down at her place at the table. A chill settles into my heart. The look was one of fear, of pleading terror, a silent entreaty for help.

My eyes flick back to Gordyn. He watches Corna as she struggles to elegantly sit in the chair for her meal, but it's a pitiable attempt. Something of the wolf deep in his eyes rises to the surface as he looks at her, looks at her as if she's a particularly succulent and appealing prey. He slowly turns back to look at me, and there is little human left in his gaze.

"I see you disregarded my parameters for this meeting," I speak quietly. Too quietly. The words grate out of me like a serrated blade drawn from my ribcage, each word skipping across bone.

"I have followed it to the best of my ability," Gordyn answers. "We weren't aware of your rule regarding young Corna until after your meeting with Atlan. As you can see, we have done our best to be hospitable to our guest ever since we learned of your wishes."

I don't answer, staring at Corna. She sits, dully, her shoulders slumped, staring at her untouched soup, refusing to meet my eye. Where is the bright, vibrant woman of my memory? She is a doll made too lifelike; all of the pieces there, but the way they fit together wrong, abnormal, unnatural. Gordyn has done this to her. Gordyn has broken my sister.

"Now, you have something I want..."

"Here are my terms," I speak, ignoring the part of me screaming to be reasonable, to hold it together, to keep up the charade. The part of me demanding rationality is a thin candle before the hurricane of my anger. I feel like I'm speaking through mouthfuls of blood. "You are going to get up and walk away. You are going to leave here, now, without making a sound. You are going to pretend I never came into your life, and I am going to do my best to forget you exist. Corna and Timo and I are going to follow when we damn well please. In return, I won't make you my personal canvas, my knife the paintbrush, until you beg me to stop practicing my art on your flesh. Are we agreed?"

Gordyn sits, impassive, through my entire speech. He doesn't respond, either in expression or words, his look one of disappointment rather than fear. He obviously has no idea what I'm capable of.

"Are you done?" he asks in the same tone as before. I simply stare, beginning a mental countdown in my head before I end this negotiation permanently. "Good. We are negotiating, and I have come here in good faith. I will let this… fit… you are throwing pass, but my patience is wearing thin."

"Enough," I say, standing abruptly from the table. My chair crashes back and to the ground. Timo rises with me, seeming to grow before my eyes into a menacing bear. "I gave you your chance. Send my regards to the Creator, Jon Gordyn, if he will have you."

I summon the shadow, and it roils up out of my clothes, forming into a slender sword. I leap forward, urging the shadow on, gliding into an unnatural dive that easily clears the dozen paces between us. I bring my blade around, narrowing it, thinning it, focusing that edge into the sharpest I can imagine. It will be quick. Gordyn may deserve pain, but at least this bitter business will be over. I strike, my own reflection growing in Gordyn's eyes as he recognizes his death.

Aurelion slides smoothly between us, his own sword rising to meet mine. It won't matter. No blade of steel has ever stood up to focused shadow. But his hand is empty. Why has he sacrificed himself for Gordyn? He doesn't even have a means of defending himself.

A light appears out of thin air, brighter than fires, shining as the sun. His glowing blade meets mine and they clash there, darkness and light intertwining and writhing against one another. I stumble back, shocked. He doesn't press the advantage, but merely sweeps his blade down in a smooth arc, standing at the ready. The Master of Light? In Gordyn's employ?

"Stand down, Kettle," Aurelion says, his eyes pleading even as his body is relaxed and ready. "You can still walk out of here."

"What you have done to Corna is unforgivable," I spit out. "If you would stand with him, die with him."

I fall into a crouch and hold my blade behind me. The shadow doesn't think, not as people do, but it still *feels*. Right now, despite my anger and determination, the shadow only exudes fear. I almost run, knowing that my greatest ally, my constant companion, does not wish this fight. But Corna is here. If I leave her, I may never see her again.

I dash back into the fight, darting stabs at Aurelion's eyes, his throat, as preternaturally quick and fast as my mind can think the attacks. He deflects them with ease, his glowing sword always there, always meeting mine at the perfect angle, never gracing me with anything but the barest of movement necessary to defend himself. Each clash of our weapons sends both into a wavering frenzy, the swords losing shape as the elements war directly with one another. Aurelion has two scars. He is Tempered, one small step below the Blades themselves. I can no more break his defense than I can kick through granite.

"Enough, Kraft," Gordyn snarls. "You know I want her alive, but end this charade."

"Last chance," Aurelion says, his voice steady and low, low enough that perhaps Gordyn can't hear him. "Go."

My breathing is ragged, my best attacks useless. I can feel something in the shadow I've never felt before: weakness. The shadow itself is tired, its response to my will sluggish, as if its war against the light is wearying us both. I almost listen to Aurelion's advice. I let my weight settle back onto my heels, beginning the turn to get the hell out of this fight for which I'm utterly unprepared. I tense to go…

Timo runs into the fray, his great roar shaking the structure of the Edge as surely as any earthquake.

I can't leave them both. I would rather die fighting for them than live a coward without them. Aurelion turns to engage Timo, his glowing blade darting back and forth like a golden snake. I watch Timo shy back, smoke and flame erupting across his clothing, his skin blackening before the onslaught of the light. Tears blur my vision as he staggers back, great sweeping swaths of burned flesh replacing his pale skin. The keening wail filling the space is my own.

I have one chance. Aurelion is in Gordyn's employ. If Gordyn dies, Aurelion will have no need to continue fighting. I open my hand, willing the shadow into a short dagger. Gordyn's eyes meet mine across the room. I cock my arm back to throw and pray as I have never prayed before for this blow to strike true. I snap my hand forward, the shadow little more than a dim blur through the air.

Light erupts from the side, light such as I have never seen, a twisting, glowing, *living* mass of brightness. The light weaves a cage around my little dagger of shadow, capturing it as surely as a rabbit in a snare. I growl, willing the shadow back to me to try again. The shadow, however, does not return. I feel it, as surely as I feel the rest of it pooled in the palm of my other hand, but it can't respond. It's trapped.

Then, the light begins to squeeze. I gasp, falling on my knees, as the fear in the shadow spikes to a crescendo. Pain erupts through our bond, a pain so intense I can't see, I can't hear, pain such as I've never imagined. The light constricts further, pressing against the darkness inexorably, inevitably, crushing my shadow in a noose of glowing power. Twisting ribbons of light dart here and there to keep the shadow locked firmly in its cage. The shadow in my hand quivers, trembles, weeps. The light snaps inward one final time, and the forlorn sliver of shadow disappears. The pain evaporates. I sit up, seeing without seeing the light dissipating, leaving nothing behind in its wake.

The shadow is gone.

My shadow.

Gone.

Sorrow comes as swift as an adder's strike. The remaining shadow keens a lamentation, the sound unheard, the sorrow unfelt, the despair unrelenting. Tears stream down my cheeks, all fight gone from my limbs, my eyes staring vacantly at the spot my shadow occupied but a moment before. The remaining shadow retreats, sliding under my clothes against my will, hiding against my skin. I don't try to call it back. I can't form a thought so precise. I've failed in the one vow I swore when I took up R'hea's mantle.

Some of the last living shadow in the entire world is dead, gone, as if it never was, as if it never can be again. I shoved my element squarely in the face of its most feared and hated enemy. forced it to continue fighting a fight shadow long ago lost. And I had to watch as it suffered the same death living shadow had evaded for millennia. No one can shoulder that burden but me.

Distantly, I hear Aurelion shouting at Timo, demanding he stop fighting. My lips move, but I can't hear my own words. Some noise must escape, though, for the shouting stops and quiet falls. The glow of Aurelion's sword disappears, and the dimness of the dining room is shocking after the brilliance of his Shaping. The Creator-Cursed Master of Light, nothing but a lackey? How could I have known?

My gaze tracks dully around the room, my eyes leaden and slow. Corna huddles in the corner, her eyes wide and terrified. Timo leans against the wall near the door, breathing heavily and clutching at his blackened torso. Aurelion stands, elegant as before, the only sign of his exertion a light sheen of sweat on his forehead. For a second, it almost seems his hand glimmers in the darkness, but the moment passes without much interest for my thick and languorous thoughts. Gordyn steps back to the dining room table, righting his chair and seating himself once again at the head.

He gestures for me to resume my seat. Numb, I comply under Aurelion's watchful gaze. There's confusion in Aurelion's posture, as if he can't understand why the fight left me so suddenly. He steps forward and helps me into my chair. I collapse into it like a marionette without strings.

For a brief second, Aurelion allows his hand to linger on my shoulder, and I feel the first ripple of emotion deep in my shocked and shaken heart: anger. If I was more aware, I would have shrugged his hand off, but his touch is gone before the action registers. Instead, I shiver. The sadness, the unending sorrow of my shadow is an ocean too wide to cross and too deep to swim. The fear and uncertainty of this moment is too much to grasp. But *someone* caused this pain. A bitter seed grows in the bottom of my heart. Gordyn's orders led me to this moment. Whether it takes me a dozen breaths or a dozen years, I won't forget.

And neither will he.

Gordyn studies me from behind steepled fingers for a moment, and I feel the distant urge to straighten and regain something of my confidence from before, but the impulse can't pierce through the malaise swimming at the surface of my brain. He's already won. What purpose is there in bravado? What hope in swagger? The only truth lies buried in my soul, and of that he will get no sign.

"I truly meant this to be a good-faith negotiation," Gordyn begins, his voice the same neutral tone as before. "Your friend for my goods. I heard rumors of your abilities, always heightened and exaggerated until you were some legendary beast, a terror of the night to stalk children's nightmares. I am sorry to see that the rumors were merely that."

"You have no idea," Aurelion speaks from the side, still standing and eyeing Timo across the way. "I saw her anger, I saw her intent, and I acted accordingly. But if I didn't see this woman coming? If she could choose the arena? If she didn't have others to protect? Believe me when I tell you *I* will not sleep well if she wishes me harm."

Gordyn sits back at Aurelion's words, studying me anew.

"What do you have to say to Mr. Kraft's… opinion of you?"

I stare. As if I will give him anything. He watches me in turn, and long moments pass. Timo's harsh breathing and occasional grunt of pain mixes with Corna's terrified little gasps in the silence. Slowly, inevitably, I struggle to the surface of my shock and sorrow. Even if I've led us to this end, I have to do my best to save my Family.

"What do you want, Gordyn?" I ask, forcing my spine to lock. "You've won. You have me at your mercy. Why continue the game?"

"The 'game' I am playing is beyond your understanding, thief. But, despite everything, you may be of use yet. They say you can steal anything if you set your mind to it…" he trails off leadingly.

"I acquired a pair of boots a few weeks ago. I don't think their owner ever meant to part with them."

"Point taken," he says, nodding. "I'm going to be honest with you, Kettle, Mother of the Family. I approached this meeting with the hope of hiring you. You've forced me to reevaluate my expectations for this relationship."

"And?" I ask, impatient.

"Well, now I'm afraid I can't trust you," he says frankly. His eyes give away nothing. "So I'm going to have to keep your friend as insurance against your no-doubt clever and meticulous plan to end my time on this earth."

"Take me," I say, eyes flicking to Corna. "Let Corna and Timo go, and I'll do whatever task you ask of me free of charge."

"If I judged you before correctly, and with Mr. Kraft's assessment of your abilities, I have to say I can't imagine a world in which I feel safe without some kind of power over you. How can I trust you won't stab Mr. Kraft or myself in the back the moment we allow your friends to leave?"

"My word?" I say weakly. I know, even if I *would* keep my word, that these men will never trust it. Gordyn gives me a glimmer of a smile, as if I've told a mildly humorous joke. "You know that power over me only lasts as long as she is safe."

"Of course," Gordyn says, waving the concern aside as if the thought is ridiculous. "I would not make a lasting enemy of your abilities. I just wish you to understand: I will not be trifled with. Your friend will remain unharmed so long as you work as my ally. The second I discern a hint of treachery from you, she will die a long and painful death. Don't even give me reason to question. Now, if you do as I ask and accomplish this task, I see no reason why we can't part as amicably as you demanded at the beginning of this meeting."

"What do you want me to do?" I ask, my heart sinking like lead through water.

"I want you to steal something for me," he says, blinking once as if it's the most obvious thing in the world. Perhaps it is.

"What could I possibly steal that you can't buy?"

“Something beyond price. Mr. Kraft will fill you in on the details. When my desire is met, your friend will walk free. Until then… well. ” he says, standing and walking to the door. He turns back as he opens it to leave. “Oh, and those boots you acquired? Keep them, for now. Perhaps they will prove useful.”

Chapter 14
Jace
The Forty-Third Day of Spring
In the year 5222, Council Reckoning

"You have the potential to be one of the best swordsmen I have ever seen. You have natural speed that is absurd, personal commitment, and, best of all, timing. The difference, however, between the great and the best is a simple thing: control."

"Elaborate," I say, raising an eyebrow at Reknor's excited expression.

"You have great endurance and natural talent," Reknor says, pacing, staring at the floor intently. "Your speed is fantastic. What you lack, to put it simply, is control. Every master of every discipline can tell you about being able to control your craft, about having perfect discipline to never question your instincts, to allow your experience and talent and knowledge to merge into one single force that is seamless, as if the parts were never separate. Control. Just as a master mason needs to be able to place a chisel just so, and strike at exactly the right angle, with the perfect amount of force, to dislodge the precise amount of stone that he desires. Just as the painter places each sliver of color with deliberation and vision for the whole piece. Just as the greatest runners know exactly the stride length they need to achieve their best speed, how hard they can push themselves, exactly when to burst and use their final reservoir of energy. Control is the complete knowledge of your body, your capabilities, and the limits, or lack thereof, of your craft. You already have the natural instincts and creativity of a potential master. If you learn control, Jace, you will be unbeatable."

The tasks that Reknor created to teach me 'control' were impossible. Cut halfway through an inch-wide candle. Cut all but one strand of a hempen rope. Put out three of five lit candles with a swing of my sword, in various order, not in a row, in a single slash, with multiple attacks. Cut the straps of Reknor's training armor without being touched in full combat, as if Reknor is a slouch with the sword himself. Hang by one hand from a rope and fight. Fight Reknor hanging upside down by my knees from a pole. Fight from my back, from my knees, with one leg, with one arm. Prune a neighbor's bushes into perfect shapes with slashes of the sword. Be awoken in the night with a sword to the neck, and expect to win. Do each of the above tasks blindfolded. Spin a dozen times and complete them dizzy.

I failed time and time again. I cut through a hundred ropes, two hundred, before the first success came and the final twine was left intact. I split candles down to nubs, then melted and reformed them to start again. Over months, I started to make genuine progress in the impossible tasks. The ropes and the candles have become trivial. I'm nearly as much at ease upside down or in the dark as standing on my own two feet in the day. My right and my left hands are practically interchangeable.

For all that, I'm still terrified as I eye the stranger standing with quiet confidence in the center of the training room.

Where there had been colored poles and the various and sundry equipment of Reknor's esoteric training, a simple mat has taken their place. The stranger is small and wiry, his skin several shades darker than my own. I figure him for a Khalintari, perhaps from the far north or west. A bright green sash wraps around his wrist, but otherwise his drab and unremarkable clothing does little to set him apart.

Reknor kneels off to the side of the room, his eyes serious and calculating, two others also waiting quietly: a man with a rakish blonde beard and a shaven head dressed in a blue military cut of the latest fashion and a woman in the dark leathers of a mercenary, her clothing a shade lighter than her deep brown skin.

A scar bisects one of her eyes, brow to cheek, but the eye itself still gleams out a vibrant blue.

"Hello," I say without the faintest idea of what's going on.

The woman snorts indelicately, shooting Reknor an incredulous look.

"You told me you had a worthy challenger, not a real *ak'aia*," she snaps, loud enough for me to hear. I don't know what *ak'aia* means, but her tone says enough.

"I told you this would be unorthodox," he retorts.

"You said unorthodox, not unprecedented."

"There is precedent," Reknor answers, looking at her with some kind of hidden meaning I can't fathom. His words seem to mollify her, though she can't wipe a skeptical look off her face.

"Jace, this is Benko," Reknor continues, ignoring the woman and gesturing towards the man standing in the center of the room. "And this is James Elthe," the man nods, giving me a playful wink and a grin. "And this is Ke'sti'ra of the Rak'a'to. They are here to test some claims I've made about your abilities with a sword."

"A test?" I ask, my stomach dropping a bit. Weren't you supposed to be warned before a test?

"You will be afforded one duel with each of them," Reknor explains. "These fights are an exercise in the control you've developed. Your path to victory is through delivering a fatal strike, yet inflicting no harm upon your opponent. Any blood drawn is a sign of weakness, and you will fail the test. Your opponents will follow these same parameters."

Benko, whoever he is, does not speak at all for himself, nor seemingly react to Reknor's explanation. He simply stares at me, his eyes deep and dark. The sword he holds is thinner than mine, double edged and deadly.

"Benko of No Name, you are called to question this *um'iel* and see if he is worthy of the A'kai'ano'ri. Your sacred task is before you. You are the test," the dark mercenary Ke'sti'ra intones from the side. Question? I'm going to answer questions? I breathe an inward sigh of relief and relax a hair.

"We are the children, yet we seek to learn. We are the ore, yet we seek the hammer. We are the soul, yet we seek purification."

All four voices in the room speak the words in various accents, their cadence blending into a simple harmony. My confusion deepens. Is this some sort of ritual? Some kind of ceremony?

"Begin."

Instantly, without any sign of tension or expectation, Benko explodes into action, his blade whipping straight for my unprotected neck. I block the first three blows with my sword half out of its scabbard, backing towards the corner to give myself room. Benko matches my pace, refusing to give up the initiative, his sword an unceasing strike of lightning. Each swing moves in blurring intensity, but the sheer speed costs him his ability to feint or effectively counter. Once the man commits to an attack, he's *committed.* After a tense few seconds where I'm almost trapped against the corner and kept from effectively maneuvering, I finally see an opening. He steps forward, his weight transferring to the ball of his forward foot to put more force into his next strike. I step in with him and have the satisfaction of watching his eyes widen in surprise as I close suddenly inside the arc of his weapon and plant an elbow squarely in his solar plexus. His breath leaves him in a quiet wheeze, and he staggers backwards. I give him no time, closing ground and ending the fight with the tip of my blade against the inside of his groin. He steps back, struggling to regain his breath, and bows his head formally. I nod in return.

The rakish man Elthe continues to smile, but the dark mercenary of the Isles wears something of a stunned expression. Reknor appears stoic, but his smugness radiates from across the room. Just as my breathing returns to normal, Ke'sti'ra speaks again.

"James Elthe, you are called to question this *um'iel* and see if he is worthy of the A'kai'ano'ri. Your sacred task is before you. You are the test."

Elthe stands, stretching his shoulders and patting Ke'sti'ra on the head as he passes. She scowls, but otherwise doesn't react. He draws his rapier smoothly, the thin blade ending in a gleaming point. Grinning a confident grin, he winks again, but I can see the seriousness in his eyes as he takes on a ready stance. The casual facade is nothing but a playful mask.

"We are the children, yet we seek to learn. We are the ore, yet we seek the hammer. We are the soul, yet we seek purification."

A brief moment of expectant silence.

"Begin."

Unlike Benko, Elthe doesn't move as the fight begins. Instead, he makes an arrogant 'come here' gesture, planting his feet and angling the point of his rapier so it aligns with my throat. I have no intentions of doing what the man wishes. I circle, stepping carefully to the side, wary of how far or fast the man can lunge with his long weapon. He pivots smoothly, his feet always in perfect balance, his posture relaxed and steady. When I've circled about halfway around him, slowly closing the distance between us, he lunges out of nowhere, the point of his sword rushing towards my eyes faster than thought. I sweep my blade up to deflect the strike, but his sword is gone, darting instead for my vulnerable groin. I twist to my left, bringing my sword down in desperation to block the blow, but again he's years ahead. His sword is an adder, striking and retracting so fast I can't even blink. The tip of his sword gently, almost apologetically, pokes my right shoulder just where the muscle would suffer the most damage. The strike is surgical, the control precise.

I step back, frustrated with myself. The man's speed is startling, but I should have been ready for it. His smile turns almost rueful as he spins on his heel to walk back to our waiting audience, but Reknor holds up a hand.

"What are you doing, Mr. Elthe?" he asks, furrowing his brow in confusion.

"This fight is over. He would have lost all use of his arm if this fight was real," Elthe says, shrugging.

"Does he not have another arm?" Reknor asks in response.

Elthe frowns, glancing back at me. I promptly put my right hand behind my back, presenting my blade in readiness with my left. His eyebrows rise, but then he belts out a short laugh, straight from his belly.

"Well, you can't say the boy doesn't have pluck," he mutters, assuming his ready stance and waving me forward again.

This time, I do come on, driving firmly into his range. He strikes, his moves coming with the same casual grace and liquid speed, but I press forward. He retreats, still in control, but I move with him, keeping inside the range of his long and deadly lunges. He counters with a series of short and darting feints, the tip of his sword a scorpion's tail. My urge to retreat roars under the absurd speed of the attacks, but I force myself closer, my sword reacting only to genuine strikes, my instincts picking up on clues my mind could never read. Before long he's pressed against the wall, his sword working furiously just to keep mine at bay. The signs of desperation blossom in his face, his movements more abrupt, his control slipping, his eyes roving. He almost gets me with the sheer reckless audacity of his final strike, surrendering all defense to send one last bolt of lightning hurtling at my throat. I move my head, just enough, feeling the air move across my cheek from the blow, cleanly resting my blade across his throat in the same movement.

His smile is gone. In its place, his eyes smolder in anger. With a careless flick, he cuts my cheek as he retracts his sword. The urge to do likewise on the side of his neck swells in me, but I manage to lower my blade without giving in. The weight of

Reknor's heavy gaze rests on me, and I desire his disappointment less than I desire death. So I step away, ignoring the stinging cut and the thin sheet of blood working its way down my neck. Elthe seems to relax, coming back to himself, a ghost of his former smile gracing his lips.

He nods towards me once, sharply. I nod back.

"Sorry, boy. I was careless. You're too good for me," he says, attempting to adopt a flippant tone.

Careless? Please. The man had executed a brilliant surgical strike on my shoulder, in perfect control, without even damaging my shirt. My blood is on his blade because he desires it to be.

"Of course," I respond, waving my hand as if it doesn't matter. It doesn't. I've suffered far worse. "It's nothing."

"Jace of Donir, you are deemed worthy of the A'kai'ano'ri," Ke'sti'ra says, wonder and no small amount of surprise in her voice. "The Process, in your tongue. The Path. The Forge. The Ascendance. Your skills and your control, both in combat and out, are deserving of the title *Nori,* the Man, the Blade, the Zenith. You have earned the mark of our order, and all will recognize you for your rank."

With a flourish, Ke'sti'ra and the other two whip off the colored scarves on their wrists, revealing unique markings. Each has what looks like a single short line, as if a numeral denoting 'one,' tattooed along the inside of their wrists, clear and bold and black against the various shades of their skin. Next to that one line, however, are a trio of scars as if three identical lines have been cut away.

The terms she uses, some mixture of Isles speech and Donirian translation, all go sailing past me. The Process? The Ascendance? What are these people talking about? And now they want to mark me? What insanity has Reknor brought me in to? It's with a start that I realize Reknor holds out his own wrist, revealing a similar tattoo. He had the same original markings, but two matching dark numerals are paired with two scars. Despite everything we've been through, all of our time spent together, I've never seen him out of long sleeves. Has he been hiding this the entire time?

"The cut on my face," I say, suddenly realizing. "Another test?"

"Just so. A *Nori* must control her emotions in addition to her body. It seems my questions are not necessary," Ke'sti'ra says, somewhat regretfully, as if she most definitely wanted to test herself against me. "I will admit to some surprise, boy. How many Winters have you seen?"

"Seventeen."

"So young. I survived above the Depths for twenty-five Winters before I dared try my hand at joining the A'kai'ano'ri. Thirty before I was *Nori.* I was wrong, my old friend, to doubt you," she says, turning to Reknor.

"There is no offense. Your questions were not necessary, Ke'sti'ra, but would you do him the honor of asking them anyway?" Reknor asks with a smile.

"He is no longer *um'iel.* The decision lies with him," she answers, turning to me. "Do you wish to test one another, young *Nori*?"

"What does *um'iel* mean?" I ask in response.

"Stranger. One who is not of us."

"And I am, now? One of you?"

Whatever that means.

"You are. If you show this mark to another, you will be honored as a *Nori,* a Blade. For those with knowledge, they will understand that you have an uncommon gift. If you seek to eat from your blade," she pauses, fingering her own mercenary sigil, "you will find that employers will honor the mark of your ability in accordance with your rank. If someone does not recognize your skill, they are unworthy of your services."

"Are we mercenaries then? Skilled fighters for hire?"

"Have you taught him nothing?" she asks Reknor, her tone chiding. "We are the A'kai'ano'ri. We seek nothing but the End, the telos, the perfection of our bodies, minds, and souls. We know we will never finish. We will never achieve our goal. But still, we strive for perfection. Our skills are merely a product of that search."

I think back through the thousand lessons Reknor taught me, the endless books, the absurd tests, the ceaseless search for mastery, for control… I've been following that idea ever since Reknor began to teach me, whether I knew it or not.

"I would love to answer your questions, then, Ke'sti'ra."

"Good," she says, standing and drawing not one, but two blades sheathed side by side. One sword she holds in a traditional grip, the other curves downward towards her forearm. Immediately my stomach sinks. What the hell kind of style is that? "The A'kai'ano'ri are ever seeking tests."

I want to say that I put up a good fight, but she humbles me in the span of ten heartbeats. I not only fail to even threaten her once, but I have the feeling she could have disarmed me twice in that span, but took pity on me. I shudder to think about anyone who has to face her in real battle. With a solemn nod from Benko, a pat on the shoulder from James Elthe, and a magnanimous smile from Ke'sti'ra, the A'kai'ano'ri take their leave.

I have a thousand questions, but Reknor cuts me off before I can speak by brandishing a piece of crafted vellum covered in gold ink calligraphy. The piece of paper itself probably costs as much as my sword, so I can't imagine what's written on it. The grin on Reknor's face, however, fills my gut with unease.

"What do you have planned this time?"

"Me?" Reknor says, too innocently. "I don't have anything planned. Two nights from now, however, you do. A unique opportunity, if I say so myself. You can get your tattoo marking you as *Nori* when you return."

"What opportunity could that be?" I ask, sheathing my blade and stretching out my fingers for the note. Reknor snatches it away with a scowl.

"You'll damage the ink," he huffs. Puffing up to his full height and throwing his chest out, Reknor coughs pretentiously and declares: "To the Lord Hollenzar of Hollen, on this Most Special Occasion at the Height of Spring, an Invitation to the Ball of Kings at the Royal Palace of the Kingdom of the Sea, Helikos the blah blah blah."

"Who in the Creator's name is the Lord of Hollenzar?"

"Can't you guess?" Reknor asks, lone eye glinting in amusement.

***

My carriage comes to a mild, lurching stop and I bend over. I can't see anything but darkness, and my stomach convulses as I taste bile. A young nobleman who has never been to court might be nervous, but that excuse will only go so far. I ruthlessly push down my emotions and take a long, deep breath, reaching for the stillness. I don't find it, but the action calms me anyway. I summon up what little knowledge I have of noblemen's sons and knock imperiously on the door to the gilded carriage. The footman opens the door immediately, and I sweep out, struggling for the proper balance between arrogance and humility. I'm not known at court, so I can't be full of confidence, but I'm still a noble. My short cape swishes behind me as I walk, and I smile. As the first servant to see me bows low, I know I have the walk right, at least.

I stride up to the palace gates, approaching the wide and inviting double doors. The warmth and music from inside is muted from the threshold. I listen, slowly trying to fall into my role, absently presenting the invitation to a guardsman who nods and welcomes me. The King's Ball is not a place where you want to be exposed as a fake.

The palace is largely functional rather than opulent, and the cut stone mildly forbidding as I walk under the portcullis. Glancing up, an eye glints from an arrow slit above as a soldier peers down at me. I hastily face forward again and follow the line of rich and wealthy to an ornate pair of double doors.

The doors themselves are a work of art, wrought in what appears to be pure gold. Each panel depicts a different cardinal element: waves and crashing storms for water, roaring flame around a volcano for fire, proud mountains and sweeping plains for earth, and a swirling, mesmerizing pattern for air. In the center connecting each panel is a deep hourglass. The doors swing wide, and the couple at the front of the line strides through, heads held proudly as their names echo throughout the packed ballroom.

I'm supposed to be a young nobleman from a distant and inconsequential province, forced out on a grand tour of the world to become a better man. I'm making a stop in the High Court, gaining in 'culture' and experience. The Hollenzars do have a legitimate young son, who Reknor assures me will not show up at the dance.

The line moves forward, and I straighten my brilliant white jacket and half-cape once again, fighting to keep a scowl off my face. Even my boots are polished in such a way that they look to have an off-white sheen. The only color on my outfit comes from the golden buttons adorning the right side of my tunic. Reknor claims it's fashionable, but all that I've seen so far from the other guests are muted colors. The doors open for the couple in front of me, and I groan inwardly. The vast majority of the crowd is dressed in greens, blues, and reds to honor Spring. No white at all.

The hall itself is filled with perfect mosaics of crashing waves and oceans, each precious and semi-precious stone carefully wrought and arranged. A balcony surrounds the entire room, with space underneath separated by glittering pillars shaped like water spouts. High overhead a massive orb of water floats over the crowd, flowing and churning, spinning around itself in a slow dance that matches the music. There are no attachments I can see, no glass or wire. The orb is levitating of its own accord, and lanterns float inside of its depths, bobbing around in the water and casting a dim, dappled light over the crowd and the glittering walls.

Somehow, the king is Shaping the water into the awe-inspiring chandelier without even being in the room. It's my first experience with Shaping up close, and it sears twelve colors of fear into my soul.

The walls may glitter, but they have nothing on the guests. Each dress in attendance is a work of art, and, although many are in shades of green or blue and largely unadorned, each woman has on enough jewelry to feed me for years on the streets. Gems I don't recognize rest boldly on top of cleavage or dangle like magic from earlobes. Men are dressed in muted blues and greens in honor of the Sealord and every guest possesses a noble's bearing.

A polite cough sounds to my right, and the majordomo looks at me expectantly.

"Teldaran Hollenzars, first son of the Lord and Lady of Hollen."

The man nods and bows for me to enter, slamming his staff three times against the marble. Dozens of pairs of eyes turn to me, and I force myself not to wilt. It feels like my stomach is trying to escape through my bowels, and the shaking in my knees has to be obvious. I've stolen from these people, attacked them, hated them, and resented them. Now I have to act like I'm one of them.

"Elder Son Teldaran Hollenzars of Hollen," the majordomo calls, and several people whisper fiercely to one another.

As soon as I start down the steps, however, the crowd turn back to their conversations, the music comes up, and I manage to relax slightly. I am, for the moment, forgotten again. A smile works its way on my face. I don't have to be me. I'm not the sullen thief of before, or even the proud scholarly ward of yesterday. I'm the eldest son of a noble family, and the court had better watch out.

My fears disappear like dousing a torch. I saunter forward, my brilliant white clothing shimmering in the lights from above. I ignore the surreptitious glances from the crowd and walk with my head held high. The vibrations from my boots reverberate off of the polished marble floor, but I can't hear them over the music. The other guests have drinks in hand so… there. On my way towards the servant with drinks, I pass into an open pocket of people. A conspicuously open pocket, the second I notice who stands in its middle.

The Lord General towers over the crowd, his muscular arms folded firmly across his chest. He wears a simple matte black tunic with matching pants and utilitarian boots. The only thing impressive about him, aside from his unnatural size and stature, is his sword. The weapon is absurd. Easily as tall as the gigantic man himself, the hilt has room for four of my hands to close around it. Ornate, delicate gold tracings work their way around the hilt, but I can see that some of them have been damaged or flattened. That sword isn't just for show. Somehow, Kranos has found the need to use it. Or the desire. He's larger than any man I've ever met. His shoulders are broad and powerful, his face strong and charming. Despite that, there's something… off about the man.

His eyes focus on me, and he beckons.

Shit.

I sweep down into a low bow, my hand out to the side in the manner of the eastern provinces. He grunts as I straighten.

"Hollenzars, eh?" he says, his voice coming out as a melodious, warm baritone. I'm shocked by the pleasant deep rumble as it cuts through the other chatter. "Pretty country, for a pretty people. I remember conquering you."

I straighten further, my spine locking, shocked. Some part of my mind knows he's trying to unnerve a new face, but another part of me feels the anger that the real Hollenzar heir would have felt. Kranos' eyes glitter with a cold intelligence that makes my skin crawl. I struggle to keep my face under control, but I redden as the warlord smirks.

"Lord General, I am glad you have… fond memories of your time in my lands. My father sends his regards," I say with forced civility.

"I'm sure he does. If he didn't, I might be forced to replace him."

"You could very well try, my lord."

Even as the words leave my mouth I try to will them back. Kranos, for his part, doesn't move. His eyes are like flint, and I struggle not to take a step back as they narrow. The man's absurd musculature ripples as he moves forward in a forbidding pose, looming over me like a mountain granted life. He bursts into sudden laughter, his head falling back and bumping against the pommel of his sword. He continues to laugh, and I don't have any idea what to do. All of the etiquette training that Reknor has given me goes out the window in the face of a powerful ruler laughing in my face. I force myself not to look around as the conversations die throughout the room.

"Perhaps the pup has more bark than his sire. But can he bite?" he asks, and his tone makes the question rhetorical. I simply bow my head, my arms at my side. "Well, then. I like you, boy. You've got balls, I'll give you that. Tell your father I'll send those reinforcements he's been waiting on. We can't have so interesting a future threatened by some crazy barbarians, now can we?"

"Thank you, sir. We will put them to good use," I say, having no idea what the man's talking about.

"No doubt, no doubt. Perhaps you should lead them, eh? Ah, well. Go enjoy the party."

"A pleasure, Lord General," I say, bowing in the elaborate eastern way once more.

I fade back into the crowd and travel quickly to the nearest wall to beat my head against it, silently praying into the air above me that my luck hasn't run out yet. For a moment, I thought he was going to kill me on the spot or invade a land I've barely heard of. The sound of the music is muted along the sides of the chamber.

An open, arched doorway nearby elicits the echo of voices. I don't pay them much mind, too busy breathing deeply through my nose, until I begin to make out words.

"... don't know why we keep throwing these worthless dances. A portion of my mind dies each time that one of these sycophants fawns over me. How can a man be expected to think straight with this much perfume in the air? The palace smells of it for weeks afterwards," the deep voice says, smooth as butter even as he complains.

"It's good for morale, my lord. The nobles need to see your presence, to see their leader. They also need to be reminded of who that leader is..."

"Pah, I know the reasons, Graevo. I'm just complaining, as usual."

I freeze, my heart racing. Torlas is here, and the Sealord is with him. If I'm recognized, I'll be following Jonah to the chopping block. I set off towards the nearest group of guests to lose myself in the crowd, cursing.

Too late. Helikos and Torlas walk out of the entryway just as I glance back towards them. My eyes pass quickly over the king, flicking towards Torlas just as sees me. I wince as recognition blossoms in his eyes, and my mind races through the possible exits if I'm forced to make a hasty retreat.

Ah, well. There's nothing for it. I step forward and bow, holding the bow for several long seconds as Helikos and Torlas no doubt look on. Straightening, I meet the King's gaze solemnly.

"Teldaran Hollenzar, elder son of the Lord and Lady of Hollen, at your service, my king."

The king looks me up and down, then smiles with an inviting grin.

"Teldaran, it is a pleasure. Is Jenaras well? I regret that we haven't been able to help with that barbarian problem, but with the growing dissent in this province, we have problems of our own. I assure you that we will spare the troops at the earliest possible convenience."

I nod once, sharply.

"The Lord General has promised the troops presently, your majesty. The matter has already been resolved. I thank you for your generosity."

"Wonderful," the king says, his voice warm again, though his eyes go cold. "The Lord General would know the disposition of our armies better than I. Regrettably, I can see a line forming for my attention. Send my regards to your father."

I bow again, holding the uncomfortable pose as the king sweeps by me.

"My lord," Torlas calls. "Will you excuse me for a moment? I would have a word with the young Hollenzar."

I close my eyes, praying without even knowing what I'm praying for. The king grunts once.

"Yes, yes. Don't be too long. I'll need you to give me some breathing room from time to time."

"Of course, my lord. I'll be with you presently."

I stand up, turning back and meeting Torlas' eye. He's struggling to contain his laughter as he steps up to me. He glances around, making sure that no one is watching, before grinning widely.

"Jace, Jace. You know that impersonating nobility is considered treason, right?"

"Hush, Graevo. My name is Teldaran Hollenzar. Is my bow not recognizable?" I ask, grinning back.

"Did Reknor get you in? That old rascal would pull those kinds of strings. Nice… outfit?" Torlas says, arching an eyebrow at my pure-white ensemble.

"Reknor, too," I say with a laugh. "He obviously has great fashion sense. And a great sense of humor."

"So," Torlas says as we move over to the wall and lean against it. "Who have you had the pleasure of meeting so far? How many dukes and earls and duchesses and puppet kings and queens have you bowed to this evening?"

"So far? Just a general, a king, and one sniveling duke whose company drags ever onward."

Torlas shoots me an arch look before laughing.

"Splendid. Now, I can give you an idea of who you should meet before you ever have to bow…"

Torlas accurately and hilariously describes the privileged few in attendance at the King's Ball. Men and women from all over the Kingdom of the Sea have traveled to take part. Torlas points out an Earless of a province not too distant from Hollen, and I immediately make a mental note to avoid the woman if at all possible. Most of the attendees are nobility of some sort or another, but many are noble through the benefit of wealth. Dignitaries from both the Isles and the Khalintari Republic huddle in separate corners, rich merchants lucky enough to be invited to the ball. They stick out almost as much as I do, but the sheer weight of the gold dripping from their fingers, clothes, ears, noses, and even toes would allow them to stick out wearing black to a funeral. Torlas impresses me time and again with his knowledge of the court, and with each introduction comes a sardonic little quip.

"And she, well, Countess Taloon is the most lecherous woman on the planet. And, due to her station, she can surround herself with even more lecherous servants. If you ever make it to her home, watch that you don't get invited into the study," Torlas says, winking at me.

"And who is that?" I ask, pointing across to a slender young woman in a green dress. She's pleasant to look at, and only a simple string of pearls decorates her elegant neck. She turns at a comment from the man next to her and smiles, and I smile back. Okay. She's more than just 'pleasant.'

"Ah, that…" Torlas trails off as he realizes I'm not really paying attention. "Jace. Jace."

"Huh, what?" I say, shaking myself slightly and looking at him.

"That, my friend, is entirely off limits. That is Helikos' daughter, Iliana. She is worthy of any man's admiration, but that admiration can only come from a distance," Torlas says in warning.

"That is the princess of the kingdom?" I ask, slightly incredulous. The girl is pretty, sure, but she doesn't seem as... *impressive* as she should be.

"Watch your words, or you really might get accused of treason," Torlas says, his tone more serious than I expect it to be.

"I feel like I know her…" I start to say before realizing I don't know her whatsoever.

"I have to say that seems unlikely..."

"Sure," I say slowly, but I can't shake the feeling. "All the same… Torlas, would you do me an enormous favor?"

"How enormous?" he asks, eyebrows raised.

"Would you… introduce me? To her?"

"Right… I don't know how enormous a favor that would be, but, as a friend, I'll humor you. Then, however, I have to go. The king will be needing my presence."

He sets out, and I fall in behind him, trying to swallow back my nervousness. The time across the marble floor is an eternity, but when I look up into the waiting eyes of a half-dozen powerful women, it feels like we've appeared over there instantly.

"Ladies, I am pleased you were able to attend," Torlas begins, sweeping into a deep bow.

"Please, Graevo," Iliana chides. "We have to be here."

"All the same, lady, I thank you."

Iliana leans back and gives Torlas a sad, simple smile. She's suddenly stunning, and I ache for whatever sadness lies behind her eyes. She reaches out and brushes his arm, but neither notice. The silence draws onward, and I open my mouth and give a slight cough into my hand. At the same time, a dainty cough sounds from next to Iliana. A pretty girl with brown ringlets and green eyes her hand over her mouth in the same way I do. Our eyes meet, and we both drop our hands and smile sheepishly.

Iliana and Torlas seem to start, coming back to themselves and talking all over each other at once.

"Ladies, I would like you to meet..."

"Torlas, what are you..."

They stumble to a jerking halt, and everyone laughs at their expense. To Torlas' credit, he laughs along with them.

"Lady, if I may?" he asks, dipping his head in respect.

"Please, proceed, my lord," she responds, dipping into a curtsey. I find myself smiling broadly, the tension gone.

"My lady, this is the esteemed first son of Hollen, Teldaran," he says.

I step forward as gracefully as possible. She holds out her hand, and I bend over it, stopping short of pressing her hand to my lips, but only just. I straighten smoothly, and she graces me with a smile.

"The talk of the ball," Iliana says, even as her brow furrows. "I'm sorry, but have we met before?"

Strange, that she feels it, too. Something about her face, the structure, the smile, reminds me of someone. It feels less like a memory, and more like a... I can't place it, so I simply shrug.

"I would be lying if I didn't say I feel the same, but I do not recall ever meeting someone such as you. And, surely, I would have remembered."

"Ah, Graevo, you've made a friend with a similar tongue to your own," Iliana says, half-smiling.

"So, Teldaran," the girl next to her begins. "What is Hollen like? We've heard so much about your country, and I've always wanted to visit."

"Ah," I say softly, and I hope the uncertainty doesn't show in my eyes. "There is little to be said, other than for the mountains. When you see the peaks rising into the sky, there is something inside of you that… stirs."

"They are beautiful," Iliana says, her gaze far away. "I passed through with my father when I was a child. I don't think you were in attendance at the dinner. Too young, my father said. But the mountains are indeed breathtaking."

"Thank you, my lady, for honoring my country," I say, bowing slightly to hide my alarm. She knows far more about my supposed homeland than I do.

"Drop the 'lady,' Teldaran. Among friends, I remain simply Iliana."

"I am honored to count myself as such," I respond, smiling.

"We shall see," she says, smirking. "Now, Graevo, I have a royal command for you."

"Yes, my lady?"

Iliana looks at me and rolls her eyes.

"No matter how many times I tell him, he doesn't ever drop the act."

"If it were only an act, my lady," Torlas says, his eyes dropping. I would throw his comment out to the banter of the night, but something like truth rings in his words.

"Duke Graevo, I command you to dance with me," Iliana says, tilting her head imperiously and holding out her arm.

Torlas smiles as he takes her proffered arm. He only glances once towards the king, who is engrossed in a conversation with the knot of Khalintari men. The couple disappear into the crowd arm in arm. A blonde woman in an extraordinarily intricate dress of garish green folds her arms and glowers after them. She would be pretty, but her broad chin and her ugly demeanor prevent her from being described as such. You must be Eleanor, the Duke's betrothed. I would probably dance with Iliana instead, too.

I drift over to a servant and finally find the drink I've been looking for, staring after my friend. Iliana and Torlas match each other in elegance, the picture-perfect sight of nobility as it should be. Their dance captivates the crowd, many of the others pairs halting their twirl to admire the two gracefully spinning about the room. Everyone applauds as they finish, the sound startling them both out of a seeming reverie. Smiling and nodding, Torlas confidently, Iliana somewhat ruefully, they walk under the balcony together.

From my vantage, their faces remain clear. He looks at her with such tenderness that my heart goes out to him, and her eyes are shining in response. Torlas suddenly looks up, and his eyes harden. Even from across the room, I can tell something is wrong. Iliana's face falls, and my smile evaporates as Torlas turns sharply and walks away. The Lord General strolls up and puts his arm around Iliana. Her face reflects a quiet melancholy, but she reaches up and pats his muscular arm familiarly.

Iliana and Torlas obviously love one another, but even the power the couple wields, perhaps second only to the King and the Lord General in the entire kingdom, can't bring them together. I find myself hating the man, personally for once instead of as a faceless entity. In meeting Kranos, in seeing the coldness in his eyes, in seeing the wedge he drives between Torlas and the woman he loves… A distant part of me realizes that he probably ordered the attack on the Simply. My rage awakens into a screaming, aching knot of ice and fire. The Lord General heads away, and my eyes burn holes in his back. I should be cautious, I should be afraid, but I glare after him until he disappears behind a pillar.

A soft hand comes to rest on my arm. I jump and turn, meeting stunning eyes that shock me with their intensity. They are a deep, vibrant shade of blue, like the sky at noon. I'm frozen, caught in their depths.

"Again, Teldaran," Iliana says softly. "I feel as if I know you."

"My lady, I believe that you do."

Her brow wrinkles prettily, and she gives me a confused smile.

"I'm afraid I don't understand."

"Looking into your eyes, I simply feel... known. It isn't a feeling I can explain," I respond, suddenly embarrassed.

"Well, I can't explain my feeling, and you can't yours, so we'll just have to live in perpetual confusion," she answers in a reasonable tone.

"Naturally," I laugh. "Iliana, would you do me the honor of a dance?"

"Teldaran..." she glances over at Torlas, who smiles at us briefly from amongst a knot of people. "Very well."

I pace with Iliana out to the center. We stand the awkward moments of a couple who has entered the floor at the wrong moment, waiting for the previous song to end and for the next to begin. I fidget with the buttons on my jacket, surreptitiously check the laces of my boots, and generally try to appear nonchalant. Failing utterly, Iliana and I look at each other and laugh at our own awkwardness. The music comes up, and I step close to her. It's a slower song, the measured pace of a waltz.

I place my hand on her hip and the other out for her to grasp. Her fingers light on mine with little more than the flutter of a hummingbird, and the warmth of her radiates through the thin silk of her dress. We dance slowly, precisely, and smile together at the ease of our sway. We're nearly directly underneath the massive orb of water that serves as the unbelievable chandelier, and I glance up at it apprehensively from time to time.

I'm nervous underneath the damn thing, so I'm not surprised when a drop of water strikes my shoulder. Another hits the top of my head, and one mars Iliana's silk dress, ruining the cloth. Suddenly, Iliana is wooden in my arms. Her feet stutter to a stop, and she spins away from me, searching the crowd.

"I'm sorry," I start. "Perhaps we should move out from under the water, I didn't mean to ruin your dress..."

"The water never falls," she says, waving me to silence. More drops cascade down, and soon other couples notice, voicing quiet complaints in the buzzing room. Iliana stiffens next to me. I follow her gaze to the Sealord himself. He stares at her. At me. At us. His look is intent, piercing, evaluating, but above all surprised. What's the problem? Why is he riveted on a slow dance between a stranger and his daughter? Have I done something untoward?

I blink, and he's moving towards me, his eyes staring and intent. Iliana's brow furrows, and she moves to meet him on his way. Just as his eyes turn to meet hers, I duck aside and behind others in the crowd, breaking our line of sight. Whatever the king wants with me, I'm not going to stick around to find out. Damn Reknor's remaining eye, I never wanted kings or generals to notice me. I just want to live my life. Rushing to the shining golden doors out, I slip through the tunnel and out into the night, too quickly for any orders to detain me. I don't look back.

***

I can't really be in trouble, can I? The King thinks I'm Teldaran Hollenzar, son to a distant and minor noble. I have no idea what his interest in me might be, but, surely, I'm safe. Every time I think of the Sealord's stare and the cold water working its way down my back, though, the icy claws of fear skitter across my stomach and I'm less certain. Reknor doesn't show any undue concern when I tell him. When no one shows up to arrest me after a few days, I start to breathe easier. I return to my training with the sword, though I lack something of the focus I dedicated to the art before. The ache of the single line drawn in black ink on the inside of my left wrist doesn't help matters. Reknor assures me I won't have to get the scars, as the others did. As to why, he's less forthcoming.

Weeks pass, and my fear of the Sealord dissipates. Spring winds down, heading towards the clear heat of Summer. My mind and body settle into the dull slog of training without fervor. I stop getting better. Soon, in fact, I feel like I'm regressing. Cutting through seven candles and half of the eighth becomes a difficulty instead of a warm up. I get the feeling I've exhausted Reknor's creativity with swordplay, and the tasks are beginning to grow dull and repetitive because of it.

After everything he's managed, why do I doubt him?

One hot morning, I'm left to sit in the library, reading another dull, uninspired volume about how a beggar rose to prominence in a kingdom and won the heart of a princess.

"What drivel," I mutter, slamming the book closed. "How could a princess ever love a beggar?"

I hear Reknor return, but I don't stir myself, staring listlessly at the cover of the leatherbound volume and idly running my hands along the title. My eyes don't leave the cover when Reknor walks into the room, but they leave pretty quickly when he smacks me on the back of the head.

"Ow."

"Wake up, my lovely," Reknor says. He has a wide grin on his face. Shit. "It's time for another stage in your quest for control."

"Eternal's broken bones, there's another stage?"

"Always. Now get up, or more than the Eternal will have some broken bones."

Reknor leads me out of the house carrying a basket filled with a hard sourdough bread and a sharp aged cheese. We walk through the Pennies and into the Palace District, threading our way through the noonday crowds with practiced ease. I catch myself as my hand makes a leap towards a passing man's purse, contenting myself with patting it gently before moving on. I still have to fight the old instincts Jonah drilled into me as a child.

We stroll into a park with vivid, almost impossibly green grass spreading out in waves of brilliant viridian. The wealthy cruise the park in their beautiful best, courtiers and ladies wending their way among ancient oaks. Small ponds dot the landscape. Reknor leads me straight to one of the ponds, stopping by the edge and turning back to grin at me.

"Alright, Jace, here we are."

"Why am I armed for a picnic?" I ask, frowning.

"Draw your sword, remove your shirt, and jump in the water."

"What?"

"You heard me. Do I have to explain everything to you? What happened to your commitment?"

"In public."

"Ignore them. They're fawners. No one likes fawners anyway."

I look around, and none of the lords and ladies have taken notice of us yet. With a muttered curse, I whip off my shirt and slide into the water. The late Spring sun has warmed the water to a pleasant level, and I wade out until I'm about chest deep.

"Now what?" I call to Reknor.

"Kill me a fish," he shouts back, pointing down into the water. "The more you kill, the more you get to eat tonight!"

My lowered gaze reveals dozens of fat, lazy fish swimming sullenly around, disturbed from my entrance. I sigh. I lift my sword out of the water, poised to thrust down at one of the fattest, when Reknor shouts.

"No, no, no. All under water. Start your attack underwater, finish underwater. Think of the colored poles," he says, giving me a thumbs up.

My cursing isn't nearly so quiet as I slowly lower the sword into the water. Seeing a particularly slow and juicy specimen gliding past, I swing down at the creature with everything I have. My sword moves slowly, gaining speed like a lumbering elephant. The fish is two feet past when my blade cuts through where he was, and the motion doesn't even disturb him.

"They can feel you coming!" Reknor calls lazily as he lays down on the blanket.

"Thanks," I growl back at him.

Slashing isn't going to get me very far. Whenever I do manage to anticipate a fish's path and it looks like I'm going to connect, the swelling of the water allows it to dart aside with ease. My arms burn from forcing the sword through the water, and my legs ache from taking the impetus of the attacks. The colored poles were a difficult mistress, but the water is swiftly kicking my ass.

When I switch to thrusting, some of the fish look a bit nervous instead of just blithely ignorant. They start to avoid my section of the pond. With a growl, I chase them, sloshing mud about and ruining my sight of them in the murky depths. I thrust blindly in frustration, ten or twenty times into the silted water.

The last time, I pull my sword out of the filmy water with a fat fish skewered neatly on the end of my blade. Pure luck. Reknor laughs at me from the shore, and I glance over to see him miming my frantic attacks. When his eye closes for a particular motion, I bring the fish up stealthily, take aim, and flick it out of the water. The fish strikes him squarely in the face, and his laughs turn to a surprised shout as our bloody, wriggling dinner bounces to the ground.

It's my turn to laugh, neck deep in a pond in the middle of a public park. Reknor's horrified expression as he dabs at the guts on his tunic only spurs me on. He motions me out of the water, shaking his head in disgust. We didn't bring a towel, so I settle onto the blanket and let the late Spring sun bake my skin dry. The bread and cheese are the perfect complement to the day, and I'm content to lazily spend the afternoon with Reknor, talking and laughing.

"What's wrong?" Reknor asks after a while. Of course he's realized something is off about me. "Is it a girl?"

"More like the lack of one," I say.

"What are you waiting for? You're young, handsome, a fearsome swordsman, and witty to boot. How are you not swimming in ladies?" Reknor asks, waggling his eyebrows.

"What?" I ask, more to stall than anything. "I, well, that's… really?"

"Or is there a particular girl?"

"Particular? Maybe. But… I doubt she'll ever notice me."

Like the fool I am, my mind jumps to Iliana. The impossible quarry.

"Women like to be chased. While the patient hunter waits for his prey, a real hunter knows when his prey needs to be stalked."

"Maybe I will," I mutter, but I know I'll never approach *her*. Princesses and beggars just don't mix.

"There you go. All is right again. Now, if this Juliet stomps on your heart, I have an entirely different remedy, which involves a tavern and that—"

"Who?" I ask, frozen in shock.

"Hmm? Oh, you mention Juliet at times when you're sleeping. Don't be alarmed, but you do talk in your sleep from time to time."

"Juliet..." I sigh, remembering my promise to see a leper girl nearly a season ago. I made that promise easy as breathing, and I've broken it just the same. Guilt washes over me. How could I have forgotten her? My heart drops to my toes.

"Well, go find her," Reknor says. "Be back for dinner, and I'll have Pies do this fish up nicely."

But I can't just go back to her. Guilt weighs me down far too much for me to just walk up and apologize. Juliet has to be light on trust and lighter on friends, so it doesn't make sense just to pop back into her life. I need something that'll surprise her and make her happy, a gift fit for the girl she used to be. Wracking my brain, I can come up with only a single person I know that can help me.

***

Though I've called on him a half dozen times before, this time, my palms are sweating as I knock on the sturdy oak door in front of his offices. Every time before, I came to Torlas as a friend, a confidante, but now I'm here to ask him something. For something. And I have no idea how he's going to react. The door opens to Watkins' careful somber expression. I nod merrily to him, grinning. It's a constant competition to see whether he can keep a straight face looking at me. Well, I kind of figure it's a competition. He still hasn't smiled, nor even had a twitch of the mouth, but the sparkle in his eyes tells of a man begging for a smile.

"Master Jace," he says in his typical butler voice. "The duke is expecting you."

"Is he? I do so hope his legs work this time," I say with a wink.

The joke is getting a bit stale after all of this time, but, at Torlas' urging, we convinced Watkins three times that Torlas lost the use of his legs. It gives the poor old man a heart attack every time, but Torlas just thinks it's hilarious. For Watkins' part, he doesn't alter his behavior at all, though even his infinite patience has to be tested by our rambunctious pranks. Torlas and I are like twelve-year-old street rats. We figure out a scam to run on someone important or of a particular dislike to Torlas, and, well, we run it.

Watkins leads up the four flights of stairs and through the well-furnished hallways, ignoring the paintings that inspired awe in me the first time through the building, ignoring the doors that branch on either side, opening to judges and lawyers that all work under Torlas to ensure justice is upheld in the city. We come to Torlas' door at the end of the hall, and I struggle not to gulp as Watkins knocks twice, opens the door a fraction, and then swings it wide to permit me a view of the third most powerful man in the city.

He glances up from a piece of parchment he's reading and brightens, grinning at me like a child. As I step into the office, I can't help but pause to admire the view. The room has more windows than Reknor's entire house, revealing a wide, panoramic vista of the city that always makes me struggle not to gawk. Just the dozens of Stars of Donir visible from his office are breathtaking. Apparently, it was his father's office before the late duke's death last year, some kind of illness that struck suddenly when he was far from Kranos' healing hand. Torlas' original office was a 'dank cave,' as he described it.

"Jace!" Torlas exclaims, setting the paper down and coming to his feet. "No need to plan today, I've already got something in the works. Just come…" he trails off as he notices the serious look on my face. "Is something the matter?"

"I would love to hear about your plan, Torlas," I say evenly. "But perhaps later. I have come to you with a… serious request."

Torlas sits back down, his smile wilting slightly. He gestures wordlessly for me to sit. As I lower myself into the gorgeous leather chair, Watkins clears his throat behind me.

"If I may sir, I told you—"

"Watkins, that will be all. I'll ring if I need you."

"Yes, my lord," Watkins responds, his voice stiff as he bows his way out of the room. A glint of anger blazes in his eyes as our gazes briefly lock, and I wince. What's that about?

"Watkins believes that you are only cultivating a friendship with me to curry favor with a powerful lord," Torlas explains as I turn back around.

"Is that what you believe?"

"No," Torlas says succinctly. He doesn't have to add *or you wouldn't be sitting here*. "What can I do for you, Jace? If it's within my power, I'll do my best to grant it."

"Well, Torlas, I have a friend, and, well…" I trail off, squeezing my fingers into my palms nearly hard enough to draw blood.

"Creator's breath, Jace, you weren't nervous when we snuck into Lord Frayen's manor and stole his statuette of the Mind Razor, and he had thirty guards defending him. What could this possibly be?"

I close my eyes, taking several deep, solidifying breaths.

"Torlas, what do you think of lepers?" I ask softly.

"Lepers? As in those poor diseased folk living in the fenced colony in the Corpses? I pity them."

"But what do you think of them? Do they scare you? Are you frightened of the idea of coming in contact with one?" I press, leaning forward.

"No, no more than I fear the plague or a sudden fever. If such wrongs are to afflict me, then so be it, but I can't live my life in fear of them," Torlas answers easily.

"Good," I say in the same soft tone. "That will make this easier. I have a friend, among the lepers in the colony outside the walls. She is… dear to me."

Torlas sits back, his expression one of confusion.

"I see…" he says in a probing tone.

"Her condition is very advanced, and I fear for her life if she remains in that filthy place any longer."

"I can't just ask them to let her out of the colony, Jace. I'm sorry, but the populace—"

"Let me finish," I cut in. His eyes narrow slightly, but he gives me a nod to continue. "She was once a known acquaintance to the Lord General, a student of medicine under his care. I believe she may still be known to him, at least as she was before the disease. I was wondering, hoping, that you could speak to him, entreat him to heal her…"

I trail off as Torlas slowly shakes his head. The sorrowful determination stamped on his face leaves little doubt as to his answer. I slump, head down.

"I wish I could Jace. Really I do," Torlas says sincerely. "But there are a very few truths that are to me unshakeable. My life, my position, my betrothed, these are all potentially fluid truths. They can be changed. But a rule I have lived by for the last ten years is that I will never allow myself to go into debt to either the King or the Lord General. As soon as that happens, I'm a slave. I don't know if you quite understand how much such a favor would cost me. I would spend my entire life trying to repay it. I'm sorry, Jace."

I look up at him, meeting his eyes and nodding once.

"I understand, Torlas. I wouldn't want to put you in that kind of situation. It was just a hope, and a faint one at that."

"Jace, you are a valuable friend. My most valuable friend. You keep me sane when all others are struggling to drive me the opposite direction. If there was anyone in the world I would do a favor for, it's you. But what you ask for is beyond my ken to give."

"I understand. Thank you for even thinking about it. Though..."

I trail off suggestively. Jonah once taught me an old bargaining trick to convince your mark agree to the term you genuinely wish for. You start out astronomical, a shot in the dark so high that your client can't reasonably accept. Now, if you're as blind lucky as it gets, they agree, and you have your wildest dream achieved. Otherwise, you back down, ask a much more likely request, and seem like a reasonable human being.

"Yes?" Torlas asks, looking hopeful. It feels bad to manipulate him, but the man is brilliant and extraordinarily powerful. Friendship aside, I need his help.

“This friend I spoke of, she is fascinated with a particular artist. A 'Caldero.' I want to find one for her so I can brighten her life at least that much.”

“First you ask what I cannot do, then you ask the impossible,” Torlas says, shaking his head.

“What?” I ask, indignant. Surely a piece of art can’t be that difficult to obtain.

“Caldero is the most reclusive and eccentric man I’ve ever heard of, and no, I haven't met him. He’s a master, head and shoulders above any of his contemporaries, and he’s created less than a score of paintings in his entire life, despite approaching seventy Winters. Each Caldero is hanging in a different museum or private collection, or is under the Sealord's personal care.”

I sit back, a bit deflated. I had no idea the man is so revered, or that he’s been so spare in his gifts.

“Now, come to think of it,” Torlas says, tapping his chin. “I do remember that I was going to present a plan for us to execute when you walked in. It involved a certain duke and stealing his favorite dog, but perhaps the target can be changed to his single, solitary, priceless painting created by a certain master...”

“Yes,” I say, practically bouncing in my seat. “Pick me.”

Torlas laughs and stands, coming around his desk to clap me on the shoulder.

“Now, come with me so that we can spend the day on the town and plan our victory.”

“So what? We'll be sniveling young nobility?”

“What, in your opinion, makes us sniveling?” he asks like he’s wondering if he should be offended.

“Oh, you know, the usual for powerful nobility. Walking into stores and refusing to pay for anything, saying that a retainer will be along. Humiliating everyone we see who is lower than us, which is everyone. Looking down on people's clothing, whispering loudly behind their backs so that they can hear, causing a ruckus like we're a small natural disaster.”

Torlas waves his hands in surrender. I give him a cocky grin as one of his eyebrows slowly rises upwards. His head slowly drops down to meet his hands, and he stands like that for a long moment.

"So that's what you think a duke would do, eh?" he says through his fingers, his voice muffled.

"Just the sniveling ones," I say with a shrug.

"Right. I think that your education is sadly lacking in this particular measure," Torlas says, raising his head. "It's my duty, here and now, to educate you otherwise. Walk with me. You don't have any other pressing duties today, do you? Or are you afraid we'll cause enough of a ruckus to give the wealthy a bad name?"

"A bad name? The wealthy?" I ask skeptically.

"Okay, okay," Torlas admits, standing and turning me to the door again. "Most wealthy people give wealthy people a bad name. But there is only so much good a man can do to outweigh the idiocy of his class. Still, being a sniveling duke has far greater privileges than the rest of the populace get a chance to see."

We walk out of his office and down the hallway. Every door we pass, eyes drop respectfully. Torlas' strides are purposeful as he grabs his coat and shouts for Watkins to bring the carriage around. We ride out of the city a short distance into the countryside, and Torlas shows me what it really means to be a duke. He takes me to his summer cottage (castle), and we proceed to go hawking and riding, before we feast and laugh the night away. All the while, we plot the downfall of Duke Paloran, fifth arm of the council of eight. They say that money can't buy happiness. I fully believe that. But there, with Torlas, I'm happier than I ever was in the gutter.

Maybe it's just luck. Maybe I've found the few wealthy people who actually have hearts. The money and the surroundings probably have nothing to do with it. Well. They probably don't have that much to do with it. I'm not saying that I wouldn't love to spend time with Torlas if we were living on the street and begging for coins. We probably would laugh less, though.

Chapter 15
Iliana
The Fifty-Sixth Day of Spring
In the Year 5222, Council Reckoning

"How's Eleanor?"

Torlas shifts in his seat, clearly uncomfortable.

"She's… fine, I guess," Torlas says. "She went to her father's lands for the rest of Spring. I haven't seen much of her the past few weeks."

"They're still looking for Teldaran, you know," I say, watching Torlas' reaction as he stuffs a large bite of biscuit into his mouth.

He coughs, choking on the crumbs and pounding a fist into his chest. A faint glimmer of a smile ghosts across my lips, but I'm too worried to really feel the humor. I take a sip of my coffee to give him time to recover. I glance around, but no one looks in our direction despite the early disturbance. My weekly breakfast with Torlas is my one regular venture into the city proper. It's the only time I feel like I can be something other than the princess of the kingdom, the one time in which the responsibilities of my station don't weigh quite so heavily on my shoulders. The endless negotiations and judgments and policy… I need the breaks these visits provide.

"Really?" he says when he can speak again, his voice still raspy.

"Teldaran Hollenzar. The phantom noble. An imposter, so it seems. Messengers have been dispatched to Hollen, but Father and Uncle are certain he's not the son of its lord. They believe he's still in the city."

"They are that interested in punishing someone who crashed the King's Ball? Still? After ten days, wouldn't you assume he would already be long gone? I mean, did he steal something?" Torlas asks, his expression totally sincere. Too sincere.

"I don't know why they're still so concerned," I answer honestly. "Father hasn't been very forthcoming when I ask him about it. He's interrogated me twice on everything I can remember about Teldaran."

"He did the same to me last week. I haven't seen him so interested in something since the last battle against the Vengeance's rebellion. And that was ten years ago! I remember him shouting at my father, something about damning him for being cautious and letting them escape," Torlas says, frowning. "He questioned me with something almost like…"

"Like what?"

"Desperation."

"I didn't quite get *that* impression. Are you sure you told him everything you know?"

"Of course," he answers, but he doesn't meet my eyes. "I met the boy looking terrified under the balcony awning and tried to perk him up. He stuck to my side like glue, and I gave him advice about the court and etiquette. He appeared an earnest young noble with something to prove until I introduced him to you. The rest of his actions are public knowledge. He danced with you, and shortly thereafter fled the Ball. From all my knowledge, he seemed to be the person he claimed to be. If he was an imposter, he was well trained."

"Very," I agree, my heart sinking.

Torlas definitely knows something he's trying to hide from me. I thought that Torlas and I were beyond deceptions, but I was clearly wrong. Even though I've bared my soul to him, trusted him with everything I've done, all of my mistakes... he still keeps this from me. The betrayal hurts worse, knowing what secrets of mine he holds.

"I still can't believe you faced off with the Vengeance," he says, clumsily changing the subject. "And you're still breathing."

"I shouldn't be. He made me look like a child playing with a wooden sword," I say, sighing.

"But you drove him off, right? He ran!"

"I don't really know how. What I did… the power I called… Father told me I nearly died. That using up so much of my soul nearly made my body shut down. I have no memory for twelve days, Torlas."

"You can… kill yourself? By Shaping?" he asks, his brow furrowing in concern.

"Apparently. Yes. Normally, a Shaper would lose consciousness long before approaching death as our souls grow weary, but I was desperate and called on everything at once. The margin was… razor thin," I say, glancing down at my lap. My fingers are twisted into a snarl of white knuckles, and I force my hands to relax.

"What about your other mystery? Did you ever find out what really happened to your messenger?"

"No. Uncle claimed something about the messenger being delusional from his incarceration, but I'm not so sure."

***

I wake in an unfamiliar bed surrounded by unfamiliar curtains. The darkness is unnatural, sunlight peeking through a crack between the edges of a set of thick drapes. The twittering of birds drifts through the curtains, but their sweet song turns grating as my weary mind struggles back towards sleep. I fight the urge to return to unconsciousness, rolling over and pushing the curtains aside. An open window looks out on rolling green pastures and a herd of distant horses. My mind claws back into clarity, the memories of my fight with the Vengeance filtering back. This is Calladan's estate. Either I'm in the most beautiful prison I can imagine, or something odd is going on.

I stagger to my feet, a strange, ill-fitting nightgown clinging to my form. As I reach to open the door, a maid jumps in shock, the bowl in her hands splashing broth onto the wooden floor with a wet smack. She turns and darts from the room, her voice raised in alarm. I glance down at myself, trying to figure out what in the Creator's name could have frightened her so. My hair definitely looks a total mess, but probably not enough to terrify. I hope.

Poline sprints into the room, her clothing immaculate and her sword sheathed at her side, a look of such relief in her eyes that I stare in wonder. She even looks to be blinking away tears. A member of the Tide, crying?

"You woke up," she says, her voice shaking.

"Yes..." I respond in a leading tone.

"It's been twelve days. After three, I started to panic. After eight, I was terrified you weren't ever going to wake up."

"Twelve days?" I repeat dully. I've slept for twelve days. The thought seems so absurd that I almost dismiss it entirely, but Poline's reaction is far too genuine for me to doubt.

"An entire contingent of the Tide led by the Lord General himself is a day away. I didn't know what to do, so I commandeered one of Calladan's messengers and sent to the capital." Poline said, looking down as if she's afraid to meet my eyes. "I'm sorry, my lady."

"Why are you apologizing?" I say, trying to recover some of my humor despite the fog saturating my thoughts. "I would have left you for dead after three."

Poline offers a wan smile, then launches into an explanation about the past twelve days. She's maintained control of the entire property by herself through a mixture of mystery and the threat of Markis Calladan's death. He's locked in a closet of a bedroom not far from mine, and Poline has held a constant vigil outside our respective doors for two long weeks. I can see the strain and the weariness hanging on her proud frame like a leaden cloak. When she blinks, her eyes open just a hair slower, and her steps are far from certain.

"Sleep, Poline," I say, patting her on the shoulder.

"But, my lady, what if you grow tired again?" Poline asks, though I can tell it takes everything in her being not to collapse into a bed instantly.

"Honestly, I feel fantastic," I say, surprising myself to find it true. There's a vigor in my limbs and a spring to my step, and the fog of my long sleep burns away the more I move about. I'm fresh and focused, as if I've been remade, or at least renewed.

"But—"

"Poline, you have watched my back long enough. It's time I watched you. Perhaps you can sleep easy for once."

The question is how to watch over my friend while also getting up and moving. I don't want to stand guard outside her and Calladan's doors like some kind of sentinel. The screen of duet I used in inn the night before—or perhaps a few weeks before—should serve. The dust jumps directly into line, invisible and swirling. The earth answers my call more readily than it ever has before; I hardly feel the need to concentrate.

Walking down the hall, I leave a part of my concentration back with the screen of dust, but the strain doesn't grow with distance. It seems that I can stand watch and explore without worry. Which is a good thing, because the house calls to me in a way I can't resist. The rustic woods and natural growing trees speak to my soul in a way that's fundamental. It reminds me of my garden at the palace. I miss that space more than I ever thought I would.

The rampart of earth filling Calladan's study hasn't been altered. Between the massive split in the natural beams and the sheer tonnage of earth that moved at my desperate command, it's hard to fathom how I survived the effort. The echo of that terror wells in my heart, the unfiltered fear for Poline's life, and the earth trembles in response. The grasses outside are rumpled beyond repair, and several shrubs and small trees fell in the near distance when the earth suddenly abandoned them. At my call. I can barely believe my will caused this level of destruction.

My other purpose for being in Firdana floats to the front of my mind. Where is the messenger? Has he been slain? Are there even dungeons in an idyllic place like this? I'm struck by the quiet of the house. When we arrived, the estate had been populated by half a dozen guards and several servants. Their presence is no longer in evidence. The kitchens are silent, the fires cold and the counters immaculate. A creak from the hall draws me back towards the front of the house, where I find the maid who was bringing me broth. She immediately starts in surprise and hurries away from me.

"Wait," I call, but she doesn't slow. "Stop!"

I growl in frustration. Just before she can turn the corner, I draw the earth from a nearby potted plant and throw it in her path. She screams to see me bearing down on her, cowering to the side and covering her face with her hands.

"What is the matter with you?" I ask, more confused than angry. "You look like you've seen the Eternal returned."

The girl peeks up at me through trembling fingers, her chestnut hair falling messily across her face. She meets my eye for the briefest moment, but then squeaks in fright and covers her face again. I get the distinct impression the girl believes she may indeed be seeing the Eternal once more.

"What is your name?" I ask, trying to make my voice kind. She doesn't respond, but instead continues to cry into her hands. Creator, she's starting to annoy me. "Girl, what is your name? I won't ask you again."

She peeks up at me again, terror in her gaze.

"Elle," she says, almost too faintly to be heard.

"Elle, listen to me. I'm not going to hurt you. I just want to ask you about this place."

"You hurt the master. You destroyed the house. You even made… him… run," she says, her eyes wide and searching.

"Well," I say slowly, shocked to realize that everything the girl said is true. From her simple perspective, maybe she's right to be afraid

of me. She certainly would mean less than nothing to Father or Uncle. "It would seem wise to answer my questions then, yes?"

Elle nods furiously.

"Good. There was a messenger who came here from the King. A soldier sent to deliver a missive to your master…" The blankness in the girl's eyes is enough to end that particular line of questioning. She has no idea what I'm talking about. What would she know about matters important to the Earl? "Elle, if someone got in trouble here, like serious trouble, where would they go? Say, if they stole something."

"That hasn't happened in Firdana in years," Elle says, her eyes clearing. "No one does bad things here."

"No one has committed a crime in years?" I ask, skeptical.

"Nothing worth locking up," she answers, a hint of pride for her town rising to the surface. I pause for a moment, considering this strange piece of information. How can this girl believe no one breaks the law here? Donir's jails are full to bursting.

"Right. Well, say someone did commit a crime. Where would they be put?"

"Well, the old jail in the town proper is empty. But—" she cuts herself off before she finishes the thought.

"But?"

"I'm not supposed to say."

"Do I have to remind you who you're speaking to?" I snap, tiring of the game. "Tell me what I want to know."

"It's just, the Earl didn't want anyone to know, and I'm not supposed to know, and I'll get in trouble if I say, but he would be dead if I hadn't been sneaking him some water and food when no one was looking, ever since the Earl—" she breaks off, sobbing, seemingly unable to decide whether her terror of me or the thought Calladan's harm is a stronger emotion.

I call on the earth, the symbol of my power flaring emerald in the hallway, and she tells me. It still takes me half an hour to find the stables they modified to house the imperial messenger, as it's almost half a mile out in the pastures. Farmhands and grooms take one look at me and grow far more interested in their work than wondering what I'm up to. My connection to the earth watching over Poline doesn't waver despite the distance. What was once difficult is easy as breathing.

The stables are conspicuously silent as I slide aside the bar and open the doors. It's dim, a few beams of sunlight filtering through cracks in the wooden slats. A distant scraping, rhythmic and unnatural, carries over the faint sounds of horses running. I follow the noise, stepping carefully and quietly in the darkness. The scraping emerges from the far corner. The dimness is strangely unsettling, and I mentally curse myself for forgetting a lantern. But why should I need one in broad daylight?

Makeshift bars have been hammered into the wood in and around one of the stalls in the back, barbed and cruel. A gleam of light falls on a sliver of the bars, and I wince to see old blood caked to the dull iron. They've been torturing him.

"Locke?" I call softly.

The scraping immediately ceases. A man's face appears at the bars as if by magic. I fight not to jump, my pulse suddenly galloping along. He has narrow features, his cheekbones high and his eyes cold and hard. He's not wearing a uniform, but instead a dark and tattered form-fitting set of silk. The clothing hangs off of him, far too baggy for someone so small. Clearly, he hasn't been getting enough to eat.

I almost step close to try to find a way to get him out, but something in me whispers a quiet warning. The way he's standing, the look in his eyes, the strange way he holds his hand, almost as if concealing something…

"Locke?" I ask again.

"My latest minder," he suddenly speaks, his voice rough from disuse. "How did you learn that name?"

"No, Locke. The Lord General Kranos himself told me your name. I'm here to rescue you."

"Kranos? You'll have to come up with something better than that," he says, his eyes tightening at the corners.

"But it isn't a lie!" I say, stepping forward. "He told me of your plight and—"

His hand is in my hair before I can react, spinning me around. The point of a blade presses against my throat. Eterna's cursed name, why did I ignore the warning of my instincts? This man, whether Locke or some other assassin, has been waiting for just such an opportunity.

"You're going to get me out of here, whether you know it or not. Struggle, and I'll cut your throat before you can scream," he hisses in my ear. "Do you understand?"

"Yes," I whisper, ignoring the horrifying feeling of the blade moving in time with my words.

"You should have told a more believable lie. Kranos would never spend resources on a failure."

"I didn't lie," I say, trying to inject as much sincerity in my voice as I can muster. "I'm not foolish enough to ask you to let me go, but can I show you who I am?"

"Nothing funny," he answers, tightening his grip in my hair.

I draw gently on the earth, allowing the symbol of my power to glow in the dimness. Either he's going to let me go, or he's going to kill me, here and now. After a brief hesitation, he sets me free. I stumble forward, rubbing the back of my head. I turn back, trying not to scowl. The man has obviously been through a lot. I don't know why he's wearing such a ridiculous outfit, nor how long he's been trapped and tortured in the dark.

"Princess," he says, his voice that of a ghost.

"Yes. The Lord General genuinely did tell me about your presence here. I know you're just a messenger. You didn't fail. Calladan's treachery is completely to blame."

"Calladan's treachery… yes," he says, his voice drifting. "I couldn't deliver my message. Not the one I meant to."

"It's all going to be okay. Let me figure out how to get you out of these bars. The Lord General will be here tomorrow, and we can take you home."

"Kranos? Here?" he says, his voice suddenly filled with fear.

"Yes, he's coming to make sure I'm okay," I say, trying and failing to come up with an excuse that makes me sound less helpless.

"Princess, what few stories escape about you are mostly of kindness," Locke says, his eyes locking on mine. "Will you do me one kindness?"

"Anything," I say, smiling.

"Kill me."

***

"Well, that's one mystery only you can solve," Torlas says between bites of biscuit. "Those aren't the kinds of questions I can ask around the palace."

"Who would I talk to? The messenger, whoever he is, has probably been long since deployed again. It's not like I can just look up a registry and find out the barracks he's assigned to."

"Are you sure he is what he says he is? What if he isn't a messenger at all?"

"I don't know," I answer, shrugging. "He seemed so scared of Uncle; it was strange."

"Perhaps there's one place you could check," Torlas says thoughtfully. "If the man was so frightened, maybe he had a reason to be. What if you went to the dungeons?"

"Surely not."

I mean the words to come out flippant, but they end up like a question. Even as I asked Locke why he would seek death, a rushing presence disturbed the dust guarding Poline. I left him and sprinted back to the manor to find that Uncle had ridden in far earlier than expected. His horse was lathered and gasping, almost stumbling from the cruel abuse he forced on it to reach Firdana. He'd given me a crushing hug and lifted me from my feet as I rushed into the estate.

The arrival of a waiter interrupts our conversation. On a platter rests two steaming cups, and Torlas' eyes light up at the sight. He grins a boyish grin as the cups settle in front of each of us, filled to the brim with warm chocolate. The grin recalls the days of our childhood, the mischief and mayhem we spread throughout the palace, the laughter and the joy. I smile, more for his smile than for anything else, but it feels wrong on my face.

So much of what I've learned the last few weeks refuses to add up. The older I get, the more mysteries surround the palace. Perhaps they've always existed, and I was too young or blind to notice. The desperation of the people on the Way of the East. The rebels earning good will with nothing but bread. The betrayal of Markis Calladan, a wealthy man with everything to lose. This messenger, so afraid of my uncle he would rather die than see him. The falling water at the King's Ball, all due to a dance with a stranger, a stranger Father and Uncle are devoting resources to find weeks later, without any discernible reason why.

And now my best friend, one of the only people I can trust, has lied to me. It's time to solve some of these mysteries.

The moments when Torlas' arms surround me, brief as they are, always make my heart beat a little faster, my breathing come a little more difficult, and my blood warm. He's grown strong and solid, and his arms are a safe harbor in an uncertain sea. This time, though, as Torlas and I part, our hug is awkward as it's never been. I'm tired of people hiding things from me.

The Spring day is perfect, the feeling of life drifting on a light breeze, the colors of the city brightening in the burgeoning Summer air. It should be a perfect day to stroll back to the palace. Instead, I keep my hood up, feeling the gaze of strangers, skin crawling as men glance at me in passing. I still use the loose bar to escape to the city, but only with a purpose. The last time I let my guard down in the streets… needless to say, I don't exactly trust the common man any longer. The palace is fully awake and bustling when I replace the bar and return to my gardens. Some of the tension leaves my shoulder blades walking amongst the beauty of life. I gently caress my white lily on the way past. Poline falls into step with me as soon as I enter the palace proper. The stress eases out of me further to hear the familiar ringing step of her gait as we walk through the halls.

She and Uncle had a long conversation in Firdana, one I was not privy to, and she left it chastened but determined. It hadn't taken much to get her to tell me he's furious she allowed me to engage the Vengeance in the first place. He knows, above all others, how powerful and dangerous our enemy is. They fought to a stalemate shortly after the Liberation. They being Father *and* Uncle together, against the Vengeance by himself.

"Poline," I begin as we reach the door to my chambers. "What is on my agenda for today?"

"You're due at the High Court for judgements at ten, and you have an appointment with the Khal of the Ram and his son at five for an early dinner."

"Ugh," I groan. "More men looking to use my title to come up in the world."

"You could give them a chance, my lady," Poline says carefully. "You will have to marry eventually. If you want any choice in who, you need to look around and, well, *choose*."

"No, Poline. I… I'm not sure I have it in me to marry," I say, fighting against a blush.

I most definitely don't wish to marry a stranger based on nothing but his wealth or lineage. There might be one who could convince me… but he's already bound to our kingdom. Father would never allow it, when my virginity could buy so much we don't already possess.

"Tell that to the king," she mutters at my back.

I ignore the comment, listening to the distant ringing of bells instead. Only eight. Perhaps I have time to do a little research. Turning right instead of left at the next fork in the hall, I head towards a set of stairs leading deeper into the palace instead of towards the throne room.

"My lady?" Poline asks, her step hitching slightly as she follows me down the stairs. "Why are we heading to the dungeons?"

"Something Torlas said. It might be a long shot, but he thinks we might find more information about the messenger—or the messenger himself—in the dungeons."

Poline doesn't say anything, but her silent skepticism is apparent in every returning echo of our footfalls in the stairwell. We wind our way down the spiraling stairs, our steps the only sound in the enclosed space. Soldiers of the Wave stand vigilant as we approach the door leading deeper. It's an impressive sight, the four members of the Wave stiffly at attention, their armor gleaming despite the early hour. I nod to them, and one strides smoothly to the thick wooden door and opens it for us without comment, either recognizing me or Poline despite our scarcity in this part of the palace.

"Your diligence will be noted," Poline says quietly to the men behind, but I continue forward. I have perhaps an hour before I'm due at court, and I need to cover some ground.

The first cells are, again, largely full, but I ignore the petty criminals contained therein. I move on and descend further, reaching the second level. My steps slow on this level as I peer into more cells. There are many prisoners here, though none are given the freedom of those above. These are traitors, the treasonous and the seditious. They're chained to walls, their groans audible over the guttering oil lamps placed at intervals throughout the dungeon. I expect to see Markis Calladan here, but we reach the end without finding him. The begging of the desperate is easy to ignore. People only end up in the second level if they deserve their fate.

The stairwell leading down to the final level looms dark ahead. I slow to a stop without really realizing it. A chill travels down my arms, my pulse growing erratic despite the deep breaths I force through my nose. I try to take another step, to continue my search, but my legs lock up. The darkness of the open doorway grows, its opening a black maw waiting to swallow all that would dare…

"My lady?" Poline asks quietly at my elbow, her voice strained.

I don't answer.

What am I afraid of? Nothing in these cells can harm me.

You are not afraid of what is there, a part of me whispers, the voice scraping against the rough edges of my mind. *You fear only what you bring. What you've done.*

As I stand, frozen, my ear tracks the pleading of a woman in the last cell next to the door.

"Please, my children, I just wanted to know where they were taking my boys, please, where were they taking my boys, my little Adam, why would they take Adam? Surely he wasn't big enough to hold a sword, please, give me my Adam…"

The litany is unending. The uncaring stone swallows the woman's hopeless voice before it can travel past this meager distance. My heart doesn't move for her, but my brain latches on to her words and compels me to listen. With a titanic effort, I drag my eyes from the waiting portal and over to her cell. She's in her middle age, and her skin sags on her frame, as if she was rotund and matronly once, but her trials since have burned away much of what she was. Her hair, gray and thin, clings to her head as if by chance more than purpose. Her eyes are vacant, and I can tell her pleas would fall on the deaf stone regardless of my presence.

When I step close to the bars, Poline immediately comes to my side, her hand on the hilt of her sword. But the woman doesn't react. It's not like her chains will stretch far enough for her to harm me anyway.

"What happened to Adam?" I ask, my voice shrill in the dim prison.

Poline glances at me in alarm. I clench my eyes closed and shove the doorway from my mind, swallowing to clear the dryness in my throat. Unsuccessfully.

"Lady," I begin again, my voice more controlled. "Where are your children?"

"This is a waste of our time," Poline says, but the woman's eyes suddenly focus.

"Princess?" she says in wonder. "I came here to find you!"

"Me? Well," I answer slowly. "You've found me. Why did you seek me out?"

"I came…" Her eyes glisten with tears, but they don't fall. "They took my children. Theo I could understand, but Adam was but ten years old. He couldn't even lift a blade if he tried."

"Who took your children?"

"The Wave," she answers simply. "They told me they were needed, that my boys would become brave soldiers, but they didn't want to go and I needed them on the mill, what with their Da passed two Winters ago. Last trip we'd made to Glorwen, there was a line of young folk out the door seeking to join the Wave, and many had been that were turned away, men and women twice the age of my boys."

"Wait. Glorwen?" I ask, frowning.

"Yes, the mill my husband built is less than a score of miles down the Ripple from the city," she says with a mixture of pride and sorrow in her eyes. "I've kept it up, but it's been hard these last few seasons. Without my boys…"

"How did you end up here?" Poline asks, curiosity awakened by the woman's story.

"I came to Donir to ask for them back. The princess is a nice lady, so all the people say, so perhaps she could help. The worst she could do was say no, right? But I never got to see the princess. They brought me here instead. I just wanted my boys back. Sweet Adam, he's too small to hold a sword, and Theo's needed on the mill. Please, just give me my boys…"

I step back as her litany resumes, the brief moment of clarity already fading from her eyes. Poline and I exchange concerned glances.

"I know that area," Poline says. "Shepherds and scrubland, for the most part. They're hardy folk because they have to be. The Winters are deep, and the raiders are ruthless. Even south of Glorwen, they aren't safe from the tribes."

"But seriously, 'the Wave is taking my children?' What is going on in our kingdom?"

"I wish I knew," she says, her eyes troubled. "You may be the only one who can get away with asking the king."

"I'd be surprised if he told me anything," I mutter, feeling like a frustrated child and hating it.

"Do you really think he would be down there?" Poline asks, eyeing the final stairwell with more than a bit of trepidation herself.

The sound of our voices awakens more of the prisoners, their desperate entreaties and calls for aid rising in the cramped corridor. A part of me—a large part of me—wants to say no. There's no reason to check those cells, so deep down in the darkness under the earth. But the absence of Calladan from the second level concerns me, and I need to be thorough with what little time I have to devote to this mystery. And I'll be damned to the Eternal's prison before my fear controls me.

"I don't know. But let's hurry," I say, striding to the stairs and grabbing an unlit torch from a waiting sconce.

I dip the tarred end into one of the oil lamps, and a guttering and smoking fire springs fitfully to life. The light only seems to deepen the shadows, each step illuminating the new in front, darkness swallowing the old behind. The fear stirs in me as we descend, our eyes squinting forward into the gloom.

You enjoyed your time here, the voice rasps again in my brain. *His squirms, his pain…*

I draw on the earth instinctually, here surrounded by its vastness, and the feeling comforts me, quieting the whispering shadow in my thoughts. The final level holds the same four cells, each unique in their own way, each crafted to hold a being of greater power than any normal prison could restrain.

It's silent. The last sounds echoing through this space are those of screams, and the silence now feels close, unnatural, like a presence hovers over our shoulders, judging us for bringing such cacophony to a place of stillness. I almost turn back immediately. There's nothing here. This place of uneasy quiescence does not welcome us because we do not belong. Without Father and his soldiers, without the assassin and his screams, an oppressive peace fills the space and leaves no room for us.

I turn to Poline, whose eyes echo my own disquiet even if she would never say it, and we tacitly agree to head back to the world of the sun.

"Is someone there?"

Poline's sword springs out of its sheath before I can finish jumping, the voice so unexpected and shocking in the quiet that my heart skips two beats. No one appears, however, and we glance at each other sheepishly. The voice is familiar, one heard not too long ago, though spoken with far less confidence and strength than when he walked the surface.

"Markis Calladan," I say, stepping up to his door and peering in through the barred slit at eye level. The room looks nothing like the cell the assassin had been held in, but the comparable size of the cramped prison makes me suppress a shudder. Of eagerness or dread, I can't tell.

Calladan hunches opposite, a chain about his neck keeping him crouched against the wall. The tight chain holds his throat at just such an angle that he can't sit, but neither can he stand. Instead, he's forced into an awkward half-crouch, unable to easily wake, impossible to effectively sleep. It's a cruel and effective form of torture. His body has been degraded by more conventional means as well. The crusted stumps where his fingers should be are still wet and glistening in our dim torchlight. He catches sight of me and smiles through a mouthful of fresh blood.

"Princess Iliana," he says, offering a tiny nod. "How kind of you to grace me with your presence."

"An accident," I say honestly. "I see you have received your due."

"Spoken like a true believer," he says, still smiling his bloody smile. "Tell me, princess, do you genuinely believe this is my due? Do you think I've earned this?"

"You betrayed your king. You suborned necessary supplies, food that would go to hungry people. You consorted with the Vengeance, of all people!" Creator knows why I'm shouting.

"True," he says conversationally. "I admit to each of these things."

"Then yes," I snarl. "You have earned this."

"Remarkable. He's raised you well. Tell me, what do you call him? Does he make you call him your majesty? Your grace?"

"I call him father, which is the only title that has ever mattered between us."

Calladan looks startled for a moment before he bursts into laughter. The laugh clearly pains him, but he persists regardless, his mangled hands poorly covering his face and smearing his skin with old blood. He subsides after a while, his breathing still uneven, and stares at me with glittering eyes.

"That man is no more your father than I am," he finally says.

"How dare you," I spit, drawing on the earth. A shard of glass forms in the air beside me. I ignore Poline, who turns to me in concern, pleading with her eyes. "My father is a great man—"

"Your father *is* a great man. Which is the only reason your Tide still breathes," Calladan answers, jerking his chin at Poline. "Masterful swordwork, by the way, Tide. My shoulder still aches."

"Why would Poline have anything to fear from my father?"

"You know its name? Remarkable. No wonder your fear brought on such a strong... reaction."

"Answer the question."

"I didn't realize Helikos raised you to be dense, as well. Perhaps that was his intention, to keep you from growing too curious," Calladan muses.

Frustrated, I snap. The glass shoots through the bars, slamming into Calladan's thigh and lodging deep. He yelps like a kicked dog, staggering and choking on the chain about his neck before he can recover his balance on his remaining leg. The glass reflects the torchlight in shimmering red as his blood leaks out of the wound.

"And he raised you to be cruel," he says, his voice clear… and sad.

"Answer the question!" I shout hoarsely through the bars. "Why would Poline be in danger?"

"Your Tide is safe. Your father spared her the moment he realized you cared."

The implication of his words slowly permeates my brain. The idea is so absurd I laugh before I can hold it in.

"The Vengeance? *My* father? What kind of preposterous absurdity will you throw at me next? Poline is my daughter?"

"Ask him," Calladan says wearily, dismissing me with a wave of his three-fingered hand. "Ask Helikos about Nadine. Ask him how she really died."

I tear the glass from one leg and jam it into the other. Blood spurts from the first wound and begins to leak from the other. He groans, slipping down to his knees, choking on the chain about his neck.

"My mother's name is too sacred to be heard from your lips. I'll watch you die here, choking on your own spit," I growl.

"My lady…" Poline begins.

"Enough, Tide," I snap in annoyance.

She looks as if she's been slapped, her eyes hurt. In this moment, I don't care. I have no memories of my mother, and this traitor won't sully what little I know of her with his lies. He struggles to stand on wounded legs, his words echoing weirdly in the strange cells as he chokes.

"Look him… in the eyes… when he lies. Altos told… me long… ago," Calladan gasps. He struggles mightily, standing on trembling legs as tears stream down his cheeks and blood rushes down his legs. "He's a fantastic liar. But… when he lies... he never looks away, never blinks. Ask him."

His legs give way, and he starts to choke in earnest. The sound of footsteps vibrates on the stairs, and I spin back, raising my hands and summoning more earth and glass to my fingertips. Uncle turns the corner, alone, his expression stormy.

"What are you doing down here?" his deep voice grumbles. He doesn't wait for an answer, but pushes past me and looks into Calladan's cell. Making a short sound of disgruntlement, he pulls an ancient key from around his neck and opens the door. "We cannot break our toys, little one. This one still has use."

"I'm sorry, Uncle," I say, chastened. Only the giant man can get away with calling me 'little one' anymore without annoying me. "He was telling horrible lies."

Uncle shoots me a look over his shoulder, his expression strange.

"You can't believe vipers like this one," he says, reaching out with his hand and lifting Calladan off the chain by his hair. Calladan's bruised throat gasps for air, his larynx jumping up and down in a feverish fight for survival. "They will fill you with poison. Aren't you late, little one? Court began a quarter hour ago."

"Oh!" I gasp. "I'll hurry!"

I turn to go, my skirts rustling as I hurry away.

"Ask him."

I glance back, meeting eyes with Calladan for the briefest of moments before Uncle's bulk blocks me from sight. Scowling, I dart up the stairs.

***

For all that I hate and despise traitors like Markis Calladan, I can't shake his words from my thoughts. They burrow deeper and deeper, and the harder I try not to think about his words, the more they stick in my brain. The thought of the Vengeance as my father is still more a joke than anything, but the bit about my father lying…

I'm a distracted mess at court. Yrena barely combs my hair into a semblance of tidiness after I run up to the doors, and I perch on my small throne to the left of Father with no care to the proceedings. He dictates a dozen decrees, handling disputes with a cold logic that I don't know if I can match, should my time come. He glowers in disapproval at my tardiness, but afterwards ignores me as usual. I'm expected to be learning how to handle the important members of the populace, and normally I do my best.

The High Court is only for the wealthy and the nobility. Peasants and laborers bring their disputes before any of the lesser courts in the kingdom, run by the noble magistrates who work under Torlas at his offices, but no one but the royalty can settle disputes between the nobility. Prior to the Liberation, the High Court had been run by a tribunal of Shapers from the Council, Father included. His experience adjudicating disputes was invaluable when he assumed the throne.

"Where is my husband, my lord?"

"He is awaiting trial for his crimes, Lady Calladan," Father answers. I snap out of my distraction, eyes focusing instantly on the woman before the court. "Crimes you accused him of, if I recall correctly."

Whispers break out on the edges of the crowd and in the waiting line beyond, the sibilant hiss of rumor already spreading far beyond the room. She's young, but somehow mature, her face not a classic beauty but definitely striking nonetheless. Her elegant black dress hangs from her shoulders below the black veil of mourning. She appears small and forlorn, alone in the middle of the throne room, but her face scowls in defiance.

"Transgressions I suspected, but could never confirm. I came to you in confidence, seeking aid. Now my husband is gone, and no one has laid eyes on him since the Tide brought him here. Where is he? Until Markis is proven guilty by trial, he deserves all the rights accorded him as an earl of the kingdom."

"He was found in conversation with the Vengeance himself," the king responds, his voice mild.

"Since when has a conversation been proof of treason? What man could refuse the power of the Vengeance if he desired conversation, even you, my lord? Are words enough to condemn a man in this kingdom?" she calls, her voice clear and strong. "What proof do we have that Markis ever saw the Vengeance, other than your word?"

"My own daughter walked in on his conversation," Father says, raising an open palm towards my throne.

I shrink back as the woman's fiery gaze rakes over me, and her lip curls with scorn.

"Princess or no, she is nothing but a child. How can the word of a youth be enough to ruin a man of Markis' standing? What world is this that our lives are determined by the stories of children?"

"I saw the Vengeance," I shout furiously, half rising from my chair. "He and your husband were meeting together. They were planning sedition even as I listened!"

"Control yourself, princess," Lady Calladan says, raising a mocking eyebrow. "You make my argument for me."

"I fought him! The Vengeance and Calladan fought together against me."

"Now your story stretches belief, princess. My husband is an accomplished swordsman, and the Vengeance… if half the rumors are true about him, he would crush you like an insect."

"But—"

"Enough, Iliana," Father cuts me off. "Your words achieve nothing but making us appear foolish."

I sit down, my mouth snapping shut and blushing furiously. To be publicly chastened…

"You want to see Markis, Nariah?" Father says, his voice smooth as a windless sea. "Very well."

"He is unharmed?" she asks, her voice suddenly trembling.

After the collected and confident performance she managed prior to that moment, the relief in her voice is palpable. The Sealord leans forward, his eyes intent. A flicker of disbelieving recognition springs to life in my breast. The posture, so familiar, so natural, brings my stomach to clenching. I've seen that posture far too often. Those moments when I asked a difficult question, moments even in the recent past, such as when I asked him about the desperation of the people on the Way, such as when I asked him what had happened to the messenger Locke. As then, he doesn't blink.

"He is unharmed. We can take you to him now, but only if you end this disrespectful spectacle. You are better than this."

She almost sags as a pair of guards in the gleaming armor of the Wave come to escort her out. As the next dispute is led before us, I school my face into a stoic mask. He did not blink as he told Nariah Calladan the most blatant of lies. Just as Calladan claimed. The next hour passes in an instant, the freezing inferno inside my breast overwhelming all else. When the High Court is adjourned, I'm gone before the last supplicant exit. I need to hide the tears in my eyes.

Poline finds me a few hours later in my room, Yrena stroking my hair as I try to stifle my sobs into a pillow. I don't look up as the door opens, but I hear Poline's voice as she orders

Yrena out of the room. Yrena huffs, but does as she's bid. Poline takes her place. She doesn't touch me, and I can feel the stoniness in her without looking. I hurt her, I know, and I yearn to reach out to her and ask for forgiveness. Creator knows, I need her friendship more than I need her to guard me. Just as I work up the courage to speak, she begins first.

"I have news, regarding this Locke," she says, her voice colder than I've ever heard it. I sit up suddenly. She doesn't meet my eyes, but sits stiffly on the end of the bed.

"Oh, Poline, that can wait. I'm so sorry! I should never have spoken to you like that," I cry, lurching forward and throwing my arms around her.

She can't stiffen any further, but I can feel her surprise as I squeeze her wooden form tightly. After a long moment, she softens, loosening her arms and giving me a quick hug.

"Alright, alright," she says awkwardly. "Let me go. I'm not happy about it, but I forgive you."

I look up and smile, and she smiles back, more amused than happy. It'll have to be enough.

"So what news?" I say, just glad she isn't mad at me anymore.

"Well… I tried to track down a member of the Wave named Locke. I called in a favor with one of my old squadmates who has risen up in the ranks and asked him to go through the records for me right when we got back from Firdana. He sent me a message an hour ago. There are two soldiers named Locke who enrolled in the Wave. One is still serving faithfully… as a guard at a dock in Itskalan. His career has been unremarkable, and reports of him bear that out. The second received glowing reviews from the officers in charge of his training, advanced to training as part of the Tide… and then died. In a 'training accident' that is remarkably light on detail."

"Died?" I ask, skeptical.

"I wondered the same thing. One of the trainers is stationed at the barracks in the city, and my squadmate went to ask him about this Locke. He doesn't remember him dying, just disappearing one day. He assumed he washed out."

"Definitely strange," I murmur, musing.

"At the end of the message, he wrote something... kind of cryptic," Poline says, frowning. She offers a piece of parchment for me to peruse. The contents of the letter are as she described, but the words 'even those amongst the tide should shun the deep' are scribbled at the bottom after the signature. I shrug, having no idea what it means. "Honestly, if this was anyone else... I would think it a joke. But he seems to be warning me about a legend."

"What legend?"

"The Deep."

"I'm going to need a bit more than that," I say, elbowing her gently after she's silent for a long moment.

"Rumor, legend, what have you, there have always been whispers about a third division of the army beyond the Wave and the Tide. The Deep: assassins, spies, people with no record and no name. They are a scary story for soldiers to laugh about, a ghost story for people who have little to fear."

"And this... friend... is warning you off? From some clandestine organization that probably doesn't exist?"

"Possibly."

"Well, I can tell you, from being invited to many of Father's private conferences, their name has never come up even obliquely."

"They wouldn't, though, would they?" Poline asks, looking at me sidelong. She shakes her head. "It's ridiculous. I'm a soldier of the Tide tasked with guarding the princess of the kingdom. What do I have to be afraid of? Anyway, I asked around, quietly after I got this message. The guards on duty at the dungeons the day we returned claim that a figure matching Locke's description was hustled into the dungeons, but has not been released."

"The dungeons? But we were just there. Locke is most definitely not in the dungeons," I said with certainty.

"Then where is he?"

***

It takes me a few weeks to find the opportunity to head back to the dungeons. Poline thinks it's a fruitless endeavor, but I figure I will, at worst, waste an hour glancing into the nooks and crannies of the prison. Locke was led down, but never checked out? Is this another 'training accident' where the only trace of Locke will exist in the memories of a few guards? I want to ask, well, *someone*, but who can I talk to? My trust in receiving a straight answer from Father is shaken to say the least, and, by extension, Uncle as well. The guards won't tell me anything they didn't offer Poline, and I don't exactly want it known that the princess is poking around the dungeons.

I leave Poline 'guarding' my door in case anyone comes looking for me. It's convenient to have a shadow follow you everywhere: people start to become so accustomed to your shadow always being at your side that they forget you can separate. When you can choose a moment to do so… that assumption leads to a remarkable amount of freedom.

The servant's dress I've stolen fits poorly, but my hair is pulled up into a tight bun, a basket of linens balanced precariously and conveniently in front of my face. I feel a bit ridiculous sneaking around my own palace, and I'm certain someone will find me out before I can get anywhere. I pass quietly to the entrance to the dungeons, though, unremarkable and unremarked. Four soldiers stand in the same position, their armor cerulean in the lamplight. This time, unlike before, they hold up a hand.

"What is your business here, girl?" a woman's voice calls.

I lower the basket to the ground, revealing my face. Her eyes widen, and she steps back, her hand falling down to her side.

The other soldiers all shift in their stances, the only sign of their surprise the sound of jingling armor.

"Wave," I say, glancing around. "Come here."

They aren't going to refuse a direct order from the princess. They gather close, but not too close. I look them in the eye, taking a moment to gaze at them each directly.

"I have something to ask of you," I say quietly. They lean in closer. "I'm not going to command, but rather request. I'm searching for something, down here among these dark cells. I don't ask your help, but I do ask that you tell no one I'm here. If my secret remains quiet, I'll have the Tide who guards me reward you handsomely for your trouble. All I ask is for silence."

The members of the Wave look at each other briefly, but they don't speak. After a moment, the woman who addressed me before stares directly into my eyes.

"Princess, we need no reward. We'll tell no one. I hope I'm not overstepping my bounds, but can you give us any more to go on? Some of us have been assigned here a long time. We may be able to help."

"Right," I say, considering. I'm already trusting these soldiers with the secret of my presence. What's the harm in stepping farther into the sea? "A man was brought to the dungeons recently. There are no reports of him being released, nor has anyone seen him leave. Yet when I was here two weeks ago, he was not in a cell. Even the deep cells."

This time, the silence is lengthy, as the guards look at one another out of the corners of their eyes. They shift uncomfortably, and tension sparks in the air where none had been before. One of the men on the end, a younger man, probably only a year or two my senior, opens his mouth, but the leader shoots him a stern look. He closes his mouth for a second, but then he scowls.

"This is the princess," he says to his captain. "If we can tell anyone, it would be her, right?"

“Is it worth your life? Or worse?” she asks, the question as solemn as it is pleading.

“What could be worse than death?” I cut in. The soldiers look at me and fall silent again. “I will hold your secret to my grave.”

“Even from the Lord General and the King?” the guardswoman says.

My skin chills. What do they know?

“What are your names?” I ask instead of answer.

“This is Terin, Rillow, Wix, and I’m Lorna,” she answers, pointing to each in turn.

“I am Iliana. A pleasure to meet you all,” I say. They all smile, clearly a little surprised. “I’m not going to tell you some line of nonsense about immunity or protection. If you tell me a secret, especially one of *theirs*, and are found out, I’ll not be able to save you. But know, in this room here under *my* earth, they will never hear it from me.”

“There is a place in the dungeons,” Terin says immediately, his youthful features earnest. “A single cell on the second level. We are ordered not to place anyone in it, save for those the Lord General himself commands. The next time we patrol, that cell is always empty.”

“Show me.”

The other three stay and Terin leads me back, his steps loud in the quiet of the first floor. The minor prisoners don’t bother calling out, their eyes remaining down and their shoulders slumped. Some have been beaten, though many of the injuries appear old.

Terin leads me past the groaning masses, his step quickening and the tension in his shoulders evident even through his armor. I shake my head at his back. He isn’t made for a posting like this one. I send a brief prayer to the Creator to give him another soon. My stomach drops as he brings me to the cell where the old woman had been, endlessly calling for her sons. It's empty, as silent and empty as a tomb.

"Open it," I command. He steps forward hesitantly, turning the key in the door. The bars swing aside. I run my hands along the stone, but nothing seems amiss. Pressing my ear to the wall, I jerk back as if burned.

"What is the matter, my lady?" Terin asks.

I don't answer. Instead, carefully, I place my ear back to the stone. The same sound reverberates through the wall, muffled and yet distinct: screams. Screams of agony, of such total anguish my heart aches to hear them. I shudder against the cold rock, my fingers grasping at nothing. The screams continue, on and on, until abruptly they end with a sharp jerk. I gasp.

The stone begins to tremble in a regular cadence, vibrating to a rhythm I quickly realize is the fall of heavy footsteps. I dart out of the cage, silently and frantically motioning for Terin to close the door. He swings it closed far too harshly, and the bars rattle against one another in a violent explosion of noise.

I'm halfway down the hallway when I hear the sound of grinding stone. Terin frantically works the key in the door, but fumbles with the release in his panic. Finally, he jerks it free, and turns to follow after me. Just as he does, his limbs freeze. One moment, he's living and moving and breathing, and the next he's flesh made stone. He teeters, unbalanced and tipping towards the floor, but invisible hands steady him before gravity can finish the job. His frozen body lifts a few inches off the ground, and his terrified eyes meet mine. He blinks rapidly, grunting frantic breaths through an immovable jaw.

It's all he can do.

He jerks to the side, flying through the air and slamming into the bars of the cell, his armor screeching in discordant protest. Out of his control, his head turns slowly, deliberately, to face the occupant of the cell. He lets out a whimper as his face moves forward and presses against the bars. I can see his muscles straining to run, to hide, to flee, but nothing happens. Nothing can resist the power of the Master of Beasts.

"What are you doing here, little man?" Uncle's rumbling voice echoes down the hall.

As quietly as I can, I turn and run, closing my ears to the sound of Terin's pleas.

Chapter 16
Bastian

Some time near the end of Spring
In the year 5222, Council Reckoning

It begins in Donir. The streets are bustling, busy, the heaving multitudes of the populace darting here and there, their worries important for a few brief, final moments.

A carriage drives by, the coachman shouting angrily at passersby to move aside. He will die hating his life.

The peddler on the corner begs a man for a coin, and the man grants his request. That kindness will be his last.

The spice merchant set up his wares a few paces down, but spice is a common commodity in Donir regardless of what his brother said, and he's never made much money. A curse against his family will be his final words.

The end, when it comes, is so sudden that few have time to scream. A light, a distant glow, the sudden sound of rushing wind, and then… nothing.

Nothing but ash.

The view shifts. I'm flying, chasing the massive wall of flame. The fire spreads shockingly fast, all the more terrifying because it ignores all laws of nature. It plunges underwater, consuming the fish and sharks and whales and plants as easily as it incinerates dried tinder. It climbs mountains, racing up their slopes faster than the melting snow can fall, tongues of flame snapping forth to consume birds just as the edge of the wall passes on. The flame spreads, one long growing ring of destruction, until it meets on the other side of the world and dies as swiftly as it lived. The bright sparks of life, the creatures fighting for their children, clawing just for the right to breathe for one more moment, the humans and their petty hopes, their worries and their fears.

Nothing but ash.

I wake with a gasp. The same dream. The same horrifying dream of fire and ash, of... *the end.* I don't know where the words came from, but they seem fitting. Sometimes, the dream begins in other places, spreading out from the middle of the wilderness, or from the heart of Coin, or from the Broken Isles. Most often, though, it starts in Donir. Regardless of where or when it begins, the result is always the same.

As if my life isn't shit enough, now I've started having consistently depressing nightmares, as well. The strange dreams of conversations with disembodied strangers ended abruptly, replaced completely by the repeating end-of-days narrative. It's so shockingly regular, so strangely repetitive, that I begin to wonder if something unnatural is happening to me. Has the shock unhinged my mind? I liked it better when I had some control over the dreams. At least those people had spoken back.

Now... I sigh as the first glimmer of sunlight crests the horizon. It's going to be a bad day. Most of them are.

The worst days, such as this one, are when Te'ial is occupied elsewhere. The captain flatly refuses to tell me where she's going or what business she's about. While she's softened to me some over the season of tender treatment, she still makes it evident as often as possible that she despises me with as much of her being as she can muster. Still, she knows I'm weak as a newborn lamb, and, while I regain strength by the day, I need her to survive. The instant she larks off into the jungle, though, her lithe arms pushing aside low-hanging vines with a careful confidence, Ton'kapu appears as if by magic, his broad grin presaging more torments.

The man is an absolute terror. The first time I accepted a bowl of food from him, it was filled with maggots. He laughed uproariously as I made frantic and ineffectual attempts to shove the writhing worms away from my weakened body. Every time he passes, even when Te'ial is around, he smiles, walks close, and spits on my face. You figure you'd get used to it after the fifteenth or fiftieth repetition, but the unending insolence is maddening. The little savage only has power over me because I'm trapped in a cage surrounded by idiots with spears that would kill me if I so much as step out of place again.

The rare times anyone else of the People passes, they watch me with wary eyes. I get the feeling that, though they've hated Shaping their whole lives, they haven't been faced with a Shaper in the blossoming of his powers before. They hate and fear me… and the longer I'm stuck in this cage, the more terrified we all become. We. Not just they. Because something is wrong.

I can't Shape.

The thoughts of others, so distinctly available to me before, are now as unfathomable as the bottom of the sea. It isn't just that my body is weak. I've reached the stage where I'm able to get up and move, to walk around the tight confines of my cage for hours, pacing the same one and three-quarters paces thousands of times. I can jump and squat, and I've started lifting myself up to the top of the cage, only relenting when I can kiss the twisted wood holding me in check. Honestly, I'm probably in as good or better shape than at any other time in my life. Despite my body's recovery, though, my mind can no longer reach out.

The first time Ton'kapu spit on me, I reached for his thoughts so instinctively I was shocked when my power failed. He laughed and walked away, his wizened little back hunching with each shake of his shoulders. I'm Ton'kapu's favorite joke, and I never get old. Between the nightmares and the absence of my powers I'm terrified something is seriously wrong with me.

Te'ial left the day before, and I peer eagerly into the morning light, searching the jungle for her return. My first clue to Ton'kapu's sneaky approach is the spear butt he slams into my kidneys. I cry out and fall to the ground in agony.

"Lok'ahnae pai'wia, Eo!" he shouts joyfully. *Fed by the world's excrement, Eo.* I don't know why he keeps calling me Eo. His own personal little pet name for me, apparently, since he uses it so often.

"Thanks, Ton'kapu," I mutter from the ground. I don't insult him in return because he hates it the most when I dare to use his name. As if the sounds coming from my tainted lips are a disgrace. "Getting real creative with that one."

I hear motion behind me, but I can't turn because my back hurts so much. A thick stream of warm piss splashes onto my back. I dart up, fighting back vomit, the stream tracking down my leg as I lurch away. He smiles, tucking his penis back in his trousers, and ambles away. I finally lose the battle against my stomach, vomiting everywhere, the thin stream of bile all that remains in my stomach from the early morning breakfast Te'ial gave me yesterday. Of course, Ton'kapu gives me nothing when she's gone.

"Ton'kapu," I spit at his back, probably too far for him to hear but meaning every word. *"Nio'pele'stina." Make-death comes, Ton'kapu.*

The *I'wia* is a tricky language of nonsense, as far as I can tell. Even after listening to the People speak for nearly half of Spring, I barely feel any closer to understanding how the language actually works. After a dozen days in a row of wheedling and cajoling, I managed to get Te'ial to at least tell me the basics. Apparently, the *I'wia* isn't a language, but one long word which describes everything the world contains and all emotion and thought. If you said the whole word, it would take you perhaps two minutes without a breath, but no one bothers to speak the whole word. Instead, the subtleties of life and the world can be described by taking the relevant portion of the world-word and breaking it up into smaller chunks.

Thus, *Lok'ahnae* roughly means "excrement-fed," because the overall portion of the *I'wia* "Alokahnae" means Food of Life.

When broken up, the letters can variously mean breakfast, lunch, dinner, shit, bitter, sour, sweet, spicy, disgusting, vomit, diarrhea, taste, energy, starvation, hunger, sated, delicious, salty, savory, nauseating, stomach, and a dozen other food related words. All meaning exists in where and when the nearly imperceptible pauses occur between the sounds of the world-word. To make matters more interesting, the People use shortcuts and abbreviations for commonly used words, which serve to complete the confusion of anyone not raised on the twisted and absurd language.

I've learned perhaps a dozen of the most common portions on the *I'wia*, from food to sleep to weather, as well as some of the variations off of them, but I sound less like a child and more like a disabled war veteran struck dumb by a hammer. Perhaps because of that, Ton'kapu speaks his insults in the most basic terms he can manage. He still creates new and unfortunate combinations of words that degrade me in a unique and depressing manner anyway. If I didn't literally dream of taking a long needle and pushing it slowly through both his eyeballs, I might be impressed with his creativity.

I spend the day alternating between exercising and languishing against the bars dreaming of lobster dipped in rich melted butter. I go to sleep hungry, Ton'kapu ignoring me aside from the pair of times he strolls by to spit on me, shout a gleeful insulting epithet, and walk away.

It begins in Donir…

Nothing moves. Nothing breathes. Clouds of grey and black drift listlessly over mountains melted into smooth and undulating hills, seas smothered in an opaque rain of unmoving grey.

Dawn brings the same vain search for Te'ial in the dense jungle undergrowth. I start to grow worried the longer she's gone. Ton'kapu hasn't bothered to bring me water, and my joints ache as my mouth dries. My stomach, once soft and smooth, now lean and hard, exists in a small knot of pain. Spring is passing quickly towards Summer, and the days are growing hotter. As the sun reaches its zenith, I stop sweating. Two long days in the sun without water... the heat picks up, the tropical sun blazing overhead, and I can't tell if my vision is swimming or if the heat is shimmering in the air.

"Ton'kapu!" I call, my throat dry and rasping. "Ton'kapu!"

The man's ridiculous hunched back doesn't appear, and I gasp. The heat pours down, the sun an unbearable burning brightness…

The flames spread, consuming, destroying, mountains melt, seas boil…

I blink, the jungle in focus one second, aflame and smoking the next…

Ash, unending tides of ash, swirling, choking….

I cough, my swollen throat desperate to breathe, to drink…

It begins in Donir, in Coin, in Isa, in the center of the sea…

My heart beats fast, my lungs surging for air so hot my blood boils...

"Creator, help me," I call into the void or into the air, I can't tell. "Save me, Creator. By your forgotten name, by your wisdom, please, save me from this hell."

"And what have you done to deserve my aid, Bastian of Coin?" a voice asks from the cloud of ash. The voice is a multitude of voices, the intertwining of dozens at once, their echoes in perfect unison, yet their voices distinct. The voice of the Creator, just as I've always imagined it.

"Nothing," I answer honestly. "I've done nothing but live and wish to keep living."

"What will you do to earn my aid?"

"Anything," I say desperately. "Anything."

"When I call, you will answer?"

"Yes," I say, but a warning echoes under the surface of my thoughts. Something… some instinct... My desperation fades, suspicion

creeping to the fore. The Creator's voice… exactly *as I imagined it? "I swear it on my blood."*

"Blood you hold cheap, Bastian of Coin. I know your heart. Hatred for those who birthed you. Pity for a brother who does not know you. Your heart is known only to yourself, and trust is a concept foreign to you."

The longer they talk, the more I begin to realize 'they' is a better pronoun than 'he,' and the more familiar the voices become. The same voices I've heard before in my dreams. The moment I recognize the stuffy woman, Ulia, I pick out several others, Jynn leading them all.

"Why should I trust when I have been constantly misled, Jynn?" I ask.

The voices break into a babble of noise, shouts and panic. Even as their voices clamor, I catch a glimpse of Jynn, much as I've seen her before, her armor shimmering amongst the clouds and dust coating the air. She darts away, her soul disappearing into the darkness of the drifting ash. I give chase as fast as I can think, blasting through the ash and catching sight of her braid curling around one cloud, her foot as she dives into another, the tip of her sword as she hides behind a melted mountain. Every time I close, she breaks at just the right moment, or moves just a hair faster, my outstretched will inches from her trailing back. No matter what I try, no matter the angle, she is just a step ahead....

What the hell am I doing? Chasing the physical form of a spirit? Through an imaginary dream world? I growl, the whispering will of another suddenly audible in the back of my mind as I become aware of it.

"Get the fuck out of my head!" I scream, throwing everything I can at whoever whispers in my mind.

The voice ceases and vanishes with a cry, the distant sounds of pain echoing through the soundless space. I reach for Jynn's spirit, just as I have before, but something blocks me. A wall, invisible and boundless, edges beyond imagination and yet solid, holds me back. I scrabble at its edges, gouge at its mortar, ram into its center. I feel it buckle, crack, the tenor of panic rising in their voices as I fight to free myself from whatever unnatural magic holds me at bay.

"Wake up, Bastian," Jynn says, her voice a calm center amongst the raucous storm.

I hear it, the call, the urge to head back to my waiting body, but I growl, resisting the temptation and slamming again against the invisible wall.

"Enough," Jynn says, her voice reverberating with power on this mental landscape. The voices cease as one, and I stop fighting, my mind exhausted. I might yet break through, maybe, but I don't know what it will cost me. I'm weak, and the efforts of my struggle make me weaker still. "Bastian, wake up."

I can't resist this time, the command so much more potent, her will so powerful—

The heat hasn't changed; the sun is still a torrent of fire, but my mind is clear, my soul revitalized. Standing, I sense the thrum of reawakened power. My body still needs water and food, but the energy of my soul burns those needs away for the time being. My sight is sharp when it has been blurry, my mind awake again.

Ton'kapu strolls around the corner, carrying a skin of water in his hand loosely. He grins his shit-eating grin the second he sees me awake. I stare at him, my gaze steady, my body urging me to beg for the life-giving water he grasps in his hand. I try to ignore the voice, but it's impossible. Slowly, calmly, I raise my hand for the skin. Ton'kapu stops, grinning, before taking a long drink. Exaggerating the sigh of satisfaction, he allows water to drip down his chin, wasted amongst the rivulets of his sweat. I simply stare, hand outstretched. My serenity makes him angry, his surface thoughts as clear as day.

Ton'kapu lifts the water skin and begins to turn it upside down, but then cocks his ear as if he hears something. He frowns and glances behind him. I allow my senses to spread farther into his mind, and suddenly the desperate whispers of Ulia become audible, her clear voice begging Ton'kapu to reconsider. I smile.

"You should never have shown me such useful abilities," I call out to the aether. Narrowing my focus, it's my turn to place a wall around Ton'kapu's mind. Her voice disappears.

Ton'kapu makes peace with the strange voice in his head almost immediately. It's not the first time he's been afraid he's hearing things that don't exist, and he figures it probably won't be the last. Instead, his joy for my torment rises to the surface like a child seeing a favorite toy. Through his eyes, I look weak, but not frail enough. My calm demeanor infuriates him. His next action is his own, purely and completely. His malice is his own. His hate is his own.

His punishment will be mine.

He tips up the skin and pours the remaining water out onto the moist earth. Taking control of his body from his simple brain isn't difficult. He's perplexed as he kneels to the ground against the commands of his feeble mind. His confusion grows as he scoops up the wet earth with his bare hands. He only realizes fear when I speak.

"Niope'lesti." Death-wishing. Suicide.

He pushes the dirt into his mouth, the fistfuls of moist soil immediately choking him. Even as his lungs spasm in an attempt to clear his throat, he pushes another handful of dirt into his mouth, and another, and another. Worms wriggle in the earth as he digs the hole deeper, cramming handful after handful of dirt into his waiting mouth. He tries to cough, tries to swallow, but his body will not, cannot respond. His stomach fills with dirt, his throat and lungs packed tight. His lungs can't move anymore, their expanse filled to the brim. His last moments of life are spent staring into my eyes. I don't let him blink.

I stare at his cooling corpse for a long moment. Distant shouts and the sound of hurrying feet drift on the wind. Six warriors, each dressed in armor half-covering their muscular forms, sprint into the clearing. Two immediately fall to their knees next to Ton'kapu, pointlessly checking him for signs of life. The other four shout at me, fanning out and brandishing gleaming spears. I ignore them and take a seat in my cage. They're terrified, but are under strict orders not to harm me under any circumstances. Though the idiot on the far right is tempted, he doesn't have the balls to disobey a direct order from the Seer.

I close my eyes. I want to sleep, but the needs of my body are insistent. Shaping used to cause exhaustion, especially when controlling obstinate minds. Not Ton'kapu. I held his mind in my hand like a violin and played a symphony. I should be drained from the experience, but instead I'm invigorated. My thoughts drift, sharp and dull, clear and cloudy, the needs of my body warring with the exultation of my soul.

"That was evil!" Ulia shouts into the darkness.

"The method was evil," Jynn responds. "The act was not. Ton'kapu was a horrible man, who had already committed murder before, if you'll remember."

"So the ends justify the means?" a foreign voice asks.

"That depends, and you know that as well as I, Eligio," she answers. There's a momentary pause. "He was pushed. Could you, could any of you, have taken Ton'kapu's torments if you had the power to end them?"

"Of course not," the Khalintari responds. "But the brutality of the punishment… his satisfaction afterward..."

"He is what we have Seen," a new voice cuts in. It is a woman's tone, older, colder. "Why argue over that which is necessary? Your approval is immaterial."

"What else have we, Kimi, but our voices?" Ulia answers. "What can we do but weep to know the devil of our nightmares first hand? Even in the best of futures, his deeds tarnish our future. I refuse to do it. I will not aid that monster."

"In order to have a future in the first place, he is our only chance," Jynn says, her voice sharp. As always, they fall silent to listen.

"Ulia, you aren't doing it for him. You're doing it for all of us. When the time comes, you can rest. You know this. But we cannot hesitate now. Not this late in the game."

"I know my place," Ulia answers stiffly. "I also know how eager you are for my rest. You may come to miss my voice, as aggravating as you find it now, Jynn. Nothing is certain, especially not this treacherous path we walk now. Your impulsiveness could kill us all."

"And it is the only hope we have," Kimi responds quietly. "The time for debate is over. The time for action is at hand."

"Wake up, Bastian," Jynn says.

I scowl into the darkness.

"No."

"We've sent people with water. Your body is failing as we speak. This sleep is not one of your making, but of your body shutting down. We'll answer your questions, soon. You're to be brought to the Seer, and she will speak for us."

"Who in the Eternal's blasted name are all of you? How are you speaking in my mind?" I growl. There are several flickers of emotion from the edges of the void, flashes of sorrow, hints of humor.

"Soon, Bastian. You'll die. Tick tock," Jynn urges.

"Fine. But only if you tell me who you *are at least."*

"My name is Jynn Dioran," she says, a sigh in her voice. "I fought for the Eternal more than five thousand years ago as her Master of Thought. They called me the Mind Razor."

"What?"

"Wake up, Bastian."

I cough on the water streaming down my throat. Before I finish convulsing, I grab the skin greedily, bloating my belly but leaving me woefully unsatisfied. Te'ial's familiar muscular calves crouch next to me holding the skin, and my first emotion is relief. She's back. Ton'kapu won't be able to torment me again... I remember suddenly that he's dead. I killed him. I glance over at Te'ial, but she refuses to meet my gaze, her eyes sliding away. It seems what little rapport we had is destroyed.

"Te'ial," I begin, but she waves her hand at me irritably.

"I am not interested in your words, *thriska* Cursed. For me to believe Eo to have changed, even some, was the hope of a child."

"Is anyone going to tell me why you keep calling me Eo?" I ask wearily.

"Eo is the soul in your body," she surprises me by responding. "Well, I guess Eo is you."

"Going to have to set a new course, Captain. I have no idea what you're talking about."

"Barbarians," she says, rolling her eyes. "Eo is the man who stole the Creator's thoughts."

"But—"

"Shut *up*, Cursed. I am not finished. The Creator you so blithely curse about and pray to was real. All peoples know this. But he did not *bless* us with this power to control the elements. The power was taken from him. Sixteen men and women ripped him to pieces and took the power for their own, raping the elements—"

"There are only fifteen elements," I interrupt.

"Barbarian," she says, gritting out each syllable as if each is a new word. "Shut up. Your knowledge of the world is less than a *chela*. The men and women destroyed the Creator, stealing his powers, and for that crime they are Cursed to take new bodies, Cursed to live out countless lives of suffering as penance for their—your—crimes. Each time you die, you are born again in a new body, forgetting your past and living the same cycle of destruction and hate over and over again. You are both your own Curse, and humanity's."

"You think," I say slowly. "That Shapers are the souls of the people who murdered the Creator. You think I am the same man from thousands, tens of thousands of years ago."

"Of course you are, Eo. You are living what appears to be a particularly evil life, even for you."

"You people are insane," I say, burying my face in my hands. I look up again as a thought occurs to me. "How could they kill the Creator? Wasn't he all powerful?"

"He trusted the early men and women more than he should have. We were a wicked creation, but he believed he could fix us. He brought the early kings and queens to speak with him, to reason with our leaders. He did not know they plotted long to surprise him. In his trust, he allowed them close, and in his love, he refused to fight back. He gave us free choice, and accepted the fate his knowledge of time offered. He gave himself up for humanity, and we are unworthy of his sacrifice," she answers, somberly staring off into the distance. I don't need to see her thoughts to know she believes every word. As unbelievable as they are.

"You realize how ridiculous this sounds. A literal god, master of all the elements, capable of controlling time itself, was murdered by normal humans? He gave up literally everything so that creatures little better than worms could live? Impossible."

"You are so full of yourself that humility is a foreign concept. You know nothing of sacrifice."

"I may not know sacrifice, but you have taught me loss," I say, gesturing broadly to the cage.

"What have you lost? Two years? In the life of a Cursed, a pinch of dirt. In the scope of your many long lives, Eo, less than nothing," she scoffs.

"You pretend to know me," I answer with my eyes closed. "But you see only what you wish to see."

"I see what you are, regardless."

"You want to know what I lost in two years? You took my only family from me. You took the only thing good in my life and left me with this… existence. I'll be damned if I let you judge me when you are the cause of all my problems."

"Lav is not lost."

"What?" I snap, sitting up and pressing my face against the bars. My heart races, my skin tingling in sudden anticipation. I drink in the strong lines of Te'ial's face. She appears sincere. "What do you know of Lav?"

"The Seer told me you would respond to this name, and there I would see something different about you. That I might begin to understand you."

"Tell me of Lav, damn it. Did the Seer tell you more? Where is he? How has he managed without me?" I ask desperately.

"I see nothing different," Te'ial says, her lip curling. "Only the same greed and desires."

"Please," I say, fighting back the urge to shout at her. Anger will get me nothing. "Please, Lav is my brother. He can't take care of himself. I'm the only one in all the world who loves him, and I'm the only one who looks after him."

She doesn't respond, but merely studies me. Her face remains closed, her eyes narrow.

"Te'ial, when you told me it had been two years, I lost control. It wasn't because I was angry or sad. I was terrified," I say, willing her to understand. "I was terrified for a brother who needs me more than anything. All I could think was to get back to him. I'm… I'm sorry I did that to you."

"My head still hurts, some nights," she says, her gaze softening. "I am afraid I feel you there."

"That's not how it works," I try to explain, searching my brain to figure out a way that will make sense. I've never done it before. "At least not this time. I was barely conscious of what I was doing. I just wanted to leave. I didn't mean to hurt you."

"Come," she says abruptly. With a deft move I can hardly follow, the cage opens, twisted and hardened vines swinging aside without a sound. Without the bars, the scene of the jungle is somehow more appealing, the breeze refreshing and true where nothing was before. I breathe deeply, my lungs filling and the free air sweet.

So they're setting me free. I didn't lie to her. Not one moment. But if these idiots think a month in a cage has tamed me, they are fools. With my power returned, my body free and healthy, I'll take the first opportunity to get even with these blasted savages.

Te'ial leads me a short distance through the jungle, cautioning me to step only where she steps. Barefoot and bedraggled, I dodge away from insects and animals, doing my best to keep my vulnerable skin away from everything that might think me a meal or a host. We walk for perhaps ten minutes when the sound of laughter rings from ahead. High and long, it's the kind of laugh that can only be produced by children.

A clearing breaks into the mud and thatch huts of the People. There are perhaps a dozen of the rudimentary buildings in the little village, set against the backdrop of a jagged cliff covered liberally in vines. The top of the high expanse is lost amongst the low-hanging clouds, and the houses look tiny before the dark grey rock. Cooking fires tended by women perch here and there amongst the dirt paths between the huts, the smell of the spicy broth of my captivity reminding me how Eternal-damned hungry I am.

"Your stomach speaks for you, but you are too disgusting to eat amongst civilized people. Behind there is heated water waiting for you, and all you may need to groom yourself," Te'ial says, jerking her chin at a hut off to the left. "When you have finished, walk through the door in the back and we will have food waiting."

She doesn't need to tell me twice. I practically skip around the corner, almost crying in relief as the sight of a dozen steaming buckets of water greets me. A thick drying cloth hangs on a railing nearby, and I'm shocked to see a plate on which rests all of the necessary tools I need to shave, including a gleaming razor.

My beard has grown long and bushy, and I grimace as I try to rake my fingers through its matted strands. The whole thing will have to go.

I douse myself carelessly with the first two buckets of water. The feeling of dirt, grime, sweat, and all manner of other detritus cascading from my skin is divine. In that moment, I know Te'ial has to be wrong. The Creator definitely still lives and keeps an eye out for his Shapers. I take my time despite the hard ache in my stomach demanding food. I scrape every seam and wrinkle, my nail finding tiny parasites and layers of dirt in every nook and cranny.

The final bucket is reserved for the shave. The tiny mirror is barely large enough to fit my face, but the sharp razor cuts cleanly. I sigh in pleasure at the luxurious lightness as my face feels the first touch of breeze. Despite taking my time, I nick myself at the edge of my chin, a small spot of blood welling along my jaw. I consider taking the razor for the briefest of moments, but they never would have given me a weapon if they were afraid I could use it.

Looking into the mirror, I meet the eyes of a stranger. The softness of my jawline has disappeared, my hollowed cheekbones prominent and striking against skin tanned dark by the sun. My eyes are heavy and serious, my hair long and wavy, hanging past my shoulders and curling in on itself.

I don't realize my predicament until after I've finished toweling off the water: the only clothing I have to put on are the disgusting rags of my incarceration. I don't even want to step closer to them, let alone let those repositories of filth touch my clean skin. Shrugging, I wrap the drying cloth around myself and enter the back of the hut. Two women with frightened eyes wait for me. Their skin, several shades darker than my own, gleams in the sunlight arcing in through the open window. They hold what looks to be an armful of scraps of cloth in various colors. We stare at each other dubiously. I'm all the more self-conscious to be wearing a towel in front of strange women, and it doesn't take much to deduce why they are wary of me.

Te'ial walks in and takes charge, luckily for all involved. She snaps some orders in her native tongue and darts over to me. Before I realize what she's planning, she grabs the edge of the drying cloth and jerks it out of my grasp. I yelp and cover myself as best I can, rolling my eyes as the women giggle. Te'ial offers me a smirk and saunters out of the room. The women step forward to offer up scraps of what appear to be silk. They are dressed in roughspun clothing of linen the neutral color of wool, the dozens of crossing straps traditional to the People covering their chests. I frown. Where have they gotten this beautiful silk? How on earth is it clean in this barbaric place? Why are they offering it to me?

They hold various colors up close to my face, finally settling on a deep forest green. They weave the straps around my arms and across my chest, leaving a generous portion of my chest and my forearms bare to the wind. One leaves and returns with a pair of loose silk pants, the opening for my waist clearly far too large for me. I don't have time to protest or feel awkward as they lift my feet one at a time and slide the pants smoothly up to my hips, expertly tying a dozen intricate knots between the loose bottom of the straps trailing across my belly and the top of the pants. Before I can blink, my feet hug a pair of sandals, the straps decorated with shining gems. Surely they are just colored rocks. Surely they aren't emeralds.

They step back, admiring their handiwork. They make a few minor adjustments before they exchange a look, giggle, and prance out of the room. I don't have a mirror, but looking down I feel a bit ridiculous. The silk is both too revealing and too confining, and the color is never something I would choose for myself. I square my shoulders. Even if they've dressed me as a clown, I'm not the primitive here. I was raised in Coin, the beating heart of commerce in all the world. I will carry myself accordingly.

That attitude lasts right up until I pass into the next room and behold the veritable feast laid out for me on a low table. There are no chairs, just a few woven reed mats to cushion my knees, but I don't care. Flatbreads and ground pastes are in abundance, dried and salted fish spiced in the vibrant way of the People, three separate bowls of various broths swimming with seafood and meats I can't name, roasted chicken and vegetables doused liberally in cream. There are no utensils, so I fall to my knees and grasp the edges of one of the bowls, bringing the tangy liquid to my lips and sucking greedily at the delicious soup.

"Barbarian," Te'ial remarks casually as she walks in, kneeling gracefully at the opposite end of the table.

She helps herself to a piece of the flatbread, tearing it daintily and scooping some tan paste covered in translucent red liquid into her mouth. I don't care what she calls me. It has been three days at least since I've last eaten and more than two years since I could eat my fill of whatever I want. I'm damn well going to enjoy it. Which I do wholeheartedly until my stomach, unused to such largess, cramps. I run out of the hut to vomit most of the food I've eaten back into the grass. When I return, Te'ial hasn't moved, but simply continues to eat in small and careful bites. I force myself to match her deliberate pace, eating slowly, savoring every bite. My stomach rumbles questioningly, but seems more content with the second meal of the last ten minutes.

"You are lucky you did not ruin Arir and Ple'ti's handiwork. The rumor of the terrible beauty of the Cursed is already spreading through the women like locusts," she says, nodding at my clothing.

"I am terribly beautiful, aren't I?" I say, grinning for what feels like the first time in a long time. "They haven't dressed me up as a joke, have they?"

“We would never dishonor a guest, no matter how much it pains us.”

“What?” I sputter. “I just spent a month in a cage! I was spit on and pissed on and starved!”

“Then you were a prisoner. Now you are a guest,” she says, shrugging, as if that statement makes all the sense in the world.

“Just like that?” I ask, snapping my fingers. “How did my status change so quickly?”

“The Seer gave me the choice,” Te’ial says. She doesn’t elaborate.

I stare at her for a long moment as she eats. Te’ial was given charge of my fate… and decided to release me? The Seer gave her the option *after* I killed Ton’kapu? I open my mouth to question her further, but she stands abruptly.

“Come, Cursed,” she says, her mouth twisting as if what she’s about to do is distasteful. “You are to meet with the Seer.”

She leads me out of the hut and back into the streets. Tiny faces peek out of doorways as we pass, the whispers and giggles of children a constant counterpoint to the soft sounds of our footfalls. A boy of perhaps six summers darts out ahead of us, his face locked in a terrified grin. He runs past me, touching my hand briefly with his. I smile in confusion as he lets out a triumphant whoop, which sparks the admiration of his little followers.

“They’ve never seen someone with skin so light,” she says, shaking her head. “They have no idea who or what you are.”

We continue on, the whispering gaggle of children close behind. I frown as Te’ial motions for me to wait and ducks into the last hut in the village. I glance around, noticing the lack of any male presence in the village. In fact, there are no people at all aside from children and their mothers. Where is everyone else? The Seers are supposedly a wealthy, if primitive society. I think to reach out to the thoughts of the nearest women when Te’ial emerges with a sturdy cloak made for traveling. She throws it to me and sets off again at a swift pace, heading out of the village.

The sun is hot, but I don't exactly feel up to arguing about the cloak, so I reach out to her thoughts. They rest on an ascent towards the cliff. Apparently, the drifting mist soaks everything near the rock's face. Recognizing the sensibility of protecting my new clothes, I throw the cloak over my shoulders. Te'ial's hardy leather version of the People's garb is clearly up to the challenge of protecting against a little water.

I crane my neck up as we close with the cliff, my eyes tracking twisting vines a hundred yards long, their green tips swaying in an unfelt breeze so far above. Misty clouds fall off the cliff and pool high on the rock. Birds dip in and out of the mist, brief flashes of brilliant scarlet and viridian against the white clouds and gray rock. We wind our way through moss-covered boulders and around vine-laden trees seemingly at random. At first, I slip often, but the longer I follow Te'ial, the more I get the sense of a well-worn path. Her steps are sure and certain, the places she sets her feet always firm and reliable no matter how uncertain the footing appears. Her thoughts are squarely on the path at hand, never straying to the future or where our final destination could be. It's almost as if she's deliberately keeping me in the dark on the off chance I'm reading her surface thoughts. I am, of course, but I do feel vaguely offended.

She moves in silence, and I'm fine with the quiet. Though boredom drove me to work my muscles into something resembling fitness in the cage, I lack the lungs to keep up with her pace for much longer. We've been traveling for perhaps an hour, and the air cools the closer we get to the wall of rock. The low-hanging clouds of mist close in about us, and the sun's rays disappear so suddenly I blink in surprise. The temperature plummets, the lack of sunlight and the drifting mist transforming the late Spring day into a chill Autumn night. I shiver as the light sweat of our climb cools on my forehead, but Te'ial doesn't react.

I glance down to see where to step, and when I look back up she's gone. I stumble to a stop. Checking behind and above, all I can see is drifting mist and unforgiving jungle. I open my mouth to call when her head appears out of the solid rock ahead.

"Hurry up, Cursed. We will be late."

The crack in the rock wall is thin, its contours constantly turning in and around itself. From outside, you would never know it's there. The fissure was caused long ago by some kind of massive trauma, an earthquake or some other titanic gouge in the earth. It isn't an enclosed cave; glancing up, clouds drift far above in brief patches when the curving path turns just right. It's as if some thin, colossal razor gouged a jagged line in the mountain. Te'ial stops me just as the passage widens.

"Know you look upon wonders not seen by any outside the People in a generation. If my course of action had been considered, we never would have brought you here. Our secrets are our own. But the Seer told me this is necessary," she seems to sag a bit, weary or defeated, and moves aside. "Welcome, barbarian, to Isa."

On our right, the earth ends abruptly, falling into a smooth oceanic bay. On the distant horizon, nearly invisible, a massive rocky escarpment encircles the calm, sheltered stretch of water. A dozen of the massive Seer ships bob on the water beside a long dock stretching out into the center of the bay, and another ship sails through a distant crack in the distant natural walls.

On our left, however, a city spreads out from the opening in the rock, a city the likes of which the world no longer contains. The walls of the dwellings share only an unnatural smoothness to their construction, each building in shapes and contours that defy the senses. Some buildings tower nearly as high as the walls of the rock itself, sharp spindles and undulating waves married at platforms floating above the streets. Structures of smooth stone, of bright wood, of gleaming emerald, of sparkling sapphire, each seems to bend against the will of nature and spurn the physical laws of the world. Pathways stretch across boulevards dozens of feet into the air, the entire city its own dizzying riot of angles and shapes. A single tower of glittering glass stretches higher than all the rest, its tip lost amongst a low-hanging cloud.

As I gaze in wonder, however, I begin to feel a kind of harmony to the structures, as if the whole city has been constructed to a tune beyond normal hearing, as if the entire confusing array is in fact only confusing because the larger picture can't be seen, as if my perspective is so miniscule that I can't see the purpose for what it is. An ache forms behind my eyes as I look at the city. I turn again to the bay, needing the relative normality of the docks to ground myself.

"What is this place?" I ask, utterly failing at a nonchalant tone.

"I have told you," Te'ial answers. "You look on Isa."

"Isa sank below the waves thousands of years ago. The Breaker completely destroyed it, and the last remnants of the Eternal's power with it. That isn't just legend. That is history."

"Lyna did destroy the city, as you claim. The ancient kingdom of the Cursed was broken perhaps a dozen miles to the north," she gestures towards the crack in the distant wall of the bay. "But the destruction was not complete. Isa was built by dozens of generations of Cursed, at the same time they constructed the unnatural Ways your cities cling to like tumors. The efforts of one Cursed, even Lyna, could not completely undo the powers of so many others working in harmony. This small section survived the Breaking. The water you see before you… Isa once encompassed the entire span, and more besides."

"What?" I gasp. The bay stretches nearly beyond sight, practically an inland sea. Isa filled… all of it? All of Coin could fit four times into the space, and the buildings of Coin do not tower so into the sky. "Impossible."

"It has been the home of the People for many long years since its discovery. There are records, censuses from time long past. Isa alone held millions of people in her walls, and the surrounding countryside many more. Lyna has untold seas of blood on her hands. But come, we must be moving," Te'ial says, setting off towards the city.

My feet crunch on what feels like a mixture of gravel and sand. As we follow the path, I glance behind me, noticing again the jagged fissure in the rock… which aligns with the edge of the docks near the water. Am I walking along the literal line of the Breaking of Isa?

The path turns left and winds up stairs hewn into the rock, and the echoes of life begin to drift back to me. The sounds of haggling, of laughter, of shouts and cries become more distinct with each passing step. The second we step off of the stairs, I pause. Dozens of passersby walk in the same vibrant and gleaming silks they've dressed me in, rainbows of vivid color. Jewelry decorates the ears and throats of every person, man or woman, the display of opulence so casual it's off-putting. The People laugh and argue, cajole and joke, all in the staccato fits and bursts of the I'wia. Hearing the language from all sides jars my ear, understanding nothing but snippets and tone.

A couple is the first to notice me, dressed in identical silks of the deepest purple with gold and amethyst ornaments perfectly matching their attire. They stop in their walk, stunned. A trio of men, dressed in black leathers akin to Te'ial's and walking with long curving blades similar to Talan's, run into them and good-naturedly call out for them to move along. When they don't, the men follow the line of their gaze and light on me. Instantly, the leader of the men, an absolute giant of a man, drops his hand to his blade and marches forward, his companions at his back.

"*Itlo'ka'enia,* Te'ial?" the leader says, his tone aggressive.

His face, handsome at rest, quivers into a lopsided scowl. A scar, so thin as to be nearly imperceptible, cuts through the edge of his mouth and along his cheek to the ear. A small portion is missing, as if some impossibly-fine blade drew a perfect line through his flesh. His eyes, though, speak double for any lack in his face. Rage and hate, so much more potent and *personal* than Ton'kapu's, burns so brightly I flinch.

"Are'lentiel'e, Sanar," she responds, raising a hand in warning.

Their conversation flows too rapidly to follow, but the growing crowd of onlookers makes me uneasy. Several men finger weapons, and the looks of curiosity are quickly being replaced by stares of cold hatred. The continued anger of the giant and his black-clad brethren is only inciting them further. Te'ial says something, but the only word I follow isn't a word at all but a name: Eo. Fierce whispers erupt through the crowd at the name, anger rippling like a stone thrown into a pond. The man gestures sharply for Te'ial to move, sword appearing in his hand. She snaps something in response, and his face goes stony. He steps aside, reluctance and anger evident in every movement.

"Didn't the Seer tell people we were coming?" I mutter quietly to her back.

"Shut up, Bastian," she says, the first time my given name has ever passed her lips. "Do not speak. Do not look up. My People hate you and fear you, tainted as you are. Many believe the Seer has lost her way in bringing you here. That I chose it has divided them further. I can't protect you if enough decide to rid the world of your taint, however temporarily. If you value the skin you wear, follow my steps exactly, say nothing, and do not look up."

My first walk through Isa is thus dreadfully terrifying and dreadfully boring at once. The People move aside, however reluctantly, as Te'ial and I walk. I don't see any of it, however, because I stare as diligently as I can at the street. Aside from the hems of gaudily colored silk dresses and the ornate sandals of their wearers, my eyes only track the whorls and inconsistencies of the wooden street.

I have to remind myself to keep walking as the thought hits me. The streets of Isa are constructed of… wood? The floor upon which the city is built isn't stone or earth, but smooth and unbroken wood. We've walked for many minutes, and I haven't seen a seam. Somehow, the entire street was constructed of a single sheet of unmarred wood. What forest… what *tree* could produce such a plank?

The People don't speak as I pass, nor do they spit on me or throw things. The silence, however, is all the more damning. I disregard drawing even the tiniest bit on Thought, terrified one of them will notice the glimmer from the symbol on my leg. The walk ends as my sandaled feet pass over a threshold in the wood, transitioning smoothly to a perfect marble floor. The light brightens as we enter, as if a shade has been raised from a lamp. I glance up despite Te'ial's commandment.

We're inside the gleaming tower of glass I glimpsed before we entered the city. Up close, though… it's not glass at all. It's diamond. The filtered sunlight refracts and grows on itself as it passes through the glittering wall, the interior of the tower brighter than direct sunlight. The sun itself is just beginning to arc towards the distant horizon, and, for the briefest of moments, it peeks out from the clouds that hover over the city. The entire wall blazes as if aflame, a cascading, brilliant torrent of light arcing through the tower. I gasp.

The sun tucks itself behind the clouds again, and the gleaming light resettles to its normal hue.

"It never gets old," the Seer's quiet, strong voice speaks at my elbow. "No matter how many times you see it. Of all that survived the Breaking, I am most glad for the shrine to Light."

"This is a temple?" I ask, incredulous. We're the only two in the tower. Te'ial has closed the doors and retreated. Even though the tower appears translucent, I can't see outside aside from a hazy blur of color.

"The only to withstand the Breaking. The others were all lost."

"The fifteen others?" I ask sardonically. I feel comfortable speaking for the first time since we entered the hostile city. "For isn't that what you believe, that there are sixteen elements in the world?"

"Of course. The records we found here list them, along with the location of their shrines throughout the known world," she answers calmly. "The knowledge of one has passed from the world, and the element of the other has long been dormant."

"What are they, then?"

"That would be telling," she says, a faint grin decorating her lips.

"I'm just about tired of being kept in the dark. I'm going to need you to start telling me what's really going on," I say, reaching for my power. Her smile doesn't falter, and her thoughts remain as unreadable to me as her native tongue.

"You need to learn patience, Bastian. Do you think I brought you here for riddles? Why do you believe I've allowed you to wake up? To torture you?"

"It's starting to feel that way," I snarl. "Are we ever going to get to the point?"

"You want answers, Master of Thought? Come with me."

She strides over to a glimmering diamond staircase cut or formed out of the edge of the tower itself and begins to ascend. For a moment I hesitate. I'm damn tired of being led about like a dog, but what else am I going to do? Go back to the crowd of people who want to kill me? Sighing, I follow.

By the time we reach the top, my breath is little more than gasps, and the view robs me of what little I still have. The streets do follow a great pattern, the strange peaks and valleys of the alien architecture harmonious when seen from above. There is a truth to it, a value, but it's incomplete. As eyes naturally track a subtle pattern through the city, it ends abruptly at the bay. Each time I'm able to discern something that seems to make sense out of the chaos that is Isa, it ends inevitably at the broken line of the lost city where it meets the water. What had Isa been? Was it more than just a city? Did it once reveal something grand, something hidden, something now lost?

"We can speak freely here," she says, her voice almost lost to the stiff breeze blowing off the water. "The top of the tower is my sanctum; too high to be overheard, too far to be seen."

"Do you have so much to fear from your own people?" I ask, gazing out over the myriad buildings and streets.

"All leaders do, regardless of how much they are loved or feared. But no, I don't have anything to fear from them. They trust me completely, regardless of what they debate or whisper in the streets. Even so, you and I have to talk about matters beyond the scope of my People."

"Are you going to tell me, or are we just going to stand up here in the breeze until sundown?"

"Before the Eternal's fall, the world knew quite a bit more about Shaping and all that came with it. They knew what they were capable of and bore that responsibility gravely. They could avoid events like the Desolation of two decades past, when the souls of Shapers exploded into the aether and so many lives were lost. They had methods to contain the destruction or eliminate it entirely."

"Why are you telling me this? Are you planning on killing me?" I ask bluntly.

"Not today," she answers, smiling. "No, I am enlightening you. The Shapers of old had a process they called Ensoulment. They could give up their lives and enter an object, something the hand of man had shaped. It could be anything created by another: clothing, houses, weapons, or, most commonly, jewelry. In doing so, their bodies and their powers passed on without the deadly explosion current Shapers create when they die. In doing so, they also earned the right to continue to exist, at least in a limited form."

"Exist? You mean they didn't die?"

"They died as we know it, yes, but their souls lived on in the objects they inhabited. Their memories and skills and personalities could be called on to serve as both advisor and warning to any with the ability to listen. Before you speak," she says as I open my mouth. "Do you dream, Shaper of Thought?"

"Rarely," I answer, but the implication of her words hits me even as the word leaves my lips. "You don't mean… Jynn? Ulia? You're trying to say…"

She holds up her right hand, on which rests a ring of silver: simple, elegant, the surface inlaid with a few subtle, delicate markings that swirl and eddy around one another. My soul feels light, staring at that pattern, the moorings of my body less solid, less sure. That feeling only derives from one thing in this world: the symbol of my power. Of Thought.

"Open your mind, Bastian, as you do when you Shape. Use your power and *see*."

I reach out, as I so often have before, but not towards a human mind. Instead, I mentally call to the ring, as silly as it seems.

"I already regret this," Ulia says, her sulk clear even disembodied. *"We can't go back after he knows."*

"We reached the point of no return long ago," Jynn says, the impatience in her voice clearly for Ulia. *"Hello, Bastian."*

"Uh," I answer. *"Hello?"*

Vertigo strikes me. The Seer catches me as I stumble, trying to balance between the world of the spirit and realm of the flesh. Even as I listen to voices in my head, I stare into the eyes of the woman in front of my physical eyes.

"Don't push so hard," she counsels, standing me back up. "Just open yourself to the power."

I take a deep, steadying breath and let the tension go, easing towards my power as if it is a colt I don't wish to startle. The barest trickle of awareness is all I need.

"It'll get easier with time," the Khalintari says. *"I am called Asimir, young one. I am glad to meet one of my blood."*

"A... pleasure?" I answer. *"How many of you are there? Are you all in this ring?"*

"There are twenty-seven of us, though some have been here so long that they sleep more than they are aware. Even the Ensouled require a will to live in order to do so," Jynn says.

"How long? How long have you been here?"

"I am the youngest," Jynn answers. *"I became Ensouled three years before the Eternal's fall. We are the Shapers of Thought from the time of Queen Elitrea, the woman your legends call the Eternal. And we need your help."*

Chapter 17
Kettle

The Final Day of Spring
In the year 5222, Council Reckoning

The gaudier the get-up, the less they see you. That's the plan, anyway. As we saunter, cavort, tumble, and spin our way to the servant's entrance of Duke Paloran's estate, however, I swallow back some nerves. My costume is my own design. I've taken the traditional silken garb of the People and simply removed two thirds of the interwoven strips of silk. The only concession I've made to utility is the scuffed leather boots I stole from Gordyn. Polished to a black shine, the scuff remains despite all efforts to remedy the scar. I would dearly have loved Corna's input on the costume; she always knows exactly how much skin to show, exactly how to move to attract the gaze of men and convince them to forget you all the same.

The only benefit to this costume, as far as I can tell, is how Aurelion's eyes follow me wherever I walk. Others might believe it's because Gordyn sent him to watch over our efforts and ensure we aren't attempting anything untoward, but the gleam in his eyes tells a far different story. He makes me want to cover up and strut both at once, and I have to work to keep my breathing even whenever I catch sight of him out of the corner of my eye. It doesn't help that he's revealing far more skin than he normally would as well, his physique as honed and primal as his skills suggest.

Aurelion and Timo wear matching costumes, Timo's rippling muscles in proud display as well, his powerful frame covered by a thin vest and loose silk pants tucked in at the ankles.

Theirs is the prototypical 'exotic' look of the far western Khalintars, or at least the exaggerated Donirian view of it. Corna once sewed and hemmed all of our costumes, but of course we've lost that resource, so we're forced to head to costume shops meant to cater to the wealthy of Donir. Thus, we are caricatures of the races and cultures we're supposed to represent.

Rather than question us and our absurd attire, however, the guardswoman at the front wave us in, laughing as Timo spouts something charming. I love seeing him like this. Even though we're in a desperate race for Corna's life, even though we're neck deep in a job we would never wish to pull ourselves, still Timo is confident, swaggering, his exuberance for life shining through. My heart hums a tiny melody of contentment despite the constant tremulous note of tension for Corna.

"You people lack nothing in confidence," Aurelion murmurs at my shoulder just as we parade through the entrance to the estate. His breath tickles the side of my neck, and I can't hide the goosebumps as my body gives an involuntary shiver. "I thought the plan insane."

"We know our business," I say, glancing at him briefly over my shoulder. I make sure not to let my eyes travel down his oiled and gleaming body. Not that his piercing eyes are much better to stare into. "That's why you hired us."

He doesn't respond aside from giving me a quiet nod and a half smile. I turn back, flustered and inwardly scowling. The man needs to stop being so Eternal-damned enticing. I can barely focus when he's close, and, despite the ease of our entrance, dozens of unwitting enemies surround us. I can't afford a slip, as all our lives potentially hang in the balance, Corna's most of all.

For this task, I've called all of the Family together for the first time in more than two years. It isn't as if the Gordyn job hasn't already been as compromised as it's going to get, and I need them all for our 'insane' scheme to succeed. When Aurelion told me we would be stealing something from Duke Paloran's estate, I expected to utilize a small team, perhaps only a solo job, mainly due to the inordinate number of highly trained professional guards the man employs. Paloran's holdings include the mountainous regions of the kingdom, from Hollen and Ardinland all the way to the top edge of the Claw Mountains bordering the Baldinlands to the north. Though the land itself is hardly worth the effort of maintaining, the Duke's territories contain nearly all of the lucrative gold, silver, and iron mines of the entire Donirian continent. His wealth is legendary.

Paloran also has a strange quirk: he trusts absolutely no one with his belongings. He does not make use of Gordyn's Imperial Bank, and he most definitely doesn't trust the money counters in Coin. Instead, he keeps all of his considerable wealth in his own sprawling estate. His is a house many thieves long to plunder, but none have succeeded outside of rumor.

Unfortunately, Gordyn has no use for any of the money or priceless art. He wants something else: an heirloom, an old artifact of the Paloran line. Best of all, he could provide only the vaguest descriptions of what it is, what it looks like, and where it could be. An amulet, which may or may not contain a ruby, which will most likely be in the private museum Paloran likes to show off for his friends, though it might be in his personal rooms, or somewhere else entirely. And Gordyn demands I steal it without anyone realizing the Family is involved at all. The plan will clearly have to be… fluid.

I need time, a cover, and a reason to slink about without interruption. Luckily for us, Paloran throws notorious parties for each major holiday, inviting everyone who is anyone onto his estate for a grand feast graced by dozens of entertainers. And Summer's Dawning is tonight.

We're ushered into a waiting room larger than most houses, cleared of all furniture or ornament. They need the space, too. A dozen other performers mill about: jugglers and acrobats, bards and singers, knife swallowers and fire breathers and magicians. Many eye each other with the hostility of rivalry, having performed similar acts throughout the city and competed for patronage. Others simply practice their craft. A member of the nobility has to recommend you in order to even get consideration for Paloran's celebration of Summer's Dawning. Faking that letter had been all the more difficult without Corna.

All the performers turn to see us as we enter, a large troupe of unfamiliar acrobats and jugglers showing far too much skin and far too much athleticism for the average act. I let the others take the lead: Rina in her absurdly salacious barbarian furs, Inia, Koli, and Ezil in the pale silks of the legendary courtesans of Coin, Hom and Yelden in our simplest costumes as mere well-dressed duelists. Aurelion and Timo, though neither fit the skin tone of the Khalintars, do pull off the silk costumes well. I wouldn't allow Sario or Ret to be involved and leave the Temple of Shadow undefended. The other performers view us skeptically, what with the overstated costumes and caked-on makeup. We look like pretenders, if capable ones. It's remarkable, however, what obscure skills thieving for a living will teach you.

As the others settle in, our fake courtesans stretching, Hom and Yelden darting at each other with fake rapiers, each thrust more flamboyant and intricate than the last, I catch Aurelion's eye and flick my gaze towards the pair of guards in Paloran's red and white livery waiting at the doors leading farther into the house. He walks with me, taking the lead as we close. Due to the sheer number of guests and the multitude of questionable performers, Paloran has hired dozens of extra guards. The places of genuine value will be protected by Paloran's normal retainers, but less important things like the doors to hallways are guarded by mercenaries only interested in the money. These two definitely appear to be the latter.

"Kettle," Timo calls quietly behind me, and I turn. He beckons me over solemnly. I ignore Aurelion's look of impatience and walk back to him. He enfolds me in a deep hug, and I lean into his strength. My bear.

"When this is over," he murmurs above me. "We should get away. Travel. Maybe try our hand in Coin. Maybe not. Maybe just..."

"What?" I ask him quietly.

"Corna always pushed us to bigger and better. But look where that's landed us. I think we need to back off. Take the children and go west. Find a quiet place and settle down."

"This isn't like you. Where's the excitement?" He doesn't respond, but only hugs me a bit tighter. "But I agree. A vacation could be nice."

He squeezes my shoulder one last time and nudges me towards Aurelion.

"Let's get our girl back," he says with a wink.

Aurelion and I approach the guards, he with confidence, me with deference.

"Stop," the one on the right calls, raising a hand. "Wrong way."

"Of course, my friend," Aurelion answers. "We still have some time yet to pass before we perform, and my companion needs to tend to an unfortunate necessity of life."

"What?" the man asks, scowling. Aurelion leans in close.

"She has to pee," he whispers.

"Why can't she talk for herself?"

"She is from the Isles, fresh from them, if you catch my drift. I can scarcely understand her jabber, but what can you do? Talent is talent," he says, casually throwing an arm around the guard's shoulder. "And she has plenty."

"I see what you mean," the man says in a husky voice, his eyes raking over my exposed skin and forcing me to suppress an entirely different kind of shiver. I smile at him invitingly and, hopefully, vapidly. "I can take her to a place where she can... go."

"She gets scared when she's left by herself. Do you know what it's like to talk a native down from the ledge? I'll need to accompany her."

"Hum," the man mulls it over, scowling. "Nothing funny, right?"

"In the Creator's name," Aurelion says, bowing with his hand over his heart.

"Alright," the guard mutters reluctantly.

He leads us farther into the estate. We take two turns down sumptuously furnished hallways before the clanks and clatter of the kitchens grow loud enough to cover our steps. The guard motions to a door off to the left just before the warm and inviting door of the kitchens, and I smile at him again, ducking inside. The second I close the door, Aurelion talks the guard up, his voice muffled but understandable. He's smooth, I grant him that. Before a few seconds have passed, he has the man talking about his life, his job, his family. I crack the door, and the guard glances back at me. I frown, motioning at my stomach.

"What's that mean?" he asks suspiciously.

"Let me check," Aurelion says, walking up. He presses himself against the crack, his hands on the wall and the door to either side. In the brief moment his body blocks me from the guard's view, my hands dart into his pants. His conveniently loose and flowing pants. All manner of things can be hidden in loose and flowing pants. He winks at me, and heat rises in my cheeks, but I don't have time to scowl before he closes the door.

"Shit," Aurelion says blandly. "She has to shit."

"Eternal's saggy tits, we aren't supposed to be doing this," the man curses.

"She'll be a while. Nasty shits, that one has," Aurelion says. "Where are you normally stationed in the house?"

Aurelion asks another question, and the men's voices begin to fade as they move off down the hall. I quickly unwind the bundle of cloth, revealing an emerald dress appropriate for just such an occasion as this. My shadow darts out from under the thin straps around my body, exploring the dimly lit room and all its nooks and crannies. The second I have the dress on and adjusted, I will the shadow under the skirts. It goes, albeit reluctantly. With a deep breath, I slide out of the toilet and walk briskly down the hall.

The guard's voice resonates from the left, punctuated by Aurelion's charming laugh, so I head right. As soon as I turn a corner, I walk the casual, confident walk of someone who belongs. The darker shade of my skin will stand out, sure, but the People are not so exotic that one might not end up at Paloran's gala. When the first pair of patrolling guards pay me no mind save to incline their heads in respect, I know I have it right.

Following my mental map of Gordyn's sketches of the estate, I make the turn towards Paloran's private collection alongside a pair of giggling women led by an equally obnoxious set of what passes for gentlemen in this city. It's easy as breathing to fall in behind them, my pace matching theirs as I become a part of their little group. The men brag about their exploits as officers in the Tide, which makes me roll my eyes. If these men are in the Tide, one painfully short and the other waddling around a belly conjured from an excess of wine, then the standards of the kingdom are slipping. They prove a rather compelling distraction, as my presence at the back of the group goes unnoticed by either the idiots themselves or the ubiquitous, vigilant guards defending the wealth Paloran puts on display.

Paloran's little museum is, unsurprisingly, quite magnificent. Exquisitely crafted statues depicting legendary figures in history are placed tastefully throughout the room, each given enough space to be enjoyed as a single piece of art. Beautifully realized paintings from a dozen different cultures decorate the walls, the vibrant colors of some offset by the muted beauty of others. A master created each piece, and I have to ignore the itch in my fingers to swipe some of the ancient figurines from the early rise of the Khalintars resting on a nearby shelf. I know a collector who would practically die to get his hands on those little bits of history.

I break from the group as I notice another door leading farther in. The idiot nobles continue on, blathering loudly enough to attract the attention of the guards strategically placed throughout the room. I pause in front of a statue, something in me compelling me to look closer. The engraving at the bottom claims it to be a depiction of Jendo the Mind Razor. His features are aristocratic and strong, with a strong jaw and high cheekbones. A solemn look graces his face, blank eyes cast to the distant horizon. Despite the beauty of the sculpture, an abrupt spike of anger and shock lances through my chest.

How could they possibly have gotten this so wrong? Didn't the artist know anything of history?

The feeling disappears as swiftly as it came, and I wince as my head begins to ache.

What in all the Depths was that?

"Ma'am," a stern voice speaks from behind me. I jump, spinning around. "Is there anything I can help you with?"

I open my mouth to respond, but then snap it shut. Aurelion Kraft's handsome grin is not supposed to be gracing the uniform of a Paloran guardsman. The fool. What is he doing?

"You can only be escorted into the exclusive collection by one of us," he says loudly. "You'll need an invitation from the Duke."

He steps close, winking cheekily at me. I'm sure my face is stone as I pretend to hand him a paper.

"Ah, everything is in order. Follow me," he says, leading towards that closed door in the back. None of the other guards react as he pulls a key from his inner pocket and unlocks the door. I blink in surprise. Where did he get the key? The door opens into darkness lit only by a rectangle of light shining in from the lanterns in the museum behind.

"You fool," I hiss as the door closes behind us and plunges us into darkness. "Where did you get that uniform?"

"Our friend was extraordinarily talkative," he whispers back. "I realized you would never make it back here without my help. He was also quite receptive to coming with me to check on you in the bathroom. And taking a nap soon afterwards."

"How could he possibly have had these keys? Isn't he a temporary?" I wonder aloud. Strange. Why would the undisciplined mercenary have keys to Paloran's most valuable assets? "He'll be discovered soon regardless, you idiot. His fellow saw us leave with him."

"Then we'd better hurry, hadn't we?" he mutters, unconcerned.

He raises a hand, light shining from it as if he holds a torch aloft. I ignore the pang of sadness that creeps through my heart at the reminder of Aurelion's power. And what it has done to my shadow. The glow illuminates another, smaller museum. The pieces here are farther apart, but each feels like a shrine to some forgotten deity. I would whisper in this space even if we weren't trespassing. I kill my natural curiosity to poke around at the priceless works, though, and quickly survey the room for our particular prize.

It isn't here.

How would you know? I snap.

Gordyn wants something old. Something like me, but from long before. Something more powerful, my boots respond.

Who were you? Eo? The Shaper of Thought? How do you know what Gordyn wants?

He wore me for years, Tecarim says. *He's desired the Ensouled for decades. From what I've taken from your thoughts, the common knowledge of our existence no longer exists, but Gordyn knows. We are his obsession. The amulet you seek is beyond your understanding. His, too, if I am to be honest.*

How do you know it's not here? I ask again, continuing to scan the room.

We can feel each other, talk to each other if we're close. Nothing Ensouled exists in this room.

My spirits drop a hair as I surmise that Tecarim is correct: nothing remotely resembles a locket or necklace. Everything on display is a larger piece, from archaic miniature replicas of ancient cities to a hideous painting covered in scrawling lines and colors. Aurelion seems to come to the same conclusion, turning back to the door and reaching for the handle.

Just as it begins to open.

I grab Aurelion and throw him down next to the replica of the city, landing on top of him and putting a hand over his mouth before he can make a noise. The reaction is instinctual; I realize the second we hit the ground that we have a perfectly reasonable excuse for being in the private section, and that Aurelion even wears a guard's uniform. Aurelion smiles against my hand, and I glare at him from an inch away.

A servant walks in, young, his face strangely familiar in the dimness, the way he walks… I can't tell, and I almost ask Aurelion to brighten the room so I can know for certain. Surely not. It can't be him...

My thoughts scatter as Aurelion's hand comes to rest on my thigh. My heart skips a beat and I turn back to him, eyes wide. His eyes are hungry and locked on the curve of my lips. The overwhelming urge to kiss him rises in me, the unrelenting *need* to bend my mouth to his. I fight the urge, trying desperately to stay focused in the moment, to remember where we are, what danger we're in…

Our lips meet. I don't remember taking my hand from his face or bending down to him, but my blood races in my veins, my skin hot and bright, his right hand cupping the back of my head, the burning warmth of his left as he tracks up my leg, sliding under the hem of my dress…

The door closes with a quiet thump, and I jump off of Aurelion like he's a poisonous snake. The room is empty. In fact, the room is emptier than even a moment ago. The ugly painting from the wall is gone, a faint dusty outline on the wall the only sign of its resting place. I think again of the way that servant moved, the furtive grace, every step on the balls of his feet. He was a thief, sure as the sun will set, and Aurelion and I will be the clear suspects if we're found here. How the thief didn't mark us in the dark is beyond me.

Aurelion stands slowly, shakily, shaking his head as if in a daze. I beckon for him to leave, but he raises the tips of his fingers to his lips, his expression an equal mix of wonder and confusion. It's been a long time since I've kissed anyone, but his reaction certainly doesn't match mine. My heart is racing practically out of my chest, the fear and adrenaline and desire each beating their own staccato rhythm against the inside of my ribs. His eyes clear, and he frowns at me. The corner of my mouth tugs upward, but I kill the smile when I see his expression.

"We've got to go," I hiss, darting over and dragging him back to the door.

I straighten his uniform, smoothing my own dress as he brushes my hair back into place. Our eyes meet, and my stomach drops in the worst of ways. His gaze is full of confusion and a hint of anger. He most definitely does not look happy to have been kissing me a moment ago. It hurts, seeing that. I thought he was enjoying the kiss in the moment, but obviously I'm wrong. I turn away suddenly at the tell-tale prick of tears.

By the Forgotten Depths, you fool. Are you a lovestruck teenager? Pull yourself together.

He is not what he seems, Tecarim says as if answering my inner monologue.

I wasn't talking to you, damn it.

Aurelion Kraft is not the Master of Light. He simply bears an Ensouled ring. They have hidden themselves from me, for what end I cannot tell, but I recognized their presence when you brought us so close together.

My cheeks burn as I face the door, thinking about *why* we were brought so close together. Inwardly I snarl, the hurt and embarrassment evaporating as I make the conscious choice to be angry instead. I yank the door open and storm out into the museum proper. I push past the two men blocking the door, and they don't have the balls to protest after they see my face. One of the guards asks Aurelion what the hell he was thinking trying to tumble a rich lady in Paloran's estate. I'm gone before I hear his reply.

The bathroom next to the kitchen is still blessedly unoccupied, the faintly snoring man propped against the toilet in nothing but his skivvies. It's nothing short of a miracle his compatriot hasn't come looking for him or a cook hasn't come to relieve himself, but I'll take the Creator's pull over the Eternal's push any day. I slip off the dress and stuff it efficiently into the waiting maw of the toilet, sauntering back down the hallway to my waiting troupe. Aurelion waits outside the door with a stormy expression on his face, but I ignore him, opening the door myself and passing back into the waiting hall. We've made it back just in time: the Family is next in line. Aurelion doesn't follow me through the door. No doubt the guard, as oblivious as he has been so far, would recognize a stranger taking his partner's place.

The doors swing wide as I walk to Timo's side. He raises his eyebrows in question, but I simply shake my head. He shrugs, turning to face the massive banquet hall. We tumble in like the performers we aren't, contorting and cartwheeling and flipping, the stage set up on the left side of the hall our destination as we dance our way through the widely-spaced tables. Dozens of wealthy guests sit at the decadently decorated banquet tables, their best jewels and silks on full display. I barely get a glimpse of heaped platters of pastries and cakes as I sprint past. Dessert already. The meal is nearly over.

Yelden casually plucks the wine glass from an intoxicated noble as we pass, his sputtering of outrage provoking a quiet ripple of laughter. As soon as we reach the stage, he throws the wine into Hom's face, and our pair of duelists commence in a ridiculous display of sword fighting. They range throughout the room, using the backs of occupied chairs for leverage, tumbling over and through the various platters of dessert. The duel is honestly impressive, both in the skill and athleticism required not to kill themselves, or any guests, and in the extemporaneous touches they throw into the performance. Hom takes two slices of cherry pie to the face, tumbling backwards and flicking a bowl of thick mousse squarely onto Yelden's chest. By the time the men finish by loudly calling that 'honor has been satisfied' and stiffly bowing to one another, their clothes are a myriad of colors and the audience is breathless with laughter.

A man rushes into the room in servant's livery just as they finish. I'm up next, but I narrow my eyes at his hurried movements. He leans over Duke Paloran's shoulder at the head of the largest table and whispers into his ear. Paloran's laughter falls from his face, and he hisses an angry response. The man flinches, but nods, turning and hurrying out of the hall. Either our unconscious guard or the painting's absence has been discovered. Luckily, it seems that Paloron doesn't want to disrupt his party, so he forces another laugh, turning and speaking loudly to the elegant young woman next to him. She wears a silver dress, her features recalling typical Donirian lineage save for the darker shade of her skin and the upward tilt of her eyes. I read his lips from across the room, my eyes flicking back to the girl. Princess?

The young man beside her leans across and speaks to Paloran, eliciting another laugh, and my eyes follow his hand as it comes to rest in the princess's lap. She doesn't react, so he has to be a potential lover. Well, then. It turns out our performance is for more than just the merely rich and powerful. Royalty looks on.

Timo steps up to the fore, the practiced step of trained entertainers, the step which draws the eyes of the audience regardless of their distraction. His time training on the stage has been put to good use. The audience falls silent as Inia, Koli, and Ezil contort around him before turning themselves into rings, their backs bent so that their feet and hands meet in a near perfect circle. Timo casually lifts one of the women by the small of her back, spinning her around the broad muscle of his arm. The audience gasps as he flings her upward, catching her just before she strikes the hard wood of the stage and continuing to spin her taut form. He stomps his foot. The signal.

I sprint forward, calling on the shadow to draw me farther than I could ever leap. Just as he releases Ezil into another throw high into the air, I soar over him, my arms out straight as if diving into the sea, darting through the circle Ezil's body makes as she spins through the air, the quiet rustle of silk the only sound in the room as I emerge unscathed out the other side. The audience starts to applaud, then several begin to shout as I simply… don't fall. Those in attendance will believe it's a parlor trick, thin wires or some other illusion. They'll explain to themselves how the dark woman from the Isles defied gravity, floating there above their heads. They'll never connect me with an element no one has heard of in millennia.

The attention snaps back to Timo as he picks up the three women and begins to juggle them. The small bits of shadow I left under their clothing allows me to control their ascent and descent, keeping their bodies in perfect lines for his waiting hands. The strength is his own; the control is mine. We have the audience mesmerized. They'll remember the feats of strength, the impossible tricks. They won't remember our faces.

Timo breaks from the performance early, far too early, catching the women on one arm like three horseshoes perfectly thrown. Perhaps he tires… but then I follow the line of his eye. To the servant, the thief, the square canvas of the painting firmly on his back, covered in a dark cloth... and I know him. I realize why he was so damn familiar, even in the dark.

"Thief! There is a thief in the hall! Stop! Thief!" Timo shouts, his arm pointing unwaveringly towards the servant.

Towards Jace of the Simply.

I almost don't recognize him in those clothes, his hair clean, his face mature. Where the little bastard disappeared to still haunts Timo. He's never forgotten Grace, never forgiven the rogue thief who inadvertently caused her death. If he gets too far into his cups, Timo still talks about how much he disagreed with letting the boy live, one of the rare occasions he's questioned my decisions. Now, it appears, he's going to get his chance at revenge after all.

The audience turn as one, their heads spinning and chairs scraping. We had them riveted, and Timo's call uses that attention to great effect. The uproar is instantaneous, the entire room bursting to their feet. Lowering myself to the ground, I catch Timo's eye. He is viciously satisfied as the nobles and guards converging on Jace.

"Was dooming Corna worth your revenge?" I ask him, just audible over the shouts in the room.

He has the decency to look chagrined as I turn and run for the doors. I doubt another opportunity like this will present itself, but the entire estate is now on full alert. We have to get out of here.

The tenor of the shouts change, and a look over my shoulder reveals Jace sprinting full on in my direction, feet racing atop of the main banquet table, the nobles stumbling over one another to follow. The second I see crossbows being hefted, I want to duck out of the room, but a tug in the back of my mind roots my feet to the ground. A feeling, almost a premonition. I need to be right here. I need to see something.

"He has the Caldero! The Caldero! Creator's blessed name, stop shooting at him!"

The cloth covering the painting has come free, the hideous tangle of colors flopping about in the thief's haste. Timo races past me, darting out the doors with the rest of the Family.

"Kettle, let's go," he calls, but I ignore him.

The Duke shouts commands, the crossbows lowering as the foot race rages on, but a flash in the brightly lit hall catches my eye. Amongst all the glittering jewelry, the chaos, the screams, the bejeweled ornamental swords, a glimmer of red catches my attention. Around the throat of the Duchess Paloran.

Is that it? I ask my boots.

Perhaps. We are too far for me to know.

I thought that urge to stay came from you.

Urge? What urge? Wait, Kettle, close—

His voice cuts off abruptly. He doesn't answer when I call to him, but I can feel his energy still there, crackling behind the invisible walls in my mind. His energy roils, straining against its bonds. Despite that, he remains silent. I'm on my own. Jace nears the exit, his trail of angry friends stretching behind him.

I dive back into the chaos, jumping into the side of the pursuing crowd to slip closer to my mark. I reach her as the crowd thins, and just as the wealthy ladies around her begin to relax. Had I arrived a moment before, the distraction of the rushing pursuit would have been total, but instead my window snaps closed. I'll have to create my own.

"I'll simply die if the Caldero is harmed," the Duchess says, her simpering friends practically fawning to be the welcoming voice of comfort.

She's perhaps forty, cosmetics and money doing enough to keep her passably attractive despite the unhappy influence of far too much wine and far too many decadent desserts. I consider bringing the shadow to bear, but sometimes the simplest, oldest methods are best. Feigning a stumble over one of the overturned chairs, I fall into the Duchess with all the grace of a drunken cow. Which is what she calls me before realizing I'm one of the performers and shoving me forcefully off of her. Her friends laugh as I stumble away again, this time the falter in my step real. The necklace seems to writhe in my grasp, a similar energy to Tecarim's boiling just beneath its metal surface, but many times his strength. Buzzing energy crackles just under my fingertips. Tecarim doesn't respond to my thoughts, and neither does the necklace. But I know I have what we're seeking. How did the Duchess wear the necklace? How could she stand the feeling?

I start to tuck the necklace away, but stop as a pair of dainty white and silver slippers appear, peeking out from under the hem of a silver dress. My eyes slowly track up the slender body, past the delicate silver chain around her waist, and finally meet the eyes of the princess. Her face is stone, her sapphire eyes glimmering in warning.

"Helping yourself, Islander?" she says, one slim eyebrow rising elegantly over her deep azure eye. We aren't far from the Duchess and her cohort, but the princess keeps her voice low, low enough to go unheard in the quieting room.

"I have a feeling no one is going to pay me after tonight," I answer, finishing tucking the necklace into the band of my pants. It's a lie, and yet it isn't. If she's speaking to me quietly, though, she has a reason.

"So you'll pay yourself? That doesn't seem entirely honest," she answers, studying her fingernails casually. The man who sat beside her at dinner stands off by the door looking stricken. His eyes are wide, his face in agony. Something most definitely went sideways between them in the last five minutes.

"What happened to your boy toy?" I ask, jerking my chin at him. The princess glances behind herself briefly, turning back to me with a black look.

"He lied to me," she says evenly, but the words are edged to cut diamonds.

"Why did he lie?"

I probably should be running as fast as I can for the nearest exit, but something makes me stay. Something tugs me towards her, a quiet sense that this woman needs someone to talk to. I scoff at myself internally. The princess of the Kingdom of the Sea? What am I thinking?

"It doesn't matter," she growls.

"Doesn't it? I've been told lies by people I love," I return, glancing around. Servants are fast reassembling the pristine dining hall, the bustle of their movements the only activity in the place aside from the pair of us and the Duchess' group. We are conspicuous: the only dark-skinned performer and the princess. Someone will grow curious sooner rather than later, and I can't be recognized as the last performer seen before the Duchess' necklace disappeared. I need to go, now. Even so, I think of Talan, of his lies, lies meant to protect me, meant to give me happiness. "Some lies are hurtful, some wonderful. Some, honestly, have nothing to do with you. Figure out which is which."

She seems taken aback by my words, her eyes clouding. We stand in silence for a long second. Making a decision, I walk past her, and she makes no move to stop me. I sigh in blessed relief, throwing a prayer to the Creator.

"You're lucky," her voice comes behind me. I glance back. "I have somewhere to be… and I never liked that woman in the first place."

"You're lucky, too," I answer. "That man loves you so much he's dying over there. It's so obvious it hurts. Be careful, princess. Love like that is rare."

Her eyes narrow like she wants to be offended. I can almost hear the words: you overstep yourself, Islander. But she doesn't give them voice. Instead, her eyes find her lover over my shoulder, and her mouth twists in an unfathomable expression. She looks back to me and gives me a tiny, fragile nod.

I don't reply other than to nod in return, getting the hell out of there before I can run into any other important people. The doors are all heavily guarded as I make it out of the hall, and I feel more and more like everything is descending farther into the Depths the longer we're here. Just as I start to consider cutting my way through a window, though, I spot Aurelion, still in the guardsman's gettup, the lone man in charge of one of the side servant's entrances.

"How do you keep showing up in the perfect place at the perfect time?" I ask him as he opens the door for me and bows as if I own the place.

"Honestly? Tonight has been one of the strangest..."

Aurelion trails off at the scene awaiting us in the courtyard. The guards at the gate question everyone as they try to leave, examining their clothing and checking them for any ill-gotten gains. My heart drops. In my scandalous attire, there's nowhere to hide the amulet. Even as we watch, a temporary guard is accosted and led back into the estate, his indignant curses falling on deaf ears.

"I'll make a run for the fence," I say quietly. "I can make it over and be gone before they can stop me."

"They'll recognize you," Aurelion answers. "You're too distinctive in that outfit. No one can know you, or we, were involved."

"What do you suggest then?"

"Something… something is guiding me," he responds, his eyes unfocused. "Tonight, as no other night, I've had hunches, feelings, urges… and they've all turned out to be correct. All of them."

"Do you realize how crazy that sounds?" I ask incredulously.

"We're going to walk out the front gate," he says, his eyes clearing. He reaches up and grabs my arm as if I'm a thief and he's my captor. He marches purposefully towards the gate, dragging me along behind. "No one is going to stop us."

“What? Let me go, Kraft, or I’ll geld you,” I snarl, clawing at his hand.

Before I can pull away, though, we come in sight of the guards at the gate, striding past the waiting line of performers and mercenaries trying to leave. I stop fighting and meekly follow along. My stomach clenches as we approach… and pass through the gate. No one stops us. No one so much as glances our way. We’re out of sight in less than a minute, and Aurelion releases my arm.

“How?” I ask, dumbfounded. “How in the name of all that dwell in the Deep did you do that?”

“I have no idea,” Aurelion answers honestly. “I don’t know how I knew… I just knew.”

***

We ditch his uniform in an alley the second we’re out of the Palace District and back into the relative safety of the Pennies. He tries to engage me in conversation several times, but I offer him nothing. Despite having saved me—repeatedly—the kernel of anger in my heart drives me to ignore Aurelion. We head to the inn chosen for our rendezvous in case of shit heading south. Which of course it had.

“Kettle,” he finally says, grabbing my arm.

I snatch it out of his hand, a blade of shadow at his throat before he can react. The only potential witnesses are a trio of drunk young men out on the town, but they’re too absorbed in their own nonsense to worry about us. I back him against the bricks behind, and he keeps his arms wide and unthreatening.

“Don’t touch me,” I hiss.

“Kettle, listen to me,” he says. The bobbing of his throat draws a small bead of blood, but I don’t lower the thin blade of darkness. His eyes trace the dark symbol of my power as it winds about my face. “What happened before, between us…”

“What of it?” I snarl into his face. “You’ve lied to me from the beginning. You are not the Master of Light.”

He blinks in surprise, his expression going confused.

"I never said I was," he says honestly. I think back through all our experiences. Damn if he isn't right.

"Then how?"

"Your boots are not the only thing with a silent voice," he answers. He deliberately leaves off which item he might possess that gives him power.

I told you he possessed the Ensouled, Tecarim suddenly speaks again. *He draws his power from the soul of another, not from his own.*

What happened before? Where did you go?

What are you talking about? he responds in confusion.

We were talking, and then… you cut off. Right when I needed you.

His only response is a quiet hum of contemplation.

"Listen, I'm sorry. I am a professional. I can't believe I lost control on a job. I've never allowed myself… I'm sorry that happened."

"It is nothing," I say, though the not-so-tiny wound in my heart says otherwise. "It was a convenient bit of… ugh. I hate this inelegant language."

I step away from him and continue walking. He hurries to catch up.

"Bit of what?" he asks curiously.

"A word like hiding."

"Camouflage?"

"Close enough," I mutter, thinking of the long days hidden in the jungle smeared with mud, waiting for the passing wild boar, Talan a steady and reassuring presence at my side. The memory saddens me, my heart aching around a wound I thought to be scarred over. We walk for a brief moment in silence, the warm air of Summer—for it's past midnight, and Summer has begun in earnest—a pleasant melody against my skin.

"I don't regret the kiss," Aurelion speaks abruptly. He studiously stares at anything but me. "The timing, yes. I don't know what came over me, why I let my discipline lapse. But I don't regret it. It was one of the wonderful moments of my life."

The statement, spoken so simply, so honestly wrought, erases the sad thoughts of Talan from my mind. I smile without realizing it, the knot of tension in my stomach disappearing as if it never existed. In its place, my heart races. I can tell he notes my smile, his expression relaxing as well. My head grumbles of the idiocy of growing close with a potential enemy, regardless of how attractive or talented. But the reassuring weight of the amulet tucked into my pants allows my heart to take the lead. I've done as Gordyn asked. Despite his reputation, he's treated me honorably, and none of his words have rung false. Soon, Corna will be safe with me, and I can be free to explore whatever ends I desire. With whomever I choose.

I walk a bit closer to him, closer than is strictly necessary. Close enough that our hands can touch, if he wants them to. His fingers brush mine, and we walk.

Together.

***

Three nights later, I dress comfortably for my second meeting with Gordyn, not bothering with the fancy dress or the elegant hair. The comfortable black leathers of my trade are plenty enough, my hair bound tightly as always when I work. The only cheek I dare give is wearing Tecarim openly to the meeting. I'm not certain if giving the boots back is part of the deal, but they weren't mentioned in our agreement. The thud of Timo's reassuring footfalls allows me the leisure to let my mind wander as we head to the meeting place, which is when a thought strikes me.

Tecarim?

I was a Master of Voices, he answers my unspoken question. *Yes, with the right time and training, you can call upon my power, command the sound and vibrations of this world. Your mind, its loneliness, its particular workings coincide with shadow. Tones require… a different sort of thought.*

Did you work with Gordyn? Did you teach him these things?

No. He did not possess the correct frame of mind, the trust needed to Shape. Otherwise Kraft would never have been given an Ensouled of Light.

If we stay together… perhaps we can learn more about each other, I offer. *Even though you tried to steal my body.*

Perhaps, he answers drily. *Since I was selfish in life, I'm having to learn another way to operate in this life after death.*

The Falling Edge is its usual lavish self, the beautiful facade opening out onto the depths of the Abyss still as breathtaking as before. Aurelion links his arm with mine as soon as we enter, leading us through the expansive courtyard and under the gaudy chandelier. I squeeze his arm, and his eyes twinkle. I'm excited to see Corna again, healthy and whole after the weeks she's had to heal from her ordeal. At least she damn well better be healed. Creator help Gordyn if a hair has been harmed on her head.

The winding staircase lasts forever and passes in the blink of an eye, my eagerness warping time in strange ways. The door swings wide, and Corna is in my arms before I can blink, her happy laugh vibrating through my body, her tears of joy and relief bathing the skin of my neck. I squeeze her back, and she doesn't pull away, in pain or for any other reason.

"It is so good to see you, *chela,*" I whisper into her neck, ignoring the prick of tears in my own eyes.

"Likewise, little girl," she says as she pulls back and jumps into Timo's arms, revealing Gordyn sitting at the head of his table, smiling indulgently.

"As you can see, I've kept up my end of the bargain," he calls. "And yours?"

I reach back and pull out the necklace, the bright red ruby set in the amulet flashing in the light from the lanterns. I make to toss it to him, but he holds up a hand to halt me.

"Mr. Kraft, if you would be so kind," he says, nodding at Aurelion. Aurelion takes the amulet from me gently, his eyes briefly unfocusing, then he nods in confirmation. "That will be all, Mr. Kraft."

"Sir?" he asks, sounding confused. The startled expression on his face matches his tone.

"Take the amulet and return it to my office in the bank," Gordyn commands. "I have some further business with the lady Kettle here, but I do not wish to risk the amulet being out in the open any longer."

"But—"

"That will be all, Mr. Kraft," he says in the exact same voice, but he sounds suddenly dangerous. His expression doesn't change, but the wolf rises in his eyes once again. Aurelion shuts his mouth and turns to go. Our eyes meet, briefly, and warning and fear are plainly written in his copper eyes. The door closes with a quiet thud.

"What is this?" I demand as soon as the door closes. Gordyn holds up a finger, quieting me until the sound of Aurelion's footsteps fades away.

"A fair proposition for one of your talents," he says, gesturing towards the seat opposite him.

"Our business is done," I say, turning to the door.

"Won't you at least hear me out?"

"No," I answer, turning the handle.

"If that door opens, you and all your friends will die."

I freeze. Corna gasps behind me. Fear tries to find purchase in my heart, but I push it aside. I'll be damned to the Eternal's prison if I give up Corna again. Gordyn's chair scrapes as he stands. his soft footfalls move to the opposite side of the room and pull a chord. The sound of the distant bell is inaudible. I turn back to him slowly, calling my shadow to the surface.

"Do you think Aurelion is enough to contain me again?"

"Mr. Kraft is far too honorable a man for moments like this," Gordyn says amicably. "If he were present, he would perhaps precipitate an unfortunate series of events. As is, he is far too valuable an employee to waste on a useless gesture. Know, Kettle, that I never intended for this to fall out as it has. I am a man of honor. But some forces are beyond my control."

"What are you talking about?"

My answer comes in the form of vibrations. The heavy footfalls of something massive, or many people walking in unison, shake the structure slightly with each reverberation. The steps stop just outside the door, and the three of us back away as the handle turns. The form of a veritable giant stands silhouetted against the distant darkness of the Abyss. He has to duck to enter the doorway, and even then his head comes close to ringing on the threshold. He dwarfs Timo, both in height and girth, but every inch of him ripples with muscle. His face is beautiful at first glance, but the beauty only an artist would imagine. There is nothing natural in his features. He studies us in silence for a moment, his eyes piercing over the simple vest and trousers he wears.

"Which one is the Shaper?" he rumbles in a pleasant baritone.

"The Islander in the middle. The other two are the leverage," Gordyn answers from behind.

"Piss on that and piss on you, Gordyn," Timo growls. "We held up our end of the deal."

"That you did," he responds mildly. "After you broke into my personal vault and stole from me. Did you really think I would, how do they say, forgive and forget?"

"We're walking out of here, big bastard or no," Timo snarls. "He's large, but you told little Krafty to go. Big mistake."

"Do you know who I am?" the titanic man asks from the doorway.

"Do I care? Get out of the way before we cut you down."

"Timo, wait," I say, something tickling at the back of my mind. As if this giant is familiar, somehow. As if I've seen him, at least at a distance. As if I *should* know who he is.

"Bah," Timo says. "I'll move him if you won't."

"Timo, no," I cry, sudden fear rising in my chest as the pieces click into place. "Don't—"

But Timo has already stepped forward. He cocks back his fist, the fist which has always loomed so large but is now oh-so-small in the face of this giant, and delivers a towering haymaker. The punch connects on the man's strong jaw; the man makes no move to dodge. It's a blow I've seen send men into unconsciousness instantly, the kind of blow that can kill a lesser man. The giant accepts it. Casually. His face turns less than an inch. He continues to stare down into Timo's eyes, his gaze turning hungry. Timo steps back, shocked, his hand dangling at his side.

"I do not need two leashes for one dog," the giant rumbles.

The room lights up red, light the color of arterial blood bathing the room. The edge of a sinuous symbol of Shaping glows crimson from underneath the man's clothes. The bright scarlet power of the Master of Beasts.

The Shaper raises a hand and holds it over Timo's chest. Timo lurches, his hand clutching at the fabric of his shirt. He groans, some pain beyond imagining lancing through him. He throws several punches, powerful haymakers that the giant swats away as if fending off an annoying insect. Timo falls to his knees, gasping, trembling. His shirt, clean and white, bulges once, twice, then bursts open.

His heart hits the giant's palm with a wet smack.

The fight leaves Timo instantly. His face turns towards me like a child seeking answers, forlorn and lost. The giant places his other hand on Timo's shoulder and gives him a gentle shove. My brother's body flops backwards, his head hitting the floor, his eyes lifeless. His heart is tiny in the huge man's giant fingers.

Corna screams.

I stand, stunned, my mind in such shock I can't move. The giant—the Lord General Kranos—steps carefully over Timo's body, dropping his still-warm heart in my hands. I catch it reflexively. It moves, slightly, as if still trying to beat. The Lord General walks over and sits at the head of the table, Gordyn making no move to protest. The silence is broken only by Corna's pitiful sobs.

"You work for me now," he says into the stillness.

Chapter 18
Jace
The Final Day of Spring
In the year 5222, Council Reckoning

It's one of the most hideous things I've ever seen. If it wasn't for the fact that I received a detailed description of its location and surroundings from Torlas, I wouldn't look at it a second time, save to wince. The 'master' Caldero has taken shapes and colors, those that an infant might draw in their first explorations of a straight edge, and stuck them together to create a meaningless mash of... yeah, shapes and colors. Having gone to the trouble of being here, standing in a hostile noble's house, ready to steal the painting for Juliet, I kind of figured I'd take a moment to savor this moment. Instead, my head slowly lowers in defeat.

There's nothing for it. I stride up and lift the frame swiftly from the wall, throwing a dark cloth over the painting before I can convince myself to forget the scheme and leave it. Looping small woven cords around the painting creates an easy set of shoulder straps, and I swing the thing on my back as I turn to go.

Getting to the painting has been easy as breathing. Torlas had already been shown Caldero's painting in a previous visit to Paloran's manor, so he was able to let me know exactly where to go. On Torlas' recommendation, it was beyond simple to hire on as one of the staff.

Hopefully, the Duke won't get it into his head to show his Caldero any time soon, at least not until I've made my escape. I walk back out the ornate entrance, ignoring the various sculptures and other works of art in my haste to be gone. A rustle near the entrance sends me diving to the floor behind a statue. The sound continues, almost as if silk slides against silk, whisper light and breathy like a breeze. I creep around, slipping quietly from statue to statue. The sound grows louder, then a gasp accompanies a male grunt. I risk a peek. the entwined limbs of two no doubt powerful nobles thrash about on the ground. Her dress wraps up around her thighs; their lips are locked together.

Blushing in spite of myself, I slip past them quickly and make it back to the main museum. Engaging my mental map of the palace from my explorations as the cook's helper, I take a winding, laborious route to the nearest exit so that I can avoid the majority of the guests in the main halls. The guards look at me curiously, but make no move to stop me as I walk with the clear confidence of someone on a mission for my master. A servant can get away with murder on a night of this kind of drunken debauchery. Turning a corner, I duck back. Two alert and belligerent-looking guards stand at the servant's entrance to the kitchens. Their words drift back to me, and my stomach drops. An unconscious guard was found in the privy, his clothes stolen. They're interrogating a line of servants as they try to pass through.

As I hurry back along the side hallway, I hear murmurs ahead of me and around a bend.

"Hey, what's this?" a gruff voice asks.

"This? It is a steak knife. I am returning it to the kitchen to get another for Lord Sinole," a haughty, high-pitched voice answers.

"That looks a bit sharp for a steak knife. And, come to think of it, we finished the steak almost an hour ago," the man says suspiciously. Suddenly, the second man gives a squeal.

"What is the meaning of this?" he gasps. "I have worked here a dozen times. Lord Paloran himself would vouch for my—"

The heavy sound of a meaty fist striking flesh echoes down the corridor, and the servant moans and sags to the floor in a rustle of cloth.

"Take him away. If he's innocent, fine. We can't take any chances," the first man's raspy voice scrapes. "The Duke's property is paramount. Keep questioning the servants, report on any suspicious activity."

"Aye, sir," chorus several men and women.

Boots immediately tramp down the hall towards me. There are doors back down the hall that lead deeper into the servant quarters, but the guards are right around the corner. I take the only option that isn't an entirely guaranteed discovery: I silently slide into the great hall where Paloran hosts his guests.

I'm not entirely sure what I expected, but when I turn around, I'm surprised to see a circus set up in the great hall of the Duke's estate. A man stands, holding up three contortionists each balanced atop one another's intricately twisted frames. One woman floats above the crowd, no wires or support in evidence. The nobles sit at various tables around the hall, enthralled by the performance.

The sight fills my heart with the sudden innervation of fear.

The Family.

What are the odds? Timo and Kettle working a job the same night I attempt my first bit of genuine thievery in years. The Creator is somewhere laughing his ass off.

I slink along the back wall, hyper-conscious of the fact that I have a giant black object strapped to my back in servant's livery. I pray for the invisibility of servants to hold true. The guards are no doubt on alert because the thieves are there, not because I am, but that fact gives me no satisfaction and leaves my job just as difficult.

The audience gasps as Timo begins to juggle the contortionists. I stop moving and stare at the performance. Timo has always been a heavy hitter and powerful, but the level of strength is shocking. Somehow, he has the three women twirling through the air as gracefully as swans, spinning and flipping and landing in his large hands to be thrown up into the air again, costumes a brilliant blur of sparkling greens and blues in the lamplight. The display is remarkable, his face showing not a hint of the massive strain that has to be weighing on his arms. I shake myself, realizing that I'm staring with the rest of them. It's the perfect time to make my escape, and I'm wasting it. I head towards one of the front windows, ready to slip it open and get out into the night to safety.

Moving at that instant, however, is a mistake. Timo's performance is such that no one in the entire room moves. They all stare, enraptured, including Torlas at the head table next to a florid man with gray mustachios that has to be Paloran. My movement is slow and sure, and none of the guests notice it. Timo, however, looking out over the crowd and grinning like a fool in his pride, locks onto me across the dim room.

I freeze, but it's too late. Through the haze of smoke and perfume in the room, across the dim light and past dozens of flowers in full bloom, despite juggling live human beings, Timo's eyes find mine. Recognition flickers across his face, replaced soon by shock. Then, however, he smiles, and the smile chills my gut to the bone.

He catches all three contortionists on a single arm, smooth as silk as if he practices every day, points at me, and shouts.

"Thief! There is a thief in the hall! Stop! Thief!"

The guests were so enthralled by Timo's performance that every single eye was on him, and his sudden proclamation causes every head to spin around and lock on me: cowering against the wall and carrying a black-wrapped rectangle on my back that couldn't be more obvious against my white and red servant's livery. I freeze. The whole room joins me.

Silence.

One heartbeat.

Two.

Uproar.

The reaction, when it comes, is like a physical blow; the nobles all scrambling, the women screaming, the men climbing over tables to get at me or to defend their own valuables, the guards trying not to push over the most powerful people in the kingdom even as they hurry to my position.

Through the chaos, Torlas stands slowly and looks over at me, his unhurried movements a calm eye in the whirlwind. He's shocked and shrugs helplessly. I do what comes naturally to me in situations like these. I grin. The princess rises next to him, another person I never wished to see again. And she, too, recognizes me across the room. Our eyes meet, and her brow furrows, eyes narrowing. Her arm begins to glow green over the elegant silver dress she wears. I turn to run as I realize she's Shaping something at me.

The guards, probably wisely in a conventional sense, are dividing between closing on my position and making for the nearest doorways to block off my escape. Along with the guards come a small horde of angry, ornamentally-armed nobles, red in the face and shouting. They run into one another, hindering the guards and stumbling over chairs as they come.

There isn't a hope of reaching the far end; men and women in Paloran's livery are already pouring through the doors. Instead, I need to improvise. Shooting directly forward into the surprised crowd, I punch a noble in the face, leap onto a table, and sprint across the long surface as men and women try to grab me and pull me down. The painting flops on my back, slowing me like a sail, but I duck my head and drive harder, soon outpacing the majority of my pursuers as they turn and stumble over one another to get back at me. I stay ready for whatever earthy end the princess has planned for me, but it never comes.

Several of Paloran's guards, dressed all in red and white, anticipate my path and move to cut me off. Not breaking stride, I dive directly towards the man in front of me, planting both feet right into his surprised face. He drops like a corpse, and I'm up instantly, darting towards the gap in their line. Someone tugs at my back, but I rip myself away and keep running. Glancing back, I see the frame of the painting instead of the black cloth and an angry guard left holding the fabric.

I weave through the tables, now empty on this side of the room as people are either after me or fleeing the scene, throwing tables and chairs around in an attempt to hinder the pursuit. Angry voices and pounding feet beat the music of that little dance, and it's cacophony. A crossbow bolt slams into a chair next to me, and I duck as another flies close overhead. Out of the crowd, a sudden, horrified scream cuts through the noise.

"He has the Caldero! The Caldero! Creator's blessed name, stop shooting at him!"

I risk a glance back during the tirade. Paloran's wife, practically fainting with fear, screams the words.

"Don't harm that painting, on your life!" the Duke himself shouts, knocking aside a crossbow that discharges into a nearby chair, ruining the rich wood. "That piece is worth more than all your lives put together. Stop his escape, but do not let the Caldero come to harm."

I turn and dart through the open doors at the end of the hall, taking advantage of the momentary respite as the couple dictates to the crowd and their guards. I make for the nearest door, but four men and women settle the locking bar in place. I recognize them for thieves, wincing inwardly as the wooden beam drops down, far too heavy for me alone to move. The Family is actively helping my pursuers. Damn Timo to the Eternal's forgotten tomb.

I spin in place and sprint back down the long hall towards the servant's entrance, hoping against hope that I'll be able to make it through. I'm willing to risk even unreasonable odds at this point, because my options are quickly running out. Flying through the kitchen, I knock over several servants in my run. The door is open!

I duck my head and burst towards the welcome glow of the Stars of Donir in the darkness. But my heart drops through my stomach as the light cuts off. I slide to a stop, eyes coming up on a muscled man, dressed in absurd gypsy clothing and covered in oils.

"It had to be you," I say, spitting to the side.

"Who else?" Timo responds, settling the locking beam into place with a final click. His voice is more educated, more formal than the last time I saw him.

"You really have been moving up in the world, haven't you?" I say, stalling as I back slowly away. I don't really fancy a tumble with Timo on my best day, but with a ravenous crowd following me and a painting on my back, I figure my chances fall to zero. If only I had my sword.

"I have, haven't I?" he answers, smiling like a wolf. "I would say the same, but I have no idea where you've been or what you've been up to these last years. I tried to find you, trust me I did, but you put on quite the vanishing act after that old man saved you. At least you are aiming for bigger targets than the pennies you pinched on the street," he finishes, nodding at the painting on my back.

"So, me and you, eh? Just like old times," I say, hearing the approaching tumult of the mob at my back.

"Ah, little Jacie," Timo says, clucking like an old mother hen. "I don't have to fight you. I just have to prevent you from getting the door open until they get here. Not that I wouldn't love to break you over my knee."

The first of the guards runs around and into the kitchen, shoving serving staff aside much as I had. I look around frantically, but there are no windows, no routes of escape. Guards approach me, swords drawn, and I glower at Timo as he smirks.

The guards begin to hem me in, and I glance at Timo as he makes a swift move in my peripheral vision, but it's just to dart out of the room and away from scrutiny now that I'm caught. Timo's exit distracts me, and a flash of silver off to my side has me ducking and lunging back, but I can't get out of the way in time. I close my eyes and turn my back, bracing for an explosion of pain. I'm disappointed.

Nothing happens.

I scramble back. The sword hovers over my back, but doesn't finish the blow. Why did he stop? He had me dead to rights... wood slaps gently against my back. The painting. Grinning, I swing the Caldero around in front of me, catching it in my hands. The guards are so afraid of hurting the priceless artifact, so frightened of the Duke's pronouncement in the dining hall, that they won't dare damage it.

This, I can work with.

The guards circle me warily, and I match them. Every time one makes a move towards me, I thrust the painting out at him, threatening, and he backs off. Improvising, I back into the kitchen, deeper into the house, the frail canvas my only shield. More than a dozen guards surround me with more crowding the entrance every second. Snatching up a cleaver, I hold the blade close to the Caldero.

As I continue to pace around the room, I struggle not to laugh outright in spite of my fear. I'm holding hostage, of all things, a painting. Every time I jab the cleaver at the painting threateningly, the guards flinch and back up. It isn't exactly a tenable situation. Eventually, someone will figure out a way around it, or Paloran will say to hell with it and have me killed, painting be damned.

Warning prickles at the back of my neck, a sixth sense I've always trusted. I spin quickly, but no threat looms. Instead, my eye catches a small window in the back of the kitchen that opens into darkness. Heading back towards the party proper doesn't seem like a possibility, and the guards will swarm me if I try to lift the beam on my own. The little alcove is the only option. I back myself into that corner, jabbing the knife at the painting occasionally to let them know I'm serious.

The dimly-lit cubbyhole contains the rope pulleys and stable platform of a simple hoist for carrying food up and down in the mansion, supported by a thin shaft heading upwards into the walls of the Duke's residence. The contraption is normally reserved for platters and little else, either coming down dirty for washing or rising hot to feed the upper reaches of the castle in a timely manner. Eyeballing the size of the box, though, I figure I can fit.

I turn back to the guards, who relax some now that I've cornered myself. Smiling at them, I lift my right leg back and slide into the hoist, backing into the tight space. Riding the small platform to an upper level swiftly and before the guards can make it up the stairs, it'll be easy to find a convenient window and make my escape.

Clunk.

I can fit, sure. The Caldero? Just fat enough to cling like a dockside whore and twice as rude besides. I turn the frame, spinning it a full circle, but the large wooden rectangle has the perfect dimensions to refuse entry. The guards laugh outside, and I can't blame them. I would laugh, too, if it weren't so damn tragic.

Hearing the guards shift towards me, ready to come in and snatch the painting, I make a snap decision. It isn't worth my life, and it's definitely turning into too much trouble just to apologize to a leper girl I hardly know. I wince even as the thought crosses my mind. Juliet deserves better. With more than a little relief and a teensy twinge of guilt, I let the painting drop to the floor, grab the ropes, and speed myself upwards to safety. As my cover falls away, the Duke storms into the kitchen. He sees me, his face purple with fury, and points as I disappear.

"Into the upper reaches!" the man shouts, such outrage in his voice that it's practically comical. "If you let that man escape, I will have each and every one of you hanged. How do the cretins dare?"

As I pull on the ropes, a thought worms its way to the front of my consciousness. An idea; a way around all this nonsense. The third floor door follows suit, and the fourth and final floor's opening is soon ajar. Let them guess where I've actually exited.

As the fourth level's door opens, I gape at the Duke's private bedchambers. Gold and silks decorate every surface, and a massive bed that easily took five or six entire trees to build lolls like a daisy in a field compared to the size of the room. My instincts practically throw me out of the elevator to snatch up everything that I can carry on the way out, but I restrain myself. Barely. I sit in the box, holding the ropes, counting slowly and steadily as I wait. My heart jumps as the door opens far faster than I expect anyone to be able to reach me. Instead of a soldier, however, the princess ducks inside, her movements furtive. Is she… sneaking? She walks to Paloran's desk, rifling through the papers before opening his drawers.

"You don't have much time." The words leave my mouth before my brain catches up to the thought.

Shit! Where did that come from? She jumps, her cheeks blushing red, and I'm shocked again to feel like I recognize her, like there's something more there than just the brief time we've spent together. The room is immediately bathed in green light, and spinning glass glitters around her.

"Who are you, imposter?" she asks, scowling.

"Men will be here soon, looking for me. They know I've come up this hoist," I say, ignoring her question. "You have seconds at best."

"Perhaps I'll just join the hunt, and we can find out who you are and what you know…"

Glass darts towards me, sharp edges glittering, faster than I can think, faster than I can… my hands open of their own volition, and the hoist drops away just as several speeding shards of glass crunch into the back wall. I don't have time to celebrate by survival, though. My weight, easily more than the hoist normally lifts, sends me free falling back down with the speed of a striking falcon. I fly past the third and second floors, barely getting a glance at empty hallways as I careen past.

Breathing deeply through my nose, bracing myself for the pain, I grab the speeding ropes, squeezing with everything I have.

It's like gripping liquid fire.

The skin on my palms bakes away as the speeding ropes begin to slow, and I bite through my lip trying not to scream as the ropes rake my hands again and again. The termination of my descent is abrupt. The hoist and I hit the bottom of the shaft with many times the force the makers intended. For the briefest second, I'm stunned, my lungs frozen, the world strangely quiet. When I blink, my eyes focus, and all of my pain evaporates or, well, at least fades, as the tiny hope in my heart blossoms into reality.

Standing in front of me, less than five paces from the exit to the hoist, stands the Duke and a single servant. The two of them are a brilliant tableau of perfect surprise, staring at me with mouths open and eyes wide. The guards are nowhere to be seen, all scattered around the mansion looking for me. Just a scared noble and his frightened servant.

I scramble out of the contraption and dive forward before they can recover. Snatching the cleaver off of the ground where I dropped it, I jump forward and grasp the Duke by his graying brown hair. He doesn't cry out when I lay the cleaver gently along his neck, and the servant doesn't move, mouth agape and shock written across his face.

The Duke draws in breath to speak, no doubt to plead or threaten or shout for help, but I pull his chin up higher with the cleaver.

"No, my lord," I say quietly. "We're just going to walk over to that door, the pair of us, and you aren't going to make a peep. Not even a quiet whisper. You, boy, pick up that painting and come with us."

The servant does as he's told, lifting the painting like it's his firstborn child. I walk Paloran over to his own servant's entrance, the same one Timo blocked from me just moments before.

"Help me lift the bar, Paloran, or you and the painting join the Eternal," I punctuate the threat with the slightest prick to the neck.

"That's Duke Pal—"

He cuts off as the cleaver comes around and hovers in front of his eyes.

"Not a whisper, I thought we agreed," I tease. "Now open the door."

Paloran grunts and crouches under the bar with difficulty, but he manages. I motion for the servant to do the same. He sets the painting down carefully and puts his own back into the effort, and the bar slides up and off of its slots, falling to the floor with a crash as the men stagger underneath it.

Before they can recover, I strike each man at the base of the neck with the pommel of the cleaver. They slump onto the dirty kitchen floor, motionless. Sounds of shouting and footfalls echo through the corridor, coming closer as they follow the commotion, but they only find a door swinging open in the moonlight, partially blocked open by the unconscious form of the head of the house.

***

Three days later, I jog through the streets, eager to get my errand run and be on my way. The news of Duke Paloran's treason is afire in the streets, and the rumor of my escapades stealing the painting are fading in its wake. My adventures became a curious oddity compared to the news that the Duke himself was arrested for funneling money to the Vengeance. His arrest allows me to breathe a little easier.

I slip through the wrought iron gate at the back of the restaurant, hardly glancing at the statues as I practically run up the stairs to knock on Miranda's door. The door opens a crack, then swings wide to reveal Miranda in all of her splendor. Even at the early hour, the sun hardly peeking above the horizon, she's resplendent in finery, not a hair out of place above an intricate, brocaded ruby gown sewn up at the back.

"Good morning, my lady," I say, stepping up to her and kissing the back of her hand.

"Ah, what a dear you are," she says, grinning broadly and faking a blush. "You don't have to treat me like that. Those of us with red blood know one another."

"You are more worthy of the title than any of those with the blue," I respond, winking. "Is my order ready?"

"It should be ready presently. Do you have time to stay and chat? We need to catch up."

"Regrettably, I have to go. I'll be sure to stop by as soon as I can, though."

Having stared starvation in the face, I know that food is both necessity and luxury. When you encounter the best food of your life, it sticks with you. Torlas ruined me by showing me this place, setting off an addiction that hasn't faded over the season hence. A side benefit to the perfect food is my budding friendship with Miranda herself. I often come at off hours, so we generally have time to chat, at least for a while.

"I'll go kick the hornet's nest then," she says, turning and bustling off. "A boy in a hurry can only mean one thing."

"And what's that?" I call after her.

"A woman!" she shouts, laughing.

I hang near the threshold, refusing to actually enter the house, for I know I won't be able to leave. She'll press some sort of unholy dessert pastry on me, and I'll spend an hour learning what exactly she's done to create such a work of art. The very thought of what might be in there almost breaks my will, but I persevere because I know I'll get plenty soon enough. Miranda returns, a force of nature filling the entire hallway, a small cloth-wrapped bundle in her arms.

She grins, handing me the package gingerly, and I realize that the bundle isn't small, I only had the massive woman in front of me for scale. I heft it, cocking an eyebrow at Miranda.

"This seems a bit heavy."

"Oh, I couldn't resist throwing in some surprises," she says, tittering. "I didn't think you'd mind."

"From you? I would blindfold myself and trust anything you feed me would be divine."

The big woman blushes for real this time, bending down and hugging me quickly.

"Well, whoever she is, don't let her break your heart, you hear?" she says, fixing my hair for me as we stand on her front doorstep.

"I don't think that's an issue," I respond, winking and hefting the package.

I set off at a quick pace. It'll take me at least an hour to make it to the colony. I'm concerned about passing through the Corpses while dressed well and holding a bundle of food that costs more than most of the people there will see in a lifetime, but I don't hesitate. My fortune is my own, my luck and life earned. As Jonah always said, you get the luck you deserve, and damn anyone who hates you for it.

It's difficult to climb the fence into the colony with everything that I carry, but I manage just before a patrol rounds the corner to spot me. My steps carry me up the rise and to her door. I don't bother knocking; she won't be here. On a normal day, Juliet makes her rounds in the morning, so she'll be off tending to the other members of the colony, away for another few hours at least. Part of being a thief is knowing your target, so I've watched her through the fence for two days so that I can learn her routine. She moves even slower now than she did before, barely shuffling. Watching her move, I fight something dark scraping along the edges of my heart, something deep and despairing.

I slide to a stop at her table, placing the bundle on top and slowly unwrapping its contents. The white wrapping becomes a tablecloth, the coarse wood hidden easily under its folds. Fresh, thick toast with a chocolate-hazelnut spread, small, wrapped bowls filled with fresh strawberries, blueberries, raspberries, and some kind of exotic fruit called mangoes, and Miranda's breakfast specialty: eggs lightly cooked in a skillet, white with the yolk intact, only the yolk has been sucked out and replaced with a spiced sausage that makes my mouth water just to smell. At the bottom, wrapped in a strip of cloth with Miranda's golden seal stamped firmly on it, lies that unholy, holy dessert breakfast pastry I dreamt about. With a soft sigh of appreciation I rewrap the gift.

Pulling the painting from my back, I carefully place it on the table, angled so that the light catches it just so. Then, I sit back to wait.

I hear her long before I see her, the shuffling gait instantly recognizable. The door creaks open, and I smile broadly as she turns to face me. Her eye moves past me, roving over the assorted goods that I've brought for our lunch. Only through familiarity am I able to ignore the portions of her face that leprosy has devoured. One of her eyes and the left half of her face is devastated, and wrappings of relatively clean cloth cover her from head to toe to hide the rest.

I lean forward and strike a match, lighting the golden candelabrum in the center of the table and standing aside respectfully so that she can admire the view.

"Who's there?" she asks, her voice quavering. "If you need help, I'll be down tomorrow to look after you."

"Juliet," I say warmly. "It's me. It's Jace."

"Jace?" Juliet says softly. She shuffles forward and sits down heavily, her hands sliding over the back of the chair as if she feels her way into the seat. She moves her head around vaguely, not focusing on anything, as if... "I didn't figure you for a liar, but you sure like to keep a lady waiting."

What joy I had at her arrival crumbles under an unexpected and extraordinary weight. My breath leaves me with a soft, long exhalation. I collapse heavily into the other chair at her table, the food forgotten, the plan disintegrating before my eyes. I glance over at the painting, the ugly riot of color and geometric shapes, and my vision blurs. The disease, already unfair, has claimed one of the last luxuries she had left.

Juliet is blind.

"Don't weep for me," she says, her dirty, wrapped hands gently brushing my shoulders. I didn't hear her get up. "It happened sometime near the middle of Spring. I've come to terms with it, and I still get around to my patients. My life hasn't changed, really."

Her words just shatter me further, and my face slackens under the onslaught. I look up with clear eyes at the painting in front of me, forcing down the sharp, instantaneous stab of sorrow that accompanies the sight. She'll never get to enjoy it, never even get to glimpse it. I stayed away so long that I didn't realize the mistake I was making. And *she* is comforting *me*.

"Juliet," I begin, gently lifting her hands away and standing up. She waits quietly, expectantly. "I've brought... brought you something."

I can scarcely get the words out, but she simply smiles with a sudden joy.

"A gift? What is it? I can smell something divine. Did you bring me something to eat?"

"I... yes," I say softly. "I have brought you food fit for the Creator himself. Delicacies that would have graced the Eternal's table thousands of years ago, and she would have been impressed beyond speech. Sit, please, and eat while it's warm."

We settle into the table, and I slide Juliet plate after plate of Miranda's fare. Juliet consumes each with a look of such rapture on her distorted features that I smile even as tears roll quietly down my cheeks. The entire time, she comments on the food, asks me how my life is going, and probes about my own health and physicality, as if she is the doctor that she once aspired to be. Throughout the meal, the painting looms close to my left like a specter of death.

She finishes the food, sitting back in her chair with a grateful sigh.

"Creator's holy name, that was perfect, Jace," she says, laughing.

Her voice still possesses the elegant tones I remember. I study her face, looking at the lines that might have been, imagining what this young woman looked like, how lovely she must have been. Because there, in a dingy hut, face wasted by a ravaging disease, single eye dull and unfocused, I can't help but find her beautiful.

"I brought you something else," I say quietly.

"Two gifts in a single day?" she says, patting the table with a smile. "Good. You had better make up for some lost time, because it's lonely here without any new blood. I have the others, sure, but moments of happiness are few and far between in this place."

"That's exactly what I figured. This is my apology," I say, heart breaking anew.

"Yes, well, we're just getting acquainted. You'll know better in the future. Well, what is this second gift? It's not like I'm going to refuse it," she says mischievously.

"I remember a comment you made, about how you loved a certain artist, how he occupied your thoughts. So, in apology for my absence, I decided to get a painting for you, created by Caldero."

"Caldero?" she asks incredulously. "No, you haven't. There are seventeen on the entire planet, and each of them priceless."

She carefully ignores the tragedy lurking under the surface.

"I... acquired it from one Duke Paloran. He was loathe to part with it, but I was able to convince him after a time."

"'The Lost Girl'?" Juliet gasps. Of course she knows exactly which painting I've taken. I didn't even know its name. "You brought me 'The Lost Girl'?"

"Yes."

The word falls on silence. It seems to echo in the tiny room, bringing back with it the stillness. The stillness grows heavier the longer we hold our silence, and it binds us, holding back words and emotion and leaving us in a quiet, electric tension. As still as marble, her breath hardly moves her frail chest. I bite my lip, struggling not to shout to break the moment.

"I'm so sorry," I gasp out, fighting the turmoil in my chest and losing. She comes forward again, comforting me even in her despair.

"No, Jace, no. How could you know? Please, Jace, do not weep for me..."

After long, indeterminable moments of sorrow, silence descends again. This time, it feels better, more whole. Juliet strokes my back one more time, then points her face towards mine.

"Jace, would you... will you... describe it to me?"

Her voice is so sincere and hopeful that I don't question. I immediately turn and begin to speak. I speak for hours, my voice growing hoarse, my imagination stretched to its limit. My words touch on the colors, the shapes, the brush strokes, the feel, the image. The gentle curve of blue, achingly delicate and recalling the horizon. The sharp angle of white, a space of order amongst chaos. The delicate splash of subtle red, a hazy mist of drifting life. I paint the painting again and again, words the color, pauses the lines, metaphors the thoughts and the girl and the lost.

It's dark outside when the candles gutter out, but I continue to speak, my eyes having long remembered each contour and delicate intricacy of the art. Finally, I subside, my voice falling silent and my throat aching from the effort. My arm wraps around Juliet's thin shoulders, and her head rests lightly on my chest in the dark. We lay in the straw, the words still burning between us like a ship's beacon calling for aid in the midst of a towering storm.

"That's better," she says quietly, wonder in her voice.

"What? What's better?" I ask in a whisper.

"That's better than seeing the painting itself," she says, putting her arm around me and squeezing gently. "Thank you, Jace."

Lying there in the darkness, cradling a broken woman to my chest and barely holding my own fractured soul together, I recall my first reaction to the painting. I believed it hideous, without sense, without thought. How was I so foolish? When you look closely, when you take the time, the true image, the true message, the true exquisite beauty rises to the fore, the chaos and sadness just another infinitesimal part of the seamless whole.

It is beautiful.

It is her.

***

My feet hit the earth with a soft puff of dust as I leap the fence. I head back home, hardly looking left and right as I walk. The morning was a quiet one. I woke with the small, fragile bundle of rags under my arm and lifted her gently to the thickest part of the straw. She didn't move aside from raising a hand in gentle farewell. I stroked her hair once, softly, and left the colony behind me.

No more words were necessary. The previous night held everything that needed to pass between us. Even as I walk away, I know I won't ever see her again. It's okay. In fact, it's perfect. The closeness we've shared is greater than anything I've ever experienced, and watching her deterioration would only destroy this transcendent moment. That hand opened in a wordless goodbye echoed my sentiments exactly.

As I near the house, I get an odd feeling along the back of my neck. My hairs stand up in the way that tells me I need to duck. I glance around, but nothing appears out of the ordinary. Soldiers tromp down the street, wagons trundle through the muck, and the pedestrians pointedly ignore one another. All normal.

As I take another look, though, it hits me. They are *all* soldiers. Many of the pedestrians look to be armed in some way or another, each obviously muscular and in shape, hair cropped close. The riders all sit with a bit too much precision, the wagon flaps all drawn closed in an identical manner. And, of course, the soldiers marching in unison are hiding in plain sight, a common spectacle throughout the city.

It takes all of my willpower not to head for the nearest rooftop. There are any of a million reasons why soldiers would be impersonating everyone in a crowded intersection. If only I can think of any good. I try to shake off the feeling, but my reflexes are itching like mad. Are they after me? Or Reknor? Surely they wouldn't go through so elaborate a hoax because they discovered that I crashed the King's Ball. Duke Paloran is in prison, isn't he? Did the thieves rat me out?

I think about climbing up and going in through a window and into Reknor's house, but the soldiers have already seen me. Stealth is out of the question. I walk up like nothing is wrong, taking Reknor's front steps two at a time and sliding into the house quickly.

"Are you entirely blind? Or just stupid?"

I almost jump, but I catch myself and glance up at Reknor leaning over the railing on the stairs to the second floor.

"The question seems a bit rhetorical, all things considered," I say, shrugging. "Obviously, you already know. I was coming here to warn you."

"Jace: the only man I know who would knowingly enter a deathtrap surrounded by half an army in order to warn me. Literally, half an army."

Suddenly he turns and goes back to the front window.

"Here they come," Reknor calls, a frown in his voice. "I was wondering what they were waiting on. It's been hours. But I guess they were waiting for both of us to be in the same place."

"Whoops," I say, but there isn't any remorse in my voice. "Why are the King's soldiers coming for us?"

"I may be involved in certain activities that would tickle their fancy. A great many such activities, in fact."

"What does that mean?"

"Well, I may or may not be meeting with the Vengeance and plotting the downfall of a tyrant," Reknor responds easily as he walks down the stairs and buckles on his sword.

"What?"

"We don't have time to hash everything out, but, in short, yes. I've hated Helikos longer than you've been alive," his voice shakes for the first time, not in fear, but in anger. "I tried to be careful, tried to keep you out of it, but you appear to have ended up facing the same fate. Or, well, blast. You would be."

"You have a plan?"

"Damn if you being here doesn't ruin the original plan. I guess that you go through escape plan number one, and I go through number two. The exit tunnel is behind the big door." He doesn't have to specify which door. There can only be one. He pulls the key off of his belt and tosses it to me. I catch it deftly, sliding it into my pocket as I jog up the stairs past him. "And where are you going? You know that dozens of soldiers are about to kick in this door, correct?"

"Of course I do," I say cheerily. "That's why I'm going to get my sword."

"Sensible," Reknor says. "But you won't need it. Go to the tunnel now so that we can be sure you make it out."

Something in his words leaves me abruptly and totally afraid.

"What about you?" I ask, the forced cheer gone from my voice.

"I'll manage. Damn, all that I thought I would tell you, and now I don't have enough time. Couldn't they have waited an hour before they just charged the front doors?" Reknor says, moving over by the door and glancing through the window.

The door begins to shudder under blows from outside, but like everything in Reknor's home, it is well-built. I turn back to grab my sword, but Reknor raises his foot dramatically high. I can't help but watch. He slams his boot down on a certain floorboard, which depresses. Screams of men in perfect agony erupt from outside, and the shuddering abruptly ceases.

"What was that?" I ask conversationally.

"You think I haven't been waiting for this? Well, that should give us enough time to chat. Listen, boy. Everything that you can carry from the house is yours. The rest I'm sure will end up in Helikos' coffers, so we'll have to do something about that. By we I mean me."

"You're planning to die here, aren't you?" I cut in. "Don't."

"Jace, don't be a child. All men die. I am dying so that you can live. All of our secrets preserved. A whole future there for you to take, to seize."

The door shudders again, more heavily this time.

"Why can't we both go out the tunnel? Isn't that the point of an escape tunnel, to escape?"

"Ah, my boy. They will be through and chasing you in moments, and there is more to hide than just your escape. I *can't* let them find that tunnel. So I'm going to delay them long enough for you to collapse it."

"I still don't get it," I say, panic clawing at me at my soul. "Why don't we collapse the tunnel together? They can't follow us then."

"They have to believe that there wasn't ever a tunnel at all. And the only way for me to ensure that is to stay behind," Reknor says regretfully. "If I could have chosen a different way to say goodbye, I would have."

"What is so important about that tunnel? Why is it worth your life?" I ask desperately.

"The answers are down there. Waiting for you. I love you, Jace," Reknor says, walking over and pulling me into a hug.

I cling to him like a sailor to a piece of driftwood, the last hope on an unforgiving planet. It's the first time Reknor has ever told me that he loved me. Tears well in my eyes, and I struggle to let go when he loosens his grip. The door finally splinters behind us, and Reknor turns and draws his sword.

"It's about time to go, Jace. Down the tunnel and pull the lever at the first door. It is low, near the ground, just as you pass through to the right. Let go of your fear, if you're still holding on to it. I'm sure you'll find the right path."

"I love you, old man," I say quietly, desperately, to his back.

"Remember," he says, half glancing back at me. "These men do not ask questions."

The door bursts in.

Reknor spins, his sword lashing out and almost decapitating the first man who stumbles through. He engages the second, disarming and slicing a neat hole in his throat. The sword work is brilliant, but more men press in from behind. I reach down at my side, but my sword still waits upstairs, useless.

Reknor engages the fourth man, the third lying on the ground with a deep wound in his groin, blood gushing out too fast to follow. It is all happening so fast. And here I am, gawking like a frozen fawn.

"Are you still standing there?" Reknor thunders as he cuts down another man. "Go. Go!"

I jump, spinning and running for the door. I turn the corner frantically, fingers fumbling with the key as I struggle to work the intricate lock. Windows shatter to the side, and I stop as men shout a battle cry. I listen, hard, but the sounds of battle continue. I finally manage to get the counter turn and pull the giant door open, slipping inside before I can think. The door closes behind me with a soft thud, and the swordplay becomes muted like I've fallen underwater. I look around, surprised to see that the room is little larger than a closet. A trap door waits in the center, and a chest sits in the corner. Curiously, a lit torch burns in the corner. Where does the smoke go? Who lit it? Reknor?

I walk over to the trap door squarely in the middle of the room, reaching down and yanking the handle. The door flips up with startling ease. A ladder descends into darkness. Grabbing the torch, ignoring the tiny voice that tells me to drop the live flame, I put my foot on the first rung. The floor is hardly ten feet down, and I drop the last few feet to land in a crouch.

The tiny room is built out of solid stone, a sole exit leading into further darkness. After a hundred yards with the torch my only company, I come to a door, which opens easily at my touch to reveal an old sewer, so ancient that it doesn't even stink anymore. A channel runs down the middle of a large, curving hallway made of the same cut stone as the room behind me. Some murky, filthy water still fills the bottom of the trench, but I can tell that nothing has been emptied into the area in a long time. I half-expect to see the bones of forgotten urchins lining the walls, one in particular with brilliant red hair. But the corridor appears empty.

The expected lever, low on the stone wall of interlocking bricks, waits for me just where Reknor described. I glance back at the small tunnel, imagining the house that was a home, the man who was a father. Gone. Taken from me by a tyrant king and his soldiers. Swallowing thickly, I grasp the lever and pull.

The rock groans, the sound as if the very earth cries out in pain, and the tunnel collapses in a cataclysm of noise and stone and dust. The torch gutters and blows out in the explosion of dust, plunging me completely into darkness. As the last rock settles, I close my eyes and fight back tears.

"Too soon," a voice, quavering and yet steady, resonates from the darkness behind me. I spin around, my eyes straining from their sockets to see in the dark, but to no avail. "The man should know better."

Chapter 19
Iliana
The Final Day of Spring
In the year 5222, Council Reckoning

Ours is the last carriage to arrive, the servants gathering in a swarm to help us out of the door, lead our footman aside, unhook the horses and lead them to the expansive stables, and finally provide a long line of people to bow us up to the doors. We're fashionably late, the kind of late that only men and women of our stature can afford. The excessive greeting is the kind of expense that only fools like Paloran would indulge in, but I hardly notice. Though I haven't made many public appearances in my life, I know they had damn well better bow when they greet their princess.

Torlas' arm flexes firm and strong beneath my hand. I try not to notice, but I can tell he hasn't been skipping fencing practice. My face is warm as he leads me through the glittering gates of Duke Paloran's estate. The banquet hall is already full when we arrive, but every person in attendance stands as a man calls in a loud and clear voice.

"The Princess Iliana of the Kingdom of the Sea, escorted by Duke Torlas Graevo."

No one meets my eyes as we walk to the table to be seated at Paloran's right hand. A gigantic and intricate display of late Spring flowers in a dozen hues decorates the hall, each placed so carefully as to feel like a small piece of a grand and greater whole. Flowering garlands drape from the ceiling, and the heady scent of gentle blossoms hangs in the air. As soon as we're seated, servants enter with crystal carafes of wine in a variety of colors, dyed to match the exact shades of the flowers throughout the room. Each tray appears to be a flower itself, the glasses arranged to fill in the color of the petals. I take a pale yellow from the tray, impressed in spite of myself at the presentation. The movement restarts the conversations that our entrance stilled, and the hall soon buzzes with conversation.

"My lady," Duke Paloran speaks from my left. He's a burly man, the genetics of his warrior line apparent in his figure despite never having wielded a sword himself. His florid cheeks complement his extravagant mustache, and his belly is the only thing more impressive than his estate. His voice is both rich and unpleasant at once, its power offset by a wheeze that can only be derived of sickness or inactivity. "I cannot tell you how pleased—and surprised—I was to learn our humble gathering would be graced with your royal presence."

"Humble, Duke?" I say, smiling sarcastically as I gesture around. "The wine alone could keep an army in its cups."

"As I have invited a veritable army, I have need of it," the Duke responds, unashamed. "I'm glad you managed to secure permission to attend. Our King keeps you so tightly to his side that I can't recall the last time I've seen you outside the palace."

"I was recently in Firdana, or didn't you hear?" I ask innocently, staring into his eyes, begging for a sign. But his eyes stay steady as he speaks.

"Ah yes, young Markis, led astray by the Vengeance. How foolish of him to set himself against the King."

"Indeed," I reply evenly.

The first course interrupts our conversation, luckily. I can feel a heat in my cheeks that has nothing to do with the wine. We didn't accept Paloran's invitation for the fun of it, of course. The spectacle and enormous cost notwithstanding, I'm here with a purpose, one our host would find more than a bit alarming if he knew. And here I am, waving around Markis Calladan's capture like a threat. Despite my court upbringing, I'm not exactly the most adept at deception.

The food surpasses my expectation, everything intricate and complex, too complex for my experience to fathom. For all its quality, the palace kitchens cook simple food perfectly. This is exotic food cooked… well, hopefully perfectly. Or not at all, as it turns out. The first course is raw, some fish delivered a thousand miles from the coast and prepared in an esoteric fashion with rice and other fillings. I look at it skeptically for a moment, but Torlas just shoots me a mirthful look and pops a large bite into his mouth. Rolling my eyes, I follow suit with a more modest portion. The taste is divine, but something about the consistency of the fish and the knowledge that it's raw prevents me from fully enjoying the experience.

As soon as the Duke's table finishes, the plates are whisked away as if by magic, another glass of wine replacing the empty one at my side. The banquet hall quiets unnaturally. Torlas and I glance around in confusion, but the guests all look towards the doors in hushed anticipation. Just as I resolve to ask, the doors burst open and a dozen men and women in flashy attire come tumbling into the room, setting up a circus show right there in the hall. Two women loop long ribbons over a hook high overhead as the men perform feats of unbelievable strength, lifting one another into ever more precarious positions. One of the men flips into the air and strikes another in the head, and I wince even across the room. But, impossibly, he sticks there, upside down, his bald head flush with his fellow's, his feet splayed wide for balance. I applaud with everyone else, Torlas letting out a cheer in appreciation.

The women climb the ribbons, like they're horizontal, their movements sinuous and sure. I gasp as, together, they let go of the ribbons and hang, only a thin sheet of fabric suspending them from certain death high above the floor, no ties or ropes evident. They perform several acrobatic feats up there, graceful as swans, arms flung wide, their bodies spinning and contorting. Without any discernible signal, they both drop into sudden freefall. Several members of the audience scream as they spin towards the floor, uncontrolled, their limbs flashing. I'm half out of my seat, the earth answering my call to arrest their fall, but I'll be too late… they snap to a halt less than a foot from the ground, their smiles wide as the terror of the audience turns to thunderous cheers.

"That was unbelievable," I shout to Torlas as we clap, and Paloran overhears me. I should be tense, expectant, cautious. I have a job to do that's more delicate than anything Father has trusted me with before. Somehow, though, I find myself relaxing and enjoying the show.

"They were simply the first act, my lady," Paloran answers from my left. "We have many more courses to share, and many more performances to enjoy."

Though a boast, it's a truthful one. Each course is more exotic than the last, each performance more breathtaking. Bards with fingers of lightning and voices of thunder sing tales of heroism and sorrow that break our hearts. A troupe of players perform a satirical scene of the Vengeance that leaves us holding stitches in our side with laughter even as we boo the player stomping around and pretending to conjure gusts of wind to defeat his foes. Eventually he resorts to bending over and producing… another type of gust. All the while, some prescient artist paces the courses, the food and entertainment following each other so smoothly I'm never sated.

"Ah, we are coming to the main event," Paloran says over dessert. "I had never heard of these performers before, but they came so highly recommended I saved them for last."

"Let us hope they live up to their reputation," I answer honestly. Even if I have another task to complete, and soon, I lean forward in my chair as the doors open a final time.

A pair of duelists strut out with all the arrogant grace of peacocks. One smoothly snatches the goblet from the hand of the new Earl of Firdana, Edwin Beck, who is so inebriated or shocked that he hardly has a response. The first throws the glass of wine into the other's face, and they're off. They twirl up and over and around the tables, fight fish to fish, and even use the arms of some of the guest's chairs as a tenuous place to dart a dozen brilliant jabs and slashes at one another. It's part showmanship, part comedy, and all breathtaking skill. Those men are more than just trained swordsmen; they have the balance and timing of acrobats as well.

"Not entirely what I expected from the main event, Hoiran," Torlas says, leaning across me. He uses Paloran's given name, a calculated move. Perhaps a half dozen people outside his family can call Paloran 'Hoiran,' and each is more powerful than he. Torlas' hand rests on my thigh, the contact casual... until it lingers. I try to ignore him and keep my eyes on the performance, but my eyes flutter involuntarily, hyperaware of Torlas' hand. Paloran turns back from speaking to a servant in hushed tones, and I blink at the angry face he makes an effort to control. He forces a laugh.

"Nor I, Graevo," he answers with good cheer. Forced cheer, but still genuine. "Though I think it is just getting started. See, look, princess!"

Our attention returns to the stage as a man steps up in the stylized attire of the western Khalintars, a vest and overlarge pants his only covering. His massive and toned physique gleams with oil in the lamplight. The only person I've ever seen more impressive is Uncle, and he, well, he cheats. A woman in thin veils and silks slides between his legs, and the man catches her wrists, flexing and flinging her flipping into the air. She arcs gracefully, her body in complete control, hovering longer than seems possible before falling elegantly back into his arms. Two more women enter in equally impressive fashion, their nimble and disciplined movements balletic.

One of the women forms a ring with her body, bent backwards so that her feet rest on the crown of her head. The strength and physical control necessary to maintain that form is outlandish. The man lifts her and launches her spinning higher than any have gone before. A flash of movement, a shimmer of green silks, and a dark-skinned woman of the Isles dives through the spinning ring of her partner and… freezes. By the Creator, she should fall to the ground after the impossible leap, but instead she hangs in the air as if gravity can find no purchase on her skin. There are no strings I can see, no apparatus. Only a woman, her face serene, her attire a scandalous and revealing series of silk ribbons. On her face twists a tattoo of black whorls and undulating lines reaching from her forehead down the left side of her face almost to the jawline. It's dark even against her skin, and it shimmers in the light as if alive.

The man below begins to juggle the women, their bodies contorted into compact and intricate shapes. I gape, having no idea if even Uncle could perform that particular feat of strength. The enthralled audience watches in silence, the absurd feats of athleticism bordering on mysticism. Surely, this isn't happening. Surely, it isn't possible. Surely, something will happen to break the spell, to reveal the trick, to open the door again for normal thought and expectation…

"Thief! There is a thief in the hall! Stop! Thief!"

I blink in surprise, my head turning with all the others in the hall to see a boy crouching against the wall on the other side of the hall. Dressed in Paloran's colors, he has a large rectangle of cloth balanced on his back like some strange pack. His expression is shocked, his mouth open, his face strangely familiar.

The imposter. Teldaran Hollenzar.

It appears we will be solving a mystery tonight. I reach for my power, drawing in the residual dust from the hall, forming it into a tendril of earth, reaching out to grasp the boy before he can run. Torlas grabs my arm and tugs me around just before the earth can grasp him. I scowl at him.

"Let me go," I growl, turning back to the imposter as he sprints along a tabletop towards the doorway the performers entered from. The fool launches himself at a group of guards, tumbling into them and coming up sprinting. The cloth tears, and the unmistakable frame of a painting slaps on his back as he sprints away. "I can stop him."

"No," Torlas says desperately. "Please. He… I know him. He is my friend."

"That boy is your friend? You know him *well*?"

"Yes, he's my friend," Torlas answers reluctantly. "I met him nearly a season ago, and he is here on my invitation. My suggestion. If he can escape, then please, let him."

"These weeks my father has been looking for him, you've known where he was all this time, and you didn't tell me?" I ask the question low, quietly.

The thief makes it out of the hall, the majority of the guests in hot pursuit, hindering the guards as they attempt to do their duty.

"Yes, I've known, but what would you do? Would you betray a friend for crimes that can only be described as harmless? He crashed a party, so what. He... well, he is currently stealing a painting, but Hoiran has more money than he knows what to do with. What is one painting?" Torlas speaks rapidly, as if to prevent me from getting a word in before he finishes, but I simply hold up a hand, and he subsides.

"I'm glad to know you're loyal to someone. Because you have shown your *kingdom* no loyalty. You have shown your *king* no loyalty. And you have shown," I speak over him as he tries to interject. "No loyalty to *me*."

"Iliana, that's not true," he says quietly.

"You should have trusted me," I say. I keep my voice low and steady so my simmering rage doesn't boil over. "If you were my friend, as you claim, if you would have been my partner, as you wish, you would have trusted me. Know now you are neither."

"Iliana—"

"Enough," I make a cutting gesture with my hand. "Enough."

I turn and stalk away. The anger in my heart burns hot. A reaction, I know, to the betrayal, but I let it have the reins. I'll feel the hurt and the loss later. I still have work to do, and at least I don't need to come up with a distraction of my own to slip away. The exit to the hall that leads deeper into Paloran's estate is near the back, and a small crowd of self-important women block my path. I plan to skate by with the excuse of heading on to be certain the rest of Paloran's art is secure, but another woman beats me to it: the Islander in the green silk who so ably levitated above the floor. She stumbles as she reaches them, and I stare in shock as she turns and stumbles away, the ladies tittering after her graceless exit. The theft was so smooth I never would have noticed without my angle and the brief glitter of the jewels in the lamplight.

My feet move of their own accord, and I'm in her path before she can move far. Her eyes track up my dress and stop on my face, showing surprise but no fear. She's younger than she appears from a distance, but still older than me by a few years. Her eyes shine a deep, liquid brown and her hair a smooth and luxurious black. A scar on her cheek only highlights the delicacy of her features.

"Helping yourself, Islander?" I ask, raising an eyebrow. I keep my voice low. The audacity of the theft is so impressive I don't feel like giving her over quite yet. Normally, I wouldn't condone anyone breaking the kingdom's laws, but I feel strangely forgiving.

"I have a feeling no one is going to pay me after tonight," she answers, the necklace disappearing somewhere amongst the gleaming emerald ribbons.

"So you'll pay yourself? That doesn't seem entirely honest," I say, glancing at my fingernails to hide the widening of my eyes. I need a moment to process. Something's different about the woman, something important.

"What happened to your boy toy?" she responds, flicking her chin over my shoulder. I glance back to see Torlas near the entrance, all the sadness of a beaten puppy on his face. I'm not ready to see him yet, haven't processed my anger, and the look he's giving me pushes a strange mixture of rage and sympathy deep into my belly.

"He lied to me," I say.

"Why did he lie?"

"It doesn't matter," I snap.

"Doesn't it? I've been told lies by people I love," she says, and her eyes are sad. She glances around. Her movements are a little slower, a little less certain. She speaks from somewhere that matters to her. She meets my eyes again with a wan smile. "Some lies are hurtful, some wonderful. Some, honestly, have nothing to do with you. Figure out which is which."

Her words strike a chord in my heart, a resonating thrum that vibrates through the haze of my anger. Why did Torlas lie? To protect a friend. After what I saw in the dungeons, what Uncle is capable of, the hopeless screams of pain down past that particular cell… I can't say I entirely blame him. Even so, he owes me honesty. I've given him everything, unadulterated, uncensored, so that we can understand each other. He can trust me to keep a secret, even from my father.

Can't he?

The woman walks past me, brushing past so close I feel the warmth of her skin, so much darker and yet more beautiful than my own.

"You're lucky," I call softly to her back. She pauses. "I have somewhere to be… and I never liked that woman in the first place."

"You're lucky, too," she answers. "That man loves you so much he's dying over there. It's so obvious it hurts. Be careful, princess. Love like that is rare."

Anger lances through my heart. No one tells me how to act, no one save Father, Uncle and… Torlas. The thought brings me up short. Even as the idea begins to worm its way beneath my skin, I shake it off. Eternal's tomb, I don't have time. I file away her words for later. Whatever that strange Islander saw between Torlas and me may be significant… but not now. Now I need to accomplish what I'm here to do.

I brush past the Duchess and her cohorts with a flimsy excuse, but they don't dare question. It isn't until I reach the doors that I realize exactly what was different about the Islander. Her face, so striking and pristine aside from the scar… it was tattooed before. An intricate, complex tattoo, one that seemed to gleam black in the bright lights…

I spin back around, my breathing coming sharply as my dress swirls around my legs. The hall is empty save for the Duchess' crowd and servants. The Islander… the Shaper… she's gone. I almost resolve to run after her, but I force myself to continue on. What kind of world are we living in? A Shaper, blessed by the Creator above all others, reduced to thieving and acrobatics?

But what is she the Shaper of? What element has a black symbol?

The halls are empty in the back of the estate. I pass a few frantic guards as they scurry from one place to another, but one look at my face is enough to hurry them along. I'm aiming for stern, but it's coming off frightening judging by the reactions of the guardsman. There will be no doubt in anyone's mind I wandered throughout Paloran's estate tonight. There are far too many witnesses. What I need is a moment to myself, a moment unobserved to find what I'm looking for… or leave something behind. Creator, what a frustrating mission.

***

I was nervous for days after my narrow escape in the dungeons, shying away from contact with Uncle and Father, certain the guardsman gave me up under questioning. When the summon comes, I'm so terrified I can hardly move, and the expression on Father's face does nothing to smooth over the rough edges of my fear. I almost burst out with an apology, my mouth opening, the words beginning in my throat, but Father speaks first.

"Hoiran Paloran is a traitor," Father says quietly, his voice as grave as I've ever heard it.

I blink once, surprised. He stares down at the maps laid on the table, the markings of hundreds of notations scribbled across the length and breadth of the world. The war room brightens in the late Spring evening, the stark and severe chamber illuminated by the rays of the rising sun. Father leans over the table, his powerful frame sagging wearily. For the first time in all the years I've been alive, he looks tired. He looks like the burden of his position, the responsibility of being king, finally grows heavy.

"Paloran?" I gasp. "But why? What does he stand to gain? What more can he desire?"

"Apparently, his greed knows no bounds. Perhaps being duke is not enough, but instead he wishes something more. A return to the days of the Council, when normal men ruled and the Shapers were... subservient," his face twists in disgust at the final word.

"But the Council was corrupt," I protest. "They were leading in all but name, influencing and threatening..."

"I know, daughter. Trust me, I know. But not all view the Council as we do. Some miss the days when men were kings instead of dukes."

"So he is in league with the Vengeance. Just like Calladan."

"How do you think we discovered his treachery? Paloran first came under suspicion years ago. We placed him in charge of our trade negotiations because he was viewed as such a shrewd businessman, but he signed us into a ruinous deal with the Khalintari Republic that I

nearly had to threaten outright war to renegotiate." Father says bitterly. "Markis's servants and retainers were very forthcoming after his capture. Both of these traitors have been very meticulous in hiding their involvement. There hasn't been a shred of hard evidence. If they keep any records of their support for the rebels, we haven't been able to find it. We weren't completely certain about Markis until you saw him in conversation with the Vengeance himself."

"If Paloran is a traitor, then we can arrest him. He's here in the city; his house guards would be no match for the Tide."

"It is not as simple as that. He is well-connected, his wealth and influence deeper than perhaps any other noble in the kingdom. He has a stranglehold on all the iron of the Claws. I can't just remove him. If his people went wholeheartedly over to the Vengeance, if his allies turned on us, we would have to gut half the kingdom before we could regain control. For us, it would be nothing but an inconvenience, but thousands, perhaps tens of thousands, would die, and our economy would be in ruins."

"So we just let him continue to support the Vengeance?" I ask incredulously.

"Of course not. But we need evidence if we want to arrest him without causing an uproar. We need proof. I think you can help me with this."

"Father, what happened to Lady Calladan?" I ask abruptly. The question has been burning through me for weeks. He seems taken aback by the sudden question, and his expression doesn't turn to anger or surprise, but sadness.

"She asked to be with her husband," he says somberly. "I told her she could return as the Earless of Firdana and rule in her husband's stead, that she was blameless for her husband's treason. She refused to go. She demanded she be placed in the same cell."

I study him as he speaks. He doesn't stare at me, as he had the Earless of Firdana. He blinks, he rubs a hand over his face, he sighs. The tell I received from Calladan is nowhere to be found. Is he telling the truth? Was I mistaken that day in the High Court? Is Calladan the liar?

Father reaches out and draws me to his side, his body solid and strong. I feel safe, despite everything. Love radiates through his quiet embrace. This man is my father. How did I ever trust a traitor over my own father? How could I have believed a word he said after that nonsense about the Vengeance? I think about Lady Calladan in that dark and lightless cell and try to feel sorry for her.

"What can I do?" I ask.

"That Hoiran is guilty is beyond question. There were too many witnesses who corroborated that he and Markis were in constant correspondence, that they had business dealings far tighter than an earl from a different dukedom should. Several spoke of shipments of iron gone 'missing,' redirected to the Vengeance and his followers. Despite that, we need proof. Hoiran throws a massive banquet for the celebration of Summer's Dawning. I want you to go and investigate."

"What could I possibly find at a party? What am I supposed to do, ask him directly?"

"No, daughter," Father chides, squeezing my shoulder. "I expect you to be creative. Solve the problem. How will you get time uninterrupted with the Duke's personal effects? Your reputation with the nobility remains sterling, especially after discovering Markis meeting with the Vengeance himself. I haven't been able to get anyone close to his estate."

"Even members of the Deep?" I ask. Rather than showing any surprise, Father smiles broadly.

"I don't know if you will be able to find anything in writing that shows Hoiran's guilt," he answers as if I haven't spoken. "But his guilt is without question. So we may also need to... manufacture some evidence of our own."

He hands me an envelope heavy with parchment.

"Perhaps, if you're successful, we can talk more about the Deep when you return."

A servant bustles out of a stairwell ahead down the hall, interrupting my mindless walk. He doesn't glance left or right, but heads off with a purpose. For a blessed moment, the hall is empty. I can't see any guards, and the corridors are quiet.

Now, a voice whispers in my mind.

I dart up the stairs, moving on the balls of my feet. I brace myself to run into someone, anyone, but the passages stay blissfully empty. Either the chase has concluded or it's restricted completely to the first floor, for I pass unbothered. It isn't difficult to find Paloran's suite of rooms; I simply have to follow the opulence. The Duke's rooms themselves are so lavish in their luxury I have to be quietly impressed. The man certainly understands what he wants from life.

A desk stands at the far end of the room, and I hurry over to look through Paloran's personal correspondence. Certainly, if he's a traitor, something will be here. I need proof of his guilt, because I have no desire to use the documents strapped to the inside of my thigh.

"You don't have much time."

My instincts react even as my mind registers the words, the glass slivers woven into my dress leaping forth as I spin towards an unoccupied portion of the room. Or so I believed. Teldaran Hollenzar, or whoever he is, sits in a dumbwaiter of some sort. His hair is disheveled, his servant's uniform askew, but it can be no one else.

"Who are you, imposter?" I demand, scowling.

"Men will be here soon, looking for me. They know I've come up this hoist. You have seconds at best."

My mind barely registers the words, instead consumed by the dull roar of anger his sweating face ignites in my stomach. This boy is the reason Torlas deceived me, the reason I have to doubt my best friend. Whoever he is, I'm damn well ready for answers.

"Perhaps I'll just join the hunt, and we can find out who you are and what you know..."

Just as I direct the blades of glass to hurtle through the air towards him, he disappears. Like a magician revealing his trick, the boy is there one instant and gone the next. I blink, the speeding ropes the only sign of how he possibly could have vanished so suddenly. He's insane. What in the Creator's name possessed him to let go like that? A resounding crash echoes up the thin shaft, and I wince. If he's not dead, he's close.

The seconds I stand dumbfounded prove costly. Guards pound up the stairs. I turn back to the Duke's letters quickly, examining them as closely as I dare. All generic, all filled with platitudes and little else, nothing of note, nothing incriminating, notes between friends and business associates. The sounds of footfalls grow closer. I have to make a choice.

The packet of incriminating evidence rests in my hands. Is he truly guilty? The door slams open. I drop the letter amongst the others and storm towards the guards, who look terrified to see their princess angrily stomping through their master's apartments.

"I was tracking the dust on his clothes," I lie angrily. "He is back on the first floor, injured, crippled, I'm not sure, but we have to hurry. You, stay here and guard the Duke's personal quarters. The rest of you, with me."

I lead the charge back down the stairs. I didn't find anything. Creator, I barely tried. But at least Paloran will pay for his treachery.

He deserved it.

He deserved it.

The litany keeps me walking as guilt trails along behind me like a leaden weight.

***

Torlas waits for me on the street. I'm tempted to tell him to go to hell, but his damnable beaten dog routine is strangely arresting. The carriage waits for us both, but I walk past, knowing he'll follow. He orders the driver on and hurries to catch up. Part of me knows I should be more cautious, that my enemies would gladly take an unguarded opportunity to send my power back into the world. But I'm too angry to care.

"I'd like to have the opportunity to explain, completely, without interruption. If you still feel as you do when I'm finished, then at least we will understand each other," Torlas says, glancing at me sidelong. I don't respond, but merely continue to walk.

"His name is Jace, and he is a ward of the Historian," he begins. I frown. Torlas speaks as if I should understand who that is, but I've never heard of the man. He seems to catch on to my confusion. "He's an elder statesman who does scribing for most of the noble houses in the city and beyond. They call him the Historian because he's always talking about compiling the true history of the world. The task is beyond him, as it is beyond anyone, but he still claims to be making the attempt. Honestly, if it was anyone but Reknor, I'd laugh in his face, but the man is sharp. Everyone who speaks with him feels out of their depth, including my father."

The former Duke Graevo's likeness wavers into memory, his strong jaw, his hearty laugh, his bombastic attitude towards life. I smile to think of that man ever being out of his depth. No one celebrated on the day of his death. Had he not been traveling so far south, Uncle could have saved his life, but the sickness claimed him too quickly for any aid to reach him.

"Regardless, I met Jace under unusual circumstances. I might have hit him with a chair during a brawl at a coffee shop, which sounds absurd when I say it out loud, but... blast it. How do you describe friendship? He talks to me like I'm a person. I am a man with no peers, aside from the other seven dukes, and each desires my position far more than my companionship. Jace laughs, Iliana. By the Creator he laughs. We do things, not because we have to, not caring about what it looks like, but just because we want to. It's so... liberating. I've never enjoyed life so much as with him. You and I both know the king wants him for more than just crashing the party. That look the king gave him at the Ball... I fear for him," Torlas says, looking at me fully for the first time. I stop in the middle of the street to face him. "He's my friend, Iliana, the only one I can claim aside from you. I would protect him with my life. I never wanted to deceive you."

His words strike me like knives. What can a woman with no peer do for friendship? It's easy to desire power; to wish for the wealth and benefits of the nobility. But the lofty heights of power are lonely. This friendship… I can't understand. I don't know what it's like. How can I? How could I even find someone? Torlas is the closest thing to friendship I possess, but we never get to just… live. It isn't fair. It isn't right. A kernel of jealousy ignites in my chest, ugly and black. I struggle to push it aside.

"You should never have lied to me," I say, but there isn't any venom in it.

"I won't," he says simply.

"Don't," I try to say, but my voice breaks.

"Iliana…" he says, stepping close.

My heart twists at the pain in his voice, an echo to the anguish in my heart.

When his hand comes up to my cheek, I lean into the touch, so foreign, so strange. It feels like the only contact I've had with anyone in the past few years has been violent. His hand is warm and gentle. His eyes meet mine, and the Islander's words echo through the quiet recesses in my mind.

Love like that is rare.

As he leans in, fear claws at my belly, but it finds no purchase. Instead, my blood rises to meet him, my face tilting up and to the side, my heart taut and quivering. The first touch of our lips is feather-light, the mere brushing of one hopeful soul against another. He presses closer, and my fingers wind into his hair, drawing his face to mine, claiming his lips as my own. His arm slips around my waist, his lips parting, our breath intermingled.

I pull away, my hands coming to rest on either side of his face, my erratic breath matching the erratic beat of my heart. His eyes are shining, a combination of love and triumph. I lose myself in his gaze for a time, brief or long I cannot say. A spark of raucous laughter from a wandering group of men brings me back to myself and where we are. I turn and begin to walk again, tearing my eyes from his face and staring fixedly at the cobblestones. He walks beside me, his footsteps off kilter with mine, his steps slower but longer, mine short but swift. Even so, we walk in time.

***

Two long days are spent with task after bureaucratic task, with both Father and Uncle taking extensive time out of the palace on business for the crown. I'm anxious for a dozen reasons, most notably I'm practically bursting at the seams to tell someone about the Shaper I encountered at the party. She was exotic and beautiful, mysterious and foreign. Her symbol of power rose so prominently on her face that she must be careful how she uses the power in public lest her secret become common knowledge. She's clearly adept at hiding that power; we would have heard about her long since otherwise.

Who is she? What does she care about? Why is she nothing but a performer and a common thief when she's blessed by the Creator with unimaginable power? The nature of her power remains a mystery. I rattle off the list, counting through the altars in my head much as the priests taught me at temple. Earth, Wind, Fire, Water, Stone, Thought, Lightning, Roots, Beasts, Voice, Ore, Light, Force, and Time. The fourteen elements of the world, the forces and matter that make up existence, with the Unknown rounding out the number at 15. Which would allow her to fly? Force? Had she reversed the gravity of the world? But no one else was affected. Could she be so precise? The Unknown? But no one has discovered that power in millennia. Most believe the element was extinguished long ago, even the Temple. I settle on Force, but that seems wrong. The forces are metallic colors. Force is bronze, thought is silver…

The briefest flash of dark, mocking eyes and music tinged in silver light. Behind, a mosaic… crashing waves...

My head aches immediately like my brain is clamped in a vise, but I refuse to shy away from the pain. I force the memory to the front. A man, older than me, but not by much. His skin darker, his hair nearly black, his handsome face twisted into a smirk.

Put your shiny toy away, girl. You might hurt yourself.

The scribe. At the Liberation Ball. He was…

A faint symbol in silver gleams through the silk, beautiful and mesmerizing in its shape. My eyes trace the lines, intricate and weaving, and I start to feel dizzy. I tear my eyes away, meeting his dark gaze.

Blast it. I encountered the Master of Thought himself. Not only that, but he used his power against me. He covered over the memory of our meeting so completely it has taken me years, dozens of inexplicable moments of anger and recognition that made no sense at the time. My head throbs as more and more pieces of the memory fall into place. I have no idea how, but I get the feeling the scribe intended for me to uncover this memory, some day. He could have destroyed it utterly, burned it out so I would have no recollection of our meeting. Instead...

"Perhaps, when you're older, you can come visit, neh?" he says, reaching out and patting me gently on the head. "I will be there. In the heart of the Coin. Until then..."

Oh, I'll be paying him a visit. Of that there can be no doubt. A scribe in Coin. What is with the Creator's chosen hiding themselves in anonymity? These people are Shapers. They have the strength to change the very fabric of society, to alter the motions of the world, to take their personal destiny into their own hands. And what are they doing with that power? A scribe and a street performer.

The thought sends a tremor of disquiet through the dark corners of my mind. The known Shapers of the world are all fewer in number than they should be. The Mason and the Vengeance. The Sealord and the Healing Hand. Me. A mere five of the fourteen Shapers have risen following the necessary death toll of the Liberation from the Shaper's Council. Why have no others risen? Where are they? Father and Uncle are always watching, always waiting, looking for signs another Shaper has discovered their power. They have so far been unsuccessful.

Perhaps the Shapers exist after all, and are not unaware of their strength. Perhaps the Shapers of the world do not wish to be found. Perhaps they fear they will share the fate of their predecessors. If I could find them, I would tell them how welcome they would be. How much their power would be appreciated, how blessed they are to be chosen by the Creator himself. Our kingdom reveres the chosen. We do not harm them.

***

I preside over High Court the day of Paloran's arrest, because both Father and Uncle are busy. The last petitioner is a wealthy landowner in Firdana demanding repayment for the loss of sheep he incurred in order to feed the contingent of the Tide who came to bring me back to the capital. He claims more than a dozen were commandeered for an impromptu feast, and they only took from his best breeding stock, the fattest and plumpest and the healthiest. I wearily agreed to reimburse the man for half his lost stock, for the Tide often step outside the boundaries of decency. He leaves with a sour face and a begrudging acceptance of my ruling.

Duke Hoiran Paloran was arrested earlier this morning. Incriminating documents were intercepted, signed by his own hand, each more than enough to reveal his connection to the Vengeance, his systematic subversion of rare metals and iron, and his clear intention to seize the throne after the Vengeance deposed the 'tyrant' king. His trial is set for a month hence, and no one protests his guilt aside from his wife.

The High Court is tense, frightened, the few members of the nobility in attendance often shooting me furtive and uncomfortable glances. Clearly, they've heard of Paloran's treason. I can't wait to call the court concluded and be on my way. A messenger's arrival, demanding my presence before Father, is a blessed relief. This trip to the war room begins with a nod from Father and a hug from Uncle, my feet fluttering through the air as he spins me in a wide circle. I laugh, feeling for a brief moment like the little girl he once sent flying into the sky, terrified, only to be caught by his steady hands. His presence is reassuring, his strength so immense that nothing can possibly hurt me so long as he protects me.

He sets me down with a grin, stepping back and taking a seat next to Father at the table. A third chair is set for me. I settle across from them, the two most powerful men in the entire world. Between them they've walked for more than three hundred years on this earth, though neither appears a day over thirty. Some part of me notices for the first time how comfortable they are with one another. They combined their strength to uproot and overthrow a system of government which had lasted more than five millennia. I'm lucky beyond imagination to have them as mentors and role models. I'm seated at a table of strategy with these men who have literally shaped—Shaped—the world.

"How are the nobles taking Paloran's fall?" Uncle rumbles without preamble.

"From what I gather, they're terrified," Father answers as he flips through reports. "Some fear us and the control we're exerting, but many fear Altos and the nobility who have fallen under his sway. They believe we may be losing control."

"Are we?" I find the courage to ask. "Losing control?"

"No," Father says. "Though powerful, Calladan and Paloran have been contained, and the danger of their influence is already waning. When Paloran is found guilty and executed before the rest of the High Court, what little dissent exists will disappear with him."

"Iliana," Uncle begins. "Did you notice something at Paloran's banquet that would make you question? What is the disposition of the nobility? Did you overhear anything?"

"Nothing on that front," I answer. "But I uncovered more than one mystery. Such as the identity of the imposter Teldaran Hollenzar."

"What?" Father drops his papers so quickly it's like he has been stung. "You spoke with this boy?"

"More like confronted. He escaped, but I was able to learn that he is actually a ward of the historian Reknor. He goes by the name Jace."

I ignore the twinge of guilt that uneasily wends its way through my stomach. This boy is clearly leading Torlas astray. Defying the kingdom, hiding information… this isn't the Torlas I know. He shouldn't need anyone but me. Torlas shouldn't *want* anyone but me.

"We will investigate immediately," Father says, sitting back in satisfaction. "This is a boon for us. I think the boy could be important."

"How?" I ask, honestly curious. "He is just a boy."

"If my suspicions are confirmed, I'll tell you, but until then they are merely baseless conjecture," he says. He stares squarely at me when he says it. I fight the tense note of disquiet that squirms out of the back of my mind. Calladan is the liar. I've chosen to trust. "You mention another mystery uncovered."

"I met another Shaper," I say, holding up a hand to forestall their questions as they both open their mouths to speak. "It was a woman, an Islander, who was a performer at the banquet. I watched her float in the air without aid, almost as if she were the Vengeance herself. The symbol of her power was there on her face. I thought it was a tattoo at first, because her symbol was black, like oil. What power is represented by darkness?"

The two men share a look, but eventually Father shakes his head. They both appear at a loss.

"Do you know anything else about her?" Father asks, leaning forward. "Any other abilities, defining features, what have you?"

"She was a thief," I say, shrugging. "An Islander, though lighter skinned than most. She stole a necklace from the Duchess herself."

"Which necklace?" Father demands, his face contorting into an expression both intense and fierce. "What did it look like?"

"I only saw it in a flash of light, but I think it was… ruby?" I say, staring off into the distance as I try to remember.

"Gordyn," Uncle rumbles immediately, and he does not sound pleased. "He has sought the amulet for years."

"Jon Gordyn?" I ask, confused. "The banker?"

"The very one," Father says absentmindedly. "I knew he had been in some quiet war against a collection of thieves, and it appears he won."

He turns to Uncle, who nods.

"The rumors of this thief were not so far-fetched as we believed. The power of the Unknown, rising again in our time," Uncle declares quietly, a note of awe in his voice. I've never heard that tone from him. He always seems so sure, so certain of himself. It honestly scares me.

"Perhaps you should pay Mr. Gordyn a visit, Kranos."

"The Unknown?" I ask quietly.

"Iliana," Father says, as if noticing me again for the first time. "We're proud of you. You've grown in the last few seasons from the little girl of our memories to the woman seated before us now. Kranos and I have agreed that you are ready to assume more responsibility."

"Of course, Father," I answer slowly. I see the deflection for what it is, and I scowl. He can clearly see the anger in my face, because he frowns in return.

"You have to learn to control yourself, daughter," he lectures, his finger coming up like the Creationist who once schooled me in the faith. "If you wish to ever sit at this table as an equal, you can't allow your emotions to rule you. Some secrets, even mentioned in passing, could disrupt the very fabric of our civilization as we know it. We risk much just by allowing anyone with the knowledge to live."

"I can keep a secret," I mutter, but I can hear the petulance in my own voice. Deliberately smoothing my irritation away, I replace it with a stoic mask. "Should I tell you the last of my revelations?"

"Another?" Father asks incredulously. Uncle sits back and looks at me in surprise.

"The Shaper of Thought is, or is at least pretending to be, a scribe in the Khalintar of the Coin. He came to my coming of age, and used his powers to block the memory from my mind. I have just now managed to fight through whatever wall he put up around the memory."

Uncle and Father exchange a long look, a look of both relief and realization, as if this knowledge has solved a dozen mysteries at once. Father glances at me, his eyes leading, and Uncle turns to look as well. They seem to be evaluating me, sizing me up again and perhaps finding something there they didn't before.

"It is growing impossible for Kranos and I to control the breadth of this kingdom we created," Father says quietly. "There is too much to manage, too many fools and rebels and dissenters. Would you like to be a part of how this fragile kingdom stays strong? Tell me, daughter. What do you know of the Deep?"

Chapter 20
Bastian
The Final Day of Spring
In the year 5222, Council Reckoning

"What? What the hell?" I ask everyone and no one in particular.

"There is a way to transition from one life to the next. We gave up our lives so that we might serve future Shapers as the Ensouled," Jynn responds. *"Instead, our world collapsed along with the kingdom we all lived and died for."*

"Some of us lived for it," Asimir grumbles. *"Some of us fought against it. Keep your zealotry to yourself."*

"And yet here we all are," Jynn snaps. *"Fighting to fulfill Elitrea's dreams."*

"Don't speak as if you knew her," he growls. *"She had fallen into the trance a dozen generations before you even existed."*

"I stood at her side and listened to the—"

"Enough," Eligio says, his accent still eluding me. Though I know he speaks in another language, I'm still surprised not to be able to place it. *"Forgive my companions, Bastian. This is an old argument, one which neither side has ever acceded so much as an inch. You do not recognize my voice because my people were extinguished so long ago that your histories have no mention of us."*

"I'm sorry," I say lamely.

"The wound is so old I can only see the scar; I can't even feel it. But I thank you nonetheless."

"Where did you live? You and your people?" I ask.

The chorus of voices falls silent, the murmurs and whispers of the others dying down. Why would they stop speaking for this man?

"We were the A'kai'ano'ri. Isa was originally our land, these environs you call the Broken Isles our domain. But our lives were lived in a time before the Ways, a time before the great sea, a time before even the Eternal. We began as many civilizations do: warlike, exonerating fighters and generals and burning the collected knowledge of any who did not agree with us. As we matured, however, we turned introspective, scholarly. We began to pursue the spiritual realm, to study the nature of the world and the workings of those you call Shapers. We created the Voice of the World; the People still speak a form of the language that originated with my people. We started the Process: the path to becoming Human, the path to becoming a Blade, the path to reaching the Zenith. We believed we had ascended beyond the mortal concerns and the failures of our species. We were mighty, and no other people in the world could challenge us."

"Then what happened?" I ask. *"Why are we not all speaking the I'wia?"*

"The dissent came from within, of course. The debate that tore us to pieces was the same that people still argue today. Who was the Creator? We—each civilization which has arisen throughout time—each know of the Creator's existence. It is accepted as fact. Why? How do we know he lived? Why does no one question his existence? Where did he go? What did he care about? If he existed, how could he cease to be?

We took centuries to study the past, using our own Masters of Time to peer deep into the veils of the distant past rather than following the maddening strands of the future, as Queen Elitrea did. What we ran into was quite shocking: eventually, the past has an end. Or, really, a beginning. This world, and all that it is and was, started in one moment. Man was created and placed on this earth whole and aware. The Shapers were there from the beginning, the tools placed into their hands to tame the wild and lush land of our ancestors. But how? How could we have been given these tools of creation? Are there others like us? Other worlds, other species, other timelines? Where does the power of the Creator stop?"

"Did you find an answer? To any of this?" I wonder.

"We had our… hypotheses. But our own questioning of the fabric of creation led to our downfall. As we peered into the past, Shapers concerned far more with the present arose to power. They were elected; we had no form of government so barbaric as a monarchy. But the true A'kai'ano'ri fell out of politics. How can you care about the goings on of the present when the secrets of all that we are drift just out of reach? By the time we realized we needed to care, our laws and policies had been replaced. Our knowledge had been deemed heretical. The Temple of the Creationists had taken over."

"The Temple? The priests?" I ask incredulously.

"The very same. They had formed an entire religion based upon one of my ideas: that the Creator was still alive and well and cared for his creations. The paper I published was more satire than fact; how could any being with the might to create all that ever was and is care about the fate of his creations? What would possibly possess a being of unlimited knowledge and might to busy himself with our petty squabbles?

Be careful, Bastian, of the most dangerous force this world has ever known: hope.

The A'kai'ano'ri had achieved what we believed to be physical and spiritual perfection, but some of us were not satisfied. There had to be more, they said. There had to be something better for those who reached the Zenith. What use was the Process if it didn't lead somewhere? They did not understand the journey was the goal, and the journey would never be completed. Instead, they grew fearful of the journey's end instead of welcoming its peace. These men and women needed hope, and my brief and ill-considered treatise ignited that for them." Eligio falls silent for a time.

"What happened to you?" I prompt.

"When the assassins came for us, no one wept. They slaughtered us wholesale. I briefly considered fighting, but I knew my efforts would only further destroy what little chance we had of our knowledge surviving. So I gave myself up. I entered into this ring, shucking my mortal coil in the process. The Creationists found me and placed me on a pedestal in their first temple; the power of my soul an offering to the Creator they believed still looked down on them. There I languished for centuries, until finally I was graced with companions."

"The time approaches," Ulia breaks in, her voice frightened.

"Yes, Bastian," Jynn continues. *"It is time for you to help us."*

"What can I... what could I do for you?" I ask the waiting collection of souls. The sun drops towards the horizon, the tower's summit the perfect place to watch the fiery orb set the waves ablaze.

"We have reached a crux in the fate of the world. Our future, the fate of all that lives and breathes on this earth, will be determined tonight," the Seer's rich voice is grave.

"Uh, what? Isn't that a bit dramatic?"

"No, it isn't," she answers solemnly.

"Queen Elitrea fell into a trance that lasted centuries," Jynn says. *"Many believed she had gone insane, that the weight of untold centuries of life had broken her mind once and for all. They believed that the burden of knowledge was too much, that no one person could safely peer into the ever-mutable, ever-shifting river of the future. They didn't listen when we told them otherwise."*

"The queen was not broken," Ulia picks up the tale. *"She was searching. The Masters of Thought who stood at her side could listen, for a time, our power allowing us glimpses into the vast and endless tide of possibility Elitrea explored. We understood the terror that drove her to continue the search, the humanity that drove her to follow an endless number of strands to their inevitable conclusion. In every single future she followed, every branch, no matter the choices, our world ends. In fire."*

"My dreams," I start slowly. "The world burning, the fire feeding on life..."

"*The future,*" Jynn agrees. *"We decided to show you the visions of the Master of Time so you could come to understand the gravity of this moment. The importance of what we do tonight."*

"If it all ends in fire, what's the point? To delay? To put off that end?" I ask skeptically.

"She found a strand, there amongst the myriad ends of our collective life, in which we do not die. We do not fail. We fight, we thrive, and we continue to exist for so long she abandoned the strand for the centuries grew too long even for her patient sight. There were a handful of futures that led to that one shining strand, each balanced upon a knife's edge. Our lives and deaths hang on the most inconsequential of decisions: actions taken or not, thoughts voiced or withheld, anger kindled or forgiveness granted."

"Why didn't she tell the world what she was doing? Why allow them to believe her broken?"

"There were no futures in which her kingdom could save us," Jynn answers. Ulia's sorrow hangs as a palpable weight in the nothingness that is their existence. "*She gave herself up so that we might live. And even now, her efforts may have been completely wasted. We are ever in a game against the capricious and uncaring nature of history and the turning of the world. Over the past five thousand years, those dim candles of hope have been snuffed out one by one."*

"Let me guess," I say sourly. "There's one left?"

"Yes and no," Jynn hedges. *"There are several futures after tonight in which our world has a hope for continued survival. But all of them, each and every remaining future in which we exist, can be extinguished tonight."*

"Over centuries, the Eternal was able to pinpoint a few particular individuals in a few significant moments in history who would determine our fate," the Seer says, her face a stoic mask. "If we wish to keep the flame of hope alive, we must act. Tonight. We have lost futures we thought would never go dark due to the decision of a man to turn left on a leisurely stroll instead of right, thereby missing the one chance he had at laying eyes on the woman he loved, and so their child never existed, which annihilated an entire line of altruistic and brilliant people who would have steered the world towards unity and strength. We lost entire swathes of possibility because he turned left. Now, tonight is everything. Every. Single. Future."

"What am I supposed to do about it?" I ask, shaken.

"There are three souls at stake tonight, three individuals of such significance the events that transpire tonight will strengthen or destroy the last hope of our future. One must be saved, one must be broken, and one seek vengeance," the Seer gestures at the ring on her hand and seems to encompass me in the motion. She says the list as if it were a litany, but somehow, it feels unfinished, like she deliberately ended the chant before its conclusion. "We are going to keep the flame of life alive."

"What do I get out of it?"

"What?" the Seer responds, clearly stunned.

"What do I get out of it?" I repeat impatiently. "Despite your cleverness and deliberate obfustication, I can sense from dear Ulia's surface thoughts that the end of the world is quite a ways away. I could die tomorrow, having never seen nor worried about the fire of the future. You could kill me the second I finish helping you because 'it's necessary for the future.' Oh no, you manipulative little pricks, I am going to need something in return if you want me to stir even one metaphorical finger to help you."

"The fate of the world isn't enough for you?" Ulia speaks as if in a daze. *"You would let all life cease?"*

"I won't be around to see it, neh?" I answer, smiling. For the first time since I woke up in that damned cage, a flicker of the confidence which was so thoroughly stolen from me by these people returns. "No, I think I quite have the power here. You need me far more than I need you. I have some things you're going to need to do for me if you want to see it done."

***

"Does it bother you?" I ask the Seer as she leads me down. The starlight sets the diamond walls glimmering with a soft muted light. "Lying so blatantly to your people?"

"It had to be done," she answers without turning around.

"What? You have raised your people on a false religion that, surprise, you've known all along is false, and all you have to say is 'it had to be done'?"

"The People believe as they believe for a reason, one which I will not explain to you now. Just know… it was necessary," her eyes cloud, the warmth draining from her voice.

The Seer's personal chambers are a strange kaleidoscope of styles. Sumptuous silks drape right next to ascetic stone chairs, and brightly colored lamps hang beside tragic tapestries of long forgotten battles. It's as if a dozen people have all been given free rein to decorate, and none of them can agree an ounce on how the rooms should look. There are figurines from a dozen periods in history, tribal masks, a pair of short, curving knives, an ancient helmet corroded by salt. It is chaos, splintered, anachronistic and entirely unrelated. The crystalline walls are translucent, but not transparent, and the oddness of the structure and the lighting only adds to the eccentricity of the rooms.

Her bed is the only piece of furniture that does not embrace the disorder. Well-made and austere, the bed exists as a small piece of order amongst a storm of chaos.

"Lay down," she commands.

"But Seer, we've just met," I shoot back. "How forward of you."

The Seer ignores my comment and lowers herself onto a nearby cushion, crossing her legs and straightening her back.

"I'll be fine on my feet," I say, feeling strangely awkward as the woman closes her eyes.

"*Sit, you arrogant fool,*" Ulia's voice growls in my mind. *"If you lose control and fall, you'll break the trance."*

"It's the worst when bitches like her are right," I mutter sullenly as I sit down on the Seer's bed. It's remarkably comfortable. Whatever woven reeds they use to cushion the Seer are both soft and well-worn.

"It's the worst when assholes like you are the hope of the world," Jynn puts in drily.

Ulia seems mollified, but I can sense Jynn's laughter behind the words. As much as she wants to hate me, Jynn likes me more than she cares to admit.

"That is one point we can all agree on," I send back. *"Now, how do we even do this?"*

"I know how you're going to feel about this," Jynn begins. *"But you're going to have to let us take control. We don't have time to explain the how and why behind everything we're doing. Your strength and power are necessary when we get there, but let us do the heavy lifting to start."*

"Fine," I say. *"But I'm pulling out at the first sign you're trying anything funny."*

"No," Asimir says quietly. He hasn't been quite so friendly since I called them all manipulative pricks. I have no idea why. *"We've agreed to your demands. Until you have fulfilled your end of the bargain, you will follow every order you are given to the letter. As much as it may pain you to admit, this is not your story. This is the story of the world, and you are merely one tiny soul among a vast multitude of souls."*

"I'm not very good at following orders."

"Time is running out," Jynn declares. *"Bastian, close your eyes and shut up. Remember exactly what we need them to do, what we need them to achieve, what we need them to choose. We go. Now."*

Without warning, an invisible force seizes my mind and thrusts it out into the void. Before I can begin to feel the edges of my panic, I lose all sense of time, of movement, of self. My physical body is forgotten, discarded, useless.

Darkness and silver light, flashes of sea and sun and cities, vast distances devoured instantly, sounds heard for decades, hate and love and unending pain. For an eternity and no time at all, I drift, my focus flitting from one moment to the next in arbitrary fits and starts, dark eyes here, sunlight lancing through clouds there, everything and nothing experienced in an instant.

I open my eyes. My body is unrecognizable, lithe, lean, fit, all dark skin and slender deadliness. My skin prickles as a cool breeze from the swinging doors kisses my skin, the laughter of a big man ahead of me bringing warmth and joy, the longing eyes of the man at my side burning against my exposed skin.

I open my eyes. My fist is sure and certain, my muscles powerful, twisted chords of iron. I need to hide my strength, to appear small, frail, insignificant. I hunch, the tailored uniform still feeling somehow loose, and raise my fist to knock on the polished wood door.

I open my eyes. The sheer silk sheathes my body, its delicate softness delicious as I slide one leg over another. The man seated across from me in the carriage smiles that small, personal smile he reserves for me. I ignore the spread of warmth and the kernel of anger in my belly both.

It's too much. What am I? Who am I? Where am I? I fragment, the parts of me that make up Bastian shredding before the weight of three personalities so foreign and strange, so different from one another, each living a separate life in the same moment as I live mine, the same moment stretched to bursting by the awareness of all of us…

"Breathe, Bastian," Jynn speaks in my mind, her voice gentle as I've never heard it. That high voice has only ever been spoken in command, in sarcasm, in scorn, never gentle, never understanding. For a moment, the difference threatens to destroy me further, but I hold on to the sound of her voice. *"Let us help you. You are not alone. We are here. Calm, now. One at a time. Kettle needs us first."*

We dive back into the eyes of the woman in the silk strips of the People. We walk down a corridor, the back of a guardsman ahead, murmured voices… Distantly, I feel the sorrow of the Seer, some distant tragedy that lurks with this woman Kettle, her past, her childhood, a thin, gangly girl, her face serious despite her youth, the childlike wonder robbed from her eyes far too young, her skin, too pale to be normal, standing out sharply against a black tunic, the sign of her pride and acceptance…

With an effort, I pull myself out of the Seer's memories, her melancholy separate and yet a part of each of us as we trail along a new corridor, an emerald dress covering our attire, seeking something, something old, something Gordyn wants. Even as we walk, I feel pulled back down the corridor, awareness of Kettle fading as we come back to the man and the guard talking.

"She needs us now. If she goes into the museum alone, she'll be caught, and all is lost. Aurelion needs to be there," Jynn says, directing us towards the man in ostentatious Khalintari attire. Asimir and I suppress twin measures of disgust as we witness this pale man in a caricature of our culture.

"I'll take the guard," Jynn says, her presence deviating from our collective so abruptly I'm stunned. She's there one moment, her thoughts flickering under the surface of our presence, and the next we're one fewer, her presence gone as if she never existed.

"Bastian, you must be subtle," Ulia says, her voice serious and strange. *"He can't know what happens here."*

I dive into Aurelion's thoughts, his mind both simple and breathtakingly complex.

My muscles are powerful, disciplined, my control perfect, which is the only way I can resist the urge to glance over my shoulder as I hear Kettle's footsteps in the hall behind. The guard's eyes go vacant for a moment, and I reach out and pat his shoulder. I—Bastian—struggle to maintain my own independent thoughts as I merge with another foreign mind.

"What did you ask?" he mutters in a distracted tone.

“I asked where you’re normally stationed in the house,” Aurelion—we—repeat.

“The museum,” he says dully. The personality of the man has changed somehow in the last few seconds, his jovial cursing and good-natured complaining gone as if he’s been kicked by a mule. “They station me at the second door, you know, the one to the expensive pieces.”

“Second door?” we ask with concern. I heighten our sense of concern. Kettle needs us.

“Yeah,” the man answers, his voice still dull. “You have to have a key. That part of the museum is closed off tonight. Too many strangers about.”

“Do you have the key?”

“Of course. Hey, shouldn’t we check on your Islander?” the guard says, setting off down the hall without warning. Aurelion jogs to keep up.

“No, surely not, I told you she takes a while,” we say, following along.

I take the moment to urge him to consider the possibility. The opening. The grateful look that will ignite Kettle’s eyes as she realizes how we’ve saved her. All we need is a good cover. Perhaps a guardsman’s uniform, one that seems strangely the right size to fit, a man who already possesses the key… We leave Aurelion just as he hustles the guard into the empty bathroom, darting straight back to Kettle. Jynn rejoins us before we dive into her mind.

We are in the museum proper, wealthy fools laughing and drawing the attention of the men stationed in the room. Statues are placed tastefully so each can be viewed separately. We lay eyes on a statue of marble depicting a young man with a strong jaw and high cheekbones, his eyes cast heroically to the horizon. I feel Jynn subtly exerting some will so that Kettle turns to look at the plaque beneath. “Jendo, the Mind Razor.”

"What?" Jynn's voice is acid. *"How could they possibly have gotten this so wrong? Didn't this artist know anything about history?"*

Kettle's mind reacts to the anger, her body bristling at the affront even though she has no reason to be angry.

"Jynn, please. You will ruin everything," Asimir says.

They have a minor battle of wills, their minds twisting and writhing against one another. Jynn backs off, but I get the impression that she came to her senses more than Asimir was able to contain her.

"I'm not even female?" I hear her snarl to herself, but she keeps her emotions contained this time. *"Idiots."*

Kettle doesn't notice as another guard approaches, having seen her interest in the door leading deeper into the museum. Aurelion hustles up just before the man opens his mouth to question her, and the man returns to his post as Aurelion loudly proclaims that her invitation is in order. We enter into the dim room, the artifacts and ancient works quiet as they rest on their shelves and tables.

It isn't here. A stranger's voice, disembodied just like ours.

How would you know? Kettle snaps into her mind, almost as if she's addressing us.

Gordyn wants something old. Something like me, but from long before. Something more powerful.

"Her boots?" I ask the group. *"Are they Ensouled?"*

"Yes," Jynn says shortly. *"And we don't like him."*

"Why?"

"Later."

Who were you? Eo? The Shaper of Thought? How do you know what Gordyn wants? Kettles asks.

He wore me for years, Tecarim responds. *He has desired the Ensouled all that time. From what I've taken from your thoughts, the common knowledge of our existence no longer exists, but Gordyn knows. We are his obsession. The amulet you seek is beyond your understanding. His, too, if we are to be honest.*

How do you know it's not here? Kettle asks again, continuing to scan the room.

We can feel each other, talk to each other if we're close. Nothing Ensouled exists in this room.

Aurelion turns to leave, and the door handle twists. We tackle Aurelion onto the ground, landing on him quietly behind a display. We look up, and we begin to feel something, a recognition…

"Distract her, now," Jynn cuts in urgently. *"She can't recognize him yet!"*

Kettle's mind is too tight, her focus narrowing too close for us to easily break in. Aurelion, however, is far more distracted, a beautiful woman lying on top of him, her body pressed tightly to his own. His hand becomes mine, and we reach up to slide it along the silk of her skin. She stiffens, turning back to look at us with wide eyes. Her full lips quiver as her eyes meet ours. Our lips join, our hands exploring her body, our breaths coming in gasps.

"That's enough, Bastian," Jynn's voice echoes wryly in my brain. *"The danger has passed."*

Reluctantly, I let my mind separate again from Aurelion's, his hands losing confidence, his lips no longer so eager, his breath growing hitched with confusion. Their kiss breaks apart.

"Where's Asimir?" I ask, suddenly realizing his absence. *"And Ulia?"*

"Holding off the man sent to find the guard in the privy," Jynn answers. *"Quickly now. Asimir has let them through to find the guard. Ulia is with the princess."*

We jump to Jace's eyes. We walk slowly down the hallway, our steps quiet, but the sound of conversation ahead brings us up short.

"Hey, what's this?" a gruff voice asks.

"This? It is a steak knife. I am returning it to the kitchen to get another for Lord Sinole," a haughty, high-pitched voice answers.

"That looks a bit sharp for a steak knife. And, come to think of it, we finished the steak almost an hour ago," the man says suspiciously. Suddenly, the second man gives a squeal.

"What is the meaning of this?" he gasps. "I have worked here a dozen times. Lord Paloran himself would vouch for my—"

The heavy sound of a meaty fist striking flesh echoes down the corridor, and the servant moans and sags to the floor in a rustle of cloth.

"Take him away. If he's innocent, fine. We can't take any chances," the first man's raspy voice scrapes. "The Duke's property is paramount. Keep questioning the servants, report on any suspicious activity."

"Aye, sir," chorus several men and women.

"Through the doors," Jynn whispers in Jace's mind.

We comply, darting into the banquet hall just before the guards can round the corner.

"Now comes the hard part," Jynn whispers to me.

We're suddenly alone, just Jynn and I. Distantly, I can feel the others, their subtle alterations to the scene a quiet melody of manipulation. Ulia rides with the princess at the high table, and I inwardly frown as I catch hints of her surface thoughts. She's enjoying the show with the princess, watching the acrobats and comedy with a melancholy nostalgia.

"Shouldn't she be...?"

"Her part is yet to come," Jynn answers. She sounds strangely somber. *"We have to keep Jace alive in the next few minutes."*

The man juggling acrobats on stage suddenly comes to a halt, catching the three women and pointing squarely at us.

"Thief! There is a thief in the hall! Stop! Thief!"

We all freeze in surprise. In the pandemonium, I struggle to maintain my grip on Jace's mind. His actions are lightning quick, his reactions born far more of instinct than any rational thought, and the speed of his decisions is too much for us to keep up with. Jynn falls off with me as we float free.

"The canvas. We have to expose the painting!" Jynn says desperately.

Already, I can feel the malicious intent of several men gathering crossbows at the far end of the hall. Jace is up and running on the tables, his feet finding balance despite the chaos and cutlery. He leaps off the table into a waiting group of guards. Jynn dives into them in a whirlwind of emotion and false reaction, distracting their gaze, spasming their fingers, cutting through their intentions. In the chaos, I pick out the one man with a chance to genuinely grab onto Jace. I exert all my will, feeling my soul drain away at the sudden expenditure of strength, and the guard's hand falls on the cloth instead of Jace's back. Jace rips away from the group, and I let go of the guard's mind as he throws the cloth down in frustration.

"No! I can't stop him!" Jynn shouts into the aether.

I spin in the darkness that makes up this half sight, searching for the source of her anguish, jumping along the bright sparks of light that are the minds of the guests, settling on a guard. Competent, focused, his crossbow levels between Jace's fleeing shoulder blades. I claw at the edges of his concentration, but his focused will is too tight, too complete, my own power too frail after the efforts I've made so far.

"Take of me," Eligio says, his foreign voice warm next to my own. *"And remember."*

I reach out and seize the energy Eligio offers, the flaming torrent of his soul burning through my consciousness as I slam all the power I can into the guard's mind.

- a cityscape of angular buildings, each like the blade of a knife cutting into the sky -

- the setting sun silhouetting the form of a woman staring off at sea, her arms wrapped around herself and her green eyes filled with sorrow to match my own as she turns -

- the ring, that familiar ring from the Seer's finger, balanced on the palm of my hand, my skin dark, the sound of screams and terror in the distance -

I crack through the guard's focus, spasming his muscles just as the crossbow releases. The bolt flies wide by inches, crashing and through the back of an expensive wooden chair. I tear out of his mind quickly, Eligio already gone, no doubt on to some other task in this symphony of uncontrolled chaos. Jace sprints through the doors leading back towards the kitchens. For the moment, Jynn and I are adrift. The frantic thoughts of the mob chasing the young thief fades second by second.

"It's not over yet," Jynn mutters. She sounds tired, faint, her voice losing the vibrant energy to which I've grown accustomed. We dart over to Kettle, over by the doors to the banquet hall. I'm vaguely familiar with her thought patterns, so I slide into her thoughts easier this time. *"She can't leave yet. She needs to see the Duchess. Her necklace, the ruby…"*

I manage to convince her to stop, to continue looking. No one is going to be worried about a little Islander performer, we have time, we can continue the search. Kettle's eyes scan the mob surging past her position near the doors... I allow her eyes to roam, filling her with a quiet certainty that the flicker of red on the Duchess' neck is indeed what she's searching for.

Is that it? Kettle asks the Ensouled in her boots.

Perhaps. We are too far for me to know, he answers.

I thought that urge to stay came from you.

Urge? What urge? Wait, Kettle, close—

"Ugh," Jynn's voice is quiet, exhausted. I can feel as she wrestles her will down into the Ensouled below, burning an extraordinary amount of her energy to take over his mind, however briefly, sending him down into dormancy and erasing the memory of our presence. *"They can't know. It has to be…"*

Her voice fades. I can still feel her, clinging to my energy, and I let her, too tired to care.

Ulia's voice, quiet and whispering in the ear of the princess, echoes through my thoughts.

"How dare she? Stealing from the nobility in their own home. But talk to her, don't turn her in just yet."

For the moment, I'm without direction. Jynn is quiet and trying to recover, but the others are all scattered to the various rooms and minds in the estate. The conversation between Kettle and the princess sparks mild interest, but I allow myself mostly to drift.

"You don't like Duchess Paloran anyway, the Islander could be right..." Ulia's voice continues to breathe into the back of the princess' mind, her power so much more subtle than the rest of us, her urgings coming almost from the person's own mind.

"Jace will not escape too soon, and the princess' path to the Duke's chambers is open," Asimir's voice returns to us. The Seer's energy burns next to his, still strong, still bright. She doesn't have the power, so she wouldn't be tired, would she? She's merely an observer on this extraordinary adventure. *"Ah. Jynn has exhausted herself already."*

"Quickly now," the Seer breaks in. *"We need to keep moving. Find Jace."*

He's higher than I expected him to be, and rising, his hands strong on the ropes of a dumbwaiter, the regret at being forced to leave behind the painting prominent in his thoughts.

"He needs that painting," the Seer reminds the others. With a weary sigh, Asimir departs again, flying down towards the waiting mind of the duke.

Our heart jumps as the door opens far faster than we expected anyone to be able to reach us. Instead of a soldier, however, the princess ducks inside, her movements furtive. Is she... sneaking? She walks to Paloran's desk, rifling through the papers there before opening his drawers. What is she looking for?

"They must meet," the Seer's strong voice breaks in. I narrow my focus for what has to be the thirtieth time tonight. What truth can we tell her…

"You don't have much time."

She jumps, her cheeks blushing red, and we're shocked again to feel like we recognize her, like there's something more there than just the brief time we've spent together. The room is immediately bathed in green light, and spinning glass glitters menacingly around her.

"Who are you, imposter?" she asks, scowling.

"Men will be here soon, looking for me. They know I've come up this hoist," we say, ignoring her question completely. "You have seconds at best."

"Perhaps I'll just join the hunt, and we can find out who you are and what you know…"

"I can't hold her," Ulia's voice cries out weakly to us.

The fear and the tension spikes alarmingly as we become aware of the princess' intent, her shards of glass already beginning their deadly flight. We will never be able to dodge in time, the box far too small to maneuver. But the box… the box itself can move. With the last spike of my waning focus, I push Jace's fingers open.

"What have you done?" the Seer cries out in horror.

We fall, free-falling, the speed of our descent accelerating with each passing second. I'm at a loss, the seconds passing too quickly, time slipping through my fingers. I saved him from one death and cast him directly into another… by the Creator, all of this effort, wasted… luckily for us, Jace still has some agency in his own fate. He grabs the ropes, the skin from his strong hands burning away instantly, the ropes slicking with blood, but he holds. We hit the bottom with a mighty crash, alive but shaken. Asimir has done his job; the Duke and his servant look on us in horror.

"One last task," the Seer practically shouts. *"Jynn, take us to Kettle. She can't be seen, can't be remembered."*

Kettle prepares to make a run for the fence. Asimir guides us into Aurelion.

"Where's Eligio?" the Seer declares. *"We need his strength."*

Silence greets her. She seems to peer about, even though our eyes mean nothing in this state of spiritual freedom. She sighs, the sound weary, accepting.

"No, Min'dei," Asimir says, but his protest sounds weak even to me. *"There must be another way."*

"We knew this was a possibility," she answers quietly. *"Talan will be—must be—ready. Bastian, use me. Blank the minds of these men and women in the courtyard. We will guide Kettle and Aurelion out."*

Her energy mingles with mine, her soul powerful and strong, certain and yet questioning. I don't bother arguing, but dive forward, spreading my focus like a net, erasing the knowledge of the passage of the pair as they walk right out the gates of the estate. My energy expended, the voices of the collective fallen silent, I stray into darkness.

***

Opening my eyelids is the trial of a lifetime. A decade after they open, my limbs twitch, as weak as when I woke in the cage all those days ago. I can barely lift my head, my neck trembling under the weight of my skull. I recognize the chaotic intricacies of the Seer's personal chambers through my wavering vision. The Seer slumps next to the cushion by the bed, her arm cradling her head in the picture of peace. She looks younger with her face relaxed, her wrinkles smoothing and the severe furrow in her brow easing. I let my head flop back onto the bed.

"*Did we win?"* I cast into the darkness.

For a long, long moment, I think no one will answer. Distantly, almost beyond the senses of my hearing, Asimir's voice comes back, almost unrecognizable after the ordeals we faced.

"Partially," he says quietly. *"Meddling with the future is neither art nor science. We guess as much as know. As far as I can tell, hope remains. Though how many strands perished and how many remain… impossible to say. We must rest now. And mourn."*

"What is there to be sad about if we succeeded?" I ask fuzzily, having trouble focusing through the tide of my weariness.

"Do you hear them?" he asks, his voice despairing. *"Where is Ulia? Jynn? Eligio? Even the slumberers are gone, used up, their strength spent to get us to the estate. I am all that remains. I am, truly, alone."*

Confused, I reach out, but there is no answer. The space of the ring is quiet, unnaturally so, the voices and murmurs and surface thoughts of the souls stored there strangely absent.

"They didn't… surely they can't have… died?"

"The cost of the future is always the past," he answers bitterly. *"I couldn't even save Min'dei."*

My eyes snap open, and I find the strength to sit up. I look over at the body of the woman once known as the Seer. The lines on her face have not smoothed in sleep, but in death. Her chest is still, her peace eternal. I lie back, what's left of my energy evaporating as mist before a strong breeze.

That same old feeling, the same knowledge of my own insignificance, consumes me as sudden as a storm. I've been running from it my whole life. The despair. The meaninglessness of our lives, our hopes, our dreams, our loves, and our hates. How long did Ulia cling to her pretentious ways? How long did Jynn fight to keep her fire burning? And Eligio… the last soul of a civilization so ancient history has forgotten it, wiped away after thousands upon thousands of years of existence. I didn't know these people for long, but the sheer history and experience the world has lost… these people have been around for thousands of years. In a single night, untold millennia of knowledge, of life, has been destroyed, and the only people who know it are the sorrowful soul of a long-dead man and me. When we finally pass on, there will be no one to remember.

The same fate that one day awaits us all.

***

The knocking at the door turns to urgent shouts as I claw my way back to consciousness. My weary mind still needs rest, my power nearly used up. The angle of the light filtering in through the windows shows it to be past midday, though I've no idea which day it can possibly be. The Seer still lies curled on her side. Physically, I'm recovered, my eyesight sharp, my limbs strong. I rise and look down on the corpse. Part of me admires her. When the time came to stand or to fall, she gave herself unflinchingly to the cause. I still don't know if I honestly believe all of the nonsense these souls espoused about the tangled web of the future, but *they* most definitely believed it with all the fervor in the world. And they paid with their lives for it.

"Seer? Bastian? Open this door!" Te'ial's muffled voice calls in time with the incessant pounding against the ancient wood.

I open the door before she can hurt herself. The smile of relief that eases onto her face falls away when she sees my face. She'll probably never look at me that way again, not after what awaits her. My lips press into a line as I meet her eyes. Sudden fear fills them, and she pushes past me. I ignore her frantic calls to the Seer and the panic that laces her voice as she tries to awaken a soul that has long since departed. Her keening cries of sorrow chase me out into the hall, Te'ial's agony an assault on my anguished spirit which I can't endure. I walk until I can't hear her, ignoring the sound of rushing feet and the first angry lamentations as Isa learns the fate of its beloved Seer. The spiral staircase seems the only escape, so, ignoring the complaint in my limbs, I push up to the rooftop of the brilliant diamond tower.

Safe on that high vantage once again, my lungs gulp the fresh salt air, struggling to regain balance here in this city filled with enemies. I'll need my focus and my strength.

The Seer was my only ally among an entire nation made up of uncompromising zealots. The deal we struck was silent, and there were no witnesses. My stomach lurches as a new thought strikes me. Of course there were no witnesses. Of course she agreed to whatever terms I asked for. She knew that she wouldn't be here afterwards, and not a single soul will trust me or listen to me now that she's gone. When they learn that I was alone with her the night she died, they will probably try to kill me. And most likely succeed.

The wily bitch manipulated me masterfully. I try to be bitter, but my admiration for her grows instead. How she hid all of this from me while our thoughts and souls intermingled is beyond my understanding. I'll learn from her, if I can live long enough to use her lessons.

Gazing out over the sheltered bay where Isa once stood, the business of the People continues for the brief moments they have left before the nation descends into anger and sorrow. Young couples walk together, fingers intertwined, a few early merchants preparing their wares for the coming day. A new ship sails into the mouth of the bay, its sails strangely familiar. A shock of recognition lances through me. The *Mason's Fall.* Even as they close, I pick out the proud figure perched on the bow, guiding the ship into dock. His broad chest and powerful shoulders stand out miles away. Fear rises in my throat despite our distance. He is the cause of all my troubles, the reason I'm trapped in this Creator-forsaken land.

"Talan will be—must be—ready."

As he steps off onto the docks, I hope he is. Because I really need him to have a long conversation with Asimir before he decides my fate.

The expected party of angry tribesmen stomps around the winding staircase waving curved weapons. They shout at me in their foreign tongue, their faces locked in a collective of rictus rage. I open my hands quietly at my side. I haven't recovered enough to affect this many, let alone pierce through the haze of emotion that grips them. If the moment of my death has arrived, there's nothing I can do about it. At least their hate will ruin them. The explosion of power my death creates may well cripple the minds of everyone within the walls of Isa. At least I get to spit in their faces even as they drag me into oblivion.

I wish the thought brought me any satisfaction.

So I ignore them, turning and looking out over the bay again. The view steals my attention, here in the middle of the mightiest city the world has ever known, the broken capital of the most powerful kingdom the world has ever seen. The gentle breeze carries the soft scent of the sea, overwhelming any stench of human corruption from the world. I breathe deeply, the sigh rushing forth and taking all my tension and fear with it. If it happens, it happens.

They continue to shout at my back, the only word I can pick out from their gibberish *thriska*. Tainted. I take another deep breath, and just as I let it out, they fall silent. Talan strides up the stairs with the grace of a hunting panther. He doesn't acknowledge me, but joins me at the edge of the platform to gaze out over the city. The deep resonance of his voice reverberates through my chest in the *I'wia*, and the people leave, filing silently away.

"She did not expect to survive," Talan speaks quietly, his voice cutting through the breeze. "When I left this last time, she said goodbye in such a way I knew it to be final."

"She sacrificed herself for the future she believed in," I tell him honestly.

"Did she succeed? Has the Worldfire been averted?" he asks, turning to me with terror and hope mixed in his gaze.

I guess I shouldn't be surprised that the heir to the Seer knows of these things, but I am. As I search his face, little remains of the selfish man who placed his search for a sister over the well-being of his people.

"For now," I say. "The cost was absurdly high, but the futures, some of them at least, appear to still be alive."

"Then we are blessed indeed," he says sincerely, turning back to the bay. "Even though I know you were not willing, I thank you for your part all the same."

"So you know, then," I say, turning to him in shock. "You know that your beliefs about the Shapers are nonsense."

"I have been educated, since last we met," he answers, his mouth curving up into a half smile. "It is remarkable, how you can see so much of the world and yet remain so blind. It gives me hope for all of humanity. The Shapers may one day serve the Creator's purpose again."

"Who is Aea?" I ask suddenly, my mind jumping back to the Te'ial's memory in the ship's hold. I don't know why the question slips between my teeth. I scowl, thinking Ulia is manipulating my thoughts, but then I remember. She's gone.

"My sister," he answers, his smile growing. "Not tainted. Not R'hea of Darkness. Simply Aea. I have not found her, but I will, now that the future is secure."

"You mean Kettle?" I blurt out, some pieces clicking into place.

"Who?"

"Nevermind."

So what if it's petty. The man punched me in the face, and his people held me captive for years. Why should I give him this truth? Let him suffer.

"I'm glad you've come around," I say instead, slapping him on the back and smiling a free smile for the first time in a long time. He loses his smile and glares at me.

"Do not forget, fool, I would have killed you for daring to touch Te'ial. Your taint… your gift," he corrects himself, his mouth twisting. "Was the only reason I spared you."

"I'll take what I can get," I answer, not losing my smile.

"You asked for a ship," he says, his gaze intent. "You wished to go home. You wished to find your brother, who the Seer told me to assure you still lives. The *Mason's Fall* has returned to take you back to Coin, so long as you swear on the life of your brother to tell no one of Isa. The People honor our agreements."

***

As Summer dips into Autumn, the *Mason's Fall* cuts through the choppy waves as we skirt along the Way of the West. Standing solidly at the rail, arms crossed, I stare steadily at the horizon. The salt spray is a blessed balm on my face, a welcome relief from the relentlessly beating sun. Apparently, spending more than a year unconscious on a ship gave me the sea legs I couldn't find in my first voyage.

My first moments on the *Mason's Fall* were occupied by a surprising reunion: Tana had joined the crew two years before, cheerful and helpful as she is, now tanned nearly as dark as the People she works beside. The scar where her slave mark once rested is almost imperceptible after the long years spent in the sun upon the waves. Somber, she stands at the rail beside me. They told us that we would be sighting land today. The rooftops of Sail should be visible any moment.

"I haven't been back," she says in a small voice. "Not since… you know."

"Thank you," I say quietly. "If I never thanked you before, you're the only reason I'm standing here. I won't let Cortola take you back, if the man still lives. You're safe with me."

"I know," she says simply, her eyes still intently watching the horizon.

"If you don't protect her, I will," a voice cuts through my thoughts. *"I like her."*

"Jynn?"

Epilogue
The Eternal
The Seventh Day of Winter
In the Year 5204, Council Reckoning

She hasn't spoken in eighty-seven years.

The thought is slow to come and slower to leave, the languorous stretch of a long-dormant psyche. The present is as foreign to her as the sun; she once traced the moment she went blind in a childish fit two hundred years after Sherrine. Not that it matters. The sun never casts its rays deep enough to pierce the impenetrable darkness of her existence. Nothing that lives there has need of sight. The pressure at the bottom of the ocean was unbearable for the first decade, or would have been, but she hadn't spent a moment in the present, knowing how awful those times would be.

The man at her side suffered through each and every one of them. She almost reaches out to touch him, to wake him, to begin. But no. Let him sleep a little longer. His dreams are pleasant, she knows. He cannot remember the forests, the sun, the sky. But he dreams in emotion and golden light, and she remembers from long examination that these dreams, these particular, final dreams, will be lovely.

It nears midnight, directly above. The sun just rises for the Khals. The evening stars twinkle over Donir. She has studied this day so often she knows the vagaries of the wind and the sorrows of the people. She can *see* as her eyes will never see again, the tension in the shoulders, the fear set deeply in the lines of the face of the man she set on this course eighty-seven years before. The orders have been given, the pieces moved into place, and all that remains is to see if he will succeed. If he can dethrone a government that has spent five thousand years ruling.

He had been young, idealistic, so full of wonder and life that her heart sought to break for him the moment she opened her mouth. Finding part of Isa had been the triumph of his young life, the broken remnants of the unbreakable city there under the ocean's waves. His excitement led him deeper, down, past ruins lit only by the soft blue glow of his power, past creatures with no eyes to see him, deeper than any had gone before. He hadn't believed it, at first, the moment his straining eyes caught the glimmer of golden light in the darkness. It was impossible, that light, that soft golden glow there so far from the world of light. Of course he had explored onward, never expecting to find what he found. He had been so excited, so happy, so young. He didn't deserve the fate the future—the future she created—had in store for him, but the sacrifice of one is worth the salvation of many.

Though she plans to sacrifice far more than one.

Perhaps I should change that phrase, she considers briefly.

The sacrifice of many is worth the salvation of *any.*

Even as she prepares her muscles to move, to stretch, to strain, she keeps a part of her mind's eye on the rest of the present. The tent flutters in the cold Winter air…

"Are you going to defend yourself, Telias?"

Still a few moments yet. She's moved past regret, past fear, past what little humanity remains to her. Her unseeing eyes nevertheless move around the archways of windows filled with glass of such beauty and strength the world will never again see their like, the floors so intricately carved as to beggar belief, a twisting mosaic of all that makes up the world, the high vaulted ceiling so distant all sound echoes. The throne she graced for millennia still stands, a grim monolith three paces behind. She can see none of these things, and yet each is more vivid to her than if she had eyes to witness them now.

This moment has played out in all its infinite variations before her mind's eye. It always seemed so distant, so impossibly distant. Racing over the infinite realm of possibility, witnessing the death of each world, all worlds, an infinite number of ends to an infinite number of lives, it was easy to forget that this moment approached. Yet now it has arrived.

They called her mad. Perhaps she is. Mad to fight, to strive, to search for all the untold centuries of life she has been granted. Mad to give up the present for the future. Mad to sacrifice everything that made her human so that humanity might, *might*, live.

"It is forbidden for a Shaper of the Council to lead and govern men. This army you have raised is a clear breach of our laws. It is forbidden for a Shaper, but not for a man."

A pause. The dull sound of a dagger slamming into wood echoes through the soundless space.

"Become a man."

She tenses, the crux upon her faster than she expects, the pivot in history upon which all rests. She moves, slowly, her muscles protesting from long disuse, yet still responding, still supple and young, still strong despite the uncaring turning of the world. She crouches over him, silently, bathed in a golden glow her unseeing eyes can't register. Her hands come up, preparing to squeeze, to twist, to… end. She calls on her strength, long passive, this one final time… awakened.

Existence holds its breath. The world's turning slows. In this moment, however fleeting, time eases its passage to a crawl.

"I would have faltered, wouldn't I?" he says quietly, his voice a melody of song in this place of silence. She pauses, surprised and yet not. This future is rare, this present unexpected. It almost breaks her. Maybe it does.

"Too many times to leave to chance," she whispers, tears unfelt sliding down her cheeks.

"Good, then. We can't risk failing now," he answers, content. There is a brief pause. She slows time further to give him the chance to speak. "Was it worth it? Us? This?"

"Yes," she lies quietly, bending low and pressing a kiss to his furrowed brow. It smooths, his expression clearing. She knows his hair still bears the rich brown of his youth, his eyes still soft and young. She knows the golden symbol of his power still glows strong and bright on the back of his left hand where it rests against her leg. "It was worth it."

She makes it painless. The end of her last subject, the last living soul under her rule.

Existence exhales. The world turns again. Time resumes its inexorable march.

And Elitrea, the Eternal, now queen of nothing, buries her face in her hands to weep.

THE ETERNAL DREAM WILL CONTINUE...

If you enjoyed this adventure and wish for more, the best way you can support me is to tell every human you've ever met about this book and leave a detailed review so that others can share in the experience!

Acknowledgments

I'd first like to acknowledge you, the reader, for your eyes are the reason these words exist. For making it this far, thank you. Hopefully it wasn't too painful to get here. There will be more.

The two people who helped most in the creation of this book would require a novel unto themselves, so I'll keep their acknowledgement short. Pop, thanks for listening to a hundred thousand ideas, some of which are related to plot points that won't be relevant for ten flipping books, and doing your best to understand and follow along. Your love and pride has always inspired me to keep fighting. Ellen, thank you for your endless support and love. Your belief in me allowed me to believe in myself. Thank you for reminding me that love exists. And for kicking me in the ass when I needed it.

To my beta readers: Mom, Wells, Meghann, Elizabeth, Mark, Neal, Caitlyn, Emma, Raven, Rich, Evan, Meagan, Brittany, Dickie, Jeff, and Leila (if I forgot someone, I will accept your everlasting anger). Your contributions allowed me to see where my wayward brain was, well, wayward. Thank you for taking the time to make this monster so much better.

Thanks especially to Evan Chabot and Emma Kenemer, without whom the lovely map and cover art for this story would not exist. Your talents constantly amaze.